England's Fury

Book Two of the Ironside Trilogy

Alfred Read

Cover design by ebooklaunch.com

To my uncle, Barry Charles Poole, 1954-1993.

Character List.

(* after name denotes fictional character.)

Alfred, Aetheling. Son of Æthelred and Emma. Brother of Edward and Godgifu.

Alston*, Thegn.

Bede*, horse.

Bertram*, gaoler.

Brandon*, son of Æva.

Cenric*, Captain of the Ealdorman Ælfric's hearthweru.

Cnut, son of King Svienn. Brother of Harald and Estrith.

Cuthbert*, steward to King Æthelred.

Dog Face*, dog.

Eadgyth, Aetheling. Daughter of Æthelred and Ælfgifu, wife of Eadric, sister of Æthelstan, Edmund, Eadwig, Eadred, and Wulfhild.

Eadric, Ealdorman of Mierċe, husband of Eadgyth.

Eadwig, Aetheling. Son of Æthelred and Ælfgifu, brother of Æthelstan, Edmund, Eadred, Eadgyth, Wulfhild.

Eadwulf*, Thegn.

Ealdgyth, wife of Sigeferth. Mother of Ælfwynn.

Eamon*, warrior.

Edmund, Aetheling. Son of Æthelred and Ælfgifu, brother of Æthelstan, Eadwig, Eadred, Eadgyth, and Wulfhild.

Edward, Aetheling. Son of Æthelred and Emma. Brother of Alfred and Godgifu.

Estrith, daughter of Svienn Forkbeard. Sister to Cnut and Harald.

Ælfgar, Thegn. Son of the Ealdorman Ælfric.

Ælfgifu. Daughter of Ælfhelm. Sister to Wulfheah and Ufegeat.

Ælfgifu (deceased), wife of Æthelred. Mother of Æthelstan, Edmund, Eadwig, Wulfhild, Eadgyth, and Eadred.

Ælfhelm (deceased), Ealdorman of Southern Norþanhymbre. Father of Ælfgifu, Wulfheah, and Ufegeat.

Ælfric, Ealdorman of Hamptonscir. Father of Alaric and Ælfgar, father-in-law of Æva, grandfather of Brandon.

Ælfmær, Abbot.

Ælfnoð*, commander of the Snotingeham garrison.

Ælfweard, Reeve.

Ælfwynn*, aunt of Æthelstan, Edmund, Eadwig, Wulfhild, Eadgyth, and Eadred. Widow of Æthelstan.

Ælfwynn*, daughter of Sigeferth and Ealdgyth.

Æthelflæd (deceased), wife to King Edgar, mother to King Edward.

Æthelmaer, Ealdorman of Dæfenascir.

Æthelred, King of England. Son of Ælfthryth and Edgar, father of Æthelstan, Edmund, Eadwig, Eadred, Wulfhild, Eadgyth, Edward, Alfred, and Godgifu. Husband of Emma. Widower of Ælfgifu.

Æthelstan (deceased), Aetheling. Son of Æthelred and Ælfgifu, brother to Edmund, Eadwig, Eadred, Eadgyth, and Wulfhild.

Æthelstan (deceased), Thegn. Son of the Ealdorman Thored. Brother of Ælfgifu. Brother-in-law of Æthelred. Uncle of Æthelstan, Edmund, Eadwig, Eadred, Wulfhild, and Eadgyth. Husband to Ælfwynn.

Æva*, widow of Alaric, mother of Brandon, daughter-in-law of the Ealdorman Ælfric.

Ginger*, a ginger bloke.

Godgifu, Aetheling. Daughter of Æthelred and Emma. Sister of Alfred and Edward.

Godwine, son of Wulfnoth.

Harald, son of Svienn, brother of Cnut and Estrith.

Harold*, Thegn.

Hereward*, Thegn.

Knud*, Jarl.

Leafstan*, Thegn.

Leofwine* (deceased), captain of Canterburie's garrison.

Morcar, Thegn, brother to Sigeferth.

Olaf Haraldsson, associate of Thorkell.

Osbert*, personal steward of the Ealdorman Ulfcytel.

Osmund* (deceased), warrior and best friend of Alaric.

Østen*, Jarl.

Richard II, Duke of Normandy. Brother of Emma, brother-in-law of Æthelred. Uncle to Edward, Alfred, and Godgifu.

Sigebryht*, Thegn.

Sigeferth, Thegn, brother to Morcar and husband to Ealdgyth. Father of Ælfwynn.

Svienn "Forkbeard", King of Denmark, father of Cnut, Harald, and Estrith.

Thorkell "The Tall", leader of the Jomsvikings.

Thurcytel, a former Captain in the Ealdorman Ulfcytel's army.

Ufegeat, Thegn. Brother of Wulfheah and Ælfgifu. Son of Ælfhelm.

Uhtred, Ealdorman of Norþanhymbre.

Ulfcytel, Ealdorman of Eastengle, husband of Wulfhild.

Wilfrid*, warrior.

Wilfrid*, priest.

Winfrith*, monk.

Wulfheah, Thegn. Brother of Ufegeat and Ælfgifu. Son of Ælfhelm.

Wulfhild, Aetheling. Daughter of Æthelred and Ælfgifu, sister of Æthelstan, Eadwig, Eadred, Eadgyth, and Edmund. Wife of Ulfcytel.

Wulfnoth, Thegn, father of Godwine.

Wulfstan, Archbishop of Euerwic.

Wystan*, innkeeper.

Place names.

Abbendone = Abingdon.

Arewan = Orwell.

Aultone = Alton.

Beamfleote = Benfleet.

Bebbanburg = Bamburg.

Bernecestre = Bicester.

Buccingahammscir = Buckinghamshire.

Cantebrigie = Cambridge.

Canterburie = Canterbury.

Cantwara = Kent.

Chipeham = Chippenham.

Cocheham = Cookham.

Dæfenascir = Devon.

Derbei = Derby.

Eastengle = East Anglia.

Esledes = Leeds (Kent).

Estreham = Streatham.

Euerwic = York.

Execestre = Exeter.

Exsessa = Essex.

Gainesburg = Gainsborough.

Gipeswic = Ipswich.

Hametuna = Ampton.

Hamptonscir = Hampshire.

Hringmere = Ringmere.

Humbre = The Humber.

Isle of Wit = Isle of Wight.

Lindesi = Lindsey

Lodeburec = Lothbury

Lundenburg = London.

Malduna = Maldon.

Malmesberie = Malmesbury.

Mideltune = Milton.

Mierċe = Mercia.

Norþanhymbre = Northumbria.

Northantone = Northampton.

Noruic = Norwich.

Offetuna = Offton.

Oxeneford = Oxford.

Oxenefordscir = Oxfordshire.

Porteceaster = Portchester.

Reddinges = Reading.

Remmesgate = Ramsgate.

Sancte Eadmundes Byrig = Bury St Edmunds.

Sandwice = Sandwich.

Sceftesberie = Shaftsbury.

Sciropesberie = Shrewsbury

Snotingeham = Nottingham.

Sūþsēaxe = Sussex.

Suthhamtunam = Southampton.

Tæeseford = Tempsford.

Temes = Thames.

Theodford = Thetford.

Trente = Trent.

Wadetuna = Watton.

Westceape = Cheapside.

Westseaxe = Wessex.

Wiltunscir = Wiltshire.

Wiltune = Wilton.

Wincestre = Winchester.

Wirecestre = Worcester.

Miscellaneous.

Aetheling = A member of the royal family, title generally reserved for eligible heirs.

Breecs = Trousers.

Boss = Central point in a shield, usually fashioned from iron.

Ceorl = A small holding peasant, often enjoying at least some status and/or independence from the local thegn.

Cyrtel = A type of dress.

Ealdorman = Person of significant authority, appointed by the monarch and responsible for a specific region.

Fuller = A groove running down the length of the blade of a sword.

Fyrd = Militia forces raised in a specific locality.

Hearthweru = Elite troops answering to a specific notable, quite often an ealdorman.

Heregeld = Army tax.

Huscarl = Elite Scandinavian troops generally employed as bodyguards for kings, jarls etc.

Jarl = Scandinavian noble, loosely equivalent to an English ealdorman.

Kirtle = Long tunic fashioned from wool or linen. Word applies to garments worn by men and women both.

Reeve = Senior official, again appointed by the monarch to carry out a specific administrative task within a specific area.

Rönd (Danish) = Round shield.

Scir = Shire/district.

Seax = A short sword or knife/dagger.

Thegn = Nobleman, usually holding lands in obedience to the local ealdorman.

Witan = Council of notables, meaning "wise men". Generally made up of the monarch and his ealdormen/thegns for the sake of dealing with matters of import to the realm.

PROLOGUE.

I stare at him, looking deep into those panic-stricken eyes. He speaks, imploring me to listen, imploring me to do the "right thing." He even quotes Scripture, asking me, "What does it profit a man to gain the world and yet lose his soul?" Harold is young, a father to a newborn, with little experience of war or politics. His paraphrasing of the Bible shows that, burdened as he is with petty concerns of loyalty. It doesn't matter what he thinks. I have leverage over him, significant leverage. He's powerless in this situation, and he knows it.

I don't reply to his waffle, not at first, hoping he'll come to the correct conclusion of his own accord. We break eye contact, the battle to the south calling my attention. It's terrifying, this broiling clash of men and arms, being enough to almost seize the breath with the witnessing of it. Hundreds have already fallen, and thousands more are set on killing each other, their rage impossible to quench in the face of their most hated foe. The English are brave, but it won't be enough. There is only one way this can end. Thorkell the Tall has come to Eastengle and will brook no obstacle to his passage, not from me,not from the king, not from anyone. He has the numbers, and he cannot be stopped. The Battle of Hringmere was over before it had even begun.

Few saw this, but I like to think I had the distinction of being one of them. I'd argued with the ealdorman, almost begging him to think clearly and consider his more realistic of options. As always, he wouldn't listen. He never did. His mind was set on violence, and he wouldn't be dissuaded. I had no other choice. I made a deal, one that would ideally salvage something from the slaughter to come and ensure my future wasn't cut short by a Norseman's axe. Many would throw their lives away in service to the ealdorman, but I wouldn't be one of them. I had things to do. Ambitions to see fulfilled.

We approach the critical moment. The English lines are starting to fragment under the pressure, the sheer size of Thorkell's army proving too much to bear. The ealdorman's men are fighting on, thinking that I, of all people, will be rushing in to save them. I can't fault them for that. It had been agreed that I would lead the charge south, using the force entrusted to me to move around the lake and smash into Thorkell's flank. It was a fool's plan. Even if we did as the ealdorman intended, we'd still lose in the end. I give the order to retreat. I won't be a party to stupidity.

Harold looks at me again. He doesn't want to go, nor do the rest of them. None of them understand, these brave fools, but they must do as I ask. I grab Harold by his mailed collar, hauling him towards me until his bearded face is but inches from my own. "Do as I command," I snarl, knowing he'll have little choice. "Do not make me remind you of certain things."

He stammers, his hand rising up to grab at mine so that he might free himself. "This is Eadric's doing, isn't it?! You and he made a deal to..."

The blow cuts him off. I didn't strike him hard, but I did it with accuracy, the slap from my left hand returning him to his senses. He gives the order, embellishing it with some convincing falsehoods to secure their obedience. Our men start to fall back, slow and unwilling, mutterings of confusion and outright objection emanating from the ranks. It doesn't matter. They do as I say. I look back one final time, gazing upon the slaughter as Ulfcytel's dreams come undone.

I see something, or someone, staring back at me from the battlefield. Ulfcytel himself, his eyes aflame, his face a mask of blood and teeth and rage and then… something else…sadness and shock as he sees me leaving. I try to tear my eyes away, but I can't. He sees through me, into my heart, into my soul. He knows what I'm doing. What I'm about. What I've already done and what I may yet do. I can't stand it, but I can't look away. He sees me. He sees…

"Do you understand everything I have said to you?"

The voice snaps me out of my memories and forces me back into the present moment. This Dane had brought certain issues to mind, but I shouldn't have allowed my thoughts to wander. There was no sense in dwelling on the past. Hringmere is already ancient history. Things have changed since then. Eadric and I were successful. I have Porteceaster. I have my fortress. And apparently, we have a new king.

I look the Dane right in the eyes, hoping he can't read me like I hope to read him. His story is surprising, but he doesn't have the look of a liar. Falsehoods are easy to spot, in my experience. I'd know that. I'm an expert in them, in the telling and the noticing.

"I require an answer."

He shouldn't rush me. He's not in charge here. This fortress is mine, and I have many a man to call on should I wish it. He should watch his tone. He's a foreigner and a stranger, and I say what happens within these walls. He's a guest, at best. He should behave as such.

"If what you say is true, then I will look forward to a visit from King Svienn himself. Hamptonscir has long been without a capable king. May God bless and guide him."

I like that. My choice of words doesn't give too much away. That's important. He looks satisfied. Tired, too, he and his two cohorts in their mud-splattered armour and identical blond hair. All these Danes look the same, but these are at least halfway civilised. They haven't tried to kill anyone yet. That's a novelty. They'd simply ambled up to my gates and demanded entry. I didn't care for their demands. But I do care for what they might know.

So Lundenburg has fallen. They'd been very direct about that from the start, and it was for this reason I'd allowed them inside and fed and watered them. They told a remarkable tale, some of which I was already familiar with and some that was new. We'd all heard about the invasion. Svienn Forkbeard had returned, sweeping in with a great fleet to take England by storm. It was inevitable that such a day would come.

Yet to hear of the capital falling so quickly was a shock. Even more surprising was the news of King Æthelred's flight. Nobody had said where he'd escaped to, but he wasn't in the country, and he'd apparently taken his pet Dane, Thorkell the Tall, with him. Æthelred had always been a coward, but I'd hoped Thorkell might instil some vigour into his old bones. That was too much to ask for, as it turned out. I shouldn't be so surprised.

I stand up, rubbing at my temples as I try to clear my mind. The Danes on the other side of the table remain as they are, finishing off the abundance of bread and cheese I've so graciously provided. These past few months have admittedly been easier than they might have been. I was left control of Porteceaster, as agreed, and imbued with the authority of the Ealdorman Eadric to act on his behalf and, by extension, King Æthelred himself. That last point seems a little moot now, considering what has happened. Svienn is the new power in England. Eadric and I will treat him accordingly.

But where is Eadric? Once he'd handed this place over to me, he'd said he'd be sending word on a regular basis. He sent a few letters at first, informing me the king was satisfied with our work in apprehending the Ealdorman Ælfric and was content to let me remain here as custodian of the fortress. It wasn't and isn't good enough. Men of power cannot depend merely on the contentment of others. I require surety and title, something to bind me to this place by right. I have no such thing; just a few hundred Miercian warriors and a county full of resentful people. But I remain. And I will not be dispossessed easily. Porteceaster is mine. Hamptonscir will follow, if this new king is just.

One of the Danes looks up and lets rip with easily one of the most obnoxious belches I've ever heard. His comrades all laugh, and my guard over at the door struggles to suppress a chuckle. I glare balefully in his direction, but in all fairness, I should be used to vulgarity. Ulfcytel had been amused by such things, and I'd spent years in his service, suffering his foolishness and despising him for it. He never saw it, thinking me loyal, yet despite my dislike of him, I'd still felt a great deal of trepidation when agreeing to assist in his defeat at Hringmere. A lot could have gone wrong, and had we been discovered, the fearsome ealdorman would have certainly killed me. It was for this reason I'd been more than apprehensive to hear he'd somehow survived the battle and escaped Eastengle. I'd been petrified at first, thinking him likely to seek me out, but then I'd heard about the siege of Canterburie. That must have been his end. Nobody could survive that kind of fighting. I sleep easier thinking it so.

Eadric had promised a lot in return for my cooperation. I'd trusted him, to an extent, as it was foolish to presume our alliance would entail any degree of actual friendship. We each were a means to an end, and when it came to the Battle of Hringmere, Eadric's had been directed towards ensuring Ulfcytel met his own end at the hands of Thorkell. It had been difficult to do, for Ulfcytel had placed me in charge of a good chunk of his men, none of whom were too eager to just retreat when we were supposed to be doing the opposite. The ealdorman needs us, they'd said. The battle will be lost without us. They'd soon changed their tune. I can be very convincing. People fall into line quickly if you know where to push them.

Harold had helped. He'd not been happy about it, but blackmailed men are rarely happy. He'd barked convincing falsehoods, saying Ulfcytel himself wished them to fall back and defend Noruic. It was a good ruse, and it had worked, allowing us to escape the battle with the minimum of fuss. We'd moved north at some speed, the men grumbling all the way, their suspicions of me and Harold growing with each moment. I did the sensible thing by sneaking away, albeit not before killing Harold. That had been a risk, of course, and so I'd waited until we'd made camp and he was fast asleep. I cut his throat, and he'd thrashed about in his own blood as expected, but he'd eventually stilled, and nobody had heard him. It was necessary. He'd known too much about me, and his death tied up a few loose ends I didn't want to be burdened with later. I'd then fled into the night, leaving my men to their fate so that I might join Eadric in Mierċe. There was nothing left for me in Eastengle. The real prize was always here. A stepping stone, if you will, to bigger and better things. I'd looked forward to it. I still do.

"Is there anything else you have to tell me?"

The lead Dane looks up from his food at the sound of my voice. He's got bits in his beard, and he's making an irritating sloshing sound as he chews, like he's intentionally attempting to breathe through his mouth whilst shifting saliva about with his tongue. It's repulsive, and I'm inclined to think the man's trying to push me. He's the envoy of a conquering king, here to demand my obedience. A certain attitude, a certain arrogance, is to be expected. He confirms it by what he says next.

"Give us ale. It's been a long journey."

"Of course," I reply, nodding slightly. "You're my guests. You only need ask…"

"We do ask."

A second Dane had spoken, looking at me like he thinks I'm frightened of him. I have no idea why he would think that, and I don't much care. He appears as a fool, his eyes vacant and his beard even more unkempt than those of his two friends. I'd like to cut it off and jam it down his throat, but that wouldn't make the best impression on King Svienn. I'll play along. I instruct the steward lurking behind me to bring us a keg. He returns within the space of a few minutes, another man helping him with his burden. That was fast work. I've got these people well trained. They know what happens when they displease me.

My servants pour out three flagons for our visitors. The lead steward passes me my drinking horn, full to the point of spillage, before withdrawing towards the back of the room. I hold the horn aloft, hoping the Danes will get my meaning. I don't even know if these people drink to the health of anyone, but I decide to chance it. It can't help but make at least some kind of impression.

"To the health of our new king. May his rule be long and prosperous."

They get it, returning the gesture and then drinking as I drink, the senior one quaffing almost his entire flagon in one go. If he thought to impress, he was dead wrong. He's spilled a good deal all over himself, the amber fluid saturating his beard and splashing off his mail shirt to drip onto the floor. It looks downright foolish as well as messy, but he seems pleased, as do his twin companions on either side of him.

"How long until you return to Lundenburg?"

I ask the question because I want to know. I've done everything they could ask of me, and I'm not in a mood to put up with the three of them if they insist on getting hammered in my hall. I like this place, and this room in particular. It was the Ealdorman Ælfric's chamber, and it serves me as such. I may not have his title, not yet, but I've sacrificed a lot to get this far, and enjoying his home as if I were already an ealdorman seems perfectly fair to me. It's not like anyone here is in any position to object.

"We'll be leaving in the morning," says the third Dane, this one looking like he's taken a blade to the face at some point, what with the significant scar running down his left side.

"But we'd like to get the measure of you in the meantime," says the one who has done most of the talking thus far. He's staring at me with a strange expression now. I don't know if I'm being scrutinised physically, but I don't care for it. They want the measure of me? I'll show them. There's one way I know. I'll see if they're up for it. King Svienn would approve, if he's any kind of man worthy of being called such.

"Do the men of the North hunt?"

It might sound like a stupid question to some, I know, but I'm not asking out of ignorance. I want them to think me sincere, perhaps ill-travelled and less worldly than I am. I'm perfectly sure the Norsemen hunt well enough. They'd have to, in those frozen wastes they call home. They all answer in the affirmative, looking at me over their drinks as if I'm the fool and they have every advantage. That's what I wanted. I give voice to a proposition.

"Then will you join me tomorrow morning? I like to bag myself a deer or two when I have guests. Perhaps you can teach me how your people go about such things."

They laugh, sniggering like they can't quite believe I'm capable of killing anything. "We agree," says the leader, "but we'll drink tonight, you and us. Show us how the English drink, and then come morning, we'll ride and kill."

I nod eagerly before downing what's left in my drinking horn. I make some excuses as to why I have to leave, claiming I have some business elsewhere in the fortress but assuring them I'll return soon. They fall for it, assuming a man such as I must be very busy. I'm not, actually, and wasn't until they arrived. I have a plan, and it's a good one. I can't match them drink for drink, at least not in a way that would still ensure I retain even a flimsy hold on my wits. I'll need my own supply of ale. I gesture for my head steward to accompany me and stride from the room, my personal guard following as I brush past him into the corridor beyond.

I say nothing as we move, my pace brisk and determined for the sake of expediency. I didn't want the Danes drinking here, but if my plan works, the annoyance might be worth it. We exit the hall, but I share a few words with the men on duty in the vestibule. I want at least two guards placed outside the chamber hosting the Danes. I don't bother to explain why. It's obvious. Danes are dangerous enough. Drunken ones are even more so. The precaution is so necessary it doesn't require further elaboration.

My fortress is magnificent, and doubly so on a day like this. The sky is clear, the afternoon sun gentle yet brilliant as it shines down upon my thatched roofs and sheer stone towers. I always appreciate the view from this courtyard, positioned as it is upon a smooth, slight incline that allows me to survey the settlement and the inescapable walls surrounding us. I sometimes wonder if Ælfric enjoyed this place like I do. He cared for his hall and his impressively high tower, that I can tell, filling the former with works of art and the latter with books the like of which I'd never laid eyes on before. Yet it was outside where the real beauty lay. Those walls. Like the ones around Lundenburg, and yet different. They were things of functionality, but also something else, an enchanting quality I've sadly never been able to put into words.

Fear was a part of it. They inspired fear, and when I'd first seen them I'd felt it for myself. I'd been right to be apprehensive, and as I walk from my courtyard I'm reminded of such things. The inhabitants of my stronghold are out and about, but as usual they are cowed and subservient when catching sight of me. It wasn't always so. They'd had some spirit in them when I first came here, and for a while I'd suspected Eadric's little siege of this place would end in our defeat. It had gone that way initially. Old Ælfric had not been a welcoming host, and with that red-haired daughter-in-law of his, he'd berated us from his battlements and rained arrows and spears upon us until we'd had no choice but to fall back. Eadric was a clever fox, though. He knew Ælfric had a weak heart, and so we'd brutalised his people, dragging them before his walls and gutting them like fish to aid him in coming to the right decision.

Did it work? Yes and no. I walk in through the front door of the public house, ignoring the fact everyone within has immediately fallen silent. This is a humble place, the raw earth floor strewn with rushes, the tables and chairs fashioned from the same cheap and accessible oak currently burning away in that soot-stained hearth. I speak with the fellow who owns it all, a paunchy man whose name I never cared to remember, stating my special requirements and how he is to fulfil them. He listens carefully, his brow beading with apprehension. He nods and vanishes into a back room. I appreciate his efficiency. He's acting out of fear, but I still appreciate it.

I like to think Ælfric had felt fear when he'd made the decision to abandon this place. I'd not seen that coming, but Eadric had, and so Ælfric had been apprehended easily enough in Suthhamtunam after travelling there by ship. We'd made ourselves busy here whilst all of that was going on. We'd taken the walls that morning, in fact. It had been easy. Luck had been with us. A lot of luck.

Not everyone who carries a weapon has any business doing so. Some men look the part on the outside but remain soft within, and the man Ælfric had left to command his garrison here was one such individual. He might have held out, ignoring us as we butchered yet more people in front of the walls, yet fortune smiled on us. His wife had somehow fallen into our clutches, his young son and firstborn daughter, too. What they'd been doing outside the walls I have little idea, but the sight of them in our tender care had sent the poor fool over the edge. He'd opened the gates, and we'd flocked in, taking his people by surprise and disarming them. We'd disposed of his family regardless, and in his despair, he'd made an effort to fight us. It had done little good, and he'd ended up hanging outside with a number of other hotheads who wouldn't step into line. It had sent a nice message to the others. They'd certainly quietened down after that.

The sweaty innkeeper returns, bearing a keg of my "special request" in his trembling arms. My steward takes it from him, both men grunting with effort as one hands the weight over to the other. This will do me just fine. The Danes can drink the real stuff, thinking themselves superior, as they always do. They'll have sore heads and heaving stomachs in the morning, whereas my concoction will see me hale and hearty. They'll never find out. My steward is diligent, and will know when to refill my drinking horn and from where. I'll remain largely sober. And more than capable of humiliating the Danes on tomorrow's hunt.

Some might think me petty. They'd think wrong. In my world, not all communication is by speech or letters. Men see and respect strength. Come morning, these Danes will be expecting to surpass me in skill and blood lust, and had I been drinking the same brew as they, that might indeed prove to be the case. But I've ensured I'll outshine them, leaving the distinct impression I'm a man of capabilities. Who cares if it's all deception? None of that matters. Results matter.

This isn't just me showing off. I admit I want to upstage these coarse oafs, and that'd perhaps be enough to amuse me for a while. But these men are envoys from King Svienn himself. If he's wise, he'll want a full report, including their assessment on what kind of man I appear to be. I'll be the gracious host as I'll be the skilled huntsman, and with any luck the king will hear of it. It may seem trivial, but such things could be the first steps towards a flowering relationship. It doesn't hurt to try.

We make our way back outside, my steward struggling to keep up with my precious cargo. We re-enter my hall, depositing the keg in a room close to my chambers. My steward can take my horn from me as needed, refilling it here and returning. The Danes won't notice, as they'll be increasingly drunk on the stronger stuff I've provided them. It'll be perfect. I laugh to myself. I'm going to enjoy this.

The night passes as expected. My visitors are even more boorish when intoxicated, regaling me with tales of their King Svienn and his many raids upon English shores. It's all tremendously dreary, but I find my interest piqued when they come to the subject of Thorkell the Tall and his brother, Hemingr. They hate Thorkell, thinking him a fool and now a traitor following his decision to go over to the former King Æthelred, but there's some respect for Hemingr, as he'd apparently fought alongside Svienn years ago during the burning of Execestre and Wiltune.

I nod along, supping my drink slowly, and I'm nicely drunk by the time the Danes pass out, one face down on the table, the other two tangled on the floor. I've knocked back much of the watered bilge I'd reserved for myself, but I also indulged in a little of what the Danes were drinking for the sake of appearances. They've drunk a lot, polishing off the first keg and a good portion of a second. That would be impressive, if not for the fact they've compromised themselves badly and left me every advantage. Tomorrow shall be fun.

There's one single annoying drawback to this situation. I'll have to find somewhere else to sleep tonight. I can't slip into the bedchamber just beyond. Not with these three animals here, belching and farting and snoring to themselves. They disgust me, and there's always the chance they might wake up and take to violence, inebriated as they are. I can't be killed in my sleep by a drunken Dane. It'd just be embarrassing. I have too many plans in motion for that kind of nonsense.

I move to the tower, taking care during the climb up its long, winding stairs. My guard follows, but he doesn't assist me, knowing I won't take kindly to being seen as incapable. The rooms up here will more than suffice for my needs, at least with my own chambers so occupied. I fall asleep, entangled in the linen sheets of the bed of whichever spawn of Ælfric once lived here, knowing I'll almost certainly wake before the Danes do. I was right in that. What was unexpected was the dream.

I'm back there again, in Eastengle, as I was the day I abandoned Ulfcytel for better times and better prospects. He's in the thick of it, surrounded by friends and foes as they continue the bloodletting, their blows splintering shields and hacking through mail and flesh alike. Harold isn't with me, nor are the men I was supposed to lead in a glorious charge, leaving me very much alone. Ulfcytel somehow sees me from amidst the battle, his look halfway between heartbreak and murderous rage. He begins moving towards me with that purposeful stride, the blood and fury parting to let him through. I don't understand. But he's getting closer, and I feel something. Something bad. Fear.

It gets worse, for I suddenly cannot move. Somebody has a hold of me, their strong, calloused hands gripping me by the shoulders. I look to my rear, staring into a pair of green, cold eyes. Something looks almost familiar about this man. He's older than I, but powerful, his silver-flecked beard and hair having a wild quality to them as they catch the breeze. He's all scarred up, his facial hair failing to hide it, making him seem like a veteran of a lifetime of battles and near-death experiences he somehow always managed to walk away from. He's no friend to me. There's no affection in those eyes. He's with the ealdorman, and he won't let me go.

My attention is drawn back towards the battle. Ulfcytel is somehow right in front of me, having covered hundreds of yards in just a few seconds. He stares into me, like he did in reality, searching for something, some explanation, some answer on why I betrayed him. I can't move. I can't speak. I wish I could just wake up. He sees it in me. He sees the fear, but no regret. He doesn't like that. He thinks I should be remorseful, but I'm not. It makes him angry, very angry. He raises his sword, heaving it back for the killing blow...

It never comes. I've woken. At least, I think I have. I scratch at my legs, pushing my nails into the skin, good and hard. It hurts. I am awake, for certain. The dream was just that, a dream, born of bad memories. I don't feel regret for what I did. It was all necessary, and nobody is coming for me either. Nobody is coming to avenge Ulfcytel. He's dead and done. Canterburie saw to that.

I swing my legs out of bed, gasping quietly when my bare feet make contact with the hard, cold wooden floorboards. The first rays of morning are pouring through the still-closed shutters, and like anywhere else in this fortress, I can hear the sea crashing and rumbling to the south and west. When I first arrived here, I thought little of it, for I'm no admirer of the water, but I soon came to appreciate the sound's soothing qualities. It's even more appreciable this morning as I'm, to my surprise, a little hungover. That stuff I fed the Danes must have been more potent than I thought. It's good I didn't have too much of it, instead relying largely on my own watered-down brew to keep myself sensible. It will all pay off today.

I dress myself in the clothes I'd discarded last night at the foot of the bed. It's nothing special, just my high boots and breecs with the long-sleeved beige tunic I don't actually care for. I'm fond of my belt, however, for it's decorated with silver studs spaced at tight intervals; a "gift", so it was, from a local merchant who seemed to think it might prompt Eadric and I to spare his home. I've kept it ever since, using it to attach my scabbard, the likes of which contains one of my most prized possessions. It's a seax, of middling length, with a purple jewel of some sort worked into the pommel. Now that really was a gift, from my late father, so I'm told, not that I ever knew him. I keep it close, and I should be in the habit of sleeping with it, especially now. Many would entertain the notion of killing me in the darkness of night. A few might one day try.

All is soon ready, and I make my way downstairs, my guard lurching into activity when I pass him at the door to my bedchamber. He follows me, surprisingly alert and on form considering the duration of his watch. I knew there was a reason why I half-trust him. He's one of Eadric's Mierčians, and he doesn't care about what I've done or might do as long as there's something in it for him. I could tell he was that kind of man the first time I laid eyes on him. I recognised it, like a certain cool pragmatism. A quality we both share.

As expected, I find the Danes where I left them. They are sleeping soundly, and snoring loud enough to wake my dead mother. I stare at them awhile, scrutinising their stupid, drink-addled faces. It's hilarious. What's even funnier is the reaction when I pick up one of the tankards from the table only to send it crashing to the floor.

They all leap up as one, their warrior's instinct serving them well despite their unbalanced state. They are swearing, their weapons drawn also, both blade and axe on full display. I'm not unsettled by any of it. I grin at them, and their scowls begin to soften when they remember where they are and who I am. Then I remind them of our agreement.

"A hunt then? Or are you feeling unwell?"

I can tell how they feel, but I also know they won't refuse me. "We will hunt!" blurts the eldest, although judging from his bleary eyes, I think his enthusiasm may be misplaced. His companions too are trying to put a brave face on, but that's a tough act when you already have the face of a man still drunk from the night before. These men could do with some more sleep. I don't have the patience for that.

We eat together, not out of respect for them but simply because I'm hungry. They tear into it, slurping the porridge down with neither dignity nor restraint. They then start belching to themselves, acting like the vulgar display is the peak of good humour. I try to ignore it and eat at my own pace, grateful my guests have thus far not attempted to redecorate the floor with what they've just ingested.

I get up and leave, my guard still at my side and our new friends shambling after us. I laugh when one of them almost trips, the poor fool careering into a wall and nearly dislodging the tapestry of the Battle of Brunanburh. He apologises, sounding remarkably polite for his kind, and his eyes then drift over the depiction of war he'd so nearly defaced. His brow creases in thought. I wonder if he even knows what it signifies. I wonder if any of them could know just how heavily we defeated them that day. I decide not to mention it. I don't think they'd be able to appreciate it.

We're outside in no time, my delicate companions wincing before the morning sun. I slow my steps, not wishing to humiliate them too much, the inhabitants of my fair stronghold predictably giving us a wide berth as we amble through them. They hate me, and they hate the Danes; I know all that, but I do find myself wondering whom they hate more. I'd ask one of them if I thought I could get an honest answer. Fear has some drawbacks, I suppose. People will say anything to avoid your wrath.

I find my horse in his usual spot. He's a spoiled one; cared for by an ever-diligent groom and kept in the finest stable he's ever likely to experience. We're all saddled and ready in short order, and we ride out into the middle of the settlement at a trot, the Danes following me on their own rugged-looking beasts. We turn north at the market, the people parting around us like water, and head towards the northern gate. We're almost forgetting something. The dogs. We can't have a hunt without hounds.

They too are right where we left them. They are excitable beasts, howling and leaping about as we approach, undoubtedly knowing already that something is afoot. I keep their kennels tucked away beside the eastern wall, for they are savage if provoked and require somebody special to handle them. He's a bastard of a man, my master of hounds, but so am I, and so we understand each other in the ways that matter. He doesn't need to be told what to do. He gets the dogs ready and hurries after us on his own mount, somehow managing to keep good order as he goes. The dogs are excited. They should be. They'll be tasting blood this day.

My guard moves up alongside me on his black nag before leaning over slightly to converse. He looks worried. I hear him out, and as usual he talks a lot of sense, at least for somebody of such humble station.

"I would feel better if we obtained some extra men from the barracks," he says, keeping his voice relatively low to perhaps avoid the Danes listening in. "It doesn't hurt to be better protected. I might not be able to do everything myself if…"

I understand what he means. The Danes can't be trusted, and if any of them decided, for whatever reason, to turn hostile it'd be two against three, assuming you don't count the dogs or their master. They may all still be drunk, but I don't like being outnumbered. We do as my man says, stopping briefly to pick up three additional warriors of his choice. He knows who to choose and what he's doing, and they accompany us at a jog, apparently unfazed by such exertion even under the weight of their mail and shields. They are of hardy stock. They'll be well-suited for dealing with any unpleasant contingencies.

The men on watch at the gate nod as we come closer, turning a few seconds later to unbar the substantial double doors and heave them inwards so we can pass. I take the liberty of relieving them of their spears, taking one for myself and three others for the Danes. We'll not be able to take down boar without spears. The men can have them back when we're finished with them. It'll make a good impression if they're bloodied. They'll be reminded yet again of what I'm capable of.

We move out, riding two abreast through the gate and into the crisp morning air. A lush, sun-drenched vista of meadow and woodland expands before us, the green of the grass streaked purple and white with heather and daisies. I inhale deeply, relishing the sight, only to spy the line of gibbets arranged along the roadside to the east. It's about time somebody cut those people down. They've been there for months and are now little but bone and rags. I think everyone has fully understood the message they were intended to convey.

I urge my horse into a canter, enjoying the sensation of the wind rushing through my hair. My guard keeps up, as is his job, and the Danes flock after us, the men on foot having to almost sprint to not be left behind. We reach the tree line and the hounds are already on to something, leading us through an emerald thicket of maple and ash for what has to be the best part of a mile. I'm getting impatient. Something needs to die today, and I don't particularly care what as long as it isn't me. The dogs had best lead us to something appropriate rather than some overgrown hare. I don't want to look foolish in front of my guests.

My guard suddenly spurs his steed off to my left, crying out about how he believes he saw a stag. I can't see anything of the kind, but I don't have reason to doubt him, so I hurry after him in my thunderous fashion, my horse's hooves crushing through ferns and budding wildflowers as we go. The Danes stick close, moving with all due haste, the fresh air presumably clearing their heads and sobering them up. I don't care about the hounds. They'll come back when they've finished chasing whatever it is that has them so animated. Their incessant barking is already growing faint. A good thing. The dogs can be so very trying when excited.

We burst out of the undergrowth to enter a large clearing. It's like an ancient grove, or something our heathen ancestors might have regarded as sacred, and its thick and abundant grasses would reach the knees were we to dismount. The hound master is somewhere else, probably chasing after his beasts, but the three warriors on foot are still with us, breathing heavily and sweating, it's true, but still with us. My guard ahead eases his horse to a halt. There's no stag, nor does there appear to be any sign of one. I'm confused. I don't like being confused.

He stares at me, my protector does, like he's looking at somebody he's never met and could never possibly care for. I suddenly hear a cry from behind me, and I turn my head just in time to see one of my men impaling a Dane through the side with his spear. He slides out of the saddle, hissing and groaning through bared teeth, and lands face-first in the grass, apparently as dead as can be. His companions howl with outrage when they see it, but their mounts have started to buck and whirl in a panic, so alarmed are they at the sudden violence.

One of the surviving Danes screams something about "betrayal" and makes a move as if to hurl his spear into my chest. His aim looks good, despite the antics of the frightened beast below him, and just as I think he's about to throw, he's stabbed through the small of his back by another of the men on foot, the point of his spear exiting the Dane's stomach in a welter of blood and viscera. I turn, afraid and unsure, only to see my guard is right there alongside me. He still has that look. I shouldn't have trusted him. He confirms it when he grips me by the shoulder and hauls me from my horse.

I land on my hands and knees, the grass, fortunately, absorbing much of the shock. I rise and clutch at my guard's mount, hoping to lay hands on the reins, but he kicks me in the chest and knocks me back, his animal whinnying disagreeably. My other supposedly loyal guards have finished off the Danes and are now advancing towards me, their spearheads slick and red. These are not my people anymore. Something has gone wrong. Eadric's men were supposed to protect me.

There's only one thing to do. I run for it, heading north to escape the clearing, my legs whipping through the grass. My guard, or would-be-assassin as he now appears, isn't expecting it, giving me precious time to skirt around his lumbering horse and make a mad dash away into the woods. I can hear the other three coming after me, but I'm lighter on my feet than they are, and they struggle to close the distance. I've also dropped my spear. It's for the best. Such a weapon wouldn't speed my escape. I still have my seax, at any rate.

I'm charging through an uncomfortably stubborn patch of ferns when it hits me. It's a solid mass, metal, leather, and sinew, and I know there's another assailant before I even manage to twist my head around to look him in the eye. I wish I hadn't. Those eyes. Those cold, green eyes. The same from the dream last night. It's all the same, his entire face, down to the last scar. It's him. And no resistance is possible.

He drags me back into the clearing, his arm locked around my neck. I get hold of my seax and pull it free, but he's suddenly got me by the wrist, as if some warrior's instinct told him what I had planned and urged him to act. He hits me, not with his hand but with his head, that damnably hard skull causing my nose to crack inwards. I drop my seax in shock, the taste of blood sharp upon my tongue. A shame. I really liked that weapon. I liked my nose too.

"Good work, Cenric."

I recognise the voice, and it's nice to be able to put a name to the man who's done me an injury. I'd say Cenric has every reason to be pleased with himself. I've never been so rapidly overpowered in a physical contest as I have here, and it doesn't wound the pride to admit that. The one speaking is more of a concern to me, though. I'm twisted around to face him, Cenric's unbearable strength holding me in place as my "guard" and his three men draw closer to witness the whole sorry spectacle. I know who they all serve now. He's standing right there. I can't look away. Cenric is too strong. I do the only thing I can do. I return the stare.

"I won't beg for my life, Ulfcytel."

I mean those words. As terrified as I am, I'm not about to humiliate myself before the ealdorman. He doesn't look angry to hear it. I can see the man I know him to be. He still has that same look he had when I left him at Hringmere. He's sad. He still can't believe what I did to him. He'll want to know why.

"Just tell me," he rumbles, his typically unkempt beard looking even wilder than I recall. "Why did you do it? I must know."

"You'll have guessed," I say. I've given up struggling against Cenric. It does me no good. "You were bound to lose at Hringmere," I add with a smirk. "I did what any sane man would do."

"You betrayed us. For him. For Eadric."

"Looks like you worked it all out yourself." I'm being evasive, but Ulfcytel must have had help to find out Eadric was involved. The ealdorman is not a clever man, in my opinion. He's a brute and a bore and liable to lose track of his own legs if not reminded. I wonder who he's had advising him all this time, or at least keeping him alive so he could somehow walk away from Canterburie. He wouldn't have been able to do all that on his own, would he?

"Why, though?" he asks. "Why target me? And why use you to do it?"

"It's a story as old as sin," I retort. "You were in his way. He wanted somebody he could trust in Hamptonscir once he'd dealt with Ælfric. It was a good deal. We stood to benefit greatly. We still might."

"You won't," he says flatly, his characteristic anger strangely absent. "I trusted you. We all did. We were fighting for our homes."

"Then you were a fool. My home was next to nothing. A duff village in a duff county with a duff ealdorman. Hamptonscir offered more." I jerk my head to the left, indicating my "guard" and his murderous associates who'd dispatched the Danes. "I thought I could trust these men. I couldn't, obviously. Both of us are capable of being fooled, Ulfcytel. Don't feel too bad about it."

"Good men died because of you."

His statement is accurate, I suppose, and he still sounds strangely calm, which is remarkable given how he'd act when insulted in the past. "And you did the same here," says Cenric this time, right into my ear. "Tell me, frightened one, was it you who hanged the man I left in charge of the fortress? Cuthbert was his name."

I nod weakly. It's no good denying it, for it was his family we used as leverage to get him to open the gates. Cenric doesn't reply, not with words, but he does tighten his grip on my arms, his horrifying strength causing my joints to crack and grind in helpless protest. He knows he won't get the killing blow. That'll go to Ulfcytel. But he can make me hurt in the meantime. And he does. He really, really does. I'm surprised I don't cry out.

More people have appeared, stepping into the clearing from the direction Cenric tackled me. I look over to them, the hundreds that have come, each of them edging out of the forest beyond to judge and witness. They are villagers, the regular people of Hamptonscir, armed with reaping hooks and the odd spear, a few also attired in flowing ring mail with stout linden shields. Ælfric, the old ruler of Hamptonscir, is leading them, with his red-haired daughter-in-law at his side. I remember them well and how they'd hurled insults at us from the walls of Porteceaster. They must have got free, somehow, and returned here with Ulfcytel, having these commoners join them to unseat me. Eadric and I should not have been so cruel to these people. That way, I might not have been undone.

I turn back to Ulfcytel, having grown uncomfortable staring at those hundreds of hard, unforgiving eyes. Nothing is improved by looking to the ealdorman. He has that sword in his hands, the one he always fought with, and it's obvious what he intends. It's a large, brutal thing; more hammer than blade, but it suits him, and it does a wondrous job of cleaving a straight gash across my jugular. Cenric lets me go, and I stagger forward several steps, unsure of what's even taken place. Ulfcytel walks away from me like I'm of no consequence, Cenric and the others following after him, several spitting upon the grass at my feet. I just stand there, confused, my hands reaching up to my throat. I think it's fine. Then the blood starts to flow, abundant, unceasing, unstoppable. I can't breathe. It's choking me. I fall to my knees. I'm afraid. This cannot be.

Ulfcytel looks back over his shoulder, his eyes locking with mine. There's anger there now, not heartbreak like before. He hates me, utterly, for my betrayal. He's right to. I understand how he feels, betrayed as I am, also. I made a grab for greatness, turning on my countrymen for the sake of personal power. I deserve what's happened, and I'm strangely at peace when it all goes dark, my last feeling that of the grass brushing my cheeks and my own spilt blood cooling upon my skin.

My name is Thurcytel, and I was a thegn of Eastengle and confidant of the Ealdorman Ulfcytel. When we gathered an army to oppose the invasion of our lands, I conspired with Eadric of Mierċe to encourage my lord to attack Thorkell's camp at Gipeswic, knowing the enemy had been warned in advance. I then betrayed my lord again, leading a good portion of his army away after he'd trusted me to command the flank attack as he met Thorkell's horde head-on. My reward for this was to be Porteceaster, once we'd seized it from the Ealdorman Ælfric, that is. We did so, of course, and as instructed, I held it these past months, hoping my services to Eadric might ultimately gain the good graces of our now absent King Æthelred.

Such prospects are out of reach now. They appear foolish; the ambitions of a man who lost himself to honeyed words and promises of power. As I die here, now, only one thought occurs to me. I should have listened to what poor Harold said to me upon the fields of Hringmere. For truly, what does it profit a man to gain the entire world and yet lose his very soul?

I

The abbey appeared as he'd expected, managing to look both impressive and humble at the same time. The stone chapel was the main feature, its narrow windows of stained glass drawing the eye, its outer walls darkened from the recent rain and yet no less beautiful for it. There were several outbuildings branching off from there, each of shorter stature and fashioned from thatch and clay brick, the smoking chimney that arose from one giving the impression this would be the monks' living quarters. Judging from the size of the place, there couldn't be too many of them present at any one time. That was good. Fewer people could only increase their chance of succeeding here.

It might not all be plain sailing, though. A wall encircled the whole site almost haphazardly, looking like it had been put together in ages past to give the monks a semblance of security. He was sure he could climb it if he had to, but he'd still rather use one of the two gates like the inhabitants would. Besides, if he vaulted the wall in a hurry, he'd land in those gardens and crush the leeks and carrots he could see growing there. That wouldn't be right. Most of the monks here had done nothing wrong. They didn't need him trampling his way through what was to be their next meal. It'd be rude.

As comforting a sight as the chapel was, the same couldn't be said for its surroundings. The village, Esledes, spilled out from the abbey wall, providing quite a contrast with the ordered and serene appearance of life there. It was overpopulated and dilapidated, the inhabitants at times subsisting in decaying wooden shacks with grass roofs. Many wandered the streets – if muddied paths topped with gravel could be called such – and were apparently without purpose, their threadbare rags doing little to comfort their emaciated flesh. There was at least some vigour here, the smithy and guest house looking like they still did a little trade from those passing through, but a bad feeling lingered over the place. War had taken its toll on England, and the people of Cantwara had paid a hefty share of it.

"It's a sorry-looking dump, but in a way that'll make this easier. The abbot won't be inclined to mix with these impoverished locals. He'll be in the abbey, like the oh-so-holy man he is. Now we just need to think on how to get in."

Osbert turned to look at Eamon from their vantage point amid the trees. They'd been scrambling through the woods for the better part of a day to reach this place. They'd avoided the roads, thinking them unsafe now that Lundenburg had fallen and Svienn would be looking to extend his grip over the surrounding scirs. What they had planned required a certain subtlety that wouldn't be served by lumbering about in the open. Stealth and deception were their methods now. He wished it wasn't so.

"We should go down then," said Osbert, pulling the hood of his cloak further forward over his head. "I'd like to scout the place out so we're prepared if anything goes wrong."

"What do you think is going to go wrong?" Eamon asked gruffly.

"I don't know...but it pays to be prepa..."

"You're overthinking it," said Eamon. "Our success here depends on us fitting in like we're any other poor bastard refugee on the road. If we're seen wandering around for the sake of it, we'll attract unwelcome attention."

Osbert pondered his words. Eamon was a quiet one, and sometimes he didn't know what to make of him, but he did tend to talk sense. Alaric had always seemed to respect and trust him, and as far as Osbert was concerned, that meant he should probably do the same. Alaric had been a fine man. A kind man. Osbert could attest to that. Their gentle conversations had helped him a great deal after his own…trauma…at Hringmere. He would be forever grateful to him for those small mercies. He wished he'd had the chance to tell him that.

"You're not wrong," Osbert conceded. "We shouldn't waste time then. Let's just…well…what shall we do?"

"We'll sit in the guest house and look miserable," said Eamon. "We have enough coin to give ourselves a good feed before we get down to business. If anyone asks, we can say we're from Offetuna."

"But we have come from Offetuna."

"Exactly, we won't be telling lies then, will we? No need to go to confession and all. That's a real win for us."

Osbert smiled, but Eamon just stared at him, his face blank apart from an almost imperceptible smirk twitching at his mouth's left side. That was as good as it was going to get in terms of Eamon actually laughing, and his expression soon returned to its usual slab-like solidity. That was that, then. There was no need to waste any more time. They broke cover, emerging from the tree line with easy, confident steps, their cloaks and hoods wrapped tight against the damp chill. They had work to do, and it couldn't wait.

The village somehow managed to look even worse up close. The huts and hovels had a stagnant air to them, and the people were about as piteous as one could imagine, each man and woman looking as if their sorrow had been carved onto their faces to age them beyond the measure of their days. Osbert felt nothing but regret and lamentation. It was one thing to be in this situation and be young and fast and well-armed, as he was, but something else to be unschooled in war and ill-prepared when it came calling. These were such people, and they'd had no option but to flee to wherever they might find safety. Apparently, they'd decided Esledes might be such a haven.

At first, Osbert had been surprised at that. From what he could tell, this place had been close to Thorkell's line of advance as he'd marched to attack Canterburie last year, and so it was a mystery why the village and abbey were even intact. He didn't know and didn't want to know how a murdering monster like Thorkell might think, but he could only assume he'd become so intent on reaching Canterburie he'd simply passed Esledes by without bothering to burn it down. That struck him as strange. The Danes always, always targeted holy places if they could, and not purely because they often contained valuables of a material nature. They meant something to the English, and to see them despoiled hurt in ways that were beyond physical. That was why they did it. Only a fool would claim it was merely about gold and silver.

They reached the guest house, the two men gazing up at its modest, tumbledown structure as if suddenly unsure of venturing within. Eamon snapped out of it, striding forward and through the open entrance with his usual confidence, Osbert following after him with all necessary haste. It was gloomy inside, but it wasn't too crowded, and its four soot-smeared walls at least provided a modicum of warmth. It was unusually cold for this time of year. Osbert didn't care for it.

They sat in the corner, facing the door and doing their best to look as tired and unapproachable as the rest of the patrons. The one who owned this place was an absolute rake of a man, all height and no muscle, but he was pleasant enough and more than willing to take a few coins in exchange for a half-decent meal. Eamon tucked into it, slurping his porridge like he'd not eaten in days, although his eyes never ceased to flit back to the entrance whenever opportunity arose. Osbert understood. They had work to be done here. They couldn't get comfortable just because they had food and warmth to soothe them. Once they'd eaten, they'd set themselves to their task.

Osbert took a sip of ale. It was foamy but refreshing, having a somewhat aggressive bite that reminded him of a local brew he was quite partial to back home in Noruic. He pushed the thought to one side. Noruic was gone, as was the cheerful old man who used to make such a beverage. Thorkell hadn't shown any restraint after he'd smashed their army aside at Hringmere. Noruic had burned, and there had been nothing they could do to save it.

He liked to think that things might be different now. They'd suffered defeat after defeat, it was true, and a foreigner had seized Lundenburg to dare call himself king, but all wasn't lost. They had Edmund. Edmund was an Englishman, through and through, with the blood and right to claim the throne and hack Svienn's head from his shoulders. His father may be the coward who had gotten them into this mess, but Osbert could see well enough how Edmund was cut from a different cloth. He was a man of destiny, and with the indomitable Ulfcytel at his side, he simply could not lose. Good things could only come of this.

He started to think on Ulfcytel, wondering how he could be faring. They'd been on the road with him just days ago, him and Eamon, all heading south with Ælfric, the Ealdorman of Hamptonscir, and his daughter-in-law, Æva, who was also the widow of their great friend, Alaric. They'd taken just a few people with them from Edmund's entourage at Offetuna, hoping to travel fast to skirt around Svienn's forces in Lundenburg and get into Hamptonscir. Edmund was to head to the Five Boroughs, recruiting himself an army once he got there, but Ulfcytel and Ælfric were to raise Hamptonscir's people against a man named Thurcytel, who was a pawn of the villainous Ealdorman Eadric.

Osbert couldn't guess as to their chances, but he knew it was important that Edmund gain another base of support if he were to fight Svienn and take back his throne. Returning Hamptonscir to the hands of Ælfric would be a start. He'd been quite vocal about his loyalty and hope for Edmund, and he'd also apparently displayed some bravery in their escape from Lundenburg. He'd grieved for Alaric, also. They all had. His death had been a great shock, and Osbert still wasn't sure how to handle it. The pain was so fresh, burrowing into his vitals and refusing to leave. He couldn't think of it for long. Not when he had work to do. He'd mourn his lost friend when opportunity came.

That, sadly, might not happen for a while. The name Thurcytel was a hateful one to Osbert, and it was for that reason he'd been particularly enthusiastic about catching up with him. Osbert had been at Hringmere, and he could well remember how Thurcytel had droned on about history and heroism in Ulfcytel's pavilion the night Eadric had come and encouraged them to attack Thorkell through stealth. Osbert had thought it impressive at the time, but then Thorkell had led his army north to face them anyway, having survived Alaric's attempt to end him through assassination. Osbert wasn't privy to Ulfcytel's plan for the ensuing battle, but whatever he'd intended, he was quite sure it hadn't involved Thurcytel leading his men in retreat at the critical moment. To think he'd been working with Eadric all along wasn't too hard to believe, and thus the news that he'd resurfaced as the man of authority in Porteceaster was too convenient. Eadric must have rewarded him for his services. He'd get another type of reward now. Ulfcytel would see to that.

Yet Osbert wouldn't witness any of it. He and Eamon had a different task, one given to them by Ulfcytel himself and one both of them would take no small measure of satisfaction in completing. They'd been wanting to get even with the abbot. Now they might have that opportunity.

It had all begun a couple of nights ago. They'd halted in the woods, Ulfcytel and the others, hoping to rest awhile before resuming their mad dash south through what was left of Cantwara. Osbert and Eamon had been sent on ahead to scout the road, hoping to discover any travellers who might have information or had perhaps heard talk of Svienn's actions in the capital. They'd discovered an inn on a narrow, broken path, the soot stains on its walls and fresh thatch upon its roof implying it had recently been set on fire. They'd ventured in, intending to mix with the locals and pick up any useful gossip. What they'd heard had changed their plans altogether. Abbot Ælfmær was alive.

Osbert hadn't at first wanted to take the monks seriously. They were drunk and yammering on, complaining about how the abbot had taken over their abbey at Esledes and wasn't "an easy man to like". Eamon had talked to them awhile, acting as casual as he could, and before long both he and Osbert were satisfied there was some truth to what was being said. Ælfmær, the traitorous bastard who'd allowed Thorkell entry into Canterburie, was alive and within striking distance at Esledes. This was too good an opportunity to miss. Ælfmær had to die. There was no forgiveness for what he'd done, and now they had the means to get to him.

Ulfcytel had agreed. He'd been quite boisterous when they'd told him back at their camp, and he'd at first wanted to head out immediately, storming into Esledes with everything they had and dragging the abbot outside for a summary execution. Old Ælfric had awoken and approached, his well-reasoned words allowing tempers to cool and the bigger picture to come into focus. Osbert was glad he'd spoken up when he had.

They should press on to Hamptonscir, Ælfric had said, yet send a smaller force of perhaps one or two men to Esledes to confirm whether the rumour of the abbot was even true. If it were, justice could be done, and they need not risk upsetting their whole plan by coming out into the open and perhaps alerting Svienn to their presence. A full intervention in pursuit of the abbot was likely to do that, and they couldn't raise Hamptonscir for Edmund if they all died causing chaos in some village for the sake of old scores.

Ulfcytel wasn't a stupid man. Passionate, yes, and prone to anger, but he'd discerned the wisdom in Ælfric's words. They would send just two men to deal with the abbot and see Canterburie avenged. Osbert had been proud to be chosen as one of them.

And why would he not have been? He'd served Ulfcytel for years, and he and Eamon had both fought at Canterburie and lived to endure the horrors of captivity there. They'd seen Ælfmær outside the cathedral after the battle, free to walk among the Danes, and all who saw it had known him for the traitor he was. His death was owed. Too many had suffered because of him. Blood would be shed. His blood, ideally, and lots of it.

Osbert took another swig of his ale, looking again to Eamon and how he never seemed to stop scrutinising their fellow patrons, even whilst he ate. He was a mysterious man, Eamon was, and despite their travels together, Osbert knew little about him. He'd fought with them in Eastengle, and fought well, as he'd been one of the warriors Alaric had brought with him when he'd first rushed to their aid just before the Battle of Hringmere. He'd been all hate and rage during their imprisonment in Canterburie, and he'd been grieved to hear of Alaric's death during Svienn's attack on Lundenburg, but apart from that Osbert had never known him to display much emotion. There was a blankness to him, a numbness, almost, and Osbert felt like he could on some level understand it. War and death hardened a man. Osbert knew all about that. He'd never again be the callow youth of days gone by, not after what he'd been through this last year. From appearances, Eamon had been changed also, albeit perhaps a long time ago, his heart breaking and hardening over and over from one horrific experience after another. Osbert didn't envy him. He hoped that perhaps one day he might speak of it.

They finished eating, necking the last of their ale a moment later. Osbert was just about to stand up and head outside when Eamon bade him wait, nodding towards someone who'd just wandered in.

It was a monk, from the abbey, and they were sitting down at a table close to the doors, the innkeeper already rushing them a flagon of mead. He drank, pulling back the hood of his dark habit to reveal his face. He was young, with fair hair and complexion, yet he looked troubled, as though he was hoping to numb himself to his sorrows before heading back to face them.

"I had a feeling it would be like this," murmured Eamon quietly, having leaned in slightly so Osbert could hear him. "Those drunken monks we encountered on the road…I didn't think they'd be the only ones here to indulge. When an abbey has a problem with vice, it rarely stays contained. I'll wager a lot of the monks here enjoy a tipple, if you know what I mean."

Osbert nodded, still observing the monk, who had somehow already finished his flagon and was gesturing for another. "It's a sad sight," Osbert eventually said. "Do you think the abbot has driven them to drink? He is a proper bastard, after all."

"It's possible, but my instincts tell me this is a long-running problem," sighed Eamon. "Life is hard here, and sometimes God can seem very, very far away, even for those who you'd think would be closest to him. The good abbot is undoubtedly a headache for this poor young man, but he won't be the sole source of his problems."

"So what shall we do?" asked Osbert, feeling awkward to be talking about this fellow as if they had any right to judge him.

"We buy him a round," said Eamon as he got to his feet, his voice suddenly at a normal volume. Osbert went to object, but Eamon had already begun moving away from their table and on a direct course for the monk. Osbert followed, feeling unsure, and before long they were sat facing across from the monk, who was staring back at them like he was caught between deciding to fight them or run for the hills.

"Pardon the intrusion," said Eamon confidently, signalling also for the innkeeper to come serve them. "But we are new here and would speak with someone from the abbey. You are such a man, yes?"

"What gave it away?" smirked the monk, gesturing slightly towards his roughly-sewn habit. "Did you think I dress like this because I enjoy it?"

"I have no idea," said Eamon quickly, Osbert feeling a little shocked by the monk's peculiarly irreverent manner. "But I would ask if it's possible for us to visit the abbey, we..."

"Nobody is permitted to visit," said the monk darkly. "And no, there'll be no exceptions. The new abbot is very strict. He survived Canterburie, so he's as tough as old leather, and about as easy to talk to."

"Canterburie, you say?" breathed Eamon, doing well to feign shock. The innkeeper had by now appeared, bearing three additional flagons, the monk having again somehow finished his drink already. They all supped for a moment or two, the innkeeper scuttling off to add to their tab.

"Yes, Canterburie," said the monk, placing his flagon down, his pale moustache now covered with foam. "And thanks for the beer, stranger, but if you're thinking this will get you into the abbey, I'm afraid the answer is still no. Like I said, Abbot Ælfmær won't allow it, and after surviving what happened at Canterburie, he's not the kind of man you'd be wise to cross."

"Just how did he live through that?" asked Osbert, thinking he'd been silent for too long. "We'd heard the siege was terrible, and few were able to escape. God must have been smiling on your abbot that day."

"It's a hard thing to imagine," said the monk, his smirk returning. "The abbot isn't a...he's not a kind man. Not a charitable man. Intense, is the word I'd choose. I'd say that helped him get away from that whole situation. If God was involved...well, the Lord works with what he has, sinners and bastards included. Perhaps Ælfmær is more than he appears."

Osbert took another mouthful of ale, wondering if the monk was implying something or just thinking aloud. "Then I think it's only fair we tell you that is not the case," said Eamon suddenly, Osbert's eyes widening as an unsettling feeling rose from his stomach. "You see, we were at Canterburie too, right in the thick of it...and somebody betrayed us to the enemy, allowing them inside the walls. We think your abbot had something to do with that."

Osbert did his best to contain his angst, fearing Eamon's sudden bout of honesty might cause the monk to turn hostile or raise the alarm. "I have heard that rumour," said the monk after taking another long draught from his tankard. "So if you're thinking to shock me, you can think again. Everyone can work out there's something wrong with the abbot just from meeting him. That's why people are leaving. Well, two, at any rate."

"Your brothers are fleeing the abbey?" asked Osbert, relieved for the moment that nothing had escalated.

"Two, as I said. A few nights back, so it was...they just left. They were a right pair, drank more than I did, even...but I hope they are safe wherever they end up. They didn't like Ælfmær. They thought it odd the way he turned up here with an escort right after Lundenburg fell to Svienn. Felt like something was up. I don't blame them."

"We met them on the road," said Eamon, Osbert again alarmed at his habit of being so honest. "They didn't seem happy with the situation. Neither are we. Something has to be done. Your abbot did things at Canterburie, things no man should just walk away from. If you care about what's right…"

The monk turned pale, like he was finally seeing Eamon for what he was and what he intended to do. "You want me to help you kill him, is that it? I can't. He's here because of the Danes…King Svienn…he left…"

His voice fell to silence, and he suddenly rose and made a dash for the door, his face a mask of worry. Eamon and Osbert pursued, trying to be subtle about it lest they alarm their fellow drinkers. The innkeeper shouted an objection as they slipped through the door, bellowing something about their tab, but they otherwise made it outside, the monk hurrying on ahead, the village now bathed in the fading orange of twilight.

"You shouldn't have been so damn blatant about everything," hissed Osbert, keeping pace with Eamon as they continued to follow the monk through the streets and back towards the abbey. "What good did it serve telling him who we were? He'd have been able to work out what we wanted easily enough. No wonder he's terrified!"

"I miscalculated," replied Eamon, his voice flat. "I thought if he hated the abbot, he'd want to help. Now I fear…"

Eamon suddenly accelerated, rushing ahead of Osbert to accost the monk and drag him out of sight down a narrow alleyway. Osbert ran after them, shocked again at Eamon's recklessness, only to find him with his arm around the monk's neck as if to choke the very life from him. Osbert protested, his voice hushed, fearing this sudden violence would only draw attention, despite the cover provided by the shadows. Eamon ignored him, and the monk promptly passed out, his face as red as clay and his body entirely limp. Eamon laid him out upon the earth, his movements now deceptively gentle.

"Don't worry, he's alive," he said quietly. "Now just wait there and…"

Eamon got to work, relieving the unconscious monk of his habit and sandals, leaving him almost entirely naked. "Put all this on," he said, pressing the clothes into Osbert's unwilling hands. "Be quick! This is an opportunity for us to get into the abbey and do what has to be done."

Osbert wasn't happy about any of this, but Eamon was right on that last point. They did have an opportunity here, and so Osbert quickly stripped down to his undergarments, having not the time nor will for modesty. He hauled the monk's habit over his head, allowing the dark, roughspun fabric to cover him to the ankles, and slipped his bare feet into the rather large sandals. He pulled his hood up and partially over his face, knowing he'd do well to keep his visage concealed once inside the abbey. He kept his belt on underneath his robe, his seax also hidden there for safekeeping. He'd need to kill once inside, and his bare hands couldn't be relied on to make it quick, clean, and quiet. A proper blade was a must.

"Now go, brother!" said Eamon, deadly serious. "I'll mind our friend here. You get into that abbey, find that bastard Ælfmær, and take his damn head off for what he did to Canterburie!"

"I just want to say…"

"Don't bother," said Eamon, suddenly pulling Osbert closer to speak into his ear. "I know I fouled up here. It was a risk to just think this man would hate Ælfmær enough to help us. I'll make it up to you. But for now…do what has to be done. For Canterburie! For Alaric!"

Eamon's hold lessened, and Osbert stepped back from him, his face flushed with emotion at the mention of Alaric. He nodded once and set off, traversing the alley's entire length to take him out of the shadows and back into the light of the dwindling sunset. The abbey was just about visible to the north and east, so Osbert set off, trying to look casual, hoping he appeared as any other monk returning home for the sake of vespers.

He made it to the wall and its western gate, his journey thankfully unremarked by the relatively few people still out in the streets. He passed within into the vegetable gardens he'd spied earlier, moving past rows of carefully tended carrots, the abbey itself casting yet deeper shadows as the sun continued its long fade to the horizon.

He reached the main entrance to the chapel, the muffled, gentle sound of a choir drifting out into the evening air. He tried the doors, half-expecting them to be locked, and true enough they were until somebody suddenly opened them up from the inside. The monk had a hedge for a beard, erupting from his face in a wild tangle of silver and white, but he otherwise paid Osbert no mind, permitting him to enter without so much as a single word of inquiry. He mumbled his thanks, his hood still up to hide his face, relieved he'd at least gotten inside without any more trouble.

The scene that greeted him was truly something. There were more monks here, standing in rows facing a cross and altar, their heads bowed whilst they sang in gratitude to the Lord for another day as part of His flock. The chapel was more spacious than he'd assumed, yet it was still a humble place, lacking much in ornamentation aside from several holy icons placed to the right and left of the altar. The scant light from several large candles flickered across them, illuminating an image of Christ and what looked like Saint Edmund, the Patron Saint of England. The place was otherwise dark and getting darker, yet the gentle glow of the candles seemed all the more precious because of it, creating a very palpable sense of sacral mystery. He'd have liked to have stayed and joined the monks in prayer, if he could. Sadly, he hadn't the time, and his situation required him to avoid anything that might lead to undue scrutiny. His disguise would only go so far.

Things became a little more complicated when he realised the abbot wasn't here. Osbert remembered him well, especially his irritatingly sharp, nasal voice, and he wasn't present with the others now, which meant he'd have to search the place and find him. He turned right, skirting the edge of the congregation and sticking close to the shadows, hoping his decision not to join in with the singing would go unnoticed. A smaller door appeared out of the darkness before him, and so he passed through, heading into the western wing of the abbey, the corridor he was now shuffling down looking like it hadn't been dusted properly in years.

Osbert took a left and then a right, wandering up another stretch of dusty hallway until he came to an unusually well-polished door set into an equally well-chiselled stone archway. It had a feeling to it, like there was something significant just beyond, or perhaps a person of repute had decided to take up residence here. It made sense. Most of the abbey was all dust and bare stone, but this door was almost sparkling, as though somebody had gone to great efforts to clear it of the grime and neglect so common everywhere else. There was likely only one reason for that, Osbert thought. These were the abbot's living quarters. He was lucky to have found them so quickly.

He eased the door ajar and slid through. A warm glow emanated across his path from the fire smouldering in the grate to his left, the view immediately ahead of him also illuminated by a trio of candles placed atop a desk pushed back against the far wall. A robed figure sat there, hunched upon a stool and keeping its back to him as it read from what looked like a sizeable tome perched on a stand adjacent to the candles. Osbert took a step forward, a glimmer of recognition stirring in his memory. That had to be the abbot up ahead. He couldn't see his face, but he had a bad air to him, just like he had that night he'd come to argue with Ulfcytel, Alaric, and Archbishop Ælfheah about how Thorkell was somehow God's instrument. Osbert could recall all of it, just as he recalled the sick feeling Ælfmær had left in his stomach long after he'd departed. He had that same feeling now. This would hopefully be over quickly.

He took another step forward, then another and another, and reached inside his robe to rest his hand on the hilt of his seax. He felt reassured at its touch, and by the time he'd reached striking distance, he'd already removed it from his belt. The abbot didn't react, lost in thought and peering at his pages, his only movement the lifting of his right hand to his mouth as he went to clear his throat. Osbert placed his blade there, the keen edge pressing tight against yielding flesh. Ælfmær froze, staring straight ahead at the wall. He then spoke, his voice low but as sharp as Osbert remembered.

"Canterburie, yes?"

He'd come to the point quickly. A guilty conscience, that was, and it would do him no good. "If you'd speak a final prayer, abbot," Osbert whispered through bared teeth, "then I would not stop you. If you cry out for help, I'll make this considerably more painful than necessary."

"I believe you," he said sadly. "And you were there, I assume? I know there were at least some survivors and something about a prison break afterwards. Thorkell is quite chatty at times, believe it or not. For an instrument of God, he certainly is stra..."

"Silence, you blasphemous dog!" snarled Osbert. "I still remember the rot you spoke that night when we all thought the Ealdorman Ulfcytel might tear you apart for it! God is just! Not a puppeteer for savage killers!"

"I won't bother to turn and try and look at you," sighed Ælfmær. "But I think I know your voice. I have an excellent memory. And I don't hate you for hating me. I understand. It's a hard message for some to hear. Did our Lord Jesus also not face rejection when he..."

"Enough, heretic! A final prayer and then I'll open your throat! Another word and I'll have your guts spilled over this desk!"

"A kind offer...in that case..."

The abbot began to mutter softly, his hands held up and pinned close to his chest. Osbert kept his blade pressed against the side of his neck, the sharp iron digging into the skin, blood already welling up around its edge. The muttering kept on and on, growing in intensity, Osbert wondering if he were reciting multiple psalms from memory.

"I'm finished," said the abbot with some considerable finality. "And so are you."

Something smashed into Osbert from the side. He staggered and spun, trying to regain his balance, only to crash into the wall close to the hearth. Somebody else was in the room. He didn't know how he'd not spotted them, but they were here, now, and with every advantage. They lashed out again, kicking him in the stomach and striking him across the face, a third blow seeing his seax slip from grasp and clatter to the floor. He was then grabbed by the throat, and what felt like a head-butt catapulted him into a state of semi-consciousness. He tasted blood. His legs went limp. It was too hard to stand. The old wound in his collarbone hurt. Why couldn't he have just killed the abbot as soon as he'd been within reach?

He was hit again, something solid and metallic cracking him across the head. He saw the abbot, standing there like he was presiding over Mass, his eyes empty. Osbert still couldn't see his attacker properly, but he could make out a burly figure at the edge of his sight, and then something more. The glint of mail in firelight. A flash of blond hair. Cold sapphires for eyes. A Dane. Like any other he'd fought, but here in the abbey? As some kind of bodyguard? Ælfmær's dealings with these people must have been more involved than he'd thought. Perhaps King Svienn had heard of what he'd done at Canterburie and been pleased by it. It stood to reason he'd also think the traitorous bastard would need protecting. He'd been quite correct in that.

"I'm sorry about this, young one," said Ælfmær, the slightest hint of regret entering his voice, "but God's plan for both myself and England didn't end with Canterburie. There is much work to be done, and I will not be dissuaded from my task by the likes of you. I suggest you use this moment to reflect on whether God really would approve of murdering me here, given how things have turned out. Then prepare your soul for what lies ahead. I fear an accounting is about to be demanded of you, and it will not be gentle."

II

"I baptise you in the name of the Father..."

The bishop fumbles, nearly dropping the Norwegian backwards into the water. He gets control, dipping him somewhat awkwardly into the elongated wooden tub and then out again for the next immersion.

"...and of the Son..."

The second time is perfect, or as close as it possibly can be to perfection. The bishop is quite strong, despite his deceptively slight figure. It was good that he was. Olaf isn't the smallest of men. Not by far.

"...and of the Holy Spirit."

That was enough. Olaf Haraldsson struggled from his grasp, his face wrinkled inwards in irritation. He coughs and gasps and then sneezes twice, the latter likely a result of some water vanishing up his sizeable nostrils. He looks annoyed, but it passes, and he soon stands up and away from the tub to gaze on his audience. So very many had gathered here in the cathedral to see him become a Christian. From the looks of it, he appreciated them.

And well he should. This was a spectacular venue, and the nave was filled to bursting, occupied by what looked like almost the entirety of Duke Richard's court and whoever else had managed to squeeze in here. The Danes were an object of curiosity to the Normans, Æthelred knew, and as French as they otherwise liked to think they were, none of them seemed to be able to shake off a fascination with their more northern forebears. It was understandable. History and ancestry mattered, even if the average Norman today was as French in customs and mannerisms as anyone else further south. They had an interest in where they thought they'd originally come from. That interest had been piqued even further by Olaf's decision to be baptised. None of Rouen's wealthy and powerful wanted to miss this, and Rouen had a lot of wealthy and powerful people.

The cathedral was impressive, at least to Æthelred. It reminded him somewhat of Canterburie, before Thorkell's army had torched it, but the Normans had a certain architectural style that he wasn't sure he favoured. There was an almost brutal edge to what they made, and this place of holiness was no different, being of a form to overawe the senses in a manner that wasn't entirely pleasant. Like Canterburie, it echoed over and over, every move of the body or word of mouth seeming to reverberate about its vast interior so that everyone always knew what was happening regardless of where they stood. Olaf's sneezes had thus had an almost apocalyptic effect on the ears. He was thankfully quiet now. And he was looking straight at Æthelred.

Æthelred studied his face from his vantage point at the front of the crowd. He looked as he had that day Thorkell had introduced them shortly before the battle at Bernecestre. There were some differences, of course, as then he'd been attired in mail and furs, casting a far more imposing figure than he did now whilst he shivered in his white gown. He still looked young, but not too young to be a man of war, and he retained a certain air of innocence that was totally at odds with the fearsome deeds he was already renowned for on the battlefield.

"He seems happy. God is with him."

Æthelred stared down at his son, Edward. He didn't return his father's gaze, instead keeping his eyes on Olaf as he shuffled towards them. If Olaf hadn't changed, then Edward certainly had. He'd grown, physically and otherwise, both of which came as a surprise considering they hadn't been in Normandy long. He kept making strange claims, too, like he had just now, and Æthelred wasn't sure what to make of it.

Thorkell was the first to congratulate Olaf. He intercepted him before he could reach Æthelred, the mail-clad giant offering the younger man his hand. Æthelred noted how the bishop was keeping his distance, as if he knew Thorkell remained dangerous and it would be wise to give him a wide berth. Æthelred frowned when Thorkell and Olaf embraced, the two men hammering at each other's backs in what he presumed to be some kind of display of affection. He couldn't get over how pleased Olaf seemed to be. Was the man actually sincere in his conversion?

The crowd started singing, filling the cathedral to the rafters with a somewhat discordant rendition of Psalm 51. Olaf knelt for another blessing, and the bishop obliged, coming as close to Thorkell as he dared. The latter remained as he was, looking strangely curious and perhaps wishing to find out more. Æthelred could hear Emma's voice from just behind him, sounding sweet and delicate in contrast to the hoarse racket emitted by several others. She was easily the best singer here and possibly the only reason his ears hadn't detached from his head in a bid to make their escape. She sounded beautiful, but her countrymen were a strange, dry, and aloof people, and their singing was much the same. They made him miss England. Not being king of it, no, but he missed the land and those who called it home. He hoped he'd get to see it again before his end.

Olaf had made his way over to him, Thorkell predictably at his back. The crowd eased away slightly at his approach, Æthelred, Edward, Emma, and their protector, Hereward, being the only ones to hold their ground. Æthelred was used to them both now. They were his men, paid to do his will during his time in exile, whatever that might be. They'd proven they could be trusted if given enough reason and, most importantly, enough money. The time of struggle and strife between them was over.

"Do I meet with your approval, king?"

Æthelred paused a moment, wondering if Olaf was intending to mock him. He wasn't a man who needed the approval of others to do something like this. It had been an unusual thing to request, yes, but he hadn't needed approval. He'd answer him as such.

"I didn't know that you needed my approval, Olaf. Do you wish for my blessing?"

Thorkell sniggered to himself, his arms folding over his vast barrel of a chest as he loomed menacingly over Olaf's shoulder. Olaf, for his part, didn't find anything remotely amusing about the situation. "If you will, king, I would hold such a thing close to my heart," he said, and then actually knelt before Æthelred and Edward both, his eyes averting to stare at the stone slabs at their feet. The singing stopped. All had turned to look, each and every witness bemused by the spectacle. Æthelred just stared for a moment. Sincere or not, Olaf had put him in a peculiar position here. He had to appear to do the right thing, even if he didn't quite understand the reason for it.

"I...welcome you to our Christian brotherhood," Æthelred began. "May God bless and keep you now that the Evil One's hold upon you is broken...and may you remain safe in the embrace of our Lord until the end of your days...and after."

A few moments passed, the cathedral remaining strangely quiet. Olaf finally looked up, a grin on his face and his eyes sparkling in genuine elation. He was back on his feet in an instant, his head bowed slightly as he stood before Æthelred. "Thank you, good king, for the blessing...and for taking me into your service to give me the opportunity to be here today."

Æthelred nodded, acknowledging Olaf's words and hoping he'd stomp off somewhere to celebrate. If he was confused by all this, he wasn't alone. Thorkell also looked a little perplexed, wondering perhaps why Olaf had wanted such a blessing and why indeed he'd wanted to become Christian to begin with. The crowd, however, was visibly moved by all this, and was enthusiastically applauding like their exchange was the highlight of the afternoon. Perhaps he'd been wrong about these people. They did have souls, after all.

He felt Emma prodding his back urgently. He turned, trying not to be irritated whilst he leaned in so she'd whisper into his ear. "My brother is leaving!" she hissed urgently. "I know the look he has...he's angry."

Æthelred stared out across the throng, hoping to lay eyes on the duke and catch him for an exchange of words. He felt he knew what the issue was. Richard was a jealous man, and Olaf had made a blunder by approaching Æthelred first rather than prostrating himself before the duke. It was petty, but Æthelred could somewhat understand it. It would be to their benefit if he could catch Richard and smooth his feathers. They were dependent on his hospitality, after all.

He also wanted to get back to his chambers. He was cold, and Edward would need something to eat, and as fascinating and welcome as Olaf's baptism was, he really didn't care all that much about it, especially when he could be spending time with his family. He turned away, taking Emma by the arm, and moved back through the crowd towards the cathedral's narthex. Hereward lumbered after him, his powerful, mailed figure drawing a few anxious looks. Æthelred quite liked the attention he provoked. Hereward reminded everyone he still had some strength and wasn't afraid to display it, even in a place such as this.

They exited the cathedral, passing through one final imposing stone archway to make it out into the main street that cut through the city on its way to the river. Emma was prattling on about the need to hurry after her brother, but Æthelred still couldn't see him, even without the gossiping crowd they'd just escaped obstructing his vision. He took a deep breath before easing himself down the stone steps into the street, noting how the air in the city always seemed so fragrant. Rouen was clean, or at least cleaner than many other comparable places, its well-tended byways and gardens looking out of place and out of time in contrast to what he'd been used to in Lundenburg. He missed his city, but he didn't miss how it had suffered in the last years of his reign. This place was a breath of fresh air, literally and figuratively.

That, of course, wasn't the whole picture, and Æthelred knew it. This was the "good" part of the city, far away from the hustle and bustle of the riverside docks and whatever dubious items were offered there. Rouen had in the not-so-distant past been a focal point for the Danes and the North in general, with many a raider and reaver looking to offload the spoils they'd only just recently looted from England. Slaves had been brought here, snatched from English hearths to be sold openly in Norman markets, and as far as Æthelred was aware, the practice hadn't been stopped for long. He was glad his marriage to Emma had finally prompted better behaviour from the Normans. He hadn't wanted to consider another military expedition to try and compel them to close their ports to the enemy. He'd tried that before. The cost had been great.

Æthelred had a feeling he knew where their easily offended duke had gone. Indeed, after a short journey through the streets they'd reached his keep and passed within, predictably finding him perched atop his modest throne and leafing through a book, two stony-faced guards on either side of him. His "keep" was an ugly thing, like a square, squat lump of darkened stone, but it was large and easily defended, and it was for this reason Æthelred was glad to be able to now call it home. It was an absolute warren inside, full of passageways and side chambers that boggled his mind, but the duke's throne room was quite pleasant. It was a shame that couldn't be said for him.

Duke Richard looked up as they approached, their footsteps echoing loudly on the polished wooden flooring. Æthelred stopped in front of him, staring into his eyes in the hope of gauging his mood. Richard was a vibrant fellow, energetic and youthful, with a sharp voice and a sharper gaze that at times reminded him of Emma. His throne was positioned on a narrow dais, and the walls immediately behind it were decorated with banners, some of them so elaborate and garish Æthelred couldn't begin to guess why anyone would think to have made them, let alone display them.

They had something to do with Richard's family history, that he could recall. He was proud of that, so Emma had said, but Æthelred personally had little interest in Richard's lineage, thinking it likely his kin were or had all been snakes, aside from Emma, naturally. Æthelred's relationship with the Normans and their duke had been strained in the past, and as much as he loved the man's sister, he just couldn't bring himself to entirely trust him. He was egotistical, dressed in his flamboyant, unnecessarily expensive robes, and quick to judge, thinking his own voice always had to take priority over all others. He mistook it for decisiveness, most likely, but Æthelred knew better. Richard was arrogant and prone to anger. His sudden departure from the cathedral was just another example of that.

And yet there appeared to be a sad quality to him today. His green eyes were faded, and his mouth, strangely small for a man of his size, was bent downward at the edges, his trim, dark beard doing little to conceal it. Hardly anyone else was here for him to lord it over, his loyal subjects seeming to have remained at the cathedral for the time being. Judging from the look on his face, he wasn't too happy about it. He needed cheering up. Æthelred would try his luck at it.

"You look sad, brother," he began, doing his best to appear jovial. "Why did you leave? After all, you were Olaf's sponsor, were you not? Surely he would have liked to honour you…"

"As he did with you?" asked Richard with a slight shake of his head. "That was not a proper display back there. I was due foremost respect as his sponsor. Kneeling before you like that, without so much as a glance in my direction…"

"Don't take it personally, Richard," Æthelred counselled. "Olaf helped destroy much of my kingdom before he finally saw sense and came over to my service. I've tried to forgive him for it. If I can forgive something like that, I think you have it in you to forgive a certain…breach of protocol."

"I sponsored him, my own brother baptised him," Richard said, his complaints aimed at nobody in particular. "This is just odd, Æthel…Æthel…"

"Æthelred."

"Yes, I know!" the duke spluttered, his habit of mispronouncing English names a peculiar one, given its longevity. "But what I am saying is this is not how we do things in Normandy. Your man, Olaf, shows promise, and I see that in him and work to bring it out, yet he ignores me like that in public to greet you first as part of his new life in Christ. I do not understand. You tell me how this makes sense."

"I think you're reading too much into it," Æthelred said frankly. "Olaf and Thorkell know nothing of courtly life here or anywhere else. This world to them is largely alien. Olaf almost certainly wants to speak with you and would have, had you remained. He meant no harm."

"I don't know who these people are supposed to be, aside from a massive headache," Richard continued, his complaints still plentiful. "I can barely understand them much of the time, if ever. Why did you bring them here after they'd caused you so much…upset?"

"They served well enough during the siege of Lundenburg," replied Æthelred. "Besides, Olaf is Thorkell's man, and we all can agree, I'm sure, that we need to keep Thorkell happy. He's so troublesome when he doesn't get what he wants. You've noticed this, yes?"

"I noticed you were unable to defeat him," Richard said acidly, his honesty a little too much for Æthelred to bear. "And then once he'd caused as much chaos as possible, Denmark just sweeps in and takes your throne. Did it not occur to you that Thorkell and Svienn were working together in some capacity?"

"Of course it did!" Æthelred simmered, relieved at least that Emma had appeared at his side to rest a reassuring hand on his arm. "But I fancy I know more of the situation than your good self, and, as I said, Thorkell did prove his worth to me in defending my capital. For that, I think it best to keep him around."

"But you forget, English king, that it is not up to you who is "kept around" in this city. I rule here. Not you."

Richard really was in a foul mood. He'd said the words "English king" with particular venom, like he thought the title on par with the inept or truly ridiculous. Æthelred had no time for this. He was grateful to Richard for taking him in, but he wouldn't be insulted. He had a retort in mind when Emma suddenly spoke, her voice serving to soothe some of the tension from the room just when it was most needed.

"Brother, nobody meant to cause you upset," she told Richard quietly yet sternly. "Nobody forgets for a moment how gracious you've been in allowing us to stay here. We're always so grateful. You've given us a safe refuge. I can't think of anywhere I'd rather be."

"Given you've been in England for so long, that's unsurprising."

Richard's jibe wasn't too sharp, and his eyes had a mischievous sparkle that Æthelred was inclined to think a good sign. Emma's attempt at disarming his temper had worked, at least partially. He'd have to thank her for that later. She clearly thought Richard's "joke", if that's what it was, was amusing, judging by the smile she now wore. Richard spoke again before anyone else could interrupt, his timbre a little less aggressive this time.

"In all seriousness though, Æthel...brother-in-law...how long do you intend to stay here with this army of Northmen you have? Do you not wish to take back your throne?"

Æthelred paused before answering, his mind working strenuously on how best to respond. He couldn't tell him that he didn't want to be king. He couldn't tell him how much he'd grown to hate his responsibilities, nor could he tell him anything about the dreams of his mother, his half-brother, and the enigmatic Alaric who'd ultimately convinced him to flee the country for the sake of his family. Richard would likely think him insane if he knew the full story about how he'd come to be here, and he couldn't afford to lose face. A proper response from a man who considered himself a proper king would have to suffice, even if it was a touch dishonest.

"I do, of course, wish to see Svienn dead for what he's done," said Æthelred carefully. "But the military situation is difficult. I can't just head back there with the men I have. We'd be overwhelmed and defeated, for certain."

"Then get more men," Richard said bluntly, his right hand flapping dismissively.

"There are none. None I can trust anyway. Mercenaries are difficult to handle. They need assurances, otherwise their loyalties tend to waver."

"Yes, very true," concurred the duke. "Which is why you need to find them something to do. They'll get bored just hanging around here, even with you paying them. They are of the North, my friend. They need blood and battle like we need air and water."

He wasn't wrong, but Æthelred wasn't sure what to do about it. Did Richard expect him to let them go, or lead them back to England to raid and pillage now it was under Svienn's dominion? He couldn't see himself doing that, but it had to be said Thorkell would likely jump at the chance. It would keep them mollified for a time, but the original problem would undoubtedly remain. It also didn't address why Richard had decided to bond with Olaf only to become agitated at his inadvertent snub in the cathedral. Just what exactly was he thinking?

Edward must have been somehow hearing his thoughts, as he suddenly asked his uncle that same question, or something more or less the same. Up until this point, he'd remained passive at Æthelred's side, but he'd been listening and understanding much of what he'd heard, which was another sign of his unusual intelligence. Most lads his age wouldn't care for any of this, wanting instead to get outside and do something physical. Edward was a different sort, and his next words proved it once more.

"Just what is it that you saw or no longer see in Olaf? Why spend so much time with him and sponsor him only to get so upset because he wanted my father's blessing first? Was it prudent to behave in such a manner in public?"

Æthelred restrained a smirk as he realised Richard didn't know what to do. He was gazing at Edward, his eyes wide and jaw clenched, before looking to both Æthelred and then Emma. Æthelred could tell he thought Emma might have some explanation to offer, but she said nothing, and so Richard decided to answer Edward himself. At least he hadn't taken further offence. Æthelred wouldn't have stood by and let him berate his son.

"You have a certain bravery, my very small friend," Richard said. "Many would not be so bold and direct with such a man as I. But I know your mother would pierce my ears with her voice were I to treat you harshly, so instead, I will simply answer your question. Olaf is a useful man. I want him to continue to be a useful man. To be useful, we have to make him our friend, and ensure he remembers that we're his friends when he goes back to Norway."

"Wait, what?" interrupted Æthelred. "He wants to go home? Why?"

"I'm surprised he didn't talk to you about this yet," Richard said, appearing pleased that Olaf had shared something with him whilst keeping others in the dark. "He intends to take his men, those he has left anyway, and..."

He fell silent, his eyes wandering over Æthelred's shoulder. Æthelred turned in time to see both Olaf and Thorkell entering the way he'd come, their path flanked by a clutch of their own warriors. Olaf had changed out of his baptismal gown into some modest grey and white breecs with a matching cloak and tunic, but Thorkell was as he always was; armoured and intimidating.

Olaf grinned as he approached the still-seated Richard, his relief at seeing him unmistakable. He knelt before the throne, Thorkell standing a way off, and spoke, his earnest tone suggesting he'd been genuinely bewildered by the duke's sudden departure from his baptism.

"You left the cathedral so early, my good duke. I had hoped for your blessing alongside that of our noble King Æthelred. Do I no longer hold your esteem?"

Æthelred stared at Richard, his eyebrows raised slightly in an "I told you so" fashion. The duke, however, was blind to all but the kneeling form of Olaf and evidently touched by this apparently sincere display. He was a foolish man, Æthelred thought. Richard didn't just want Olaf's acknowledgement. He needed it, and he'd made it obvious for anyone who cared to notice. It was unjust that somebody so idiotic and immature sat on a throne whilst Æthelred himself had lost his. Life was full of injustice, though, and always had been. Æthelred could endure this one if he had to. All he cared about was his family. Thrones, or rather the lack of one, was something he'd learn to live with.

"You have my blessing, dear Olaf," announced Richard, rising to stand over the kneeling Norwegian. "Come now, and let me embrace you as a Christian brother."

Olaf did as was asked of him, embracing Richard in a hug that somehow managed to look both awkward and affectionate at the same time. The two men stayed intertwined for a few moments before finally parting, Olaf's grin having still failed to pass from his face. He really was a happy man. Æthelred envied him.

"Can we drink properly yet?"

Thorkell wasn't trying to be funny. He was serious. In his mind, this day had been an occasion like any other and was thus just another excuse for him to become intoxicated. He'd been doing a lot of that lately. Peace didn't suit him. Æthelred would have to find something for him to do lest he lose his edge.

"We can!" Olaf announced eagerly, apparently unaware that the great Apostle, Paul, had explicitly stated that drunkards would not enter the Kingdom of Heaven.

"Don't you first have something to tell our kingly friend here?" said Richard to Olaf, the look in his eyes implying something significant was on the agenda. Æthelred did his best to appear calm, hoping that whatever Olaf had to say wouldn't prove too burdensome.

"I suppose it's only just that I tell you, king," said Olaf, his manner serious. "You and I are friends, are we not?"

"Yes," replied Æthelred, unconcerned for the moment with the blatant lie he'd just told. He had no idea why Olaf would think they'd developed some kind of personal bond, but since he did, he'd play along with it. It wouldn't be wise to upset him. Not with Thorkell standing right there.

"Then send your boy away first, king. Grave words of war would be lost on him, and I'm sure he'd rather be doing something else, eh young one?"

Edward looked up when Olaf addressed him, his brow thoughtful. Olaf didn't suspect that Edward would likely be very interested in "grave words of war", as he put it, but he was right about sending him elsewhere. He'd be hungry, and Æthelred wanted him to grow strong. He nodded towards Emma, placing a gentle hand upon her hip to usher her and their firstborn son away from their presence. She took the hint, taking Edward by the hand and vanishing down one of the side passages that Æthelred knew led to the kitchens. She was a good wife.

"So now they are gone, you'll be sharing words with me?" Æthelred hoped Olaf would be as direct as he'd been. He didn't like having things hang in the air like this. People should speak their minds and be done with it. Anything less was a waste of time. He'd had enough of courtly intrigue during his years as king. He sought a more direct, less dramatic approach to life now.

"Yes, Æthelred," replied Olaf, his voice strangely gentle. "I have decided I can no longer remain in your service and will depart with my men to seize the throne of Norway."

That was unexpected. Æthelred wasn't sure how many men Olaf could possibly have left, but he imagined he had some plan in motion to grant him additional troops once he returned to his homeland. What did surprise him about all this was the timing. Why now? Did he not like being here with him in Normandy? Why become a Christian only to just leave?

"Have I offended you?" Æthelred sincerely hoped he had not. He liked to think he could read others, at least to some extent, and Olaf hadn't seemed upset with him at any point recently.

"No, you have turned from an enemy into a most dear friend," came Olaf's peculiar response. Æthelred still couldn't fathom why he thought they were close. The Norwegians must have a different perspective on friendship than the English.

"So why now?" Æthelred asked. "Is this the best time for an adventure? There is war and turmoil almost everywhere we turn. Why stir up yet more?"

"This is the opportunity I've waited for," Olaf said triumphantly. "King Svienn has overreached himself. He's bled Denmark dry conscripting every man he could to wage war on England. His power over my people will have…slackened. I will take advantage of that. I will strike whilst he is distracted."

Despite his initial anxieties, Æthelred was starting to like the sound of this. He'd been wondering if he might find something for Olaf and Thorkell to do other than drink and sit about in Rouen, and this sounded ideal. He didn't know the political situation in Norway as well as some, but he did know it was a weak point in Svienn's plans to establish Danish control over the entire North. If Olaf could succeed in making himself king of his own people, it would open up another front against Svienn. He'd be forced to pull troops from England to face off against a potential threat from Norway. It might even permit Æthelred to take back his throne.

Yet was that what he wanted? In his heart, it was not. He wanted to stay here, safe and with his family, forgetting the troubles of the past and the burdens they'd placed on him. Some might say that was cowardly and negligent, arguing instead that his people needed him and it was his duty to return. Alaric had spoken along similar lines when they'd met to pore over his troubled dreams. But Alaric had also told him it was too late for him as a ruler and that he could only succeed now as a father. He'd been right. It was a tragedy indeed that Æthelred had been forced to order his death. He'd seemed like a good and wise man. He could use somebody like that now.

"You disapprove?" asked Thorkell suddenly, his voice snapping Æthelred from his thoughts.

"I do not," he answered quickly, hoping to appear decisive. "If this is what you want, Olaf, then I wish you the best and every success against our common enemy."

Olaf grinned yet again, his hands reaching out to embrace Æthelred like he had done recently with the duke. Æthelred allowed it, feeling oddly intimidated whilst Olaf squeezed and slapped at his back. Olaf eventually relented, thanking Æthelred for his "support" before striding from the chamber with Thorkell in tow. Some ale house somewhere was about to be drunk dry, Æthelred suspected. He hoped they'd keep any brawling to a minimum.

"There are also things we must discuss, you and I."

Richard had spoken, his tone giving the impression he had dark news that couldn't be shared in the company of others.

"More grand plans, is it?" Æthelred asked, hoping to make light of things. "I have to say, Olaf's news wasn't that terrible. I thought from the way you two were acting that he might be about to tell me he intended to murder me or some such."

Richard didn't laugh, and Æthelred felt stupid for having attempted to provoke it. The duke instead beckoned for him to join him as he moved towards a passage heading into the western quarter of his keep, a solitary guard detaching himself from his position by the throne to trail them. Hereward also followed, and together they made their way down yet another dark and draughty passageway, their footsteps echoing gently off the bare stone walls.

They soon passed into a small chamber overlooking an interior courtyard. There was a tall, narrow glass window here, allowing Æthelred a partial view of the southern half of the city. The weather had turned sour, the drizzle obscuring what might otherwise have been a splendid vista, but he could see the river well enough, as well as his own vessels clustered in haphazard tangles along its banks. That was his navy, bolstered by what was left of Thorkell's fleet. It was all he really had in terms of military power, yet he was grateful for it. It might still be a potent force, if needed. It certainly looked like it could be from where he was standing.

"Do you remember your little raid against us not so long ago?" Richard had sat down, parking himself in an ornate wooden chair close to a presently empty stone hearth. His guard took up position just behind him, but there was nowhere for Æthelred to sit, and he noted with some irritation how the duke had a glass of something, most likely wine, in his hand. Nothing had been offered to Æthelred. Richard was being rude to him on purpose. This wasn't a good sign.

"I do remember, yes," Æthelred admitted, hoping the subject would soon shift to something less controversial. The "little raid" he'd mentioned had actually taken place years ago, shortly after he'd been wed to Emma. They'd received word that Richard was still allowing the Danes access to his ports, in stark and unpardonable contravention of the agreement they'd come to when Æthelred had married his sister. Merely asking the Normans to honour their own agreements didn't seem like much of an option, and so, despite Emma's pleas, Æthelred had decided on a stronger approach. Invading Normandy with a raiding expedition had seemed like a good choice.

But it had been a disaster. They'd landed unopposed at Cotentin, hoping to set the peninsula on fire before pushing down south and ideally doing more of the same. The local viscount, or whoever he was, had been a canny strategist, however, and he'd rallied his men to counterattack with such a speed and ferocity that the English had been beaten back to their ships. Æthelred remembered the sorry sight they'd made as they hurried aboard, their morale shattered under the iron hooves of the Norman cavalry. It wasn't his most harrowing memory as king, but it was still one he didn't care to revisit. He'd gotten an earful from Emma when they'd made it back home, too.

"I don't recall ever asking you why you did it," said Richard, sipping his wine. "Why did you?"

"You'd been dealing with Svienn for years. You'd agreed to stop assisting him when I was betrothed to Emma. You broke that agreement. Words were not enough. I felt a stronger message was necessary."

"A stronger message? That Englishmen can't fight? I knew that already."

Æthelred put his hands on his hips and straightened out his spine. He knew his brother-in-law was a petty man, but he hadn't been aware he still harboured resentment towards him over Cotentin. Mocking him over this was unfair and unproductive. He didn't care for it, and he'd make his displeasure known.

"You've never had to contend with what we face," Æthelred said pointedly. "You'd let the Danes come and go, doing as they please. We decided to fight them. You can't tell me my people don't know how to fight when you do nothing but talk your way out when danger comes calling."

"Hah! Did you really just say that to me?" Richard scoffed, his face twisting into a mocking sneer. "I suggest you mind your words, King Æthelred. You are still dependent on my goodwill for protection and sanctuary here. But I will say you are partially right. I do prefer to talk than fight. It was the right thing to do when it came to the likes of King Svienn. Which brings me to my next point…"

"Which is?" Æthelred snapped. He wanted to end this exchange as soon as possible. He imagined Hereward felt the same. He noticed he'd tensed slightly when Richard had insulted the English people. The man likely wanted to teach the duke a lesson of his own. Æthelred understood him perfectly.

"I have made an agreement with Svienn," Richard said. "Don't look so surprised, Æthel…don't look so surprised. He is the power in England now. We have to recognise that reality."

"But what does this mean for me?" Æthelred spluttered, his anxiety rising. "Are you going to hand me and my family over to him?"

"My sister? And her children? Given to that monster? No. But I felt you should know the truth. Svienn came here just prior to invading your shores. He wished to re-establish economic ties between his realm and mine. Trade relations and such. Buying and selling."

"You mean he wants to offload in your ports what he's seized from my land!" shouted Æthelred, his anger fresh, vibrant, and entirely justified. "And what kind of plunder are we talking about here? Slaves? My people taken from their homes to be sold to whoever can afford to pay? Are you still claiming to be a Christian, Richard, or shall I assume you take your faith as seriously as you do our friendship?"

"You are getting emotional…"

"You get a piece of all this, don't you?" Æthelred interrupted, his ire still flowing hot. "Everything Svienn sells here…every captive he brings to a Norman market…it'll all be taxed, won't it? And that revenue will go straight into your coffers…Duke Richard the Second…the man who made himself rich from the enslavement of Christians!"

Richard leapt to his feet, the wine spilling from his glass to saturate his tunic. "Do not seek to test me, Æthelred!" he declared, his tone venomous. "This situation is not of my creation! I must do what I feel is right. There is no defying Svienn. Not now. He's a powerful man. Too powerful for me to resist. I do what I must."

"And doing what you must involves profiting from the despoliation of my country?" snarled Æthelred. "How very noble of you, brother. I'm impressed."

"I had not wanted it to come to this," replied Richard, his manner calming somewhat despite the continued provocation. "But I have no choice. I encouraged Olaf to return to Norway for a reason. His actions will decide our fates. Yours more than mine, it's true, but what he does in the next few months will decide the destiny of many."

"Speak sense, Richard, there's only so much of this I can stand to hear."

"I'll make it nice and simple so even an Englishman can understand," Richard jibed, his sneer returning in all its noxious glory. "If Olaf becomes King of Norway, then Svienn will intervene there, giving us space to breathe. If he fails…Svienn will dominate the North, and England, and by extension…Normandy."

"Then we must do more to help Olaf." Æthelred didn't consider this a complicated issue. He'd tried to wrest Norway away from Svienn in the past, with some admittedly brief success. He didn't see any reason why they couldn't try again.

"I will," nodded Richard. "But you should know something…if Olaf fails, we'll be surrounded, and I won't be in any position to refuse Svienn should he make certain demands. I'll never give my sister up, nor her children. But you, Æthelred…our relationship has changed back to what it was. You are not my friend, just as you were not when you attacked us at Cotentin. As such, you will remain here in my keep until…"

"Until what?"

"Until I can be sure of the situation in light of Olaf's success or failure. If he wins in Norway…things will look brighter for you. If he doesn't…I will use you as a bargaining chip. I will use you to placate Svienn. Even if that means handing you over to him."

III

"We have nothing left to give. What treasures we held were sold off to care for the refugees from your war. That is the truth of it. Depart now in peace."

Cnut stared at the abbot, wondering if he was intentionally insulting his father or if he were just an unfortunate fool. He'd chosen his words poorly in any case, and he now feared for him. He looked over at his father, hoping to gauge his response. For all he knew, they could be moments away from bloodshed. He'd seen it happen for more trivial reasons than this.

"I do not believe you," said King Svienn, the abbot's failure to address him by his proper title having thankfully failed to provoke him. "We know you have a rich abbey here, and it is only just that you share your wealth. Do the right thing, and do not lie to me again."

The abbot squinted at him, his aged face pained and unsure. Cnut hoped that was fear in his eyes, and from his fear might come the desire to capitulate and do as he'd been asked. His hopes were dashed by what the abbot said next. This fellow wasn't afraid of anything. It would be his downfall.

"I think not. Like I said, what we have is for the poor and desperate. Many have fled your harsh rule over Lundenburg. We will keep what we have for the purpose of God's work. I'm sure you..."

The abbot collapsed onto his knees. Cnut hadn't seen his father strike, but he'd successfully doubled the English monk over with what must have been a weighty blow to the guts. Svienn reached down and hauled him upright by his habit to speak directly into his face. It was a harsh sight to see, but Cnut had grown used to it. The English were an awkward, disobedient people, from their greatest warriors to their most humble of holy men. This monk was living proof of that. He'd need to acquire a little wisdom in the next few moments. His life depended on it.

"Listen to me, your king!" seethed Svienn, his pointed words laden with menace. "I have given you a command, and I will see it carried out, one way or another. If you wish to see your bastard Saint Edmund respected and your place of worship left intact, you'll do as I say. Defy me, and I'll keep you alive so you can watch us kill your brothers and destroy your saint's remains before I finally dispatch you to hell."

"You speak unjustly," replied the abbot, his face now as white as his wispy, fist-length beard. "A true king of this land would never make such a demand upon..."

"I am not of this land," replied Svienn, "but I am a true king. Submit to me, for God put me here and gave me authority, as our Apostle Paul made clear."

"You twist the meaning of Scripture..."

"I do not! I am king! God appoints kings! Now obey me or suffer the consequences!"

Cnut shifted on his feet, adjusting his weight from left to right. The abbot was in a tight spot, and he didn't see any way out for him other than surrender. Cnut could also see from here that the rest of his flock had come out to see what the fuss was about. They were all dressed alike, their dark robes giving them an almost sinister appearance, but their faces said it all. They were overcome with worry. Not one of them had the courage their abbot had. He could tell that by the fact they hadn't even dared approach. Pathetic is what it was.

By contrast, the monastery they'd emerged from was a splendid thing. It was larger than most he'd seen, and by the look of its weather-beaten stones, it was of an age that would conceivably date its construction to some considerable time prior to the life of Saint Edmund himself. It had been looted by Thorkell when his army had rampaged through here as it pillaged the rest of Eastengle, but it was otherwise untouched, its neat, greying walls looking appropriately venerable in light of the relics that lay within. Cnut was glad. He really wanted to see the inside. He'd never looked upon the remains of a saint before.

Such reverence was not shared by his father. Svienn had by this point struck the abbot several more times, and Cnut winced at the sharp crack of a nose breaking, but the abbot's spirit was undimmed, and he continued to babble defiance through split and bleeding lips. Svienn threw him to the ground and strode past him, Cnut and the rest of their party lurching into motion in a bid to keep up. He could tell his father had come to a decision. He'd take what he wanted, and there was no one on earth who could stop him.

Cnut gazed behind him, looking back toward the rest of their army waiting amidst the wood and thatch buildings of the surrounding village. They had hundreds of troops here, but they really were not needed. Eastengle was in no state to resist them, so battered as it was from Thorkell's own marauding. The settlement of Sancte Eadmundes Byrig belonged to them now, and nobody could argue otherwise. He just hoped he could calm his father down before he did something foolish. Desecrating the remains of an English saint would provoke nothing but trouble. He was surprised he didn't see that.

The other monks began to panic as the Danes approached. One broke ranks and started to head towards them, babbling something about the need to "listen to reason", only to be pushed back by Svienn's armoured huscarls. The Danes then smashed their way through the front doors of the monastery, the timber yielding to the weight of their axes, and entered within. The place was silent, deserted, the only sound heard the muted wailings of the monks outside as they were dispersed under a deluge of threats and the odd kick to the posterior. They really didn't possess even a fraction of the courage displayed by their abbot. A shame.

The view in here was as expected. This was some kind of chapel, austere and unadorned. The air was musty, the odd sunbeam pouring from an opening set into the stone just above an altar some distance ahead. The walls were ancient and plain, the altar before them devoid of ornamentation aside from a single wooden chalice. Nothing in particular caught the eye, yet one didn't always perceive things of import with the physical body. This was a place for the heart and spirit. You could feel the reverence, thickening the very air with its presence. This chapel was a vantage point for what lay beyond this world, for the monks and villagers alike. For all England, most likely.

Svienn didn't appear to sense it, or if he did, he still didn't care to stop and ponder its significance. He stormed forwards, loping past the altar to duck through a narrow archway at the back of the nave. Cnut followed, his instincts telling him he was approaching something of escalating importance. As he passed through the archway, he saw his suspicions had been only partially correct.

This was most likely a reliquary, or at least it had been. It was empty, its bare stone walls appearing strangely sorrowful in their aged starkness. A short dais just in front of them had until recently held something of relevance, for he could see from the way the dust had fallen that an object of some length had been placed here. There were holders for candles also, positioned around the dais in a broad circle, yet the item they were supposed to illuminate was conspicuously absent. Cnut could venture a guess as to what had been here. The remains of the Patron Saint of England. The martyred King Edmund himself.

He'd heard the story a few times. The Ealdorman Eadric had also told him before they'd left Lundenburg, advising him to be careful when it came to anything associated with the saint. The English were capable of being defeated like anyone else, he'd said, but being physically bested was different from humiliation. A people who felt like they were hated could only hate back. Respect worked both ways, and anyone who sought to rule England would have to be seen to respect it on at least some level. Venerating the remains of their saint would be a powerful image to convey, should Cnut and his father wish to be seen as legitimate rulers. Failure to do so would only encourage further resistance.

Cnut felt that he understood. Edmund had been a king in his day, perhaps a hundred and fifty or so years prior, and had done his utmost to retain his kingdom even as Cnut's ancestors did their best to despoil it. He'd failed, of course, and unlike his southern neighbour, the great King Alfred, Edmund had not lived to see the tables turn on the invaders as they had so decisively at the Battle of Ethandun. Edmund had died, shot full of arrows by those under the command of the pagans, Iva and Ubba, his last words thick with defiance as he again refused to renounce Christ, as had been demanded. It was a striking story, and even Cnut could see why the English would continue to revere his bravery. There was great dignity in a death like that.

His father didn't feel the same way. He'd clenched his fists, his anger palpable upon beholding the empty dais. He then spat; a length of spittle suddenly erupting from his mouth to splatter the clear space where the box containing the saint's remains had presumably once rested. Cnut scowled, confused and irked by the display. It would be ill-advised to let any Englishman see him do that. Behaving as such in front of his own countrymen was one thing, but an English heart would only rage at the brazen irreverence. He was surprised his father hadn't worked that out. He was old enough to know better. Just what was wrong with him?

"Bring me the abbot," Svienn said, low and severe, Cnut wondering if he had bloodshed on his mind. The huscarl immediately behind him nodded and headed back the way they'd come, moving at some speed. He returned within minutes, the still numb and bloodied abbot held firmly by the shoulders.

"Explain to me what you were storing here," said Svienn, not wasting time with preliminary threats. "This was where you had the bones of your Saint Edmund, yes?"

"It is," said the abbot, his words slightly slurred by the fresh bruising across his mouth and face.

"Then where have you taken them?!" thundered Svienn, his temper breaking in the face of such brevity.

"You'll never know. We sent them away when Thorkell came calling…and I'm not going to tell you where. I won't have you legitimising your Godless usurpation by pretending to respect our martyred King Edmund."

"Don't mistake me, monk! I came here for a reason and will not be thwarted by the likes of you! Tell me where his remains are, or see your life end here!"

"I'll not tell you anything. You are a man of violence, you've made that known over and over. You'd as likely desecrate the saint's body on a whim…and your disgusting presence would remain unworthy even if you were of a mind to offer respect. I will not cooperate with you."

Cnut stepped forward, hoping to place himself between his father and the abbot so that tempers might cool. He was too late. His father moved fast for his age, and the monk had no time to so much as whimper before he was cut down with a swing of his axe. Cnut flinched as the weapon sailed past him, its razor-sharp edge missing the tip of his nose by mere inches. Svienn laid into the expiring abbot, hewing his axe up and then down with both hands to split his rib cage. Blood seeped from his torn and splattered robes, its metallic taint rising to befoul the air. This was not such a holy place now. Base murder had been done here.

Svienn turned and strode back into the chapel, his guards following. Cnut just stood there, trying to comprehend what had happened. The abbot was dead, and there was no changing that. Cnut didn't feel sorrow for it. They'd come here as conquerors, as was their right, but he still couldn't understand what his father was doing. He'd told him when they'd taken Lundenburg that he'd be magnanimous. He'd told him he intended to keep England and rule it so that he, Cnut, would learn from him and one day do the same.

Something had changed. He couldn't tell when or how, but those noble sentiments had dissipated within days of Svienn sitting on the throne. Nobody would respect him, he kept saying, if he "turned soft." The English were a "rebellious and duplicitous people", he'd also said, and a gesture would be needed to bring them into line. Eadric had agreed with him, suggesting he gather those thegns and ealdormen who were compliant so they could publicly affirm their submission. Svienn had concurred, but said he also had other things in mind. Harsher things.

He'd started with Lundenburg. Far from reinvigorating the city, he'd had his men begin ransacking the place, taking what little was stashed or hidden and placing it within the treasure vault beneath Æthelred's hall. Cnut had expressed confusion, asking whether it would be wiser to allow the city's economy to recover and thus regain its status as a focal point for maritime trade. Svienn had not relented. He'd said lessons had to be learned and the treasury needed to be filled. It was only right that the defeated pay for the cost of this war, but something had clearly gotten under his skin. Cnut couldn't tell what it was. He'd hoped his behaviour would not become yet more aggressive and ill-advised.

He was to be disappointed. Svienn soon turned his attention to the "notables" who'd first surrendered to him that night they'd stormed the city gates. He'd threatened them, promising to cut off their hands and feet if any of them attempted to hide valuables. They'd quickly complied and given up what they had, every one visibly rattled and fearful. Cnut couldn't help but notice the looks they'd given Svienn once he'd turned away. They'd hated him. They hadn't hated him at first. They did now.

Cnut hurried to catch up with his father. They left the monastery, passing through the shattered front entrance to again behold the village beyond. Their men looked up, hundreds of blue eyes glancing in the direction of their king. They could tell something was afoot. All of them could read Svienn by now. Violence was on his mind. He proved it with what he said next, his thunderous tones echoing out for all to hear.

"Burn the monastery. Don't let anyone leave the village. Question the monks... question everyone. If they refuse to tell us where the saint's remains were taken, kill them."

The village flew into uproar. Danes grasped at those commoners attempting to flee, wrestling them to the ground and subduing them with enthusiastic brutality. Others tried to barricade themselves in their homes, hoping to hold out within, but Svienn's warriors had no patience for their theatrics and simply broke through their doors to drag them outside for a beating. Those monks who had been scattered previously were rounded up, whilst the chapel and buildings immediately behind Cnut were surrounded with bracken, dry grass, and assorted detritus, and set alight. He stood there, hands on his hips and gazing upon the blaze, the sounds of panic, despair and the crackle of flames rising up around him.

In his heart, he knew he didn't care. These were inept, fragile people. They were not the issue. What mattered was how others would react when word of this got out. A lot of fuss would be made, and somebody more capable than these weaklings would want to avenge what had happened here. They'd lose good men then, wasting lives in a fight that could have been avoided. Cnut made a promise to himself that when he was king, he'd think before acting, using violence as a tool rather than a hammer to crush and destroy everything in his path. That was a more kingly approach, he felt.

He nonetheless ignored the bawling monks Svienn and his bodyguards were leading away into the village square about fifty paces away. Cnut remained where he was, his own men gathered around him and looking on as the captives were killed, one after the other, their severed heads rolling away with a certain horrifying lightness that almost turned the stomach.

Cnut could tell his father was questioning them before introducing the axe, but judging by their expressions, none of them really seemed to know much on the saint's whereabouts. One shouted out a couple of names, his voice strained with fear, saying something about a Sigeferth and the Ealdorman Ulfcytel. Cnut would have liked to question him more on that, yet his father wasn't in the mood to hear a name as hated as that of Ulfcytel. He would remember well enough how the man had nearly bested him, years back when Cnut was still a boy. They'd all heard the stories, the old and the new. This Ulfcytel was a man of fierce and heroic deeds. If anyone stood a chance of unseating his father, it was him.

The monk fell to his knees, his voice an enfeebled whine whilst the huscarls held him so their king might slay him. Svienn applied himself to the task, his axe removing the unfortunate man's head. Cnut folded his arms, thinking this more than foolish. If the monk had been taken somewhere secure and allowed to calm down, he could have collected his thoughts and told them something half-sensible. They'd get nothing out of him now. This was all a waste of time. He wished a real reason to fight would present itself. Brutalising unarmed men didn't earn you great renown as a warrior and ruler. He wished to be known as such and not just another Danish murderer.

His thoughts betrayed him. A bestial roar erupted from the swaying tree line of oak and maple just beyond the village outskirts to the west. Men appeared from the woods, hundreds of them, all dashing forward with wild abandon and wilder shouts to fall upon the Danes like wolves. His own warriors flinched, a second later forming a circle around him to shield him from the attackers. Something was wrong. They'd had no reports of a resistance force operating in this area. This was entirely unexpected. It looked like Cnut was going to get his chance to prove himself. It wasn't like he had much choice.

The man next to him fell, twin arrows protruding from his throat and chest. Cnut heaved his rönd up and over and knelt down, anxious to protect himself from any more projectiles. Something heavy smashed into it from the other side, his whole frame shaking from the impact. He ventured a look, glancing up to see the tip of a spear protruding through splintered wood. He'd nearly died. If the man who'd hurled that spear had aimed just a few inches lower, Cnut would have taken that in the side of the head as it smashed its way past the boss. That wouldn't have been right. It wasn't his destiny to die from having things thrown at him. That wasn't how legends were made, was it?

Cnut looked over to his father in the village square. He was in his element, his face red with rage as he roared for his men to charge the new arrivals. They obeyed, forgetting the villagers for the moment so that they might meet the enemy head-on. It was chaotic, and they hadn't formed a line or cohered themselves into any formation to speak of; each warrior rushing into the fight like he alone in his bravery might prove the deciding factor. Cnut admired it, but it wasn't ideal, and as far as he was aware, that hadn't been how they'd won in the past. This would be a bloody affair for all concerned.

He realised he had no right to think like that as long as he was cowering behind his shield. He stood up, peering over its rim just in time to face his first opponent. Cnut's guards were beset, each of them now fighting their own battles, and so this man had slipped through them in an effort to take his head. He didn't look like a warrior and wasn't dressed as such either, but he had a frenzied manner to him, akin to one who had lost everything and thus had nothing left to fear.

He threw himself into Cnut, kicking at his shield and slamming his body weight against it repeatedly. Cnut staggered back, his right hand reaching for the sword at his belt. The man wouldn't let up, raining down blow after blow with a worn, heavy axe. He didn't have much skill. Yet that kind of determination could still kill.

Cnut drew his sword and lashed out in a great sweeping arc, finding his efforts rewarded almost immediately with a cry of pain and a splash of gore. The Saxon fell, his splintered forearm gushing red, his eyes still lit with a blazing fury. More Danes charged in, hoping to defend Cnut and win acclaim, yet these wild English kept coming, ripping into their number with a furious enthusiasm. They were not all as ill-equipped as the man Cnut had just killed, and at least some of them were properly attired in full ring mail with shields and helms also. Not everyone here was an irate woodsman, then. Somebody had professionals organising all this. It was important they kill them to break the spirit of those who followed.

It wasn't going to be easy. More Danes fell, slain by English iron, and the smoke from the burning monastery was spreading across the battlefield, enveloping the whole bloody spectacle in an ashen embrace. The stuff was bitter and cloying, as one would expect, but it wasn't affecting every man in exactly the same way. The Saxons seemed to be drawing a certain strength from it, their already great rage intensifying as the flames and smoke spread further. It was as Cnut had feared. They knew what the place had contained, and were outraged King Svienn had come here with anything but reverence in mind. This was the price they were paying for their bloodlust. It need not have happened. Once they got out of this situation, he'd have words with his father.

Cnut killed again, avenging the huscarl who'd only just been cut down a few feet from him. Another cry rent the air, and yet more English appeared from the woods, this second wave rushing into the fight with redoubled fury. Cnut caught sight of somebody in the melee, the sight of them drawing the eye. It was a man, broader than most and noteworthy for his skill, his heavy armour and brilliant sword marking him out as someone of significance. He fought like one who'd been trained from a young age, and the other Saxons looked to him with elation, rejoicing at his presence and following him to cut a bloody swathe through Cnut's men.

Who he was remained a mystery, but one thing was beyond clear: he hated the Danes. He really hated them, displaying a degree of furious malevolence that Cnut had never seen before. His hatred gave him the advantage, providing a rare and savage energy that powered him forward as he cleaved men apart, his visage a snarling, twisted mask of unleashed rage.

His sword shimmered whenever it caught the light, its metalwork reflecting the sun's rays even as the blade was increasingly marred with gore. It was a fine piece of work, thick and presumably heavy to use, and it worked well as both sword and cudgel, cutting men down or smashing them into the earth. Its owner kept on, unstoppable in his fury, his men following his example in their quest to punish the Danes for what they'd done here. Cnut knew it had been a mistake coming to this place. One did not trespass against a saint. They were paying for it now.

Cnut's eyes met those of this mystery warrior from across the smoke and carnage. The man grinned, his teeth white against his reddened face, his cloak and mail likewise splattered with blood. He pointed his blade directly towards him, like he was issuing a challenge or making some kind of declaration of intent. He must be the leader of these men, and he'd noted Cnut's own superior arms and armour as evidence of his authority. He wanted to fight him, one commander against the other.

Something fluttered in Cnut's chest, and so he forced it down, clenching his teeth and obliterating it through sheer willpower. He would fear no man. Not even one as terrible as this. He would face him and prove himself once more to his father. He would be a wiser king than he. None of this would have befallen them if he'd had his way. Cnut would put things right. He'd correct his father's errors.

He stepped forward, hoping to ease the tremors from his limbs. He looked around for his father, hoping he'd still be fighting and prevailing. He wasn't. King Svienn was nowhere to be seen, and the furious English were pushing the Danes out of the village and back past the main road to Lundenburg. That was their only point of escape. They couldn't just flee into the wilderness. They'd be hunted down, and recent events had proven beyond doubt that England was nowhere near as submissive as Cnut had first thought. They had to win here, or at least keep an avenue of escape open. He didn't want to go down in history as the Danish prince who'd died alongside his father after desecrating a monastery. Nobody would sing songs of that. People would think his fate well deserved. He wouldn't entirely blame them.

He turned back towards his nearest foes just in time to see their berserk leader fall upon another huscarl. Cnut's man put up a good fight, and he could tell the Englishman had to concentrate to defeat him, but his ferocity won through. He kicked him, in the legs and then the guts, his sword soon piercing his chest and erupting from his mid-back in an outpouring of fluids and rupturing tissue.

More Danes died, their bodies falling like felled timber, and the English warlord was at the centre of it all, killing and maiming without pause or remorse, his cohorts too taking their share of lives. More huscarls rushed in, trying to protect Cnut, trying to turn the tide, but it wasn't enough. The Danes were collapsing. Everywhere he looked they were dying, cut down, pierced, or torn apart by these barbarous men of the forest. He still couldn't see his father, and Cnut himself was rooted to the spot with fear. The English leader was closer now, standing tall and advancing over the bodies of the slain, his sword again pointed straight at him. Words thundered from his mouth, his great jaw spitting them out like they might flense the flesh from Cnut's bones.

"You should pray for a clean death, foreign dog! After what you've done here, I'll make you BREAK! I'll make you BLEED!"

His voice was horrific to the ear, the pain and hatred hanging off each syllable unlike anything Cnut had ever heard. He recoiled at the sound of it, but it snapped him out of his fearful trance. He wouldn't die a coward. He'd go down fighting and be remembered as such. Damn the songs, there'd be at least one verse, he hoped, that would tell of his bravery. He wouldn't wait for his father. He wasn't a boy anymore and shouldn't assume he'd always be around to protect him. For all he knew, he was dead already. The thought hurt his heart, but it made him hate. He'd use that hatred. He took a step forward, his shield raised and his sword held high.

Cnut didn't like being on his back. This had happened before, just weeks ago, actually, when he'd charged into Lundenburg after they'd breached the gates. A brave man had knocked him down as he'd tried to get to grips with him, and the same had happened here, making Cnut wonder if he was fated to be skilled at arms but just terrible at standing up. He lifted his head, groggy and confused, thinking somebody must have somehow tripped him whilst he closed for the contest. It wasn't so. A horse, pale and muscular, filled his vision, its rider lashing out with a great spear. Other mounted men were pouring in, scores of them, their charge bisecting the battlefield as if to smash into the English and get between them and Cnut.

Pain flared in his side, his freshly tender ribs protesting at his attempts to sit himself up. He managed it regardless, but his legs were numb and refusing to cooperate with his efforts to rise and rejoin the fight. Hooves and human legs stampeded around him, making the battle appear even more chaotic now their mystery allies had appeared to scythe through the enemy. These men were unexpected. They were English, judging by the look of them, yet they were attacking their initial ambushers and driving them back towards the forest. It wasn't going entirely their way, and some were dragged from the saddle and butchered, but they had the enemy flanked and were enjoying all the advantages that offered.

Horns blasted from somewhere, the disturbing, eerie sound pealing out over the smoke and corpses. Their attackers began to retreat, scurrying away into the woods, their expressions surprised and resentful as victory turned swiftly to defeat. Cnut caught sight of the warrior who'd marked him. He was gazing back in his direction, if only for a moment, yet his eyes remained sharp with malice. He was atop a horse, one he must have taken just now after killing its rider, and he looked strangely calm in contrast to his earlier display, his defeat here meaning little to him after he'd already wrought so much death. That's what he wanted, Cnut thought. He wanted to kill Danes until there were none left to kill. This surprise ambush was just a setback to him. He wouldn't stop. He wouldn't relent.

Somebody heaved him upright and deposited him onto his feet. Cnut wobbled slightly, his legs unsteady and the pain in his side increasing the more he struggled to hold his weight. His men were roaring in triumph around him, their bellowing cries splitting the air. They had no business being proud of themselves. From what he could see, they'd lost a good half of their people here. They'd been caught totally off guard, and all because of his father's sudden drive to humiliate the English by desecrating the resting place of their patron saint.

Svienn appeared, hobbling out of the mayhem at the head of a dozen battered and bloodied warriors. He had mud all down his front and up into his beard, and he was limping heavily, his left hand also clutching at a wound extending across the right side of his stomach. Cnut admired how he was still up and walking, even after the beating he'd taken. He may have blundered and led them into unnecessary strife, but he was still a king. It was his right to rule this land. The English would have to accommodate themselves to these bitter truths.

"Are you all right?" Svienn asked, his breath ragged. "I worried for you there," he added before Cnut could answer. "When they rushed us, I reacted on instinct…but when I saw more of them swarming you here, I tried to get back to you. One of them caught me off guard, and…" Svienn patted at his wound in emphasis. So he'd been injured in some mad scramble to reach him and render aid. Cnut didn't know whether to be pleased or not. He wanted his father to see him as capable in his own right rather than a liability in need of rescue. Yet he was touched that he cared for him like that. He wouldn't want it to be otherwise.

"Are you both well, my lords?"

The rider who'd accidentally knocked Cnut over had ridden up to address them. Both Svienn and Cnut looked up at him with curiosity, hoping he'd remove his helm and thus reveal his identity. He did so, unleashing a mess of blond curls, cascading down to his shoulders, and grey, hard eyes, the likes of which were quite unsettling. His skin was soft, like a woman, flushing pink with exertion, a not inconsiderable amount of sweat on his brow. They knew who this was. Eadric. The Ealdorman Eadric had come with his own men to rescue them. Cnut would have preferred his rescuer to at least look like a man. To be saved by a warrior so…unconventional in his appearance didn't sit well with him. And yet he could fight, and fight well. He'd shown both skill at arms and tactical acumen today. But he shouldn't be wasting time asking after them. He'd let him know how he felt about that.

"Why are you not pursuing them into the woods?" Cnut snapped. "They are on foot, you have horses! Get after them and end this!"

"Sending cavalry into rough terrain to engage infantry…no offence, my lord, but I consider that ill-advised," answered Eadric. "My ploy here worked because they'd moved out into the open and were not expecting me to appear on their flank. I've already taken losses from doing it. We don't have the numbers to do as you ask."

"He's right," said Svienn. "Those men fought like beasts, even when surprised like that. Wisdom dictates that we return to the safety of Lundenburg, and that is what we shall do. Eadric…you have my thanks. I will not forget what you have done here."

Cnut simmered, unsure about this "wisdom" that had been offered. Eadric nodded towards his father in recognition of his words, but none of that explained what he was even doing here. How had he known to come to their assistance? Was there something awry elsewhere in the country? He'd have an answer from the man, and quickly.

"Why did you follow us?" Cnut demanded. "I left you in Lundenburg and didn't tell you anything of our business here. Explain yourself."

"I appreciate your well-founded question," Eadric said without resentment. "But I am a man who likes to keep himself informed. I have people everywhere…even amidst those who might claim to oppose your reign."

"So you have a spy with the men who just attacked us?" Svienn asked admiringly. "I wasn't sure about you at first, Eadric, but if that is so, you again have my compliments. We'll need such cunning to hold this land."

"As you say," nodded Eadric, Cnut noticing that he hadn't really admitted to anything. "Now, I would recommend we depart in some haste. It's not safe here. I'm sure you've worked out who led these men. He's a resourceful man and not to be taken lightly."

"Who?" asked Cnut, genuinely curious. He'd assumed the leader of this force had been the one who'd screamed at him, but as to his actual identity, he was entirely in the dark. Was he some dissatisfied thegn? Was he Ulfcytel himself? He fit the picture in terms of bravery and skill, but he'd always imagined the famous ealdorman to be an older man. The one who'd attacked them here had been young, perhaps only a little older than Cnut himself.

"It was the Aetheling Edmund," answered Eadric. "You saw him there, yes? Fighting like a madman? Grief will do that to one such as him. He grieves still for his older brother, Æthelstan. He'll kill you all for that alone. I thought I had him there for a moment, but…"

"Wait, who?" spluttered Cnut, confused and irritated. "The Aetheling Edmund? A son of the English king, you mean?"

"You are correct," answered Eadric with a cold smile. "The eldest living son of the former King Æthelred. As you have learned here today…some still hope to see him take the throne. And there'll be more of them. You've won many a man of import to your side, but I fear Edmund will win the hearts of the commoners. I didn't think it would start so soon, but there you have it. A rebellion is what we have on our hands."

"What does he get out of it?" groaned Svienn, his patience for conversation wearing thin. "He can't possibly think to prevail. Almost everyone who matters answers to me. I have Uhtred in Norþanhymbre, I have you in Mierċe, Æthelmaer in Dæfenascir…I have Lundenburg. I have England. It's over. Even his father saw that. Attacks like this are futile gestures."

"I fear we may be misunderstanding him," Eadric cautioned. "As you saw, these men fought to stop you from harming the remains of their saint. They didn't choose this battle. They just reacted because they had no choice. That's dangerous. Edmund might not be fighting to sit himself on a comfortable throne. He's fighting because he has nothing left. He can either live in humiliation like his father, or die killing as many of you as he can. He's chosen the latter. And as long as he thinks that's his only real option, he won't desist. I'm sorry, my lords, but you have not seen the last of that man."

IV

It was long past sunset when they finally dared stop and a fair while after that until he could convince at least some of his body to cease shaking. He'd emptied his guts, vomiting behind a tree where he thought nobody would see, and then moved to sit down on a fallen log, inhaling and exhaling in a deep, deliberate rhythm. That had soothed him somewhat, but his right arm was still trembling and jerking spasmodically, his fist clenching and unclenching across his knee. This made no sense. It was over. There was no sign of pursuit. They were safe. He wished his body would understand that.

Wulfnoth reached to clasp his hand, holding it shut. He could feel it protesting, his tendons twitching as they endeavoured to resist. He felt ashamed. He didn't think he'd ever been seen like this before. Nothing rattled him, not until today. Was this what all men went through at some point? Was this the icy clutch of fear or something else?

"It's all right, Edmund," said Wulfnoth gently, still grasping his hand. "Don't be hard on yourself. I know the signs. I've never seen you like that, but I've seen others experience something similar...it wasn't fear, was it? You fought your heart out, I know."

Edmund stared into his eyes, trying to detect any hint of emotion there as they huddled amidst the trees. Wulfnoth was hard to read, his eyes seeming to shrink into that narrow face of his, but he was an old friend and one of the few in his father's court that he trusted. He was a strange-looking man, his large nose and small forehead seeming to be at odds with each other, but he was a hardened warrior, his flowing black and grey hair and beard adding a touch of ferocity that suited him well.

They had a history, he and Edmund. Wulfnoth had always taken Edmund's side and that of his lost brother, Æthelstan, knowing they needed guidance as their father succumbed more and more to paranoia and eccentricity. Edmund had long been grateful for that, but Wulfnoth had paid for it in abundance, falling victim to false accusations that had seen him go on the run for the sake of his very life. Edmund was glad they'd eventually found him. Their reunion was one of the few bright points in what had otherwise been a time of unceasing troubles.

Edmund looked past Wulfnoth's shoulder to take in the sight beyond. His men were scattered about, bruised and exhausted from the battle at the monastery, the waxing moon breaking through the trees just enough to illuminate them in their plight. They were all trying to be quiet as they caught their breath, but there was only so much just over a hundred men could do. Edmund's heart sank at the realisation of it. They'd been almost two and a half hundred the day prior, not counting the non-combatants they'd taken during their escape from the capital. He still didn't regret giving the order to attack. They'd had to stop those bastards. They'd had to stop them from getting hold of the saint. Yet the cost of it all was hard to bear. Edmund hoped he'd never get used to losing men in battle. If his heart hardened to such things, he'd be lost. There were too many callous rulers in the world. He had no intention of becoming one of them.

"I think you may be right," Edmund grunted, sliding his hand from Wulfnoth's grip and relieved that it was, at last, relatively still and obedient again. "I've fought before but never like that. Something came over me. I had to do something. We couldn't let them just...you know."

"I do know," nodded Wulfnoth sagely. "Nobody here blames you for anything. We all followed you willingly and still will. I do find myself half-wishing we hadn't got word of what they'd planned, though. Another defeat doesn't do us any favours."

Edmund sighed, the sound turning to a low, frustrated growl that rumbled in his throat. It was true they'd been defeated, but when they'd learned that an enemy force was active in the area and heading for Sancte Eadmundes Byrig, they'd had to intervene. Edmund didn't even know if the saint's remains were still there, but they couldn't afford to risk it. They hadn't known they'd be facing King Svienn himself, but even if they had, Edmund would have still been up for it. If those horsemen hadn't intervened, they'd have likely killed him and saved the monastery. It would have been a great victory, with nothing to regret.

"I don't suppose now is the time to point out that the horsemen who came to the Danes' aid were of Mierċe?" said Wulfnoth cautiously. "They had a banner. And Eadric himself. I saw him. I was less...lost in the moment, shall we say."

"Mierċe?" hissed Edmund, his teeth grinding in barely restrained disgust. "So Eadric goes over to Svienn as soon as my father isn't around for him to bleed dry? Damn it all, Wulfnoth, I wish you'd said something. I'd not have ordered a retreat had I known he was around and asking for a sword through the gullet."

"That's why I kept this quiet," came Wulfnoth's reply. "We needed to fall back. We had a good start, and the Danes will be mourning their dead tonight, but we couldn't keep on with Eadric hitting us in the flank like that. I suspected had you thought he was present, you'd not have retreated. We'd have all died then. You know it."

"I do," sighed Edmund, noting how both his hands had clenched into fists. "I'd have wanted to kill him and risked everyone by attempting it. It's not good enough. Æthelstan would have kept his senses. He always did. He always..."

"Then this is about Æthelstan, after all?" Wulfnoth murmured. "You still grieve for him? Why did it come out just now? You fought the Danes in Lundenburg, am I right, and still retained control?"

"I did," whispered Edmund, his eyes filling with tears. "But they killed my brother, Wulfnoth. He died, speaking his last to me in that monastery near Bernecestre ...and there they were today, the Danes, at another monastery, burning and killing and desecrating. I couldn't have it! I couldn't bear it!"

"I understand. There is a time for all things, it's true. The Bible says there is a time for peace and a time for war, a time for love and a time for...you know the rest. You did that today. It's nothing to be ashamed of."

"Isn't it?" asked Edmund. "Truth is, Wulfnoth, it scared me. I always remember fighting, but I can't remember much of what we just did. It's a blur. How many men did I kill? Did I...Lord have mercy, I didn't lash out at any of our own, did I?"

"Put that thought to rest," assured Wulfnoth, his head shaking gently. "You were a marvel to behold. They love you, the men do. You knew that already, but they flocked to you in that fight. It was grief and hatred, Edmund, for sure, but also a fury that was righteous. Righteous fury. Remember that and be vindicated."

Edmund inhaled deeply, filling his lungs with the cold, damp air of the forest. He thought he was going to be sick again, panic rising slightly when he pictured performing such a shameful display in front of his men. It passed, much to his relief. The shakes had stopped. He felt calm. It was time to take stock of their situation and move on.

He sat up, rising to his full height, Wulfnoth doing likewise. They began to walk between the trees, checking on their men and exchanging a few words with those who looked like they needed it. They'd been defeated, and there was barely a man who wasn't at least bruised and shaken from the fight, but you'd never be able to tell from their spirit. They were defiant and resolute, all possessing the look of those who knew their duty and were quite prepared to die in the performance of it.

Edmund felt a strange reverence in the face of it all. So many here were commoners, woodsmen, hunters, farmers even. They'd taken up arms purely because they'd judged it right, leaving their homes to seek him out as he led his company of ragged survivors away from Lundenburg. Some part of him couldn't fathom the faith they had in him, but they all saw him as the man to resist the Danes and continue resisting no matter what. He didn't think he could ever repay the honour they did him. If he were to become king, it would be because of the heroism and sacrifice of people like this. He could never balance that debt.

Such sentiments proved to be truer than he'd initially thought. They found Wilfrid breathing his last and surrounded by his men after they'd done their best to make him comfortable. He'd taken an axe to the chest and head during the fight, but someone had dragged him clear of the Mierčian cavalry so that he might live to fight again. Edmund had been startled to see him so wounded, but at least he'd still been talking as he was carried along, the helm upon his head ensuring he'd been spared instant death when the enemy huscarl had struck him. He looked up at Edmund now, his eyes focusing on him as he approached.

"I'm sorry," he whispered, Edmund kneeling at his side to hear his final words. "I was supposed to bring you back to your father. I don't think I can do that now."

"You did, though," Edmund insisted. "You saved me from the mob and brought me home. Cenric and I would have been killed without you."

"But you never made your peace with the king," wheezed Wilfrid. "It's a sorrow of mine to…see you so estranged. Loyal to your father, I am, despite everything. Loyal to you as his son…"

His eyes froze over, turning blank and empty. His arms flopped at his side, a final rattling exhalation concluding his last breath. Edmund reached out and gently closed his eyes, taking both his hands and folding them neatly across his stomach. His companions remained as they were, their heads hung low in sadness. Edmund stood up, Wulfnoth patting his arm reassuringly, and beheld those around them. A few words would be needed here.

"I'm sorry this happened," Edmund began, looking to each man in turn. "I owe Wilfrid, and I owe you. What you did for me in Lundenburg has not nor ever will be forgotten. We'll take Wilfrid with us. We'll take all of them with us. Not one of our fallen brethren will be without a proper burial. You have my oath on this."

Edmund was aware of Wulfnoth nodding at his side. He approved of his words, and from the looks of it, so did the men. It wasn't a ploy. Edmund meant what he'd said. Wilfrid and company had saved his life in Lundenburg. Those rioters would have torn him and Cenric apart if Wilfrid hadn't led them to safety, and his expertise at navigating Lundenburg's ancient sewers had ensured they'd been able to ultimately rescue Æva and the Ealdorman Ælfric. They'd had to shed blood to do it, and not all had walked away unscathed, but they'd never have made it there to begin with were it not for Wilfrid.

His quick thinking had also enabled Edmund to catch up with his father as he fled the city, but the reunion had not been as Wilfrid might have wanted. Edmund was sorry for that, but it couldn't be helped. He cared for his father deeply. He just couldn't forgive him. Not yet. Not after he'd allowed Eadric to lead him to ruin. Not after what he'd done to his uncle, Æthelstan.

Regrettably, several more men who'd been wounded had expired now that they'd stopped. Edmund did his best to console those close to them, telling them they'd be taking the bodies with them when it came time to move. Their plan was as it had been after they'd laid Alaric to rest outside Gipeswic. Edmund would return to the Five Boroughs and have Sigeferth and Morcar raise the fyrd. They would then do a forced march into Norþanhymbre and unseat the traitorous Ealdorman Uhtred. Following that, they'd rally the entire region into a mighty host before heading back down south to wage unrelenting war on King Svienn. It was a simple plan. Simplicity was good, in the abstract. It sadly didn't tend to last long when reality came calling.

The first complication had arisen shortly after Alaric was in the ground. Ulfcytel was a tempestuous one, and famous for it, but he'd been devastated by his friend's death and braying for revenge almost as soon as he'd finished giving his eulogy. The lady, Æva, was grieving too, and more so by far, but Ulfcytel's wound, whilst not so deep, was festering visibly and unwilling to let him rest. Edmund had begun to worry about him. It was in part for this reason he'd agreed to his plan to head south to Hamptonscir, as mad as it was, and attempt to unseat a certain traitor named Thurcytel, who had apparently turned on them at the Battle of Hringmere and fallen in with Eadric. Edmund had his doubts as to their chances, but Æva and Ælfric both were looking to follow him, saying this Thurcytel had been present when Eadric had attacked them at Porteceaster. He deserved death, and eliminating him would weaken Eadric, which was something Edmund could certainly get behind. Gaining control of Hamptonscir would also be a valuable win.

It had been Æva, however, who had really added some weight to their arguments. She had a way of speaking, one that was far more pleasing to Edmund's ear than the dry, measured tones of Ælfric or the menacing rumblings of Ulfcytel. He suspected this was because of the situation he'd found her in when they'd first met. She'd been imprisoned then, and helpless and desperate to be reunited with her son, Brandon. Edmund had been moved by it and shown her mercy, thinking his father cruel for separating them without cause. When he'd seen her again, she was free, but her husband, Alaric, had been killed and Brandon again lost. Edmund had reunited them for a second time, confronting his father in the process, but he'd had to do it quickly and with stealth to prevent bloodshed. If Ulfcytel and the others had caught up with him, it would have likely become violent. He couldn't have that. He couldn't have his father dead. Family always mattered, even when you were burdened with a father like Æthelred.

Æva's joy at having Brandon back had been overshadowed by Alaric's demise. Edmund had barely known the man, but he'd apparently come close to moving heaven and earth in Ulfcytel's desperate campaign to defend Eastengle and Canterburie, so Edmund wasn't about to question his worth. He also knew Alaric had saved Ulfcytel's life when they'd attacked Thorkell's fleet at Gipeswic. Acts like that created unbreakable bonds, especially in men of passion like Ulfcytel. It was no wonder he'd grieved as he had.

He wasn't the only one with such a tale to tell. A young man, named Osbert, had said Alaric had saved him from certain death when the Danes had breached Canterburie's walls. Cenric, also, had told him how Alaric had taken over the defence of the city when Ulfcytel had been wounded, ordering him to escape with the ealdorman whilst he and the rest of the garrison fought to the death. Yet another man, Eamon, if Edmund remembered right, had said Alaric had continued the fight even as they sought refuge in the cathedral and the city itself burned around them, only surrendering under pressure from the Archbishop Ælfheah and Thorkell's threat to desecrate the holy relics.

His heroism hadn't stopped there. The word was he'd attempted to save the archbishop himself when he'd come under attack from Thorkell's men, apparently doing his utmost to reach him and fight off his captors barehanded. He'd failed, sadly, but that hadn't broken his spirit, and when Wulfnoth had sprung him from prison, he'd been quick to lead his friends in escape. They'd headed to Remmesgate, thinking they stood a chance of rescuing some of Canterburie's enslaved citizens, only to spot Svienn's invasion fleet far out upon the seas. Rightly seeing the threat for what it was, Alaric had departed from his companions and rushed off on their single available horse, intent on warning Lundenburg before it was too late.

Edmund knew well enough what had happened next, and the thought of it shamed him still. Rather than rewarding Alaric for his timely warning, King Æthelred had ordered him imprisoned. Edmund still didn't understand what Alaric was supposed to have done to Æthelred nor why he'd become so obsessed with him, but they'd later exchanged words, that he did know, and they'd had a profound impact on his father. The details of what had been discussed were still a mystery, unfortunately, and since Alaric wasn't in any position to enlighten him, Edmund feared they would long remain so.

That just left the sorrowful matter of Æva. Edmund usually had no idea about the ways of women or how they thought, but he'd found himself wishing he could snatch her pain from her and cast it into the sea, such was its baleful weight upon her shoulders. Her husband was dead, it was true, and none but a callous fool would begrudge her for grieving, but Edmund found her almost hard to look at, so troubled was her bearing. This Alaric must have been as devoted a husband as he'd been skilled as a warrior. Men like that were rare. Edmund wished he'd had the opportunity to get to know him properly. He liked to think they'd have been friends. His tenacity was an example to follow.

And so he'd allowed Æva to head south, with Brandon, Ulfcytel, Ælfric, the mighty Cenric, and a host of others. Edmund wanted Æva healed, wanted her happy, and her home at Porteceaster seemed like the best place for that. There was danger ahead, of course, and Ælfric and Ulfcytel's arguments about the need to "raise the people of Hamptonscir" in rebellion had made a lot of sense, but ultimately Edmund had made the decision with Æva foremost in mind. She meant a lot to him, somehow, and her words had a certain persuasive gravitas to them, something Edmund wasn't sure he could even explain. He'd let them go, but he'd watched them all as they'd disappeared over the horizon, his mind and heart beset with a strange ache that just wouldn't desist.

Edmund shook himself free of the recent past and called his men to order, barking commands for them to assemble and follow him onward through the woods. They did as he asked, rallying to him for the journey ahead, the dead and wounded carried with them. It wouldn't be too long now. Soon they'd find refuge and be able to plan the next stage of their campaign. Even without the ealdormen, Ælfric and Ulfcytel, Edmund still held influence, and if his friends were successful down south, he'd have all of Hamptonscir on his side. With the Five Boroughs also in his pocket, Edmund's rebellion would be off to an excellent start. Svienn would then be made to regret the day he'd ever come here.

By the time morning came, their ragged column had broken free of the forests and byways of Eastengle and begun rushing westward towards Cantebrigie. They avoided the city, knowing it to be a ruin, but were surprised to discover several outlying villages had been rebuilt and repopulated already. Some of the locals even joined them, bringing what they had in terms of money and arms and swearing allegiance to Edmund like he was already king. Wulfnoth looked on, his eyes agleam, Edmund doing his best to appear the gracious ruler. He was constantly surprised by how many were still so eager to resist the Danes. With men such as these, much could be done.

Night descended quickly, the ensuing dawn bringing some summer showers that fortunately failed to impede their progress. More recruits came to them, as individuals or in small groups, all ready and willing to fight. They were more than welcome, but Edmund had begun to wonder how word had spread that he was even in the area, let alone intending to drive the Danes into the sea. People talked, he knew that, but he was also aware that if the locals knew he was here then there was a chance his enemies would also learn of it. It was for that reason he made a point of hurrying on, never staying put for more than a few hours, even for sleep. They could all rest properly in Snotingeham, where safety would allow such things.

Another day passed, and then another after that, before they reached Snotingeham. Edmund led them through the streets, feeling proud of his men despite their dishevelled, irregular appearance and the hobbling non-combatants that followed. They'd done what they'd set out to do. Lundenburg had fallen, but they'd escaped, and they'd bloodied the enemy with it. Hope could spring in even the most barren of soil, and whilst much of England was a devastated land, Edmund was still of a mind to give it hope.

There was one thing he had to do before he got down to business with Sigeferth. Wulfnoth wanted to see his old friend. He wanted to see Æthelstan. They walked there together, Wulfnoth kneeling at the sight of the grave and clasping his hands together in silent prayer. Edmund remained on his feet, thinking how different the place looked from last winter. He'd spent so much time here then, huddled in the snow, unwilling and unable to depart from his brother's final resting place. It pained him still to think on it, and it saddened him yet further to see the normally unflappable Wulfnoth so moved. Edmund closed his eyes and hung his head, his hands lifting to his chest as he began a private prayer of his own. He loved and missed his brother. He'd have the Lord reminded of it.

Somebody approached from behind, their hurried footsteps revealing their presence before Edmund had even turned to look. He peered over his shoulder, smiling slightly when he beheld the familiar form of Sigeferth. He had a worried manner today, his wrinkled countenance appearing almost severe. That didn't stop him from smiling when his eyes met Edmund's. They embraced, the gesture long and full, their relief palpable at seeing the other unharmed.

"We feared the worst!" Sigeferth finally said, easing from Edmund's grasp. "When we heard Svienn was heading for Lundenburg, we tried to get word to you, but..."

"It's fine," said Edmund, still smiling. "We had a little trouble getting out, but we managed it."

"And you brought friends," nodded Sigeferth, his hand gesturing lightly towards the now-standing Wulfnoth. "Lots of friends. Who are they? Survivors of the siege? How did you get so many out?"

"It's complicated," replied Edmund. "But you'll know my friend Wulfnoth here, and his people in Sūþsēaxe are prepared to declare for me once I announce my intention to become king. With your support, we can raise an army and make..."

"Wait, Edmund, please," implored Sigeferth, his voice strained. "This is a lot to take in. The last time we saw each other, you were riding with your sister to convince your father that Morcar and I were not responsible for your brother's death...but now you intend to make yourself king?"

"I do. My father has fled, as I'm sure you've heard, and Svienn Forkbeard rules from Lundenburg. I will not live under a foreign yoke, and from what I've seen, I'm not alone in that. I will be king. It is my right."

"Then I have some sad news," sighed Sigeferth, his eyes mournful. "I'm afraid you're too late. Almost everyone of note has declared for Svienn, and so when his envoys reached us, we had no choice. We've submitted to him. Svienn is our king now, and I will not fight all of England and Denmark both in resisting him. I'm sorry, Edmund. I truly am."

V

"Do you remember when we first met?"

Æva looked over at Alaric, thinking he had that far-away look in his eyes that came on whenever he got sentimental. "I remember," she answered softly. "Your father had brought you over like he had some grand surprise to reveal to my parents."

"Was I that much of a disappointment?" Alaric asked, a soft chuckle following his question.

"Never," replied Æva, reaching out to take his hand. "You were never a disappointment. Not to me."

Alaric nodded, his gaze wandering slowly over to the horizon. They were sitting at one of their favourite spots in Wiltune, atop a hill overlooking the town. The warm red and orange glow of the sun was sinking towards the west, and if you looked intently enough, you could see faint traces of the heavens beginning to reveal themselves through the thinning clouds. Birdsong echoed from the woods behind them, and the fields immediately below and ahead were awash with the swaying, golden hue of barley in bloom. The wind tugged at her hair, its caress warm and soft, the trees at their backs sighing and rustling as they, too, rejoiced at its touch. These late summer evenings lifted the heart, such was their splendour. Life was good here.

"I love you," Alaric said quietly, his smile implying he thought himself mischievous for stating such a thing so casually.

"You do?!" replied Æva, deliberately feigning shock, the flat of her palm upon her chest.

"I do!" said Alaric triumphantly. "Did you not notice? I thought you'd have noticed that whole marrying thing we did...and all that stuff we did after that..."

"Shhhh," said Æva, raising a finger to her smiling lips. "My father might hear, and he doesn't know what a fiend you are. He thinks we adopted Alfred, or that he just turned up on our doorstep one day. He doesn't know how these things are actually done."

"Are you quite sure about that?" Alaric asked quizzically. "I mean, the very fact you exist would seem to indicate he knows exactly what he's doing when it comes to..."

"Eww!" shrieked Æva, a light fist slapping Alaric playfully across the arm. "I don't need to have that image in my head. I'm quite content to think my father is entirely innocent of such matters, thank you very much."

"I see," nodded Alaric sagely. "So, does that mean you'll answer my question?"

"What question?"

"As to whether you've noticed that I love you?"

"I noticed," she said happily. "I can tell by the way you keep hanging about the place...and for some reason, I end up cooking for you every night. And morning, for that matter."

"Does that mean you love me too?" asked Alaric, still playing the sincere fool.

"I think so," came the reply, Æva leaning over and kissing his cheek. "I think so very much, very much."

They continued as they were, enjoying the last of the sun as it made its inexorable descent to mark the closing of another day. Æva enjoyed summer evenings immensely. There was often something in the air, harking back to her childhood, perhaps, that never failed to touch a part of her soul, impressing upon her the preciousness of life and the good fortune she enjoyed in living it. There was nowhere else on earth she'd rather be than right here, and no one else she'd rather have the company of than her husband. This was what life was all about, and her heart was fit to burst with the sheer contentment of it all.

"How long do I have?" asked Alaric suddenly, the beginnings of a frown emerging across his forehead.

"What do you mean?" Æva asked, confused and fearful at the same time. Her husband looked troubled, and her breath caught in her chest when she noticed his wound. She had no idea how she'd missed it, but he'd somehow lost an entire eye, the flesh around the now empty socket looking like it had been knitted shut in a most cumbersome fashion.

"How long do I have?" he repeated, gazing straight at her, his beard and hair matted with sweat. "How long do I have until they take me from you?"

"What are you talking about?" she cried. "Who is taking you? Why?"

Alaric opened his mouth like he meant to answer but only managed to emit a pained sigh. He slumped at his hips, his whole body leaning towards her as his strength suddenly left him. She laid his head in her lap, noting how his face was now marked with a dozen additional cuts and bruises, his broken nose and split lips making it appear like he'd just come from a tavern brawl in which he was undeniably the loser. His chest rose and fell, the pace of his breath gradually weakening.

"I'm sorry I had to go so suddenly," he whispered, his remaining eye brimming with tears. "I didn't mean to just go like that. Don't forget me. Please don't forget me."

Æva tried to respond. She couldn't speak, her voice fleeing from her, and Alaric's breath gave out, his eye glazing over and his life ending not a few hundred yards from their home. He stared up at her, limp and lifeless, the look on his face speaking of a tremendous yearning and sorrow all rolled into one. Pain welled up inside her, overcoming her defences and clutching her heart. It strained and shuddered, buckling and now breaking under the terrible pressure. Æva looked up from her husband's mournful face, tears streaming from her eyes, her mouth opening and closing erratically. This couldn't be. This shouldn't...

"I can't sleep."

Æva snapped her eyes open and sat upright. It was dark in her chamber, so dark she couldn't see even an inch in front of her, but she'd heard a voice, and that voice had thankfully roused her from her troubled dreams. She'd been sweating, saturating her nightdress yet again. A cool, tender breeze drifted in from the shutters she knew to be on her right, but it did little to dispel the stuffiness that prevailed. There was no lightening the atmosphere. She'd tried. Sadness reigned here, and wouldn't be dissuaded from maintaining its hold on her for as long as it wished.

"Brandon?" She'd spoken into the darkness, her voice alert despite her sudden awakening. She knew it was him. It couldn't be anyone else, unless an assassin had infiltrated the fortress to complain about his sleep pattern. Considering how unlikely that was, it had to be her son. She felt some relief. She wasn't entirely alone.

"Can I sit?" She didn't know why he was asking, and he didn't appear to have waited for her to respond, as the weight on the opposite side of her bed shifted a little, indicating he had indeed sat down. "I can't sleep," he repeated mournfully, Æva wondering if it pained him to now sit in the space his father, Alaric, had once occupied.

"I'm troubled too," Æva said softly, hoping the notion of shared lament might somehow bring him some solace. "The dreams come on...sad dreams. I'm sad, Brandon. Tell me why you're sad?"

"Why are we back here?" he asked. "There were dead people outside. It scares me, and father...he's not here and..."

"I know," Æva whispered, trying to catch and restrain a sob before it could manifest. "We had to leave him in Eastengle. He'll rest there with Osmund. It's right that they remain together."

"I don't understand," said Brandon, his voice meek and fragile in the pitch blackness. "I thought they went to fight a war, and they'd be back. Why did we leave and why did..."

"It's difficult, I know," she said, hoping to cut him off before the poor boy lost himself in a thousand questions. "He died fighting for us. Both he and Osmund died fighting for us. So many others have died fighting for us."

"Why?" came the inevitable response, the bed again creaking as Brandon hunched over to rest his elbows upon his knees. Æva shifted and reached, arm outstretched, her fingers clawing at the dark until she made purchase on her son's shoulder. She shuffled over to him and lay half-upright on her side to rub his back. She could feel the cold sweat through his gown. He'd been having nightmares also.

"Men fight because they care for people like us," she said, hoping to phrase and explain such matters in a way a young boy without a father might comprehend. "No good man in his right mind fights for the sake of it, but they can't stand by and see those they love being harmed. They have love in their hearts, and the courage to show it and stand for it. That's why they fight."

"Were we going to be harmed? He left for Eastengle before those men came for us."

"Yes, he did," said Æva carefully. "But Alaric loved his homeland as well as his family. He knew he wasn't alone in that, and so he had to fight for the country...to protect the families of all Englishmen, not just his own. He couldn't do otherwise."

"Why not?"

"There would be no love there," she kept on, wondering if Brandon was simply too disturbed to comprehend what she was attempting to say. "Love isn't selfish. Love is patient and kind, so it's said...but also fierce. That's how you know somebody has love in their heart...because it won't just be sweet talk for them. It won't just be pretty words and an empty smile. They'll be willing to sacrifice, to fight, to give their very lives for their friends...their countrymen...there is no greater love than that."

"So that's what my father did? And Osmund?" Brandon was crying now. It was muffled, likely by his own hands and his efforts to control himself, but the sound was unmistakable to a mother. Æva shifted over to him and sat upright, her hands again fumbling in the dark until she was finally able to ease the boy into her embrace.

"He did," she whispered. "I miss him too. I miss him so much. I'm so sorry this happened."

"Will I have to do that too?" he asked, his question catching Æva off guard. "Will I have to fight?"

She thought for a few moments before answering. She knew of mothers who encouraged their sons to think of themselves as warriors, even approving of their bad behaviour when they bullied or outright attacked other children just for the sake of it. Æva was no such mother, and she'd always thought the mark of a true hero lay in the reason as to WHY they fought, not simply because they were capable of doing so. Alaric knew that, and he'd been a better fighter than most. Only Cenric was better from what she'd seen, and it was Cenric who was largely responsible for his training to begin with.

"Will you want to fight?" she asked, still holding him as she turned his question back on him.

"I don't know," sniffed Brandon. "Will people say I'm a coward if I don't? I don't want that."

"You don't need to worry about such things now," she soothed. "You have your whole life to live, but I will say this...enjoy it and appreciate what you have. You'll put down roots. You'll grow close to others and find a place for them in your heart. You'll see this land of ours...this England...and you'll find yourself loving it as your father did."

"And then I'll fight?"

"That will be the why of it, Brandon. That will be why you'll fight, for the sake of what we have here. For the sake of your country and its people. That was why your father did what he did."

"So it's not about being the best fighter and making a name for yourself?" Æva wasn't sure where Brandon was getting these ideas from. It was other children, almost certainly, and their parents were feeding it to them, but it was annoying for her to have to hear it. It was also distinctly un-Christian, and she'd have words with anyone she caught talking such nonsense.

"That's how our enemies think," she said sternly. "It's different with them. They act for themselves, not caring about who they hurt and deluding themselves with pride. Your father never did that. And he would have defeated many a man of such mind. Do you remember your friend, Boden?"

"Yes."

"You remember when that other lad knocked him down and wanted to hurt him for no good reason?"

"I remember," said Brandon, some pride creeping into his voice. "I scared him off. I didn't like what he was doing to Boden."

"Then you understand your father better than you think," she said happily. "The Danes are that cruel boy, and England is Boden. Your father did what you did for the same reason, that same care you had, but extended over all of England and everyone in it. He couldn't stand to do nothing whilst those he cared for were hurt. Just as you couldn't either."

"So that's why men fight?"

"Good men, yes," Æva clarified.

"Is King Edmund like father?"

She hesitated, the fingers of her left hand now playing with a strand of Brandon's hair. It was still too dark to see anything of him, but she thought she might be able to pick out just the slightest trace of brilliant blond in the otherwise inscrutable blackness. The lad's hair would never darken. It would have happened already if it were to be so. He'd look like his father. His real father. Hemingr. She could see it in him now that the man's face was fresh in her memory from their encounter in Lundenburg. There was something in the eyes, the jaw and forehead…a similarity that gave her pause.

Then she smiled. Brandon had called Edmund king. The boy was sharp to have a sense for these things, and it was likely evidence he wouldn't grow up to be a mindless killer like the thankfully dead Hemingr. He had emotions, too, deep and gentle and sincere. He wouldn't be here otherwise. She was glad of it. Her broken heart would be so much harder to bear without him.

"I think Edmund is like your father," answered Æva thoughtfully. "He was kind to us. Your father was kind…and Edmund fights FOR others, not just for the sake of it. He sees England like Alaric did, and he can't do anything but defend her. To do otherwise would be a betrayal of himself."

"Why a betrayal?" mumbled Brandon as he lay down on his side, his back to his mother. He was tired, she could hear it in his voice. She pulled her blanket over so it covered him, hoping it likely he'd drift into sleep.

"Men like Edmund and Alaric, Cenric and the others…they can't live just to get up and eat, please themselves, earn riches and the like. They have things they live by that they keep deep inside. Call it faith, or a code, honour and such, something they can never turn from, lest they cease to really be themselves. I think I see that in Edmund. I think…"

She fell silent. Brandon didn't inquire why she was no longer talking. He just lay there, his breath easing back and forth, apparently at peace. A moment passed, and then another. Æva slowly relaxed her head down upon her pillow, relieved that her son was at rest. She kept a hand on his back, the rising and falling of his torso oddly comforting as she closed her eyes. She was glad how things had turned out tonight. The dreams had been harrowing, and she'd never get used to them, but she liked to think she'd done a half-decent job of explaining a few things to Brandon. It was important he understand. It would hopefully serve him well in handling his own grief.

Light filled the room, dispelling any trace of the shadows that had held sway just seconds prior. She realised she'd fallen asleep again, missing the dawn and only awakening now the sun was in full ascent. Brandon was gone, but he'd been quiet about it, ensuring the blanket remained snugly around his mother as he headed off to who knows where. She'd best go look for him.

Æva got up, removing her nightdress and taking her deep-red linen cyrtel from her wardrobe. She dressed herself, donning her cyrtel before fastening a belt of polished leather around her waist. She spent a modest amount of time brushing her hair, knowing it would be untameable otherwise, before tying it up and back and concealing much of it beneath a white and gold threaded headscarf. She fixed a scabbard to her belt, glancing apprehensively at the slender seax that lay within. It was a gift from Cenric so she could protect herself if he were not around. It was a nice thought, and she'd wear it as such, but she didn't like weapons and wasn't sure how effective she'd be if the situation ever called for it.

She moved back to her bed, stripping her sheets and blankets and depositing them in the corner so they could be properly washed later. She'd always done this, every morning, more or less, provoking mirth from her husband, who saw no need for such exactitude when it came to hygiene. She'd sent him the odd jibe in retaliation, joking that he'd spent at least half of his life sleeping outside with other men and was thus barely suited to civilisation to begin with. For some reason, he'd found that funnier than she had. She'd do anything to have him laughing with her now. Instead, a mournful silence hung heavily over her chamber. She'd best leave. Brandon would be wanting breakfast.

Æva stepped over to her door and tugged on the worn iron handle, the hinges groaning a little as it was opened. She stepped through, letting the door slowly close behind her. Brandon hadn't gotten far. He was here by the empty hearth, fully dressed and sitting in the same chair that Cenwynn had usually occupied whenever Æva had needed her to watch him. Æva missed Cenwynn. There had been no sign of her when they'd retaken the fortress, and she feared the worst. Something had to be done about that, and she knew just who might be able to help.

"Come, let's go and see Cenric," Æva said brightly.

"I don't want to," he said brusquely. "He put that man outside who won't let me pass. I don't like that."

"What man?" Æva asked, apprehensive. If there was somebody hanging around her living quarters, she should have been told.

"See for yourself," grumbled Brandon, his bottom lip sticking out so much he looked vaguely ridiculous. "He's still there on the stairs. I don't like him. He won't let me leave!"

Æva stepped forward and away from the entrance to her bedchamber, passing both Brandon and the hearth to fling open the heavy oaken door to the stairwell. A fully armed and mailed man spun to face her, his expression, what she could see of it from beneath his helmet, a little startled by the sudden movement. "Who in God's name are you?" she demanded, her heart rate increasing slightly in anxious expectation. "Why are you here? For how long?"

"I've been here all night and this morning, lady," rumbled the rather large and quite intimidating fellow. "Cenric's orders. The fortress still isn't entirely secure, and he won't have you left alone."

"Do we not have men barring the entrance to my father-in-law's hall?" she retorted. "Any intruder would have to fight through them to access the tower and get to me. Why bother assigning you to watch my door?"

"Not sure, lady," he replied. "Cenric tells me to do something, I do it. That's how it works. I'm to safeguard you and the boy at all times until he says otherwise."

"Do I have any say in this?" Æva asked, somewhat annoyed but also strangely flattered that Cenric was so eager to keep her safe.

"Not sure, lady," said the warrior again. "Ask him if you like. He'll most likely be in the barracks at this time. Eating breakfast."

She frowned, noting how this dutiful man had laid a peculiar emphasis on the words "eating" and "breakfast". He must be hungry. If what he'd said was true, he'd been standing here for hours, without sleep and most likely without a proper feed. She'd see him put right. She called Brandon to her side, closing the door and setting off with him down the tower steps. The guard followed cumbersomely, his spear and shield occasionally clipping at the stonework around them.

They reached the ground floor and began the long walk through the Ealdorman Ælfric's great hall. It felt good to think of it in such terms again, and she was also glad the paintings and tapestries that lined its walls were largely unmolested. This Thurcytel had been a cruel and boorish man, but he'd had the good sense to leave these treasures as they were. She somehow doubted he'd appreciated them as much as she did. Anyone capable of doing what he'd done couldn't have an eye for art.

The guards at the gate nodded to them as they wandered out into the courtyard. Porteceaster spread out before them, and they moved to greet it, Æva still feeling a sense of elation that she was back here after spending so long imprisoned in Lundenburg. The walls still stood, majestic as always, and its people remained, busy and industrious as they cleared the streets after the frenzied melee that had seen them finally take back their home.

They moved through the old market square, Brandon continuing to eye their newfound guardian with great suspicion. Æva was lost in thought, thinking on the battle that had recently been fought here and how the common people had risen up on hearing Ulfcytel's booming demands for the garrison's surrender. She hadn't been able to see what was happening at the time, but the sounds of battle from within had been loud enough. She'd feared for the people, thinking it possible that Eadric's men were cutting them down, so she was beyond relieved when somebody had thrown open the gates and begun screaming for them to rush in and help them.

It had been obvious what they should do, and so they'd seized the opportunity. Ulfcytel had gone first, charging ahead of everyone else, but Ælfric, Cenric and those they'd been able to recruit on their journey had followed, rushing into the fight without hesitation. The Mierčians who'd remained loyal to Thurcytel, or at least the memory of him, were fighting back, but they were outnumbered and leaderless, and with the gate breached they were hard-pressed. It was all over within minutes. Victory was theirs.

Some had surrendered rather than die for Eadric, and Æva had listened intently to their explanations when they'd knelt before Ulfcytel and Ælfric. Thurcytel had been a cold and merciless master, they'd said, and Eadric himself had overstepped the bounds of decency when he'd used them to terrorise the local population in a bid to compel Ælfric to surrender the fortress. Æva remembered that episode well enough. Eadric had killed a woman and then a boy, cutting their throats before the walls so that all might witness the sheer horror of it. She'd wondered then if any of his men had been disgusted like she was. It was a relief to see some of them had ultimately followed their conscience.

They reached the barracks; a low-lying stone building with an abundantly thatched roof tucked into the eastern wall. They passed within, their escort muttering something to himself upon seeing about a score or so men eating at several long, battered wooden tables scattered about a wide, spartan hall. Cenric rose from the throng, approaching with a brisk pace, and patted Æva's guard on the shoulder before whispering something into his ear. The man nodded eagerly, grateful for whatever had been said. Æva had a feeling she knew what it was, finding her suspicions confirmed when he parted from them to snatch himself a large bowl of freshly cooked porridge from a great cauldron bubbling over a log fire. She watched him sit down with his comrades, unsure if she'd ever seen a man so happy at the prospect of porridge. He deserved it. He'd had a long night.

Cenric had too by the looks of him. His hair had greyed even further since they'd last been here, and his scars, whilst always visible through his long, silken beard, looked oddly jarring in the light, as if they were the marks of recent trauma rather than the etchings of battles long past. He'd aged, the past few months undoubtedly taking a toll on him, but as noticeable as that was, she was relieved to see his eyes were the same. Green, of course, with shadows of fatigue, but still glowing with that same spirit of duty and courage she'd grown accustomed to. She felt safer from being near him. It was just a shame the choice of words for his greeting was a tad unexpected.

"Brandon, lad! What's with the sulks? You've a face like a slapped arse!"

Æva gasped, surprised at Cenric's vulgarity, only to find Brandon struggling to hide his mirth. She shook her head, exasperated, her heart softening when she beheld Cenric's apologetic expression.

"I'm sorry," he said swiftly. "I've grown used to rougher company, and I wasn't thinking right." He turned to Brandon and patted him on the head affectionately. "Sorry about that, young man. You've a fine face, completely unlike a slapped...but what's bothering you? You look displeased on this fine morn."

"You placed a guard on our door who wouldn't let me leave," said Brandon sulkily. "Why wouldn't he? I've a right to go where I please here. It's my home."

"All right, I apologise again," said Cenric patiently. "But as much as it is your home, it was until the day before yesterday overrun by some rather bad men. The place isn't entirely safe yet."

"Do you mean to say you don't trust the Miercians who came over to our side?" asked Æva.

"We should talk about this in private, lady," Cenric said quietly. "Follow me, please."

He turned, heading towards the back of the hall and through another door that led into a draughty corridor. They followed him, Æva and Brandon, observing how the men in the barracks were largely unknown to them. Most of those now either eating or resting here hailed from the villages that had risen up in their favour when they'd passed through just days prior, all of them suitably stirred into action by Ulfcytel and Ælfric's appeal for them to come settle accounts with the fiendish Thurcytel. She was glad they were here, but she did wonder what had happened to the original garrison that had been manning the walls that fateful night they'd snuck off to find refuge in Suthhamtunam. Then she remembered the line of gibbets they'd seen outside the gate. It hadn't been the entire garrison hanging there, but it did indicate just how unlikely it was that any of their old friends might resurface. She was glad those poor souls had now been cut down and given a proper burial. It was all they could do for them.

Cenric turned again to usher them through a stone archway, his long, bulky figure hunching slightly as he moved ahead to pass through another doorway and enter yet another spacious hall. He closed the door behind them once they'd stepped through, Æva soon noticing the unmistakable form of the Ealdorman Ulfcytel sitting at a narrow table. He was conferring with someone, a black-haired and bearded man she hadn't spoken with, and from the looks of him he wasn't in the best of moods. She wondered why they'd never brought his wife, Wulfhild, on their journey south. She had a calming effect on him. Perhaps it was for everyone's benefit that she be kept around.

Ulfcytel rose at the sight of Æva, almost knocking over the bowl of porridge he'd been spooning into his mouth. He was a messy eater, and quite a few oats were stuck fast in his beard, but he still cut an impressive figure, his mailed chest and shoulders making him as broad as a barn door and likely twice as durable. His grey beard had grown long and full, giving his appearance a wild, primal quality, and his bald head and hard, simmering eyes intimidated friend and foe alike. It was with some relief that Æva realised he counted her among the former.

"Tell me, lady," he rumbled joyfully, "how does it feel to be sleeping in your own bed again? Good, yes?"

He didn't wait for an answer, instead turning to Brandon, a wide grin cracking his jaw. "And what about you, young sir? Good to be back here, no?"

Brandon looked at him, a little hesitant after being addressed by somebody so fearsome. "It's...nice," he replied, his voice a tiny squeak when compared with Ulfcytel's. "It's just sad my father isn't here."

The ealdorman's face crumpled, his smile vanishing into that thicket of a beard. "I know, lad, I know," he said, quietly now. "We miss him, all of us, but it must be doubly hard for you. Tell me..."

Ulfcytel had stopped talking. He was staring, leaning forward ever so slightly like he wanted to focus on every detail of Brandon's face. "You have the look of..." he said, his voice barely a murmur, "the look of..."

"The look of his mother," Cenric suggested quickly.

"That's it, that's what I was thinking," burbled the ealdorman, Æva noting how he shot Cenric a strange look, as if he was conveying gratitude for helping him out. "You look just like your mother, that's it," he said, turning back to Brandon, his grin again on display. "Just like her, just like her..."

He trailed off. This was awkward. Ulfcytel was renowned as a great leader of men, and from that, Æva assumed he had a mind for details and spotting inconsistencies. She felt strangely paranoid now because of it. The ealdorman had gotten to know Brandon a little on their journey down here, and he'd never once questioned that he was Alaric's son, despite the startlingly obvious fact they looked nothing alike. Æva had thought him fooled, like everyone else, but now she was not so sure. She hoped he'd be decent about it. She didn't want to have to deal with gossip and hurtful rumours.

"So you think we're not as safe as we could be, Cenric?" asked Æva, hoping to converse on anything other than Brandon's appearance.

"Let's just say we have work to do," he replied, "but I wouldn't worry unduly. What we pulled off here was a miracle. It shouldn't have worked...I still can't quite believe it..."

"Believe what?" Ulfcytel asked. "That we took the fortress? A bastard like Thurcytel was always going to make mistakes. It's fortunate for us his mistakes led to the people here hating him enough to let us in."

"I don't think that was all his doing," said Æva. "I was here when Eadric came with the rest of them. They were savage, murderous...as bad as Danes. The people of Hamptonscir would have learned to hate them from that day onwards. They were probably always looking for an opportunity to shake off such a yoke. You gave them one."

"Me?" asked Ulfcytel, suddenly acting like a man of modesty. "All I did was walk up to the gate and shout about what I'd done to Thurcytel. How was I to know it would all kick off just from that?"

"Well, what would you have done if it hadn't worked?" asked Æva. "The Mierčians could have just shot you full of arrows from the walls. Had you prepared for that? Could you have?"

"I had prepared for that possibility," said the dark-haired man still seated at Ulfcytel's side. Æva could tell who he was now. He'd had a full helmet on before, back when they'd seized Thurcytel in the forest and put him to death, and this man had been the instigator of it all, using his position as his personal bodyguard to lure him into a trap.

He'd been clever to pull that off, it's true, but he seemed to be faintly troubled, his small, fierce eyes suggesting he'd seen more than his share of unpleasant sights in his time. "You had sympathisers on the inside, my lady," he went on. "You just didn't know it. My Lord Wulfnoth wouldn't have advised you head down here if it was a fool's errand. How could you have prevailed otherwise? You'd have been shut outside, with no help, no support...Wulfnoth saw to it that it wouldn't go that way. His plan paid off, as they usually do."

Æva stared at him, wondering who he really was and who he might be to this Wulfnoth. That man was a strange one. She'd barely spoken with him back in Offetuna, but she was rapidly getting the impression he was a fount of information, and not all of it gleaned via honest means. She didn't know how she felt about that. Scheming and double-dealing sounded like something a cur like Eadric would go in for, and the men who indulged in such things were inevitably tainted by it. On the other hand, Edmund seemed to like Wulfnoth, and he'd apparently had a hand in saving Alaric from the ruins of Canterburie. That said a lot for his character, and yet she just couldn't bring herself to trust him. There was something in his eyes, and as she continued to think on it, this man who'd just spoken had the same look to him.

"It's all true," said Ulfcytel with a contented sigh. "I kept it to myself, but Wulfnoth let on a few details to me. He had a spy inside the walls here, providing him with information, information that was crucial to us catching Thurcytel when we did and also opening the gates when we made our move. A most resourceful man, are you not, Dunstan?"

"I do as I'm told," came the response, this Dunstan, if that was even his real name, appearing unmoved by Ulfcytel's flattery. "When my Lord Wulfnoth told me to expect you, I made preparations. It was easier than I'd feared. People here hated Thurcytel. He was not kind, not even to me and the other Mierċian warriors he relied on. Eadric also recalled much of the garrison some months ago. I suspect he wanted all his forces on hand to defend his own lands should Thorkell continue to prove a menace."

Æva reached out to take Brandon's hand, knowing he'd likely be getting bored at all this talk he couldn't hope to understand. What Dunstan had said was of interest. When Eadric had come here last year, he'd had hundreds upon hundreds of warriors with him. They hadn't faced anywhere near that number of men when the fighting had started days ago, and they'd never have been able to prevail if it were otherwise. Eadric had clearly gambled on Thurcytel's ability to keep order on his own terms, and lost. That was good. What was concerning was Wulfnoth's apparent habit of placing spies about the place to keep tabs on his rivals. Intrigue was afoot, and she wouldn't have it so close to home.

"How long have you been in Wulfnoth's service, Dunstan?" She thought she'd be as direct as she could be. There was no sense in being diplomatic with dishonest men.

"A long time," he grunted, his left eye twitching slightly with the admission.

"So how long have you been in Eadric's service, or at least pretending to be?" she continued, ignoring the concerned look from Cenric. Dunstan didn't reply. He just sat there, his hands folded neatly on the table and his eyes level with hers.

"Does Wulfnoth have other spies? Here? In my home?" she pressed, hands on hips, her voice as stern as she could manage.

"All right, I'll say that's enough on this," interjected Ulfcytel with a flick of his hand. "Dunstan, I'll catch up with you later. Leave us be now, if you please."

Dunstan rose from his chair, ignoring Æva to make his way to the exit and escape her questions. She glared at Cenric and Ulfcytel both for a few seconds more, the echo from Dunstan's rather forceful closure of the door gradually subsiding. Ulfcytel might not care about Wulfnoth placing a spy within Porteceaster, but she did, and Cenric at least should. Otherwise, what was the point in his attempts to keep any of them safe?

"I will not be dissuaded from this," said Æva, her voice quiet yet determined. "How do we know Dunstan is the only spy here? He certainly didn't act alone when it came to dealing with Thurcytel. Does this Wulfnoth and his intrigue not bother you? You, in particular, Cenric."

"But he helped us," shrugged Cenric, as though a little exasperated. "We'd not have been able to prevail without Dunstan. We'd not have caught Thurcytel outside the walls had Wulfnoth not told Dunstan in advance to prepare for our arrival."

Æva shook her head, annoyed that nobody else seemed to share her suspicions. "And how did Wulfnoth get word to him?" she asked. "We left Eastengle quickly enough. Does Wulfnoth communicate with his people through magic?"

"He sent a rider on ahead of us," said Ulfcytel. "He had orders to make contact with Wulfnoth's people here and tell them what needed to be done."

"And where is this rider now?"

"Around here somewhere. I saw him just yesterday. He'd taken a slight wound to his side during the fighting, but he was alive. Trust me, Æva. We have nothing to fear from him or Dunstan."

"I can understand you worrying," said Cenric, like he was really putting some effort into making her understand. "But Wulfnoth has been a friend to us. We know Eadric is one to employ base treachery in his designs. It makes sense that Wulfnoth is attempting to counter him by his own methods, but I will say…"

"It doesn't matter anyway," snapped Ulfcytel impatiently. "Edmund trusts Wulfnoth, and his assistance has been invaluable in allowing us to take this place. The ends have justified the means, and I'll…"

"You shouldn't interrupt people," said Æva lightly. "Cenric was speaking, and your authority here is superseded by that of the Ealdorman Ælfric. As his daughter-in-law, I'll have you reminded of this."

Ulfcytel gave her a look, something halfway between annoyance and amusement, if she were reading him right. "I should mind my manners, yes," he admitted grudgingly. "But let's think on what we've gained. You have your home back, and Edmund has Hamptonscir, or we've made a solid start in getting him it. That's what matters."

"But for how long, in all seriousness?" she asked. "How many fighting men do we have here? A few hundred?"

She looked to Cenric, hoping he might provide answer. He nodded his head, his brow creasing as he affirmed her statement.

"That's not enough to hold back Svienn," she continued. "And how much of Hamptonscir is really ours? Remember what happened in Suthhamtunam. Eadwulf rules there, and he is Eadric's man…he betrayed us when we sought refuge with him and handed us over to Eadric…and if Eadric is with Svienn, then we're still in serious trouble. We're surrounded by enemies, even in victory."

"You have a mind like that of your husband," muttered Ulfcytel. "But you're not as optimistic. I prefer that. I like solutions, not a list of problems."

"What solutions can we obtain if we don't speak on the problems we have?" she replied. "I will bring this up with Ælfric. I'm sure he's already given it some thought. I know Eadwulf's betrayal would have cut him deeply. He'll be wanting to set things right."

She didn't know that for sure. Ælfric had not spoken much on the journey here. That was to be expected, considering what had happened to Alaric, but Æva had a feeling there was some other issue that was troubling him. Ælfgar had also remained unapproachable, albeit not for the usual reasons. She'd seen first-hand how he'd feared for his life when that despicable Hemingr had tried to get him and Alaric to battle one another for sport. Ælfgar had been beyond terrified, but he was also humiliated, the latter, she suspected, posing more of a problem for him than anything else. She'd like to talk to him when she could. He hadn't always been a disagreeable man, and he was truly suffering now.

"I can attest to the fact my Lord Ælfric is indeed planning to seize Suthhamtunam and deal with Eadwulf," announced Cenric, a look of satisfaction on his face, like he was hoping to please Ulfcytel with something positive. "That will be a real boon for us. Eadric will have lost an ally, and by association, so will Svienn. We'll also have our vengeance. I'm looking forward to it."

"But how will it be done?" asked Æva, bemused at his over-confidence. "Do we have the men to overcome Suthhamtunam's walls? They are not like the ones we have here, but they are good and sturdy. How do we deal with that?"

"No disrespect, lady, but this is all beyond your expertise," Cenric said, looking very serious now, as if standing up to her was something he didn't do lightly. "We are men of war, and these are matters of war…and the Ealdorman Ælfric is well aware of our predicament and the resources he has at his disposal. I'm sorry if my words have caused any offence."

She couldn't be angry with him. He was absolutely right. All of her knowledge on military matters stemmed from things Alaric had mentioned from experiences he'd had when she was generally very, very far away. She wouldn't win any friends here by assuming she knew best regardless of the subject under discussion. A little modesty would serve her well, and it wouldn't benefit anyone to alienate and demoralise the two undoubtedly brave and decent men before her. She was better than that.

"I have something to show you, Æva," said Ulfcytel suddenly, wanting to head off any argument before it could get started. "Cenric, my man, would you accompany the young Brandon here back to his rooms?"

Æva went to object, thinking it improper for the ealdorman to just order her son to be taken elsewhere. Brandon looked quite happy with the arrangement, though, moving over to Cenric and looking up at him expectantly. She knew what this was about. He wanted a male role model in his life. Æva understood that, and just then, she couldn't think of a better one than Cenric.

"I would ask a favour before you leave, Cenric," Æva said, hoping she hadn't somehow offended the man to the point he was ill-disposed to listen. "There was a girl here whom I knew before we were taken by Eadric. A good young lady who used to watch Brandon for me. Cenwynn was her name, and for the life of me, when we retook this place I couldn't find her nor her parents. Will you see if you can find anything out?"

Cenric asked her for a description, Æva then going to some lengths to describe Cenwynn, from her hazel hair and eyes to the gap in her front teeth that became more evident when displaying one of her many smiles. Cenric claimed he remembered her, but, like Æva, had not laid eyes on her with their return. He promised to "make some inquiries" before turning to leave, an aged yet powerful hand clasped around Brandon's. They departed. Æva and Ulfcytel were alone.

"I once asked your husband if he trusted me." Ulfcytel sounded thoughtful, a faint trace of grief creeping into his tone at the mention of Alaric. "At Canterburie it was, before the big fight. I knew he did, but I wanted to make sure, for his sake as well as mine. Do you understand that?"

"I think so," nodded Æva. "He thought highly of you, before you'd even met, that I knew. Your reputation is quite something."

Ulfcytel ignored the compliment, instead angling his head slightly downward as if to stare at her feet. He wasn't actually doing any such thing, and the look in his eyes suggested he was reliving some not-so-distant memory and pondering whether to share it with her. He was still grieving for her husband, Æva suspected, but in ways that were a mystery to her as a woman and widow.

"Follow me, if you will," he said, his sizeable bulk meandering its way around the table to pass through the doorway and out into the corridor beyond. She moved after him, noticing how the main dining hall of the barracks was now more or less deserted, the warriors who'd feasted here having presumably marched off to their duties. Ulfcytel moved fast for a man of his size, his legs propelling him forward and out of the barracks with a swiftness that defied her expectations. She could see a slight limp on display, for reasons she was unsure of, but if it caused him discomfort he made no sign of it. It certainly didn't stop him from getting about.

They walked for some time, Æva feeling a little awkward whenever the locals stopped and stared at her and the purposeful ealdorman. She liked that they were happy to see her back, but sometimes she could see them looking when they thought she wasn't aware. There was pity in their eyes, of the genuine sort, but still something that only reminded her of her loss. Their reaction to Ulfcytel was very different. He was a legend to them, an invincible figure, unstoppable and ferocious in his pursuit of the enemies of England. She didn't envy him, thinking such renown would prove itself a burden, if it had not already. From the look of things, it didn't bother him. He was a leader, and a good one, knowing full well how to play up to expectations and reassure those around him. Of that she was glad. They didn't need anyone panicking about how difficult their situation really was.

They came to the southern wall and began to climb up a narrow, well-trodden stairwell to bring them atop the battlements. They reached the summit, Ulfcytel pausing for breath before continuing along to the west until he finally came to a halt overlooking the harbour.

There were ships out on the water, some leaving, others coming in to dock at the jetties below. The sea was reasonably calm, the crash of waves on the stony shore soothing rather than calamitous, and the summer sun was making the water sparkle in resplendent hues, from deep blue to golden green and then everything in between. The breeze tugged at her headscarf, forcing her to reach up and secure it lest it blow away and leave her exposed. She inhaled deeply through her nostrils, savouring the freshness and the sights beyond. Ulfcytel was leaning slightly forward, his hands gripping the edge of the wall to give Æva the fantastical impression he fancied himself capable of flight and was desirous to prove it.

"I'm afraid of the water."

She blinked, unsure if she'd heard right. Ulfcytel was reputed to be one of the most, if not THE most, formidable leaders England had. To hear him admit to being afraid of something typically feared by children was more than unexpected.

"I never used to be," he said, gazing out to the horizon. "It was after Gipeswic I knew something had changed. You know how Alaric saved me there?"

"I heard, yes," affirmed Æva. She had indeed heard this story shortly after they'd fled Lundenburg. It was a magnificent tale, undoubtedly, but she sensed the ealdorman had remained silent on a few things he'd not have felt comfortable admitting in public. It stood to reason that his fear would be one of them.

"I was in the water, and I was cut," he said. "A spear in the leg, hurled from onshore. Alaric comes hurtling out of nowhere, churning up the water like some maniac to grab hold of me and pull me…you heard all this before. But I panicked. We were done for, and the Danes knew it. They hurled more spears at us, laughing at me as I tried to stay afloat. They thought my pain amusing, you see. They are like that."

Æva stayed silent, drawing herself up alongside Ulfcytel so as to listen properly over the sound of the wind and waves. She enjoyed stories of Alaric, wanting to hear each and every one to better remember him.

"Alaric pulled me below the surface of the river. Right down, deep, heaving me along through the water so the Danes couldn't see us. I worked out what he was doing and tried to cooperate, but…I thought…I think I passed out. I recovered my senses aboard one of the ships we took as we rowed away, with Alaric staring out from the prow like the bloody hero he was."

He laughed softly, Æva smiling at his recollection. Ulfcytel held out his arm over the wall, holding his hand flat so his palm faced the shingle and mud below. There was a tremor, almost imperceptible at first, but it was there, extending from his fingertips and up into his shoulder. He held his hand like that for a time, his expression serious, before he relented and turned to face her.

"I was never quite the same. The limp is nothing, but the fear is inside me now, churning away. I can't get rid of it. I thought I was going to die, I was sure of it, and it petrified me. I've seen death before, in the eyes of men trying to kill me…it didn't bother me the way this did, when I was bleeding and suffocating in the dark waters of the river. I felt so…"

"Helpless?" Æva suggested. What Ulfcytel was telling her made a great deal of sense. With a weapon in his hand and enemies to fight, he would always be a force to be reckoned with. Being trapped and vulnerable, bleeding out and also used for target practice by those mocking him from afar was a different scenario altogether. She wasn't surprised it had rattled him. She was perpetually grateful that her place as a woman shielded her from having to endure such horrors.

"Helpless is the word," nodded Ulfcytel. "Helpless, terrified, humiliated, they all apply. I survived because of Alaric...and he and Cenric saved me again at Canterburie. I couldn't save him even once. What kind of a friend does that make me?"

"Why are you telling me this?" Æva asked gently, hoping he'd not take offence at the question.

"Because I want you to trust me. I felt I should share something of myself with you to achieve that end. Like I said...I asked Alaric to trust me, and it matters to me that you do, also. I repay my debts, and I owe your husband a great deal. I won't leave what's left of his family in a tight spot. I'll see you all safe and secure before I return to Edmund."

"How can you do that? You've already helped us take back our home. What else remains to be done?"

"I can give you back all of Hamptonscir," he answered grimly. "I can give you the one who turned on you to hand you over to the loathsome Eadric."

"Eadwulf?"

"The very same. But I have to face my fears, Æva. The Ealdorman Ælfric has drawn up a plan for us to attack Suthhamtunam. It's a good one, but we'll be going in by sea. One of those ships out there will take us under cover of night to infiltrate the town and catch Eadwulf unawares. I admit I'm not looking forward to it."

"You could always ask Ælfric if you could stay behind. Tell him how you feel and..." she stopped, realising how foolish she sounded. There was still some kind of tension between Ælfric and Ulfcytel, and it was thus doubly unlikely either of them would be sitting down to talk about their feelings with the other. Ulfcytel knew the value of reputation. He wouldn't stand to see his sullied by admitting his frailties to the wrong people. She felt strangely honoured he'd taken such a risk with her.

"Ælfric and I don't always see eye to eye," he said gruffly.

"You told me that too," said Æva, "but there was no need. I can tell something is wrong just from seeing you both together. I know you didn't want me to ask, but what is the situation with you two? Why do you mistrust one another?"

"I told Alaric all about his father and his past misdeeds. It was a difficult conversation."

"You make it sound as if he killed somebody," breathed Æva, aghast and frustrated at his reticence to talk. "Why won't you tell me? I need to know what happened. Does it have something to do with me and Alaric?"

"Partly," came the rather sullen answer. "Along with your son."

"Brandon? Why?"

"Not him. The other one. Your firstborn. Alfred."

"What?! How? You have to tell me! Please, if you told Alaric, then tell me!"

"I...I..." he was stammering, the great Ulfcytel actually lost for words. She didn't know if that happened often, but she doubted it. He was suffering, and she felt shame for that, but she deserved to know. She'd waited, as he'd asked, back when they'd spoken on this after fleeing Lundenburg, but the mention of Alfred had rekindled her curiosity. She had to press on until he relented.

"Please, Ulfcytel," she implored. "Why play this game with me? You were quite content to keep quiet about all this on the journey down here. What's changed?"

"Your boy, Brandon," he admitted tentatively. "There's something about seeing him here, in this place, with you but without Alaric. It cuts deep, right to the heart. I keep thinking I should confess what I know, to do what's right and reveal all as I did with Alaric, and yet I'm…"

"Afraid?"

"I'm not afraid for myself, lady. I'm afraid for you. That's why you have to trust me. These revelations reduced Alaric to tears. I feared he might hate me, thinking I was telling him lies. I don't know what he ultimately intended to do about what I told him, but I'll ask you this…think on what Ælfric means to you and what your life here in Porteceaster provides. Because if you still want to know the truth when I return from Suthhamtunam, then I shall tell you. Yet think long and hard, Æva. The truth can seem so very fine and noble, but sometimes the weight of it can be too much to bear."

VI

Darkness, true darkness, was a much-unappreciated thing. In folklore and Scripture, it was often used as a synonym for evil, something that was to be feared or otherwise avoided as the domain or characteristic of infernal powers. For years he'd thought nothing of that, treating the night as anyone else did and only feeling discomfort in its presence simply because he couldn't see. It was only now, when darkness was so absolute, that he'd developed this new perspective. This darkness was something else, not necessarily evil, nor capable of malice in and of itself, but so utterly enveloping when undisturbed. This here was a darkness that had overwhelmed his entire existence, reducing him to a single lonely point in a void that was as vast as it was featureless. At times he found it strangely comforting. At other times it was downright terrifying.

He cleared his throat, the sound of it impossibly loud in his ears. He liked to think he was defiant by breaking the silence, proving that he did indeed still exist and this blackness did not wield full dominion over him. The sound echoed, not just in his ears but around his person, making him think he was surrounded by rock or stone to the point it was pressing in upon him. He felt some apprehension at that, fearing himself buried alive as punishment for his supposed crimes. If that were true, it was beyond cruel. He'd never have wished such a thing on anyone. Not even his enemies. Not even traitors. Not even Abbot Ælfmær. He thought on that for a moment. No, not even him. No crime could justify such a fate.

He began to panic, his breath filling his ears with a sound akin to the frantic working of bellows. He tried to focus, hoping to master his fear, telling himself that he hadn't been buried and these anxious thoughts were just that, thoughts. It didn't work, and his angst started to overwhelm him, his chest aching and his heart hammering in revulsion at his terrible predicament. He couldn't move, for his hands and ankles had been bound tight, confining him to an uncomfortable sitting position upon what could only be hard, unyielding rock. Another thought stirred, born of his keen mind, informing him that if he were buried here in such a confined space, he'd have been lacking in breathable air for some time now. He wasn't a learned man by any means, but something told him this was truth. He hadn't been buried. He wasn't going to die. Not yet.

The darkness shifted, the impenetrable blackness suddenly lightening so that his eyes squinted half-shut in instinctual apprehension. A light source was coming closer, likely a torch, the glow just enough to turn his perspective from one of total blindness to a kind of oppressive, charcoal grey. Moments passed, the glow slowly intensifying along with the sound of approaching footsteps. He really hadn't been buried alive. It was rock that surrounded him, yes, but on three sides, with what looked like a carved salient or corridor heading off to his right. Time would tell if...

"This is him?" said a voice, a faint glimmer of recognition stirring in his mind at the sound of it.

"Yes, I remember him. Don't you?" This voice was also familiar. A hateful sound. An enemy. One he'd like to kill. Justice and all that good stuff demanded it.

"I think so. One of Alaric and Ulfcytel's underlings. A survivor like the rest of them, so it looks."

Osbert wrenched his eyes fully open. The pain was intense, but he forced his way through it, ignoring the tears trickling down his cheeks in protest at the searing light before him. The unwelcome spectacle that was Abbot Ælfmær came into focus, his torch held aloft and his dark robes as menacing as his sharp, angular features. That was bad enough, but yet another man was standing alongside him. One he'd seen before. One who also deserved death.

"Eadric," Osbert growled. "Of course you two would wind up working together. Evil attracts evil. Bastards attract other bastards, or some such."

"Charming little fellow, you are," Eadric said smoothly, unmoved by the vulgarity. "Let's get straight to it. You located and tried to kill the good abbot here. I doubt you managed to plan such a thing all on your own. Did Ulfcytel have a hand in this? Edmund? Alaric?"

"Alaric is dead."

He realised as soon as he said it that he shouldn't have. Eadric would take some satisfaction from knowing of his death. He didn't want to give him cause for that, but he hadn't been able to help himself. There was something intolerable about hearing Eadric say Alaric's name. A loathsome, honourless dog like him shouldn't be permitted to even think on such a man, let alone talk about him.

"Alaric is dead." Eadric sounded flat, like he was repeating Osbert's words to test their authenticity. "Alaric is dead," he said again, still without emotion. "How?" he demanded, his pitch sharpening. "I saw the bodies of Hemingr and his men. Alaric was not among the dead. Reason would suggest he'd murdered his would-be-executioners and escaped the city."

"Hemingr?" Osbert wasn't familiar with the name. He'd heard Ulfcytel speak of the tragic brawl in Lundenburg that had ultimately taken Alaric's life, but Osbert was unaware of the details or the exact names of the antagonists. If this Hemingr had meant Alaric harm, then it was a good thing he was dead.

"Of course, you won't know," muttered Eadric, to himself as much as anyone. "Alaric came to Lundenburg alone just before Svienn arrived to lay siege. So who were you with all this time? How did you escape Canterburie? I saw you there, remember, when I came to pay for the unfortunate archbishop. I don't forget a face."

Osbert twisted his hips, making his spine straight and long before unleashing a globule of spittle in Eadric's direction. He aimed well, all things considered, and Eadric's otherwise stoic demeanour cracked for a second as he gazed down at his now-wetted boots.

"That wasn't the best idea," he growled, stepping forward close enough to kick Osbert in the face and onto his back. His head rang with the force of the impact, the sensation doubling in intensity when his skull impacted upon the hard rock floor.

An image stirred in his memory, the pain shocking something into motion. He remembered the abbey in Esledes and how he'd been about to cut the abbot's throat. Somebody had attacked him from the shadows, beating him bloody and then…nothing. He couldn't remember. He had no idea how they'd brought him here, nor what had happened to Eamon. Had he escaped, or was he captured also? Or perhaps killed? His anxiety compelled him to ask.

"What did you do with Eamon?" Osbert snarled, his bound wrists tensing and flexing as he instinctively tried to bring his hands up to shield his face from further blows.

"What are you talking about?" demanded Eadric, his patience already exhausted. Osbert shuffled backwards, eventually bumping his head into the cold, hard rock that he correctly assumed to be the rear wall of his cell. He sat up, using the rough and unyielding surface behind him as a prop. He looked down at himself, noting he was still dressed in the habit of a monk, albeit one dirtied and worn from the beating he'd taken and whatever journey they'd forced him on to get him here.

Eadric was still staring at him, Ælfmær too, both apparently wanting an answer. Osbert wasn't inclined to tell them about Eamon. If they hadn't caught him, then the less information they had, the better. "Was there a second man?" Eadric asked, turning to the abbot. Ælfmær frowned as if thinking on it before shaking his head. Eadric turned back to Osbert. "Was there a second man?" he asked him this time. "Did you have help? You were not sent alone to kill Ælfmær, were you?"

"I'll tell you nothing," Osbert croaked, his head throbbing.

"It's irrelevant now anyway," said Eadric with a slight shrug. "I had a feeling somebody would turn up and try to kill Ælfmær for what he did at Canterburie. I saw it as an opportunity, as the assassin would almost certainly be connected to either Alaric or Ulfcytel. I was correct to think that."

"I don't care," said Osbert. "You'll get nothing out of me, even if this was all just a ploy to get your hands on somebody who knows the ealdorman. I'll not speak with you."

"I think you will. I've broken fiercer men than you. Alaric was one of them. Did you know that? I put him to the question when he came to us. I broke him, not in this cell but another. He told me where to find Wulfnoth."

"Where is he then?" laughed Osbert, thinking Eadric's claim difficult to believe.

"He's…he was…" Eadric was lost for words. He'd been caught out, his idle boasting exposed for what it was.

"He didn't tell you anything, did he?" Osbert exclaimed triumphantly. "Or if he did, it was intentionally false information…that's what happened, yes? Played you for the fool you are." He rested his shoulders against the wall, gazing at Eadric and drinking in his flustered bearing. He might be in mortal danger right now, but he could still enjoy himself. The fact it was coming at Eadric's expense was sheer delight.

"So you used me, Eadric?" Ælfmær breathed. "You used me to lure Ulfcytel into making a move?"

Eadric turned back to the abbot, an eyebrow raised in irritation. "I did," he admitted. "You didn't think I was just trying to protect you for the sake of it? After what you did? You cost our lost King Æthelred one of his greatest cities."

"It was God's will!" spluttered Ælfmær, his face flushing with indignation. "You know it was! The fact King Svienn now sits upon Æthelred's throne proves that! God deemed Æthelred unworthy, and the English were to be chastised for…"

"Yes, yes, all that," Eadric said impatiently, his interruption thankfully serving to shut the abbot up. Osbert continued to gaze up at them both, noting the differences between them. Eadric was the cold, calculating bastard he'd always been, but Ælfmær was actually mad enough to think his crimes were justified. From where Osbert was sitting, that somehow made him worse. There were plenty of evil men in the world, willing to sell out their own for money and prestige. That wasn't unusual, yet to do all that out of some twisted notion that God desired it was truly repellent. It was heresy.

"Look at the pair of you," Osbert chuckled. "You're at odds over the right reasons for being traitorous dogs! What other tricks do you do, I wonder? Don't be shy now. I could do with a proper laugh."

"You've certainly come a long way since I first saw you in that tent at Hringmere." Eadric didn't sound like he was mocking him. It was true, in any case. Osbert had come a long way since then.

"You could say that," Osbert concurred. "Life has a way of grinding a man down to his true self. Were you always rotten, Eadric, or was that a blessing ill fortune handed you?"

"I'm not interested in your jibes, Osbert. Like I said, you were serving drinks for Ulfcytel when we first laid eyes on each other. You were his underling, a glorified servant, regardless of how you might like to pretend otherwise. You don't have to be. I know potential when I see it. Tell us where Ulfcytel is, and you'll want for nothing."

"Are you attempting to bribe me?" It was a good sign if he was. Eadric wasn't stupid enough to think such a ploy had much chance of succeeding. This was desperation on his part. If he had indeed tortured Alaric in captivity only to have his efforts rewarded with misinformation, then Eadric likely wasn't confident that brutalising Osbert would yield a different result. He was trying something new here. Conversion. It wouldn't work. Osbert would die before betraying Ulfcytel. That's just the way it was.

"It's not a bribe," said Eadric, his attempt at a smile making him look even more untrustworthy. "Many men learn to put themselves first when the chaos of our times threatens to overwhelm them. I did. I served one king, and now I serve another. I made the right choices precisely because I refused to be weighed down by abstract burdens of right and wrong. Such things are illusions. I make my own truth. Why not do the same?"

"Because the burdens of right and wrong are a little more than that," sneered Osbert. "And the truth is just the truth…you don't opt out of it…you can't remake it to suit your own perverse fantasies, your own selfish interests. You'll be remembered by history, Eadric, as just another evil man doing what he could for himself and using any means to try and justify it. Ulfcytel will be remembered differently. Edmund Ironside will be remembered differently. I serve them! Never you! Nor that murdering foreign bastard who dares call himself king!"

"Ironside?" Eadric asked, raising an eyebrow. "What's this now? Is that how he styles himself whilst scratching about in the woods? How fearsome."

"You wouldn't understand," simmered Osbert. "It's a name born of heroism and brotherly love. Æthelstan himself gave him that name as he lay dying, telling him to fight on and claim the throne that's now his by right! Do you understand that, Eadric? The love of a brother? Is that something you can ever relate to, as wretched and pathet…"

He'd hit a nerve. He couldn't say exactly how, but Eadric's face twisted in the blink of an eye, going from bemused curiosity to absolute fury. He stepped forward, kicking Osbert in the face yet again, the force of the blow even greater than the last. He then knelt down, striking Osbert repeatedly with a closed fist, his teeth bared and his eyes flashing with hatred.

Osbert twisted and strained, trying to work his hands out of their restraints, his efforts at pulling his knees up to defend himself proving fruitless. The beating kept on and on, and Osbert eventually slipped into the darkness he'd only just been contemplating earlier. He snapped out of it suddenly, a sensation of icy cold shocking him back into awareness. He was soaked. Eadric had thrown a bucket of water over him. So he'd passed out from the battering he'd taken. Not his proudest moment. Yet the lion's share of shame belonged to Eadric.

"I give you one last chance," Eadric said, his voice laden with bitterness. "Tell us where the Ealdorman Ulfcytel is. Edmund's resistance depends on an experienced man like that. Do the right thing and tell us everything you know before more people die."

"I will not." Osbert's voice was quiet yet determined. He was scared. He didn't want to die or suffer further physical punishment. His mind, however, was made up. He wouldn't betray the ealdorman. He wouldn't betray his king, the real king, Edmund Ironside. He could face God in the full knowledge of that and stand tall. That was something Eadric could never do.

"Very well. You've made your choice." Eadric stood up and left the way he'd come, the abbot following. Just as Osbert thought they'd left him altogether they reappeared, this time in the company of two Danes. They were imposing men, fully armoured in burnished mail, their hair flowing to their shoulders from beneath heavy iron helms. They seized Osbert, lifting him to his feet and dragging him from his cell and down a similarly dark corridor into what eventually came to be open air.

He blinked, the warmth and brightness of sunlight a shock to his senses. They hauled him on, ignoring his struggling efforts to right himself so he might at least stay on his feet. Eadric and Ælfmær kept the pace, both of them stony-faced and impassive. Osbert glanced about. They were in some kind of garden, the trees full and heavy with leaves and even fruit. The place wasn't well-maintained, the flower beds, in particular, appearing overgrown and untidy, implying that whoever tended this place was either negligent or absent altogether. Osbert inhaled deeply, determined to enjoy the fresh summer air despite his perilous situation. He then realised where he was. The view to the south made that clear enough.

It was Lundenburg, although not quite as he remembered. The garden was enclosed on three sides, but anyone looking in the right direction was treated to a splendid view, their elevated position allowing them to see virtually the entire city and over the walls beyond it. Osbert could see the Temes and its sparkling bluish-grey waters, and there were a few ships out there too, moving slowly and almost languidly away from the riverside docks to head out for parts unknown.

This was as good as it got. The city itself was a mess, many of its buildings looking like they'd either been destroyed or at least partially burned down. He couldn't see clearly, such was the haste with which he was being dragged, but he fancied there were fewer people out on the streets than seemed normal, their figures hunched and forlorn whilst they went about their business. Lundenburg had suffered terribly. The rule of Svienn Forkbeard had not brought an end to it.

He was indoors now, his captors strong-arming him down a spacious stone corridor, his bound feet still shaky and unsteady. They came to an intersection and then another after that, Osbert for a time thinking they intended to deposit him in some labyrinthine maze where he'd be condemned to wander aimlessly for the rest of his life.

Fortunately, it was not to be, and he was soon dragged through a pair of sizeable double doors and out into what looked like the city beyond. This was ideal. There'd never be a better time to try and escape.

His hopes sank in his chest. He was outside, yes, but in another enclosed area. A wall encircled the place, high and smooth, and there was a large gate to the south, sealed and guarded by several spear-armed Danes. A menacing stone tower also lay to the west, something that left Osbert with an unsettled feeling whenever he looked at it. He was pulled along still, past what appeared to be some stables, a single grey horse peering at him from within. Just when he thought he was destined for the tower, his captors came to a stop. Eadric gazed at him briefly and then nodded to the two guards, who promptly drove Osbert to his knees with a flurry of blows, his wrists and ankles still tied with rope.

Osbert struggled, trying to lift himself up and onto his feet, but both Danes were now pressing him down, ensuring he remained kneeling, his arms back and his head pitched forward. Osbert then heard something; the tell-tale sound of a sword leaving its scabbard, and so he looked up and to his right, as much as he could manage, expecting to see Eadric. Sure enough, he was there, sword in hand, a smug, reassured look on his face. He knew Osbert was helpless, and he knew he was afraid.

"Do you have anything you'd like to tell me?" Eadric asked quietly. "Know that your life now hangs in the balance...know that this is your last chance."

"I have nothing to say," Osbert replied, making sure he kept his gaze on Eadric. He wouldn't look away. If this was to be his death, he'd face it full-on. Let this wretched traitor see how a true Englishman might die, defiant to the end. It would do him good.

The Abbot Ælfmær started muttering to himself, apparently deciding now was a good time to "pray for the young man's soul." Osbert bared his teeth, incensed by his hypocrisy. Eadric, however, didn't want to wait, and he took a single step forward, sword in both hands, to bring himself close enough to the bound and kneeling Osbert for a decapitating strike.

So this was it then, thought Osbert. He was to depart this world; killed by a traitor in the ruins of his homeland's capital. There were worse ways to go, but he'd have preferred to die fighting at Ulfcytel and Edmund's side in some heroic drive to push these heathens back into the sea. Sadly, like so many things that had taken place in his relatively short life, he had little choice in what was happening. He'd make the best of the situation. He could do nothing else. He began to pray, the words flowing out of him like the purest water, their sweet sound cleansing him of fear and apprehension:

"Lord Jesus Christ

Son of God

Have Mercy Upon Me

A Sinner."

Eadric readied his blade, heaving it up high over his head, his grey eyes flickering with cruel purpose. Osbert inhaled sharply, knowing he was seconds from death. He breathed out with a half-roar, his rage forming the words "God Save King Edmund!" His statement echoed across the courtyard, his defiance repeating back at him several times over. That was a good choice for his last words, he thought. He closed his eyes. He was ready. He'd face his Lord and Saviour now. He was at peace.

"What's the meaning of this?"

Osbert looked to his left, hoping to catch sight of whoever had spoken. He craned his neck as far as he could, spying a tall, young man, around Osbert's own age, dressed in a flowing, sparkling long mail byrnie, a heavy black and grey fur cloak cascading down to the backs of his knees. He wore his hair free, and his flaxen locks extended past his shoulders, a modest beard of a similar hue hugging the contours of an almost delicate jawline. He had blue eyes, typical of the Danes, but they had a greenish tint to them, a certain depth also suggesting he was not just another base, violent animal like so many of his brethren.

"I asked you a question, Eadric." He sounded displeased. This probably wasn't a man who was accustomed to having to repeat himself. There was an air of authority to him, also, and the effect he was having on Eadric said it was probably best not to defy him.

"I am carrying out an execution, my lord," Eadric said, lowering his sword. "This man is a rebel, an associate of the renegade Ealdorman Ulfcytel. I would..."

"Ulfcytel, you say?" interrupted the mystery Dane. "The same Ulfcytel who came so close to defeating my father all those years ago? Surely one of his confidants should be questioned first rather than killed?"

Recognition dawned. This must be Cnut, son of Svienn Forkbeard himself. It could be no one else, since he'd clearly referenced the battle where Ulfcytel's reputation had been won fighting Svienn to a standstill, close to Theodford, back when Osbert was just a lad. That the Danes remembered this battle brought Osbert some comfort. It was important they realise England was still capable of resisting them. It was important they realise they hadn't won.

"He won't talk," sighed Eadric, his eyelids fluttering with obvious anxiety. "I can tell when torturing a man would be a waste of time. This one is that rare type who won't crack. Death is all there is to be done with him."

"How close were you to Ulfcytel?" Cnut asked, staring down at Osbert with a faint smile. "You fought at his side? You shed blood together? The blood of my people?"

"I did," growled Osbert. "I was at Hringmere and Canterburie."

"So that's it?" replied Cnut with a slight shake of his head. "Two battles? Both of them losses? Not too impressive."

"How many battles have you fought?" demanded Osbert. "Real battles, that is, not murdering innocent people and burning their villages. Real battles against real warriors."

"We're both still in our youth," said Cnut, his smile fading. "I have plenty of time to make my mark on the world, but at least the battles I've fought were victories. Think on that."

"Edmund will kill you." Osbert knew he was pushing his luck with that last statement. He was still being held in place by the two guards, and his shoulders and knees were aching fiercely, but he had no reason to think he'd escaped death just because this Cnut had appeared to blather at him. It could all be a game, and he wouldn't do him the service of playing along. Besides, he hated him, and he wanted him to know it.

"You may be right," Cnut said quietly, his eyes flicking away from Osbert and back over to Eadric. "I saw him just recently, Eadric and I. A fearsome warrior. Very fearsome. We defeated him and sent him fleeing into the woods."

"He'll be back," Osbert said triumphantly. "Whatever victory you think you had over him won't last. He won't give up."

"So I keep hearing," said Cnut. "So tell me, young man, what is your name?"

"Osbert."

"And will you tell me, Osbert, how close you really were to Ulfcytel? You knew him before Hringmere? He valued your service? Did people associate you with him?"

"He values me. He values all of his men. I owe him much."

"Get this man up and cut his bonds," ordered Cnut, his tone sharp and authoritative. The two Danes did as they'd been told, pulling Osbert upright and cutting the ropes around his wrists and ankles. Osbert began rubbing at his knees whilst shifting his weight from right to left, trying to ease the numbness from his feet. He was only partially successful.

"I can't believe a man as cunning as you, Eadric, would seriously consider executing a close ally of Ulfcytel." Cnut's tone was now light, suggesting he was unconcerned with how Eadric might take his statement.

"Like I said, he wouldn't talk," said Eadric, sheathing his weapon. "There's no point in indulging him if he won't cooperate and…"

"You never intended to kill him," Cnut said firmly. "This was a ruse to make him panic and start talking. Such a ploy only works on those who are weak. This one," he gestured towards Osbert, "is nothing of the kind. I would have thought it obvious."

Osbert looked over at Eadric, his left hand rubbing feverishly at a sore spot on his wrist where the ropes had cut into his skin. From the look on the man's face, Cnut was right. It had been a ploy, intended to terrify him into telling Eadric anything he wanted. Osbert sneered, unafraid to show his contempt. Eadric and Ælfmær were fools to think him so easily frightened. They were fools to think he'd betray England.

"It's been known to work in the past," Eadric said sullenly. "Physical punishment doesn't always yield results. The breaking of a mind through fear rather than force has its advantages. We could…"

"Yes, yes," Cnut snapped impatiently. "I understand all that, but you failed here. You misjudged the situation, and now your position is weakened accordingly. I will do what I must."

Cnut looked around and gestured to the two nameless Danes that had dragged Osbert from his cell. "You men, follow me and bring the prisoner," he commanded. They reacted quickly, Osbert feeling his arms twinge in protest when the two warriors again seized them.

Cnut turned and began to stride back the way he'd come, Osbert finding himself hauled along when the Danes fell into step behind him. They passed through the doors into the hall, retracing their steps from one echoing corridor to another before Cnut suddenly took a left turn to ascend a narrow staircase. They followed, Osbert grateful he was free to climb the steps under his own power, his escorts otherwise taking up position in front and behind him. Another empty corridor soon presented itself, and Osbert was again pushed, prodded, or otherwise forced into motion, his captors apparently eager that they should keep up the pace and not risk displeasing their purposeful master. This continued for a few minutes more before they finally eased to a halt, their journey ending at a single, unadorned door set into a similarly modest stone archway.

Osbert saw Cnut fumbling with the door handle, as if he didn't possess the wit to operate such a thing and would require help. He finally managed to work it out, pushing the handle downward and using his right shoulder to force the wooden frame inward so it swung back on its evidently aged hinges. They moved inside, Osbert again feeling a push from the man behind him that sent him stumbling into the chamber.

It was a strange place, that was certain. It had an atmosphere, like weighty and perhaps dark things had been discussed here. The northern wall was dominated by a large window, the likes of which appeared to open up over the city itself. Shelves, solid and durable, lined the stone walls elsewhere, each one burdened with an impressive array of books, the nature of which Osbert could only guess. An elaborate crimson rug covered much of the floor, and there was a stone hearth built into the far wall that was large enough to keep the place comfortable in the deep winter months. Two wooden chairs were placed nearby, a short, unadorned table tucked between them. This was a place of learning and contemplation, Osbert surmised. King Æthelred's study then. It must be. It wasn't like the Danes would have brought any books with them.

Cnut sat in one of the chairs before beckoning Osbert to sit across the table from him. The Dane behind him half-shoved him into it, but Osbert was secretly glad to get off his feet and resume rubbing at his still-aching wrists and ankles. Cnut addressed the second guard, instructing him to head to the kitchens and bring them mead and food. The man turned and left, shutting the door behind him, his compatriot taking up position nearby in watchful readiness. It was just as well. If Osbert had been left alone with Cnut, he'd have fancied his chances at strangling him. He'd be discovered and killed, of course, but Cnut's death would break Svienn, giving Edmund every advantage in his war against him. Cnut also had it coming. He was a Dane, after all.

A few seconds went by until he realised Cnut was staring at him with thoughtful eyes. Osbert was initially nervous under his protracted gaze, but it wasn't long before he realised he was looking at the assortment of books perched past his shoulder. Why a heathen bastard like him would be interested in such things, Osbert had no idea.

"Do you read?" Cnut asked, still peering at the books.

"Sort of," Osbert replied quickly. "I doubt I could sit with one of those tomes, though. Big ideas for big people, by the looks of it."

Cnut nodded, his expression a little crestfallen. He'd probably hoped Osbert could translate the works, perhaps even recite them to him, given he was almost certainly illiterate himself. Moments passed, then minutes, the passage of time seeming to slow as Osbert did his utmost to avoid displaying any unease at Cnut's unsettling presence. A bump was finally heard at the door, and the warrior on duty heaved it open to allow the guard Cnut had sent to the kitchens to pass within. Osbert had never been so pleased to see a Dane in his life. He'd brought food.

He tucked in, snatching a hunk of bread from the tray that had been gingerly placed on the table. The guard-turned-servant took a step back, his eyes glowering within his helm as Osbert insisted on eating before Cnut could take his share. If the man was offended, he made no display of it, and Osbert didn't much care, hungry as he was and more than happy with the rich, warm quality of the crust he was gnawing on. Cnut snatched at a jagged slice of seared meat and wolfed it down, his hands then finding themselves a flagon of mead before he rested back into his chair.

"Drink and eat all you like," Cnut said, a faint smirk on his face at the realisation Osbert would do just that. "There's plenty more where this came from. The dark days of starvation are over. My father rules the waves, and our ships have opened the city to trade and wealth once again."

"Stolen wealth," Osbert said from behind another mouthful of bread. "You trade in what you take from others. Like this food. It's from English barley grown in English soil. Don't pretend you're doing me a favour by letting me eat what's mine to begin with."

The guard who'd served them shuffled uneasily, his gaze darting from Osbert to Cnut and then back again. Cnut looked over to him and nodded once, and Osbert nearly choked when the guard's heavy, gauntleted hand gave him a hard slap across the back of the head.

"Don't assume because I let you eat in my presence, I'll put up with any insolence," cautioned Cnut. "Understand that if you push me too far, I will kill you myself before my men have to do anything. Am I clear?"

Osbert nodded once, his teeth grinding with barely restrained rage. Cnut took a swig from his tankard, unconcerned by the recent violence and content to go back to playing the gracious host. Osbert followed his lead, snatching his own tankard from the tray and pressing its edge to his lips. It smelled heavenly. Proper honeyed mead, of a brew he couldn't quite identify. It didn't matter. It would take the edge off. He quaffed half of it in one. It was as good as it smelled, and then some.

"My father has a great spectacle planned," Cnut said quietly. "Most of your leading thegns and ealdormen have already declared their loyalty to him in some fashion, but we understand formality and ceremony are important. Every English notable willing to swear allegiance is to gather at Gainesburg in a week's time. My father will go to them there, and they will submit to him."

Osbert stared from across the table, doing his best to keep the ale he'd just swallowed within his stomach. Talk of submission made him sick, and talk of Svienn prancing about in Gainesburg as yet more treacherous, fake Englishmen bent the knee before him was easily the worst thing he'd heard in some time.

"Why tell me this?" asked Osbert resentfully. "Who am I to such people?"

"That's what I want to find out," said Cnut eagerly. "Tell me what you mean to Ulfcytel. How long have you been in his service?"

"Years," answered Osbert with a shrug. "He found me on the streets in Noruic. My parents had been murdered in another of your raids, my brothers too and my sisters taken. I had nobody. Ulfcytel was kind to me. He gave me a purpose."

"Strange that a man of position and prestige would bother with a common orphan," Cnut exclaimed, his callous disbelief rankling Osbert further.

"He's a Christian," Osbert replied forcefully, making sure to lock eyes with Cnut. "He did the right thing. He gave me a purpose, as I said, to serve him and my country."

"To seek revenge?"

"Much is owed," Osbert agreed. "So much. For my brothers, my sisters, my parents…all my country. Much is owed."

"You'd like to kill me, wouldn't you?" Cnut didn't seem upset, instead making a statement that was entirely factual, as far as Osbert was concerned.

"You know I would," he replied, letting his words stand in the silence that followed.

"Then I'm glad you have not yet tried," Cnut said. "It's good to be in the company of an Englishman who knows what he's about. Eadric is a clever and useful man, but he's..."

"A damn traitor," Osbert interrupted. "You can't trust him. He betrayed his own king. He betrayed us at Hringmere, all to see Thorkell run riot through our lands just so Æthelred could pay him off."

Cnut nodded, his look turning thoughtful. "I've heard much about that," he eventually said. "About what happened at Hringmere and Æthelred's unwise decisions. Tell me, though...what did Eadric have to do with Hringmere? He's not offered up such a tale to me, not yet anyway."

Osbert told him, thinking it a harmless narrative that would hardly help Cnut in his struggle against Edmund. He went into some detail, giving him a first-hand recollection of the meeting in Ulfcytel's pavilion that night Eadric had come to demand they move their army south instead of defending their own homes. Cnut listened, his frown deepening at Osbert's account of the ensuing battle and their betrayal at the hands of the dastardly Thurcytel. He gestured for him to continue, his manner still attentive as Osbert described their retreat into the woods and their final mad dash to Gipeswic to attack and steal Thorkell's ships.

"So you and Ulfcytel made off with Thorkell's own ships and used them to reach Canterburie?" There was admiration there. Cnut approved of their audacity, respected it even.

"We did," Osbert confirmed, "and Alaric saved the ealdorman that day. I'll never forget it. I've never seen such bravery in all my life."

"Who is Alaric?"

Osbert paused, the sadness spreading up through his chest catching him off guard. "Just another good man," he said glumly, unwilling to honour Cnut by telling him of Alaric's exploits. He didn't deserve to hear them. None of them did.

"So it's fair to say people have gotten used to seeing you with Ulfcytel?" Cnut asked, his curiosity about Alaric thankfully fleeting. "They'd know you, if they saw you, and associate you with the ealdorman?"

"I was his steward," answered Osbert. "Many know how he helped me and how I respect him. There's nothing secretive there."

"I'm glad you told me," Cnut said eagerly, "because now I know I was right to save you from Eadric and his foolish monk. You'll come with me and my father to Gainesburg. The English thegns will witness you at my side and take it as a sign that even those closest to Ulfcytel can betray him. They'll think his days are numbered along with Edmund's. Whatever defiance...whatever hope that might be left in them...will crumble to nothing. And you'll have my thanks."

"But they've already submitted," Osbert shot back. "What's the point in having me be seen by such men? If they were worth anything, they'd be fighting alongside Edmund right now."

"It's the spectacle that matters," answered Cnut. "People have to understand this is how things will be from this point on. The memory of the England that was can either be fresh in their minds or gradually fade. I would prefer the latter...and that people like Ulfcytel fade with it. You can help speed that process along."

"I won't!"

"I only ask that you…"

"I will not help you!" shouted Osbert. "Listen well, Dane, for I will not play any part in whatever schemes you've set in motion! None!"

"Do not interrupt me!" Cnut roared, his temper exploding as he rose from his chair to smash aside the table with a furious sweep of his arms. It flipped over entirely, scattering the bread and ale with it, and Cnut charged through the space it once occupied, his right fist delivering a savage blow to Osbert's jaw.

He fell, dazed by the punch and surprised by the sudden escalation. He was soon heaved upright by Cnut's men, each of them again seizing him by the arms and holding him in place. Cnut struck him twice more, the Danes on either side laughing at his helplessness. Cnut leaned in close, his snarling visage mere inches from Osbert's face. He spoke quickly yet surely, his ultimatum all the more sickening considering the stench on his breath.

"I humoured you for a time, little man, but hear me well on this. I am your lord here, and I will tolerate your defiance no longer. You will do as I ask and accompany me to Gainesburg. You need not speak, you need not perform, you need only be seen and allow your fellow Saxons to draw their own conclusions. Because I will kill you. If you refuse me on this, I will kill you, and take my word for it…the method I'll devise for your execution will make you wish Eadric had taken your life back there."

VII

About five miles or so from Snotingeham's eastern outskirts lay a copse of ash trees. They were old, very old, their towering, gnarled forms presiding over the road to provide a well-known landmark for travellers and locals alike. Their roots went deep, stretching down and out in all directions, their mossy trunks thick and durable as they maintained a watch that had already spanned more than a century and would likely continue longer still.

There was a narrow trail that snaked between them, branching off from the main road to skirt past the trees and into a dark and rather ominous thicket. The vast majority of those who passed by were uninterested in this mystery path, preferring to push on to Snotingeham, or, if they had come from there, continue east to find the main route from the Five Boroughs into Eastengle. Those who did take this trail out of curiosity soon gave up and returned to the road, finding the thicket difficult to traverse and the dense, shadowy terrain somewhat threatening.

To two boys from the South, that was half the fun. To them, the trees were guardians set there to watch over and protect some secret place that was just asking to be discovered. They braved the beaten path, passing through the trees and onward into a mess of tangled briars, their efforts seeing their cloaks torn and their breecs muddied before they'd made much headway.

It didn't deter them. They strove on, plucking the brambles from their clothes, their eyes locked on the increasingly elusive path weaving ever onward. Hours seemed to pass, the sound of bees and songbirds filling the air, the light and warmth of the sun filtering down through swaying, golden-green boughs. There must be a reason for this trail to be here, and their imaginations ran wild supposing what it might be. Had it been laid by the Romans in ancient times, connecting to some now-forgotten redoubt or mustering field? Was it the work of wizards, their powerful magic cutting a now overgrown swath through nature so they might access some secret trove of knowledge? Were witches responsible, putting their thralls to work in carving out a route to a forbidden place of power far from the prying eyes of righteous men?

There were many possibilities, some benign, others terrifying, none of which dissuaded them from attempting to find out the truth. The path soon dipped at random into a narrow, gloomy gully, the earth rising up around them to reveal the tangled roots of trees set into the slopes now looming to their left and right. They crept on in this shadowed world, moving forward and never back, and when they finally began to ascend into a broad, forested clearing they were sure their courage had paid off.

Their optimism soon faded. The path seemed to gradually vanish, disappearing into a thickening carpet of grass and wildflowers. They'd lost track of time, for the sun had almost gone down entirely, the lengthening shadows obscuring the route they'd used to get here. The lads looked around, trying to locate the path in case it had started up again to lead them deeper into the woods. There was nothing, or at least their eyes failed to detect anything. It was quiet, and neither bird nor beast made its presence known; the only sound to reach them the hissing of the wind through leaves and the creaking of ancient wood.

"I think we should go back," one whispered nervously.

"There'll be a reason we were led here," replied the other, his bearing more confident. "We just have to find out what it is. Are you afraid?"

"I am not," insisted the first boy, younger in years and meeker in manner than his companion. "I just think father might get worried. Mother will be upset, and when she's upset he doesn't like it. He has enough to worry about as it is. He says that."

"He says that a lot. We should do him a favour then by finding out the truth of this place quickly. He'll be pleased we did. He doesn't like secrets. He says that too."

The first lad would have replied were it not for the commotion made when he struck his foot, hard, on something fixed into the forest floor. He hadn't seen it in the gloom, but it was enough to make him fall, the soft flesh of his palms tearing open as he slammed into the uneven ground. He grit his teeth and got up, his forearms rising to his eyes to wipe away the tears of pain he knew already welled there. He didn't want to look weak, even if he couldn't avoid looking clumsy.

"You've found something," said his brother as he knelt, his hands brushing at the earth excitedly. The boy bent over, peering at whatever it was that was of interest, seeing then how he appeared to have tripped on some kind of pale stone in the shape of a brick. He leant down further, eventually dropping to one knee as he saw yet more bricks caked into the earth, each one worn and weathered and brazenly out of place in this wilderness setting. There seemed to be a broad layer of them, the earth and bracken of the clearing covering only an inch or so over the top of what looked to be an entire stone surface deliberately worked into the ground.

There was something else in there with them, loose and circular, like tiny slivers of metal that had been rolled in dirt and scattered among the strange rocks. He picked one up, digging his thumbnails in to scrape aside the mud, his efforts revealing a single silver coin that sparkled in the fading light. There was a face on it, long and angular, with some kind of wreath set upon its head. There was writing just below it, a few words of an alien tongue, but one not so strange that he didn't recognise it. Father Dunstan spoke this language, he knew that. He'd heard him speak it and had suffered through his efforts to teach him it. It was Latin. The language of the Romans.

"I knew it," said the second lad, sounding giddy. He started clawing at the earth, his scraping and scratching revealing several more coins. "I knew we were right to come here," he continued, his excitement close to mania. "You found it, Edmund! You found us treasure!"

"We found it, Æthelstan," Edmund said magnanimously, his eyes still on the coin. "We found it together."

Edmund inhaled slowly, his memories leaving him with a sense of melancholy. He was stood in the clearing once more, the birds singing and the twilight's long shadows again at his heels. He poked at one of the remaining bricks with his boot, noting sadly how it seemed to partially fragment under his weight. All things faded in time, even the works of a people as mighty as the Romans. The best and bravest, too, would suffer the same, some living long and fruitful years whilst others were unfairly snatched away before even reaching their prime. Edmund would know about that. It had been that way with his mother. It had been that way with Æthelstan.

"So, was your father angry that you'd both gone off alone?"

"Of course," replied Edmund, his boot still scraping over the earth absent-mindedly. "He didn't want to know about the Roman coins. I brought the first one I found, thinking to make it a gift to him."

"And how did he react?"

"He told me I was a fool and then ignored the coin completely. He scolded Æthelstan worse, telling him how he'd taken us into danger and how we'd be punished for it."

"Did he punish you?"

"Sort of," sighed Edmund wearily. "He was shouting so much…the noise of it hurt my ears, so we hid in Æthelstan's chamber, barricading the door with his bed so father couldn't get at us. We thought he might hurt us."

"Did he ever do that?"

"Sometimes. But even when he didn't, he'd say he would and acted like he might. It's the confusion that does the damage. To think a parent would be pleased with you, only to have hope replaced with fear in the blink of an eye…"

"I hope I've never acted like that with Godwine."

"Where is your son?" asked Edmund, tearing himself away from his fixation on the rock to look Wulfnoth straight in the face.

"He's safe," came the answer, "and far from our lands. Nobody in the South has been safe for years, so I had the children moved elsewhere. It made sense at the time. It still does."

"He'll miss you," said Edmund. "Being away from him must be difficult."

"It is, Edmund. Very difficult. Yet we do what we must. Duty demands it."

Edmund nodded, wanting to cut the conversation short now it was drifting onto subjects as vaguely defined as "duty" and likely "honour". It wasn't that he disagreed, but his heart was aching at having returned here, his memories of his brother and their elation at finding buried treasure bubbling to the surface. He turned around, looking out from the clearing and what awaited him to the north west.

It was quite a sight. Hundreds of men, grim and soldierly, were camped out amid the trees, the smoke from their cookfires drifting up into the branches. His men. His army. All that was left of a free England.

They'd all followed him from Snotingeham, marching out in his wake without question and their numbers swelled with yet more volunteers. As always, the newcomers were a mixed assortment of farmers, commoners, and a few warriors, and most were under-equipped, coming armed with little more than a spear and the clothes on their backs. They had absolutely no chance of victory in the open field, and they all knew it, but it wasn't the expectation of an easy win that had brought them here. They were stubborn, proud, and loyal with it, something that had spurred them on to continued resistance even in the face of apparent defeat.

It sounded noble, and it was, but there was also a darker edge to it. All of them had suffered, each and every one, from years of Norse attacks on their shared homeland. They were full of stories of such things, all bloody and tragic, and they'd developed a fondness for sharing them over their campfires in the depths of night. At first, Edmund had been worried, thinking it ill-advised for them to sit up and dwell on the past, but he'd come to welcome it. It hardened them, keeping them bold to their task, the hate kept fresh and alive in their hearts so it might be vented upon the enemy in furious retribution. Svienn might have Lundenburg and every cowardly noble in the country in his pocket, but he doubted his warriors could ever hate like these people could. It wasn't possible.

He knew some of their stories already. Old Ælfsige over there had once had a family. They'd been his world, and he'd loved his wife, four daughters, and three sons with a depth and intensity that had softened the hearts of all who saw it. That had all changed after Svienn had overpowered the English at the Battle of Malduna and his daughters had been carried off and his sons murdered. Ælfsige had been away with the fyrd at the time, but he'd returned to find his wife and boys dead and half-buried in the ashes of their home. He'd never found any trace of his girls. They were gone. Every Dane he'd slaughtered since had been for their sake, and those who knew him believed him when he said he'd never stop killing them as long as he walked the earth. He could do nothing else.

Cerdic sat across from Ælfsige, enjoying their fire and talking on matters Edmund could not hear. He was a younger man, but he too had his own tale of loss and lamentation that had set him on the path of vengeance. He was from Theodford, yet he'd shamefully declined the summons to muster at Hringmere to resist Thorkell, thinking he'd be better served by sequestering the wealth from his blacksmithing business somewhere safe. He'd made it out of Eastengle to seek refuge in Cantebrigie, only to be trapped in the city when it came under attack from Thorkell's armies. His modest fortune had been of no help to him then, and he'd lost his wife, brothers, sisters, and all of his children, either to a heathen axe or the slaver's lash. Edmund wasn't sure how he'd escaped, but he'd been fighting well from then on, killing Danes wherever he could find them. It was no idle boast. He'd butchered several when they'd attacked Svienn at Sancte Eadmundes Byrig, his zeal for bloodshed easily matching that of anyone else in their little warband. He may have once been a dishonest man, but now he was a warrior, fighting for his country. Edmund respected that.

There was a third fellow sat with them whose story was so horrific Edmund had at first been shocked to hear it. He bore his father's name, Æthelred, and they were alike in some ways, for this man also possessed that perpetually haunted look that Edmund had sadly become accustomed to seeing at home. He'd been one of those who'd rallied to Ulfcytel's call to defend Canterburie, bringing his entire family within the walls and volunteering to serve in the garrison. He'd fought in the battle, but had been captured when Thorkell's men had somehow infiltrated the city to take the defenders by surprise. He'd been tortured as the Danes took the place apart, and they'd burned his wife and newborn son alive, in their cruelty making him watch before dragging him to Remmesgate. There were ships there, taking on loot and captives, and they'd forced him aboard one of them with a batch of other prisoners, the vessel then departing into the open sea for parts unknown.

Edmund had been astonished at what had happened next. God must have been with Æthelred, for he'd somehow broken out of his fetters. He'd acted fast by shoulder-charging the Norse captain from behind, the impact sending the bastard flying off his own prow to sink under the weight of his armour. The rest of the crew had tried to kill him for that, of course, but he'd gone berserk, defending himself with a single spear until the deck was awash with heathen blood. He'd admitted he wasn't sure how he'd managed to achieve such a feat, but he'd heard his wife and son's screams as he fought, making him think he was fighting to save them from the flames. That was how he'd bested so many men. The love for his family. It was just tragic it was already too late by then.

Æthelred had then freed the other captives on board, and through their combined efforts, they'd managed to steer the ship back to the coast and head inland. They'd soon heard Edmund was in the area and correctly guessed he'd be heading for Snotingeham. They'd joined up with him there without hesitation. Edmund had been moved by such loyalty, as always, but he'd started to notice a pattern. Those who had lived lives of comfort would not support him, thinking it better to adapt to the changed situation and see what they could make of it. Those who had suffered until they'd almost broken were flocking to him, eager to resume the fight and kill as many Danes as they could. Edmund understood why, on some level, because he understood their hate. He shared it with them. The Danes had killed so many, including his brother and his beloved uncle. He'd never get over that. He'd never forgive that.

Edmund turned away, thinking it better to give Wulfnoth and their present troubles his full attention. "Has there been word from Sigeferth?" he asked, knowing the answer already in his gut.

"Nothing," replied Wulfnoth, "not since we left. The supplies were welcome. That's all I'll say for him."

Edmund nodded, feeling his shoulders tense in recollection of the recent altercation with his supposed friends. Sigeferth and Morcar both had argued their case, offering pitiful platitudes as to why they'd had to submit to the enemy. "Svienn's force is too large", they'd pleaded, claiming any war against him would be a war against every thegn in every scir who'd already come over to his side. Their solution to that was apparently to become one of those thegns. It had made no sense to him.

He'd told them that in no uncertain terms. Sigeferth had continued to blather on, arranging several cartloads of food and weapons to go with them so they'd at least be better provisioned. Edmund hadn't wanted to listen. He'd thought better of them, thinking them loyal, believing without doubt that, of all people, they'd be the first to rush to his side in his bid to take back his father's throne. To hear them speak as they had, like opportunists and cowards, had angered him beyond words. The best thing he could do was leave. He didn't want to burn all his bridges. Harsh words, spoken in the moment of hurt and injury, could do that. He'd buried their dead from the recent battle and left.

"Were you surprised?" asked Edmund, hoping Wulfnoth might provide some salve for his wounded pride.

"At their capitulation? I had wondered. Svienn's armies spread across the country with a speed I've never seen before, and Thorkell's lot hadn't left much standing. Many people would have had no choice but to submit. Sigeferth is right on that score."

"I get the feeling you have more to add," muttered Edmund.

"Your intuition is right," Wulfnoth affirmed with a humourless laugh. "This isn't the South. These lands are not all devastated. If Uhtred in Norþanhymbre had not betrayed us, Sigeferth would be in a better position to help us. A combined army of the North and the Boroughs would have made a difference."

"Uhtred is a product of my father's reign," said Edmund quickly, "and he's a product of Eadric's scheming. It's no surprise a creature like that would betray us."

"And I fear Eadric remains a thorn in our side," Wulfnoth said. "We'd have killed Svienn at the monastery if it were not for his sudden reinforcements."

"You speak true enough," replied Edmund sadly. "We still know so little about him. Even I can't say I really know him, and I saw him more often than most others. What motivates such a man? Are some men simply evil? Born bad?"

"That's an easy answer to offer, Edmund. Yet in my experience, the truth is a little more complex. Eadric is a monster born of a very specific environment, and I fear he'll continue to act as such until he's put down. Permanently."

"Let me guess…you know his past? His motives?"

"I'll be blunt," said Wulfnoth, his foot kicking at a stone as if to illustrate the point yet to come. "I recognised Eadric as a threat years ago, before he was even an ealdorman…we just called him "Eadric of Sciropesberie" then, because that's all he was. That changed, of course. He became dangerous, and he needed to be watched. That's why I have such a spy network."

"To keep an eye on him?"

"On him and his own spies. He sets them up everywhere, recruiting the greedy or downright malevolent, promising gold and favours for whoever will supply him with information or perform yet darker deeds when called upon. He's very good at it. Fortunately, it seems I am too."

"It didn't work to your advantage, Wulfnoth, not always. My father suspected you of placing people behind the scenes to conspire against him. I would say that's why it was so easy for Eadric and his brother to level such accusations against you."

"Yes, that was unexpected," Wulfnoth sighed. "I knew something was coming; some pointed fingers or whispered words that I was a traitor or corrupt or some such. I just didn't think your father was foolish enough to believe it so readily."

"Are you saying my father is a fool?" Edmund arched his eyebrows, uncomfortable even now that anyone should be so bold.

"Yes," Wulfnoth said without hesitation. "Look at England. Look at the state we're in. There's your answer."

Edmund's brow softened. Wulfnoth was right. It was difficult to hear, but his father had simply done too much, or failed in too much, to be safe from censure. There was no excusing some of his actions, and his decision to try and arrest Wulfnoth was one of them. It had been ill-advised, and that was always the problem with him. He listened to the wrong people. He listened to Eadric. Try as Edmund might, he couldn't see how his father shouldn't be considered a fool for that act alone.

"So, what have you learned about Eadric?" Edmund asked, hoping to change the subject away from his father and onto something more productive. "Is he the true villain in all this? Because I like simple solutions, and from where I'm standing, it certainly looks like he is. Svienn is a murderer and a savage, like the rest of his kind, but he's no traitor. Eadric is, and there is much blood on his hands."

"Old Morcar's been telling you what he knows, has he?"

Edmund grunted in acknowledgement, remembering how both Morcar and Sigeferth had told him and Æthelstan what they knew of Eadric before the two brothers had headed to Lundenburg to try to talk their father out of taxing the realm into oblivion. They'd intended it as a warning, correctly thinking they should know what Eadric was capable of before they faced him in the capital.

It had made for a grim and troubling tale. Eadric had killed their kinsmen, Ælfhelm, paving the way for Uhtred to become ealdorman of all Norþanhymbre. This had been on Æthelred's orders, so they'd said, but Eadric had also benefited in that Ælfhelm's influence in Mierće had been an impediment to his ambitions to become ealdorman there. Ælfhelm's death was a means to such an end, and Eadric had proved himself to the king in the process. His power had been in the ascendant ever since, and nobody had been able to constrain it.

"It is as it's been for years now, Edmund," Wulfnoth continued, taking Edmund's silence for approval. "We fight for the seat of power, or to ensure the right man gets to sit on it. Eadric has the same ambitions as me, he just wants a different man on the throne than I do. Somebody he can control."

"Who?" Edmund asked.

"The boys," Wulfnoth said quietly. "The children your father had by Emma. He sees them as easily malleable. They would certainly be easier for him to manipulate than you and Æthelstan. Neither of you suited him. You were both too strong and too pious...precisely why you should be king."

"Then why not flee with them into exile? If Eadric wants to control the royal family through my father's children, then why leave them to play lackey with Svienn?"

"Because Svienn has a huge army and presents opportunities Eadric probably didn't think were possible before," said Wulfnoth. "If things don't work out with Svienn, he'll probably revisit his plans for your half-brothers. Eadric is never fixed in place. He has no morals, no honour, so he's constantly on the move, flexible...and empty. There's no heart in that scrawny chest of his, just desire, appetite, ego...be wary of such men, Edmund. When a man cannot help but put himself before all others, he's dangerous enough...but when he has a mind as sharp as Eadric's, he becomes a special kind of menace."

"How do you always know so much, Wulfnoth?" It was a fair point to raise. Wulfnoth seemed to know everything and had a strange habit of appearing in places where he was most unexpected. Edmund knew all about his rescue of Alaric from Canterburie. It was heroic, but also incredibly fortuitous, especially since Wulfnoth had been on the run himself at the time.

"Let's dwell a little more on Eadric and his motives," Wulfnoth said, content to dodge Edmund's question. "His background explains a few things. He's of middling birth, from a modest family, which marks him out as unusual, given the power he's accumulated. In a strange way, his humble background worked in his favour, at least in your father's eyes. He liked to say he valued ability over blood, but he was being manipulated by Eadric from the start. The question is how."

"How indeed?" asked Edmund, thinking aloud. "Eadric isn't the first rat to make himself present at my father's witan. I just never understood how he was able to maintain himself there."

"It's not because of money or prestige," said Wulfnoth. "You'll know of the murder of Ælfhelm, I'm assuming?"

Edmund nodded, his jaw tightening at the mention of it.

"That didn't do him as much good as you'd think," Wulfnoth continued. "He broke the rules of hospitality, killing Ælfhelm when he was owed all due respect as his guest. Nobody has ever been able to prove conclusively that that's what happened, but people in high places talk, and that was a step too far. Eadric may have gained position in the eyes of your father from that day forward, but he was never liked or respected by anyone else."

"So he resents his fellow notables?"

"Oh yes," Wulfnoth nodded emphatically. "He knows what we all think of him, and it's not purely because of his common bloodline. In my opinion, that caused him to cling to your father quite tenaciously. He was never satisfied with his lot, and his early life in Sciropesberie was something he'd rather forget. He fears the humiliation of being hurled back there."

"He's irked about not being accepted at court?" Edmund asked. "That's what all this is about? All the lying, all the intrigue and double-dealing?"

"Partly," Wulfnoth confirmed. "Men of power are nearly always men of great sin. Eadric isn't anything new in that regard, but it's the sheer enthusiasm and capability he has for advancing his position that's unusual. He hates and fears the rest of us for thinking little of him, believing we wish to see him toppled because of it. He's right. But that fear made him even more aggressive, even more treacherous…even more dangerous, to everyone."

"So he hated you all so much for thinking ill of him that he's been driven to accumulate yet more power so he might forestall you moving against him?"

"I would say fear was a motive of his, yes," Wulfnoth said. "Fear of me, in particular. He knew I was watching him. The same goes for Sigeferth and Morcar, which makes their decision to side with Svienn all the more foolish. If they know Eadric is with him, they should also know he'll now likely move against them to take them out of play. It's what I'd do."

"Perhaps they feel driven to develop a relationship with Svienn because of that," Edmund suggested. "Sigeferth feared my father, thinking he'd blame him for Æthelstan's death. That's how I ended up returning to Lundenburg only to be trapped there. I had to convince my father not to do anything foolish."

"If that's what they are doing, they've miscalculated. Eadric is clearly well thought of by Svienn, and will be more so following his attack on us at the monastery. The Five Boroughs are in peril, Edmund. Taking the coward's way out, as Sigeferth and Morcar have done, will not help them. It may only encourage Eadric to try to have them removed."

"He's just one man," growled Edmund, "and of low status at that. How did Eadric make his wealth? It makes no sense to me."

"He didn't," Wulfnoth said. "I don't have the full details, but I've heard rumours Eadric used your father's heregeld to enrich himself. I wouldn't be surprised if it was all his idea to begin with. He's certainly done well from it."

"How? That tax was payable directly to the royal coffers. Only official reeves were permitted to collect it. Eadric didn't have the authority to just come and take it."

"He doesn't, no, but apparently he's exploited a certain loophole in the law regarding the confiscation of property. Your father, probably under Eadric's advice, made it so that anyone refusing to pay their share would have their property seized. Anyone is then free to acquire that property from the crown on the condition they pay the entirety of the original tax that was demanded."

"So he's been buying up anything he can?" asked Edmund, amazed at how much thought Eadric must have put into this. "Just how much does he own now? Half the kingdom refused to have anything to do with the heregeld, and the other half was taxed into ruin by it."

"It's a lot, I'd say. Mostly land, as you'd expect, but some developments too and Church property also. That might explain Eadric's willingness to cooperate with Svienn. He doesn't want to lose what he's already gained."

"Off the backs of the people!" snarled Edmund, his hands clenching into fists. "It was bad enough that my father emptied the treasury before fleeing, but now this? It's like we're beset by endless villainy, and so much of it from our own kind!"

"Æthelred emptied the treasury?"

"He did. He loaded it onto his ships before fleeing. Most of it will be in Thorkell's paws by now, I think."

"You saw your father before he fled, though?"

"I did."

"And you didn't try to stop his theft? We need money, Edmund, and we have none."

"I know! But…it was a difficult situation. My father had taken the boy, Brandon, and I had to get him back to his mother. She'd just lost her husband, Alaric. She was so pained. So lost…I had to get Brandon back, and antagonising my father with further demands wasn't the way to do it."

Wulfnoth sighed, the exhalation sounding like it was one part weariness and the other exasperation. "You're fond of the lady, Edmund, and I do feel for her. I didn't know Alaric long, but I was grieved to hear of his death. But you let your heart get in the way…"

"What are you suggesting?" Edmund demanded. "I took pity on a widow. That is all."

"Is that all it is, Edmund? Are you sure?"

Edmund turned away, his face flushing as he struggled to decide whether to be angry or just embarrassed. He felt sorry for Æva, that was all it was. He'd played the noble part, and now she was out of his hands, free to live her life down south with her son, assuming they'd been successful in retaking Porteceaster. He'd never have to see her again. It was better that way. She'd only complicate things. He could tell by how he felt when he thought of not seeing her. It hurt. He couldn't afford to hurt. Hopefully, the pain would ease in time.

"It's all right, Edmund," said Wulfnoth softly. "You're of an age where you should be married by now. A woman like Æva may have a certain hold on a man in your position."

"She's freshly widowed!" Edmund cried, spinning around to face Wulfnoth again. "I'm not the kind of man to press himself upon a woman in grief! Give me some credit, at least."

"I never said you had or would do such a thing," said Wulfnoth. "That would be shameful, and you're not the kind to behave shamefully. But a compassionate heart can be a vulnerable one, and you have shown such compassion to this woman. Certain…feelings…can therefore arise."

"That's why I agreed to her proposal," sighed Edmund. "I can't have those… feelings…you mention, getting in the way. She's better off down south…and yet sometimes I think I should have kept her with me. I fought so hard to keep her and her son safe, and now she might be in danger all over again."

Wulfnoth smiled a confident, lop-sided grin. "She's safer than you think," he said. "Ulfcytel will kill anyone who tries to harm her or that boy of hers. And I also set certain things in motion beforehand…to make sure they have some help when they reach Porteceaster."

"What does that mean?"

"Just trust me, Edmund. I wouldn't have advised you let them go there if their chances of success were so low. You don't think straight when it comes to Æva. I think that's why you agreed to what she asked. She's got a hold on you. An influence. Am I wrong?"

"Let's talk about something else," Edmund asked, embarrassed and almost alarmed at how easily Wulfnoth was able to read him. "Let's focus on Eadric...just how much land does he own now, thanks to his mercilessly acquisitive ways?"

"I can't say," Wulfnoth said with a scratch of his head, "but it's interesting you call him acquisitive. Apparently, he's earned the title "The Acquisitor" within his own lands in Mierċe. His people take note of his activities, and they are not impressed."

"Is this a weakness we can exploit? Is Mierċe inclined to rebellion?"

"I wouldn't go that far, Edmund, but there's certainly resentment, particularly from the Church. He seems to be making a habit of obtaining Church property, although that may simply be because so many clergymen objected to your father's heregeld."

"It's true," said a voice from behind Edmund, both he and Wulfnoth turning swiftly to face it. Edmund's heart leapt on seeing who stood there. It was his younger brother, Eadwig, his high forehead and deep-set eyes unmistakable, despite the overly-abundant mop of hair cascading from his scalp. He was dressed like a woodsman, his dark green cloak failing to entirely obscure a light leather jerkin, the satchel of supplies at his belt indicating he'd come prepared for braving the elements. Two armed men stood on either side of him, both of them sentries whom Edmund had tasked with watching the approach to their camp. He dismissed them promptly. He had nothing to fear from Eadwig, despite the mystery of his appearance here.

It was with some shame that Edmund realised he hadn't thought of him in some time. The last he'd heard, Eadwig had relocated to Derbei with Morcar so as to learn more from the thegn-turned-monk, Wulfgeat. Edmund didn't know how all that had turned out. He'd first met Wulfgeat on the day Æthelstan had died, and despite the monk's claims to know all sorts of things about his father and certain suspicious dealings at court, Edmund had found it difficult to give him much attention. Gossip bored him, and whilst Morcar and Eadwig both appeared to think Wulfgeat fascinating, Edmund had felt it more important to grieve for Æthelstan. That had been a hard and lonely time, and he couldn't help feeling somewhat resentful that Eadwig had left him to it. He didn't feel like bringing it up now. He was too pleased to see him.

"Eadwig! I thought...you've come from Snotingeham? I didn't see you there."

"You left in a hurry," Eadwig shrugged. "And it's true what you're talking about. The seizing of Church lands by unscrupulous nobles is a time-honoured tradition in this country. Our grandfather tried to bring some stability to the situation and clearly demarcate the rights of the monasteries...you could say he wasn't always successful."

Edmund smiled. Eadwig's propensity for book learning meant he was a fount of knowledge on subjects others might disregard. "And Eadric is just carrying on with such a tradition?" Edmund asked, wanting to encourage his brother.

"I'd say so," replied Eadwig. "He's a special breed, this Eadric, but in many ways, he's behaving as a man in his position would. It's a sad thing to have to admit, but that is our lot these days. We've suffered corruption in high places for too long."

"What brings you here?" Edmund inquired, thinking it likely was something other than brotherly love.

"I wanted to see you," said Eadwig, surprising Edmund with the sincerity of his words. "I was told you were upset with Sigeferth's decision to capitulate. I didn't want you just heading off into the wilds like that. I was worried. We all were."

"I appreciate it," said Edmund, a little awkward at hearing what was easily the most affectionate thing Eadwig had ever said to him. "And yet I fear the trust I placed in Sigeferth and Morcar was ill-judged. If you're asking me to go back to them..."

"I'm not, but I wanted to speak with you, and I had a feeling you'd be here. It wasn't just you and Æthelstan who liked this place."

"You knew of it too?"

"Yes, Edmund. I still remember how father reacted to you finding those coins here. I had to find it myself. History lies beneath our feet."

"Why didn't you ask me about it? We could have all come together."

"I didn't think you'd want to...I didn't think you'd care for me poking around in search of Roman remains. So I came alone."

"You didn't have to," Edmund sighed, saddened at the thought of his lonesome younger brother scratching about in the mud. "You'd have been welcome. You were always welcome. You still are."

"I'm happy you think that," said Eadwig with a slight smile, "but I've not come here to talk about our past. Sigeferth is very upset, Edmund, as is Morcar. They feel you don't appreciate their situation."

"Their situation?" Edmund repeated quizzically. "They've submitted to the enemy. There's nothing for me to appreciate."

"Please think on what you're saying. We didn't know what had happened to you, and then suddenly, Svienn appeared with an army and demanded we kneel. There was no choice to be had there."

"But I'm back now," said Edmund bluntly, "and Svienn isn't here. I'm the rightful heir, and they owe me their allegiance."

"I don't dispute that, but I think you know frightened people may forget obligations made in better, more comforting times. They fear the war cannot be won and that resisting Svienn will result in the deaths of thousands. They are not just thinking of themselves, Edmund. The welfare of their people is their foremost concern."

"Are you suggesting I'm being selfish?" Edmund asked testily. "You were not there when Lundenburg fell, Eadwig. You were not there when Æthelstan died either. Do not presume."

"I don't. I'm just telling you how I see it. You should understand they don't mean to slight you. They'd be with you if the odds were not so overwhelming."

"A king is owed the allegiance of his subjects," said Wulfnoth suddenly. "That doesn't change when times become difficult. If anything, trying times only intensify the meaning and need for loyalty."

Edmund looked over at Wulfnoth, wondering whether he'd somehow thought Eadwig had meant to cause offence. "You're quite correct," Eadwig said meekly, uncomfortable under Wulfnoth's gaze, "but that's another reason why I've come here. I want to join you, Edmund."

"To win me a crown?" Edmund asked, again surprised. "What about you? Don't you fancy sitting on the throne? You could make a claim to it, you know. Age isn't everything."

"I fear I'd be unsuitable. You know the differences between us as well as anyone. I'm no warrior. I never had the...enthusiasm you and Æthelstan had for such matters. England needs a warrior king."

Edmund held his tongue, a brief flash of sadness catching him by surprise. Æthelstan's final words to him had been about how he had to go on and become "our warrior king". It was a surprise to hear that Eadwig felt the same, and the realisation touched his heart in ways he hadn't expected.

"Why come here and say these things?" asked Edmund, his voice trembling slightly as he did his best to push the recollection of his dying older brother to one side.

"Because a great many things have been said and done...and I find myself looking on my past and present both with little but regret. I should have stood up to father, like you and Æthelstan...I should have done something."

"Some may say you made the better choice," Edmund muttered. "Æthelstan and I didn't always make the best decisions. He's dead now because of it."

"Please don't say that," Eadwig said with a shake of his head, Wulfnoth also audibly exhaling in what Edmund assumed was shock and displeasure. "You were trying to stop father from paying yet more tribute to our enemies. It was a bold move."

"It was," nodded Edmund, "and not a day goes by where I wish I hadn't done it. I'm not the man Æthelstan was. I don't inspire others like he did. He should be here. Things would be different then."

"That's nonsense, Edmund," objected Wulfnoth, moving to stand at his side. "And I'm surprised to hear you say that. These men around us are all here because they have faith in you. Men had faith in you at Eadmundes Byrig. They had faith in you at Lundenburg. They had faith in you at Bernecestre. Æthelstan was one of them."

"As am I," said Eadwig, a slight twinkle in his eye. "I'm not as useless as some might think, and I've not simply come to offer my services, meagre as they are. I have information...something that could end this war and free England from the Danish yoke."

"You're always welcome at my side, brother," said Edmund eagerly, "and even if you had nothing to offer but yourself, I'd still make a place for you here. Believe it."

"Noble sentiments," said Wulfnoth, "but what's this information you have, Eadwig? Something from that old fox, Morcar, is it?"

"It's from both him and Sigeferth," replied Eadwig. "Or at least it involves them and every other thegn. Svienn has made a request of them. He wants them to come see him. A gathering. At Gainesburg."

"What manner of gathering?" Wulfnoth asked, his eyes narrowing.

"Some kind of formal ceremony, I think. Svienn wants them and the other compliant notables to publicly swear oaths and make a fuss over him. A horrible idea, but they intend to make an appearance lest they provoke his wrath."

"What's the purpose behind this?" growled Edmund, the image he held in his mind of bowing Englishmen and gloating Danes making his teeth grind in anger. "Because I don't care what airs Svienn puts on, or how many sycophants he can summon. If it were up to me, I'd have them all executed for treason."

"I had hoped you'd say something like that," answered Eadwig, a wicked grin on his face. "Because this is an opportunity for you, Edmund, and one I intend to help you seize. An opportunity for you to kill Svienn Forkbeard."

VIII

The sea is calm tonight, the thick clouds reducing it to one single, black expanse, empty and still. The wind is almost entirely absent, allowing the dancing light from our onshore torches to shine boldly into the dark. All is quiet across the wharves, the day's bustle giving way to a silence disturbed only by the sound of my own footsteps. It's an easy night, free of drama and strife, the peace I feel a comforting rarity in these otherwise troubled times.

I stop for a moment, standing at the head of the central jetty as it strikes out into the surf. Hardly anyone is out here, the cargo from the day's comings and goings having been hauled away and stored either for sale or transport. The town slumbers at my back, safe behind the walls that encircle it from the north, east, and west, its southern facade entirely inaccessible to anyone approaching without recourse to water.

I take a deep breath and then another, enjoying the chill salt tang filling my nostrils. There are a few others on duty with me, each patrolling his own route and always within shouting distance of the other in case anything goes awry. There's rarely any trouble, for the worst days of raiding are behind us, so it's been said, and the Danes have thankfully refrained from visiting us by ship for some years now. I wasn't here then, born and raised as I was in Wincestre, but the tales the locals tell of those days are harrowing enough. Nothing like that can happen now. Not on my watch. Nothing can get past me and mine.

Fate challenges my hubris almost immediately. I spot something, remote yet still sizeable, approaching silently on the water. You could see it only because the sea had been so calm, the mass of what could only be an incoming vessel churning the placid waters until only the blind would fail to spot it. The ship soon comes into full view, its appearance changing from an ominous silhouette pressed against the horizon to a squat, cumbersome hulk caught in the light of our watchtower. I breathe a sigh of relief as I take in its dimensions. It's no raiding ship. Only those hauling cargo for sale would invest in a beast such as this. Either way, the hour is late. They're welcome here, but I'm obliged to have words with the captain.

I wave to my men, beckoning them over whilst the ship's oarsmen try to steer themselves in to dock. The vessel is even larger up close, and the deck is covered with what look to be furs and hides, the captain presumably wishing to fill his ship to capacity for the sake of profit. He's lucky the weather is so fair. His greed could have cost him severely if it were not so.

One of my men joins me on the jetty, and the pair of us begin marching down towards the vessel struggling to heave itself alongside. I throw a rope that is deftly caught by a figure on deck, and we then throw another and yet another, making sure our ends are tied securely, our mutual efforts ensuring the ship is gradually pulled in and made fast. I nearly put my back out, so strenuous is the task, but the absence of strong winds assists us greatly, the sea itself parting without complaint as we go about our work.

Several men leap ashore, their features obscured beneath flowing cloaks pulled tight to protect against the elements. I wonder why, knowing this summer night to be more pleasant than most, thinking perhaps it was colder out upon the open water. One of them approaches me, his gait strong and purposeful, the oarsmen aboard his ship all rising as if expecting to join him. I nod to whom I assume to be the captain as he comes closer, an instinctual feeling of unease suddenly taking hold of me. Something isn't right.

"Welcome to Suthhamtunam," I say, going through the usual motions when it comes to newcomers. "May I ask what brings you here at this late hour? We like to know."

He doesn't respond, instead pulling his hood back with both hands to reveal his face. I almost wish he had not. He's scarred, severely, his lean, wiry beard doing little to hide it. His hair is long, lank, and unwashed, hanging lifelessly from his thinning scalp. Those aren't scars from some kind of accident. They've been inflicted by a cutting edge, in battle most likely, and everything about him tells me he's more than accustomed to violence. I look into his green, piercing eyes, and I feel panic, cold and unpleasant and spreading upward from my stomach.

I know this man. He was there the day we captured the former ealdorman and traitor, Ælfric, and handed him over to the king's loyal servant, Eadric. He'd escaped, killing several men in the process, and we'd pursued, eager to see justice done. To my surprise, he'd proven himself as capable in flight as he was in battle, and when he'd leapt off this very jetty to plunge beneath the waves, I'd thought not to see him again. He shouldn't be here. He…

"You!" It's the best I can manage, the shock of recognition numbing my wits. I reach for my spear, discarded upon the jetty so that I might haul ropes, but he's fast. Too fast. I'm hi…

Cenric felt a twinge of guilt when the man dropped, his knuckles already numb from the impact. It was a hard thing to knock a fellow Englishman unconscious, but he'd been going for his spear, and there was only one reason why he'd be doing that. His companion tried to cry out and ready his weapon, but it was already too late. Ulfcytel was on him, his heavy cloak falling from his shoulders as he charged forward. He beat him senseless, his fists rising and falling in their own brutal rhythm, the poor fool he'd accosted now bloodied and still upon the wooden decking. Somebody yelled something up ahead. They'd been spotted already. That wasn't good.

He heard a sequence of heavy thuds behind him as the rest of their men disembarked. The hides had been a nice touch, providing cover for their people and concealing their actual numbers, the deception making it look like their vessel was simply overstocked with valuable wares. They had a good forty men with them, hand-picked from Porteceaster, the Ealdorman Ælfric also among their number and eager for revenge. Cenric saw him now moving up alongside them, his aged features failing to hide the menacing vitality that possessed him. He wanted to lead them. He didn't want to be upstaged by Ulfcytel, but most of all, he wanted to kill Eadwulf. Cenric understood. He shared that goal.

They set off, charging down the jetty and towards the wharf with as much order and precision as space would allow. The watchtower was their first target, although a clutch of guards gave them some trouble almost immediately. They overcame them quickly, but the fight was still hard, for nobody in their party had any desire to shed

English blood. And yet they had now done so. Cenric would grieve later. Right now, they had more immediate concerns.

A bell started to ring, the sound cutting through the cool night air with the promise of ruined plans and impending defeat. They rushed the watchtower, knowing they had to silence that damn racket before all of Suthhamtunam awoke and came charging out to greet them. The door to the tower crashed inward under Ulfcytel's charging bulk, and Cenric wasted no time vaulting up step after step to leap upon the unfortunate bell ringer. He'd sequestered himself up here next to a blazing brazier, this well-lit beacon providing the light that had originally allowed them to spot the contours of the port and guide their ship in to dock. The bell he'd been ringing hung from a wooden beam erected presumably to allow a sentry to raise the alarm if hostile vessels were spotted. The man wouldn't desist, and he'd be their doom if something wasn't done to silence him.

Cenric tackled him to the floor with all the force required. He then tried to reason with him, stating he was English and in the service of the rightful Ealdorman of Hamptonscir, Ælfric. He wasn't sure if the man was thick-headed or just unwilling to listen, but the blade he pulled from his belt spoke clearly enough of his intent. Cenric couldn't take any chances. He took his life. He hadn't wanted to, but he'd given him little choice.

He sped back down the stairs, joining Ulfcytel and the rest of the men outside. They looked relieved that the bell had stopped ringing, yet there was no time to lose. They rushed on, moving away from the docks and into the streets beyond. Cenric remembered the route. He'd run it last year, Eadwulf's men hot on his heels. God had been with him that day, although Cenric had no forgiveness to offer. Eadwulf's end was nigh.

Theirs was a dangerous plan, born in part from Ælfric's desire for vengeance and the realisation that Suthhamtunam's outer wall would not fall to an attack from the few men they had in Porteceaster. An assault by sea was preferable, Ælfric had said, giving them the chance to carry out what he'd called a "butcher and bolt raid" under cover of darkness. It was a simple enough notion. They'd dock at Suthhamtunam's port, pretending to be just another merchant vessel, and fight their way to Eadwulf's hall and kill him. They'd then beat a hasty retreat to their ship, avoiding the garrison as best they could, and row back home to think on their next moves. It wasn't without risks, but Cenric felt their plan had a fair chance of success.

Events soon proved him overly optimistic. As fast as Cenric had been in cutting off the alarm bell, it had still rung out into the night, and shouts were now emerging from the darkened streets ahead. Cenric exchanged a look with Ælfric, but the ealdorman pressed on without speaking, leading them around a corner to hurry north and then east. They found themselves outside a walled courtyard, the double doors naturally barred from the other side lest intruders decide to attempt entry. Cenric knew this place. Eadwulf's hall lay beyond these walls. Now they just had to get to him before reinforcements arrived.

They could break through, but it would take time and make such a racket the men undoubtedly on high alert within would hear them and respond. Ulfcytel made a gesture before bending low, his fingers interlacing and his hands held out before him. Cenric understood. He put his right foot in his hands, Ulfcytel then using his great strength to send him scrabbling up the wall adjacent to the doors. He made it over, falling with surprising grace to land on the other side.

There was no one here, or so it looked, but the alarm and noise from beyond would soon change that if he dallied. He approached the sealed doors and unbarred them with some effort, allowing the length of solid oak to clatter to the ground. He winced at the noise he'd made, but he'd achieved what he'd set out to do, and the doors came flying open almost immediately, his compatriots rushing inside. They crossed the courtyard in haste, Eadwulf's hall emerging from the darkness ahead, a muffled, panicked shouting sounding from within.

Ulfcytel and three others charged, their weight, strength, and speed sending the hall's front doors crashing inward. Cenric dashed after them along with Ælfric and the rest, their numbers flooding the antechamber and their weapons bared and ready. The much-hated Eadwulf was up ahead, almost exactly where he'd been when they'd come calling months prior, but he had a fearful look to him now, even with a dozen armed men standing between him and Ælfric.

"What is the meaning of this?!" he spluttered, his eyes wide with panic. He'd been asleep and was dressed in nothing but a white nightgown, a small hand axe held feebly in his trembling grip.

"It's what it looks like!" Ælfric snarled, his sword drawn as he took position at the head of their men alongside Ulfcytel and Cenric. "I've come for you, Eadwulf! Eadric can't help you now! Stand forth and submit to my judgement as your rightful lord!"

"You're a traitor, Ælfric!" shrieked Eadwulf. "Eadric told me enough! I know all of it! Just what do you intend to do here? Murder me in my own home?!"

"None of you men need die," Ulfcytel boomed, addressing the warriors that stood before them. "I am the Ealdorman Ulfcytel. You'll all have heard of me...and I tell you that the man you defend is nothing but a pawn of the real traitor in all this: Eadric of Mierċe. Put down your weapons, and no harm will come to you. We only want Eadwulf. You have my word on this."

Indecision reigned in Eadwulf's ranks. Several mumbled something in apparent confusion, and one asked Ulfcytel outright if he was indeed who he claimed to be and how he might prove it. Eadwulf then made his own mistake, sealing his fate in the process. He could have tried being clever, perhaps accusing Ulfcytel of being an imposter and branding him nothing but a liar. Instead, he panicked, and, in doing so, made it clear Ulfcytel was exactly who he said he was.

"You lost Canterburie!" he said, raving like a man who correctly saw his end at hand. "You lost Hringmere too! All you do is lose, defying your king in pursuit of personal glory! You'll lose here tonight, too, Ulfcytel! Svienn is our king now, and I'll give him your head!"

That did it. His men turned to look at him, surprise and disgust upon their faces. They stepped back and away a moment later, their assorted mutterings and exclamations indicating they found the notion of killing a hero like Ulfcytel absolutely repellent. Eadwulf stood alone, his chest rising and falling in panic. Cenric strode forward and doubled him over with a kick to the stomach, his axe clattering to the floor, and dragged him before Ælfric, a quick blow to the back of the head ensuring he fell to his knees. Cenric stayed behind him, his sword held aloft and gripped, point facing down, towards the back of Eadwulf's neck. He looked to Ælfric. He need only give the word, and justice would be done.

"Have you anything to say to me?" Ælfric asked quietly, his manner strangely forlorn even in this moment of triumph. "Do you have some case to plead, some explanation as to why you betrayed me and my family to a beast like Eadric?"

"He came on the king's orders!" Eadwulf rasped, his face deathly pale. "He told me of what you'd done, in the past and most recently! A litany of misdeeds! I did what any man loyal to his king would do!"

"Eadric paid you, didn't he?" Ælfric asked, ignoring the accusations. "He paid for your compliance, knowing I'd hope to find refuge here. It's true, isn't it? He bought you."

"I'll not admit to anything! Eadric is a loyal man, as am I! The same cannot be said of you, Ælfric! Never!"

Ælfric caught Cenric's eye and gave him a slight nod, the gesture sealing Eadwulf's fate. Cenric readied himself but then hesitated. Eadwulf's protestations had troubled his heart. Could the man really have been that gullible? Had Eadric come to him, as if he were a loyal servant of the crown, and convinced him to turn on his ealdorman through simple persuasion? It wasn't impossible, and Cenric knew that at least some of what Eadwulf had said was true. He still remembered what Ulfcytel had told Alaric in Canterburie. Ælfric remained his lord, but he had a dark and troubled past, one Cenric wasn't at ease with.

He made the kill, his blade piercing Eadwulf's neck just behind the collarbone and penetrating into his chest cavity. He fell forward when Cenric wrenched his sword up and out, a thin splash of blood coming with it. Eadwulf lay face down, a puddle of his own fluids expanding outward with unsettling rapidity, the men that had only recently been loyal to him shifting uneasily at the sight. Ælfric spoke to them, telling them they'd made the right choice and that any who'd had a part in his capture last year were now forgiven. It seemed to work, but Cenric still felt uneasy. It hadn't been Ælfric who had convinced them to switch allegiance. That man stood off to the side, his hard eyes lingering on the dead Eadwulf. They owed Ulfcytel much. Without him, they'd never have taken this place without a fight.

Eadwulf's men continued to obey them from that point on, the deceased man's household also compliant when they awoke to learn of the change in leadership. His wife howled and bawled, as was to be expected, and Cenric felt great sorrow for her, suspecting she had little to do with Eadwulf's scheming and was just heartbroken over his sudden and unexpected demise. He was about to offer words of comfort when a distraction came. Trouble had arrived. Lots of trouble.

They were reinforcements from the garrison, bursting in through the courtyard after being roused by the alarm bell. They were angry, very angry, and when they saw Eadwulf's corpse they seemed ready to attack, brandishing weapons and demanding explanations. Eadwulf's guards went to calm them, telling them of what had happened and how Ulfcytel was here in support of Ælfric. It wasn't having the desired effect, and Cenric feared they were again on the cusp of bloodshed.

Ulfcytel, fortunately, managed to cool things down before a pitched battle broke out. He strode forward, announcing his presence with his thunderous voice and equally thunderous bulk. The intruders stopped, as if they couldn't believe it was really him, some looking suddenly of a mood to turn and flee. Ulfcytel took advantage of their benumbed state and began talking, regaling them with fine prose on how Eadwulf had been a traitor and that there was no further need for violence. He kept on at them for a while longer, telling them all about Edmund's heroics in Lundenburg and that by serving Ælfric, they were serving him, the rightful king. They liked that. None of them thought highly of Svienn. It was a good sign.

The newcomers were led by the garrison commander, a stocky, balding man named Ceadda, who, as luck would have it, had a cousin who'd fought alongside Ulfcytel years ago during his heroic defence of Theodford. Ceadda was more than surprised to see Ulfcytel now, and like the rest of them he believed every word that came out of the ealdorman's mouth. Ceadda also had a few things to say for himself. Eadwulf had been a harsh master, apparently, and Eadric had indeed bribed him for reasons that, at the time, were unknown. He then apologised to Ælfric, affirming his loyalty to both him and the absent "Edmund Ironside". It had been a heartwarming display. It also removed the need for them to flee back to the docks and escape. Suthhamtunam was theirs.

By the time dawn was breaking, Cenric was once again aboard ship in the company of Ulfcytel and Ælfric. They were heading back to Porteceaster, their oars heaving through the calm waters of the open sea, the rising sun casting a gentle golden glow over their starboard side. Their vessel wasn't so crowded this time, for Ælfric had left a few of their men in the town, entrusting them to keep order and work with Ceadda so that trade to and from the port would continue without disruption.

Despite their victory, Cenric remained worried, thinking it was still possible some of Eadwulf's men might make trouble for them. Ælfric brushed aside his concerns, stating that whilst Suthhamtunam may have followed Eadwulf initially, it was only due to Eadric's capacity for deception. The people were loyal to their ealdorman, so he said, and since they now knew he served a proper English contender for the throne rather than the cruel Svienn Forkbeard, their allegiance was assured. Cenric nodded, agreeing with much of what was said but still secretly ill at ease. Ælfric overestimated himself. Ulfcytel had won them Suthhamtunam, just as he'd won them Porteceaster. That was the truth, and it was foolish to pretend otherwise. Without him and his capacity to inspire loyalty, they'd be lost. He suspected Ælfric knew that in his heart, but some hidden animosity prevented him from acknowledging it. Cenric could guess what that was about. Ælfric somehow knew that Ulfcytel was aware of his past. He hoped no drama would come from this. They had to be united behind Edmund, not at odds over bitter memories.

Stronger winds picked up and filled their sails when they were almost halfway to Porteceaster, this small piece of fortune speeding them home just as the midday sun was casting its rays across the waters of the harbour. Ulfcytel had become more and more tense as the fortress walls grew closer, like he thought some additional feat of bravery and cunning awaited him within. Something struck Cenric as off, and it was for that reason he made sure he remained at the ealdorman's side when they disembarked, hoping Ulfcytel might choose to lighten the burden he was so obviously carrying.

"You did well back there, Cenric," Ulfcytel said, their large, booted feet crunching through the gravel covering the roadway linking the harbour to the southern gatehouse. They'd outpaced Ælfric, leaving him in conversation with one of his aides, Cenric hoping he'd not take offence at his sudden departure.

"I did what had to be done," replied Cenric. "As did you. You talked our way out of a bloodbath, you know that, yes?"

"I do," Ulfcytel said. "I didn't want anyone to die. Those men thought they were doing the right thing. I'm just glad my reputation preceded me...and that Eadwulf was stupid enough to confirm my identity. I wouldn't have been so convincing had he not started raving like that."

"He knew who you were, and he knew what it meant," Cenric said, both men passing through the wide stone and timber gates and into the fortress interior. A few chickens hurried past them across the muddied path, all clucking away with a small boy in playful pursuit, the birds apparently enjoying themselves as he was.

"I suspect also," continued Cenric with a faint smile, "that had you not been with us, they wouldn't have been so inclined to obey Ælfric. I think Eadric has made his...past misdeeds...common knowledge, or at least concocted some story with it to get Eadwulf to do his bidding."

"You could be right," said Ulfcytel. "The best lies often contain an element of truth. For Eadric to tell people that Ælfric had indeed cooperated with Svienn Forkbeard years back...it would work to his advantage, I'd say."

"Is it really true, though?"

"What?" asked Ulfcytel.

"What you told Alaric in Canterburie. I was there, remember. You said Ælfric had tried to defect to Svienn and then later failed to save Wiltune when he could have. Is it true?"

"It is, Cenric. I'm sorry. I know you're a loyal man, and so this won't be easy for you, but..."

"You're going to tell Æva, aren't you?"

"Yes," Ulfcytel confirmed. "She wants to know. She deserves to know. That was her son who died in Wiltune, thanks to Ælfric's ineptitude."

"Please, hold a moment," implored Cenric, stopping dead in his tracks just outside the smithy. Ulfcytel paused to look back at him, the harsh sound of metal hammering on metal emerging from the open-air forge just a few yards away.

"Think of Brandon," Cenric pleaded. "This place is a good home for him. He can be safe here. He doesn't need any more upheaval, not since his father..."

"His father?" Ulfcytel asked, raising a single silver eyebrow. "Are we quite sure, Cenric, that the lad is Alaric's son?"

"What are you saying?! Æva is a good woman! She would never be a party to adultery!"

"She is, and she almost certainly wouldn't," Ulfcytel concurred, "but the boy looks nothing like Alaric. Nothing. Tell me you don't see it."

"I don't have a suspicious mind," Cenric replied carefully, "but I ask you again...what would telling Æva achieve? She'd be heartbroken. She IS heartbroken."

"I am, Cenric, which is why whatever it is that Ulfcytel has to tell me can't possibly make me feel any worse. And he promised me an explanation."

Cenric blinked, troubled and confused at how Æva had managed to approach without him spotting her, especially given the deep, flowing purple of her dress. There were people passing by, it was true, going about their business as was usual for this time of day, but Cenric prided himself on his ability to spy a face in a crowd and respond accordingly. He must have just been distracted by Ulfcytel. The man had uttered words that Cenric would have normally answered with a fist. He was lucky he was an ealdorman, and a friend, if Cenric were being honest. He'd also made a valid point. It was a sad thing to have to think about, but there it was. Brandon really didn't look anything like Alaric.

"Let's talk in private," Ulfcytel said, his eyes falling upon Æva. Cenric followed as they headed in the direction of Ælfric's hall, his mind racing about how he might somehow convince Ulfcytel to hold off. It wasn't that he felt Æva shouldn't ever be told. He just wasn't sure how Ulfcytel himself had come by his knowledge of Ælfric, or why he believed it to be true. He also remembered how Alaric had wept upon hearing it. He didn't want that for Æva. She'd shed enough tears already.

"Is there something I can help you with?" Æva asked, aware that Cenric was following them.

"Yes, a favour, lady," he said hurriedly, "for old time's sake, and for the sake of your husband's memory."

"What is it?" she asked, pausing in her stride to look back at him.

"Let me stay with you. I was there when Alaric heard the words Ulfcytel is set on telling you. I like to think I helped him in some way. Let me help you too. Please."

Æva's face softened. "Of course," she half-whispered, Cenric struggling to hear her over the hustle and bustle of the surrounding township. "You don't have to think of this as a favour. I'm glad to have you with me. I know Alaric would be glad too."

Cenric swallowed hard and endeavoured to blink away the tears that had sprung up unbidden. He'd always kept how he'd felt about Alaric a secret, thinking himself sentimental and foolish in his old age. He'd never let on to anyone how Alaric had played an important part in his own process of healing following the death of his wife and children. Cenric had been lost then, his entire life in ruins, and so when the ealdorman had sent him his sons to train in swordcraft, he'd taken to it eagerly for the simple reason it provided a distraction from his grief.

Yet Alaric had made it so much more than that. He'd displayed an enthusiasm that Cenric couldn't help but warm to, and he was talented; possessing an instinctual skill that was lacking in his older brother, Ælfgar. He was honourable also, refraining from the jagged put-downs and general cynicism displayed by his sibling. Cenric felt that he'd have liked his sons to have imitated Alaric, had they lived long enough to know him.

Cenric had never once told him how much those training sessions had meant to him. They'd saved his life, quite literally. He'd already tried to kill himself after losing his family. He'd made a noose, tying it to the rafters of his all-too-empty cottage, but it had snapped under his weight to send him crashing to the floor. He'd lain there in a sorry heap, sobbing and gasping and wanting nothing more than to just slip into a deep slumber and never awaken.

He'd never told anyone about that either, and he wasn't about to tell anyone now. They'd only think him soft, and people were cruel about those who tried to take their own lives. Cenric thought that odd. There was nobody in the whole world who knew despair like a man pushed to the brink. When one seriously thought it was the end and their own despair would be their undoing, it seemed logical that mercy would be the answer, especially from those unafflicted and able to render aid. Instead, people often disregarded the brokenhearted - especially when they were men - thinking them weak or silly, and those who fell further and died by their own hand were rejected outright, as if they'd intentionally set out to spite the Lord God himself. Cenric didn't understand it, but it was for such reasons he'd kept his dalliance with suicide a secret. He wouldn't bare his soul just to be condemned by those who'd never tasted the suffering he had.

They passed through the courtyard and entered the great hall, Cenric wondering where the Ealdorman Ælfric might have got to since he didn't appear to have followed them after disembarking. They continued down the length of the hall, the paintings and tapestries of past events always drawing the eye. Æva took a left to access the stairwell to the tower. They followed, Ulfcytel and Cenric both, but the climb was long, and Ulfcytel's limp and breath were somewhat laboured by the time their journey thankfully ended and they were stepping into Æva's chambers. Cenric had only been here a few times before and always for the sake of calling on Alaric. It felt strangely empty without him. He suspected Æva thought the same.

Brandon was here, watched over by an elderly woman Cenric recognised but didn't know by name. Æva whispered something in her ear, and the crone clambered to her feet to hobble with Brandon through another door that would take them out of earshot. Cenric pulled a chair away from the wall and manoeuvred it into place by the hearth, feeling surprised when the ealdorman refused to sit. Æva remained standing also, her face stony and unemotional as she closed the front door and turned to stare at them both, her arms folded.

"So tell me. What did you tell my husband about his father that was so earth-shattering?"

Ulfcytel just let the words fall out of him, retelling the story Cenric had heard him tell Alaric about how Ælfric had warned Svienn of an attack by Æthelred's fleet shortly after the Battle of Malduna. This incident was ancient history to some, but Cenric still remembered it well, just as he still wondered whether Ælfric really had tried to aid Svienn against his own people. He felt bitterness now, and anger towards himself also, thinking he'd been a coward for never confronting Ælfric on any of this. He deserved to know the truth. They all did.

Æva scowled, an unusual expression for her, but it didn't last, her face instead falling flat when Ulfcytel told her what he knew of Ælfric's inexplicable failure to lead the Hamptonscir and Wiltunscir fyrds in the defence of Wiltune. She was silent for a time, but she spoke before long, her voice a strange croak as she asked him to repeat what he'd said. Ulfcytel did so, telling her again how Ælfric had reputedly feigned illness rather than lead the armies entrusted to him into danger. The ravaging of Wiltunscir had been the end result. The destruction of her home town, the slaying of her parents, her baby son…

"You told Alaric all of this?" Æva asked.

"I did," replied Ulfcytel.

"And you heard all this too, Cenric?" There was something about her eyes now that Cenric found downright disturbing. There was a wrath there, like how she'd looked the day Alaric had died and she'd buried a blade in his killer's throat. Cenric wouldn't be forgetting that in a hurry. He hoped the look would pass, and quickly.

"I was there with Alaric at the time," Cenric affirmed. "I'll say to you what I said to him…I remember the battle at sea well enough. It was a bloody affair, and Svienn again got the better of us, and Ælfric had indeed vanished from our ranks the night before. Whether he actually had betrayed us, I cannot say."

"You never asked him?"

"I've wanted to. Many times. But he's a man of power, Æva. I'm just a man, of common blood. People like me don't confront people like you and Ælfric on anything. It's better that..."

"I'm nothing like him!" Æva's voice had risen unexpectedly, her pitch sharp and hard on the ears.

"I didn't mean to say you were," Cenric said stoically, making efforts to hide his distress at seeing her so disturbed. "I only wish to explain my inaction. If Ælfric is the type of man Ulfcytel claims he is, then it wouldn't be an issue for him to get rid of me. Nobody would notice."

"I would," she snapped, wringing her hands anxiously. "I'd notice if you were gone, Cenric. I wouldn't let anything happen to you. We're not all as cold as...what did Alaric say about all this? Why didn't he tell me?"

"Were you not imprisoned when you were reunited?" Ulfcytel asked. "If so, then that's probably your answer. Alaric wouldn't have wanted to cause you further distress in an already difficult situation."

"And Alfred?!" she asked, her tears now flowing as Cenric knew they would. "My son died because...of what? Was Ælfric scared of fighting Svienn, or was he helping him by letting him do what he wanted? What's the truth of it, Ulfcytel?!"

"I can't explain that for sure," the ealdorman confessed sadly. "I've told you everything I know. I'm sorry it came to this, but I felt you deserved to know now that Alaric is..."

"I do deserve to know," Æva sobbed, her hands waving erratically when the old woman opened the door a crack to peer through at the ongoing drama. She closed it quickly upon seeing Æva, interpreting her irritated gestures for what they were. "But, in the name of God! It makes no sense!" she continued, turning back to Cenric and Ulfcytel. "Alfred was Ælfric's grandson! I saw him grieve for him! Why would he do that to himself, even if he were in league with Svienn? And why side with Edmund now?"

Ulfcytel hung his head, his great bearded face heavy and glum. Æva had asked some valid questions, but Cenric had no answers, and Ulfcytel wasn't able to provide any either. There was no rational explanation for Ælfric's actions, especially in light of his recent decision to side with Edmund rather than go over to Svienn. So many others had done the opposite, choosing the easy path of surrender, but Ælfric had not. That had to say something about his character. He couldn't be the monster he seemed. There had to be more to this.

"I'll not get any answers stuck up here with you two," Æva announced, spinning around to open the door onto the stairwell. Cenric stepped forward, following her as she moved through the doorway to begin her descent. He knew what she was doing. She was going to confront Ælfric here and now, something Cenric perhaps should have done years ago. He'd do the right thing this time. He'd stay at her side until the whole truth was known.

Ulfcytel lumbered after them, his limp intensifying as he struggled with the steps. Æva was moving fast, uncaring as to whether anyone was trying to match her pace. Cenric went to take her arm when they reached the ground floor, hoping she'd wait and allow the ealdorman to catch up. She shook him off, heading straight for Ælfric's chambers. Cenric kept close, Ulfcytel trailing at a respectful distance.

Ælfric looked surprised and annoyed when the three of them barged through his door. He was sitting at his dining table, a parchment laid out before him, an aide seated to his right as if they'd been going over something of import. Cenric's heart was hammering in his chest. This was beyond uncomfortable. He hoped that whatever Æva now said wouldn't offend the ealdorman too much. Both she and Brandon needed a home, and Porteceaster was a better one than most.

"Is it true that you deliberately held off from giving battle when Svienn attacked Wiltune?" Æva hadn't wasted any time, getting right to the point before Ælfric could breathe a single word. He straightened his spine abruptly, his shocked expression giving way to anger and resentment upon spying Ulfcytel and the guilty look on his face.

"So you've been spreading rumours then," Ælfric said darkly. Ulfcytel held his gaze, his eyes brimming with a quiet yet pained determination. "What else did you tell my daughter-in-law?" Ælfric asked him. "That I'm some kind of traitor? Not to be trusted?"

"Don't speak to him!" Æva snapped indignantly. "Answer my question first before you start looking to blame others!"

Ælfric rose from his chair, his aide doing the same in what looked like a gesture of support. "I won't be accosted like this in my own home," Ælfric declared. "I don't need to answer to rumours, especially those voiced by a man who barely knows me."

"You could always try answering the question," Ulfcytel muttered. "She's owed that much. The king didn't have you imprisoned without reason, Ælfric. He didn't take Ælfgar's sight on a whim either."

"You know nothing of this, Ulfcytel!" Ælfric hissed. "Is this why you came to Hamptonscir? To try and turn my family against me?"

"Not exactly, but I felt the lady deserved to know. I told Alaric in Canterburie about you and your misdeeds...I'd hoped never to speak of it again, but now Alaric is dead and his son is without a father. I felt..."

"What? Like interfering in things you don't understand? Why tell Alaric this? Why re-open old wounds?"

"Assassins were trying to kill him, Ælfric!" Ulfcytel exclaimed, his recent apprehension now replaced with anger. "They kept coming, even as we readied ourselves to defend Canterburie. You know why! You know why the king would want him gone, why he'd want you and your family gone...he deserved to know what was happening."

"So now, with my son dead, you'd again whisper poison, this time into the ears of his widow? You make a strange case, Ulfcytel."

"Just tell me if it's true!" Æva shrieked, her right hand making a violent sweeping gesture in Ælfric's direction. "Did you have the chance to stop Svienn before he attacked Wiltune? Did you get my Alfred killed?!"

Ælfric slumped back into his seat, his withered hands rising to his head to massage his temples. He looked like a dying man, in more ways than one. His skin had turned pale to the point of translucence, and he had shadows under his eyes, the things seeming to grow yet darker as Cenric imagined him dredging up old memories he'd long sought to bury.

"I can't believe it's come to this," he whispered, his hands still pressed to his temples. "I hope you're happy, Ulfcytel. I hope you're content with what you've wrought here."

"Answer me!" Æva bellowed again. "Ignore Ulfcytel and everything else! Tell ME what happened!"

Ælfric made a tired gesture towards his aide, the man taking the hint and shuffling past them to make his exit. The ealdorman seemed about to order Cenric to leave also, but Æva's glare only intensified, which Ælfric correctly interpreted as a sign that she wanted him to remain. Cenric felt more than awkward, and part of him dearly wanted to go. The other part wished to linger, knowing that he, too, wanted to hear the full and final truth of all this.

Ælfric took a deep breath, steeling himself and gathering his resolve before speaking. "Svienn's movements were confusing," he began, his voice laden with sadness. "We'd been marching in all haste, trying to link up with anyone in Wiltunscir who might muster with us. We thought Svienn would push on to Wincestre. I had no inkling at the time that Wiltune would be a target."

"Why?" Æva asked, incredulous.

"Like I said, his movements were erratic. We'd received conflicting reports on where and what he was doing. Wiltune is close to Sarum, and we knew Svienn wouldn't likely attack fortifications like that if he had a choice. I'd also assumed Alaric would evacuate Wiltune and get you and Alfred somewhere safe."

"So it's his fault?!" Æva asked, her anger burning bright at the notion that Ælfric would blame his dead son. "He tried to reach you. He was attacked himself…he said you weren't there, or that he couldn't find you! Where were you?!"

"I'm sorry, Æva. I just didn't have the men."

"What?"

"I said I didn't have the men," Ælfric repeated meekly. "Even with the combined forces of Hamptonscir and Wiltunscir at my back, Svienn still had the better force. I couldn't commit to battle when our knowledge of his movements was so incomplete. He'd have slaughtered us."

"So you did nothing?" Ulfcytel rumbled, his contempt obvious. "You feigned illness so you'd be unable to lead the army entrusted to you, just because you feared defeat?"

"You weren't there!" came Ælfric's retort. "You weren't! You can't judge me, Ulfcytel! It wasn't your grandson who was killed!"

"You dragged me into this mess the moment you sent Alaric on ahead to join me at Hringmere," answered Ulfcytel. "I could hardly believe he was your son…he was so brave, and I'd rather not be here now, trust me on that. But I owed Alaric an explanation as to why the king had imprisoned you and Æva…and I owed her an explanation, too! For Alaric's sake! For the sake of his memory!"

"So that's the reason?" Æva asked bitterly, her focus still on her father-in-law. "You didn't confront Svienn because you feared him? My son is dead, my parents too…all because you were too afraid to use the men you had to defend us?"

"I thought you'd have fled!" Ælfric protested weakly. "So many others had! Why didn't Alaric get you out?! Why didn't he…"

"Your messenger never said anything about us being in immediate danger," Æva fired back. "Alaric would have told me if it were so. He'd have protected us. He came to us as Wiltune burned, his men wounded and bruised from battle…all whilst you did nothing! Because you were afraid!"

"You have no idea, Æva, none! You assume you'd have been the hero, is that it? Leading an outnumbered host against a monster like Svienn Forkbeard?! How many battles have you fought, woman? Tell me!"

"That's enough," warned Ulfcytel, his face flushing. "Your failures are your own, Ælfric. Don't make this worse by mocking the lady just for being angered by your mistakes."

"But she has no idea, has she?" Ælfric asked, seemingly rhetorically. "She's never seen a battle, never had to make the hard decisions, never shouldered the responsibilities of leadership…and yet she judges. You judge me, Æva, and you have no right. Alfred was my grandson. I grieved for him. Don't you dare say I didn't."

"But you could have saved him," Æva protested. "You could have and you didn't, all because you were afraid for yourself…and you still claim to not know why the king resented you? You kept all this from us, and for what? To spare your feelings?"

"Did you try and join Svienn after Malduna?" Cenric suddenly asked, half-surprised at the sound of his own voice. "I was with the fleet that day, my lord. You were supposed to be with us, but you vanished. Why?"

"I don't have to answer to you, Cenric," Ælfric snarled, his anger hot in the face of being challenged by a subordinate.

"I think you should," said Ulfcytel menacingly. "Let's get everything out in the open. Did you try to join Svienn? Is that why you wouldn't confront him at Wiltune? Were you his man all along?"

"GET OUT!" Ælfric roared, leaping from his seat, his sword suddenly free of its scabbard and brandished aloft in his hand. "OUT! ALL OF YOU! LEAVE ME AND SPARE ME YOUR ACCUSATIONS!"

The door suddenly flew open, three warriors armed with axes and spears filling the space behind Æva. They glanced about, confused at the scene and looking to Cenric as to what they should do. Æva was in tears, her hands pressed to her face, Ulfcytel troubled and remorseful at the sight of it. Cenric couldn't bear to see her like this. He turned to Ælfric, fearing he might order his men to attack. He was surprised to see him slumped back in his chair, his sword clattering upon the stone floor as he also lifted his hands to his face, the tears flowing freely.

Cenric saw the truth there. Ælfric wasn't a traitor, and he wasn't a coward either, at least not now, in the autumn years of his life. If he had been, it was when he was younger, perhaps back when he'd thought he had something to lose. Greed and ambition did strange things to men, and as weak and reckless as Ælfric had been in the past, it seemed likely the shock of losing his grandson in Wiltune had finally knocked some virtue into him. It was just tragic the repercussions of his foolish days had gone on to harm so many others. He was certainly paying for it now.

Æva turned, barging past the guards to make her way from the room, both Cenric and Ulfcytel in pursuit. She strode down the hallway, the long sleeves of her dress trailing in the air. Cenric called out to her, asking what she intended to do now. What she said in reply wasn't unexpected. She was leaving, with Brandon, yet she knew not where. Cenric was sad, knowing it meant a change in both their lives. His place was with her now. It pained him to think that, bound by oath as he was to Ælfric, but he had no choice in the matter. He owed Alaric a debt. He'd given Cenric purpose, years back when all he'd wanted to do was hang from a noose. Keeping Æva and Brandon safe was now the only means he had to repay that debt. He hoped that Alaric was somehow a witness to these events, because if he were, Cenric would do him proud.

IX

It was as Cnut had said, only worse. When they'd laid eyes on him, something had gone out of them, whatever aspirations of defiance they might yet have had dying there and then. Osbert couldn't abide it, being paraded around like this as some kind of trophy, the very sight of him serving to demoralise those who should, by all rights, be fighting at the side of their true king, Edmund.

Osbert had thought to defy Cnut. He'd told him back in Lundenburg that he'd rather die than help him, but the bastard had quickly worked out how to make him cooperate. He'd threatened to kill others, dragging in two hostages he'd obtained from somewhere and saying their children would suffer also if Osbert continued to prove disobedient. Osbert couldn't have innocent blood on his conscience. He'd agreed to Cnut's demands. He would be his prize.

He'd discovered later that these weren't the only hostages Cnut had taken. His father, King Svienn, had obtained a fair number of them, apparently to secure the "goodwill" of those thegns who'd already submitted to his rule. Osbert didn't know if Cnut had the authority to just kill them like he'd said he would, but he wasn't going to argue with him and risk finding out. His demands were simple enough, anyway. Cnut wanted Osbert to be seen by the thegns assembled at Gainesburg to make them think Ulfcytel had been betrayed by those closest to him. Cnut really didn't know anything about Ulfcytel if he thought he'd lose heart from something like that. The ealdorman would fight on regardless. He always had. He always would.

When they'd arrived at Gainesburg, a lot of thegns were already waiting for them, each pitifully subservient when greeting Svienn and his malevolent son. Svienn had then made a sudden announcement, claiming Cnut was to marry a woman Osbert had never laid eyes on before, called Ælfgifu. This was a curious thing, as Osbert could easily recall that had been the name of King Æthelred's first wife and the mother to England's rightful king, Edmund. Osbert couldn't work out if Svienn was attempting to make some kind of joke, but if he were it was lost on him, and the wedding ceremony had taken place in Gainesburg's own chapel, both bride and groom looking largely disinterested in the other. At least they'd done the right thing and held the ceremony in a church. It had given Osbert the opportunity to pray, silently, for the ruin of Svienn and Cnut both. He'd wondered if any other of the Englishmen present were doing the same.

The events of the following evening were not quite so civilised. Svienn had demanded that everyone of note attend him just outside of town, apparently for the sake of yet another announcement. Cnut had appeared personally to ensure Osbert accompanied him, and Osbert stayed close as he wandered through the assembled thegns, the looks on their faces suggesting they both feared and admired the young Dane. Svienn arrived soon after with a detachment of his elite huscarls, his glittering mail and terrifying battle axe making him look very much the conquering heathen he aspired to be.

Osbert caught himself in mid-thought. Svienn didn't fancy himself a heathen. As humorous as it was, he and Cnut actually dared think of themselves as Christians. Osbert wondered what God might think of that. Chances were He wasn't pleased. Osbert hoped He'd act on that displeasure and send aid and comfort to those genuine Christians still resisting these two blasphemers. He had to do something. Had England not suffered enough?

Cnut moved up alongside his father, mounting a raised dais overlooking the crowd. Osbert followed, obeying the instruction to stay at Cnut's side. He looked out over their assembled audience, doing his best to ignore Cnut and Svienn and the look of smug satisfaction on their faces. He recognised a few people in the throng, the Ealdorman Uhtred of Norþanhymbre being easily the most discernible.

They'd waited a while for him to arrive, but when he'd finally come he'd not failed to disappoint, making a great show of his supposed admiration and lavishing Svienn with gifts. He was an imposing man, taller than most, his athletic build and noble, refined countenance conveying the illusion he was a man of principle and destiny. He stood out there now, dressed head to toe in studded leathers and furs, an excessively ornate sword at his hip. He had his arms folded, and his chest was swollen with a certain impetuous pride that seemed to grate upon any who witnessed it. Osbert noticed his eyes. They were dark, almost black, and strangely lifeless. That made sense, thought Osbert. Uhtred had no soul. Anyone capable of turning on his own country like he had was dead inside.

The Ealdorman Æthelmaer was no exception. Osbert had seen him only once before, at some witan he'd attended alongside Ulfcytel years back. He'd cut an impressive figure then, but so had everyone present, since in those days Osbert had been new to power and easily awed by those possessing it. Æthelmaer seemed changed now. He'd been aged by recent events, his green and black finery and towering brute of a bodyguard failing to distract from his noticeably hunched back and rapidly greying hair. He was surrounded by a whole score of his thegns, all similarly flamboyantly dressed and yet appearing so anxious Osbert wondered if they had some plot in motion to kill Svienn and trigger an uprising. He shouldn't be so optimistic. To do anything like that, they'd need to have spines.

Eadric was close, his fellow Mierċians looking hard-bitten and astonishingly untrustworthy. Osbert noticed Eadric staring at him, his look a little different from the others. He seemed ill at ease, like he suspected Osbert of something, perhaps thinking he'd been able to win Cnut's favour. That was seriously funny if he really thought that. Osbert knew well enough that Cnut only wanted him here to create the impression that resistance to his father was a foolhardy endeavour. Once that was achieved, he wouldn't have any further use for him. Death would come swiftly. It was preferable, in a way. He didn't want to live under heathen rule. He didn't want to be like the people here.

Another stood out from the throng, this one looking like he must have spent some time styling that fine shock of hair and black beard of his before making an appearance. Osbert had a feeling he knew who this was, even if he'd never spoken with the man or known Ulfcytel to have had many dealings with him. This was Morcar, from Derbei in the Five Boroughs, and as far as Osbert knew, he was often inseparable from his brother, Sigeferth, who today was nowhere to be seen. Osbert's heart sank. He didn't know King Edmund's plans in full, but he knew his base of power was in the Five Boroughs, and he was reliant on their help to raise an army. Morcar's presence here could only mean that something had gone awry. He found it hard to imagine he could have willingly turned on Edmund, but these were treacherous times.

The clergy was also out in force, the most "pious" men England had to offer mixing freely with the most treacherous of "nobles" as if they were almost one and the same. Archbishop Wulfstan stood close by, looking uncomfortable under his thick grey robes, his rake-thin neck bearing the weight of a large gold crucifix that hung down to his chest. He was surrounded by several dozen monks and priests, their dour faces looking up at Svienn, some in fear, others harder to read. Osbert pondered what the sadly deceased Archbishop Ælfheah would make of all this. He'd been an impossibly brave man, and his defiance of the brutal and avaricious Thorkell had ultimately cost him his life. There was no way Ælfheah would have behaved any differently with Svienn. He was a true follower of Christ.

The rest of those gathered were largely unknown to Osbert, although there were many of them, this assembly looking like it was made up of several hundred very cowardly, very self-important people. Svienn had a couple of thousand men camped nearby, and a good portion of them were present now, surrounding them in a sea of grey metal. At a single command, they could deal with any disorder, and everyone knew their new ruler was not above random violence and terror if he felt it would serve him. Osbert started to wonder who was the more despicable, the father or the son, Cnut. He'd wait and see how things played out before he made a decision on that, but, for the moment, he felt they were both matching each other in malevolence.

Svienn began some long-winded speech, his bass voice carrying easily into the ears of every man present. Osbert peered off to the side and away from the dais, noting the series of long tables and freshly dug fire pits. What Osbert assumed to be enslaved locals were hauling a number of kegs and barrels into an open storage area close by. It was highly unlikely the kegs were full of water, so it seemed possible that once all this boasting and grovelling was over, drink and entertainment would be offered. Gainesburg itself could be seen off to the north east; an unremarkable settlement aside from its status as an inland port the Danes had so far used to ferry warriors and supplies from Lundenburg. Osbert had been curious about that, thinking it strange how Svienn wanted his new subjects to bow to him here rather than just visit him in the capital. Was there some reason he wanted to do this so far north?

He looked back at Svienn as he droned on, briefly toying with the idea of making a move for Cnut's weapon. He'd be killed, of course, but an opportunity might yet present itself for him to do Ulfcytel proud by slaying at least one of these murderous bastards. Osbert could die happy then. It was with some sadness he realised another scenario was altogether more likely. Ulfcytel would undoubtedly hear of his presence here and the supposed honours he'd endured. He hoped the ealdorman would see through it. He couldn't bear the thought of him thinking he'd betrayed him.

Something happened. Osbert wasn't sure what, but the crowd had let loose a collective sigh, with even Eadric looking aghast as if somebody had just threatened to murder his own mother. Svienn had said something appalling, but he carried on regardless, Osbert realising in horror that he was bragging about recently attacking Sancte Eadmundes Byrig and defiling the remains of the blessed Saint Edmund himself. It got worse, for Svienn then claimed the saint had "been a weakling and a fool" who had "failed to seize the truth of the times and died a slave to his own inadequacy." Osbert felt his face flush, noting that their assorted company was equally disturbed, Æthelmaer and his people, in particular, looking like they were about to either draw their weapons or storm off home.

Svienn laughed suddenly, deep and resonant and full of contempt. He took a breath and kept on waffling about the saint, his inability to read his audience making him appear more like a madman than a gracious king. Cnut, interestingly enough, looked almost as outraged as the English, the spreading alarm upon his face suggesting his father had not informed him of the full contents of his speech. He carried on for a while longer, claiming Saint Edmund's death somehow marked the end of "England's right to rule itself"; a comedic proposition, considering England hadn't properly existed then and King Alfred of Westseaxe had ultimately smashed the Danes at Ethandun and laid the foundations for re-conquering the entire country. Svienn was making a fool of himself. It would hopefully get him killed.

Unfortunately, he had one more surprise in store for them. He held out his arms, ordering his "most esteemed guest", whoever that was, to "come forth and be recognised in submission." Everyone below peered about the place, still confused and exasperated, even Eadric looking like he had no clue on what was happening and was deeply unhappy about it. The crowd began to part, an assortment of muted exclamations rising up when they laid eyes on a figure now advancing towards the dais. Osbert had never seen this man before, but he looked a little strange, his face oddly proportioned so that he wondered if God had given him an unusually large brain to rattle about in that bulbous skull of his. He knelt about a half dozen feet from Svienn, his eyes cast downward and his face unreadable, his rough, muddied garments making him seem out of place in this assembly of pampered turncoats. Svienn's voice boomed out again, revealing the man's identity in all his ignominy.

"You see! Even King Æthelred's own blood know the situation for what it is. Your aetheling, Eadwig, has made the wisest of decisions and now secures his future under my rule. I will honour and reward his fealty in the days to come, and all will see I can be generous as well as mighty."

Osbert shook his head, trying to overcome the cold shock seeping into his bones. Eadwig! A son of Æthelred! Younger brother to King Edmund himself! Impossible! For him to appear here and make such a public display was unconscionable! Unprecedented! Nothing like it in all of history! Osbert, to be fair, hadn't read much history, but he found it hard to imagine that incidents like this could happen too often. Only the most pitiful and disloyal of souls could countenance such a vile act. Perhaps this Eadwig was a son of Eadric's instead? He wouldn't put it past the Ealdorman of Mierċe to bed a king's wife, although he wasn't old enough to be Eadwig's father. From the looks of it, the aetheling didn't need any lessons from Eadric either in how to be a snake. He was a master at it already.

Svienn burbled on further, at one point gesturing towards Osbert and saying something about "the futility of continued resistance" by those who "don't know their war is lost." That could only be a reference to Ulfcytel, and whilst Osbert would normally bristle at such talk, he was still too shocked by the sudden appearance of an aetheling. The other Englishmen didn't appear to feel the same, and once Svienn had finished speaking they came forward, one by one, to kneel and then embrace him.

Eadric and his thegns followed their example, the Miercians easily the most compliant and downright sycophantic of the lot. Osbert felt ill. He briefly thought of throwing up on Eadric, thinking with a smirk on how the grasping ealdorman might look when splattered with vomit and covered in bits of carrot. He decided against it. Cnut would not be pleased, and Osbert wouldn't cut short his time among the living by doing something foolish. If death was close at hand, he'd use his remaining moments for something useful. Like killing Danes. Especially the ones who liked to insult English saints. Svienn deserved to pay for that, preferably with his life.

But that all depended on whether he could get a weapon. Cnut wasn't so stupid as to give him such a thing, and from what he could see, there was only a minimal chance of obtaining one small enough to conceal on his person. He looked over at the huscarls flanking the gathering on both the eastern and western approaches, beholding their assorted spears and axes with something approaching envy. He'd find no help there. Even if he were able to reach them, they'd just cut him down, and the odds of being able to snatch a spear and hurl it into Svienn's chest were pitifully small. He liked the idea of it, though. There was a desperate heroism there.

The sad spectacle finally ended. Every man who had been supposed to kneel and embrace their "king" had now done so with the required servility. Osbert hated the sight of it, and when his turn had come he'd thought to refuse. Cnut wasn't in the mood for any of that, and he'd driven Osbert to his knees with a blow to the stomach. He'd then whispered various threats into his ear, telling him to honour his father lest "your countrymen suffer greatly for your disobedience." Osbert had gone on to mumble some words at Svienn's feet, feeling sickened by the sound of his voice. He blanked out much of what he'd said, but he knew he'd called Svienn "King of England and Denmark." That was a lie, one that tasted bitter in his mouth, but in his predicament, he'd had little choice. Cnut would hurt innocent people if he continued to resist, and Osbert wouldn't have others bleed for the sake of his pride.

Svienn was satisfied, and he soon babbled on a bit more, booming something about "past grievances" being "forgotten" for the sake of a "new friendship between Saxon and Dane." Osbert almost choked at the very notion of it. Svienn and his forebears had started this historic conflict, yet he spoke as if both peoples were somehow equally at fault and in need of reconciliation. There was no blame to be placed upon the Saxons or Britons. This was their land, their island, and it belonged to no one else. That was the truth of it, as any honest man would attest.

And yet honest men always seemed so few in number. A day may come, Osbert thought, when persons of supposed learning might argue that Svienn had a point, or that the Northmen hadn't been as bad as the English had claimed. That would be a strange thing, but not impossible, and such men would no doubt think themselves terribly clever for having somehow come closer to the truth of these times than those who'd lived to witness them. Osbert hoped that wouldn't be the case, but he wouldn't be entirely surprised if it came to pass. He himself would always cleave to the truth as he saw it with his own eyes. Svienn and Cnut both were nothing but usurpers and killers, like the rest of their damnable kind. He hoped future generations would see that.

Svienn finally shut up, his guards escorting him and his hangers-on to the tables and chairs assembled just beyond the dais. Everyone filed after them, Cnut shoving Osbert to shake him from his thoughts, the crowd settling down as stewards appeared laden with flagons of ale and platters of over-cooked meat. Osbert stared at the drink placed in front of him, and before long, Svienn was again on his feet and imploring all and sundry to join him in a toast. Cnut rose, as did everyone else, yet Osbert remained seated until somebody laid hands on him from behind to haul him upright. They weren't gentle, and Cnut looked on triumphantly when the huscarl slapped Osbert over the back of the head. A few thegns glanced in their direction, wondering what the fuss was about, Osbert feeling a tad embarrassed as Cnut forced another flagon into his hand. Osbert knew that look he now had. If he didn't drink like the others, somebody would get hurt. He raised the ale to his lips and took a rather restrained sip. It was enough. Cnut's eyes softened. All was well for the time being.

More drinking followed, the food that came with it looking like it might spell the end of Svienn as he ate and then ate yet more. Some music started up, the harp sounding mournful, and an old-timer began to recite what seemed to be "Beowulf " in low, depressing tones. The stars had emerged in full across the heavens, and the drifting wood smoke from the now-lit fire pits added to the ambience, but the recitation still felt melancholy, at least to Osbert.

It didn't matter too much. He'd heard it all before, in better times in Ulfcytel's hall. The ealdorman had enjoyed poetry, which sometimes came as a surprise to those who didn't know him well. Few could blame them for that. Ulfcytel did come across as more bear than man, especially if one encountered him on a war footing. Osbert would have done anything to be at his side now. Instead, he'd likely never see him again. He swallowed another mouthful of ale, the warmth of it spreading through his stomach to dispel any sadness before it could take hold. He couldn't let heartache get the better of him. He needed his strength if he were to make his death hold meaning.

An hour passed, the night coming on full and cloudless to bathe them all in yet more starlight. The revellers were up on their feet now, dancing and laughing to themselves or engaging in mindless conversation, Svienn's supposed dream of bringing unity apparently successful, at least for the moment. Cnut had wandered off somewhere, his own personal huscarl following him, leaving Osbert alone with a smattering of Englishmen he'd never spoken with and one very drunk thegn by the name of Burgred. He was a talker, this one, and very much attached to Osbert, finding it fascinating that "one so close to a great man like Ulfcytel" could "end up here in the presence of even greater greatness." Osbert glared at him, noting his irritating tendency to alliterate, surmising this had more to do with random chance and his befuddled state than any intentional degree of sophistication. He had a nice seax, though, too thin for its scabbard by the looks of it, but very nice to behold.

Burgred, perhaps, didn't feel the same, since he entirely missed it when Osbert made a not-so-subtle effort to pull it free. He was successful, after a fashion, but in his anxiety it slid from his fingers to land silently upon the muddy grass at his feet. It glinted in the darkness, reflecting the firelight from the nearby pit, but Bugred was still none the wiser and continued to drink and babble at anyone who'd hear him. Osbert angled his arm to the earth, his face twisting in a grimace whilst he made a great show of "rubbing the ache from my bones" after their long journey north. It served well enough, and nobody thought anything of it, Burgred himself failing to notice Osbert had retrieved his weapon and stashed it in his breecs. It was uncomfortable, and the coldness of the metal against his skin made him wince, but if he angled his weight correctly, he'd be unlikely to accidentally remove his manhood anytime soon. The ultimate test would come once he stood up. He made his excuses and tried it.

It went well. Nobody raised an eyebrow at his decision to depart, apparently convinced by his claim that he needed to relieve himself. He took a few steps to the left, observing how, if he held his right hand in place, he could stop the seax from slipping down his leg. He strolled on, doing his best to seem casual, his eyes on Svienn and those around him. The "king" was looking a little addled, and he was presently spitting bits of food over his audience as he regaled them with tales about his supposed "Viking exploits" elsewhere.

It was all murderous gibberish as far as Osbert could tell, and he couldn't work out why Svienn thought himself impressive by the fact he'd killed a lot of people and stolen their stuff. The Englishmen unfortunate enough to be close by did their best to humour him, but even at this distance, it was obvious they found him abhorrent, especially when he again riled them all up by repeatedly mentioning Saint Edmund as "just another defeated king." They'd all held their tongues thus far, the heavily armoured guards at Svienn's rear no doubt discouraging open disagreement. They were a fearsome sight, and there were thousands more close by. To defy Svienn tonight meant death, and everyone knew it.

Yet that would prove a deterrent only to those who feared it. Osbert knew he was a mere tool to Cnut, and his usefulness would end with this celebration. Death was certain, but Osbert was determined to die on his own terms, even if it meant being hacked to pieces by Svienn's outraged guards. It would be worth it. This seax was going in his neck, right now, and he didn't care what happened after that. He dearly hoped Ulfcytel would hear of it. He needed him to know what had happened here. He needed him to know he hadn't betrayed him.

He moved closer, ambling between the tables and some standing revellers. He was almost within striking distance, his hand instinctively reaching for his stolen blade. He was just offering up a silent prayer when disaster struck. Somebody knocked into him, hard, their mass and trajectory almost toppling him from his feet. He flailed around, his right hand cleaving to the shoulder of his unknown assailant just as his left tried to grip the seax already sliding down his leg. Osbert fumbled and fumbled again, feeling a surge of panic when the blade tumbled from his breecs and out into plain sight. He froze, knowing that if he could see it, the man who'd knocked into him also could. He mustn't assume the worst. There was always the chance he was drunk or blind or stupid. Osbert bent low, reaching for the blade, hoping to snatch it up and hide it before anyone saw.

It didn't go as planned. He clawed at it and gripped the hilt, yet his arm was trembling so much he made a hash of things and almost dropped it. A hand suddenly clasped his own, and Osbert turned his head, staring right into the eyes of the man he'd collided with. He was squatting on his haunches, his look strangely placid, and he plucked the seax from Osbert's clutches and sequestered it within his own robes like it were of no consequence. Recognition flared in Osbert's memory. This was Eadwig, the traitor aetheling. Was he playing some game here? Was he about to give him up to Svienn?

"I thank you," said Eadwig quietly as he gently eased Osbert back to his feet. "I confess I've had something to drink this evening, and this blade of mine is in the habit of misplacing itself. You have sharp eyes to have spotted it in the grass like that."

Osbert couldn't find the words to respond. He simply stared at Eadwig, confounded and terrified, wondering if this was some cruel jest to be played before handing him over to the enemy. Eadwig looked like he was about to speak again when a great shout suddenly rent the air, Osbert's heart nearly giving out as he realised his plot had surely been discovered. They both turned, looking towards the commotion, the sight unfurling before them as strange as it was unexpected.

Svienn was on his feet, staring with wild eyes at something ahead of him. Osbert couldn't see anything there that could give reason for upset, but Svienn clearly saw it, having the look of a man who thought death mere moments away.

"I didn't mean it!" he simpered, trying to hide his face with trembling hands, his normally deep, bass voice breaking into a child's squeal. "Don't come closer!" he implored again. "It was just a monastery! I never found your bones anyway, they'd already been taken! Please!"

Everyone was up and alert now, any trace of drunken merriment fading away. Cnut appeared, barging through the crowd to stand at his father's side. Svienn's guards had also rushed to form around him, their weapons drawn. They looked about, trying to locate the source of his alarm. There was nothing there. Nothing at all, yet Svienn was still frantic. "I'm a Godly man!" he kept saying, his eyes wet and wide with fright. "A Godly man! I respect the saints! I respect you! I didn't mean…"

Svienn didn't finish his sentence. He began to make a choking sound, desperate and pained, his hands clutching at his chest. He slouched to one side, but Cnut steadied him, holding him up with both hands upon his shoulders. "Is it your heart, father?" he spluttered, Svienn turning to look at him with a mixture of horror and incomprehension. "Tell me what's wrong!" Cnut demanded, the panic in his voice unmistakable.

Svienn didn't answer. He broke eye contact with his son to again gaze fearfully at whatever it was that only he could see, that strangely pained gurgling still sounding from his throat. He then stood upright, his spine fully straight, and something ripped through him, shaking his body whilst it stood rooted in place, several onlookers crying out in horror at the flecks of spittle and vomit erupting from his mouth. He eventually fell forward, his strength apparently spent, and crashed face-first into the table, his great weight serving to almost split the thing in half.

Cnut reached for him, managing to lift his father up and onto his back with the help of a towering huscarl. Svienn's face was a bloody mess, and his breath was fading, his lips mouthing the same phrase over and over. Osbert crept closer, knowing he was taking a risk but wanting to hear what was said. He had a feeling Svienn's words would shed much light on this otherwise bizarre situation. He wasn't disappointed.

"I'm a Godly man, I'm a Godly man, have mercy. I'm a Godly man, Saint Edmund, spare me. Have mercy."

He carried on like this for a few moments more, his voice fading to a whisper and then nothing at all. Cnut implored his father to wake up, demanding he rise and tell them what he'd seen. Osbert sensed somebody behind him, his glance over his shoulder spying the form of Eadwig, a peculiar look on his face. There was something in those large eyes. A strange calm. Like he knew.

Cnut began bawling, his tears bitter and plentiful, his hands pawing pitifully at his father. Osbert felt almost sorry for him, knowing his agony to be genuine. The Danes around him, however, were soon in uproar, shock and surprise ripping through their ranks until they were almost insensible. The English, too, were confused and yet fearful, choosing to keep a respectful distance lest they fall prey to accusation. Despite it all, Osbert felt oddly tranquil. He could see how this would play out. Word would spread quickly, all across the land. Everyone would know what had happened here this night. Svienn Forkbeard, King of Denmark and would-be-conqueror of England, was dead.

X

The thin, stony trail wound on and on, vanishing and then re-emerging from behind the trunks and boughs as if daring them to follow. They did so, the trees springing up around them in greater numbers, their leaves the colour of sunset and their branches heavy with fading blossom. Birdsong came on thick and fast, these creatures of the forest appearing to serenade them with their own gentle music. Dappled, golden light shone through the shifting, bronzed canopy above, illuminating the abundance of fungi and wildflowers blanketing the forest floor. Other beasts, less sociable than their feathered brethren, made their presence known, the sound of rustling and scampering a sure indication that a badger, rabbit, or deer had just decided to depart in some haste.

Æva pulled the hood of her cloak tighter about herself, a trace of regret settling upon her heart. She was always dismayed at the fear the animal kingdom displayed towards her and others. She could understand them fleeing a brute like Ulfcytel, for the commotion made by his passing was enough to alert the entire forest, but there was something else to it that always bothered her. The Lord's creation had learned to dread humanity, and in their fear, they were unable to differentiate between a gentle soul like Brandon and the most ferocious of Norsemen. It wasn't always so. She knew her Bible well enough. There had been no violence between humanity and the rest of creation in the beginning, and the Book of Genesis was quite clear that God's original intention had been for humanity to follow a diet obtained from "every herb bearing seed" and "every tree that has fruit". Alas, the Fall of Mankind had changed that, and the Great Flood had brought with it a concession from the Lord that permitted humanity to eat the flesh of animals. She wished it was not so.

Others had scoffed at her for that, saying she had the "gentle heart of a woman", as if a statement of the glaringly obvious might dismiss her concerns. She didn't understand it herself. She didn't think a sheep was the equal of a man, but she did think it was incumbent upon every Christian to be gentle and compassionate towards ALL creation. That was how things had been in Eden. The Lord had brought the animals to Adam so he would name them, not harm them. Killing for sport and the pleasure of consumption struck her as something abhorrent, and as much as she'd been told it was God's will, she found her detractors on this issue to be more than a little disturbing. They could become so aggressive, acting like her preference for vegetable soup was some kind of moral failing or refusal to "heed the word of God". It wasn't right. She was no heretic. She just abhorred cruelty, killing...all of it. Only Alaric had understood her on this. It was yet another reason she'd never stop missing him.

She stopped suddenly, feeling as if she was being watched. Cenric stopped behind her, Brandon also skittering to a halt on her left. Ulfcytel and a half dozen others lumbered on for a few more feet before pausing to look back at them, confused at the delay. Æva glanced about, attempting to peer through the sun-drenched thicket to her right and locate whatever had disturbed her. Then she saw it. A stag, far off to the east, its form perfectly still whilst it gazed back at her from under tall, majestic antlers. There was something in its eyes, those dark, deep orbs conveying a certain substance, one very much related to what she'd been thinking on. She then saw the doe, smaller and unadorned, peering nervously from close by, her eyes also possessing something Æva couldn't quite define.

They stayed like this for a few moments, the woman and the beasts looking upon the other in mutual fascination. They knew she was gentle, like them, or so she liked to imagine, these peaceful souls recognising one of their own even in the face of their many differences. The spell broke without warning, the deer vanishing deeper into the forest at the sound of Ulfcytel scraping back down the path towards her. She looked up at him, saddened at his heavy footfalls that had ruined the moment. She shouldn't be angry. He couldn't help making so much noise. It was a marvel he was able to move as well as he did, all things considered.

"What is it?" Ulfcytel asked, his voice hushed like he feared some hidden enemy.

"The deer!" exclaimed Brandon. "They were staring right at us, but you made a noise and they ran."

Ulfcytel looked around, bewildered. Brandon pointed enthusiastically in the direction of where the animals had stood, but it did him little good. The ealdorman eventually shook his head, impatient and bemused, Brandon's attempt to explain how wonderful a sight it was provoking nought but a grin and a chuckle. Æva ushered Brandon into motion, Ulfcytel again rejoining his men in the lead. They couldn't be wasting time in the woods, no matter what marvels they held. The land was in peril, and men like those in her present company were needed. She just wished she could say the same about herself.

They'd been on the move for a week now, leaving Porteceaster with all haste and doing their best to ignore the protestations of the Ealdorman Ælfric. Even Ælfgar had joined in, demanding Æva think of her son and honour what he seemed to think were Alaric's own wishes. She didn't know what he'd meant by that, and she no longer cared. There was nothing left for her in Porteceaster. It had been a home to her once and a good one, but with Alaric gone it was an empty shell, and the revelations about her father-in-law had made it something even worse. There was no love left there. Only memories and hurt remained.

She looked back over her shoulder, sending Cenric a tired smile as he trudged on behind her. He smiled back, the shadows under his eyes showing he felt as she did, yet there was a sadness there, one she'd been pondering for some days now. Ælfric had been hard on Cenric, demanding he stay and "honour your oath" to him and his family as head of his hearthweru. Cenric hadn't had a ready answer for him on why he was leaving, and, if she was honest, Æva was surprised at his behaviour, thinking his respect for her was something given out of pity due to her status as Alaric's widow. She'd thus been astonished when he'd defied Ælfric's demands, brushing past him as he led them towards the northernmost gates, his expression a strange mix of disappointment and anger.

Ælfric hadn't sent anyone after them, and his calls for them to pause and come back had gradually faded with time and distance. They'd made it to Wincestre in quick order, the city feeling oddly unwelcoming as they passed through its crowded streets and back out onto the road heading north. Nobody had said much, and Æva was starting to find the silence burdensome. She'd tried talking to Ulfcytel, asking him why he'd decided to come with her, but his answers were brief and unconvincing, and his claim that he "had to speak with Edmund anyway" hardly explained much of anything. It also came with the assumption that Æva wanted to get back to Edmund. She'd never said anything of the kind, and when last she'd seen the aetheling, he'd been set on returning to Snotingeham to raise an army. She wasn't sure if she wanted to be caught up in all that. Not with Brandon in tow, anyway.

Cenric had been similarly terse. He'd refused to explain why he'd decided to take her side over Ælfric's, and the more she pestered him, the more solitary and withdrawn he seemed to become. He didn't sleep much, instead staying up late and staring into the embers of their campfires like he was seeking some answer to something that had long eluded him. She'd asked him about it, but he'd remained uncooperative, instead stressing that "somebody had to keep watch" and that it "might as well be me." His answer was a half-truth, if anything. Something significant was on his mind. It was a shame he didn't feel comfortable enough to share his burdens with her. Perhaps he would in time.

They stopped about an hour after dark, setting up camp within spitting distance of a narrow, white-foamed stream bisecting yet another forest clearing. The night passed without incident, Cenric doing his usual thing of staying up late to "keep the wolves at bay", as he liked to put it. It was all nonsense. There were no wolves in this forest, but Brandon seemed to like the idea, and tried to keep watch with Cenric just in case a "fearsome beast" were to visit them. Cenric laughed at that, and he was more than patient in explaining to the boy how he needed his rest and that he'd be the first to be told if any wolves appeared. Æva was relieved. The man she'd known for years was still in there, after all.

A curious sight greeted them the next day at around noon. The forest had grown sparse, the dense tree cover giving way to more open yet broken terrain covered in thick, hardy grass interspersed with outcroppings of bare rock. A single solitary hill could be seen in the middle distance, looking strangely out of place in the midst of what was otherwise a fairly featureless plain. They moved towards it, a feeling of foreboding growing in intensity as they progressed. They soon understood why. They'd all heard of the battle near Bernecestre. Now they'd found it.

Bodies blanketed the area for what seemed like miles. There were just a few of them to start with, all tattered and decomposed, some looking like they'd been chewed on by persistent wildlife despite the rusted armour that encased them. They grew in number as they came to the foot of the hill, and when Æva's party reached the summit, they saw more still, lying scattered almost as far as they could see. Thousands must have died here, the majority in some great clash in the centre of the plain. Shattered shields and broken spears were strewn about the place, some still gripped in withered, bony hands, the dead men appearing as if they were loath to give up their weapons even now their struggles were long over.

A great many others had fallen to the north, a trail of skeletal men and horses marking the entrance to a shallow, winding valley half obscured by a mass of tattered brambles. Everyone and everything had long since rotted down, the crows and other beasts scavenging what could be scavenged and leaving the rest, but something else remained, hanging heavy and thick and bleeding into the very earth. Hate and pain. Rage and loss. She could feel it. She was well acquainted with such things.

"This must be where the king faced Thorkell," said Ulfcytel quietly, something like admiration detectable in his voice. "For once, he remembered his duty, but it was too late by then. Had he combined his forces with mine in Eastengle, we could have stopped all this."

"Was it really too late?" Æva asked. "There are so many bodies...Thorkell must have been slowed here at the very least."

"True," Cenric acknowledged beside her, "but the cost was too great considering what we lost...all these men who will never return to their homes...and Æthelstan..."

"Poor boy," rumbled Ulfcytel sorrowfully. "I wonder where he fell. I knew he was a promising warrior...but battles are strange things. You can be the greatest of fighters and still fall prey to an arrow to the neck or fail to spot a surprise assailant. It must have been a great shock for Æthelred to lose his firstborn like that."

"You pity him, even after everything?" Æva hesitated to ask, but not because she thought such a thing would be foolish. She despised King Æthelred, but everything had to have limits. She'd lost a child, as had he. She knew that pain. She'd never wish it on anyone.

"I do," confirmed Ulfcytel. "Æthelred may have been a malevolent fool...but he was my friend once, and I still remember how he was in better times. He loved his children. What happened here would have broken his heart."

They moved on, trudging down the opposite side of the hill, the previously comforting sunlight now entirely absent under the sky's sombre grey. A light rain began as they moved out from the hill's shadow, the entire battle site appearing even more forlorn in the thickening drizzle. So many had fallen, so many brave and decent men, only for their king to again shower their enemy in riches and take him into his employ. She wondered what they might say if they could somehow know that, despite their heroic sacrifice, their old foe, Svienn Forkbeard, would sweep in and take their kingdom from them by surprise. It wasn't right. Something good had to come of all this. This couldn't all be for nothing.

"We have to get to Edmund," Æva said suddenly, Ulfcytel and company stopping dead in their tracks at the sound of her voice.

"Fastest way to Snotingeham is through the valley up ahead," said Cenric, "but... the lad..."

"I'll be alright," said Brandon. "I'm not afraid."

Æva looked down at her son, taking his wide-eyed, vaguely haunted expression as evidence to the contrary. To get to the valley, they would have to move through the centre of the battlefield, and that meant walking through corpses aplenty, none of which was an acceptable sight for a boy of Brandon's age. She wouldn't have it, but she also knew they had to get to Snotingeham quickly if they were to link up with Edmund. He was a decisive man, and if he now had an army at his back, he would have begun his campaign in earnest. She felt different about all that after what she'd just seen. Justice had to be done, not just for the sake of the living but for those who lay dead here. They couldn't leave things unfinished, nor meekly submit to living under Svienn. These men hadn't died for that. Her husband hadn't either.

That still didn't mean she was about to traumatise her son by making him march through a morass of corpses. They headed east and then north, away from the battle and the mouth of the valley, Æva stressing they could afford to add a day or two to their journey by taking a detour. To her relief, nobody objected, perhaps because they'd guessed she was simply trying to be a mother to her child and he was likely disturbed already by the sights they'd seen thus far. It wasn't just the bodies that were a problem. That dark and ominous feeling had only been getting stronger the longer they'd pressed on towards the epicentre of the battle. Æva couldn't bear it. Something evil had lingered here, and she wanted no part in it. She thought it very possible the others felt the same.

They wandered east across the now rain-swept plain, the grass beneath their feet turning slippery. The trail they'd been on for most of their journey had been chosen because it would take them away from the main roads and the prying eyes of the usurper king, but they'd now lost it entirely, and with it any notion of where exactly they were. The passage of time also became more difficult to gauge as rain clouds obscured the sun's light, reducing their world to an ominous grey gloom of chill raindrops and incessant mud.

Brandon slipped at one point, covering his breecs and cloak in earth, his grumbled protestations wearing on the nerves. To make matters worse, the rain suddenly intensified, coming down in what looked like great sheets of water to hammer them without mercy. Eventually, they'd had enough, and Cenric proposed they take a turn further northward, even if it meant entering a very thick and distinctly unapproachable-looking stretch of woodland. They all agreed, knowing it would take the edge off the downpour, yet they'd only made it about a half mile past the tree line when darkness fell, the blackness smothering their sight until all they knew of was the rain pattering on down from above. Efforts to get a fire going were only partly successful, and much of the night was spent in a state of half-wakeful discomfort. It was perhaps for the best. Æva had started to dream of Alaric again, her exhausted mind replaying his final battle with Hemingr in all its heart-breaking finality. She'd been glad when Brandon had woken her with yet more complaints. It was bad enough that she'd had to watch her husband die. She didn't need to keep seeing it again in her dreams.

Morning saw them find their way out of the thicket and continue north, the rain refusing to ease off. They passed several ruined and empty villages, their inhabitants either dead or missing. Not everywhere appeared as such, and some fields seemed to have been recently worked, the well-trod earth parted and flattened under the weight of both beasts and men. They soon located those responsible inhabiting a hamlet that looked to have been recently rebuilt, the thatched roofs and wattle-and-daub walls of its buildings appearing crisp and new in the sobering drizzle. They avoided it for the sake of safety, knowing full well their discretion would pay off if they hoped to reach Snotingeham undetected. Nobody knew just how firm Svienn's hold on the countryside was, but it was best to be cautious. Spies could be anywhere, and from what they'd seen on their journey down south, the Danes were hardly lax when it came to mounting patrols.

Evening came, and another restless night followed. The rain had thankfully turned to mist, which filled up the prickled labyrinth of pine trees they were currently lurking in to the point they couldn't see more than a dozen feet in front of them. Cenric insisted on lighting a fire, apparently intent on resuming his habit of staring into the flames until sleep finally claimed him. Æva struggled to doze off, and her troubled thoughts stayed with her, resulting in a truly peculiar dream where she was in this exact same place and again striving to fall asleep. She awoke suddenly, Cenric shaking her with some urgency. Æva noticed the fire had been put out. She went to speak, but Cenric put a finger to his lips to signal she should remain quiet. Ulfcytel was awake also, his eyes wide and serious in the faint moonlight. Then she heard it. The rustling, in the undergrowth up ahead. Somebody was coming.

Her heart skipped a beat when the familiar form of Osgar, one of Ulfcytel's companions he'd seen fit to bring from Offetuna, emerged into the clearing. He sounded half-winded, as if he'd moved with some urgency to get back to them. He whispered something to the ealdorman before making a few hand gestures towards Cenric, Æva noting with disappointment that their meaning was entirely lost on her. It wasn't long before she understood. Something was carrying on the wind. The blast of a horn, distant but still audible, followed by the braying of savage men. It could mean only one thing. There were Danes about.

Cenric shot Æva a look and inclined his head towards the still-sleeping Brandon. He then made the same gesture with his finger he'd made earlier, conveying the rather obvious notion that the boy was to be kept quiet, should he awaken. Æva nodded back at him to signal her compliance, and he turned and vanished into the trees with Osgar and two others she didn't know. They returned within minutes at a jog, alarm written across their faces. Cenric skidded to a halt, a strangled whisper upon his lips.

"They're heading this way! We have to go! Now!"

Ulfcytel sprung into action, his great paws scooping up the slumbering Brandon with one single movement. He woke up almost immediately, but he was a clever lad and remained silent, having understood the situation was a dangerous one. Æva was up and after the ealdorman in quick order, the rest of their party following. If there were Danes out there, it was certain they had violence in mind. A hurried retreat was the best course of action.

Æva wasn't as adept as some when it came to navigating at night. Whilst Ulfcytel simply barrelled his way ahead into the undergrowth, Æva was nowhere near as robust or capable of smashing her way through any obstructions. She found this out the hard way when a particularly sharp bramble slashed her across the face, the thing having been bent back at a sharp angle after Ulfcytel had stormed past. The shock was enough to send her reeling, and she lost her balance; the resulting trip and then fall sending a sharp, shooting pain up through her left shin. She cried out in surprise, yet Cenric was fast and heaved her up onto her feet, Æva feeling beyond foolish.

She tried to stumble on, the throb in her leg slowing and destabilising her movements. She soon tripped on a protruding root, but Cenric caught her, allowing her to drape her arm across his shoulders and steady herself. She whispered a quick "thank you" to him, hoping nobody unfriendly had heard all the noise she'd made. That hope dwindled quickly. A cacophony of shouting and heavy footfalls erupted behind them, all of it getting closer. The Danes were on to them.

Æva gasped as Cenric pushed her face-first into some bushes. She slid a short distance downward and stopped, her vision all darkness and leaves. Cenric crouched next to her in their new hiding place, his face unapologetic. Ulfcytel and everyone else followed them, rushing down into what appeared to be a natural defile that concealed them from the view of anyone traversing the clearing they'd only just fled from. Æva tried to hold her breath lest she make a sound, the pain in her leg and the discomfort of her surroundings testing her further.

They were all more or less hidden now, for the sloping ground was covered with overgrown ferns and the swaying shadows cast by the omnipresent pine trees. It was just as well. Somebody was coming, their footsteps rapid and erratic, their tempo suggesting they were running for their very lives. They all waited, trying to be silent and still, each man present ready to fight whatever or whoever might prove foolish enough to disturb them.

A single ragged silhouette appeared just above them and passed by, fleeing eastward into the forest. Another appeared, and then another, each figure little more than a fleeting shadow, each desperate to escape from something. Then the Danes came on, or what they supposed were Danes, their heavy treads and incessant horn-blasts alerting the entire forest to their presence. They hadn't noticed anyone crouched in the ferns, so busy were they with their pursuit. Æva glanced over to her left, hoping to catch sight of Brandon. He was there, looking both fearful and annoyed as Ulfcytel held him close, a giant hand clasped around his mouth. Æva couldn't begrudge Ulfcytel for that. If anyone was likely to lose their nerve, it was Brandon. Precautions had to be taken.

Several larger figures hove into view just above them. Æva couldn't see much in the darkness, but they looked to be inspecting something, a fearful thought telling her they'd likely seen evidence of her and her companions' hurried efforts to conceal themselves. Cenric tensed next to her, his hand slowly moving down to his side to grip the hilt of his sword. He lifted his shoulders slightly, his legs flexing as if preparing to suddenly launch himself upright and explode from the leaves to take the Danes by surprise. Æva closed her eyes, giving up a silent prayer as she tried to contain her mounting apprehension.

The men above were now joined by several others. She couldn't hear exactly what they were saying, but they'd worked out that somebody had passed through here in a hurry. A light suddenly appeared, a torchbearer from somewhere joining them as they continued their deliberations. This wasn't good. Without the shadows, they'd very likely be spotted.

They were Danes all right, that she could see. They were predictably brutal in appearance, their armour besmirched and soiled from who knew how long upon the road, their beards also caked in mud and sweat so that they looked half-wild. Three of them carried those long, cruel axes of theirs, another four wielding spears that they were using to prod at the ferns. Just as Æva was sure Cenric was about to leap into a full-bodied charge, they heard a scream, shrill and terrified, from a short distance to the east. At least two of the Danes jumped at the sound, the torchbearer almost dropping it as he backed away in confusion. They all headed off as one, what sounded like an even larger number of men following them in swift pursuit.

The forest quietened, the sound of hurried footfalls fading until all that could be heard was the wind through the trees. Everyone stayed silent, protected in their blanket of ferns, even the mighty Cenric looking quite content to remain here for the rest of the night should it be required. Another scream sounded, again far off to the east, a raucous cheer erupting in response. Æva didn't want to think about it. The Danes were a low, cruel people, and by the sound of it, they'd caught up with those frightened souls that had rushed by earlier. She peered over at Cenric and was surprised to see he was looking right back at her. He was thinking the same thing. He wanted to go and save those people. They couldn't. There were a lot of Danes about, judging from what they'd both seen and heard. They couldn't just go charging off to confront them. It would mean their deaths.

For some time, all remained still. Ulfcytel was in charge now, and everyone instinctively followed his lead, knowing he was their best chance of survival. He remai-

-ned motionless, like the rock he was, and when he finally moved it was merely to give Cenric a look, his eyes sharp with meaning. Cenric somehow understood what was being asked of him, and he rose into a low crouch and scurried upward and back onto open ground. She lost sight of him as he moved off towards their campsite, thinking that since only Cenric had moved, she had best remain hidden. A few minutes passed before a dark silhouette suddenly manifested at the top of the rise, the suddenness of its appearance making Æva nearly cry out. It made a gesture, beckoning them to come closer, Æva feeling somewhat foolish upon realising it was Cenric.

Ulfcytel was the first to respond, his shadowy bulk rising from the earth. He still held Brandon, but the boy had thankfully gotten used to the situation, including the fact that Ulfcytel had as yet refused to remove his hand from his mouth. Æva got to her feet and caught her son's eye, hoping the sight of her might reassure him. The rest of their company followed, their entire party retracing their steps back to where they'd been resting prior to being so rudely interrupted.

There was no respite to be had. A lot more Danes had moved through here, trampling the grass and greenery with a brutal disregard. They'd not come back this way, thankfully, and the direction they'd gone in remained quiet, making Æva think they were either far off or waiting for something. That didn't mean they could afford to be complacent. They headed north west, away from the forest clearing and back into the thicket. It was hard going, and they couldn't avoid making at least some noise, but they had to get away. Fighting that many foes just wasn't an option, even with beasts like Ulfcytel and Cenric on their side.

Another half hour passed when they heard a sound. There was laughter, callous and rough, emerging from somewhere off to the east, the faint light of a torch also making its way through the trees from the same direction. They rushed on, breaking into a spirited jog to put as much distance between themselves and the light as possible. It could only be the Danes. They'd killed whoever it was they'd been pursuing and were heading back. They were no doubt pleased with what they'd wrought. Æva knew that whatever they'd done, they wouldn't think twice about doing the same to them.

The forest abruptly ended after another few hundred yards, the night sky above coming into full view in a glorious patchwork of fast-moving clouds and glittering, almost jarringly beautiful stars. In any other time, Æva would have been pleased to see such a heavenly display, but not now, for the starlight would only further expose them to anyone who might be looking. They had to get across this open ground, and quickly. If they were lucky, the Danes would perhaps linger in the forest, permitting them to slip away without further drama.

They hurried from the woods, sharing not a word between them. Sadly, Æva soon began to feel the strain of prolonged movement, her breath wheezing and her leg aching all the fiercer as she did her best to keep up with the indefatigable Ulfcytel. She tried to think, hoping to distract herself from her discomfort, realising for the first time how she'd been somewhat negligent in getting to know any of the ealdorman's companions. She'd made the escape with him back when Edmund had led them through the tunnels to get away from Svienn's siege of Lundenburg, but she wasn't entirely sure if these men had been around then. They were well-suited to their task now, moving swiftly and without complaint, their physical capabilities saying they were all warriors and had been chosen by the ealdorman to accompany him down south for precisely that reason. It was good he had such a talent for leadership. The best men always seemed to appear at his side, drawn as if by instinct. It had been that way with Alaric. It was certainly that way now with Cenric.

Their group slowed a tad when some thicker cloud cover crept in from the south to thankfully mask the stars and intensify the darkness. Cenric peered back at her and offered her his arm, perhaps thinking she was so exhausted she'd need his strength to continue. That wasn't far from the truth, and Æva wasn't such a fool that she'd let pride come before her safety. She looped her arm around his, allowing him to take some of her weight. She felt a little embarrassed, yet she didn't have to endure it for long. The sight that greeted them up ahead put an end to that.

They'd not seen it, so deep was the blackness, the embers from the fire that had recently raged here cooling to the point they couldn't be discerned from far off. The village had been torched, the entire place consumed by flames. It was no accident. There were bodies, some blackened by heat, others hewn apart and dismembered by what could only have been a Dane's frenzied axe. A few had been strung up, their entrails dangling loose and swaying with the wind, their faces swollen and distorted from the violence of their asphyxiation. Æva felt the urge to vomit. She didn't need to see this. It was too much like Wiltune.

Brandon cried out, and so Æva rushed to him, hoping to settle his nerves lest he alert anyone best avoided. It didn't do much good, and Ulfcytel's attempt at reassurance also failed to make an impression. They should leave this place immediately. Nothing beneficial could come from lingering. Then the horn sounded. The same one heard earlier in the forest. The enemy was still out there. And they were heading this way.

Æva spun around, hoping to impress some urgency upon Cenric. She recoiled in alarm to see him struggling with a shadowed figure, the hostile newcomer looking like he'd emerged from one of the ruined buildings. He died noisily, roaring with outrage as Cenric broke his face with a flurry of blows before drawing his sword and cutting his throat. He shut up then, but he'd alerted his brethren, and there were now at least six more figures arrayed before them, axes held ready and their eyes alight with wrath.

They howled as they charged, their raw aggression causing the breath to catch in Æva's throat. She stumbled backwards and away from them, looking towards Brandon. Ulfcytel had dropped him and drawn his sword to face off against yet more enemies emerging from the darkness, the total number of assailants looking to have grown to well over a dozen. They were Danes, as anyone in their right mind could tell, and they'd obviously burned this settlement for one reason or another, their compatriots with the horn then chasing the survivors into the forest. Why they had targeted this village, specifically, was a mystery, yet it was fair to say it was unlikely to be for any cause a just man would entertain. Loot was most likely the goal behind all this, that and the sadistic glee of causing harm to others. It was their way. Nobody expected anything different.

Ulfcytel ran forward, his roar fit to shake the very earth, and drove his sword into the chest of the first enemy within reach. The man he'd impaled stumbled and started to drop, but Ulfcytel wasn't finished, grasping the hilt of his blade to tear it through his enemy's torso at an angle that saw much of his rib cage come apart in a welter of blood and shattered bone. The ealdorman didn't pause at the sight, instead heaving his bloodied weapon up and about him in a whirling arc that saw yet another Dane collapse to the earth, his neck and face rent asunder. Æva made a dive for Brandon as the rest of

Ulfcytel's people rushed in to aid him, the night air now ringing with the sounds of battle. This wasn't going as she'd hoped.

Brandon came to her, his face a mask of barely controlled terror. Æva reached for his hand only to feel herself suddenly lifted off the ground, the scent of hot, foul breath invading her nostrils. Whoever it was that held her laughed and gibbered into her ear, assuming her to be easy prey. She lashed out at him, trying to dig her elbow into his ribs, her efforts only provoking yet more mirth. He bellowed suddenly in what seemed like agony and surprise, making her fear for a moment that she might become deaf, but he'd released his grip on her, such was the pain of whatever had befallen him.

She saw the situation well enough a moment later. The Dane was advancing on Brandon, axe in hand, his eyes burning with a cold anger. Brandon was backing away in fear, his shaking hands gripped around a spear he'd snatched from the ground. He'd managed to stab the Dane in the leg, and he'd aimed well, but the boy simply didn't have the physical strength to force the tip past the scales of his armour. Even worse, his admirable attempt at protecting his mother had ensured he'd now become a target. Æva wouldn't have that. These bastards had taken her husband from her as well as her first son. They would not have another.

Anger came with her resolve, and so she threw herself at the Dane, leaping upon his back and tearing into his neck with her teeth. The heathen screamed and lurched backwards, his attempt to throw her off turning all the more desperate when she started clawing at his eyes. He eventually dropped his axe and reached up, his hands gripping Æva by the hair and pulling her forward with such force she was slammed into the earth. The air fled her lungs upon impact, her vision also blurring over for a moment as she tried to force herself up onto her elbows so that she might kick outwards with her legs. Fear clutched at her heart, her mind telling her the Dane was directly over her and death was imminent. She saw him clearly when her eyes again focused, his appearance all the more terrible with the torrent of red cascading down over his armour from the mess she'd made of his neck. He bent low, picking up his axe before placing his boot on her chest to press her into the earth.

She struck him, hoping to somehow knock him off balance and spare her rib cage from his terrible, crushing weight. Brandon made another attempt to intervene, but the Dane was wise to his feeble efforts and disarmed him, snatching his spear from his trembling hands and knocking him over. Æva continued to punch at his shin, raining down blows upon the leg pinning her in place. The Dane laughed again, the sound bitter and contemptuous, some blood and spittle erupting from his mouth. He heaved his axe upwards and back, his intention obvious. Death was now certain. Æva would die here tonight. She wouldn't close her eyes. She couldn't.

Something hit the Dane from the rear, his body shifting forward slightly as the tip of a blade emerged explosively from his chest. He fell, landing on top of Æva and spluttering his last, his breath still foul beyond compare. The weight eased suddenly, and the expiring Dane was hauled off and away by none other than Cenric himself. He took her hand and dragged her upwards, bellowing for her to take Brandon and flee. She reacted immediately, clasping the shaken Brandon by the hand to rush into the night. The horn sounded again, closer now, its cruel, piercing tone cutting through the din of battle. The Danes from the forest were returning. This fight would be over soon enough.

A multitude of emotions assailed her as she fled. She wouldn't look back, such was her terror, but shame and despair both had begun to spread their dull ache across her already tender heart. Cenric was going to die, as was Ulfcytel and all those who stood with them whilst she escaped to safety. She knew they would not have it any other way, and Brandon's death wouldn't be something any of them would want on their conscience, but still it hurt. These were good men, and in better times they'd have been gentle and kind, enjoying a peaceful life and a contented end in the twilight of old age. Now they'd just be more dead Englishmen, cut down in their own homeland by a foreigner's cruelty. She hoped they'd each take their share of Danes with them. Given what she'd seen so far, she had a feeling she'd get her wish.

Somebody screamed, the sound long and drawn-out, another horn blast followed by a cacophony of war cries signalling the arrival of enemy reinforcements. Æva ran on and on, Brandon's hand gripped firmly in hers. She didn't stop, her breath and heartbeat roaring in her ears, the sounds of battle receding behind her as the inevitable took its course. She began to weep, her grief contrasting sharply with the sounds of savage jubilation now resounding through the darkness. So that was it then. They were all dead, those few men, those brave men of England, giving their lives so that she might live. Æva tried not to picture it as she disappeared into the night, but the thoughts came on anyway, terrible and mournful, and with them something else. Something from the battle site they'd passed earlier. Something dark. Something cold. Hatred.

XI

The ring sparkled slightly, the burnished gold catching the candlelight. Ælfwynn gasped at the sight of it resting on Edmund's palm, her hand rising up to hold his. He looked down at her in her grief, his own efforts to control his emotions failing miserably as he too felt a tear trail down his cheek.

"How did you find this?" asked Ælfwynn, her voice a gentle whisper.

"A friend found him just after it had happened," Edmund said sadly. "He retrieved this ring, thinking he'd return it to you."

"And who is this friend? Where is he?" Ælfwynn asked, her mournful eyes now gazing up at him. Edmund was silent a moment before replying, his heart growing yet heavier with the recollection of Alaric.

"He couldn't be here," Edmund said softly. "He died just before Lundenburg fell."

His aunt took in what he'd said, her eyes then drifting downwards to again behold the ring. She reached out and took it, a fainter gasp escaping her lips when she held it to the light. "It's as I remembered," she whispered, "just as it was on our wedding day. Your uncle was always so good to me, you know that, Edmund?"

"We know," said Wulfhild gently from Edmund's side. She was sitting down at the table, her deep eyes sorrowful. Edmund had felt it only right that his sister come with him, feeling if anyone deserved the comforts of a family reunion, it would be her. They didn't look the part, for they were dressed in the same travelling garb they'd worn for weeks now, and their rapid march into Norþanhymbre hadn't helped. When they'd finally made it to their aunt's hall, Wulfhild had been excited, and Edmund could tell she was still more than glad to be here now despite the sombre mood. She'd been lonely. Her husband, Ulfcytel, had been absent for too long. She missed him. As did Edmund.

"We both know what you meant to each other," said Edmund. "Our brother was proud to bear his name. He said it was the only way he knew our father loved him in that he'd allowed him to be named after our uncle. He said..."

He stopped, his sadness engulfing him further. Ælfwynn placed her husband's ring on the table before moving swiftly over to Edmund so that she might hold him. She embraced him tightly, pressing her head into his chest as she rubbed his back, Edmund returning the gesture whilst doing his best to retain his composure.

"And your brother is in heaven now also?" Ælfwynn asked softly, knowing the answer already. "We heard about the battle. It must have been so hard on you, Edmund. You're so young, and life has been so harsh to you already. But I know your uncle would be proud to see you now."

"Would he?" Edmund whispered, his tears trickling further down his face and into his beard. "What have I done but fail? What have I done but neglect you and others? Alaric is the only reason you even have uncle's ring."

"This Alaric is the man who found my husband's body?"

"Yes."

"And he was a good man?"

"Yes."

"Then he'd be with you now, Edmund. He'd be one of those outside who have followed you this far. He'd be one of those already calling you their king. Just like your uncle, Æthelstan, would be, if he were with us."

His aunt wasn't wrong. If Alaric were alive, he thought it very likely he'd be one of his loyal companions. Edmund owed it to his memory to do right here. Falling into despair and talking like he was already defeated just wouldn't do. He took a deep breath, taking his aunt's words into himself to draw strength from them.

"Have you been well?" he asked, allowing her to continue embracing him for as long as she wished.

"I have," she said, "but it's lonely now. I didn't know what had happened for so long. I didn't want to believe any of it when the rumours started, but I have no choice now. I have to face the truth, as horrible as it is."

"What about Uhtred?" Edmund asked, his tone darkening. "Does he leave you alone? He's not made a nuisance of himself in these parts?"

Ælfwynn parted from him, returning to her seat across the table with a faint yet drawn-out sigh. She was a woman of means, as was proper for her station, and her abode was spacious and well-furnished, the few candles presently lit failing to do their surroundings justice. He was glad to be here. He'd not seen his aunt in years, not since the last time his father had come this far north, and a visit was long overdue. She'd aged, her previously blonde curls fading to white, the passage of years suddenly catching up with her as she learned to live a life of solitude. Edmund still couldn't fully believe his Uncle Æthelstan was actually gone. He'd been good to them all, his siblings and him. And yet gone he was.

"Won't you sit down?" asked his aunt, gesturing for him to take a seat. A servant appeared from out of the darkness around them, a platter of roasted vegetables and chicken balanced expertly in their hands. He set it down on the table in front of Edmund, the look on his aunt's face suggesting she very much wanted him to eat his fill. The servant reappeared seconds later with a flagon of what he assumed would be ale. Edmund took the drink from him with a nod of gratitude and held it to his lips. It was as he thought. He drank, draining half of it in one go, the liquid cool and crisp as it cascaded down his throat. He sat down after that. He needed to. It had been some time since he'd drunk anything so potent.

He tried the food, enjoying the scent and texture of something prepared in a proper kitchen rather than over an open fire beneath a night sky. The servant appeared yet again, placing a similar platter in front of Wulfhild for her to enjoy. They ate together, forgetting their courtly manners, their appetites taking hold after weeks of hard living.

"I shouldn't be eating like this," Edmund said grudgingly between mouthfuls. "My men don't get to enjoy this. I should bear their hardships along with them. It's what's right."

"What makes you think they won't be fed?" Ælfwynn asked, gazing approvingly at her nephew. "I inherited your uncle's lands and wealth, you know. I'll see to it that your companions are provided for."

"We won't be staying long," Edmund said quickly. "Although if there's anything you can do..."

"I will do it," she said. "But I must ask...have you heard from Eadgyth or Eadwig? I think you should be keeping your brother and sisters close, Edmund, especially now."

"Eadwig was with us until he went to Gainesburg."

"Why did he go there?"

"Politics," said Edmund simply. "He wanted to help with our situation. I felt it time he proved himself."

"So he has something to do with Svienn Forkbeard's death?"

Edmund almost choked, his surprise and astonishment prompting him to nearly deposit the contents of his mouth back onto his plate. He got control of himself quickly, swallowing hard and finding his voice.

"How did you hear this?" he breathed. "And where? When?"

"I hear a lot of things," she said. "The Ealdorman Uhtred keeps our family close, always has, and he shares things with my household. He sent a messenger just the other day. Svienn suddenly died whilst "entertaining" him and the others he'd summoned."

"I'd not heard a word!" exclaimed Edmund.

"Why would you?" chuckled Ælfwynn. "You're either fighting or marching these days, is that not right?"

He nodded. She was correct, but he was taken aback all the same. Wulfnoth seemed to know everything as it happened, but he'd had no mystery informant in play this time, or so it seemed to Edmund. His aunt's revelation did, however, shed light on something else they'd heard, a rumour that was partly responsible for them travelling into Norþanhymbre to begin with. Something was afoot at Euerwic. Something important.

Wulfnoth wasn't sure on all the details, but the word was the Archbishop Wulfstan was set to give some kind of sermon to any man of nobility who might attend him. Not just any sermon, mind. One that was intended to set England to rights and shame its inhabitants back onto the path of righteousness. It all made sense now. If Svienn really was dead, then the archbishop would certainly have something to say about it, especially after the bastard had so maligned the remains of Saint Edmund. Intriguing days were at hand.

"So he's really dead?" asked Wulfhild, her disbelief yet remaining. "Just like that? Within weeks of stealing our father's throne, he just...dies?"

"Yes," laughed their aunt, the shake of her head implying she'd not quite believed it when she'd first heard either. "If you ask me, there was something Godly at work in all this...Svienn was such a vile man. I don't just mean his years of raiding and murdering...I'm sure you both know he recently attacked the monastery where our Saint Edmund lies at rest."

"I was there," Edmund said abruptly.

"You were?" asked Ælfwynn, surprised.

"Yes, we tried to stop him. Almost did too, and we'd have killed him if our own Ealdorman of Mierċe, Eadric, hadn't intervened to save him. Treachery again foiled our plans. It's been like this for years now."

Ælfwynn scowled, the brief yet sharp expression oddly disturbing in the dim light. "I can't pretend to understand much of the politics," she admitted, "but I know your uncle didn't trust that Eadric. Said he had an appetite for advancement. Said he crossed the line between healthy ambition and something darker. I never agreed with your father's decision to marry Eadgyth to him. It wasn't right."

Edmund grunted in agreement, his thoughts turning to what he'd learned from Ulfcytel on Eadric's role in the death of his uncle. He'd been adamant that Eadric had led both Æthelstan and Alaric into a trap days before the battle at Hringmere, apparently as part of some ruse originally intended to eliminate Ulfcytel himself. This had all been confirmed some time later by Hemingr, who was none other than a brother to Thorkell the Tall, although he'd died before he could elaborate any further. It was a complex situation, and if things were different, he'd have felt his aunt had a right to know the full and complete truth of it. As it stood, he sensed there was little point in trying to explain to her just how rotten English politics had become. Her husband was dead. That was burden enough. Edmund would do the decent thing and spare her any further troubles.

"Eadric's time will come," Edmund said confidently, his sister's eager nodding strengthening his resolve. "Anyone who defies my claim to the throne will see justice fall heavily upon them. It's only a matter of time."

"So this is why you're marching to Euerwic with this army of yours?" asked Ælfwynn excitedly. "You think the archbishop will be of some assistance to you?"

"He's called for a great assembly," answered Edmund. "He'll get one."

"Were you invited?"

"Not as such," he replied tactfully, "but I intend to make an appearance, with my army outside the city so others can…ascertain the situation for themselves."

"You intend to make a show of force? That might not go down well with Uhtred, Edmund. These are his lands. I'm surprised he's not challenged you yet. Perhaps he's been busy with affairs of his own since he returned from Gainesburg."

"Do you think Uhtred will try and challenge us?" Wulfhild asked sceptically. "With Svienn dead, the Danes will be in turmoil. Edmund is the natural choice for who should be king. To attack him just for entering Norþanhymbre would be beyond reckless."

"It would," conceded Ælfwynn, "but I am actually a little surprised you'd not heard anything of Svienn's fate. Word spread quickly. Do you not have people who advise you, Edmund? People who make information their currency, as it were?"

"I do," Edmund admitted, his thoughts on Wulfnoth. "One man, in particular, is normally very adept at keeping me informed. Perhaps this time, he just missed out."

"Does that seem likely to you?" His aunt's eyes had narrowed, making Edmund feel she'd suddenly become suspicious of either himself or the situation in general. He took another swig of ale, the previously sweet taste seeming bland and unremarkable in wake of the ill feeling that had settled on him. He stuffed some more chicken into his mouth, chewing slowly as his thoughts began to race. His aunt was on to something here. It was strange that Wulfnoth hadn't heard of Svienn's death.

It was strange too that they still hadn't heard from Eadwig. He'd been the one to come up with the plan to get close to Svienn, offering himself as a distraction. It was quite brilliant, but dangerous, and Edmund hadn't wanted to risk his brother. Eadwig had insisted, though. He'd wanted to make himself useful, and Edmund hadn't wanted to disappoint him. He'd let him go, but he'd been praying every night since for the Lord to return him unharmed. He had to find out exactly what had happened. There was no time like the present.

Edmund rose from his chair, his sister glancing up at him whilst she continued nibbling her way through her meal. He mumbled his excuses and turned to proceed away down the hall, his gait a little unsteady as he tried to navigate through the now-smothering darkness. Despite this, he soon reached the front door and heaved it open, easing himself through into the crisp night air.

A reassuring sight greeted him just ahead, the light of several dozen cookfires emerging out of the black. His army was clustered around them, the men huddled in small groups for warmth and conversation, the firelight reflecting upon the armour and weapons of the sentries standing guard in a silent vigil. There must be almost a thousand men here now, every town and village they passed through bringing yet more recruits. Edmund still didn't understand why they were so drawn to him, but he wouldn't turn anyone away. He needed them, as did their country, and their service would not go unrewarded. When he won his crown, he'd see to it. He'd hand out honours and favours aplenty to those who'd been faithful. To those who had betrayed him, he'd offer the axe or exile. He'd not be dissuaded on this. He'd be generous to his friends. His foes would get no respite.

Edmund made his way through the ranks, his faithful warriors reacting to his presence with a flurry of salutations. Edmund made a point of returning each with a quick nod of acknowledgement, thinking it important he make the effort. He found Wulfnoth where he'd left him, sitting on a tree stump and staring into his campfire, his own men who'd stayed with him during his time on the run remaining close and talking quietly among themselves.

"Svienn Forkbeard is dead," announced Edmund loudly. The men he'd only just passed heard him, and Edmund's face creased into a slight smile as the word spread and the whole camp erupted in a flurry of cheers and excited conversation. Several warriors approached, begging Edmund to clarify if it was indeed true. He confirmed what he'd heard, and they returned to their comrades with a light step and beaming smiles. Wulfnoth looked up at Edmund, his face blank, his companions also glancing in his direction like he'd not said anything of interest at all. Edmund could read them well enough. Wulfnoth had known all along.

"You knew, didn't you?" snapped Edmund, annoyed.

"Yes," came the reply, Wulfnoth shifting himself adeptly off his tree stump to face Edmund on his feet.

"And you kept it from me? What about Eadwig? Is there word of him?"

"I've heard nothing of your brother yet," said Wulfnoth. "I wouldn't worry. He's unlikely to get into trouble, at least in terms of being killed outright for whatever reason. He'd be too valuable as a hostage, if they were even inclined to seize him to begin with."

Edmund felt a little relief, knowing Wulfnoth was speaking sense, at least on Eadwig. "And the rest of what I said? You wanted me to remain ignorant of Svienn's demise? Why?"

"The timing was all wrong."

"What's that supposed to mean?"

"You'd have attacked the Danish army at Gainesburg, Edmund, knowing them to be leaderless without Svienn. Don't deny it, and don't think ill of me, please. Just remember, I know you. You're a great fighter, and you have a brave heart, but you'd only have met with defeat if you'd tried to rush into battle so soon."

"How can you know that? They are almost certainly in chaos now, and we know Gainesburg was or is full of men who rightly owe ME their allegiance. Had I turned up with my army…"

"We'd have lost."

"Don't ever interrupt me again, Wulfnoth. Not ever."

Something shifted in the air, the tension from this already frank exchange sharpening considerably. Several of Wulfnoth's men had stood up, their manner uneasy as they looked from their commander to Edmund and back again. The scene behind them was as it had been, all joviality and mirth as the rest of the army celebrated the news of Svienn's death, but here in this corner of the camp it was different. Words were about to be broken, and Edmund knew in his heart he couldn't afford to back down.

"I only meant to act in your best interests," Wulfnoth said quietly, his attempts at equivocation rankling Edmund further.

"You can't serve me without honesty," Edmund retorted, "and you can't respect a man you mislead. I'm owed your respect, and I will have it."

"It's because I respect you, Edmund, that I avoid playing either the sycophant or the mindless underling. To have told you of Svienn's death as and when I learned of it would have seen you commit yourself to a rash undertaking. Your life would have been at stake and the kingdom with it. You know this."

"Don't presume to tell me what I know," Edmund simmered, his hands on his hips. "I've guided this army for weeks now, almost killing Svienn and his brat of a son when they were stupid enough to leave themselves exposed. I understand when to hold back and when to commit. You do me an injustice by making assumptions about me."

"I'll not disagree," Wulfnoth admitted soberly, "and since I have earned your displeasure, I can only ask your forgiveness. Just know that…"

"I'm not interested in your excuses, Wulfnoth. You either serve me, or you don't. We've suffered enough from thegns putting their own interests before that of the common good. If you conceal information from me again, we'll have to re-evaluate our relationship. Am I understood?"

Wulfnoth looked directly at Edmund, his expression neutral aside from a slight narrowing of his eyes. He was irritated, and his men looked equally perturbed, leaving Edmund wondering where their loyalties might lie should they be forced to choose between him and Wulfnoth. In that same instant of thought, he felt something else, something he didn't want to admit but couldn't deny. He was alone. Wulfnoth had betrayed his trust, and even if he had truly felt it for the best, it still wounded Edmund's pride. Without Wulfnoth, he had few other notables whom he could rally to his side, especially with Ulfcytel and Ælfric still down south. He needed new allies. He had a feeling he knew where he might find some.

"Tell me what you know of this meeting in Euerwic," Edmund asked, hoping to sound as authoritative as possible.

"It's as I told you before," Wulfnoth said hesitantly. "The archbishop wishes to address any man of standing who will hear him about the situation we face."

"The situation we face now that Svienn is dead?"

"Yes…and you would have found that out when we arrived, in any case. My silence would have then been irrelevant."

"But we'd have been too far north for me to do anything stupid, is that it? Like attack the Danish army at Gainesburg?"

"Something like that," Wulfnoth conceded, "although I will have it known, I don't think you're stupid. Tempestuous, yes, but stupid, no."

"I'll accept I can be ill-tempered," said Edmund, "but it's my opinion that a victory over the enemy would draw more supporters to my cause, especially now the Danes are leaderless. They'll be vulnerable. Archbishop Wulfstan can give all the sermons he likes...men will follow victories more readily. My victories."

"You're not seriously considering marching south? We're just days away from Euerwic."

"I am," said Edmund, folding his arms neatly over his chest. "And we've wasted time because of your dishonesty, Wulfnoth. Had I known Svienn was dead, we could have attacked Gainesburg and perhaps been able to attend the archbishop whilst still aglow with triumph from the battlefield."

Wulfnoth sighed, averting his eyes to again sit down on his tree stump and resume his gazing into the fire. Just as Edmund was about to take issue with such disrespect, he suddenly spoke, broaching a topic he'd not expected.

"Svienn's death doesn't mean the Danes are finished with us, and even with him out of the way, there are other powers to consider. Duke Richard is just across the sea, Edmund, and your father is with him, along with Thorkell and what's left of his bastard horde. Have you not thought they might try to intervene for their own benefit? To take back the throne, either for Æthelred or a proxy of Richard's choosing?"

Edmund shook his head quickly, his mind reeling at the possibilities being introduced. He'd never met the duke. He was the brother of the ever-irritating Queen Emma, that he did know, but outside of that relationship he'd never had reason to think of him, let alone the possibility he might attempt to interfere in the affairs of England. Would he try and do just that now Svienn was gone and the country leaderless? Surely nobody would capitulate to a Norman army, especially when the opportunism of their duke would be so clearly apparent. It was all quite far-fetched. He'd have Wulfnoth know that's what he thought.

"I can't see the duke launching an invasion just because he might have heard a rumour or two. We'd be better off focusing on what we do know and what we also know to be possible."

"Sound advice," Wulfnoth replied, his manner sincere. "But, as I said...your father is with him, Edmund. Richard may not even need to set foot here to extend his influence. Æthelred could do that for him."

"How?" Edmund asked, confused and exasperated. "What can my father do for him, and why?"

"He still has a certain legitimacy. He's the only Englishman living who has been ordained as king by a witan recognised by anyone who counts for anything. And he's completely dependent on the duke. He owes him. Richard will have all kinds of leverage over him...his safety, his wife...his children."

"Are you suggesting Richard would hold my half-brothers hostage so as to blackmail my father into resuming his throne and ruling as a Norman puppet?"

Wulfnoth looked up, a strange smile on his face. "Like I said, I've never thought you stupid, Edmund. You work things out for yourself quickly enough. You just need pointing in the right direction at times, and I think there is wisdom in what you've said here. Which is why we need to make haste to Euerwic, not to Gainesburg and battle."

"Why?"

"Because we need help. We need the archbishop to understand your father is a spent force, and a compromised one at that. The future of this kingdom has to rest on shoulders broad enough to bear the weight. You do have broad shoulders, Edmund."

"How likely do you think it is that Wulfstan will call for my father's return?" Edmund couldn't see how that could happen. Æthelred had fled the realm in disgrace, abandoning all he had just to seek refuge for his own sake and what family he could still summon to his side. It didn't matter that Edmund half-understood his reasons. Most others would just see him as a coward.

"Nothing is certain," Wulfnoth said darkly. "I'm just preparing for all eventualities, and alerting you to those you may not yet see."

"And keeping information from me when you think I won't react well to it?"

"I won't do that again," Wulfnoth said grudgingly, his shoulders slumping slightly in what looked like genuine resignation. "Just hear me when I say I had your best interests at heart."

"I'll decide what's in my own interests," Edmund replied sternly. "I'm not a boy anymore, nor am I a pawn in some factional dispute at court. I'll have you know this."

Wulfnoth nodded, a motion so slight it might have gone unobserved had Edmund not been staring directly at him. The men sharing the fire were still heeding their conversation intently, their unease ebbing somewhat as Edmund reasserted his authority. It was important he make such a gesture. Wulfnoth might be sincere in what he said, but there was no way he could have him deciding of his own accord what information was worth sharing and what wasn't. To win this war, Edmund would need to see the big picture, and he couldn't do that if he were treated like a child or, even worse, an asset to be manipulated.

"When will we resume our march on Euerwic?" asked Wulfnoth, seemingly eager to change the subject.

"First light," said Edmund. "I'll let the men celebrate the news of Svienn's passing tonight. Then we'll be on our way."

"Prepare yourself well, then. You'll be walking into a nest of vipers. The archbishop is a good man, if intense, but the rest of them…Uhtred will try to outmanoeuvre you, and if Eadric is there, the situation could be downright dangerous."

"Which is why I'll trust you to keep me well advised," Edmund said, turning away from Wulfnoth to begin walking back to his aunt's abode. The men were still festive on his way through their camp, Edmund for once thinking it a blessing they had no ale lest his army celebrate itself into a stupor and be unable to march come morning. Svienn had been the villain in England's story for years now, and his many raids and final attempt at outright conquest had brought nothing but misery and devastation. It was a weight off everyone's mind that he was finally dead. The only thing Edmund regretted was that he hadn't killed him himself. His claim to the throne would be solidified then. He'd be the man who'd killed England's nemesis. Instead, the stupid bastard had managed to expire all on his own.

He put his hand on the blunt iron handle of his aunt's front door, his gaze drifting up and down casually across the building's exterior. The outside had little to no bearing on the interior, the hall appearing more like an oversized barn than the seat of power for a family who had once ruled Southern Norþanhymbre. There were some decorations in the wooden beams that formed the supporting walls, the carvings here forming intricate spirals flowing upward towards the heavily thatched roof, but overall the external decor was largely unremarkable. Once Edmund stepped inside, there was no doubting this was the residence of somebody of note, but the darkness persisted, the splendour of mounted shields, blades, and tapestries remaining hidden in the shadows. Edmund wondered if his aunt had made it so on purpose. She could light her home properly if she wished. Did she somehow prefer the dark now her husband was gone?

Wulfhild greeted him when he returned to their table, Ælfwynn too. He sat down and resumed eating, ignoring the fact his food had cooled considerably during his absence. His sister seemed a little sad, speaking often of her husband as if he were the only man left in the world. Edmund didn't think her foolish for that. He respected marriage and the emotional ties that went with it, and despite his occasional frustrations with Ulfcytel, his sister had developed what looked like a sincere and lasting affection for him. As long as that bond wasn't taken for granted, the Ealdorman of Eastengle would always enjoy Edmund's friendship and appreciation.

"He'll be back soon," Edmund said for the third time, doing his utmost to keep any hint of irritation from his voice.

"Can you be so sure?" Wulfhild asked yet again, her hands fidgeting with her headscarf. She'd taken to covering virtually her entire head in her husband's absence, as if thinking even the slightest wisp of hair might drive a man to passion from the mere sight of it. Edmund understood she was likely feeling vulnerable, but he also wished she'd not worry quite so much. Nobody would lay a hand on her in his army. Not unless they wanted to lose that hand.

"His business with Ælfric will be done by now," soothed Edmund, "and I'm certain he's missing you as much as you are him. That'll speed his return."

"Ælfric?" asked Ælfwynn suddenly, her expression anxious. "The Ealdorman Ælfric? He's a slippery character, that one. Your uncle had little time for him."

"He's loyal enough," Edmund said, wanting to avoid any discussion of Ælfric and the various rumours that forever seemed to be circulating around him. "He's the legitimate power in the South, and since he's backing me, it's expedient we make sure he has his lands back. Father did an injustice by having him seized."

"Are you sure?" Ælfwynn asked again, her questions wearing on Edmund's patience. "Your father wasn't always the fool. He may have had good reason for making an enemy of Ælfric."

"I'll not pay attention to rumour, only facts," Edmund retorted. "My father was also the man who kept Eadric of Mierċe around as if he were a friend. That alone rules him out as a good judge of character. Ælfric professes his loyalty and has not shown me any disfavour as yet. I'll return that confidence."

"If you say so…"

"I do!"

Edmund paused and unclenched his fist. He'd slammed it against the table, almost knocking several cups and flagons straight over. His aunt had flinched, and Wulfhild was clearly upset, the lines on her forehead arching in alarm.

"I'm so sorry. That was unacceptable."

"Something more is on your mind," Ælfwynn stated, her back straight and expression neutral. "You can talk to me, you know. Yours is a heavy burden."

"It is," Edmund said appreciatively. "I just…I'm not a boy anymore. I'm a man, fighting to secure his rightful…"

"A man without a father," his aunt said softly. "You can try and deny it, Edmund, but I can only imagine how it must be to have had Æthelred just take off like that and leave you here. You're in pain."

"He's not alone," Wulfhild sighed. "It's a hard thing we have to bear…but our father had priorities in his life that didn't include us. I always suspected it, being as he was, and he's proven it now. There's not much to be done, sadly."

"I'm sorry," Edmund mumbled. "I forget sometimes how he treated you, in particular, Wulfhild. But let me just say…I don't think it was because of anything you did yourself…his animosity towards you was purely a result of his belief that Ulfcytel…"

"Was better off dead? Was his enemy? It never made any sense, Edmund, and with Æthelstan gone, it was as if he had no reason to remain with us. All he cared about was Emma and her children."

"I understand it must seem like that…but it wasn't entirely so. When I saw him as he fled Lundenburg…he asked after you. He wanted us with him. A change had come over him, like he was seeing his mistakes for the first time. It was from his encounter with Alaric…"

"He's all Ulfcytel would talk about!" laughed Wulfhild sadly. "Alaric was so brave, Alaric was so good, Alaric saved my life, Alaric…"

"…tried to bring my husband's ring back to me."

They both nodded at Ælfwynn's words, acknowledging that the man had intended to do precisely that.

"He certainly played an important role in recent events," Edmund said. "I wish, though, that I understood more about his influence over our father. He was obsessed with Alaric. You saw it, Wulfhild. You remember when he became violent at the table that time, all because I happened to mention how Alaric had survived the Battle of Hringmere."

"I do," replied Wulfhild. "I thought it was just father being father at the time. He was always unpredictable, but I suppose he got what he wanted. Alaric is lost to us, gone like so many others."

"So was he always troubled about this man?" asked Ælfwynn. "Why? How did they know each other?"

"He'd never even met him until Alaric came to Lundenburg after the fall of Canterburie," explained Edmund, "but he was fearful of him even before that. I can't explain it."

"Then I suggest we put it to one side for the moment," said Ælfwynn. "You can drive yourself to distraction trying to work these things out…and your father was always a complex man. Too complex. Let his motives be until you have the opportunity to ask him again."

"If that ever happens," muttered Edmund. He was right to be sceptical. As far as anyone knew, his father had no reason to return to England. He was rich after plundering the treasury, and he had his queen and their children along with it. He could quite happily spend all of his remaining days lounging around Duke Richard's keep, enjoying the soft living and day-to-day insincerity of life at court. Wulfnoth might believe otherwise, but as far as Edmund was concerned, his father's role in English politics was decisively over. He'd made his decision to flee. Now it was up to Edmund to salvage something from the mess he'd left behind.

Another hour went by in idle conversation. Ælfwynn began to yawn profusely and apologise with it until Wulfhild insisted she retire, arguing she mustn't try to remain awake on their account. Their aunt eventually agreed and took herself off to her chambers, leaving Edmund alone with his sister. They talked for a bit longer, but Edmund must have been less entertaining company than he'd imagined, as Wulfhild soon departed to the rooms that had been set aside for her. Edmund sat by himself for a little longer, enjoying his third cup of ale and the relaxation that came with it. His eyes began to feel heavy. It was time to rest.

He decided at the last moment he wouldn't spend the night in comfort. A bed had been prepared for him, indoors in the warm, but he'd rapidly concluded that authentic leadership involved the sharing of hardship, and it wouldn't be right to spend the night here whilst his men slumbered outside. He headed out into the dark, the cold seeming to clutch at him as he closed the front door, and made his way over to the encampment. Most men were sleeping, but a few remained at their campfires, and there was the usual number of sentries pacing back and forth and keeping watch whilst their brothers rested. They nodded in respect when Edmund strode past, seeking his own tent. He found it quickly, bending low as he dipped inside. The furs laid out for him were quite warm, and he slipped into a dreamless repose, his eyes slowly opening as dawn's light and the singing of birds intruded upon his senses.

He got up immediately, feeling reasonably refreshed, a quick gulp of cold water and a mouthful of bread serving as a suitable repast before he made his way back through his men and into his aunt's hall. Wulfhild predictably wasn't awake yet, but Edmund wasn't of a mind to indulge her, his hammering at her door eventually rousing her in a state of irritation. He ignored her objections. It was time to say goodbye to Ælfwynn and depart. Their business in Euerwic couldn't wait.

By the time he was outside again, his army was fully assembled, their tents and equipment stowed away and their arms and armour fully equipped. They let loose a scattered cheer when they saw him, making him wonder what he was supposed to have done to provoke their adulation. Just as he was thinking they were still jubilant over the news of Svienn's death, he saw another reason for their continued excitement. His aunt had provided several carts, each drawn by two beasts of burden and laden with food and supplies. Not only that, but she'd seen fit to donate an additional dozen horses, one of which was presently being led towards him by an unusually happy-looking Wulfnoth.

"I thought you should get the best of the bunch," Wulfnoth announced, coming to a halt with their new friend. He wasn't exaggerating. The horse was magnificent – larger than most and heavily muscled – and almost black in hue, sporting a thickset mane that was being tousled by the early morning breeze. Edmund made sure to be careful as he extended his hand to gently stroke the horse's muzzle in an impromptu greeting. It wouldn't be wise to rush things with such a beast.

He needn't have worried. The creature was quite sociable, and it offered not a hint of resistance when Edmund eased himself up into the saddle straddling its unusually broad back. Another cheer erupted from his men, the sight of their king atop a horse stirring them to renewed enthusiasm. Wulfhild sauntered over, expressing surprise when Ælfwynn presented her with a horse of her own. It was a pale creature, but strong and agile-looking, its manner suggesting it too was perfectly comfortable around people and not inclined to panic easily.

"So you'll head back this way once your time in Euerwic is over?" Their aunt sounded a little worried, like she was fearful the two siblings would forget her now they'd eaten her food and accepted her totally unexpected gifts.

"We will," said Wulfhild happily, her steed likewise snorting contentedly beneath her.

"We shall," Edmund said quickly, his sister's demanding gaze spurring his words. "I'll let you know what we learn there...and please know that you have my gratitude for all you've done."

"On the contrary, Edmund, you'll find I'm the one who is grateful. You brought me something of my husband that I'd thought entirely lost. Words can't convey the solace I feel."

"I'm glad," he replied, donning a pair of leather riding gloves. "We'll return soon. Until then, may God be with you."

"Wait a moment, Edmund," said his aunt quite urgently. She was fumbling with something in her robes, and Edmund's curiosity rose when she revealed an old bronze brooch, one he felt he recognised.

"You remember this?" she asked, holding it up in both hands. The metal had been shaped with some real skill, the bronze having been worked to take on the shape of a giant moth, or so Edmund supposed. "It was your uncle's," continued Ælfwynn, "and it belonged to his father and his grandfather and all the way back to...well...we don't actually know how old it is. But I think he'd want you to have it."

Edmund took it, holding it up to the light. It really did look like a moth, huge and yet beautiful, the metal seeming to glow slightly whenever it caught the sun. "I can't possibly accept this," said Edmund, his eyes still on the brooch. "You've already done so much for us."

"If that's so, then what's one more gesture?" asked his aunt, smiling. "But honestly, Edmund...your Uncle Æthelstan would have wanted this. I knew him better than he suspected, and he loved his brooch. Treasured it. And he loved and treasured you. So take it. It'll make me happy. Trust me."

Ælfwynn's smile broadened when Edmund attached the brooch to the hem of his cloak. He made sure it was properly secure before turning back to his aunt, feeling sort of strange now he appeared to have a giant metal insect stuck to his clothing. "It looks wonderful," said Ælfwynn. "Now go," she added, suddenly serious. "You have work to do, so get to it. Your uncle would wish it."

Edmund nodded and mumbled some thanks and farewells, feeling sad and yet inspired by his aunt's words. He turned, directing his steed away and towards the head of his assembling army. He did his best not to look back, thinking it important his men think him set on his task. His sister soon joined him, their two horses breaking into a trot as Wulfnoth rode after them atop his own iron-grey stallion. Their journey north then resumed, the men on foot marching in their wake, a small baggage train of extra weapons and supplies bringing up the rear.

After a mile or so Edmund gave a few orders, instructing Wulfnoth to gift whatever horses they had left to any man who'd proven himself in field craft and scouting. He had them screen their advance, these men riding ahead and along their flanks to serve as their eyes and ears. They'd not seen any trace of the enemy in days, but it would be foolish to let their guard down. These were the lands of Uhtred, who, as far as Edmund was concerned, was nothing but a traitor. It was only a matter of time until he tried something.

Another few days passed, the mood of the army dwindling to something more sombre. They were just a couple of miles south of Euerwic when they noticed something was wrong, the dark grey clouds parting suddenly to reveal the landscape in a cold, jarring light. Their surroundings were the same, the fields empty and deserted after the recent harvest, the worn stone road they'd been on for days winding ahead through a stand of bleak pine trees. Euerwic looked like any other major city from this distance, its grey, foreboding battlements appearing both aged and unwelcoming, but that wasn't what concerned him. There were men between them and their destination. Lots of men. Several hundred by the looks of it, and they were armed.

Edmund's scouts returned in a hurry, relaying the message that the Ealdorman Uhtred was with the force up ahead and wished to "impress upon him" the "importance of proper decorum whilst in my lands." Edmund scowled at the choice of words, seeing the threat for what it was. Uhtred's forces suddenly began to move, the Norþanhymbrians deploying just beyond the pines to block the road ahead. Edmund barked orders for his men to form up into a battle line facing them, knowing it was best to prepare for the worst and that to hesitate would likely invite aggression. They rushed to it, forming one great mass of bristling spear tips facing outwards towards the not-so-friendly locals. Several minutes then went by in tense silence, both armies eyeing the other over the tops of their shields.

Just as Edmund felt his patience wearing thin, the front ranks of the Norþanhymbrian host shifted slightly, allowing a group of horsemen to emerge and ride forth. Edmund bellowed for his men to hold fast but take no action, fearing some would think they were about to be charged. This wasn't an attack. It made no tactical sense. Cavalry did not rush shield walls. Something else was in play here.

The riders stopped about twenty paces from Edmund's position. There were eight of them, all similarly attired in thick cloaks and shimmering ring mail, their heavy, ornate helms hiding their features. One called out, claiming it was "good to see him again" before removing his helmet. It had been a fair few years, but Edmund recognised him. He knew that arrogant smirk. Uhtred had aged well. Power apparently suited him.

"As I told your friends just now, Edmund," Uhtred said, his loud voice carrying easily through the crisp morning air, "this is my land. I expect certain things from any visitor, even those of your stature."

"What do you propose?" Edmund called back, still unwilling to close the distance between them in the event Uhtred tried anything. "You know why I'm here. Why this show of strength?"

"I could ask you the same thing," Uhtred said, gesturing towards Edmund's army, his laugh forced and irritating. "What makes you think you can just march such a host through my lands?"

"Because I'm an aetheling?" asked Edmund, thinking his question more of a statement than anything. "And I'm the only legitimate claimant for the throne. You'd do well to remember that before you try any of your usual…flourishes."

Uhtred didn't reply, instead spurring his horse into a trot so that he and the two men flanking him were brought yet closer. "You're perhaps correct," said Uhtred, his voice softer now, "but surely an aetheling with ambitions such as yours should value courtesy? Your presence here, unannounced as it is, comes off as…rude."

"Just speak plainly, Uhtred," warned Wulfnoth. Aside from Wulfnoth, Edmund had five other mounted men to his left and right, all of them armed with long spears. Uhtred was also perilously close to their front line, making him perfectly vulnerable to any man on foot looking to unhorse him. If Edmund so wished, he could kill Uhtred, here and now, and have ample time to brace for any counterattack from the then-leaderless army up ahead. If he so wished. He'd let Uhtred explain himself a bit more before he made any final decision.

"So you've brought your spymaster with you," said Uhtred, ignoring Wulfnoth whilst referencing him all the same.

"I find him useful," replied Edmund evenly. "He understands the importance of loyalty." He studied Uhtred's face as he pronounced the final word of his last sentence. He'd said it slowly, exaggerating its vowels, wanting to give the impression he was aware of Uhtred's capitulation to Svienn and thought little of him as a result.

Uhtred twisted uncomfortably in the saddle. "Any ruler does what's right by their people," he said, "and I've always tried to stay true to those sentiments. I made a decision when Svienn returned, and look…" he gestured around him, his right arm moving up and over his shoulder as if to take in the horizon, "…my lands remain unscathed. My people are alive. I did what's right by them."

"You betrayed my father and swore allegiance to a foreign king who is now dead."

Edmund let his words sink in, feeling secretly pleased with how quickly he'd moved to deflate Uhtred's self-serving excuses. "And even if you had not," he continued, "nothing in what you've said so far explains this army you have that's barring my path. I desire to enter Euerwic to attend the archbishop. I ask you not to impede me."

"The archbishop is not here," said Uhtred.

"What?" asked Edmund, confused. "I'd been told he wished to deliver a great sermon to the assem…"

"Oh he does, Edmund. But he's still on his way. Matters elsewhere distracted him…but he's coming."

"I would hope so, Uhtred, as I'm tired of wasting time. I have a country to fight for, and I wish entry into your city. I suggest you allow it."

"Is this really the son of Æthelred?" Uhtred blurted, his hands held out, palms up, like he was putting the question to everyone around him. "You talk like a man, Edmund. You've come a long way since I last saw you. Further than your father ever came, if I may be so bold."

"You may not," Edmund replied menacingly. "In fact, you should apologise immediately. I'll not have anyone disparage my father on questions of manhood, especially from one so woefully unqualified."

Wulfnoth guffawed off to his left, the sound of Wulfhild's melodic laughter also rising up from just behind him. Uhtred's face flushed, making the situation all the more hilarious.

"Perhaps I deserved that," he said awkwardly, his admission belied by the hard, cold look in his eyes. "I respected your father, Edmund, and wouldn't have anyone claim otherwise. It's just that you have a different sort of spirit. A more direct one, let's say."

"Then will you march your army off-field and allow me into Euerwic?" Edmund asked, exasperated with this back-and-forth.

"I will, now I have the measure of your intent," Uhtred said. "Just don't presume too much about what you'll find in my city. The archbishop may not be of the same mind as you, and if you're assuming he'll make you king, I fear you're to be disappointed."

"We'll just have to see," Edmund said neutrally, hoping to appear disinterested and perhaps even bored with Uhtred's musings. In truth, they were the only subjects he really wanted to think about. If Archbishop Wulfstan wouldn't assist him, he wasn't sure what he'd do. Ever since Sigeferth and Morcar had failed him, he'd been at a loss, unsure of how to pursue his claim to the throne and increasingly bitter at his sorry situation. This meeting in Euerwic was his last hope. If things went well, he'd potentially have everything. If they didn't, he'd be just as he was, wandering the wilderness, loved by his men, yes, but still just wandering. Something had to change.

Uhtred did as he was asked, his barked orders seeing his army move off several hundred yards to the west, where it again took up a defensive position. Edmund left his own army as it was, giving Wulfnoth authority whilst he moved on to Euerwic in the company of his sister and several dozen armed retainers. Uhtred insisted on joining them, bringing a party of his own men with him. They made small talk as they rode together, Edmund feeling at least halfway reassured that Uhtred's presence would likely indicate he didn't intend to have him ambushed and killed. Wulfhild, however, was visibly tense, and as much as Uhtred was now acting the gracious host, Edmund kept his hand close to the hilt of his sword. The situation could still change at any moment. He'd be a fool to think otherwise.

Euerwic made for a strange sight. Edmund had only been here once before, when his mother had taken him to visit his grandfather, the Ealdorman Thored. He'd been too young back then to really discern much about the place, but he was struck now by how ordered and peaceful it was, its citizens going about their business without any of the fear and foreboding he'd grown accustomed to down south. Their walls were tall and strong, that was true, but there was something else in the air here, a mood that was quite different from what he'd encountered in Norþanhymbre thus far. Euerwic's people felt protected, or had grown accustomed to being out of harm's way. They were happy, and it suited them. This was how a kingdom should feel, Edmund thought. If he ruled, he'd make it so that all of England might enjoy the same.

They rode on down a wide, gravel-strewn road heading in from the southern gate. The streets beyond were spacious and clean, the chill, damp air of the North failing to subdue the atmosphere of busy optimism. The buildings were much the same, lacking any of the filth and claustrophobia of Lundenburg, every home and workshop appearing well-maintained and pleasing to the eye. Of course they were. Uhtred's lands had escaped the worst of the war, and then he'd taken himself out of it altogether by submitting to Svienn. The peace they enjoyed here was the result of cowardice and treachery rather than anything else. Edmund wondered just how many of the locals were aware of that.

"Did you pay the heregeld?" Edmund suddenly asked, cutting off Uhtred's continued efforts at conversation.

"What do you mean?" he asked, bidding his steed slow and then stop just outside a wide, stone-walled yard.

"I asked if you paid my father's heregeld when it was demanded," Edmund said again. He had a feeling he hadn't. Euerwic's prosperity was too pronounced, its people too well-fed. He wasn't sure if he could blame Uhtred for that, but it would constitute evidence that the Ealdorman of Norþanhymbre had been willing to defy his father even when he wasn't being compelled by Svienn.

"We've always paid our share," Uhtred said lightly, dismounting from his horse, his guards doing the same. Edmund followed suit alongside the rest of his party. They then all followed Uhtred, leading their horses into the yard and what turned out to be a row of well-furnished stables.

"But did you pay the recent heregeld, specifically?" Edmund asked sternly, allowing a rather rotund stable lad to take the reins of his horse.

"We did," Uhtred said again, facing Edmund directly, his arms folded. "We've always been loyal to your father, until loyalty meant our deaths. I'm sure you'd do the same in my position."

"I don't believe a word. That tax decimated the fortunes of countless people, thegns, ceorls…anyone who had anything and those who already had pretty much nothing."

"It was a heavy burden," nodded Uhtred, his expression giving nothing away.

"It was," confirmed Edmund, "but I don't see how you'd know, since you didn't pay it."

"Why do you say that to me?"

"Because I have a knack for these things, Uhtred, and it's the truth. Euerwic has to be the most prosperous city in England. There's no chance it would look this way if you'd agreed to pay what my father had demanded of you."

"You have to learn to trust somebody, Edmund," Uhtred said with a sad smile. "Going around making accusations and harbouring suspicions…it's no way to live."

"We'll see," said Edmund, knowing he'd not be able to get much truth out of Uhtred. He began making his way out of the yard, Wulfhild and their men following close, thinking he'd seen a good-sized inn near the city gate that might accommodate them. Uhtred kept on at him for a time, claiming he'd "make my own halls ready" to host him and his people, but Edmund waved him off. He wouldn't spend a night under Uhtred's roof. They'd avoided bloodshed just earlier, but he knew the ealdorman wasn't shy when it came to dark deeds. Having the son of the king he'd betrayed murdered in his sleep was certainly something he'd consider, if he stood to gain from it.

They found the inn easily enough, the place looking more than able to meet their needs. It had a wide and open ground floor, and its wooden walls kept the worst of the damp out, a staircase in the back leading up to what Edmund assumed was a second storey where guests could reside at night. He spared a thought for his men outside the city, most of whom had been sleeping under open skies for weeks. He always felt guilty that his social standing ensured he was offered comfort before any other. Once he was king, he'd be generous with those who'd stuck with him through these difficult days. He knew he thought about such things often, but he didn't care. It was the right thing to do.

There was at least one good thing about this situation. Edmund had ignored much of what Uhtred had said as they'd ridden through the streets, but he'd mentioned that Archbishop Wulfstan would be returning to the city come the morning, making Edmund's arrival quite timely. That meant he had to stay only one night in Euerwic. That lightened his heart, for he'd decided he didn't like it here. There was something distasteful in the air, as if the place had been insulated from the perils of the outside world to the point their blissful ignorance had turned slightly rotten. He shook off the thought and spoke to the innkeeper, who was actually perfectly decent, if a little overawed at who Edmund was. It wasn't their fault these people had been fortunate whilst others had not. Perhaps God simply had plans for Euerwic that had yet to be revealed.

Edmund spent the evening in patient inactivity. Wulfhild remained close, and they all moved up to the second floor right after they'd eaten, thinking it better they lie low and stay out of sight of the general public. Edmund was quite sure the archbishop would come to him once he learned of his presence in the city, and Uhtred, being a regular chatterbox, certainly wouldn't be able to keep it a secret. He had to prepare. He did so by closing his eyes, hoping a brief rest in his rooms might refresh him. That didn't turn out as planned. He fell into a deep slumber, his dreams returning him to recent events.

He was with his army outside the city walls, but Uhtred wasn't so friendly this time, and instead of parleying, he attacked Edmund and his men when they approached the gates. The blood and chaos of battle felt familiar, but Edmund was impotent in the face of it, his blows bouncing off his opponents whilst they bellowed and laughed back at him. Uhtred was cutting into Edmund's men from horseback, his normally affable face now terrible to look upon. They fought, Edmund on foot and Uhtred up high, the clash of arms and the screams of the dying reverberating around them. Uhtred was laughing at him, his sneer twisted and cruel, thinking himself better, thinking he'd outmanoeuvred the aetheling and that victory was assured. It seemed he might not be wrong.

Another figure emerged from the city, cloaked and hooded and riding a thin, grey horse. It came along at a slow, casual pace, taking up position on a slight rise upon the road so as to look down on the melée. The figure stayed as it was, its face not yet revealed, surveying the ongoing massacre whilst Uhtred continued to rain down blows upon Edmund. Something then changed; a southerly wind blowing over them to knock back the rider's hood and reveal his face. Eadric. It was Eadric there, in control of the situation, his latest plans unfurling as he'd undoubtedly desired all along. Uhtred was Eadric's man, and this slaughter was his will.

Edmund lashed out with his sword, sweeping the blade's edge across the front legs of Uhtred's horse. It reared up in a panic, sending its rider falling backwards to crumple into the grass below. Edmund was on him in a second, his boot pinning Uhtred's sword arm whilst he heaved his blade up and then down. Uhtred screamed, desperate and fearful, as the tip of Edmund's sword tore through the metal ringlets and hardened leather of his armour, but he soon fell silent and went limp, his chest cracked open and his heart impaled on sharp iron. Edmund pulled his weapon free and pressed forward, intending to fight his way through the battle and settle accounts with Eadric.

Yet Eadric was no longer alone. Another rider had joined him, this second man having the thin, cruel visage and shimmering, flaxen hair of a Dane. He looked pleased with himself, and he had an air of authority about him that Eadric seemed to defer to. The Dane lifted his arm into the air, like he was giving a signal to someone, and sure enough a great cry erupted from out of the tangled woods to the east, causing all who heard it to look fearfully in its direction. They were right to be afraid. Death was coming, their death, and there was nothing any of them could do about it. Edmund wished it were not so.

Nonetheless, he still let out a roar of defiance at the sight of the thousands of Danes storming from the trees. They reached them in a matter of moments, their frenzied movements more akin to beasts than men, and tore into the already chaotic battle, cutting men down left and right. Edmund killed one who came too close, taking his head clean off with a single swing, only to find himself again looking up towards Eadric. There was something about his fearsome companion. He felt he recognised him. The eyes, in particular, were familiar, but when he'd seen them before they'd been wide and fearful, beholding Edmund with something close to panic. Then he remembered. This man had been at Sancte Eadmundes Byrig the day Svienn Forkbeard had attacked the place. Edmund had been intent on killing him until Eadric had stormed in with reinforcements. He'd finish the job now he'd been given the chance. He'd end this fool and Eadric both.

He was hacking his way through Danes and Saxons alike when he heard a terrific hammering. Something was shaking the earth, but from the way everyone just kept on fighting, it seemed only Edmund had noticed it. The hammering sounded again, more intense and pronounced this time, Edmund realising in a single instant that he was indeed dreaming and had best awake. He did so immediately, opening his eyes to sit up on his bed just as the door to his room swung back on its hinges. His man stood there,he'd forgotten his name, but he'd been assigned to guard him as he slept. Edmund stared at him expectantly, eventually spying a second figure visible just past his shoulder. He recognised him at once. Wulfstan. The archbishop had come.

He looked different in some ways from when Edmund had last seen him. He'd then been in Lundenburg, attending his father with a whole host of parasitic thegns, all intent on living a life of leisure and luxury even as the population outside starved in the streets. Edmund had wanted to talk to him, hoping he'd be able to do something to relieve the suffering of Lundenburg's inhabitants, but such plans had come to nought. Drama and intrigue had predictably got in the way, and the confrontation between his father and Ulfcytel had left Edmund with no option but to tie his fate to the tempestuous ealdorman. He hadn't wanted to be parted from his father, yet he'd had no choice. The revelation that he'd had a hand in his uncle's death was something he could not forgive. That would never change.

Wulfstan had aged. Edmund could see that as he ushered him inside into the firelight, taking his damp woollen cloak and draping it across the chair adjacent to the room's modest hearth. His hair and beard were lank and greying, neither of which had been tended to in a while and looked to be about to run out of control. He had a slight look of old Ælfheah, the now sadly deceased Archbishop of Canterburie, but his eyes were harder, his visage more gaunt, like he was a man who bore more troubles than he'd care to admit. Edmund wondered what could be the matter. Then he realised it could be any number of things. These were sad times, even for a man of Wulfstan's standing.

"What sent you away from Euerwic?" inquired Edmund, sitting down on the edge of his bed, leaving the room's single chair to the archbishop.

"Business," said the older man, a slight groan escaping his lips as he sat and began massaging his knees with thin, bony hands.

"Anything I can help with?" Edmund asked, hoping his sincerity would be recognised.

"No," came the blunt response, "but you can tell me why your brother, Eadwig, is not with you. I'd have thought, if word has spread of what I intend to do here, that he'd be in your company."

"And what do you intend to do here?" asked Edmund, hoping to get a decisive answer.

"We need a new king, of course," Wulfstan affirmed. "It came as a surprise to me that Svienn died so quickly…he wanted to be crowned here, you see…now we need a new king. One who will return us to the path of righteousness and thus restore us in the eyes of God."

"So Uhtred and everyone else were originally going to stand and watch you crown Svienn?" asked Edmund, suddenly angry. "These men are traitors…they threw their lot in with an invader and usurper. You must see that."

"Which is why none of them must take the throne," Wulfstan said. "None. God must rule our hearts, our very lives…and God appoints kings to rule us in earthly matters as extensions of His will. We have no business putting our own interests before the Lord's. He knows best."

"So you're telling me Uhtred won't be king?"

"Of course not."

"I'm next in line. I am Æthelred's eldest, and I have an army ready to expel the Danes from England. I have the right. Will you not give me your blessing?"

"You come here with an army to make a point?" Edmund knew what Wulfstan was suggesting. He thought he was trying to intimidate him. It wasn't so. He couldn't help it that people wanted to fight for him. His popularity, if anything, should be taken into consideration. He had the people's adoration, there was no denying that. How many others could claim the same?

"I'm not trying to threaten you," Edmund insisted. "I've been on the move for some time, trying to resist Svienn's rule…those men outside the city sought to help me. They did help me. There is nothing dishonourable going on here, Wulfstan. I am not my father."

"You are not, which is the issue here. I cannot give you my blessing. You are not a valid contender for the throne, and the witan tomorrow will not see you as such."

"What are you saying?" demanded Edmund, shock and confusion upon his face. "Who else but I can be king? How would departing from the line of succession be pleasing to God?"

"Because your father is still alive, and it was wrong of us to ever turn our back on him. He was our king, for better or worse, and remains our king as far as the Lord is concerned."

"Are you suggesting…"

"I am," said the archbishop, a sickening finality in his voice. "To make things right with the Lord, we must all repent and restore to England the proper order of things. That starts with your father. You will not be king, Edmund, and you should put these ambitions away for the time being. Your father must return to us. Æthelred must rule once more…and when he does, God will see us for the loyal and pious subjects we are and have mercy on us. For we need that, Edmund. England needs the Lord's mercy, and Æthelred is the means to obtain it."

XII

The sound came out of the dark, barely audible in her sleep-addled state. She tried to ignore it, thinking it likely just an animal drawn to the warmth of her dying campfire. Exhaustion tugged at her resolve, the need for more sleep sapping her willpower until she almost slipped back into her half-remembered dreams. Then she heard it again. The same sound. She had to wake up. Something was out there.

The figure advanced, crouching low, its speed and agility surprising considering the breadth of its shoulders and the heavy mail coat protruding from beneath its frayed woollen cloak. It had come out of the trees to the south east, moving quickly through the long grasses surrounding Æva's campsite. She knew then that she'd been a fool. She was too exposed out here, and now she was going to have to fight. She hoped God would smile on her. That was the only way she could imagine prevailing.

She sat up suddenly and lurched to her feet. She brandished her seax, the weapon dull and unimpressive in the pale moonlight. The figure stopped dead about twenty paces away and stared in her direction, now entirely still. Brandon was still sleeping to her left, unaware of the drama. Æva hissed and stamped her foot, hoping to rouse him and perhaps unnerve her opponent. Both efforts were in vain. The boy kept on sleeping. The intruder wasn't bothered either.

It took another step forward and then another, its movements so sudden she felt unnerved just by the sight of it. "Who are you?" she demanded, extending her hand to further demonstrate she was armed. A strange gesture followed. The figure raised a hand, its palm extended, and then elongated a single finger like it was about to hold it to its lips. Whoever this was wanted her to remain silent. She didn't feel like obliging them. If she was to die here at the hands of some mystery assassin, she'd make as much noise as she pleased.

"I asked you a question!" That got her a reply, but not as she'd hoped. The figure made a hissing sound, the shaking of its head signalling annoyance. Just as she was about to repeat herself, the hood suddenly came back, revealing the face of her so-far uncommunicative visitor. Æva thought he looked unkempt but unremarkable, except for one thing. He wasn't blond. He didn't have blue eyes. Danes generally did, and this one's face and beard were broad and dark enough to pass for an Englishman. That was something, at least.

The stranger knelt down, his right hand pawing at the air as if wanting her to imitate him. She complied, dropping her weight to hunch on one knee, her mind racing with thoughts on who he was and what he wanted if it were not her death. Moments passed, the seconds turning to minutes, the newcomer perfectly motionless amidst the ambient shadow. Then he moved, fast and sudden, Æva again brandishing her blade as he rushed towards her. He stopped when he was just out of reach, his expression blank as he whispered urgently in her direction.

"Get your boy up. We need to move."

She did as he asked, ushering Brandon into a state of semi-alertness. He jumped at the sight of the stranger, but she calmed him down, hoping any anxiety on his part would pass before it angered their guest. That didn't seem likely. Whoever this man was, he wasn't an immediate threat. He would have killed them already if he were. There was bound to be a good reason why he hadn't. She'd like to live long enough to find out what it was.

At that thought, she heard a sound behind her, like something large and heavy was making its way through the undergrowth. The stranger lurched into action and gripped Æva's left arm, speeding her and Brandon both away from their campsite. She didn't resist. There was nothing aggressive in his touch, and they soon vanished into the long grasses. It was just in time. Whoever was back there was clearly following her, and she felt it more than likely they were not friendly.

They kept on, the stranger releasing his hold on her to better guard their backs. He stayed close, hunched and oddly comforting whilst he scuttled along behind them, his wide, dark eyes and mane of a beard a far cry from the terrible apparition she'd thought him minutes prior. He looked wild, it was true, and his hair was a tangle of knots and split ends cascading down his shoulders, but he wasn't bad. Æva could sense badness just from the feeling others gave off. This one felt faintly familiar. As if she knew him, somehow.

It was several hours until they stopped. Dawn was just beginning to make itself known, the first rays of subdued daylight seeping between the trees. They'd not heard anything in pursuit, but the stranger had hurried them on regardless, his urgency telling Æva he was no friend of the Danes. He was looking back along the haphazard trail they'd used to get here, his chest rising and falling from his exertions, his left hand pressing against the gnarled trunk of a willow tree. All was quiet for a time, the only sounds heard the wind through the leaves and the sweet song of awakening birds. Æva then spoke, her words erupting from her mouth entirely of their own volition.

"Who are you?"

He turned to look at her, his back straightening like he thought he was somehow being inspected or judged. "Eamon," he said. "My name is Eamon. I'm surprised to see you, my lady. I'd have thought you'd be somewhere more to your liking."

"Eamon?" she asked, her mind struggling to place his face within the confines of memory. "Of course!" she said, slightly embarrassed now it all seemed so clear. "You were with us on the road from Offetuna, with Osbert. Ulfcytel…he sent you away for some task or mission, if I recall right?"

"You do," he replied, his gaze again drifting back the way they'd come. "And I fought with your husband in Eastengle. I lived close to Wincestre before that. That was another lifetime, though."

"You knew Alaric?"

"I did. I saw you both, saying goodbye to each other…back when we mustered with the rest of the men at your father-in-law's fortress to make the march to Hringmere. The lad was there too. A sorrowful sight."

"How long have you been out here?" she asked, thinking he must have been stalking the countryside for some considerable time to end up looking so feral.

"Things haven't been going so well for me," he said lightly. "I've been trying to find Osbert. He was taken."

"By whom?"

"The same bastards that have been following you," he muttered darkly. "They would have had you back there, had we not gotten away in time. Did you do something to annoy our Danish overlords?"

"I escaped from them two nights ago," said Eva glumly, "but I didn't know they were following. I thought…"

"Don't worry about it," Eamon said. "We have ways of tracking people we want to find. The Danes are as adept at such things as anyone. Did you do something to them? Kill someone?"

"I did not. They attacked us. I escaped. Cenric…he…"

"Old Cenric?" Eamon asked, turning back around to look her straight in the face. "He was there? Who else was with you? Are they alive?"

"I don't know," she whispered, ashamed and sad. "I ran. They came out of nowhere. Cenric got me and Brandon and told us to run, so we did. I wish…"

"You wish you hadn't?" Eamon asked, correctly interpreting her silence. "Don't beat yourself up about it," he added. "If Cenric had decided it best you run, then it was best you run. He's no fool, that man."

"But the ealdorman," she breathed, "he was with us…it was my fault since I wanted to leave. I…I couldn't stay there anymore."

"Which ealdorman?"

"Ulfcytel," she answered meekly. "I think…I fear he's dead. They all are. All dead because I couldn't stand to stay in Porteceaster. All dead because of me."

"Where was this?" Eamon asked, his face suddenly mere inches from her own. His breath was rank, his beard knotted and sodden, but there was no hiding the concern in his eyes. He deserved to be told. She did as much, describing the events of that night and how they'd hidden from the Danes as they pursued someone through the woods. Then the ambush had come, in the ruins of that burnt, nameless village, the heathens appearing out of the dark to take them by surprise. Eamon listened intently, his expression neutral aside from his wide, penetrating eyes.

"So you just ran off into the night?" She didn't know why he'd asked her that. She'd already told him as much.

"I did," she repeated. "I had no choice. I'm no warrior. Don't judge me."

"That's not what I'm doing. But you've not seen anyone since? Nobody followed?"

"Nobody friendly. We've been lost, wandering. I give what little food I can find to my son. He's all I have now."

Eamon shifted his gaze over to Brandon, his face still blank. After a few moments, he reached under his cloak and slid a small satchel off his shoulder. He knelt down and rifled through it, pawing through its contents with urgency. He eventually let out a grunt of satisfaction, revealing a pair of fresh, if somewhat battered, apples. He threw one over to Brandon, the poor lad almost dropping it as he snatched it from the air. Eamon then handed the other to Æva. She bit into it immediately, the taste sweeter than she'd expected, her words of gratitude sounding mumbled and incoherent as she chewed away with gusto. Brandon was much the same, gnawing at his prize with an enthusiasm born of genuine need.

"So the Ealdorman Ulfcytel is dead?" Eamon had at least had the good grace to wait until Æva had finished before asking.

"I didn't see," she said, wiping at her lips with a tattered sleeve, "but I don't see how he could have escaped. I hope he did."

"If you got away, it could be that others also did," Eamon said thoughtfully. "You must take me back there. You must show me where it happened."

"I can't!" Æva objected. "My son needs rest and nourishment, and it's too dangerous. You saw what happened just earlier. Danes are everywhere!"

Eamon nodded, his eyes narrowing as he again peered at Brandon. The boy looked back at him and held his gaze steadily enough, but Æva could see the fatigue on his face. He was frightened, too. Eamon seemed to sense it, turning back to Æva with a look of sympathy in his eyes.

"I'll get you to Snotingeham," he said. "We can get your son the care he needs."

"Is Edmund there?" Æva asked, thinking Edmund may indeed be located in such a place whilst he raised his armies to take back his kingdom.

"I don't know. I was on my way there when I ran into you. I need help finding Osbert. I'd hoped Edmund might be of assistance."

"What happened with Osbert?"

"We had a special task," said Eamon, his tone somewhat hushed as if he felt he shouldn't be speaking of it. "We had a chance to take revenge for Canterburie. It didn't go well. Now he's captured, and I know not where."

"You fought at Canterburie? With Alaric and Ulfcytel?"

Eamon nodded gravely, like he put some considerable stock in the admission. "I did, and Osbert with them. It's another reason I need to find him. If he..."

He turned away suddenly to stare back the way they'd come. There wasn't anything there, the trees and bushes that had concealed them thus far revealing little of note. Then she listened, slowing her breath. A few seconds passed before she heard it; a faint sound of something she couldn't quite identify. Eamon burst into motion, ushering her and Brandon both further northward. She didn't ask him what was wrong. The man had keen senses. He was a survivor. She'd do well to follow his lead.

Hours passed, Eamon hurrying them through the forest towards what Æva hoped would be the sanctuary of Snotingeham. The going was difficult, the ancient woodland seeming to almost want to slow them with its confused trails and impassable thickets, but Eamon knew what he was doing and they continued to make progress, albeit slowly. They didn't talk, and she didn't ask why he insisted on leading them through such difficult terrain, since it was clear by now that they were being followed. She could hear them, whoever it was, rustling and trampling after them, sometimes distant, sometimes close. She didn't want to think of it. If they kept moving, they should be safe.

It was night by the time they broke cover to risk the main road in the final approach to Snotingeham. Normally it wouldn't be worth the danger, but they'd been unable to lose their pursuer, and as capable as Eamon looked, they couldn't be sure if the one following them was alone or part of a group. Haste would now serve them, and so they rushed on through what was left of the forest, making a dash towards a paved, broken road winding its way towards the darkened horizon.

Another hour went by before Snotingeham appeared out of the night. They were approaching the settlement on its southern side, an encircling wooden palisade hiding much of it from view. Several armed men bearing torches challenged them when they approached a bridge over a ditch, their voices and mannerisms softening slightly when they noticed the painfully exhausted Brandon.

They let them by, one of them even offering Brandon another apple, which he took and ate with gratitude. They passed through the southern gate of the palisade, losing themselves in the shadowed tangle of muddied streets that lay beyond. They ducked into the first inn to present itself, taking a seat close to the flickering hearth and relishing the newfound warmth. Eamon had a few coins on him, and he put these to good use, purchasing bread, water, and three bowls of a rather vivid orange soup. It tasted heavenly despite its colour, and Æva felt almost content, safe in the knowledge they'd escaped whoever had been chasing them.

Eamon left them for a while, returning once he'd obtained information from some of the locals. He didn't bring good news. Edmund wasn't here. Even worse, Sigeferth and Morcar, the two leading thegns of the Five Boroughs, had refused to support him. That meant his entire plan was now up in the air. Æva didn't know what to do. They were lost, she and Brandon, in a town without friends and their only ally looking like he was more beast than man. Things would have been so much simpler if she'd never left Porteceaster. Should she just give up now and return? Should she forget Edmund's war, go back home, and beg Ælfric to take her in again?

She flinched at the thought. Ælfric had wronged her, with deeds so callous she didn't know if she could ever be in the same room with him again. Her ties to his family were also severed, sadly, since Alaric's death had left her without status other than that of a widow people might pity but otherwise fail to take seriously. Edmund had proven himself to be a kind man, and, as much as she thought it strange, fate had seen fit to throw them together in a way that said he might need her as much as she needed him.

There was nothing romantic about that. Æva had already committed herself to the path of celibacy and solitude, and she had no interest, nor ever had had any interest, in any man other than Alaric. Edmund just had a certain quality to him, a kind of vulnerability that Æva suspected was born of his father's undoubtedly poor parenting. Edmund might need somebody like her. Somebody who would listen. Somebody he could let his guard down around. Somebody who wasn't a warrior. It might be her only option. She certainly had nothing to lose in trying to find him.

Brandon looked up at her, his bowl empty. She took his hand, a slight smile on her face, his eyes seeming to sparkle their customary brilliant blue despite the fatigue that so obviously weighed on him. Eamon was quiet, his attention focused on his soup. He let out a single belch upon finishing, his fist hammering into his guts as if hoping to expel the last of it by sheer physical force. Brandon laughed openly, Eamon shooting him a lop-sided grin that spoke of a mischievous side he'd kept hidden until now. That would make sense, Æva thought. He'd been scouring the wilderness for weeks, looking for Osbert. She couldn't imagine he'd had much use for japes and jests then. It was remarkable he could manage it now.

"Better out than in, as my grandmother used to say," said Eamon, still smiling a little. Æva raised an eyebrow. Her grandmother had said the exact same thing, but she wasn't sure it had been meant in such a way. In any other time, she wouldn't want Brandon picking up bad habits, but he looked happy enough now, appearing genuinely amused by the rather vulgar, bearded man of the wilds who sat before them. She wasn't ungrateful. He had saved their lives. It was blind luck that he'd stumbled across them when he had, and Æva simply did not have his sharp senses. Whoever had been sneaking up on her would have killed her had he not led them away. She owed him much.

"I don't think I've thanked you yet," Æva said nervously, hoping to be as precise as possible with her words. "I don't know who was following us, but it was likely nobody we'd want to meet. You saved us. I wish I could repay you somehow."

"Don't worry about it," Eamon grunted. "I'd have done it for anyone, really. Too much innocent blood has been spilled already. I won't see any more. I'm tired of it. Something has to change."

"How so?" Æva asked. "Do you mean by defeating the Danes?"

"That and more. We need to make sure this can't happen again. We had a bad king for years. Some say it wasn't his fault, or it was God's will, but I don't care. We need a man of virtue and strength, one who cares for his people yet will smite down the aggressor without hesitation. It's what's owed."

"Edmund is that man, isn't he?"

"He might be," Eamon answered thoughtfully. "I hope he is. He's gone north, so I heard earlier, but I don't know why. It's surprising Sigeferth didn't raise an army for him…with that decision, I fear our little war is going to become more difficult. What shall become of us?"

"This Sigeferth lives here?" Æva asked. "He might be able to tell us more. We should find him."

"We should. You are a lady of standing, or were…whatever…we have a better chance of getting an audience with him with you here than if it were just me, stinking and dishevelled as I am."

"You don't smell that much," Æva said quickly, hoping to spare his feelings. She felt bad for speaking falsely, even if her intentions were noble. She couldn't just let him talk like that and agree with him, despite him being right. He really did smell.

"I'm a commoner is what I mean," Eamon continued. "Even if you dressed me in the finest silks and shaved this monster of a beard off my chin, I'd still be unsuited for the company of a man like Sigeferth. And he's already let Edmund down…so I can't imagine him being overly friendly to one of his followers. You might turn his head, though."

Æva blushed, feeling suddenly uncomfortable at what she thought was being implied. Eamon seemed to sense her predicament, stressing he hadn't "meant to suggest anything improper", but she knew what he'd meant. She was a lady of noble birth, and Eamon was a common soldier who stank. It was fairly obvious who would stand a better chance of gaining Sigeferth's ear. She was their best shot at getting to speak with him. They could learn much. Perhaps he'd even tell them where Edmund had got to.

They finished eating and headed out into the street in search of Sigeferth's hall. They found it after asking around, the night watchmen leading them straight to it after a rather annoying sequence of questions on who Æva was and why Sigeferth should even care. It was past midnight, so they were told, by the time they reached the front doors of the hall, and the guards on watch were loath to disturb him, but they did, Æva putting on her most authoritative voice to obtain their cooperation. She was surprised it had been so easy. She'd been sleeping out in the open for days now, and whilst Eamon had told her she "looked alright", she couldn't shake the feeling he was just being charitable. She must look as bad as she felt. And that was pretty bad.

The guards returned in the company of a man in his middle years with a kindly yet troubled face. His beard was rapidly turning to silvered grey, and his eyes had a haunted look, but the smile lines around them said he was a man of goodwill, even if he were beset by woes he'd perhaps like to keep secret. His clothes signified his rank, his boots, breecs, and tunic all evidently fashioned with considerable skill and expense, just as the fine fur cloak flowing from his shoulders implied a status far above the armed men who escorted him. This could only be Sigeferth. He'd been awake, even at this late hour. Something must be occupying his attention. Æva hoped it wouldn't hurt their chances.

"Are you Sigeferth?" She'd blurted it out, sounding more eager than she'd intended.

"I am. And I'm told you're a lady from old Ælfric's lands in the South? His...daughter-in-law, is it?"

"That's right, Æva is my name, and this is my son, Brandon." She put her hand to the boy's shoulder, noting with an ache in her chest how he was barely able to remain on his feet. He could rest soon, she hoped.

"In the name of God, lady, the lad looks half-dead, as do you. I'd have you come in and get yourselves warm and rested."

Sigeferth turned and began walking away, the guard on the door gesturing for Æva to follow. She did, Brandon clutched at her side and Eamon just behind, all three of them surprised and relieved at how accommodating Sigeferth had been thus far. The interior of his home was something to admire. It was huge, all polished wood and oaken flooring, looking like it were fit to hold a host of men and have room left over for their horses. A stone hearth dominated the centre of the room, its sizeable chimney rising up toward the ceiling and past what could only be a second floor. Sigeferth sat at a large table just adjacent to it, the warmth from the fire much appreciated after the creeping chill of the streets.

Yet there was an air of sadness to this place. Much of it remained shrouded, the night outside intruding through the windows. Only the light from the fire in the hearth and the candle on the table kept the darkness at bay, and even that had a melancholy feel to it, as if Sigeferth had been sitting here alone and enveloped in a sadness he himself couldn't fathom. It hadn't always been this way. Æva could sense it. This place had seen joyous times in the not-so-distant past. She wondered what had caused such change.

"I have to tell you now that the Ealdorman Ulfcytel was attacked on the road," Eamon suddenly said as he pulled back a chair from Sigeferth's table and sat himself down. The thegn looked up in shock, his eyes then switching to Æva like he expected her to tell him more.

"It's true," she said. "He was escorting me from Hamptonscir with a party of men. We were set upon by Danes, and only me and my boy escaped."

"Why didn't you tell me this immediately?" Sigeferth said sharply, his expression matching his tone. Æva wasn't entirely sure how to answer him. She was exhausted and not thinking straight, and some part of her was eager to forget the ordeals of these past few nights. Eamon was right to bring it up now, but Eamon also didn't have a child to worry about. Æva would always instinctively put Brandon first, and as long as he was at risk or in need, he would remain her number one priority. She couldn't imagine that ever changing.

"The lady is very tired," said Eamon diplomatically, "and is still in shock from the stress of her escape. She was being tracked when I stumbled across her, and whoever was responsible came after us and wouldn't let up. The safety of the boy was our priority, but if you can send somebody out to learn of the ealdorman's fate..."

"Where did this happen?" asked Sigeferth. Ævа's mind began to work frantically. She couldn't remember anything helpful about the ambush. It had been in a ruined village, that she knew, and they'd just escaped another Danish search party in the forest close by. Such a description wouldn't help matters at all. Most of England now consisted of woodland and ruined villages. Then she remembered. The battle site they'd stumbled on; the one Ulfcytel seemed to know something about. That might help. There was every chance Sigeferth knew where it was.

"It started in the forest, several miles north east of a battle site," said Æva carefully. "I don't know which one. Ulfcytel said the king had fought there...and his son, Æthelstan, had fallen. We'd made it out of the forest to escape the Danes...they were chasing somebody...but they caught us soon after. Then I fled. I had to get my son..."

Sigeferth moved off to speak with the men standing guard at the hall entrance. One of them promptly vanished into the street, Sigeferth pushing the door shut as a blast of cold air snaked its way inside. He wandered back over to their table at a more leisurely pace, his look strangely apologetic.

"Forgive my manners," he said quietly, resuming his seat across from them. "I like to think I'm capable of juggling priorities, and the safety of an ealdorman is more important than idle conversation. All the same, forgive me."

"I understand and agree," said Æva sincerely. "So you're sending men out to find Ulfcytel? I fear he was overwhelmed. There was nothing I could..."

"You don't have to explain yourself to me, lady. I know how it is out there, and I'm sure there really was nothing you could do. I thank you, though, for giving us a location. I remember that battle perfectly. I was there."

"You were?" asked Eamon.

"I was indeed...with Edmund and his brother and all of our armies. We had to stop the king paying Thorkell, you see. We feared he'd bankrupt the realm. Little did we know that would come later...and we'd lose Æthelstan. It wasn't worth it. It wasn't worth the cost."

"So you were close with Æthelstan and Edmund?" Æva asked, thinking she knew the answer to her question already.

"We were," Sigeferth said glumly, "my brother and I...Morcar...we did our best for them when they were boys. Their father, you understand, was not always...attentive. A sad thing. But the damage has been done, I fear."

"Damage to Edmund?" Æva asked, suspecting again that she knew what Sigeferth was about to say.

"Yes, and a great deal of it. There's nothing I can do about that now. But I see I'm lacking in manners again. Would you be needing nourishment? A bed to rest in? Your boy here looks like he's way ahead of us in that regard."

Æva looked over at Brandon. He was asleep, his arms folded neatly upon the table to cushion his head. The poor fellow couldn't help himself. He needed quality sleep, and he wouldn't get it like that. "Do you have room for us?" she asked Sigeferth, thinking it highly likely he did, unless he had an entire army resting upstairs.

"Of course," Sigeferth said with a smile. "We don't get too many visitors these days, and my children will appreciate the company. If you'll follow me..."

Sigeferth got up, Æva following his lead and rousing Brandon from his stupor so that she might guide him upstairs. They had to pass through what looked to be some kitchens first, Eamon following at a distance, the stairs they then climbed leading them all up to a second level. It was a maze up here, the wooden corridors all leading this way and that, but Sigeferth knew where he was going and Brandon was soon tucked up in bed, several woollen blankets ensuring he was secure against the chill. They headed downstairs again as soon as Æva was sure Brandon was very much asleep, Sigeferth this time plying them with several cups of "honeyed mead" he claimed was his own special concoction. Eamon drank it all down in one, belching yet again. Sigeferth merely laughed and got him another. Either this thegn was particularly easy-going, or he was genuinely happy to have company. Æva suspected it was a combination of both.

"So what exactly brought you here?" Sigeferth asked. "Does old Ælfric need something from me? We've not had a chance to speak in a good while now."

"It's nothing like that, I'm afraid," Æva said. "I found out...the Ealdorman Ulfcytel told me some things...about Ælfric, and...I couldn't stay there. Not knowing what I know. I just regret putting anyone in danger. I wish I had stayed in Hamptonscir now, if only for their sake."

"We'll find Ulfcytel if he's out there," Sigeferth said reassuringly, "but this squabble with Ælfric...forgive me if I'm prying, but you are married to one of his sons, no? Surely he had something to say in response to Ulfcytel's words?"

"Alaric is dead," said Æva simply. "It was partly for that reason Ulfcytel felt I should know the truth about Ælfric."

"Which is?" Sigeferth had the look of somebody who knew he was pushing his luck. Æva appreciated his hospitality, but she wasn't in the mood for gossip, nor would she stoop to such a thing even if circumstances were different.

"It's complicated," she said delicately, knowing this was at least true, "and very close to my heart. I'd rather not..."

"I understand," nodded Sigeferth, "and I apologise if I seem unduly inquisitive. Like I said, I've not spoken with Ælfric in a long time, and then suddenly his daughter-in-law turns up out of nowhere looking like she's been on the run for her life...these are strange and difficult days."

"For all of us," muttered Eamon, his cup again empty. They both looked to him, Æva and Sigeferth, expecting him to say more, but he remained quiet, his eyes dark and troubled. Sigeferth poured him some more mead, the gesture causing him to break his silence with gratitude. "By any chance," he continued, his attention still on Sigeferth, "have you seen a young man pass through here? He's blond and light on his feet...goes by the name of Osbert."

Sigeferth thought for a moment before shaking his head. "I have not, but any number of men of that description could have come through here and escaped my notice. This is a friend of yours, I assume?"

"Yes," said Eamon, "but we fell afoul of the enemy some weeks ago. I know he's alive as I saw him captured, and I kept on their trail all the way to Lundenburg...but I lost them in the busy streets. I was heading north when I discovered the lady here."

"How was he apprehended?" asked Æva, hoping Eamon wouldn't mind giving her some more details.

"We were on a special mission," Eamon said.

"And what mission was that?" asked Sigeferth.

"I'm not sure I'm permitted to talk about it, but let's just say we sought to deal with a traitor, one who very much still deserves death."

"That all sounds rather dark and sordid," said Sigeferth.

"It needs to be done. If you'd fought at Canterburie...you'd understand."

"I see," said Sigeferth, unwilling to prod any further. "And I shall have to take your word for it. I heard about what happened to the Holy City. It's an awful thing, it really is. Edmund was here when we heard the news. He'd been inconsolable after his brother's death, and we..."

Sigeferth paused, like he was suddenly deep in thought or dredging up memories that were a source of profound heartache. "Are you alright?" asked Æva, feeling sadder still just from looking at him.

"I am," he said, snapping out of it. "I was just thinking on Edmund. He and I were close, and I still wish him well, despite the recent...upset."

"What's that?" Æva asked, hoping she wasn't annoying him with so many questions.

"I couldn't do as he asked," Sigeferth said after some hesitation. "I couldn't raise an army for him. We had to submit to Svienn, you see. Our forces were depleted after the battle at Bernecestre, and we had no choice. Submit or see your people die. So I submitted."

"So where is Edmund now?" Æva hoped he was all right. She didn't know much about the relationship between him and Sigeferth, but if the old man here was sitting up late, alone and troubled, she imagined Edmund also had hurt feelings. They must have been close to wound each other like that. Harsh words had undoubtedly been spoken.

"He's gone to Euerwic, most likely," came the answer. "Archbishop Wulfstan has called for us all to attend him. He wants to lecture us on the need for a new king."

"A new king?" asked Æva, confused. "Does he intend to rebel against Svienn?"

"Svienn is dead," Sigeferth said casually, "killed by an apparition of our own Saint Edmund, so they say. You've not heard of this? News like that usually travels fast."

"I have not!" Æva gasped, her shock getting the better of her. "And Saint Edmund killed him? Who says that?"

"Rumour is what it is," said Eamon, clearly unimpressed. "If he's dead, then there'll be something more mundane behind it...but it's welcome news. May he be held to account for all the evil he wrought."

"Oh, that he will," Sigeferth concurred, "but I wouldn't be so quick to dismiss the idea that our saint had a hand in this. Svienn had recently attacked his resting place and slaughtered his monks. God wouldn't have just let that go."

"He lets so much else go," muttered Eamon, his eyes flashing briefly with something Æva took for both anger and hurt.

"So what will Edmund do in Euerwic?" Æva asked Sigeferth. "And why are you not there? Don't you want to hear what Bishop Wulfstan has to say?"

"Of course...which is why my brother, Morcar, is there. I didn't want to face Edmund, if I'm honest. I can't see him like that, not like he was the last time we spoke. He was so...hurt. Like when he lost his brother after Bernecestre. He didn't understand that we couldn't help him. He wouldn't listen, and then he left. So here I remain. I can't rest because of it. I fear for him."

"He's a strong man," Eamon said bluntly, taking yet another quaff of mead. "And I'm sure he'll come to understand your position in time, just as you might come to understand his."

Sigeferth frowned at Eamon's cryptic remark. Personally, Æva was inclined to side with Sigeferth in all this, thinking it more than likely he'd been threatened by Svienn into swearing allegiance to him at the point of a sword. She could understand Edmund's perspective, but nothing would be helped by recriminations. With Svienn gone, there was an opportunity here for reconciliation. Perhaps she could help with that.

"I can go to Euerwic for you," she said suddenly, surprised at her own boldness. "Edmund has been very kind to me in the past, and I like to think he'd be willing to talk to me. I could tell him how you feel. It might help."

Sigeferth pondered a moment, taking the opportunity to sip from his cup. "Who are you to him?" he asked, staring into the fire still smouldering in the hearth to his right. Æva realised then how strange she must look. She'd turned up on this man's doorstep in the dead of night, alongside her son and a peculiar companion, with little explanation to offer other than a tale of woe and family discord. Sigeferth had no reason to trust her, and he'd been generous already in taking pity on them and letting them inside. How indeed could Æva help him heal his relationship with a man who would be king?

"I don't know," she finally said, "but he reunited me with my son, twice, and made me a promise when my husband died. It brought me comfort."

"And what promise was that?" Sigeferth asked, his voice softening.

"That he'd rule well…that he'd create a future where people wouldn't suffer as I had. Like we all have. Like our children have."

"A lofty goal," Sigeferth nodded, "and I'm sure in his heart Edmund wishes to create that future. But what do you get out of this, lady? What do you stand to gain by speaking to him on my behalf?"

"It's the right thing to do," shrugged Æva. "It sounds like you mean something to each other, and I'm sure he's still as upset as you are. If I can help, then why not try?"

Sigeferth smiled slightly, his eyes for a moment losing the troubled look they'd had ever since he'd opened his doors to them. "I can see why you two might get on," he said. "Edmund, too, has a simple nobility to him. He always did, ever since he was a boy."

"So I'll go to Euerwic?" she pressed, wanting a clear answer from him.

"I think you should rest first," Sigeferth said, his eyebrows arched and quizzical as he looked her up and down. "No offence, lady, but you've clearly had a rough time of it. Sleep and…a wash might be in order." He looked over at Eamon. "For both of you."

"I'm aware I smell most foul," admitted Eamon, his words all the more amusing given their sincerity. "But I'd ask you, Æva, if you'd allow me to travel with you? You'll need protection, and I, too, need to speak with Edmund. Osbert is missing, as you know. I need to tell Edmund what happened so we can see what can be done."

"And who are you to Edmund?" Sigeferth inquired, apparently seeing fit to ask Eamon the same question he'd put to Æva.

"I'm nobody," Eamon answered immediately. "Just another man called into service…I marched with the husband of the lady here as we hurried to aid the Ealdorman Ulfcytel in Eastengle."

"You fought at Hringmere then." Sigeferth was making a statement. Eamon nodded in response. "And what was that like?" the thegn then asked, his eyes again troubled.

"Hell," came Eamon's reply. "It was hell, or so I thought then."

"There was worse to come?" inquired Sigeferth, his face darkening further.

"Yes. I fought at Canterburie and was captured there, again with the lady's husband, Alaric. That was hell, of a sort that made Hringmere look like an argument between friends. It's one thing to face the enemy in battle and know you may die, but at least do so facing them head-on, with axe and shield firmly in hand. I had no such assurances as a prisoner. We were surrounded by death, suffering...evil. I learned then that it's possible to envy the dead. Pray, both of you, that you never have to endure such a lesson."

****

Cenric stumbled out of the nettled bushes, the top of his head catching on an overhanging branch he'd not seen in the overbearing darkness. He staggered and then fell, the wound in his stomach again opening as he slammed into the ground. The breath was knocked from his lungs, leaving him gasping for several moments until he somehow managed to stand, his breecs and armour soaked rust-red. By rights, he should be dead, but he couldn't afford such an indulgence. He'd seen Æva, in the company of some hooded stranger he didn't know what to make of. He had to reach her. He had to make sure she was safe.

He managed to put one foot in front of the other, somehow using up what he felt must be close to the last of his strength to get himself on a narrow road heading north. He'd been in the forest for what seemed like days, his escape from the battle a miracle considering he was quite sure everyone apart from him had been slain. He'd made it hard for them, killing at least three and seriously wounding two others, but numbers and surprise were with the Danes, and the outcome had never been in doubt. Ulfcytel had fallen, his bulk crashing to the earth like a felled tree. It had all been over from that point on. Hope receded with the passing of yet another hero. Cenric wished he'd never lived to witness it.

He'd made about a hundred yards further up the road when his legs gave out yet again. He lay there for a time, a few minutes, or hours, for all he knew, drifting in and out of consciousness and trying to summon some feeling back into his limbs. His wound was likely fatal, that he did know, and he remembered the man who'd done it to him, recalling well enough the sick glee that had lit up his face when he'd opened Cenric's stomach to the elements. Cenric had killed him, of course, his blade splitting the flesh of his jugular as he hammered it home with a withering scream of hate and pain. He'd gone into one of his furies then, like back in Suthhamtunam when Æva and Brandon had been seized by Eadwulf's men. He wasn't complaining. It had enabled him to somehow fight his way clear. He'd stumbled upon evidence of Æva's passing about a day later. He'd hoped to save her again.

There was not much of a chance of that now. That stranger had spirited her away just as Cenric had discovered her campsite, and he was fast, too fast for Cenric to catch up. He'd tried calling out, imploring them to stop, but his voice had failed him, the bruise he'd earned when a Dane had smashed the haft of his axe into his throat forbidding anything other than a pained gurgle. If only they'd heard him. He could have made sure Æva was safe. He'd made that promise, to God and to Alaric. Now he'd failed. He was going to die out here.

He managed a few more feet, crawling on his hands upon the hard, unforgiving stones. Blood continued to pour from his wounds, leaving a sickly, yellow-red trail in his wake. He was fading fast, and when he finally stopped, his breath rattling in his lungs, only a few thoughts continued to repeat in his mind. He'd failed Æva, but he'd tried to do right by her, and as he closed his eyes, he fancied he saw his family, his wife and girls, his two boys and then...a third. His third son, or the man who had become like a son, giving him purpose again as he watched him grow into a hero of his own making. Alaric was waiting for him. They were all waiting for him. It was going to be all right. It was all going to be all right.

Cenric died face down on the road, his body split and broken in a half dozen places. There was no eulogy to mark his passing, no heartfelt words that might otherwise honour the legacy of a man of compassion and valour both. When a group of traders rode by the next morning, they merely pushed him off the byway, taking him for just another dead Englishman on just another day in a dying England. His body rolled down a slight incline and came to rest upon a cushion of grasses, face up towards the sky, his eyes half closed and a slight smile upon his face. His right hand was held up to clutch something at his neck, and it had not strayed despite the rude treatment of his body, his fingers and palm firmly pressing around the wooden crucifix, never to be undone. Just as he had never been undone. Cenric had fought the good fight, and whilst he may not have finished the race, he'd kept the Faith. That was enough.

XIII

"…know this for the truth, dear friends…that this world is in haste, and it nears its end."

Everyone looked up, waiting for the archbishop to continue. He stood there at his oak and stone pulpit, his hard eyes flicking from face to face as if daring anyone to disagree. The austere majesty of Euerwic's cathedral stretched out behind and before him, the stark, echoing interior and soaring, venerable stonework serving to awe anyone with the good fortune to witness it. It was close to midday, and the whole place was lit up with the first rays of the winter sun, the light pouring through the cathedral's high, deeply coloured windows to bathe those within in an assortment of shimmering greens and reds.

Edmund looked further towards the ceiling, noting the forest of thick-set wooden beams that crisscrossed his vision before the heavy thatch of the roof came into view. Like many holy places in England, this cathedral was made from wood as well as stone, yet everything here still had a sense of deep permanence to it, as though the spirits of men long lost to the ages remained here for the sake of piety. This was an old, old building, with a history that went back to the dawn of Christendom in these lands. Wulfstan had been right to deliver his sermon here.

"…because it is ever worldly, the longer our world lasts, the worse it becomes…" Wulfstan continued, his grim words matched by his equally grim appearance, "…and so it must greatly worsen, due to the sins of the people, before the Anti-Christ finally comes."

That held everyone's attention, although Edmund suspected he couldn't be the only one wondering how things could get any worse. He also wasn't sure what sins "the people" could have committed that would warrant their present misery, especially since the common folk, in his experience, almost always lacked the vice and stupidity of the supposedly "higher" orders. England's problems were caused by its rulers. Wulfstan was almost certainly aware of that, but he would also know he wouldn't make too many friends by pointing it out.

"…indeed, there will be darkness throughout the world," Wulfstan said somberly. "So know now that the Devil has led this nation astray for very many years, and that little loyalty has remained among men…"

Edmund peered over his shoulder at those last words, hoping beyond hope that Eadric, of all people, might be seen in the audience. He wasn't here, as expected, but his absence was a shame nonetheless. Edmund would have liked to drag him from the crowd and have him denounced in front of everyone. He'd ask the bishop for permission before he took things further. This was a sacred place, after all.

"…too many crimes have gone unchecked in the land," Wulfstan went on, "and too few men have considered in good faith what one ought to do to remedy them. Evil after evil was piled upon the other, and injustice was spread widely…we have thus endured many injuries and insults…and if we seek a remedy to these, we must look to God with greater sincerity than we have in the past. Because we have earned the miseries that now lie upon us. We have earned them, and…"

Edmund's mind started to wander again, finding Wulfstan's predictable rhetoric on how England deserved its fate to be more than distasteful. He looked down at himself, thinking how out of place he appeared compared with the otherwise august company surrounding him. The thegns who had answered Wulfstan's call were all suitably attired, their fine clothes and regal bearing marking them out from the overworked commoner even at a distance. Edmund's party were a little different. They were all armoured, dressed as they had been on the road, and whilst they'd all left their weapons at the door, their appearance was designed to send a message. England was at war, and a nation at war needs a warrior king. He hoped anyone who beheld him now would understand that.

"...and so great is the need for every man to respect God's law and pay God's dues rightly," said the bishop, his grave words still echoing out from his vantage point atop the pulpit. "For even among heathen peoples no one would dare withhold that which is seen as due to false gods...yet everywhere we withhold God's dues altogether...in heathen lands too one dares not curtail, within or without the temple, anything brought to the false gods and entrusted as an offering...but we have entirely stripped God's houses of everything fitting, within and without, and God's servants are everywhere deprived of honour and protection."

That brought a sad smile to Edmund's face. There was nothing amusing in what had been said, but the archbishop was clearly taking a shot at his father's heregeld. He'd heard of many cases in history where churches had been ransacked of their valuables to pay off the Norse invader, and his father's reign had been no different. If anything, he'd brought such disgraceful antics to new heights. His father was the King who Paid, as much as he could and when it was demanded. It didn't seem to matter if the money was not his to give, nor who was wronged with the getting of it. It was a marvel that anyone could want him back. Edmund assumed Wulfstan would be getting to that sticky point very shortly. He'd told him as much when he'd come to see him the night before. Edmund could only wonder how the other thegns might take it.

"...God's dues have diminished too long in this land...and the laws of the people have deteriorated entirely too greatly since Edgar died..."

That was an interesting reference Wulfstan had made there. Edmund's grandfather, not that he'd known him, had generally been well thought of. Wulfstan appeared to be implying that everything had gone wrong with his death, or that the demise of Edgar had ushered in a time of general faithlessness. Given that they couldn't bring his grandfather back, was the bishop suggesting they needed to emulate him in some way?

"...widows are widely forced to marry in unjust ways, and too many are impoverished and fully humiliated...and poor, innocent men are sorely betrayed and cruelly defrauded and sold widely out of this land into the power of foreigners...and infants are enslaved by means of cruel injustices..."

Edmund looked around again, hoping to read the audience and how these hard truths were being received. He saw Uhtred a few paces back, surrounded by his sycophants, but his face was unreadable, the archbishop's words on the harsh treatment of the helpless and vulnerable moving him little. He saw Morcar a short distance behind him and to the left, but he also looked untroubled, yet that changed the moment he saw Edmund looking over at him. Edmund turned back to Wulfstan quickly. He didn't want to talk to Morcar. It was just as well Sigeferth did not appear to have accompanied him.

"...the laws of God are hated, and His teaching despised; therefore we all are disgraced through God's anger, so let him know it who is able...that that same anger will become universal, although one may not think so, to all people, unless God protects us."

Edmund did not disagree. Without God, they were lost. He just wondered how the archbishop had chosen to interpret God's anger. The Lord couldn't have wished Thorkell the Tall on them. That savage had been shot straight from the bowels of hell. There was no lesson to be learned in having such a darkness sweep over them. They'd all heard about what had happened at Canterburie. There was no way that was somehow God's will.

"...there has been military devastation and hunger, burning and bloodshed in nearly every district time and again...and stealing and slaying, plague and pestilence, malice and hate..."

Wulfstan's blood was up, his words gaining greater and greater strength the longer he spoke. Edmund was, in some ways, enjoying the spectacle, thinking a proper recitation of England's woes was long overdue, especially when delivered to an audience of those entrusted with authority. The bishop thundered on and on, raging at the injustices that had afflicted the common man, but he didn't think them faultless either, claiming with great lamentation how fathers had learned to mistreat sons and vice versa so that norms of kinship and loyalty were all but forgotten. Edmund was wondering whether that was true when he suddenly remembered the fate of his dear uncle. He was dead, killed in a plot hatched by Edmund's own father. He bowed his head, his cheeks flushed with emotion. He didn't want to think of it. He'd stand here and listen in penance. It was all he could do.

"...for there are in this nation many traitors, in both matters of the Church and the state, and also there are many among us who betray their lords in various ways...a man might betray his lord to death, or drive him living into exile...and both have come to pass! Edward was betrayed and then killed, and Æthelred was driven out of this land! And too many, too many others, innocent people, have been wronged or killed across the country..."

Wulfstan's heated words finally provoked a response from his previously unmovable audience. The thegns gasped in unison and looked about, shocked and perhaps also offended. Edmund's eyes were burning, the mention of Edward and his untimely death catching him off guard. He'd never known the boy, obviously, but he was almost a legend in death, and Edmund knew well enough how his murder had haunted his father throughout his life. He couldn't have done it, since Æthelred had been so young at the time, but that hadn't lifted the burden of angst from his shoulders. It had eaten away at him, year after year, his dreams afflicting him thick and fast as his realm descended into chaos.

And yet the bishop was wrong about Æthelred's eventual flight to Normandy. He'd fled whilst men were still fighting, and although many could argue he'd had little choice, it was the invasion of Svienn Forkbeard that had provoked his flight rather than some kind of universal treachery on the part of everyone in England. Supposed nobles like Uhtred had let him down, sure, and the riot in Lundenburg hadn't helped, but in a way both things were a product of his own making. Æthelred had not been a good king, and he was in part responsible for the promotion of the unjust and treacherous men Wulfstan was currently raging against. He doubted that would make it into his sermon. Edmund already knew how this would end.

The archbishop kept on, addressing the myriad evils that had befallen the country, his audience still shaken by the mention of their martyred King Edward and their absent King Æthelred. Edmund winced when Wulfstan again returned to England's military defeats, claiming over and over that it was the "consent of God" that had allowed the Danes to triumph over them. Edmund again looked into the crowd, hoping that perhaps the Ealdorman Ulfcytel might have somehow joined them to offer his opinion. Edmund couldn't imagine him agreeing with Wulfstan on this. Ulfcytel had been the heart and soul of the English resistance for years now. He couldn't possibly think their defeats were somehow down to God's displeasure with him and his men. Edmund shook his head sadly and turned back to Wulfstan. Ulfcytel wasn't here. Neither was the Ealdorman Ælfric. Edmund remained without allies. He hoped he wouldn't come to regret that too much.

"...men are more ashamed now of good deeds than of misdeeds, because too often good deeds are met with derision, and the God-fearing are blamed entirely too much...and men are reproached, and all too often greeted with contempt for loving what is right and fearing God..."

Beside him, Wulfhild nudged Edmund, giving him a cryptic wink when he turned to look at her. He assumed she thought Wulfstan's words somehow applied to him, perhaps thinking he fit the description of a God-fearing man who was otherwise unappreciated by his peers. Edmund pondered this implication, his mind eventually drifting to how much he admired his sister for staying at his side through all this. She must miss Ulfcytel terribly, but she hadn't allowed a heavy heart to get in the way of supporting her brother when he needed it most. Things couldn't be all that bad among families then, as Wulfstan had otherwise suggested. There was at least one loyal person in the kingdom, doing her duty as best she could. He'd make a point of mentioning that to Wulfstan if he ever stopped talking.

It didn't look like that would be anytime soon. The archbishop suddenly developed a flair for the historical, claiming that there was once a certain scholarly Briton, named Gildas, who had claimed his people's sins had "infuriated God so excessively" that He'd allowed them to be conquered by the forebears of the modern-day English. Wulfstan dwelled for some time on Gildas' account of what his people were believed to have done, listing their sins and noting by implication how similar they were to the people of today. He took exception, however, to anyone who might presume to think the sins of the past were equal to the sins of the present, saying "we know of worse deeds among the English than we have heard of anywhere among the Britons" and that therefore "there is a great need for us to take thought for ourselves and to intercede eagerly with God himself."

Wulfstan paused, his fingers drumming across the wooden lectern that held his own personal and elaborately decorated Bible. He looked tired, like he'd expended most of his energy haranguing them all, his normally skeletal appearance now positively deathly as he beheld them with his small, fierce eyes. He took a deep breath, the inhalation rattling in his throat, and continued speaking, his final words at least something all decent men could agree on.

"And so let us do as is necessary for us...turn towards the right and abandon the wrong, and eagerly atone for what we previously transgressed. Let us love God and follow God's laws and do that which we promised when we received baptism...let us order words and deeds justly, and cleanse our thoughts with zeal, and keep oaths and pledges carefully, and have some loyalty between us without evil practice. And let us often reflect upon the great judgement, to which we all shall go, and let us save ourselves from the fires of hell and gain for ourselves the glories and joys that God has prepared for those who work His will in the world. God help us. Amen."

Silence fell, Wulfstan's final "amen" only getting a murmured response from those assembled, Edmund included. When the archbishop spoke again, he seemed even more severe, his long, pointed fingers flicking through the heavyset Bible before him with practised precision.

"I would like to remind you all that what I've said here is not mere opinion. The Apostle Paul was clear enough on one's duties when it comes to earthly authority. Everyone is to submit to the governing authority, for there is no authority aside from that which God has established. Whoever rebels against the authority is rebelling against what God Himself has put in place, and those who do so only bring judgement upon themselves."

Edmund felt his ears burning, and his sense of discomfort increased when he heard several people whisper his name. He didn't turn around this time, preferring to keep his eyes on Wulfstan. He knew what he was driving at. He wasn't begrudging Edmund for failing to submit to Svienn, and those whispering behind him were fools to think so. No sane, upstanding Christian would say that Svienn's authority was valid in the eyes of God. His conduct at Sancte Eadmundes Byrig put paid to that notion. The archbishop had other kings in mind when he spoke of authority. Edmund's father was one of them.

"Authority is something we should all be thinking on right now," Wulfstan said, "especially when we ourselves have been given some degree of authority, large or small. Our moral and spiritual failures stem from a misuse of that authority...and for that, we are all guilty. And yet our greatest sin I've already alluded to...our good king, Æthelred, was driven into exile by our own doings. We must have him back."

Pandemonium erupted. Several thegns to Wulfhild's left immediately began howling in outrage. They were soon joined by others, yet Wulfstan weathered the cacophony, facing down the outraged nobles with a look of pained forbearance. Edmund scowled towards the troublemakers, hoping his displeasure would help bring an end to the commotion. He didn't understand such an intemperate display. He did not agree with the archbishop's decision either, but this kind of behaviour was unseemly. Wulfstan was owed respect, and they were standing in a house of God. To forget either was foolish.

The shouting eased off, one man looking like he was about to panic and flee upon making eye contact with Edmund's withering gaze. Edmund noticed a few things from their reactions to what had been said, all of which helped him understand a bit more about the kind of men he was dealing with. Uhtred himself had remained perfectly calm, as had everyone around him. Many of the thegns here were in some way under his authority, it was true, but he was entirely unruffled, almost as if he knew Wulfstan had intended to use this occasion to call for Æthelred's return.

Morcar was also unflustered, but that was Morcar. There was no telling what he really thought, although Edmund surmised it likely he wasn't happy. Edmund hadn't heard his father state it explicitly, but it seemed very possible he might indeed blame

Morcar and Sigeferth both for the death of Æthelstan at Bernecestre. If Æthelred returned to the throne, there would be a reckoning. As hurt as Edmund was by their sudden refusal to support him, he didn't want to see the two thegns suffer. He'd have to do something. This very moment seemed like as good a time as any.

"I would be heard, if you're willing, archbishop," announced Edmund, doing his best to appear respectful when addressing Wulfstan. The man was silent for a few moments, all eyes drifting to Edmund in apprehension at his sudden intervention. "I'm not finished," said Wulfstan bluntly, "but out of respect for your station and the mother who bore you, I will allow you to say a few words."

That was enough. Edmund moved a few paces forward, placing himself directly below the archbishop's pulpit so all could have a clear look at him. "I won't keep you long," he began, putting his hands on his hips and standing as tall as he could. "You all know me. You all know the campaign I've waged these past weeks to salvage something from the calamity that has befallen us. No man here can say I've not tried to do what is right with what little I have. Sadly, not everyone can say the same of my father. Inviting him back is a mistake. You already have a king. I'm standing right here."

Somebody laughed, Edmund's temper flaring as he caught sight of a distinct smirk upon Uhtred's face. Nobody said anything, not a single word. "Did you not hear me?" Edmund asked, the bitterness he felt impossible to disguise. "I am the heir to the throne, vacated by my father after he fled the realm after years of ill advice and ill fortune. You know I'm right. Let us make new beginnings here, rather than dragging ourselves back to the past."

Silence reigned. Edmund had gone through much in his life, but he'd never felt quite so painfully awkward as he did now. It continued, the seconds feeling like hours, not a single soul making the slightest sound in his support. It was the most embarrassing spectacle he'd ever endured, and Edmund was not one for feeling shame over what he saw as a simple statement of fact. These men were fools for not supporting him. He'd have them know it.

"Is this it then?" he said, disgusted and hurt by the reaction he beheld. "You'd go back to the way things were, with a king who reacts to foreign invaders by paying them rather than fighting them? A king under the sway of a poisonous dog like Eadric of Mierċe, who even now finds refuge with the Danes? This is the path you would choose for us?"

Uhtred suddenly broke from the crowd to make his way to join Edmund at the front of the assembly. "I fear our young friend has failed to heed the archbishop's wise words," he announced. "We've tried everything so far," he continued, addressing those before him as much as Edmund, "but neither guile nor skill at arms has kept the enemy at bay. Returning to what is pleasing to God is our only option. We need the king he appointed to rule us. We need Æthelred."

A murmur of agreement sounded among the thegns, although Edmund noted that Morcar seemed unmoved by Uhtred's words. "Are we really to believe that, Uhtred?" Edmund asked. "Are we really to believe that, after you submitted to Svienn and his army for your own sake, you've suddenly turned to God?"

"I had no choice, and I know many standing here with us went through the same. There was no resisting Svienn, but now the Lord has shown us mercy by striking him down. We owe it to God to see this blessing as an opportunity to do His will."

More agreement rumbled from the throng, this time more spirited and overt. Uhtred was playing up to them, trying to make out that this, his cowardice and theirs, was just an unfortunate accident that could be set right. Edmund wasn't going to let that slide.

"You had all of Norþanhymbre at your back. You had all that, and yet you just capitulated to the invader without so much as drawing a sword. You're a coward, Uhtred. And you are no friend to my father."

"I'm sorry you feel that way, Edmund, but I'll have you know I don't intend for there to be bad blood between us. You may want to be king, and perhaps you will yet, but this is beyond both of us now. We need to get things right with the Lord. If it's God's will, you'll be on the throne one day, and all this can be put behind us."

"My husband would not agree," hissed Wulfhild as she stepped forward to make her own surprise intervention. "Ulfcytel has promised his sword to Edmund. Even now, he fights for him down south alongside the Ealdorman Ælfric. They fight for a new dawn, not a return to the night we all endured for too long."

"A brother and sister seeking to undermine their own father," muttered Uhtred, his head shaking from side to side in forced disapproval. "Is this right, my lords?" he asked, raising his voice. "Does this sit well with all of you? This base treachery of ungrateful children? Isn't this exactly the kind of thing the good archbishop just warned us about? Will we risk God's wrath by letting it stand?"

The response from the crowd was more furious than Edmund had expected. They raged at him and Wulfhild both, pointing fingers and brandishing fists. Edmund found himself agape, unable to immediately process what he was seeing. They were so different, these men of noble birth, from everyone else in the kingdom. The honest and supposedly simple folk flocked to Edmund whenever they saw him. So many were camped outside Euerwic even now, waiting for him to return and lead them on to what they hoped would be a better future with a better king. These baying thegns had nothing in common with such men. They were out for themselves. None of them really believed Uhtred's pious words. This was rank opportunism. It stank.

Wulfstan intervened, his painfully sharp voice cutting through the outcry. "This is a house of the Lord!" he cried, his arms held up over his head in exasperation, "and I will have you reminded of it! Act properly now, or be gone from this place!"

"We shall do as you wish!" Uhtred thundered, his eyes still on their mutual audience. "But know that we will not tolerate impertinence towards our true king! If there are those who would defy God's will and refuse to support the return of Æthelred, then let them depart from us!"

The crowd again erupted into hysterics, their frenzied consensus suggesting that Edmund, Wulfhild, and their escorts should leave lest they "offend God". Edmund turned away from them to fix Uhtred with a hard stare. The ealdorman wilted a little beneath it, his eyes unsure and unsteady, like he did indeed still fear Edmund despite besting him here. The truth was in there. Uhtred owed his position to Æthelred, just as he'd owed his survival to Svienn when he'd made the decision to bow to him. There was only expediency here, not principle. Uhtred wanted Æthelred back because it suited his interests, and he'd likely turn on him again when it proved profitable. That was the way of things in Uhtred's world. Edmund might pity him, if he were not so dangerous.

He moved over to join his sister, and they began to walk back towards the cathedral's entrance, their men following. Wulfstan again called for calm, but the thegns were not listening. They continued to bellow and shout when Edmund tried to move through them, many only stepping aside at the last second as if daring him to collide with them. Edmund wasn't intimidated, but Wulfhild was unused to such things and looked close to panic. The crowd saw it. One of them was stupid enough to act on it.

Edmund wasn't sure what he'd hoped to do, but laying a hand on his sister was likely one of the more serious mistakes he'd made in his life. Edmund took that hand in his own and crushed it with all due malice, his forehead then colliding with the bridge of the man's nose to send him staggering backwards into his howling peers. Edmund stepped forward to tower over the now prone and weeping form before him, the other thegns deciding caution was the preferred option as they collectively stepped back and away. Edmund's men formed around him, their shoulders squared and fists clenched. Edmund stood there for several seconds, his breath heavy with anger, the fool he'd struck still sobbing and mewling before him.

"I came here with good intentions," Edmund simmered, his admittedly quiet words razor-sharp with intent. "But I can see now none of you wish to see this realm enjoy better days. The heathens attack again and again...and you do nothing...they return with a vast army...and you bow to them...and now you would defy me and have my incapable father return so you can again manipulate him from the shadows?"

Nobody breathed a word. They all just stared at him, some resentful, others fearful, but none with anything approaching respect. Even Wulfstan looked very much perturbed, eyeing Edmund like he and his party were common criminals. Edmund shot him a look of disgust before turning to leave. These people were all fools. Precious few of them really believed Æthelred was somehow God's king. His return would do nothing but repeat the hardships of the past. He then realised again that wasn't why they wanted him. Æthelred was to be their stooge, manipulated this way and that as just another unfortunate tool in this never-ending game of intrigue. It made him sick. He'd have vengeance upon all of them for this.

They left the cathedral, Wulfhild, Edmund, and their guards all striding out into the chill sunlight. Euerwic looked as it had done when they'd first arrived, its inhabitants going about their lives in their own myopic, carefree fashion, not one of them paying Edmund much attention even with his furious appearance. The heavy doors slammed shut behind them, and Edmund turned at the sound to see Morcar emerge from their shadow. He must have followed them without them noticing, and now he had something to discuss. Edmund wasn't sure if he could stomach it. He'd had enough disappointment for one day.

"What do you want?" Edmund growled, his appetite for confrontation unspent.

"To talk," Morcar replied, "and to let you know you're not alone, despite the display back there. If your father returns, things will just go on as they have done for years, with one difference."

"Which is what?"

"He'll have me and Sigeferth killed." Morcar looked alarmed. Edmund had never seen that before, thinking him easily the most taciturn and stoic individual he'd ever crossed paths with. His fear was genuine, and Edmund had a feeling he knew the cause of it.

"Because of Bernecestre? Because of how my brother died? I heard all this from Sigeferth. That's why he sent me to Lundenburg. He wanted me to reason with father and convince him Æthelstan's death wasn't the fault of the Five Boroughs."

"Why do I get the feeling you did not succeed?" Morcar asked, probably knowing the answer already.

"Things became complicated," Edmund said with a shake of his head, "but all this would be irrelevant if you and Sigeferth had supported me when I'd asked. Had we marched on Euerwic and deposed Uhtred...well, Svienn died of his own accord, so we'd have had half of England behind us and an empty throne to take. Nothing could have stood in my way."

"I fear you may be right," conceded Morcar, "but we had no way of knowing at the time that Svienn would prove so adept at dying on his own. We had our people to think of. A full-scale uprising would have provoked Svienn into..."

"I know!" shouted Edmund, his outburst startling several people wandering by. "I know all of it! You said! I understand! I'm no fool, despite what you might all say when my back is turned."

Morcar's face softened, his expression returning to something like his old neutral self. "Is that what you think?" he asked quietly. "You think me and my brother believe you to be a fool?"

"Don't you?" Edmund sniped, knowing in his wounded heart it was unlikely.

"Of course we don't," Morcar answered, "but now is not the time for revisiting past misunderstandings. We have to do something to tilt the balance in your favour. We have to do something to make the people see you as a worthy king."

"What do you have in mind?" asked Wulfhild.

"Svienn died at Gainesburg, trying to cement his rule with a spectacle of compliant English nobles," said Morcar. "As far as I know, he had an army with him there...not his main force, no, but still a host that could do some damage if it put its mind to it."

"I know all this," said Edmund. "Eadwig came to me outside Snotingeham, telling me as much. I sent him there to ingratiate his way into Svienn's ranks. Get him to think an aetheling was coming over to his side."

"Did it work?"

"I don't know...I think it's unlikely Eadwig killed him in personal combat, but I've yet to hear from him. I hope..."

"We hope he's alright," Wulfhild interjected, her hand finding Edmund's shoulder. "We've lost too many of our family, Morcar, and Edmund wouldn't have sent our brother into danger unless there was good reason."

"Can you be sure of your husband's support for Edmund's claim to the throne?" Morcar asked her, apparently still all business despite Wulfhild's efforts to soften the tone.

"I can," she replied. "Ulfcytel certainly has no reason to wish our father back in power. He respects Edmund. He'll do the right thing."

"I'm glad to hear it," nodded Morcar, turning back to Edmund. "So that leaves us one single task. A victory. We need a victory. I assume your army is still camped outside the walls?"

"It is."

"Then I shall send word to Sigeferth and have him meet us with a force halfway."

"Halfway where?" asked Edmund, annoyed that Morcar seemed to be making decisions for him.

"Gainesburg. We'll attack the enemy force at Gainesburg whilst they're still mourning Svienn. Kill them all, Edmund. Spill their blood, shatter their bones, and then leave the townspeople to spread word of what you did. Because, believe you me, if you handle this right, the Danes will learn to fear you…and if they fear you, the rest of England will follow."

XIV

The ships came on, four abreast, their pointed, painted prows parting the sparkling waters like spearheads through flesh. Their coloured sails had been furled, the crews preferring the precision of their oars to guide them in. Cnut thought it was no meagre feat in terms of seamanship. There had to be close to twenty ships out there upon the river, and yet they'd maintained proper formation, even now when making their final approach to Gainesburg. The men aboard knew what they were doing. He was glad of it. What came next was important.

Old Østen let out a sad rumble as one of the ships broke ranks and began accelerating towards them. Cnut glanced at him, wondering what the stout warrior could be upset about. "Are you unwell?" Cnut wondered aloud, thinking it unlikely.

"I'm not," said Østen through that impossibly thick silver beard of his, "but it's all so real now. The ships...they make for a fine sight. A moving tribute to your father."

Cnut nodded, inwardly glad that Østen approved of what had been arranged. The bulk of the flotilla was now holding position about a quarter mile out, but that single vessel was still heading towards them, its oarsmen heaving to and fro with admirable zeal. This wasn't just any old ship. It was too large for that, sitting heavy and low in the water, its prow a fearsome dragon-head that worked to signify one very important fact: this was a ship for a king. It had been so in life. Now it would be in death. Svienn was going home.

Cnut turned and made a gesture towards the men standing guard at the pavilion behind him. They saw it and acted as one, moving into the pavilion and re-emerging with his father's body upon a narrow, wooden lattice. Scores of warriors then took up position on either side of the dirt road that led past Cnut to trail down to the river bank. A lonesome jetty projected out into the water from that point on, occupied by yet more warriors in full battle dress. They were all an imposing sight, their armour sparkling in the fading sunlight, the heads of their great axes held aloft in the chill evening breeze. It was only fitting. Despite the nature of his death, Svienn would have all the pomp and ceremony that was due him. He was a king, after all, of Denmark and England both. He would be treated as such.

Østen stayed close as Cnut and the pallbearers made the long, slow walk down to the jetty. Drums sounded from somewhere, their low, rumbling beat giving the proceedings a mournful yet strangely menacing air. The sun was dipping low towards the western horizon, its deep orange rays reflecting off the surface of the river. For a moment, they seemed to directly fall on Cnut himself, half-blinding him in the process, but it soon passed, and Cnut moved on undaunted, his eyes fixed solemnly ahead whilst his father's flagship slowly manoeuvred itself alongside the jetty below.

The town of Gainesburg lay behind them, some of its braver inhabitants creeping close to watch the procession. Cnut thought on his response to his father's death as he trudged along, wondering whether he'd done the right thing in sparing the settlement and taking things as their appearance suggested. He'd immediately thought of poison as soon as Svienn had started raving, thinking one of those treacherous Saxon thegns had somehow sneaked something into his cup. Then he'd died, gibbering and frothing, his eyes wide and watery with abject terror. There was no mistake there. His father genuinely was seeing something. If it were indeed the spectre of Saint Edmund, then everyone present knew why. There had been no need to attack his resting place like that. Cnut knew at the time it had been a serious mistake.

He'd of course kept such thoughts to himself. He'd refused to grieve, instead sending word to Lundenburg to bring up ships with all haste so his father could be sent back to Denmark for a proper burial. England was no place for him to find rest, and if Saint Edmund really was responsible for his murder, then Cnut doubted he'd take kindly to Svienn's remains being deposited in English earth. Some things in this world were always due respect, and Cnut knew in his very heart that saints were one of them. They were powerful and holy men, close to God in life and now death. It was always foolish to provoke them. He wished his father had seen that.

He cast a final look at him as the bearers handed him over to the honour guard atop the jetty. He looked like he was sleeping, his beard and normally wild eyebrows now groomed and presentable, his face conveying nothing but contentment and peace. A circlet of tempered silver had been placed upon his head, the metal almost vanishing within the faded greys and whites of his hair. Nobody would have guessed from the look of him that this peaceful old man had been a ferocious warrior in life. A king, yes, but not a warrior, nor one capable of striking terror into the hearts of any who might dare oppose him. His skill and ferocity had not done him much good in the end. Saint Edmund was no mere man, and Svienn had picked a fight he couldn't win.

Cnut nodded approval when the guards passed the body to several warriors who'd disembarked from the ship, the latter bobbing and shifting slightly in the otherwise gentle shallows. Cnut felt something stir as his father was taken aboard and laid down, the men around him treating his corpse like it were the most revered and holy of relics. Østen reached out, placing a heavy paw on Cnut's shoulder, the gesture touchingly delicate despite the killing power that remained in those hands.

"Are you all right, my boy?" he whispered, not wanting to cause Cnut any embarrassment or draw attention to the tears welling up in those shimmering blue eyes.

"I am," Cnut half-coughed, his voice for the moment failing him. "Once the flagship is away, send word for the rest of his honour guard to assemble. I want them embarked and on their way home before nightfall."

Østen hesitated, his hand still resting tentatively upon Cnut's shoulder. Cnut knew why. He'd been opposed to the idea of giving Svienn such a large escort, thinking their warriors would be put to better use in England. Cnut would have none of it. England was beaten, and its people were nothing but whipped dogs, despite the resistance they'd met at Sancte Eadmundes Byrig. That was an act of desperation, so he'd told Østen and the others, and would not be repeated. His father deserved his five hundred huscarls and the ships to carry them for his voyage home. They were just fine without them. Nobody would be looking to attack them here. His father had brought many men to Gainesburg, wanting to overawe the English with his warriors. They could afford to lose a few hundred for the sake of ceremony.

Eadric hadn't agreed. He'd remained with Cnut even as the English thegns had fled, all of them eager to get back to their lands with news of Svienn's death. Eadric had been full of words on what should be done, and they kept pouring out of him without limit, a thing that had annoyed Cnut beyond measure. He'd snapped at him, telling him to desist or depart. The man must have taken it to heart, for he'd left soon after, claiming he would "be better placed to serve in Lundenburg." Cnut hadn't stopped him. Eadric was a wise man, but he was also intensely irritating at times, and he wanted the English in general to keep their distance whilst he made arrangements for his father's body. There was always something so unlikeable about them, and Eadric was no exception. He'd been glad to see the back of him.

The same had gone for Cnut's new wife, Ælfgifu. She was a fine-looking woman, and he was pleased his father had honoured him with a bride, but she was English, and Cnut presently had no time for her. He'd worked her well enough on their wedding night, thinking it more than likely his seed had taken root in her belly, and so there was no need for her to remain here. She was going to Denmark, away from this place, where she'd be unable to distract him. She brushed past him now, saying nothing, and boarded the ship that held his father. She looked back at him for a moment, her hazel eyes suggesting something between sadness and contempt. Cnut merely nodded at her, this being the only respect he was inclined to give. She turned away. She'd be safe in Denmark, and he'd look forward to receiving word of her giving birth, hopefully to a son. Otherwise, he couldn't say he'd miss her.

Not all were so fortunate. The aetheling, "Eadwig", would not be going anywhere. Cnut was no fool, and whilst he was content to allow the thegns to flee to their rat holes, Eadwig himself was too valuable a prize to let slip from grasp. He'd had him seized the night his father had died, bundling him into a makeshift prison back in town alongside the ever-defiant Osbert. Some would say it was unwise to keep men like that together, for Osbert had a rare strength to him, one that hadn't faded despite his time in captivity. Cnut wasn't excessively worried. Osbert had played his part at Svienn's gathering, hating every minute of it, but still playing his part, and as long as he was locked up he wasn't likely to cause mischief. The same went for Eadwig.

His father's favoured vessel was now pulling away, its oars slapping the surface of the river as they again began their monotonous hewing and heaving. Cnut blinked the tears from his eyes and turned to join Østen in their walk back to the pavilion, their flanks still guarded by rows of huscarls. The honour guard for his father could embark of their own accord. They didn't need Cnut to oversee everything personally. He had too much to think on.

They reached the pavilion and ducked inside, the sentries on duty nodding solemnly in respect. He'd spent all of last night here, sitting up with his father's body, knowing the next day would be the last time he'd see him. Now he was gone there was just an empty space here, something that would only serve to make Cnut melancholy. He didn't need that. This pavilion had previously served as a place of business, not sadness and lamentation. Cnut would make it so once more.

He started by heaving his father's old map table from the corner and into the centre. A fairly detailed image rested on it, the parchment admittedly dog-eared and frayed at the edges, but discernible all the same. England. Or a map of it, at any rate.

Cnut smiled at the sight. It was his father's realm by right of conquest. Now it was all his by right of succession.

Østen stood across from him, his face heavy with what Cnut assumed was grief. He was one of the old guard who'd fought alongside his father from their very first forays into this kingdom, and he was owed respect. Svienn had seen that well enough, rewarding Østen with authority and honour despite his many old wounds and even older bones. Cnut intended to keep him around. The men liked him, and he was good at what he did, although he'd long since passed his prime. He just wished he'd focus on something other than Svienn's death. Every time Cnut looked at him, it reminded him of his father. He didn't have time for grief. He didn't want it at all.

"Do you think the English thegns will remain loyal?" Cnut had tried to sound hopeful, as if by doing so he'd encourage Østen to give him the answer he wanted.

"You made them all swear loyalty to you as king," Østen said, his eyes sparkling with a certain intelligence from under those grey bushes that served as eyebrows. "They came to honour your father…if they themselves have any honour, they'll keep their word to you, as his son."

"Can a Saxon be said to have honour?" Cnut asked, eager to hear Østen's thoughts. He pondered the question, and Cnut felt some satisfaction at what he said next. They were of like mind on this subject.

"They do have it," Østen said, "but there's a split down the middle in this land. The common Englishman has always fought like a cornered wolf, snapping at us and hating us with good reason. The English thegn is something else. They are men of endless chatter and pretensions. It's a wonder how they were ever able to make themselves a nation."

"Is it fair to say they were not always like this?" asked Cnut. "They have heroes in their history. Great men we've all heard of…their King Alfred brought them back from the brink and subdued our people with both word and sword after his victory at Ethandun. That was a man, right there, no?"

"That was indeed a man," nodded Østen sagely. "But his kind are few and far between, and those descendants who followed him have been proven unworthy."

"But interesting, no? Have you spoken with the aetheling we have? Eadwig? He's a man of great knowledge."

"No," grunted Østen dismissively, "and I'll not choose to unless commanded. I don't trust him. He's thin like a woman…spent too much time reading and not enough time defending his father's lands. What kind of heir is that?"

"I agree," Cnut mused, finding it likewise odd how Eadwig had somehow managed to opt out of the martial upbringing he thought would have been mandatory. "But I'd speak with him about how he sees things. You should stay, Østen. We may all learn something."

Østen grumbled something unintelligible as Cnut called for the guards outside. They came to him, eager to serve, and Cnut instructed them to go and fetch Eadwig. They departed at once and returned within a few minutes, the very pale aetheling held between them. They let him go on Cnut's order, taking up their previous positions outside the pavilion entrance. Cnut didn't need them listening in. He needed Eadwig calm if he were to speak with him.

"I would ask you a simple question," said Cnut, hoping Eadwig would start to get some colour back in his cheeks before he passed out. "Do you think the English thegns will remain loyal to me now I've let them return home?"

"Would you be if you were in their position?"

Eadwig's words hit Cnut hard. He couldn't think of how to reply, and with good reason. Cnut wouldn't be loyal if he were them. If the English had invaded Denmark, he'd have fought them to the last, using deception and force to do so. That thought alone unsettled him greatly. He hoped Eadwig was wrong.

"You English are different to us!" snapped Østen, unsettled also by what had been said. "Some of you fight hard, yes, but your leaders are a different breed. The men who bowed to King Svienn will bow to King Cnut. It is the way of cowards!"

"Our leaders?" Eadwig asked Østen. "Our leaders are a mixed bunch. Those treacherous thegns of yours may go either way, depending on how they see the situation playing out...but don't assume anything about my countrymen. Misfortune and division have been our true enemies in this war. You Danes are far from invincible. You sweat and bleed like other men...you die like other men."

Østen's eyes widened, Cnut's too. "And what is that supposed to mean?" asked Cnut, his tone cold and even like a newly-balanced blade. "Are you planning something? Did you come here...did you come here to kill my father?"

"By what means?" Eadwig spluttered, incredulous. "I'm no fighter, everyone can see that. I came to submit to Svienn because he was king, and I desire peace. I'll not fight a man I'm incapable of fighting. That was true with Svienn. It's true with you, King Cnut."

"And are all men of your rank in agreement with you on this?" Cnut asked, still suspicious of Eadwig despite his protestations. "Will you English really follow me like you seemed willing to do with my father?"

"I can't speak for all of them," Eadwig shrugged, "but you've put on a show of force here...nobody at the feast missed the warriors all around us. England has given its all trying to resist Thorkell. By the time you turned up, we were already defeated."

"And I thought division and misfortune was your enemy?" chuckled Østen. "Why mention that mad dog, Thorkell? He's the least of your worries now."

"Why would I not speak of him? Thorkell had men fighting with him from all over the North, including Denmark. I'd wager you'd know his motives better than I. Plenty would think you were all working together to see us undone."

"You'd be mistaken in that," Cnut said quickly. "Thorkell and my father did not see eye to eye. Thorkell preferred the old ways...piracy, reaving, pillaging...he didn't understand the kind of leadership needed to build something that would stand the test of time. My father did. As do I."

"And what do you hope to build, Cnut?" asked Eadwig suspiciously. Cnut thought on that for a moment, feeling surprised at how he somehow felt the need to impress this strange little man.

"Something more than just another kingdom," he announced finally. "A union...an empire...call it what you will...but Denmark, England...all the nations of the northern seas are to be one."

"With you as ruler?"

"Who else?" sneered Cnut, enjoying the moment. "It was my father's dream, but fate has left it to me to make it a reality. I'll honour him by seeing my destiny fulfilled."

"You have not grieved yet," muttered Eadwig, Cnut's temper flaring slightly at the impertinence of his observation. "You have not grieved at all, which I find strange. You wish to play the part of a doting son, yet here you stand, all purpose and ambition, in the wake of his death. Why?"

Cnut's mouth clamped shut, tight and involuntary, the suddenness of the move almost painful. He glared at Eadwig and took a step forward, knowing with mounting alarm that the aetheling was reading him like a book. It was not acceptable. Cnut struck him, his fist careening into the side of his jaw with all the force he was owed. To his credit, Eadwig stayed on his feet, the impact instead sending him skittering off sideways to collide with Østen. The older man sensed the opportunity and gripped Eadwig by the arms to hold him in place, still facing Cnut and yet entirely helpless. Cnut grasped him by the jaw, gazing into those dark eyes with probing intent. There was something there. Something familiar.

Memories stirred, all of them unwelcome. He was back at the monastery, where his father had accosted the monks and, in his fury, killed them all for refusing to give up the location of Saint Edmund. Then the English had come, the REAL English, charging out of the woods to punish the Danes for their sacrilege. There was something in Eadwig's eyes now that reminded Cnut of the one who'd led them. That furious warrior, his face contorted with hate, his gore-slicked sword killing and killing and killing yet more. Eadwig was nothing like him in temperament, but they had the same eyes. There must be a reason for it. He then remembered what Eadric had told him after he and his men had come to their rescue. It was Edmund who had attacked them. Eadwig's brother. There was much he wasn't telling them.

"You look familiar to me now," Cnut seethed, applying a portion of his strength to grip Eadwig's jaw ever tighter. "A man attacked us weeks ago, my father and I, back in Eastengle. He and his followers got the better of us, but looking at you now, I see you have a certain likeness. You have brothers, of course? Æthelred proved a fruitful man in the siring of children, if nothing else. Tell me!"

"I have siblings!" Eadwig gasped, his discomfort piteous to look upon. "But they are scattered to the four corners of Britain, if not dead. My older brother, Æthelstan, was the only one who was a warrior...the only one who could have threatened you, and he died fighting Thorkell."

"Liar!" Cnut roared, his fingernails biting into Eadwig's cheeks. "You have other brothers! It was said by Eadric that it was Edmund who attacked us that day! Where is he now?"

Eadwig's eyes broke contact with his own, if only for a fraction of a second, the simple gesture suggesting he was fabricating a response that would get him out of this. Cnut felt a cold smile creep across his face. It was doubtful Eadwig would have given away such a thing if he were not presently terrified. Cnut really had him rattled. It was a good feeling. One he'd like to revisit many times.

"I tell you, that's it!" Eadwig hissed. "My father paid his sons little attention, and only Æthelstan was properly trained to fight and lead. Edmund is lost, dead for all I know, and my sisters are likewise scattered. Only Edward and Alfred might pose a threat, and only then in the future, for they are but boys now."

"And where are they?" asked Cnut, well aware Eadwig was trying to distract him with a half-truth.

"Normandy," came the response, "and they'll stay there for some time. They may end up living the rest of their lives there. Not all have such an appetite for power as you, king."

Cnut let him go, releasing his grip and noting the claw marks he'd left on his face. Østen did the same, removing his vice-like hands from Eadwig's shoulders and pushing him away with a contemptuous snort.

"Ulfcytel then," growled Cnut, "tell me what you know of this man."

"He's the only one who might oppose you," Eadwig said breathlessly, his hands rubbing at his undoubtedly aching jaw. "But I know not where he is. He could be dead, or in exile...my father hated him and would have wanted to settle scores before he fled. It would..."

Cnut called for his guards and had them drag Eadwig from his sight. He began pacing, his mind beset with worries. He could tell Eadwig wasn't being entirely truthful, and he felt it fair to surmise this Edmund wasn't the nonentity he'd claimed he was.

"We should kill some of the hostages," said Østen suddenly. "It will help loosen tongues, if indeed this Eadwig does know something. Even if he doesn't, they'll just be more dead Englishmen. No harm done."

Cnut thought on that. He hadn't been such a fool as to just let the thegns who'd attended his father return to their lands unhindered. He'd demanded each of them give up a retainer, a servant or companion of some sort, as a ransom to ensure their continued good behaviour. It was the custom, and there was nothing out of the ordinary in it. Cnut now had a lot of captives as a result. But more bloodshed wouldn't help. Eadwig might be a liar, but killing hostages just on the assumption it might terrify him into telling them something, anything, was a risk, and a wasteful risk at that. Other methods would have to suffice.

"I don't think the old ways can help us in this case," Cnut said. "Eadwig is a stronger man than he thinks...he's not a warrior, but he's still the son of a king, and a brother of...which brother of his was killed fighting Thorkell?"

"I don't know, and who cares? Thorkell did us a favour with his rampaging, that's all I know. We'd have faced far more resistance if he hadn't softened England up for us first."

"Resistance? From Ulfcytel?" Cnut asked, ceasing his pacing to face Østen properly.

"Of course," he replied. "He'll always be a thorn in your side until you can remove and crush him. It was always so. Our conquest won't be complete as long as he's alive."

"Just what is so fearsome about this man?" Cnut had heard all about Ulfcytel and how he'd nearly defeated his father back in the day. He knew, also, that Østen had fought in that very same battle in which Ulfcytel and his Eastenglians had almost overwhelmed them. It was for this reason Cnut took him far more seriously than any other of his supposedly learned advisers. There was valuable knowledge in that old head. He was glad to have it at his disposal.

"A number of things," said Østen thoughtfully. "It's not just his skill at arms or his undoubted courage...it's his reputation. Reputation can make a man great. It's how others see you that matters. Men will follow you if they believe you'll lay down your life for them. Few leaders will actually do that. Ulfcytel is one of them."

"Is he really so beloved?" asked Cnut, sceptical that their famous enemy could be as noble as people thought.

"Yes," affirmed Østen with a nod. "Think about it...we've had the English in a corner for years now. Ulfcytel is the only one of their leaders who has proven himself worth a damn…the only one who has fought his heart out to keep his people safe…and he keeps doing it. You'll not have peace here until he's in the ground."

"You know that for a fact? You've seen the man? In battle?"

"I have," Østen said, his voice quietening with the recalling of old memories. "I nearly fought him…wanted it more than anything…for I could see he was someone of repute even then. I wanted the honour of bringing him down. I wasn't the only one. Of course, most of those died trying."

"You think he's fiercer than the man who attacked my father and I? Eadric said it was Edmund, a son of Æthelred…and I tell you, Østen, never have I seen a more furious warrior, in the English ranks or ours. He…he…"

"Frightened you?"

There was no contempt in Østen's voice. He was a veteran of dozens of battles, the number of men he'd killed possibly stretching into the hundreds. He must have felt fear at some time, and Cnut was wise enough to know that great heroes were not men who were somehow immune to the same frailties experienced by others. They were just better at mastering them.

"It's a hard thing for me to confess," mumbled Cnut, his eyes drifting to the floor. "I wanted to face him. I did…"

"You don't have to justify yourself to me," Østen said gently. "We all feel fear. I wasn't there that day, but if you say this man was somebody of note, then I believe you. So you think it was this Edmund? That would mean Eadwig is lying to you. He should pay for that."

"I can't really say," admitted Cnut, still awkward. "But I felt something when I looked into Eadwig's eyes…like there was some similarity between him and the man that attacked us, but perhaps not. For all I know, Edmund could be dead, and I'm worrying about nothing."

"Then let's concentrate on what we're sure of. For the time being, Ulfcytel is the only one capable of opposing you, and since we don't know the identity of the man who attacked…"

"Eadric said his name was Edmund," Cnut stressed again. "He confirmed it. He confirmed he was an aetheling. He said we won't have seen the last of him."

"This Eadric can recognise a man in the midst of a melée?"

Østen had a point. Eadric had not really fought in that battle, only appearing on horseback in the last few minutes. There was always room for error in such things, and unless Eadric had the eyes of a hawk, they couldn't be entirely sure he'd got it right.

"I can only repeat what he told us," Cnut sighed, wearied by his incessant doubts. "I thought at the time he'd have good reason for what he said. Eadric has proven himself a valuable asset."

"He's a traitor to his own people, Cnut. Far be it for me to tell you what to do, but you can never entirely trust a man like that. Listen to him, perhaps, and take what he offers, but do not trust him."

"I don't," sighed Cnut again, lifting his hands up to massage his aching temples. "He is as you say…a traitor, and he and I will never understand each other on that score. But his former master was a fool, and everyone knew it. When he fled to Normandy, Eadric was left with no option but to reach out to us."

"Is that what he told you?"

Østen was becoming even more suspicious of Eadric, Cnut knew. He didn't blame him, but he wished he'd learn to trust his judgement, especially when it came to dealing with the English in any way other than killing them. They couldn't be at war with them forever. They were Cnut's own subjects now, after all.

"He did," Cnut confirmed, "and I don't see a lie there. Not everyone is suited to running away. Eadric simply seeks to benefit himself and his people in light of a changed situation."

"That's very logical of you, my king," Østen said, Cnut now wondering if he was mocking him in some way. "Although allow me to dissent a little…there are some things that cannot be understood by the head…only the heart. My heart tells me a man who can betray his own, for any reason, should never be trusted."

"And what would you have me do here?" Cnut demanded, his patience fading with Østen's insistence on repeating himself. "Turn Eadric away? He knows his people, he knows his lands. He's a resource, one I intend to take advantage of."

"You are free to do as you will, my king. Yet I will ask you…where is Eadric now?"

Cnut paused, thinking on how to reply. "He's not here," he admitted simply. "He returned to Lundenburg, with my blessing, shortly after my father died. I say it helps to have such a man in the capital. He'll keep the locals in line."

It was Østen's turn to sigh now, his great gnarled hands rubbing at his tired eyes. "He's not with you, just as he wasn't with his previous king at the critical hour…you'll have to forgive me for repeating myself, but that isn't how a loyal man behaves. Look to your own, Cnut. Foreigners only complicate things."

He couldn't disagree. As much as Eadric was useful, he wasn't one of them, and Cnut shouldn't hold him in high regard simply for doing him a good turn. In any case, Cnut was tired of discussing such matters. His heart ached persistently, demanding his attention lest it break altogether. He wasn't sure what to do. He'd never been particularly close to his father, but now he was gone and wouldn't be coming back. Cnut felt so very alone. If it wasn't for the likes of Østen, he feared he might crumble.

Cnut called for his guards again, ordering them to bring slaves and have them outfit his pavilion for a proper meeting. They did so, the English proving themselves adept servants, if nothing else, and Cnut was soon sitting at the head of a narrow table in the company of those jarls who'd originally accompanied his father to Gainesburg. There was drink aplenty, and the jarls were in agreeable spirits despite the lateness of the hour, the growing darkness necessitating the use of candles. Cnut didn't care for sleep. He wanted, needed, to hear from his seniors. He was a young king, and in his heart of hearts, he knew he was out of his depth. He needed help.

It was with some regret he realised he might not get it. The jarls soon became an argumentative bunch, and several were more intent on outshining the others than offering reasoned counsel. They didn't agree on much of anything other than that Cnut was king, and they were all grieving for his father; the latter point repeated so often Cnut began to find it suspicious.

He tried to simplify things for them, asking them directly what goals he should prioritise to consolidate his rule. That provoked yet more fragmented opinions. Some said he should return to Lundenburg, arguing it was the jewel of his new kingdom and that its people should see their new king. Others made the sudden claim that his father had wanted to be crowned in Euerwic, and that his decision to hold an audience here, at Gainesburg, had been intended to flatter the northern thegns whom he'd intended to honour above all others. Cnut hadn't heard of this, but these jarls were insistent it was the case and that Cnut himself should now head to Euerwic and demand the archbishop there put a crown on his head. That sounded like it would spark a whole new sequence of worries, and since Svienn had never mentioned such a plan to Cnut, he was inclined to dismiss it. That didn't stop the arguing, though.

Østen was a voice of sanity amid the turmoil. He agreed that returning to Lundenburg was a wise course of action, but he suggested first that they use the army they had here to put on a show of force on their way back south. Rather than take to ship and sail down the coast, as others suggested, Østen was of a mind to march the whole way, allowing the people of the countryside to lay eyes on their king as he returned in majesty to his capital. Cnut liked the thought of that, but not everyone present approved, and the "pro-Euerwic" faction, as Cnut now thought of them, were not convinced. He'd listen to everyone a little more before making a decision.

The next jarl to speak was clearly drunk, or at least Cnut hoped he was so he'd have an excuse for his foolish words. He advised they take a more direct approach and pillage the surrounding area before moving north to attack Euerwic and burn it down. Cnut asked him why, refusing to hide his displeasure, but the jarl was fixated on the necessity of terrifying the local population, as if the English hadn't already submitted and agreed to recognise Cnut as king. As stupid as it all sounded, Cnut got the feeling some of the others were sympathetic to this violent stratagem. They didn't understand. His father's plan was to rule England, not burn it to ash. Violence and terror had their place. This was not it.

The final argument he heard was somewhat better. Cnut should make haste, so he was told, and catch up with the fleet he'd sent back to Denmark with his father's body. They still had vessels out on the water, and it would do Cnut good to first secure his rule over his own people rather than play politics with the English. His brother, Harald, was also a potential threat, so it was said, and he would need to be brought to heel lest he declare himself king without Cnut's consent.

This was a difficult subject to think on. Harald was the elder, but Cnut knew their father had not favoured him, making him regent in Denmark whilst he took Cnut to seize England. Harald also wasn't the sharpest, for he'd taken this gesture as a sign of Svienn's confidence, but Cnut knew their father had wanted him and him alone to rule England and Denmark both rather than allow his lands to be divided piecemeal. Harald should and would be brought into line, but he'd need a secure power base in order to do it. England was that base, and so Cnut would, for the moment, focus his attention here.

The meeting broke up, Cnut opting to wander through the forest of tents outside of town that housed his restless army. He respected the jarls, most of them at any rate, but they were his father's men, and aside from Østen, none of them seemed to have much concern over his wellbeing or how he might be dealing with his recent loss. They talked the talk, burbling at him about how he had their loyalty, but the words felt hollow, as if they were going through the motions of fealty until he, Cnut, proved himself worthy.

That was a hard thing to comprehend. Cnut had killed his first man before leaving Denmark, and he'd fought well since then, charging into the breach with his men to win Lundenburg for his father. He was proud of what he'd accomplished, seeing himself as the fighter he was, the only time he'd ever doubted himself coming on that blasted day at the monastery of Saint Edmund.

Another unsettling thought then occurred to him. There'd been men all around him when he'd first seen Edmund. They'd have looked to him for orders and inspiration, and so some of them may have noticed his hesitation in the face of the Englishman's fury. Word might have spread, the story becoming more and more exaggerated with the telling of it. Cnut was a coward, that's what they'd have said. Svienn's chosen heir had panicked before the enemy. The jarls would have heard this soon enough and begun chattering among themselves, adding further embellishments to a narrative already based on a lie. The thought stirred Cnut to anger. No man would call him a coward to his face and get away with it. To do so behind his back was even worse.

His upset faded a little as he wandered through the camp. The men on watch greeted him with solemn nods and hushed words, their respect obvious from both their tone and demeanour. Those men who were still awake and without duties of their own were hunched around campfires, enjoying the fellowship of their brethren as they partook of yet another cup of mead or roasted freshly caught game over flickering flames. They always got to their feet when they saw Cnut approach, every one of them lowering their heads and eyes until he'd passed by. None displayed anything even approaching contempt or mockery. If a rumour really had spread as to his supposed weakness, these men had not believed it.

He stopped on the outskirts of the camp, his gaze settling on the town just ahead. It was a cold night, and the English were off the streets and safe inside their homes. Cnut thought for a moment on how they must feel, living with a foreign army on their doorstep, one that had until relatively recently been intent on their death and ruin. They'd had a painful history, England and Denmark, Cnut knew that. Unlike many of his kind, he'd always displayed an interest in such things, thinking it important to grapple with the past as a means to tackle the present and future alike. The warrior in Cnut told him the English were pathetic, that they were his subjects now by right of conquest and he could do as he wished with them. Another part of him said otherwise. They were a great and learned people, these English, and despite their present troubles, they might yet go on to ascend to even greater heights of nobility and endurance. The Danes would do well to realise that.

That would, of course, depend on how quickly the English came to terms with the new reality. Cnut wasn't going anywhere, and as indecisive as he presently felt, he wasn't about to give up his hold on the country he'd only recently helped win. He pondered going into town to visit the captives, thinking he'd talk with Eadwig and Osbert in the event they had anything of further interest to say. He decided against it, knowing he was too fatigued for another verbal sparring match. Osbert was always so defiant, as was Eadwig, in his own way, but Cnut knew there was a strength there a cunning leader could yet tap. Cnut wasn't above all kinds of violence, but he wasn't wasteful. He'd use those fate had delivered to him for the sake of his father's dream.

The night passed slowly and silently. Cnut struggled to sleep, unable to rid his mind of troubled thoughts. He'd heard in the past of warriors who'd talked of sadness or rage creeping up on them in the quieter moments when they'd least expected it, and at the time he'd wondered about that, finding it strange that great and powerful men could become so troubled. He was learning this very night exactly how that worked. He couldn't rest, not at all, and his memories of his father simply would not desist from disturbing him, no matter how hard he tried to drive them from mind. He wept openly in the darkness of his pavilion, grateful he was alone so as to be spared shame and judgement. Before long the storm passed, and by the time he'd managed to settle himself, he felt like he'd been relieved of a burden, the silent weight of his own suppressed sadness easing from his shoulders without further fuss or tribulation.

He and his father had never been close. Svienn hadn't given him much attention as a boy, preferring to fixate on war and politics rather than waste time with his family. Despite that, Cnut had always wanted a better relationship with him, hoping in his heart that one day his father might realise his blessings and love his sons as they loved him. That wasn't possible now, but he knew if his father was looking on, he'd want him to finish the work he'd started. It was for that reason Cnut would never relent. England would remain his, no matter the cost.

Cnut was up before dawn, dressing himself without bothering to summon his slaves. He took breakfast with Østen, and once finished they and several burly huscarls made a point of wandering into Gainesburg to attend morning prayers. Most of the English looked on fearfully, apprehensive about having Danes inside their church, but Cnut was determined to make a habit of this, knowing it was important his people get used to seeing him as the Christian he was. Not all of them would take his piety seriously, but that was beside the point. He was king, and kings were appointed by God. That was all there was to it.

It was late morning, and the clouds were threatening rain by the time Cnut and his brethren returned to camp. He'd made up his mind on what to do. Østen was right. He was needed in the capital, but his subjects also needed to see him and know him. An overland march south with his army would help with that. He'd then enter his great city at the head of his men and march through Lundenburg's streets to claim the throne of England. All would see his majesty and the strength that backed it. Fear and awe both. That was a powerful combination.

He was just issuing orders for his people to retrieve Eadwig and Osbert when a commotion began. He wasn't sure what it was – thinking the sound akin to that made by men who are both fearful and excited all at once – but before long, what looked like a group of warriors came into view, a single figure hauled between them. They were attired for battle, but had obviously been on the road for some time, although for what purpose Cnut wasn't aware. What was interesting was the man they had with them. He was huge, his barrel chest and thickened arms seeming to almost burst through his armour, but he'd been bound tightly across his wrists, the rough sack upon his head obscuring his identity, at least for the moment.

Østen joined Cnut just as the strange procession came to a halt before him. The leader of the group stepped forward, stating how he and his men had been part of a raiding expedition that Svienn had dispatched weeks ago to harry "English rebels" that Cnut, for one, had not known even existed. They'd all heard already how his father had died, and they all now hailed Cnut as king, appearing both mournful and sincere as they took a knee before him. Only one stood upright, the captive acting like he'd either not heard or was somehow above such things. Cnut decided to end all the drama and take matters into his own hands. He stepped forward and pulled the sack from his head.

Østen inhaled sharply, shock and alarm wrought across his face. Cnut stared into the stranger's eyes, and he stared back, his silver beard voluminous and filthy, his large, bald head sparkling in the light. He was wounded, a patchwork of bandages covering some injury to his side, and his face was bruised from what had likely been regular beatings, but he held Cnut's gaze, silent and unyielding, his spine straight and his already broad chest puffing outward. There was defiance there, and something else. This was a man of dignity and poise, of purpose and significance. He'd seen many a horror in his time, and he'd faced them all without flinching. That was to be admired.

"If you have something to say to me, Dane, then get on with it," rumbled the captive, his chapped lips curling into a broad sneer. "Otherwise, just kill me. You've all wanted old Ulfcytel dead for years now. Well…here I am."

XV

"You're wanted back home, Æthelred."

The duke had his cruel face on. He only had three expressions, Æthelred had noticed, and all were unlikeable. There was his blank look, with his eyes hard and imperious as he sat upon his throne thinking on his own majesty. Then there was his angry look, less common, thankfully, but quite unsettling when it came over him, as it had just weeks ago at Olaf's baptism. Then there was the cruel look, the rarest of all of them, but easily the most distressing. Richard had something to say that he knew would hurt him, and he was relishing the prospect. For that, Æthelred would always despise him. You'd expect a Duke of Normandy to be a bit of a bastard as a matter of course, but Duke Richard II excelled at it. Æthelred would make a point of telling him that someday.

"What do you mean?" he asked Richard, looking up from his breakfast of charred meat upon a bed of charred meat. The duke was still poring over the parchment he'd been handed a moment ago by one of his stewards, his eyes sparkling with curiosity. They were in the main hall of his keep, seated at a long table abutting the stone steps leading up to Richard's unimpressive throne. It was a cold place, in spirit and physicality, and the slightest movement tended to prompt an echo that could be as irritating as it was repetitive. They were alone, for Emma and the children were elsewhere so she might tutor them in their letters, but there were guards. Richard always had guards, lining the walls at irregular intervals, as still as statues until they were called. It would have made Æthelred even more uncomfortable if he didn't have Hereward standing close. He was the best of men and could likely beat any Norman. The thought gave Æthelred a cold smile.

"One of your Godly men, an archbishop of all things, has convened some assembly in North…Northum…Northur…"

"Norþanhymbre!"

"That's it, some God-awful place, I'm sure," Richard grinned, still unashamed of his continuing inability to speak English. "So your man, Wulfstan, his name is…he's got a bunch of your thegns or whatever you call them and convinced them to invite you back home. As king."

Æthelred breathed in, deep and slow. He reached out, gesturing for Richard to relinquish the letter. He complied, still with that damnable look on his face, Æthelred grasping at it irritably before flattening it down on the table before him. It was Wulfstan's hand, that was clear. He knew his writing, having read plenty of his myriad proclamations and admonishments throughout his reign. What was surprising was Richard wasn't exaggerating. They really did want him back.

Wulfstan didn't waste time with flattery. He started by announcing Svienn Forkbeard's death; a welcome event Æthelred had only become aware of several days prior. He then went on at some length, listing all the things that had gone wrong under Æthelred's rule and the horrors that had assailed them since he'd left. He had a flair for the dramatic, but Æthelred knew well enough the archbishop had good reason to speak of such matters. England truly had suffered, and as uncomfortable as it was, the idea that God was displeased with them was very difficult to shake. The archbishop thus wanted him home. He was "God's king", he kept saying, and his subjects had treated him most harshly by failing to see that. The good news was he'd been able to talk them around.

Æthelred paused a moment, wondering how exactly Wulfstan had achieved such a thing. Hardly anyone had followed him to Normandy, hurried as his flight was, and even some of those he'd thought would accompany him had failed to make good on their promises. Eadric of Mierĉe was the most prominent of those, and Æthelred found himself wondering how he fitted into Wulfstan's plans, given he was entirely absent from the list of men the bishop had cited as supporters of his return. Was Eadric dead? That seemed unlikely. Had he betrayed him? That, too, didn't seem likely, considering the level of loyalty he'd displayed in the past. What was clear was a lot of people did indeed want Æthelred back as king. To say that he was surprised was quite the understatement. Shocked, benumbed, and also terrified would be better ways to describe him.

He read on, his eyes merely scanning Wulfstan's incessant demands for him to be a better king and deal "more justly" with his subjects from now on. Æthelred frowned, wondering what exactly he could be referring to, but the archbishop wasn't going into too many details, instead warning quite overtly that the conditions of his return depended on him "respecting your thegns and ealdormen as if they were your own family." Æthelred shook his head, dismayed. Then he remembered a few things. He was fooling himself by pretending he didn't understand Wulfstan's warnings. He had been a bad king. Alaric had helped him see that. Was all this a chance to repay him somehow?

"So you'll be leaving us?" Richard was grinning now, the whiteness of his teeth stark against the dark hues of his beard. Æthelred glared at his brother-in-law, taking him in, in all his irritating pomposity. He was always dressed so meticulously, seeking to ape and even outdo the customs and adornments of his French overlords to the south. To an Englishman, he just looked foolish, as if he were constantly trying to prove something, an insecurity Æthelred had not yet managed to exploit.

"Your plans will require readjustment," Æthelred said dryly. "Without Svienn to threaten you, I can't be used as a bargaining chip between you and him."

"You are entirely right," Richard confirmed, that grin still plastered across his face, "but I see opportunities where they fall. Your Wulfstan is making a big show about how all your underlings have rallied to your cause, but there is no rebellion, no uprising… apart from…"

"Apart from?"

"This confuses me as much as it will you," Richard said, his face resetting into his "blank look" that was at least more tolerable than that insufferable smile. "My sister tells me you hated an ealdorman named Ælfric? That he was a traitor? Well, he's retaken his fortress in the South and, with that, refuses to pay taxes to Svienn."

That was a shock. Æthelred had assumed Ælfric dead, since he'd sent Thorkell's savage brother, Hemingr, to execute him and his family during Svienn's siege of Lundenburg. He knew Hemingr had been at least partly successful, dispatching the fearsome Alaric before apparently dying himself, and so Æthelred had hoped that Ælfric had found a way to expire alongside him. That he'd somehow escaped was a worry Æthelred didn't need.

"Ælfric is an opportunist," Æthelred said dismissively, his mind actually agog as to how the bastard could have seized Porteceaster. Hadn't Eadric left a garrison there under someone he could trust? "And surely it's a moot point about him not paying taxes to Svienn," Æthelred continued. "I mean, the man is dead. Such things can get in the way of any ruler."

"You are aware of his son," Richard cautioned. "I know this, so don't play the fool. If Svienn is dead, then Cnut will pick up the crown from his head. He'll be unsettled, vulnerable, looking to strike out and secure his position…especially when you consider how his father died."

"Tall tales," Æthelred said with a wave of his hand. "I don't listen to rumours about saints stalking people to dispatch them for perceived wrongdoings. Svienn had many enemies, and he was getting on in the world. Age or a poisoned cup would have done him in."

"Always so practical, you English," Richard murmured. "Does not a single part of you rejoice at the idea of your saint avenging his country?"

"If any of that were true, I'd simply wonder why he'd waited so long to act. England has suffered for years without any such miracle taking place. Why now?"

"Did you not read the letter right in front of you?" Richard asked mockingly. "Your Wulfstan tells you what you need to know. God was displeased when you were forced from the throne. You are His king, appointed by Him…it's time to do His will."

Æthelred narrowed his eyes, wondering if Richard believed his own words. He was capable of feigning piety like anyone else, but in actuality he was a ruthless, unlikeable chancer with precious little virtue in that blackened heart of his. Æthelred himself was more of a believer, and the only reason he wasn't as devout as he might be was because of his fear that God had abandoned him. That was yet another thing Alaric had shown him. God had apparently NOT abandoned him. The dreams he'd had were always an appeal for him to step up and serve his people, as a king should. Æthelred had tried at first to dismiss that notion, but something in his heart had told him it was true. What was being offered to him now was something very special. A second chance. By all rights, he should seize it.

Yet things were rarely that simple. As much as he liked the idea of God giving him an opportunity to redeem himself, Æthelred couldn't dismiss the feeling that something was wrong. If he became king again, he'd be dragged back into a world of intrigue and double-dealing, one that would be difficult to escape from at his age and with his temperament. He'd also come to understand he was a better father than he'd ever been a ruler, and he'd enjoyed the weight that had been lifted from his shoulders as he settled in to a life alone with his family. Richard was always a threat on the horizon, it was true, but with Svienn dead he had no reason to play politics with Æthelred's life. There was always a chance things could work themselves out without placing him back on a throne he'd never wanted to begin with.

"You are hesitant," Richard said with a nod, "so let me motivate you…this Ælfric did not retake his fortress without help. He had a certain other ealdorman with him. Ulf…Ulfcita…"

"Ulfcytel!" snapped Æthelred, wondering also just how extensive Richard's spy network in England really was. "That's very strange too," he added, "as neither of them have reason to like or aid one another. Are you sure your spies are reporting with any accuracy?"

"Oh, I'm sure," sneered Richard, untroubled that Æthelred had rightly surmised he had informers on English soil. "What's interesting is what Ælfric said when a Danish envoy arrived from Lundenburg demanding an explanation. He refused to recognise a Danish king, you see. Said he had his own king. A certain Edmund..."

"What?" Æthelred spluttered. "Edmund? My Edmund? Working with Ælfric and Ulfcytel? And to make himself king?"

"Yes, it is true," replied Richard, seeing fit to drag out his vowels as if talking to a slow-witted child. "Your boy even has a little army of his own...commoners, so I hear, but some capable men. He doesn't stand a chance, even with Svienn dead."

"He has two ealdormen backing him, one of them Ulfcytel!" Æthelred objected, surprised at how he'd almost inadvertently paid Ulfcytel a compliment.

"Of Hamptonscir and Eastengle?" Richard asked rhetorically. "Correct me if I'm wrong, but both those regions are somewhat...ruined...after your friend, Thorkell, took a nice stroll through them?"

"Villages and towns can be rebuilt," said Æthelred. "We've been doing it for years...if everyone in every settlement ever attacked by Norsemen had just stood around and waited to die, there'd be barely anyone left in England. People will return to the land and rebuild."

"That may be true," Richard countered, "but it doesn't change the fact your Edmund still has little support. Cnut's forces will outnumber his several times over. He'll lose, unless you..."

"Unless I return to England, as Wulfstan asks? And what then? Everyone will just rise up to support me?"

"Yes, you are catching on," Richard smirked. "But, just so you know, I will provide you with a force of men to make sure everything goes smoothly. We'll take back your land for you. Don't bother to thank me."

"And if I won't go?"

"Then Edmund will die fighting Cnut, and all your adoring thegns will know you as a coward. And I can't say I care for the company of cowards."

Æthelred's appetite left him, the half-devoured bird upon his plate appearing positively revolting now that his stomach had turned to ice. He hadn't been seeing things clearly. Everything was suddenly moving so fast. He knew Edmund was a promising boy, and he'd also known he'd continue to fight the Danes even in his father's absence. But he'd acted so quickly. Armies? Ealdormen? Retaking the South?! Was Edmund simply the leader England had long sought? Would he really be defeated, after already achieving so much?

His stomach told him all he needed to know. He felt sick, frightened, and anxious beyond words at the idea of losing yet another son...but was this the only way to help him? By returning to England at the head of a Norman army? Wouldn't Edmund resent such a thing, especially since he'd then be denied the throne he knew he deserved? Æthelred suspected he would, if their roles were reversed. He still couldn't understand why so many thegns wanted him back. Why not support his heroic son?

Then all became clear. Wulfstan was Archbishop of Euerwic, and that great city was the centre of power in Norþanhymbre, itself the domain of the Ealdorman Uhtred. Uhtred was a creature of Æthelred's own designs, one he'd placed in authority over the North following his decision to have the former ealdorman of Southern Norþanhymbre,

Ælfhelm, murdered. Eadric had done the deed, as he had so many times before and since, the recollection of such a vile act leaving Æthelred with nought but shame in his heart.

Uhtred would want him back as king so such games could begin anew. All the intrigue, all the treachery, all of it as a means towards further power, with Æthelred playing along as he had in the past. There was no love or loyalty there. England's nobles were not looking to welcome him home because they thought it just. This was a ploy of some kind, born of opportunism now that Svienn was no longer among the living. Æthelred didn't want to go back to that world. He'd make sure Richard understood that.

"I can't leave," he whispered, feeling frail and shaken. "I can't...I have to think of my family. Alaric said..."

"What?" Richard snapped, confused and annoyed both.

"I was a terrible king!" Æthelred wailed, his control slipping. "Alaric told me...I'm not to go back! I have to stay and be a father to my children...I have to..."

"I don't understand a word!" Richard bellowed in exasperation, lifting his hands, palms up, into the air and then down again so they slammed the surface of his table. "I tell you your own son is in danger, and yet you want to stay here with your children? What does this mean? That you only care for some offspring and not others?"

Æthelred shook his head violently, mortified at what his brother-in-law was suggesting. "Th-th-there must be a way we can help Edmund," he stammered, "I...we...we can get supplies and monies to him...mercenaries..."

"The nobles won't accept him!" Richard fired back, still annoyed and confused. "Your people want you, Æthelred! Edmund is an unknown to them...a warrior, yes, but a king? They know you, and they want you! Why are you not pleased?"

"Why are you so adamant that I must go?" Æthelred demanded angrily. "You were willing to hand me over to Svienn if the political situation remained difficult...you're getting something out of this, aren't you?"

"Yes," Richard said simply. "I'll have a puppet on the throne of England."

"What?!" Æthelred fumed, getting to his feet, his hands clenched into fists. Hereward was suddenly at his side, alert and attentive to any potential dangers, Æthelred in turn drawing strength from the man's dedication. "You think I'll be your lackey, Richard?! A King of England in thrall to a Duke of Normandy?! Intolerable!"

"Oh, but you will," Richard said quietly, several of his guards having moved over to flank him lest the fearsome Hereward turn hostile. "You'll do precisely as I say, whenever I wish. Godgifu's life hangs in the balance because of it."

"You'd use my daughter against me?! A child! Your niece, no less! Your sister would have your guts if she heard you make such a thr..."

"Enough from you!" Richard roared, his expression turning from blank to furious within the space of a second. "You take everything so personally, Æthelred, like every angry Saxon fool out there, but this is POLITICS! We have both done terrible things for the sake of securing our realms from danger...all I do here is what any good ruler would do."

"Threatening a girl to force her father into obedience? That is not the mark of a good ruler, Richard. But rest assured, I will be taking my leave with my fam..."

"Godgifu stays here," said Richard bluntly. "You will go with Edward and Alfred and my sister...all of your household, and those murderous Norsemen you dragged here with you...but your daughter stays with me."

"Why?!"

"Insurance. Once we take back your throne for you, I'll need to know we're still friends. I'd be so very disappointed if, at a future date, you were to become uncooperative. Godgifu would share in that disappointment."

Hereward stepped forward, his shoulders squared. "You threaten a princess of the House of Westseaxe!" he snarled, drawing his sword from its scabbard with a single purposeful flourish. "I'll have words with any man who does so! Dane, Norman, it matters not!"

Æthelred was close to panic. Hereward was standing tall, powerful and magnificent, but Richard's guards had stepped forward, their spears levelled and ready. The duke himself had a new expression, and it was this that had Æthelred so frightened, such was the unconcealed menace that filled his eyes. Duke Richard wasn't a man you just threatened on a whim. Æthelred would have to act swiftly to defuse the situation. Hereward's life, at the very least, depended on it.

"I will do as you ask," hissed Æthelred through gritted teeth. "I will heed the words of Archbishop Wulfstan and return to my faithful subjects…just let me take my daughter with me."

"Godgifu will remain with me, and you will agree now to everything we have discussed, or I will have your man here killed."

Hereward's eyes widened, from anger, or fear, Æthelred could not tell, although he suspected it was the former. He wasn't backing down, and he cut an admirable figure right now as he faced down the Normans, but there was little chance he'd prevail even if he killed Richard and escaped from this chamber. They'd be outnumbered, lost, and trapped in a keep full of hostiles. Thorkell might be of use if he was around, but he was outside Rouen, preferring the company of his own kind and the warriors he had left to the arrogant Normans. There was little hope to be had here. Æthelred had again run out of options. He had to submit.

"I agree, Richard, I agree. Whatever you want, whatever you need…just don't hurt my family."

"Get your man to put his sword away." Richard wasn't even looking at Æthelred when he said that. Those hateful eyes were meant solely for Hereward, not that he cared. He was still standing ready, a mighty weapon to be unleashed, should Æthelred will it. But he did not. He could not. He knew what he must do, and so he did it, giving Hereward the order to stand down and relent. Æthelred still detected a hint of hesitation in Hereward's movements when he sheathed his sword. He'd like to kill Normans, and Richard, most definitely. Æthelred knew exactly how he felt.

"You push me too far, Æthelred," said Richard casually, now strangely at ease. "I gave you refuge here…food, shelter, all of it…and now we've found a way to get you back home, you go and create such drama."

"Spare me your smug waffle," Æthelred groaned. "You took me in because you thought you'd be able to use me to bargain with Svienn. Now you've found another use for me…and you're prepared to harm your own niece to see it done."

"And you no doubt think me an ungodly man because of this, yes?"

"Richard…because of all this…I don't even see you as a man."

That prompted an interesting reaction. The duke didn't adopt any of his three typical expressions, instead looking vaguely surprised that Æthelred still had a little defiance in him. It passed, and the duke got to his feet, his manner relaxed, like he was going to take a stroll after an otherwise pleasant repast.

"Get yourself ready to travel," he said. "We'll be taking Lundenburg in one single surprise assault. You don't need to worry yourself with the details. Olaf has already given me some ideas."

"Olaf?" Æthelred asked, surprised at the mention of the man. "He's still here? I thought he was to return to Norway to fight the Danes?"

"I convinced him to remain and play his part," Richard said dismissively. "We have a small window of opportunity...whilst those Danes that remain in England move south to put down the rebellious Ælfric, we'll be landing by sea to cut them off from Lundenburg. It'll be perfect. Then all you have to do is sit on your throne. Even you should be able to manage that."

"How do you know Ælfric is about to be attacked?" asked Æthelred, wondering just how accurate Richard's information was now that Svienn was out of the picture. News could travel fast, but not that fast. Richard couldn't be getting daily reports on enemy troop movements. He was overconfident. It was a failing of his.

"It's what I'd do," Richard answered contentedly. "This Cnut...if he intends to take his father's place, he'll be moving to get Hamptonscir back under his control. He can then frame Edmund as a petty bandit of some sort, since he'll have no lands and no people willing to support him. You and I will, of course, have made our move before any of that happens."

"You really have thought of everything, haven't you?"

"I have, Æthelred. You should try it sometime. Perhaps then you won't be so...disappointed in life."

Richard turned away with that last jibe, walking with an exaggerated swagger towards a stone archway Æthelred knew led to his personal chambers. Æthelred had never been invited to visit them, but he could always tell when the duke was within, the feeling of menace that would emanate from the archway making him think of beasts and monsters he'd read about in myth. These tales often had a hero who would slay such creatures. Æthelred dearly hoped that one day he'd get to play that part. Richard was a man who needed killing, now more than ever.

"By the way, Æthelred..." The duke had stopped at the archway, leaning back against it with his arms folded casually and his twin guards on either side of him. Æthelred glared at him from across the room, wondering what this long pause was supposed to signify. "That last comment about me not being a man..." There was another pause, drawn out and tiresome. If only the insipid bastard would get to the point. "...that's the last time you get to insult me. If you speak ill of me in future, even whilst in England, rest assured I will learn of it, and your daughter will suffer accordingly."

He then left, passing from view, the silence that followed deep and heavy. Æthelred took stock of the situation. He was a prisoner now, as he had been before, arguably, but now his fate was sealed. He liked to think in his life that he'd proven himself a man who could bear a heavy burden, but what had been allotted to him now was too much, and not purely because he didn't want to be England's king. He'd never be able to rest with his daughter held in captivity. His every thought would be on her. He'd become a miserable figure again, isolated and alone upon his throne, his few remaining years angst-ridden and painful as he fretted over his absent child.

There was nothing for it. He had to tell his wife. Emma would be the only one who could possibly change Richard's mind. They were siblings, after all, and despite the duke recently implying he'd taken a dislike to her, this was still their best chance to avert an unbearable future. Emma had to step up and do her part. Æthelred hoped she'd have the strength of will to do it. Hearing about her brother's plans for Godgifu would test her to the limit. She'd need her wits about her and her emotions firmly under control if she were to make a difference. If Æthelred knew her as well as he thought, that part would pose a problem.

He left the hall, Hereward with him, and progressed down several flights of stairs and out into the main courtyard. It was cold, and Æthelred ignored everyone present whilst passing through, the clutch of young Normans who'd been practising archery all bowing to him as if he were already king again. He found Emma right where he'd thought she'd be, in a chamber overlooking the courtyard and close to the keep's main study. All the children were with her, sitting at her feet diligently as she read a book to them. They adored her, all of them, and Æthelred's breath caught in his chest as he beheld Godgifu. She was so young. He didn't know how he'd be able to say goodbye. He'd already said farewell to so many of his children, either in parting or when he'd stood, miserable and broken, as they were lowered into the earth. No father should have to bear such things. He had no intention of adding another similar tragedy to his list of regrets. Godgifu would NOT be taken from him.

She looked up, her eyes wide with anticipation at his sudden appearance. He strode over to her and gathered her up in his arms, her brow furrowing slightly at this sudden and uncharacteristic display of fatherly affection. He stayed like this for a few moments, rocking her back and forth, all those present gazing upon the spectacle with delighted bemusement. When he eventually put Godgifu down next to her brothers, Emma was looking at him intently, her expression telling Æthelred that she was well aware something wasn't quite right. He didn't know how he was going to find the words to speak on what her brother intended. But he must. They had to find a way to scupper his plans. The alternative was just too terrible to bear.

He took Emma by the hand and led her away from the children. Hereward remained, standing watch over the three of them, Æthelred trusting him implicitly to keep them safe. Emma shut the door behind them as they slipped out into the passageway beyond, the draught from the courtyard again biting at Æthelred's heels. Emma felt it too, drawing her arms up to her chest to rub at her shoulders, her gold-embroidered summer dress unsuited for the unusually chill weather that had suddenly come upon them.

Æthelred let the words flow. He told her everything, not bothering to refine or otherwise obscure the truth of what had happened. When he'd finally finished, he didn't feel any better. Emma had a look to her; restrained, cold, unimpressed. She either didn't believe him or knew something he didn't. What she said next stunned him to insensibility. She knew. Richard had told her all his plans, for Æthelred and Godgifu both. And she'd agreed.

The shouting began. Emma had betrayed him, his own queen, and here she stood now, attempting to justify herself. She insisted her brother didn't mean any real harm, that she knew him better than Æthelred and could therefore judge his true intent. She said they'd be able to get Godgifu back once they were in England, arguing they'd have their own kingdom and that Normandy wouldn't be able to resist them. It was then Æthelred saw a side to his wife he'd never seen before.

She was a fool, and worse than that, she was easily swayed. The promise of returning to England to be queen again had robbed her of what little wisdom she possessed. Æthelred had no choice. If she wouldn't try to talk her brother out of his dastardly schemes, he'd have to entertain other, less diplomatic measures. He called for Hereward.

He appeared when prompted, and he and Æthelred began walking away, Emma's calls for him to remain and "see sense" and "not do anything to make things worse" echoing after them. He ignored her and kept on, his mind racing with yet more anxious thoughts. He didn't believe Emma was actually comfortable with the notion of Richard holding her daughter as "insurance", as he'd so recently put it. That wasn't like her, and she'd never given much indication previously of being a neglectful or otherwise incapable mother. She was, however, too fond of the easy life, enjoying the trappings of power and resenting immensely their exile in Normandy. It sickened him that she'd apparently agree to just about anything to get back to all that, even if it could easily be claimed her brother was manipulating her and she simply didn't understand the situation for what it was. Emma was a dimwitted and superficial woman. Æthelred wished he'd seen it before. He'd have never put so much trust and faith in her then.

A plan hatched in his mind. He had to get out of the keep, away from Richard and away from Rouen, until he could think of a way to turn the tables on his villainous brother-in-law. Then he remembered the obvious. He had Thorkell, and Thorkell still had over a thousand men camped out and bored beyond the city walls. They couldn't attack Rouen, such was its garrison and fortifications, but they could still raise hell across Normandy, burning and looting and using what was left of their fleet to escape reprisals. Richard would crack like an egg, and it would be glorious.

He thought to turn around and get Emma, or at least the children, to come with him. He was just about to do so when he felt something stir in his mind. He had a hunch, an instinct, a premonition even, that told him Emma would now only betray him further if given the chance. If she was indeed under her brother's influence, and it certainly seemed that way, she'd sense Æthelred intended to move against him and so raise the alarm. Æthelred would have to act alone from this point on, trusting only those men he could rally to his side. He could always get his children back as part of his future deal with Richard, once he'd finished making him pay for his treachery.

They'd almost reached the main gatehouse when the trouble started. There were more Normans than usual here, all kitted out for bloodshed, and they sprung into action upon spotting Æthelred and Hereward. They rushed towards them, gabbling in that insufferable language, their faces scrunched up and indignant. Hereward drew his weapon when one of them tried to accost Æthelred, sending the poor fool crashing to the ground with a single expert blow to the hamstrings. The Norman flapped about like a dying fish, struggling and failing to get up, his blood wetting the cold stones. His comrades reacted quickly and collectively rushed Hereward, their echoing shouts suggesting outright murder was now very much on their minds.

Hereward let rip with an ear-splitting roar and commenced hacking and jabbing at his enemies in a blurred flurry of frenzied aggression. Yet another Norman was knocked over, shock and surprise upon his bloodied face, his compatriots stepping over him to try and land a blow on the enraged Englishman. Hereward was the better man, his courage and skill exceeding any of those trying to kill him, yet the Normans had the numbers, and Æthelred could tell they'd been stationed here precisely to prevent his escape. Richard must have known he'd try something and had correctly guessed Hereward would make problems of his own. The duke, as always, had laid his plans well.

One of the Norman soldiers got lucky, thrusting his spear up and under Hereward's left arm to shatter his mail and shed his blood. Hereward reacted like lightning, and the Norman dropped his spear with a cry, his hand nought but a splintered ruin. Æthelred suddenly found himself flat on his back, his ears ringing as a Norman struggled to step over him and take on the furious Hereward. Æthelred cried out in fear when that same Norman landed almost atop him, his face a broken mess and his dead eyes glazed over. Hereward was hit again, the blood from his wounds splattering downwards over his mailed leggings, but he still fought back, the Normans around him shouting and raging in their efforts to bring him down. This couldn't go on. Brave as he was, Hereward would not prevail here. Æthelred had to do something.

A voice called out, the shrill, sharp sound getting everyone's attention. It was in the Norman tongue, and Hereward's attackers had clearly understood it, for they were backing off in wary respect of the man they'd only just been so intent on killing. Æthelred got up, Hereward somehow managing to assist him despite his wounds. They both turned to look at whoever had spoken, wondering who their mystery saviour might be. Æthelred's heart sank. He thought he'd recognised the voice. It was Emma, flanked by guards of her own, standing at the intersection leading away from the gatehouse. She did not look pleased. Æthelred had a feeling her displeasure wasn't solely reserved for his attackers.

"I told you not to do anything foolish," she said with a scowl, her green eyes strangely lifeless.

"And I have not," Æthelred countered, "and I will remind you, wife, that you are sworn to honour and obey me. Come with me now, and let us leave this place so that..."

"It's too late for that!" she snapped. "You have put us all at risk with your stubbornness! I know my brother better than you, husband, and I told you he would not harm our daughter...all he wills is..."

Æthelred lost track of the words, his mind instead grappling with the novel sense of revulsion he felt for his wife. She prattled on for a bit longer, all for the sake of trying to convince him that Richard wasn't a scoundrel. She was so...stupid. She had no idea how ruthless the world was, nor how family ties counted for little when it came to the cut and thrust of high-stakes politics. Richard had really worked wonders with her mind. He was leading her down a path of his own choosing, and she was foolish enough to walk it.

The Norman warriors who'd only recently been locked in combat had by now stepped forward to seize him. Æthelred commanded Hereward to submit, knowing his brave champion would fight to the death to protect him if he so wished. Their captors began pushing them both back down the corridor towards Emma, Æthelred fixing his wife with a disdainful look. She said something, her voice soft and pleading, wanting his forgiveness for the captivity she herself was helping to impose on him. She said it would all be better once they were in England, once he was king again and she a queen. Godgifu wouldn't have to stay in Normandy for long, and then everything would be well, and all would be...

"Shut up, you damned harpy!"

Æthelred smiled at his words as he was led away. He was defeated and his future was uncertain, but the expression on Emma's face had been priceless. She'd done a terrible thing, betraying her husband and her daughter for the sake of schemes she couldn't possibly understand. Æthelred didn't think he could ever forgive her for that, and as the door to his new-found cell closed in on him, he found himself standing tall. Richard could have his day, returning Æthelred to England and forcing him to reign as his proxy. Let him have that, and let him feel smug, secure, and pleased with himself at what he'd wrought. Arrogance was a weakness, and the Normans did arrogance like no other people Æthelred had heard of. It was only a matter of time until the duke made a mistake. Then Æthelred would have his daughter and, after that, his vengeance. He was looking forward to the latter in particular.

XVI

The inside of the cottage stank, the smell from the pile of human waste in the corner smothering everything without mercy or distinction. He was trapped here, the door locked and the windows shuttered and sealed, a disused, broken chimney also choked with soot. Osbert had already tried climbing up there. There was no escape that way.

He couldn't tell how long he'd been in this accursed place. When Svienn had done the decent thing and died in front of his assembled guests, Osbert had expected to be executed, thinking the Danes would want to place blame on any Saxon within reach. He'd taken a beating, sure, and one of his teeth was now rattling about in its socket, but he was still very much alive, of that he was certain. His long-suffering nose wouldn't let him forget it.

They'd then brought him a visitor, pushing him through the door and sealing it tight behind him. Osbert hadn't recognised him at first, so besmirched was his visage, but he'd soon come to see him for what he was. A traitor. An aetheling, yes, but still a traitor. Eadwig was his name, and Svienn had made a huge fuss over him, correctly thinking his defection would make a dent in English morale. Osbert had experienced a very brief encounter with him at Svienn's awful drunken feast, but it hadn't made a lot of sense. Superficially, it looked like Eadwig had moved to save his life, snatching up the blade that Osbert, in his clumsiness, had dropped in plain sight. Svienn had started dying immediately after that, the whole spectacle distracting everyone so Eadwig's actions had been forgotten. Until his appearance here, that is. Osbert had pressed for answers.

Sadly, Eadwig had not been very talkative. He'd made some evasions, ignoring the thrust of Osbert's questions to distract him with talk of his brother, Edmund. Osbert knew all about Edmund, of course. He still served him: a point he wasn't shy about sharing with Eadwig. The aetheling hadn't been perturbed. He'd smiled, actually, and told him they'd "likely be hearing from Edmund soon" before refusing to answer any more questions. Osbert had eventually given up, frustrated, and allowed the days to pass without bothering Eadwig. If he had indeed been implying that Edmund was about to make a move on Gainesburg, then Osbert wanted to be ready. Escape was his duty. He couldn't help anyone whilst cooped up like this in a cottage full of excrement. He had no idea why Eadwig was so unfazed by it.

"Help me think of a way out." Osbert had asked Eadwig this before and not gotten much of a response. It was only boredom, if he were being honest, that had caused him to ask again.

"I can't open the door," Eadwig said calmly. He was always so patient, like he knew everything and all that needed to be done was to wait.

"I know that!" simmered Osbert. "But there must be something we can do…you helped me before, now can't you do it again?"

"You were misjudging the situation…as you are now…it doesn't always pay to rush into things. You wouldn't have succeeded in your bid to stab Svienn in front of everyone, especially since you insisted on dropping your own weapon."

"It wasn't intentional," said Osbert awkwardly, "but you know you have my thanks for what you did…I did thank you before, right?"

"No, but it's appreciated. I'm glad to see respect and civility yet remain somewhere, even in as unpleasant a place as this."

"So you'll help me again?"

"We can't escape," Eadwig said as if it were all so obvious. "We can't tunnel beneath the ground, and the chimney is inaccessible. The only possible way to do what you ask would be to spring something when the door is opened from without."

"Then let's do that!" said Osbert excitedly. "I've seen that done before…we'll take them by surprise next time they come to feed us."

"You have a weapon?"

"No, but…"

"Then your plan will likely see us killed. You're brave, braver than I…but there's no sense in taking risks when all they'll lead to is our deaths. We should wait."

"For what? If Edmund is on his way here with an army…"

"You're getting ahead of yourself," Eadwig cautioned. "I never said that. Just that we may be hearing from him shortly."

"So what does that mean?"

"It means to have hope…what should I call you?"

"Osbert. My name is Osbert."

"You're from Eastengle?" asked Eadwig.

"Yes. How can you tell?"

"Because you have the accent. I've had the good fortune to hear all the dialects and peculiarities of speech that England has to offer…and allow me to make another guess as to your origins…you're close with Ulfcytel?"

"I am," Osbert answered sadly. "He's helped me a great deal. Given me purpose, you could say. Cnut wanted me here to…"

"Show you off to everyone? Make them think Ulfcytel was a spent force and that his own people were abandoning him?"

"You're a perceptive one," Osbert conceded.

"Not really," said Eadwig. "Cnut isn't a subtle man, and he'd made it clear enough why you were with him. I suspected you were not happy with the situation, and when I saw you heading straight for Svienn with murder in your eyes…"

"You could tell all that just from looking at me?" Osbert didn't know what to think now. He knew little about Eadwig, other than that he was King Edmund's younger brother. If he was as intelligent as he seemed, Osbert thought it all the more imperative that they escape. Edmund would need wise counsellors. But could this one be trusted? He'd still not explained how he came to be here, with a welcome from Svienn, no less.

"Not for certain," Eadwig said modestly, "but I like to think I can read people. I've spent a lot of time at study…and a lot of time around others…men of importance, you understand. Men who thought I was the quiet one, who was always outshone by his brothers and wasn't worth bothering with. Their arrogance made them drop their guard. Made them readable."

"I don't know what to say," said Osbert with a slight shrug. "But I must ask you…why did you come here, to Gainesburg? Were you really looking to swear fealty to Svienn?"

"That's a very loaded question, Osbert. I think you'll find the answer you seek by referring to what I just said about arrogant men…they let their guards down. And when they do…it can present certain opportunities."

"So you planned to make Svienn think an aetheling was coming over to his side, knowing he'd be elated, distracted…vulnerable to assassination?"

Eadwig smiled coldly, his eyes appearing to almost light up with delight at Osbert's realisation. "You have an interesting mind," he said quietly. "I really can't comment on your hypothesis. Svienn was killed by our Saint Edmund, after all."

"You really think that?" asked Osbert doubtfully. "I mean…I'm as faithful a man as any other, but…is there a history of that sort of thing? Saints reappearing to strike down those who've wronged them?"

"Svienn certainly thought that's what was happening," Eadwig answered. "And he was no fool…if he saw Saint Edmund coming for him, then that's what he was seeing."

"That's what he was seeing? But nobody else did. So it was just Svienn seeing it, then?"

"Yes." Eadwig was grinning now. He was enjoying this exchange, and if he were honest, Osbert was pleased that he didn't appear to be a traitor. He was too at ease with himself, and by the sound of it, he knew a thing or two about what had happened that night the Danish king had breathed his last. Osbert paused for thought, wondering what he should ask the aetheling next. If Osbert was following him right, Svienn had indeed seen something, and from his perspective, it really was Saint Edmund. Of course, nobody else had seen it with him, so that could only mean…

"Svienn was seeing things? A hallucination? What could cause that? And one so dramatic, no less…"

"It's a good question," Eadwig said sagely, like he himself was far removed from such events. "If I had to answer, I'd say that Svienn was consuming a great deal of food and drink that evening…if some of it had spoiled, or if something had been introduced to an otherwise harmless repast…"

Eadwig stopped, letting his words hang in the air. Osbert nodded slowly, his own suppositions cohering in his mind into something more solid. He wouldn't ask Eadwig to explain himself further. It was a risk having such a conversation to begin with, what with the Danes wandering about outside. But Osbert could read between the lines. Eadwig was no traitor to the English nor his brother's cause. He'd feigned obedience to Svienn, hoping the old king would be fooled into…

The door flew open, and a large, burly figure stumbled on through with all the grace and poise of a drunken ox with no eyes. It almost fell, managing to right itself only at the last second. The door slammed with a hefty crash, and Osbert could hear the Danes on the other side bolting it shut again; their speed denying them any opportunity to break out. His mind wasn't on escape, though. He knew who this man was. What he did next was done entirely on instinct. He embraced him.

Osbert stayed like that for a good few seconds, uncaring if he was embarrassing himself or if the target of his affections might find them unwelcome. Fortunately, Ulfcytel had recognised Osbert, and he promptly returned his embrace with a huge, crushing bear hug of his own. They both held the other, no words being necessary for the moment, each man displaying their relief and joy through the most simple of gestures. When Ulfcytel finally released him, Osbert felt lost for words, a sense of awkwardness suddenly washing over him as he realised what he'd done.

"Don't be embarrassed, lad," Ulfcytel said, sensing his angst. "I've been worried about you, too. Just how did you end up here? Did things not go well in..."

"You're bleeding," interrupted Eadwig. "How are you even able to stand? Your side looks like it's been hit with an axe."

"It HAS been hit with an axe," replied Ulfcytel bluntly. "And what brings a man of your refined sensibilities here, Eadwig? It can't be the smell."

Osbert peered at the ealdorman, noting how his mail shirt was split just above the left side of his waist. It had been bandaged, and bandaged tightly, but it was an old rag of a thing, soaked and crusted with blood and the grime of the road. Ulfcytel had also taken a beating elsewhere. His left eye was swollen, and both his lips had been split, the scabs that coated them the colour of aged rust. The old wound in his leg was clearly bothering him, since he kept his weight shifted over, like he was instinctively keeping as much pressure off it as possible. The only bright side in all this was the state of his hands. They were bruised and calloused, his knuckles looking like they'd been scuffed with a stone over and over until they'd bled. Ulfcytel had been dealing out punishment as well as taking it. Osbert expected nothing less.

"Don't worry about me," Eadwig said, his expression halfway alarmed as he looked Ulfcytel up and down in all his battered glory. "Your capture will have serious ramifications if we're to resist the Danes...just how in God's name did it happen?"

"So you're on our side then?" asked Ulfcytel, his eyes narrowing in suspicion. "Because your presence here is a bit of a surprise to me. Were you attempting to make friends with Svienn, only to have him tire of you?"

"It's not like that," Osbert said, feeling he had to stop any misunderstanding before it could form. "Eadwig...the aetheling...he put on a ruse so Svienn would think..."

"Keep your wild theories to yourself," Eadwig interjected irritably. "Your words are dangerous and could get us all killed. Think such things if you will, but do not speak them aloud. At least not for the moment."

Ulfcytel gazed at Osbert for a few moments, his eyes then shifting back to Eadwig. "You always had your nose in a book," said Ulfcytel, his eyes still narrowed. "Am I to think all that reading came in useful? That it helped you become a man of guile and cunning?"

"You can think that," replied Eadwig, "and perhaps you'd be right. If we get out of here, I may tell you more, if you ask nicely."

"Oh come on, man!" snapped Ulfcytel, his impatience suddenly boiling over. "We may never leave this place! Why not tell me what happened? I could use a good story in these final hours."

"I won't," Eadwig said with a shake of his head, "and you shouldn't be talking like that. It's bad for morale."

"What makes you think we're to be executed?" Osbert piped in, alarmed. Ulfcytel seemed to think on it, a scuffed and bloodied hand pawing at his beard contemplatively.

"This Cnut is on edge, lad. He gave me a right earful when I got dragged before him...but a lot of it was for show. I can tell a lot about a man from the look of him and the sound of his voice. He's taking his father's death hard. He'll be unpredictable and looking for vengeance. He might as well take it all out on me."

"He's taken a lot of hostages," said Osbert, "and he's not killed me yet. He paraded me about, knowing people would recognise me and think I'd turned on you...I never did. I never would."

"He wouldn't," said Eadwig quietly, "that I can attest to. I had to stop him from trying to bury a blade in Svienn's neck. He'd have only thrown his life away."

"Is that so?" Ulfcytel asked, clapping Osbert on the shoulder, his grin broad and genuine. "You went to have a go at old Svienn yourself? I don't know why I'd be surprised at that. You've fought like a mad bastard on more than one occasion. Many a Dane has rued the day he met the mighty Osbert!"

Ulfcytel laughed, Osbert too snickering at hearing his name spoken like he were someone from legend. There was no mockery here, Osbert knew. It was a poor leader who didn't take his own men seriously, and Ulfcytel was anything but that. Osbert knew he respected him, cared for him. It was something that had kept him going. As sad as it sounded, Ulfcytel was the closest thing Osbert had to a father. Perhaps one day he'd tell him that. He had a feeling the ealdorman wouldn't object to hearing it.

"So, just how did you get captured?" Eadwig asked, unamused.

"I got hit with an axe and fell over," said Ulfcytel.

"Let's be serious now," Eadwig pressed. "I know you'd gone south to Hamptonscir. Edmund told me. You were caught?"

"Not exactly," Ulfcytel replied, turning as serious as Eadwig could possibly wish. "We took back Porteceaster and Suthhamtunam both for the Ealdorman Ælfric, but I…I made a mistake. I involved myself in a family squabble, thinking I was doing the right thing by an old friend. I was wrong."

"And that's how you got captured?" Eadwig asked, perplexed.

"No…no…I mean…Ælfric's daughter-in-law, Æva…there were things I told her husband, Alaric, about Ælfric's past. I thought he should know at the time, but now that he's dead…Æva was all alone, a widow…I thought perhaps Alaric would want her to know what I'd told him in Canterburie. It didn't go well."

"It all sounds very complicated," Eadwig said, "and in my experience, complicated things bring complicated troubles. And Alaric? Was this the one my father was raving about not so long ago? Something about a dream?"

"Yes and more, but that's all old news," said Ulfcytel with a wave of his hand. "Alaric is dead, and my foolishness has seen Æva…oh God…"

"What is it?" asked Osbert anxiously. "Is Æva dead?"

"I hope not! But we were all heading back north and…she didn't want to live with Ælfric after what I'd told her…she had to leave, and I thought to go with her and Cenric…but some bastard Danes attacked us in some bastard village in the middle of bastard nowhere. I got hit in the side. Fell right over and couldn't recall much until I was on the road, all tied up and surrounded by bastards."

"They would have noticed your sword," Eadwig said thoughtfully. "I'd say you were fighting with a blade suited to a man of your rank? The Danes are always looking for things of value. They'd have clocked you for an important man from the look of your weapon."

"Aye, aye, so they decided not to kill me. But none of that makes me too happy. I don't know what happened to the rest of them, Cenric or Æva or Brandon or anyone. They could be dead for all I know. And it's my own damn fault."

Osbert reached out, putting a tentative hand on Ulfcytel's shoulder. He didn't quite understand what the ealdorman was really saying, but he could tell it might not be a good idea to push him to elaborate more. Family feuds were delicate affairs, and if

Ulfcytel had involved himself in one, it was no wonder it had backfired. Such things were best left alone, even when approached by outsiders with good intentions. Osbert hoped Æva was alright. It would be a cruel thing for her and her son to have been slain in the wilderness, alone and unmourned.

"I failed in my bid to kill the Abbot Ælfmær," Osbert announced suddenly, hoping to change the subject after also realising he'd not yet told anyone how he'd ended up here. "It could have been done, but the abbot..."

"He had a guard, did he?" asked Ulfcytel.

"He did. I was imprisoned for a time in Lundenburg, until Cnut decided to show me off here so the thegns would think I'd betrayed you. I don't know what happened to Eamon. I hope he escaped."

"Let's hope he got away," said Ulfcytel softly, his eyes gentle. "He's a resourceful one. He survived Hringmere and Canterburie both. We'll be seeing him again."

"You really think so?" asked Osbert hopefully.

"I do. Trust me, lad. We'll get out of here and find all our lost friends."

Unfortunately, escape continued to elude them. There was no way out of the cottage, and despite Osbert telling him so, Ulfcytel still insisted on checking everything himself, trying the doors, windows, and even attempting to squeeze his thunderous bulk up into the chimney. Nothing worked, and Ulfcytel eventually sat down, saving his strength and also seeing the good sense in Osbert's plan to wait until somebody opened the door from without. It had worked in Canterburie, although that was because Wulfnoth had snuck in to rescue them. Osbert wondered where Wulfnoth was now. He seemed like a man who always had a way of turning up when he was least expected. Was it too much to ask for him to make an appearance here?

Eadwig sat up, his spine straight and his head inclined like he was listening. He moved over to the door, pressing his ear to the wood, Osbert and Ulfcytel watching him. This went on for a few seconds, an expectant silence settling over the room. Then the shouting started.

They rushed to the windows, trying to peer out, although frustratingly the shutters remained stuck fast. Ulfcytel tried the door, putting his shoulder and back into it to force it open. It didn't work, but Ulfcytel growled and kept up the pressure, his pride refusing to let him quit. Osbert saw the danger. The ealdorman wasn't well, and the wound in his side would reopen if he insisted on exerting himself like that. He eventually managed to convince him to stop, Osbert more surprised than anyone that his words had actually gotten through to him.

The racket outside, however, did not relent. There was more shouting now, surprised and angry, as if some kind of struggle had broken out and a great number of others were rushing to intervene. Something large and heavy smashed into the cottage door, the suddenness making Osbert jump. Whatever it was then began sliding down the outer surface, its sizeable weight finally coming to rest upon the ground. Osbert tried to get a look through the minuscule crack between the door and the frame, but couldn't make out much of anything. Something had definitely happened, though, and it was not to his liking.

Then the smell came on. This wasn't the usual stench of their prison, something none of them had so far gotten used to, despite the length of their stay. This was something else, familiar and yet all the more terrible for it. Thatch was burning. Someone had set a fire, and it was spreading quickly if the snapping, crackling sound now filling their ears was anything to go by. Osbert pulled back from the door, his nostrils stinging from the acrid fumes. He couldn't get away from it. He soon saw why. It was their own roof that was on fire.

It all happened so fast. They could hear and smell it, sure, but what was surprising was how quickly the smoke intensified, the entire ceiling above slumping and pressing inwards under a burgeoning wave of heat. Osbert tried to cry out, but the air was snatched from his lungs, his heaving breaths failing to assuage his discomfort as the temperature went from warm to hot to burning. Ulfcytel leapt into action, throwing his great weight against the door over and over, the cottage now a blazing, smoke-addled inferno.

The door was stuck fast, whatever was holding it on the opposite side refusing to budge even with all three of them hurling themselves against it. Osbert's eyes were weeping, the stinging, suffocating smoke endeavouring to dry them to cinders. This was the end. There was no escape. They'd die here and not even know who had seen fit to condemn them. It wasn't the death Osbert had wanted. He could tell from the looks of his companions that they felt the same.

Clarity then struck, born from sheer desperation. Osbert rushed over to the hearth, inserting himself again into the blocked chimney and scrabbling upwards with all his might. He'd not been able to manage it before, the layers of impacted soot, grime, and who knows what ensuring he couldn't even see the light of day, but he had no choice now. He had to make the climb and get outside. He had to free his friends. Ulfcytel was too big to fit in here, and Eadwig, for all his slight build, was probably too feeble. That left only Osbert. If he were going to die, he'd go out fighting. He wouldn't want it any other way.

He was soon plunged into darkness, the only light coming from the billowing furnace below him. He scrambled upwards, the sound of Ulfcytel's hacking, booming cough still audible over the smothering crackle of flames. The rough-hewn stones around him were hard and cruel, and they cut into his hands, drawing blood from his palms so that he left a sequence of red prints in his wake. Despite the pain, he kept on, but before long his climb was blocked altogether. There was some kind of substance above him, caked into the walls and preventing his ascent. He couldn't see what it was, such was the darkness, but the more he propelled himself into it the more he felt it yield, his fear of death and desire to save his friends adding strength to his efforts.

Something gave way, and a deluge of hard, gritty matter slid and tumbled past him, showering everything as it went. A faint sliver of daylight poured downwards, illuminating Osbert in his plight. He continued to try to push himself upwards, but it was tight and difficult, and the more he climbed the less room he seemed to have. The chimney soon felt even narrower than before, the dark, caked substance that clung to its walls still serving to slow and impede. His limbs began to ache, the cuts on his hands and shins causing his eyes to water yet more. He couldn't breathe. It was all too much. He felt weak, and his body began a slow, inevitable slide downwards, his strength entirely spent.

Then he heard the sound. Osbert didn't think he'd ever heard Ulfcytel afraid, not at Hringmere, nor Gipeswic, nor in any other battle he'd seen him fight. The ealdorman had always seemed unflappable; solid like rock, but the noise coming from below said even he had his limits. He was howling, and choking, too, the great hammering sound he was making on the door growing weaker by the second. It was desperate, pitiful, yet it moved Osbert to hear it so. Ulfcytel was a man like anyone else. He didn't want to die down there. He wanted to go home to his wife. Nobody could blame him for that. It was with that in mind that Osbert gritted his teeth and tensed, his wearied muscles contorting for one final effort. He couldn't let the ealdorman die like this. He hadn't betrayed him to Cnut, and he wouldn't fail him now.

Osbert wasn't sure how he did it. The blockage just seemed to vanish, smashed apart in one single act of furious defiance that saw him erupt from the top of the chimney and out into the open. There were flames everywhere, across the roof and beyond; a burning, flickering sea that blinded him to all else. He went to scream, but his throat and lungs were suddenly red raw, the broiling, acrid fumes choking him so severely he feared he might fall. He couldn't let that happen. He'd do the only thing he could do.

He hauled himself from the chimney, the flames licking at his skin, and began to slide and tumble down the combusting roof. The pain was intense, and his descent soon became entirely chaotic; his vision spinning around and around in a whirl of agonisingly intense yellows and oranges. It all ended so abruptly, and Osbert's almost unconscious body fell into the street with a heavy thump, his clothes and flesh scorched and seared.

Other men might have died there, expiring from the fall or just giving up and succumbing to their fate. Before Hringmere, Osbert had been a kind and gentle soul, and in a way he still was, but his journey with Alaric and Ulfcytel had taught him many things, both men inspiring him with a love of country and faith and brotherhood. He'd lost Alaric, and his heart ached to think of him, but Ulfcytel was still alive. He could hear him now, still hammering on the door from the inside, his cries frightened and feeble as he fell to heat and suffocation. Osbert wouldn't have that. That would not be happening to the man who'd taken him off the streets. That would not be happening to the man he'd call father.

He stood up, his vision still whirling, and staggered over to the cottage door, every inch of his body pained and objecting. There was a dead Dane up against it, his chest looking like it had been cleaved inward with an axe. It took Osbert a few seconds to heave him aside, so great was his weight, and he then unbarred the door and hauled it open. He fell back almost immediately, the emerging rush of heat and burning air bowling him over. A second or two went by, the smoke again clouding his vision. Nobody had come out yet. That wasn't good. Osbert would again have to do what must be done. He inhaled, getting the best breath he could before he charged inside to save his people before the entire cottage collapsed.

Fortunately, he didn't have to. Eadwig appeared, his face and clothes caked with ash as he held Ulfcytel's arm across his shoulders to steer him outside. The ealdorman was close to passing out, but Eadwig was alert, his apparently not-so-frail body still supporting him in his bid to escape the fire and get out into the street. Osbert took Ulfcytel's other arm, hauling it up onto his shoulder so they both could take his weight. They'd made it about ten feet away when the cottage collapsed behind them, the entire structure folding inwards with a great roar of burning thatch and crashing masonry. They paused to look around, all three gasping for breath. They'd had a lucky escape. But they were not out of danger. Far from it.

Flames were everywhere, extending down the street to consume all they touched. People were rushing about between them, the inhabitants easy to spot as they attempted to flee, but others fought one another with a rare fury, their brutal, frenzied movements strangely terrible in the soot-ridden air. Osbert couldn't identify the newcomers. The smoke was too thick, sweeping over the town and billowing upwards towards the sky. All was chaos, the crackle of flames raw and sharp, the uproar of the unfurling battle hammering the ears. They moved through it, Osbert and Eadwig both hobbling and unsteady, and managed to set Ulfcytel down against the warm stones of a house that had as yet been mercifully spared the spreading inferno. He was getting his breath back, and his eyes were open, their whites looking alarmingly stark against his blackened face and singed avalanche of a beard.

A man fell close by, appearing from the chaos to collapse and expire not a few feet away. He was English, for he wore a silvered, dove-shaped brooch that was unmistakably Saxon, and his helmet was a product of the more refined, skilled metalwork that was generally lacking in the armour and attire of the Northmen. His axe, also, had the look of a weapon that had been newly forged, suggesting he'd been equipped by a native smith rather than one far across the sea in parts unknown. Osbert picked it up, feeling somehow guilty to be depriving this warrior of what could easily have been one of his most prized possessions. It couldn't be helped, and if he'd been intent on killing Danes, it was fair to say he wouldn't object to Osbert having it. There was work to be done here.

Somebody else came through the smoke, bellowing and raving, their strange tongue ugly and discordant. The newcomer was Danish and evidently of some seniority, the metal rings flowing down his arms indicating he was of high rank back home. It took a few seconds for Osbert to realise he was having trouble seeing, the smoke and also a wound just below his hairline ensuring he kept having to blink both grit and blood from his eyes. He was frightened, and he clearly thought Osbert might be of a mind to render him aid. A serious mistake, on his part. Osbert split his brow open without hesitation, the head of his new axe cleaving through splintering bone without difficulty. The weapon really had been freshly forged.

Ulfcytel suddenly appeared at Osbert's side, his ordeal in the cottage now just a memory. He reached down, snatching the sword from the Dane's still twitching hand, and held it up to the menacing light cast by the flames. He grunted once, apparently content to keep the blade. He formed words, his gaze falling upon Osbert, his voice quiet yet imbued with a terrible intensity.

"We have a chance for vengeance. Follow me and let us take it."

The ealdorman strode on ahead, Osbert and Eadwig following swiftly lest they lose him in the smoke. They'd gone perhaps another twenty feet when a sudden wind blew in from the east, dispelling the bleak shroud that had only just blinded them to much of their surroundings. Osbert looked around, knowing they were close to the spot where Svienn had set up camp to regale his submissive subjects in what he thought would be his moment of triumph. That hadn't gone so well for him, and by the looks of it, what was happening here now wouldn't have pleased him either.

It was a battle, there was no doubt, and with it came all the noise and bloodshed Osbert had come to expect. The bulk of Cnut's forces seemed present here, struggling to maintain a broad line of shields that was slowly coming undone under the armoured weight of hundreds of furious adversaries. The fighting was intense, and those attacking were undoubtedly Englishmen, their full, ornate helmets and majestic flowing banners giving them away.

Ulfcytel stormed into it, bellowing and howling and shedding blood with every flick of his blade. Osbert followed, his blood up and his anger flowing hot and fresh. The Danes seemed surprised, unsure, as if they'd been caught unawares and the scale of the battle unfurling before them was entirely unexpected. Osbert couldn't understand it. Did Cnut not control the town? Had he not posted sentries to look out for an approaching force? If the fool had not, it would likely be his undoing. Osbert hoped it would be so.

They reached the shield wall and tore into it, they and the rest of this English force smashing Danes aside in a hacking, stabbing frenzy of hate and rage. The Danes, however, were not defeated yet, and one of them made a swing for the ealdorman, their heavy, brutal axe arcing through the air. Ulfcytel leaned back to allow the weapon to sail past him before countering with a sudden and precise blow of his own. Osbert had never used a sword, but he could see how deadly they could be, for Ulfcytel's strike had left the Dane without much of a neck, the blade disintegrating his throat entirely to leave his head barely clinging on by a few stubborn shreds. He fell backwards, his head finally coming free of his body, several Danes in their now splintered shield wall looking on in unashamed horror.

That didn't stop them from trying to fight back, and Osbert was almost impaled upon a thrusting spear, sheer luck helping him twist and pivot himself away. He retaliated, shattering the spear at the mid-point of its long, broad shaft, but his enemy wasn't rendered helpless, and he came after Osbert with a wicked-looking hand axe, his eyes alight with bloodlust. Osbert lashed out, fracturing his shield twice over whilst doing his best to avoid the broad sweep of that axe. They carried on like this, each man doing their best to undo the other, until Ulfcytel made an intervention by splitting the Dane's head.

Osbert didn't thank him. There was no time for that, for both of them were now fully caught up in the swirling melee that was the battle for Gainesburg. Osbert killed once and then twice, the scent of blood vivid in his nostrils. He cut down another and strode forward, stepping over the twitching corpse to seek a fourth opponent, a furious howl erupting from his trembling throat. Some brute, taller than most, flew at him out of nowhere, his axe barely missing him. Osbert was forced back, struggling to avoid the fiend's deadly reach. The huscarl was broad and well armoured, as was typical of his sort, and there were others pressing in around him in counterattack, their long axes already reaping a bloody harvest.

Ulfcytel wasn't deterred. He'd seen it all before in his long life, and he wasn't going to let the emergence of the huscarls test his courage. He rushed into them, striking left and right, a flood of frenzied admirers following after him to meet the enemy head-on. Osbert did the same, a nervous yet steady Eadwig close behind. He'd hoped to find the man who'd almost killed him just a few moments ago, yet if he were alive, Osbert could not tell, so close and chaotic was the fighting. The fires didn't help, and whilst the worst of them were dwindling, the smoke was again cloying, settling over the battlefield to choke and obscure.

The conflict rumbled on without pause or mercy, and Osbert killed once more, his axe slicing the arm and then the side of the head from another huscarl intent on ending him. Everyone, friend or foe, was now packed in as tightly as could be, this flailing mass of men groaning and cursing whilst they stabbed and hacked and fell and died in the smokey orange glow. It was hard to breathe, for the heat and fumes wouldn't let up, making Osbert wonder if he'd died and somehow ended up in Hades. He couldn't see Ulfcytel or Eadwig, and everyone seemed a stranger. He was alone; an anonymous face within a procession of the damned, all intent on shedding blood and taking lives with all the malicious energy they could yet muster.

He heard something close by: the bass thundering of heavy hooves upon earth. Men on horseback had appeared, their majestic forms emerging from the smoke. They smashed into the enemy, scattering or crushing them underfoot like they were nothing but barley before a scythe. Osbert gasped upon seeing who led them, the tears flowing freely from his eyes as he realised he was not, after all, in hell.

Edmund was there, atop a dark, muscled beast of a steed, his sword raining down blows in great overhead arcs that split skulls and shattered shields. He looked magnificent, a circlet of silver upon his head, the burnished rings of his armour catching the terrible light of the inferno. He swept on through the enemy, hacking at them from the saddle, and others followed, the cavalry's charge giving way to a mass of men on foot pressing forward in their wake.

Osbert and the others raced after them, the courage of the newcomers spreading over the rest of the English force like some great and wonderful blessing. A chant started up from the ranks, the sound steady and sure, the word "Ironside" repeating over and over. Osbert joined it willingly, his blood-sodden axe taking yet more lives as he roared the sobriquet of his rightful king.

Danes died by the dozen, crushed under foot and hoof or cut to pieces by axe and blade, this great hero on horseback seemingly immune to their increasingly desperate efforts to unseat him. They began to scream, bellowing at each other to fall back, others simply wailing like they'd suddenly realised England was not the easy prey they'd long perceived her to be. They died hard, their despair not so deep that they just gave up, their shattered bodies falling thickly upon the blasted ground.

Those able to flee sped towards the river, the smoke from the town hanging low and heavy over the tranquil waters. Osbert could see several ships were already pulling away, the oars moving quickly and with little coordination. The Danes now pressing in upon the river bank risked filling some vessels to overcapacity, yet few seemed to care, such was their fear of the vengeful English. Another ship began to move, its deck weighed down by a mass of anxious warriors, only to suddenly pitch to the right, spilling them into the river. They thrashed about in the water, some vanishing under the weight of their armour, and those not yet embarked then started fighting each other, apparently willing to spill the blood of their own kind if it meant securing a place aboard ship. The English pursued them, and Osbert followed, all still screaming the name of their king. They'd not let any escape if they could help it. Defeat and death would be the heathen's lot this day.

This really reminded Osbert of Gipeswic, where he and Alaric, Ulfcytel, and Eamon had chased the enemy into the waters of the Arewan, but this was on a far larger scale, the polluted air and the ominous, simmering glow of the fires again making him think of Hades. Edmund was still with them, his loyal retainers fighting at his side, and Osbert spied the wiry, deadly form of Wulfnoth, the man weaving his own circuit of death with that red-tasselled spear he so favoured. There was no stopping them now. Victory was at hand, and it was glorious.

Or was it? Elated as he was, Osbert couldn't imagine bringing this war to a conclusion unless one man, in particular, got what he had coming. Cnut wouldn't relent, Osbert knew. As long as he was alive, there would simply be no peace. Cnut was ruthless, cold, and also cruel if he felt he had to be, and was utterly convinced that he and his kind were entitled to England and all it had to offer. His famous father was dead, but that wouldn't slow him down. He'd be potentially more dangerous than ever now, especially if his people back home recognised him as king. He had to die. He deserved to die. Osbert owed him that.

It was with some considerable regret that Osbert realised he would have to wait. He saw something, a familiar face, out there upon the water, staring back at him as his ship pulled away to make the escape downriver. It was Cnut. The cur had fled, abandoning what was left of his army for the sake of safety. Osbert strode out into the bloodied waters, staring all the while upon Cnut's sooty, exhausted face, Cnut staring back with something akin to fearful recognition.

Men were still dying all around, some Danes struggling on even as they were speared and cut, their vital fluids fouling the waters with their foreign taint. Osbert ignored it all and waded onward, the water rising to his stomach. He stopped there, fixing Cnut with a glare filled with promise. "I will have your life," Osbert muttered to himself, "and what you've seen here is only the beginning."

The fighting behind him stopped. There were no Danes left to kill, not within reach, and the only ones alive were rowing away, the tempo of their oars panicked and disorderly. Osbert stayed as he was, watching Cnut retreat, his heart cold. The shoreline then erupted behind him. Men were screaming and bellowing, their jubilation ringing out across fire and smoke. Then came the cry again. "Ironside!", over and over, the name thundering from hundreds of throats, a triumphal chant for a people long bereft of victory.

Cnut looked away. Osbert smiled.

XVII

The smoke had finally begun to clear, the sting in his eyes fading as fresh tears washed them clean. Cnut tried to hide it, rubbing his face with what was left of his cloak, his trembling hands doing little to inspire confidence. It was all his fault. He'd sent too many men away, thinking he was honouring his father by having them escort him home. It was all foolishness. He'd have honoured him better by securing his conquests. Instead, he'd undermined what he'd fought so hard to achieve.

Cnut pushed his way to the front of the ship, hoping the view from the prow might somehow blot the images of recent events from his mind. The vessel was fit to burst, the weight from all these exhausted men causing the waterline to rise to an alarming height, but the way ahead was calm and clear. The other ships were with them, also full but still moving fast. There was no sign of pursuit. With any luck, they may yet escape.

He hadn't wanted to believe it was him. The last time he'd seen this Edmund had been in Eastengle. The man had been frightening enough then, but from the feats Cnut had just witnessed, he'd somehow grown even more fearsome. He had more followers - better equipped this time - and they loved him still, each of them gaining strength just from laying eyes on him. He'd bested every Dane that dared test him, that damnable blade of his catching the light as it killed over and over, the fires from the town making him look like some terrible image of vengeance personified. Cnut didn't believe in the old Gods, but if there was any man in the world who might just be blessed by some raging God of war, it was Edmund "Ironside". He'd heard the chant, and he could see why they called him that. Edmund wasn't wrought from flesh and bone. There was iron in him, cold and unyielding. Cnut found it terrifying.

"Who set the fire?"

Cnut turned at the sound of Østen's voice. He was talking to him, and in his shaken state, Cnut thought he heard the briefest hint of disrespect. "I don't know," Cnut answered, trying to sound as steady and unruffled as possible. "I didn't even know there was an army approaching. How did they get so close like that?"

"I know not," grunted Østen, the abundance of blood and soot that covered his already haggard face making him difficult to read. "There was no word from the sentries, or that which we did receive came too late. Their speed...their numbers..."

"It's my fault," Cnut said suddenly, surprising himself with his admission. "I allowed the death of my father to get the better of me. I should have acted quickly. I should have taken us back to Lundenburg. There was no point in just sitting out in the middle of nowhere like that. We became a target."

"Perhaps...but a warrior, and a warrior king, should learn from his enemies," said Østen, his voice quiet yet still audible over the groans and lamentations of their men. "This Englishman...the one who leads them...we need to kill him. No conquest will be secure as long as men like him are alive."

"I will face him in battle," Cnut began, wanting to put a brave face on it. "I will see him dead at my fee…"

Østen stepped closer, his hand reaching out to grip Cnut's elbow. "No," he whispered firmly, "you won't survive him. Not as he is. Not as you are. Not yet."

"What do you mean? I can fight…"

"I know!" Østen hissed, his grip on Cnut tightening. "But you can't fight that. I've seen many heroes in my years, my king. That man is one of them. The Gods are with him…"

"Gods?" asked Cnut, shaking himself free. "You forget yourself. There is only one God…and you are not to lay your hands on me again."

Østen bristled visibly, his eyes widening as if angered. "I meant no disrespect," he said quickly, "but to overcome this foe, we must think before we fight. We lost this day because we were unprepared. Just as you are unprepared still. We must learn."

"Learn what?" Cnut asked, annoyed and also fearful that their men might overhear this conversation and lose heart yet further.

"How to defeat men such as this Ironside."

"Edmund," Cnut corrected, "his name is Edmund, and his father was a weakling king. I'll beat him like any other."

"Odin's eye!" Østen exclaimed, his open frustration causing many a man to look in their direction. He seemed to regret it instantly, narrowing his eyes and lowering his voice to something more appropriate. "I admire your courage," he said apologetically, "but this is a real war now. Æthelred was a coward, and our victory over him was largely because of that. England will be a totally different beast to master now it has a man worthy of it. Please understand this."

He had a point, and Cnut was glad of his advice, even if his manner was impertinent. He could understand well enough how a people might change depending on the character of their leaders. That had been England's handicap for years now, and the fool Æthelred had done little to remedy it, relying on the same corrupt, ineffectual weaklings who'd gone on to betray him. With a fighter like Edmund in charge, the English could be different. They were different. Cnut wouldn't be fleeing if it were not so.

He scowled at the thought. The gathering at Gainesburg was supposed to have awed the newly submitted thegns, impressing on them the necessity of loyalty and what would happen to them should they prove disobedient. When Cnut had first arrived he'd thought it just another town, its people suitably fearful and the sole purpose for visiting being diplomatic. The northern thegns would appreciate a king coming so far north, Svienn had said, claiming rule from Lundenburg had not always suited them. Cnut had thought him gracious in that, assuming the gesture was likely to be well-received. The future had looked bright, yet Svienn had died that very night and the English had turned from acting as beaten dogs to ravenous wolves.

It was then that he noticed Østen was hurt. He was bloodied and covered in soot like everyone else, but it looked like a spear had hit him in the chest, shattering his mail to leave a nasty-looking wound of dark, congealing fluid. Cnut ordered him to sit, instructing others to treat and bind his injury. Østen had fought well, and Cnut owed him much. When the attack had come, Cnut had tried to fight, but the chaos of the sudden fires had made it difficult to marshal his men, surprised as they all were. Østen had demanded Cnut get to the ships, telling him directly that to remain would mean his death. Cnut had ignored him, fighting on until he'd seen Edmund atop that horrifying black beast. He'd understood then that Østen was telling the truth. The battle could not be won. Shame and defeat was their bitter repast this day, but through grief and loss, men could yet live to fight again. He wouldn't forget that. He'd learn from all this and get even.

He first had to make sure they survived. The river was treacherous, seeming to twist and turn at odd intervals in a manner he'd not observed when they'd first come here. They were having to head north, into what Cnut assumed was territory held by the rebellion, but they had no choice if they were to emerge into the Humbre and make it into the open sea. Another hour passed, the river finally broadening and then turning to permit them to head east, but it was another hour after that until they finally came out onto the coast, the air fresh and vital in contrast to the suffocating hell they'd fled from.

The sea stretched out around them to the north, east, and south, its grey, choppy waters seeming to almost harmonise with the equally grey and foreboding sky. Cnut could tell they were carrying too much weight, so he ordered his captains to stay close to the stony shore lest the worst happen and they had to swim for the beach. It was with that in mind he had everyone take their byrnies and helmets off. They'd sink like stones with those on. A warrior's death was one thing. Drowning was something else. He wouldn't wish that on anyone. Save Edmund, perhaps.

Hours passed, the sound of the oars heaving through the grey waves reassuringly monotonous. It began to rain, the drops large and heavy, but it helped to wash the soot from their hair and beards, the spray of the sea doing likewise. Daylight began to fade, the sun dipping below the horizon with all due majesty, the wind and rain increasing in intensity as night came on. Cnut didn't sleep, not that it was possible to lie down in such crowded conditions, and in truth, he didn't think he'd be able to rest even if he'd been back in Lundenburg in his own bedchamber. There was too much on his mind, his fears and troubles rising up from his subconscious like the biting wind that now assailed them. The weather calmed itself at some point, the pitch blackness making it difficult to say when, yet as dawn broke Cnut was still up, his hunched form gazing out from the prow with indifference.

He refused to eat, fearing his men were offering him what little they had out of courtesy rather than respect. Cnut was terrified of that. This had been his first battle as king, and he'd lost, and not only that, he'd had to run. It had been a truly terrible start to his reign, and if his men felt pity for him because of it, he'd have to act fast. He couldn't have rumours spreading once they reached the capital. He wouldn't be known as the king who'd fled. Nobody would really want to serve him then, even if they still felt some affection for him. They had to see him as the man he was, or at least the man he may yet become.

He wasn't entirely sure what that might look like, and judging from the sorry state of his people, he wondered if any of them would have the strength for gossiping if and when they reached Lundenburg. They were shocked, their eyes wide and alert, like they were still caught in the path of Edmund's men and the man himself might reappear to slaughter them at any moment. They were scared, and some were wounded, looking gaunt and sickly to the point death might yet claim them. This was no groundless fear, for some had indeed expired during the night, their wounds overcoming them despite the best efforts of their friends. Cnut had gruffly ordered their bodies to be thrown overboard, ignoring the muted protests this had provoked. They were still too low in the water, and if the weather turned again he wasn't confident they'd be able to stay afloat. They had to cut weight. He tried not to wince at the sound of the corpses hitting the water. It was with some regret he observed the other ships were having to do the same.

A piercing crack suddenly rent the air, and the whole deck heaved beneath Cnut's feet, the sheer force of it nearly sending him flying backwards into the men crowded behind him. Shouts of alarm sounded all around, the oarsmen ceasing their labours to look feverishly for some explanation of what had befallen them. Cnut's feet felt wet, and he soon saw why, the seawater sloshing across the deck confirming his worst fears. They were taking on water, and fast. In a few seconds, it would reach his knees. The ship groaned audibly, a palpable shudder passing down the length of the hull as if it were alive and very much in pain. They'd hit something. It was time to move.

Cnut stripped off quickly, divesting himself of whatever armour he'd kept on, his men following his example. The water was up to his thighs by the time he'd finished, and others were already scrambling overboard in panic, their ship again making that odd groaning sound as something scraped and ground against the hull. There were rocks here, submerged in the otherwise grey, featureless water, but only their ship had run afoul of them, the others further off from the coastline apparently remaining safe, for the moment. Cnut went to leap overboard, gesturing for his remaining men to do the same, but it wasn't really a leap, for the sea had now flooded the deck, pouring over the hull to drag them down into the depths.

They swam towards the beach, Cnut calling out so his warriors would follow and know he was yet with them. He'd gone about a dozen feet when he felt something pull at him, making him fear some man or perhaps beast had laid hold of him to drown him. The reality of it was perhaps more dangerous. Their ship was going down, and its great mass was heaving them with it. Cnut slipped beneath the waves, kicking and flailing his arms and legs furiously. Sea water filled his mouth and nostrils, the sensation cold and terrible. He couldn't breathe. He couldn't escape, and his whole world was now water, the stuff pouring into him like some dark and unstoppable spirit staking a claim on his very soul.

Then something else made itself known. His own voice, speaking up from his heart in defiance, telling him what he needed to hear. This couldn't be the end. He was a man of destiny; a king, worthy of his father, worthy of his people, worthy of Denmark, and worthy of England. Drowning would not be his fate.

He wasn't wrong. Somebody grabbed him from above, their almost casual strength hauling him upwards. He broke the surface, spluttering and coughing, his lungs inhaling great heaving breaths from the freezing air. He saw soon enough who had saved him. Østen. Cnut had almost failed to recognise him. He was without his armour, as was sensible, and his normally voluminous beard was trailing in the water like some kind of peculiar creature. He nodded and grinned, content to allow Cnut to get his bearings without any further assistance. He then turned and began powering through the water towards the shoreline, Cnut endeavouring to keep up. He looked back once, just in time to see the mast of their ship vanish beneath the waves. It was a sorry sight. But at least they were alive.

When they reached the beach they were exhausted, the men coughing and gasping whilst they did their best to extricate themselves from the heaving water. The beach was unpleasant, the sucking, sticky mud giving way to a hard mass of pebbles stretching on and on in either direction, but Cnut wouldn't complain. He instead stopped and began signalling to the other ships, and as luck would have it, they responded as he wished and began heading towards them. They avoided the area where their own vessel had been wrecked, as logic would dictate, but their captains otherwise made landfall in record time, the twin ships disgorging their human cargo without incident. They all stood on the beach, some armoured and armed, others freezing and disarmed like Cnut, all wondering what to do now. There wasn't enough room in their two remaining ships to accommodate everyone, and Cnut couldn't be seen to just take one and use it to get himself to safety. These men had fought with him, and he wouldn't abandon them. They'd all face this predicament together.

Cnut took a spare axe from someone, another offering him a dark, woollen cloak for the sake of his dignity. They then formed a single column, Cnut and Østen taking the lead, and began trudging up the shifting shingle beach towards an area of long grasses, coarse and hardy, to the south west. They kept this up for an hour, the men silent and tense, their view of their surroundings generally obscure. It was getting close to mid-morning when they broke free, emerging out of the grasses and into clearer terrain, their eyes falling upon something quite unexpected.

A fort of some kind, made entirely of wood, lay ahead, looking like it had been constructed on a slight rise to give a commanding view over a well-travelled road heading in from the coastline. Cnut didn't think it would stand up to much, if he were of a mood to resume the old Norse ways of looting and plunder. It was fortunate for whoever resided here that he was their king. He was owed allegiance, and violence would come only if he were defied.

Cnut led his bedraggled force onto the road, each man looking rightly apprehensive in the face of the crude wooden battlements and the warriors clearly visible upon them. Some shouts were heard on the wind, and the gates then opened, heaving backwards to allow several riders to gallop forth. They made straight for them, these mystery horsemen, and Cnut gestured for his men to hold their ground, hoping in his heart this wouldn't be the start of a fight. They'd not made it far when they'd been shipwrecked. The rebel English force that had defeated them could have moved south into this area. Edmund himself could be about, demanding allegiance from anyone of a mind to give it. That could make things difficult for Cnut. The axe would then be his only option.

The riders stopped in front of them and began gabbling, the one Cnut took to be in command demanding they identify themselves "lest they be fired on from the walls." Cnut could see they meant it, for a line of bowmen had appeared along the fortress battlements, their expressions eager as they took position. Cnut announced himself. He was the son of Svienn, and he was king here, although he took care not to mention his recent defeat lest it drive these men to defiance and earn him an arrow to the neck. Surprisingly, these English were quite amicable to what he'd said, the lead rider even bowing his head slightly in acknowledgement. It was an even greater source of surprise for Cnut that they then saw fit to invite him inside, claiming their "Lord of Lindesi would be honoured to play host" to him. Cnut was thinking of accepting when Østen again squeezed his elbow. Cnut turned and saw the look in his eyes. Going into that fortress would be a fool's decision, one that could see his head parted from his shoulders and delivered to that bastard, Edmund. Cnut wouldn't stand for that. This "Lord of Lindesi" would have to earn his trust.

He appeared momentarily, one of the riders having returned, on Cnut's order, to fetch him. Cnut remembered him from the thegns' gathering at Gainesburg, and he was glad to see him again, despite how feeble and foolish he still appeared. He was out of shape, of middling age and apparently unconcerned with his weight, his broad face sporting a wiry brown beard that was blowing about in the wind like it wanted nothing more than to detach itself from his chin. He was dressed as if for a hunt, his tunic and leggings all suitable for an afternoon of leisure, but he had an impressive sword at his belt, which looked to be the only thing that might imply this placid fellow was, in fact, a man of rank. His eyes sparkled when he stopped and gazed upon Cnut. For some reason, he was genuinely pleased to see him. Cnut couldn't think of a time when any other Englishman had looked at him like that.

Cnut kept things simple. He again avoided mentioning the battle they'd fled, but he did say there were rebels in the area and that he hoped he could rely upon the "Lord of Lindesi's loyalty" as he passed through his lands on his way to Lundenburg. That got a more than surprising reaction. Reaffirming the oath he'd given Cnut back in Gainesburg, the lord arranged for a wagon of supplies to be brought out, the food and clothing prompting a raucous cheer from the assembled Danes. A dozen horses were also delivered to them, and Cnut took to the saddle, feeling suddenly restored now he was on horseback. Lindesi even asked to accompany them all to Lundenburg with a detachment of his own troops, claiming he'd be "honoured to escort my king to his seat of power." Cnut felt a little suspicious, but he wouldn't refuse him out of paranoia.

They set off south, this "Lord of Lindesi" making for pleasant, if uninspiring, conversation, and for the first time Cnut almost felt like he was indeed King of England. Even Østen seemed at ease now, both Saxon and Dane looking as if they'd finally reached some kind of accord. Cnut hoped this would be a sign of things to come.

Days went by, this united force heading south at a decent speed. The weather stayed agreeable despite the cold, and the villages they passed through appeared free of dissent or malice, the inhabitants making themselves scarce as they went by. When Lundenburg finally came into view, Cnut was beyond glad, the city walls and the promise of rest and a good feed almost bringing tears to his eyes.

The people largely ignored him when he and his men marched through the gates. Cnut was initially angered by that, but the warriors on watch here made up for it by rushing to him. They greeted him en masse, hailing him as king, their spears and axes hammering off their shields in a riotous cacophony of acknowledgement and respect. Cnut's anger cooled with witnessing it, and he rode on through the streets in a lighter mood, Østen and Lindesi at his side. Lundenburg's citizens might be indifferent to him, but he still had the admiration of his army. For the moment, that was all that mattered. One day soon, all Englishmen would learn to be as accommodating as those from Lindesi. It was either that, or suffer the same fate Cnut had in mind for Edmund.

By the time he reached the royal halls, Cnut felt reasonably optimistic. He rode through the gates into the compound, and the men on duty hailed him with yet more shouts and shield bashing. The Jarl Knud appeared, looking well-fed and pampered in his furs, but he became emotional when he beheld Cnut atop his steed and fell to his knees, words of fealty spilling from his lips. Everyone seemed to have heard of Svienn's death, although the terrible battle they'd fled from didn't seem to be common knowledge. Cnut suspected it would be foolish to mention it out in the open like this, so he dismounted and took Knud's hands in his, accepting his vow and thanking him for taking care of his city. Knud had always been loyal to his father. Cnut was glad to have him on his side, even if he was a bit soft for his tastes.

Cnut got himself washed and dressed, ordering Østen to see that the men were settled before joining him in the great hall. By the time Cnut made it there, Østen was already waiting, his chosen attire of a long mail shirt and wolf skin cloak putting him at odds with the considerably less formidable Lindesi. Cnut, in all honesty, knew that the "Lord of Lindesi", as even he kept calling himself, had a proper Saxon name, but every time Cnut asked him what it was it slipped from memory. It was of no consequence. Lindesi was an obsequious man and, as helpful as he'd been, Cnut fancied his allegiance would likely shift the moment somebody else proved themselves the stronger. Cnut's main worry now was ensuring such a thing did not happen. He had to put on a show of strength. Sitting on the throne would be a start.

It was a good fit. Cnut had dressed for the occasion, attiring himself for war so he looked very much akin to the warrior king his father had been. Indeed, when he'd first seen his father sit here after they'd stormed the city a few months back, Cnut had felt elated, wondering what it might be like to enjoy such an honour. His father had then had an audience, a big one, made up of every coward and capitulating "citizen of note", but Cnut had no crowd of admirers, just Østen, Lindesi, and a now increasingly emotional Knud. That would have to do, he supposed.

They all bowed low, the clutch of warriors guarding the doors doing the same. They then spoke, each man present bellowing their allegiance to "King Cnut" with all proper enthusiasm. He sat there in silence, taking it in and savouring the moment. It felt right. It felt just. He was king, as his father had been and as his father had wanted him to be. England was his, and there was nothing this pretender, Edmund, could do about it. Cnut had the right to it by both destiny and conquest. Edmund was the son of a coward, victorious at Gainesburg, yes, but still nothing in the grand scheme of it all. In the eyes of God, there was only one man who should sit upon this throne, and it wasn't Edmund. Cnut grinned. He felt whole. As difficult as the past few days had been, things were looking up. Then Knud spoke and brought everything down.

"I should inform you, my king, that the Ealdorman Eadric arrived ahead of you and, after delivering the terrible news of your father, took a portion of our army and marched south to deal with the rebellion there."

"Wait! What?" snapped Cnut. "You gave him troops to march south? Why?"

Knud turned a little pale, uncomfortable at the change in Cnut's demeanour. "A traitorous lord known as Ælfric has seized lands in Hamptonscir and intends to defy us," Knud said, as if the news was well known and it was strange Cnut was unaware of it. "He's known to Eadric, and was a difficult and untrustworthy subject even in the time of Æthelred. Eadric is to bring him to battle…on your behalf."

"And you gave Eadric command of our own?" Cnut asked, bemused by the idea of an Englishman leading a Danish host.

"Not entirely. I assigned a group of my own captains to lead it with him. I would have done it myself, but that would leave Lundenburg without direction, and I wouldn't trust Eadric to be left here alone."

Whatever irritation Cnut had been feeling towards Knud began to ease. He'd made a decision, a troubling one over troubling events, for certain, but he was right about Lundenburg. His place had been here. Knud had also needed to make a decision concerning this Ælfric. Whoever he was, he'd learn to regret his actions in defying him, yet as much as Cnut understood the need to bring this dog to account, he couldn't shake the feeling that giving Eadric an army had been incredibly foolish. Dangerous days were ahead, and he would have to be both quick and ruthless to survive them. Cnut now posed Knud a question, hoping beyond hope that he wouldn't reply with the answer he most feared. He was to be disappointed.

"Just why is this Ælfric in rebellion?" Cnut asked, his back hunching to lean forward from the throne. "Has he stated some goal? Is he rising in support of someone? Does he hope to make himself king?"

"From what we've heard, he makes no secret of the fact he serves a son of Æthelred," said Knud. "Edmund is his name, and the word is Ælfric fights for him in the belief he'll be raising an army in the North to march on us here. Of course..."

"Of course it's all true," Cnut muttered. "You should know that Edmund is indeed in the North, Knud. We've already met him, and he isn't somebody who can be dismissed lightly."

"Then what shall we do?" Knud asked, concerned again. "Have I done wrong to send so many away?"

Cnut wanted to put the man's fears at rest. He was loyal, and that was a good thing, but for the moment, Cnut was unsure how to respond. If there was a rebellion in the South, it had to be put down quickly, for if Edmund gained strength as he headed down from the North, then Knud's decision might have left Lundenburg vulnerable. There could be no easy decisions here. Cnut was sure of only one thing. He wouldn't be abandoning his new capital without a fight.

He turned to his men, Østen and Knud, issuing his first formal instructions as King of England. "Give me a full account of the troops and supplies we have within the city...and then let us defend these high walls. Battle will soon be upon us, and this Edmund Ironside won't be kept at bay by mere stone and mortar. We'll deal out to him what he's already dealt out to us. Blood and hate."

XVIII

The aftermath of battle was always difficult. In defeat it was perhaps simpler, for when one was defeated, the panicked rush to escape brought on a certain clarity of purpose that allowed little time for troubled introspection. Victory was different. It was a more complex affair, and whilst always preferable to its opposite, it had in this instance left Edmund feeling estranged from his men. He couldn't quite understand why. They were happy beyond words, and they'd celebrated the carnage they'd wrought, their roaring, hammering jubilations rising up into the night sky. It was a great thing to see, and in his heart he knew he'd yearned for it. Yet there was much work to be done. Cnut was alive. Until that changed, Edmund could not rest.

Their surroundings were hard on the eyes. Gainesburg had been more or less destroyed. Nobody was sure who'd started the fire, but it was well underway when Edmund had first noticed it, and for a time he'd been fearful, thinking the smoke a deliberate ploy by the enemy to confuse and mislead. From the looks of it now, it was likely either an accident or an act of spite from the Danes themselves. They knew they couldn't hold the town, so they'd opted to destroy it instead. He'd make them pay for that. He HAD made them pay for it. The sight right in front of him was proof enough.

There were just over a dozen of them. They'd been tied by their wrists and ankles and driven to their knees, their English captors brooking no dissension. Most were injured in some way, their skin and hair blackened or otherwise fouled by the smoke and filth of battle, and from the looks on their faces they expected to die. They knew what they'd done, here and elsewhere. They'd come as invaders, and yet now they were defeated, beaten and bound by those they'd sought to harm. He wondered if any of them felt remorse. He wondered if any of them COULD feel remorse.

He approached one, demanding in a stern voice that he get to his feet and face him. The wretch seemed to understand, but once he was up he refused to make eye contact, his head instead hanging limp and low. Edmund grabbed him by the hair and forced him to look at him, the prisoner's breath coming in fast, ragged gasps. Edmund barked a few questions into his face, demanding he tell him where Cnut had gone. He got nothing but whispered denials. This fool knew nothing. He wasn't important enough to know much about his master. It was the same for the rest of them.

And yet as lowly and pathetic as they were, Edmund wouldn't allow himself to feel sympathy. These men were Danes, and it was perfectly possible they'd done grim and terrible deeds in their years attacking English soil. They deserved death, but Edmund felt spent, and the killing fury that had come over him in the battle was now entirely absent. He wouldn't murder men who had no chance of fighting back. He'd leave them here for a time, in the care of the diligent Wulfnoth. For the moment, he had other matters to attend to.

"I think it's time."

He turned at the sound of Morcar's voice. Like Edmund, he was bruised and battered, his dark armour making him look even grimmer amidst the charred, corpse-strewn ruins of their environs. Edmund knew what he was referring to. He left the captives and followed Morcar, his mind racing as they entered one of the few buildings left standing. It was large, a hall of some sort, and one that had likely served as the abode of whichever man had once held authority here. Whoever he was, they were long gone now, either dead in the fire or killed by the invaders. Edmund didn't have time to worry about such things. There was but one man here he needed to see, and sure enough he was present, sitting down at a long table. Sigeferth was his name, and Edmund had once been as close to him as a son might be to a father. Recent events had shattered that bond.

Morcar closed the door behind them as several of his own men moved to stand guard outside. Edmund didn't question it, knowing what they were about to discuss was not for just anyone to hear. He sat at the opposite end of the table to Sigeferth, not wanting to appear too familiar with the man who'd only recently let him down so spectacularly. It was cold and gloomy in here, and there was no fire to warm and lighten the mood. Sigeferth himself looked lonesome, no doubt from missing his wife, Ealdgyth, and their daughters. Edmund knew he loved them all deeply, but that didn't placate the anger he felt towards him.

They each stared at the other, Edmund hard and inscrutable, Sigeferth aged and sorrowful. Morcar joined them, his face heavy and blank, as was usual. He then spoke, his measured tones giving shape to a statement that, at any other time, would have given Edmund joy.

"The word is that…in his haste to escape us…Cnut has shipwrecked himself off the coast of Lindesi."

Edmund frowned. The men of Lindesi were a strange bunch, and he knew they had submitted to Svienn like everyone else. There was every chance they would render Cnut assistance and help him flee further south, or, even worse, replace his ships with ones of their own to permit him even greater range of movement. Anything was possible with these people, and in times as treacherous as these, it seemed very likely Cnut would still be able to call upon at least some turncoats, especially if he appeared in person to threaten them into obedience. It had worked for his father.

"Is he alive?" Edmund asked. He hoped not. For Cnut to drown would be an amusing, if still disappointing, outcome. Edmund felt his claim to the throne would be strengthened if he were able to kill Cnut in combat, although if the bastard had managed it all by himself, Edmund wouldn't object too much. A dead Dane was a dead Dane, and always preferable to a live one.

"We don't know," Morcar answered, "but there were survivors, and we believe they received some assistance from the locals. My instincts tell me Cnut has survived and is moving south by land."

"He'll fortify the capital should he reach it," Sigeferth said, his voice tired and cracked like old wood. "And even worse, he'll rally the rest of his army and come looking for us. What we faced here was but a portion of his forces. We'll be overwhelmed."

"Then why bother coming?" Edmund asked, annoyed by the pessimism. When Edmund and Morcar had rushed south from Euerwic, they'd intended to gather men from the Five Boroughs to assist them. Sigeferth had come, his hastily assembled force complementing their own, but it had not numbered much at such short notice and the fighting had been hard. It had been difficult, also, for Edmund's army to manoeuvre south of Gainesburg to meet the forces coming up from Snotingeham, but they'd somehow done it. Cnut had been distracted or otherwise negligent when it came to the need to observe the surrounding countryside. That was the only explanation Edmund could think of on how they'd been able to surprise him here. And it had been his undoing.

"I came because you needed me, Edmund." Sigeferth sounded hurt. He looked it, too, his faded blue eyes catching the light as if wet with tears.

"I needed you both weeks ago," muttered Edmund bitterly. "If you'd not bent the knee to Svienn, we could have shortened this war considerably. Loyalty pays off, in the eyes of God and men."

"You're not wrong," said Morcar, "but we've discussed this over and over on the road, you and I. We had to make a decision, and we made it…and now we must live with it. That doesn't mean we can't at least try and make it up to you, Edmund. Our men have bled here, just as yours."

Edmund nodded, wanting to appear gracious despite the continued resentment he knew still lurked in his heart. He had nothing but respect for the warriors who had come to fight with him, but the closer you were to a person, the more grievous the wounds they were able to inflict, should they decide it. Sigeferth, in particular, had hurt him greatly by his decision to recognise Svienn, and as much as Edmund knew he should forgive, the pain was still too fresh. He'd trusted him and Morcar both, and if they could turn on him once, they could do so again, despite the aid they'd recently given him.

"I would now bring your attention to other matters," said Morcar, sounding eager to change the subject. "Ælfgifu is not here."

Edmund frowned, wondering who he could be referring to, but Sigeferth apparently knew and had somehow managed to make himself look even more miserable than before. "Cnut has surely taken her with him," he said anxiously. "He wouldn't have just abandoned his own wife like that, would he?"

"Wife?" Edmund asked, confused and annoyed. He had not known that Cnut had a wife, and Ælfgifu was an English name, the very one borne by his now sadly deceased mother.

"I arranged it," sighed Morcar, looking like he was resigned to an angry outburst from Edmund. "She's the daughter of our murdered kinsman, Ælfhelm. You remember us telling you and your brother of this man, back in Snotingeham?"

Edmund remembered well enough. They'd spoken of it when Æthelstan had still been with them, just after they'd gotten word that their father was to issue yet another tax to squeeze the people of England further. They'd suspected that any monies gleaned would be used to pay off Thorkell, and they'd ultimately been proved right. They'd tried to stop it, but their decision to attack Thorkell at Bernecestre had cost Æthelstan his life. That seemed like an age ago now, and Edmund didn't think he'd ever get used to not having his brother around. Yet none of that explained what Morcar was talking about when it came to this Ælfgifu marrying Cnut.

"You tell me a lot of things, Morcar," Edmund said finally, pushing any thoughts of his brother to the back of his mind. "Tell me who this woman is…and what gives you the right to condemn her to a life of misery tethered to a brute like Cnut."

"As I said, she's the daughter of Ælfhelm," Morcar went on, undeterred. "You clearly remember us mentioning him back when we sought to warn you about the Ealdorman Eadric...Eadric murdered Ælfhelm, on your father's orders."

"And Eadric was then made an ealdorman, just as Uhtred was able to take charge of all Norþanhymbre once Ælfhelm was out of the way. My father was consolidating power in the hands of his supporters."

"That's correct," replied Morcar, "as unjust and unchristian as it all was, that's what I'd say your father was attempting to do. When I submitted to Svienn, I saw an opportunity to right a few wrongs."

"By marrying the daughter of your dead kinsman to the son of a foreign invader?" Edmund wasn't trying to antagonise Morcar. He was just saying it as he saw it, and he had no patience for political games where women were traded for the sake of gaining favour and influence. It happened all the time, of that he was sure, but he didn't like it. It was the way of cold, dishonest men, and such things he could never respect.

"As you say," Morcar nodded, unfazed by Edmund's rough assessment of his actions. "Had Svienn reigned, then a marriage between Ælfgifu and Cnut would have helped shift the balance of power...Eadric killed her father, Edmund, and then manipulated the situation to deprive her family of what little they had left. Yet with her at Cnut's side, Eadric would be outmanoeuvred and..."

"You used a young woman to make a play for increased influence when you thought Svienn was the new power in England. Don't mince your words with me, Morcar, I know well enough how you indulge in such games. Don't assume that because I'm nothing like you, that somehow means I don't understand you."

For once, Morcar looked genuinely upset, if only for a moment. "I regret that you feel that way," he said, "but I could see Eadric had already thrown his lot in with Svienn, and would become potentially even more dangerous with the doing of it. I had to take certain steps. For the safety of..."

"Your family and people, yes," said Edmund, wanting to cut this conversation short. "I understand how you would see the situation. So this poor Ælfgifu was here then? And you expected to save her from your own designs once we'd taken the place in battle?"

"It was my hope, since I put her in this predicament," admitted Morcar, "but it looks like Cnut has taken her with him. Unless you, Edmund, know something I don't?"

"I do not," replied Edmund, curious now as to why Morcar would suspect him of knowing anything about this woman. "If she was here then, as you say, he would have taken her with him when he fled. That doesn't change our plans. We march on Lundenburg. If this Ælfgifu is alive, she'll be there."

"That's good and decisive of you, Edmund," said Sigeferth, "but it's only fair to say we don't have the numbers. This was a lightning victory, yes, but Cnut clearly wasn't expecting us, and he only had a fraction of the total force he landed with at Sandwice."

Edmund sighed irritably. "So what are you saying? That we do nothing? If Uhtred and his ilk are serious about inviting my father home, then we'll have to act quickly. Unless, of course, you want him back on the throne."

"You'll remember what I said to you months ago in Snotingeham," stated Sigeferth quietly. "I stand by those words. Æthelred will blame us for the death of your brother. I can feel it. We'll all be in danger if he returns to hold power once more."

"So why play all these silly games by marrying Ælfgifu to Cnut?" asked Edmund, his attention now back on Morcar. "I mean, you sold this woman to a heathen princeling...only to then decide you wanted to support me after all? I intend to kill Cnut. You understand this, yes?"

"It was a difficult situation," nodded Morcar, his expression again irritatingly blank. "I didn't expect Svienn to just die like that...and I felt marrying into his family would not only help to counter Eadric's machinations but also mollify Svienn. Cnut, as king, is an unknown quantity, and now that the nobles are wanting Æthelred to return..."

"You felt I was your best option to avoid my father's wrath?" Edmund asked, wanting to interrupt lest Morcar try to spin him a line with his honeyed words. "I suspect, also, that you wouldn't want to risk openly siding with Cnut now that Wulfstan has convinced everyone to support my father. In simple terms, Morcar, it was one thing to support Svienn whilst everyone else was doing it, but something else to back up his son and stand alone...am I not correct?"

"Do you really think so badly of me, Edmund?" Morcar asked.

"I think you two do what you think is best for your own," said Edmund, "and that sometimes leads you down dark paths. You fear my father, I understand that, and you can't support Cnut, even with this marriage, now that Uhtred and Wulfstan are both against him. You're survivors. You want to back the side that stands the best chance of leaving you in peace once the dust settles. I'm that man."

"That's not entirely true," said Morcar. "I understand why you're disappointed in us...but when Lundenburg fell, we didn't know where you were...or what you're fully capable of. You've been fighting hard since then. You've proven yourself."

"Had I not done that before? I was no stranger to bloodshed, even before Thorkell came to our door."

"You were a warrior, yes, but not necessarily a leader," Sigeferth said. "You are now. We see how the people love you. They flock to you, like you are one of them. We've never had that, Morcar and I. There's always a gulf between us and the common folk, as is usual for men of our rank. Not so with you. You are a king, Edmund. No man here would deny it."

"You seek to flatter me now, Sigeferth?"

"I wouldn't presume to, but I'll say it as it is, Edmund. We gave in to Svienn because it would have meant death to do anything else. We now side with you because you have what it takes to rule. You've proven it. Accept our allegiance, or do not. The choice is yours."

Raised voices were suddenly heard from outside. Edmund twisted around in his chair, his attention drawn to the front door and the commotion beyond. He stood up and made his way over, only for the door to suddenly fly open, revealing the towering figure of the Ealdorman Ulfcytel. He strode forward, his movements heavy with purpose, and embraced Edmund, his joy over their reunion quite palpable. Edmund returned the gesture, only to see that the ealdorman had brought friends. Eadwig was with him, alongside somebody else who was presently a stranger. Edmund almost gasped as he realised his error.

This was Osbert. His face was partly concealed, wrapped up in bandages and the rest smeared in some kind of ointment. He'd been burnt, badly, and his wounds continued to weep, the cloth that covered much of his face appearing heavy and slick with fluid. Most of his hair was gone, singed away or otherwise falling out. His beard, too, looked so scorched there wasn't much left.

"What in God's name happened?" breathed Edmund. "And how did you all come to be here in Gainesburg, Ulfcytel?"

"We were captured, and then I got set on fire," answered Osbert, his voice, fortunately, sounding like it had been spared any damage.

"He saved our lives," said Ulfcytel loudly, like he wanted everyone and everything to know. "We were trapped, Eadwig and I. There was smoke everywhere, flames…I thought it was the end, Edmund."

"Can something be done?" asked Edmund, nodding towards Osbert's very evident and obvious injuries.

"It is done, my king," answered Osbert. "I don't want to make a fuss. I don't care what I look like. I care about getting even."

"There is something I must tell you," Ulfcytel said gravely, his eyes on Edmund. "If you've not heard already…we were successful in retaking both Porteceaster and Suthhamtunam for the sake of the Ealdorman Ælfric."

"That is good," said Edmund gratefully, "and I've also heard the rumour that Ælfric isn't keeping his allegiance to me quiet. That will get Cnut's attention. I'm depending on it, actually. If the bastard divides his forces…"

"I understand and agree," concurred Ulfcytel, "but I fear I have made an error. A serious one. Something I think may have put others in danger. We should speak on it now."

Edmund nodded and had them all sit at the table, wanting Osbert to rest easy. The young man was appreciative, and Ulfcytel helped him sit down, fussing over him as if he were his own son. Edmund called for some food, one of Morcar's men rushing off to return promptly with several loaves that seemed to have more grit in them than barley.

They ate, Ulfcytel telling them of his adventures in the South and his unexpected reunion with Osbert. Edmund asked Osbert how he'd come to be in the company of Cnut, and it was with some considerable regret he learned of the missing Eamon and their failed attempt to kill the traitorous Abbot Ælfmær. Like Osbert, Edmund didn't really know Eamon, but he knew he was one of Alaric's men from Hamptonscir and, as such, was a veteran warrior of some repute. Edmund hoped that he too was alive somewhere, waiting for rescue or discovery. They needed all the good men they could get.

That wasn't all the bad news they had to tell. Ulfcytel's face seemed to age several years whilst he spoke, painting a sorry picture of how he'd apparently caused some kind of falling-out between the Ealdorman Ælfric and Æva. Edmund didn't press him for specifics, thinking it something best left private, but his stomach turned cold when Ulfcytel told him what had happened after they'd left Hamptonscir. The ambush at night, the Danes coming out of the darkness with murder on their minds. Ulfcytel had been incapacitated, and Æva had fled with Brandon, although he had no idea where to. Cenric had been with them, as had several others, but none of them were accounted for. This was a blow. Edmund hadn't expected it to be. But it was. He felt sick.

Then came the guilt. It was his fault. It had made sense to send Ælfric south. He himself had insisted on it, and Edmund had known the man would be of use to him only if he were able to retake his lands and put them at his disposal. That had been achieved, and he was glad of it, but Edmund now considered himself perfectly negligent in permitting Æva to get caught up in any of that, especially with her son in tow. They should have stayed with him. At his side, where it was safe. He'd have been able to take care of them then. For reasons he wasn't sure of, Edmund now felt this mattered to him more than almost anything.

"This Æva woman…" said Sigeferth, his voice breaking the almost unbearable silence that had flowed in following Ulfcytel's revelations. "The name is known to me…did she, by any chance, have red hair? And this Brandon…blond, with bright blue eyes?"

"That's right!" exclaimed Ulfcytel excitedly. "You saw her? When? Was there a man with them, tall and scarred? That would be Cenric."

"No such man have I laid eyes on," answered Sigeferth with a shake of his head, "but the woman did pass through Snotingeham about a week before I received word to ready my men to meet Edmund. There was a man with her…I don't recall his name, but he looked to have been wandering the wilderness for some time."

"What did he want with her?" Edmund snapped, fearing this mysterious stranger might have meant her harm.

"Nothing," said Sigeferth. "If anything, he was acting as her guardian. They were particularly keen to get to you, Edmund. I did what I could for them in terms of shelter and provisions, and then they left for Euerwic, thinking you'd be there."

"Well, I'm not there now," Edmund muttered darkly. He should be grateful for the news, he knew, and Ulfcytel certainly was, the smile on his face suggesting Sigeferth's words were the best thing he'd heard in an age. "This man she was with bothers me, though," said Edmund. "Can you think of any other defining features he may have had? He must have introduced himself. Are you sure you cannot remember his name?"

"He was quite forgettable, but capable, as a warrior would be," shrugged Sigeferth. "If he told me who he was exactly, then I'm afraid I have forgotten, but there was no apprehension towards him on the part of Æva, nor indeed this boy…what did you say his name was again?"

"Brandon," said Ulfcytel slowly, as if he were hoping to set the word deep in Sigeferth's memory so it might jar something loose.

"That would be Alaric's son," Edmund announced. "And I think, given Alaric's role in recent events, we owe it to him to safeguard his wife and offspring, for one da…"

His voice trailed off, finding the look on Ulfcytel's face both bizarre and unexpected. "What is it?" Edmund asked, his apprehension rising as Ulfcytel struggled to find words.

"The boy is…" he began, clearly anxious now too. "The boy…he looks…I mean, I don't think…"

The door opened again, and Wulfhild hurried over to Ulfcytel, her dark, weather-beaten cyrtel seeming to suit the sombre mood here. She, however, was full of joy at seeing her husband again, and Edmund could only smile as they embraced, their relief and happiness serving to lighten his troubled heart.

"Does anyone else have anything to say to me?" Edmund asked, hoping to cut this meeting short. It was only fair that his sister get to spend some time with Ulfcytel.

Sigeferth stood up, his manner uneasy. "Just tell us what our next move is," he said.

"We head into Lindesi," replied Edmund, "to try to pick up Cnut's trail. I'll send some riders to Euerwic to see what became of Brandon and Æva…but if we can catch Cnut with our army before he reaches Lundenburg, this war will be over."

"And if we don't?" Ulfcytel asked.

"Then we attack Lundenburg with everything we have."

"We do NOT have the men for that," Morcar said forcefully.

"Then send word to your lands," Edmund said, "and get whoever it is you've left in charge there to send us more."

"You know of the losses we took at Bernecestre," Sigeferth warned. "The Five Boroughs cannot just keep coughing up warriors for the next war. It's winter, also. This is not the best time for a campaign."

"I don't care for excuses, Sigeferth," said Edmund, folding his arms across his chest. "This may not be an ideal time for a fight, but since when have we ever had the option of choosing when war comes calling? Dispatch a rider to your holdings and get me more men."

"That will take time," said Ulfcytel now. "I suggest we move with what we have and push through Lindesi on our way south. If we find Cnut, we kill him. If we don't, then we head to Lundenburg and see how things look once we're there."

"All of this depends on the Danes dividing their forces to deal with the situation in Hamptonscir," stated Morcar. "If we've been misled…if Ælfric hasn't declared himself for Edmund…then Cnut will have his entire army waiting for us. We'll be slaughtered."

"And we'll be slaughtered regardless if we just stay here!" boomed Ulfcytel. "Much must be risked in times such as these! We should move now and seize the opportunities God gives us!"

"I agree," said Edmund, his smile making no secret of his approval of Ulfcytel's brave words.

"Yet I say diplomacy is something to appreciate," said Morcar. "You'll learn this in time, Edmund, but if you recall what I said to you in Euerwic…it's imperative that you win renown in the eyes of the people so they see you as a king rather than your father."

"Have I not done that?" asked Edmund with a sweep of his hand. "Do the people not come to me wherever I go, willing to give their blood for the future of England?"

"You know what I mean," Morcar shot back. "I'm talking about men of note…people like Archbishop Wulfstan…people like the Ealdorman Uhtred…"

"A snake!" Edmund spat.

"A powerful one!" Morcar barked. "And one not to be underestimated! I urge you, Edmund, wait here whilst I ascertain how the thegns react to your recent victory. If all goes well, perhaps even Wulfstan will see that God is with us in this fight and give up his foolish notions of having Æthelred return."

"You're too much of a talker," muttered Edmund bitterly, "and I am disappointed in you. The military situation dictates that we press the advantage we've won. Waiting around to see what opportunistic scum like Uhtred think of anything will only allow Cnut the time he needs to regroup. I will not give him that opportunity."

"The archbishop wants Æthelred back as king?" asked Ulfcytel, shock and surprise upon his face.

"He does," Edmund affirmed. "He made a great sermon of it in Euerwic… everything is our fault, apparently, because of our sins…so we have to do what God wills for us and return his rightful king, my father, to his throne."

"God's king, is he?" asked Ulfcytel to nobody in particular. "What rot! We can't go back to those days, Edmund! YOU must be our king! THAT is God's will! Now do what a king would do and lead us!"

Edmund sat back in his chair, appreciative and yet humbled by Ulfcytel's faith in him. He'd already decided what to do. He ordered Sigeferth and Morcar to leave and prepare the army to march. They protested, Morcar more than Sigeferth, but they did as they were told, and when the door shut behind them, Edmund was left in the company of his brother, sister, Ulfcytel, and of course Osbert. That felt better. There was a real kinship here, one that shouldn't be neglected.

"You honour me, Ulfcytel," Edmund whispered, "as do you all. All of you have been tested, in your own way, and all of you have come through for me. To think that I deserve to be so blessed with the loyalty of such people…"

"This is why you deserve to be king, Edmund," Wulfhild said steadily. "You and I both know that many a man in your position would be overcome with pride and ambition. Yet here you sit, expressing gratitude. I believe that says a lot."

"It does," concurred Eadwig. "I know I've not always been the most... approachable brother, to you, or Wulfhild, or any of our family, but I know I've made the right decision by coming to your side. I also know that having our father back in power would be a disaster for this country, as it generally was for much of his reign. We can't have that. I can't have that."

"What have I done to earn this loyalty?" asked Edmund rhetorically. "I have an army out there largely made up of people who volunteered just because they heard I was nearby…I can't understand it. Who am I to them?"

"Do you really want an answer to that?" asked Ulfcytel.

"If you have one to offer, I would hear it."

Ulfcytel paused, the fingers of his left hand drumming upon the table. "I feel awkward saying this," he said finally, "but I suppose it's important that you know. People were frustrated for a long time with your father. That you'll have worked out already. What you might not know is how they saw your mother."

"How did they see her?" asked Eadwig. Edmund felt a little sorry for Ulfcytel. He'd put him in a troublesome situation here, as he was in the presence of three children of Æthelred, all of whom might react very differently to any revelations he had in store.

"They respected her," said Ulfcytel gently, "and saw her as a possible counter-weight to your father's…ineptitude. I don't know why they might have thought that since they'd not be privy to the real details of courtly life, but the common people often get strange notions in their heads, and once in there, they are hard to shake out."

"Don't mistake me either; your mother was a good woman," continued Ulfcytel, taking their silence as permission to speak further. "And once she…passed…the people's adoration remained. Your father's subsequent marriage to Emma was not popular, at least from what I heard. The people felt it was a slight to Ælfgifu's memory. And from what I can gather, they came to place high hopes in her children."

"For what reason?" asked Edmund. "We were so young when mother died, and father's reign was never questioned by us."

"That's not entirely true, is it?" said Ulfcytel. "Word spread about what you and Æthelstan tried to do at Bernecestre…that you attacked Thorkell's army, despite being outnumbered, all so that you might prevent your father from handing over the nation's treasure…I think that made an impression on them. A good one."

"But Æthelstan fell," muttered Edmund solemnly, "along with so many others. It was just another defeat in the grand scheme of things."

"That's not how they saw it," said Ulfcytel, "and that's not how I see it. You both showed that you cared…that you care about this country…and even after all we've suffered, you still fight on, honouring your brother's memory and those of everyone else who's fallen. There's your answer, Edmund. THAT is why the people flock to you."

"Because I care?"

"Somebody has to. A king who genuinely cares for his subjects is a rare thing, Edmund. Everyone knows that. They see what they might have in you."

"What if they knew the truth?" asked Edmund, blinking back the tears from his eyes. "…The truth that a lot of what I do is for the sake of vengeance…I loved my brother, and they took him from me. I'll kill every last heathen bastard on English soil for that."

"I don't believe that's entirely what motivates you," said Ulfcytel. "I've seen men driven solely by the desire to get even…you don't have the bearing of one. Hatred is in your heart, yes, but there's love there too. You loved your brother, as you say, but you love your people also, and you don't want them to suffer any longer. You know I'm right."

Edmund stood up, turning away from his present company to rub at his eyes with his sleeves. When he turned back around, he felt his grief subsiding, his composure thankfully retained despite the emotions Ulfcytel's words had evoked. "I appreciate your insights," said Edmund. "I appreciate all of you. It's a hard road we have ahead of us, but I'm glad I have your friendship, Ulfcytel, and my sister and my little brother."

"I'm nearly as tall as you!" protested Eadwig.

"That's not what I meant," laughed Edmund. "But we should prepare now. I've made my decision, and we have to march as soon as the men are mustered. I want to catch Cnut as he flees south, if indeed he was shipwrecked off Lindesi."

"And what if he gives us the slip?" questioned Ulfcytel.

"Then we'll march on the capital. If Cnut's not there, we can see if somebody will negotiate with us…if he is…"

"You won't be able to take the city," said Ulfcytel with a shake of his head. "You have…what…a thousand men here? There's bravery, Edmund, and then there's rushing into dangers you can't escape."

"Then let us send out scouts," countered Edmund thoughtfully. "Good men…on good horses…I want to know the disposition of the enemy as we move. If they do divide their forces to deal with this supposed rebellion in Hamptonscir, then I want to know. We can then plan accordingly."

"For what?" asked Ulfcytel. "Even with a skeleton force, Cnut could hold Lundenburg against us. We don't have the numbers to encircle the city either. There'll be no starving them into submission."

Edmund stared at Ulfcytel, his eyes hard. "Morcar told me in Euerwic that the thegns will rally to me if they see me act…if they see me as a legitimate ruler. A victory will do that, don't you think? We've had a victory here, a big one. We can make another. All we need do is seek opportunities."

"You mean to threaten Lundenburg as a means to draw Cnut out?" Ulfcytel sounded pleased, just as Edmund was impressed how he'd guessed his intentions so accurately.

"I do," Edmund answered, a grim smile on his lips. "Even if we can't take the city, we'll make a big show of our presence, and I'll wager any number of Danish bastards holed up in there will be looking to get back at us for what we did here. They'll be humiliated. With Svienn dead...they'll be wanting to hurt us. That will make them rash. They'll make mistakes."

"Some kind of hit-and-run strategy then?" asked Eadwig. "Provoke the Danes into venturing out of Lundenburg to deal with us and then lead them to a place of battle of our choosing?"

"I like the way you talk, Eadwig," nodded Ulfcytel approvingly. "You may not be a fighter, but those books of yours have taught you a few things about war. Am I right?"

"You must be right, as it all seems so obvious," Eadwig shrugged. "It's a big deal for any people when a king dies, yet to then suffer a sudden defeat at the hands of those they'd thought beaten...that's going to make an impression. I'd say we have a good chance of making the Danes do something stupid. If that happens, we ourselves will have to be clever."

"Do you have something to suggest?" Edmund was serious. In the past, he wouldn't have asked Eadwig what he thought of military matters, but his brother was proving himself quite adept in a time of crisis. It was a pleasure for Edmund to see him coming into his own.

"Say we do provoke the Danes into venturing beyond Lundenburg to attack us," Eadwig began, his voice slow and thoughtful. "We're going to be outnumbered, even if Cnut, or whoever, has sent an army into Hamptonscir. We'll have to get them to chase us...lead them somewhere where we'd have the advantage."

"I can see where you're going with this," said Ulfcytel, "and in times past, I think it may not have worked. Svienn knew England simply because he'd attacked it so many times, but he's gone, and Cnut won't have his knowledge. He'll be dependent on advice from others, but from what I can tell, much of his army is relatively unseasoned. For some, this will be their first time in England."

"So they won't know the country," nodded Edmund. "So that's an advantage to us, something that could help even things out despite our fewer numbers. We'll have to assess the situation as it unfurls...but I feel confident. God is with us. I know it."

"How do you know?" asked Wulfhild quietly.

"I just do," said Edmund firmly. "But we must pray. Pray for me, and pray for each other. Despite what some might say, it's not God's will for us to suffer like this. That's not His way...for if it were, He would be cruel and hard-hearted, and that in itself is a blasphemous notion. God will help us. He has to."

Edmund noticed they'd finished the last of the bread that had been laid out. Ulfcytel was largely responsible for that, admittedly, but it was getting late, and they all needed sleep. They said a prayer, the words of the "Our Father" spilling out of them in hushed, reverent tones. Osbert was particularly enthusiastic, saying each and every word as if they meant more to him than they'd ever done previously. It was a blessing to see. Osbert had suffered a great deal, but he'd come through, and saved the lives of his friends at tremendous risk to himself. He had a good heart, and his faith was strong. From such men, Edmund truly could build a kingdom worthy of the Lord.

They rose once prayers were over, Ulfcytel, Wulfhild, Osbert, and Eadwig moving to venture out into the night beyond. Edmund couldn't offer them accommodation of a high standard, but a good meal and a tent was something he felt they'd be grateful for after what they'd been through. Edmund stayed at the table, lost in his thoughts, hoping some time alone might reveal some sudden insight on how to proceed. Then he remembered something. He looked up, seeing Eadwig just as he was about to slip out the door. Edmund would have words.

"Stay a moment, brother."

Eadwig turned, surprised at the invitation. The door behind him was still open, and Ulfcytel and the others had wandered on, happy to give the two brothers space to discuss in private. "What exactly happened here?" asked Edmund, his hands lifting slightly off the table as if to take in all of Gainesburg.

Eadwig frowned, as though caught off guard. "It was as we'd agreed," he said cautiously. "I was to attend Svienn and act like I'd defected, then get word to you with anything that could prove useful in an assault. The goal was to kill him, as I said."

"Except he managed to get on with that all on his own." Edmund wasn't angry, and his tone didn't suggest he was. He just found recent events rather mysterious, especially what he'd heard of Svienn gabbling about Saint Edmund before expiring.

"He did," affirmed Eadwig with a nod. "We were fortunate. He would have been a difficult obstacle to overcome otherwise."

"And I don't suppose you'd know anything about exactly how he died? I know in the past, you developed a great interest in plants…potions…things that can heal…and harm. Tell me, Eadwig, did all that knowledge of yours come in useful?"

"You're a perceptive one, Edmund," said Eadwig with a smile. "You can read men, I think, as I might read one of my books. I can't hide much from you."

"It was a terrible risk, brother," Edmund said sternly. "If you'd been caught…"

"I wasn't."

"Good. That makes me happy. Yet promise me now…don't be exposing yourself to danger like that. It might strike you as strange to hear it, but you matter to me. A great deal."

"I understand," replied Eadwig, his voice softening. "And I appreciate it…I'll do as you ask."

"Excellent, now go and catch up with the others. Find Wulfnoth whilst you're at it, he'll see about setting up some tents for you to sleep in. It might not be the most comfortable rest you've had, but it's better than captivity."

Eadwig smiled again before departing, the creak and thud of the closing door seeming to linger in Edmund's ears. There was much for him to think on, but for the moment he couldn't help but grin, his grin turning to a chuckle when he thought of his brother somehow managing to poison Svienn Forkbeard. Svienn had been a menace to England for so very long, his many raids and then outright invasion bringing the country to its knees. He'd been a fierce warrior if the stories were true, and nobody had ever managed to best him. And now he was dead. All because awkward little Eadwig, who had always chosen to spend time in his father's study rather than join his brothers outside, had once read a book on concoctions or potions or who knows what. No sword had pierced Svienn's flesh, nor axe or spear or anything else. That knowledge, that mind inside that great skull of Eadwig's, had been what had laid him low, and he'd had no defence against that, none. He hadn't even seen it coming.

He couldn't explain why, but Edmund found that to be one of the funniest things he'd ever heard in his life.

XIX

The fortress loomed over the village, the shadows cast from its jagged, lichen-covered walls covering the settlement in an ominous shroud. It was an ugly, foreboding thing, fashioned from wood and stone, its squat, solid buildings and high walls built on a jagged plateau of bare rock that allowed it to rise yet higher over its forlorn, almost desolate environs.

The sea crashed and rumbled to the north east, the harsh sound of waves impacting on shingle adding to the already unsettling atmosphere. The weather was suitably dour, the air chill and yet humid, the pale grey sky overcast and oppressive as it hung low over the barren landscape. The locals appeared sombre in the face of it all, either resigned or simply accustomed to their surroundings. They went about their business as always, communicating in quiet, subdued tones, as if fearing to be overheard. This was just another day for them, something to be endured rather than enjoyed, although they all paused a moment to listen when the sound of hooves started to echo up the old coastal road. This wasn't ideal. Strangers rarely brought good tidings. They had best be on their guard.

Æva twisted in the saddle, uncomfortable after such a long ride, the grim, soldierly men riding alongside her giving little reason for optimism. She could see the fortress clearly enough now they'd crested the hill, knowing by some instinct that this was overwhelmingly likely to be their final destination. She didn't want to go anywhere near that place. There was a darkness to it, one that chilled the blood and unsettled the stomach.

Sadly, she had no choice. The rider alongside had her horse secured with a halter around its bridle, and she was flanked by men with spears, their blank, hard faces assuring her they thought little of violence and wouldn't pause before indulging in it. Eamon was somewhere behind her, bound and beaten atop some old nag, the warriors around him having made sure he wouldn't be getting any more ideas about resisting. Brandon, at least, was still with her, sitting right in front of her atop this dark brown beast of theirs, but he hadn't spoken in hours. He was afraid. She could relate to that. This whole situation was a nightmare, one she wished she'd never have to face again.

They'd all been so hopeful when they'd arrived in Euerwic. Their talk with Sigeferth had lightened her heart, and he'd been more than generous in outfitting them for the journey, giving them two fine steeds and a donkey with enough provisions to last for a week. When they'd reached the city, it had been alive with excitement, its people still gabbling openly about how Edmund "Ironside" had marched up to their walls with an army to face their own Ealdorman, Uhtred, and demand he make way.

Æva had asked where Edmund had gone, and she'd been saddened to discover nobody really seemed to know. There were rumours, as was to be expected, and the one repeated most was that he'd taken flight with his men somewhere south after the Archbishop Wulfstan had refused to declare him king. Æva didn't blame him for that.

Wulfstan was a fool if he really thought bringing the hateful Æthelred back would prove productive. She was shocked to hear how he'd apparently claimed such a thing was "the will of God". Nothing could be further from the truth, in Æva's mind. Æthelred's treatment of her and her family had been atrocious. He'd be judged by God for that and many other sins. Returning to the throne should not be his reward.

A light drizzle started when they entered the village, the chill from the raindrops making her shudder. The buildings here were all well-maintained, not one of them showing any scorch marks or other signs of desolation that were so common in settlements down south. The locals kept their distance, some giving the impression they were looking to busy themselves in the hope of not being noticed by the likes of Æva's grim-looking escorts. These were not a happy people, that was clear, and the man who lived in that fortress was undoubtedly responsible.

The fortress gates opened up, the great wooden doors heaving inward so they might ride through. Spear-armed men stared at them from atop the gatehouse, their looks strangely vacant as they passed underneath, three abreast, to enter an interior courtyard. Æva winced upon passing within the walls, feeling like she'd just been swallowed up by some dark and terrible beast. The feeling didn't shift when they stopped, the riders around her dismounting and then gesturing for her to do the same. She looked back over her shoulder before she did so, catching a glimpse of Eamon being pulled from the saddle, his look defiantly indignant, despite the bruises and black eyes. She felt so sorry for him. He'd really tried to keep them safe.

Their guards hurried them up some steps, the tread of their boots dull and heavy upon the dark, weather-beaten masonry. They passed through another pair of doors and then another, eventually entering what could have passed for a banqueting hall. Æva, however, could not imagine it being used for such jovial pastimes. It was too dark, and the atmosphere was smothering, the air so dusty and stale she wondered how anyone could stand it for long. Furs covered the floors, softening the echoing footsteps of their escorts, and there was a fire smouldering in a stone grate tucked into a corner on the right, its flickering light the only remotely wholesome thing about this place.

"I should have come to welcome you at the gate."

Æva looked around, unsure of who had spoken from the shadows. Her guards finally ceased pushing and prodding her along, allowing her to find her feet and stand still alongside a lamentably nervous-looking Brandon. Æva glanced over her shoulder again, her anxiety easing a little when she caught Eamon's bloodshot eye. He nodded to her, the gesture reassuring, despite his appearance. The feeling didn't last. A figure emerged from up ahead, lifting itself from a chair perched atop a slightly raised platform presumably constructed to allow whoever was in charge here to literally peer down upon their guests. She couldn't make out much about him, so poor was the light, but the feeling he gave off was inescapable. This was not a good man. Dangerous. Violent. Cruel.

"You'll forgive me, I hope?"

His voice wasn't unpleasant, its rich, bass timbre echoing slightly off the aged wooden walls. As he came closer, she could see he didn't seem to have any obvious scars or deformities; his dark, almost black hair pinned back to reveal a face that appeared remarkably youthful for someone of such standing. He was dressed like a man of import, the hardened leathers of his armour suggesting he liked to be prepared for anything, even within the supposed comfort of his own hall. This, she assumed, was the Ealdorman Uhtred. He had some explaining to do. He could start with why he'd decided to have her taken captive.

"I'd forgive a great deal, but you had us seized off the street in Euerwic. I would have an answer as to why and an apology for the rough treatment of my friend."

"He's your man, is he?" Uhtred asked, his eyes glancing briefly over to Eamon and his evident bruises.

"He's a friend," Æva clarified, "and your people assaulted him."

"He tried fighting us when we came for the lady," piped up one of the guards, his grey hairs and scarred visage implying he held seniority over the others. "He broke Alwin's arm and knocked Ceol senseless before I could get in there and spark him out. We had to make it clear to him not to test us again."

"I understand that just fine," said Uhtred, satisfied with the explanation. "If anyone should be apologising, it should be him. How about it?" he asked, his eyes again on Eamon. "Will you not apologise to my friends here for the trouble you caused them?"

Eamon remained silent, his hands bound at his back, but his eyes held Uhtred's gaze and did not relent. "Just tell us why you brought us here," seethed Æva, annoyed at Uhtred's perverse demand for an apology.

"I wanted to talk, that is all," said Uhtred. "When I got word that Ælfric's own daughter-in-law was nosing about Euerwic, I had to know what she was after. So why not bring you here? Don't you like Bebbanburg?"

"It's cold and grey, like the rest of Norþanhymbre."

"But safe," said Uhtred, "and you're safer still, now you're within these walls. You can speak freely. Tell me precisely who you are and what you mean to Edmund."

"How did you know I was in Euerwic?"

"Euerwic is mine," said Uhtred, like it was the most obvious thing in the world, "and I have people that tell me things. You really drew a lot of attention, wandering around asking about Edmund like that. Not the most subtle way of going about things. You should be more careful in future."

"But I'd only been in Euerwic for a day or two," said Æva with an anxious frown. "How did you manage to hear of it so fast, let alone send word to have us apprehended?"

"I give my people some freedom," replied Uhtred. "They are free to act on their own judgement if a threat to me emerges...if somebody needs to die or if somebody needs to be seized...they usually get it right. In your case, they sent a rider on ahead to let me know you'd be visiting. I was most excited to hear I'd be entertaining such a prestigious woman."

"Just get to the point then," sighed Æva, weary already of this man and his insipid meanderings. "What do you want with me? Why would you take exception to me asking about Edmund?"

Uhtred returned to his seat, or his throne or whatever it was supposed to be, his face again lost in shadow. "Edmund wishes himself king," he said, crossing his legs, "and I and many others don't really see that working out. Archbishop Wulfstan has opened my eyes to my sinful ways. I should have supported Æthelred more when I had the chance. To have him flee into exile when his own subjects proved wanting...well, it was a shame, wasn't it?"

"The only reason you'd want a man like Æthelred back on the throne is because you'd stand to gain from it," spluttered Eamon, his blunt and sudden statement catching everyone by surprise. Uhtred made a gesture, or at least Æva thought he did. His men clearly understood in any case, taking it as a signal to begin beating Eamon fiercely. Æva implored them to stop, her own fists raining down blows on the back of the man currently hammering Eamon's face, but it did no good and the punishment continued.

"That's enough," Uhtred said finally, quite satisfied now Eamon was hunched over on his knees, his hands pressed tight against his freshly bloodied face. "As you can see, Æva, I'm all about proper decorum. For a man of low standing to address me with such impertinence simply won't do. I favour tradition, you could say."

"You're a callous beast!" Æva shot back venomously. "There is no such tradition in these lands that pardons this kind of behaviour! Just tell me what's to be done with us!"

"Nothing," said Uhtred lightly. "Nothing at all. I won't kill you, if that's what you fear. I would, however, appreciate it greatly if you could explain to me why you've come this far north for the sake of Edmund. Do you have a message for him? Is old Ælfric of a mind to support him?"

"My father-in-law is loyal to King Edmund," said Æva, wondering whether she should really be telling him any of this. "After Æthelred had us imprisoned, we saw what kind of man he was…and when he abandoned the country, it was clear to us all that his son should rule. And so it remains."

"Ælfric had failed Æthelred many, many times," said Uhtred. "And if anything, I'm surprised the king had not moved against him sooner. His and your imprisonment was long overdue."

"I don't care to discuss any of that," Æva said, having knelt down to dab at Eamon's face with her handkerchief. "I just wanted to find Edmund. He's a good man. You are not."

"So he means something to you then?" Uhtred asked. "You know him well? I notice Ælfric was not with you in Euerwic…so this was a personal endeavour? It mattered to you, and you alone, that you should find Edmund?"

"I'm not interested in your witless musings!" snapped Æva. "You've kidnapped me and my son, beaten my friend, and now you sit there upon that sad throne of yours acting like you have a right to know my mind! Do what you will with us, or let us go, but spare me this tedium!"

Uhtred stood up and made his way down from his throne. He came closer, his pace casual and his shoulders relaxed, and halted just as Æva managed to finally raise Eamon back to his feet. He stared at both of them, his expression neutral, the only sign of emotion a faint narrowing of the eyes as he beheld Eamon's injuries. Æva was about to speak again when she suddenly realised she'd collapsed, the sting upon her cheek a clear indication she'd been struck across the face. She heard Brandon cry out, and Eamon lunged towards Uhtred, his hands still bound, only to be immediately dropped by a savage blow from one of the guards. Brandon rushed to her side, doing his best to help her up.

"There are always consequences for improper behaviour," muttered Uhtred, massaging the palm of his right hand. "I can tell now you don't like me, which I think is unfair, if not unexpected. I'll give you a little time to get your bearings and think on your situation. Then we can talk again."

Æva said nothing when she was seized from behind, the guards shoving both her, Eamon, and Brandon away from Uhtred and back through the double doors of his hall. They were directed left and then left again, finding themselves wandering down a long, darkened corridor that looked to be a dead end. Their escorts suddenly pushed Eamon through a narrow wooden door which was then slammed shut and locked behind him. Æva went to object, only for her and Brandon to be shoved through a similar door on the opposite side of the corridor. This was then also promptly shut and locked, the guards ignoring her continued protestations to instead stride away to whatever duties they had elsewhere. Æva took a deep breath, trying to steady her beating heart. She was a prisoner again, she realised. The question was, for how long?

Brandon started hammering on the door, demanding to be let out. She tried to calm him, but he had a strange look in his eyes, one Æva had never noticed before. He was angry, that was obvious, but this wasn't the fleeting frustration of a child. There was a maturity to it, like how a man might rage when he feels those he cares about are at risk. In a strange way, Æva was glad to see it. He couldn't be a boy forever, and whilst he still was in a physical sense, the sequence of unfortunate events he'd recently been through had caused him to mature. What was important now was that he learn to master his anger rather than become a slave to it. There were too many men walking around who succumbed to their rage, venting it on whoever they fancied and offering no apology once the dust settled. His father, his real father, Hemingr, had been one of them.

She eventually got him to relent, convincing him that he needed to wait and conserve his strength if they were to make their escape. The room they were confined to was quite spacious, more like a guest chamber than a cell, having two beds, both pushed up against the western and eastern walls, respectively. A rug lay between them, made of the grey fur of some unknown beast, and there was a small window on the far wall, facing the door and tucked up towards the ceiling so that you'd need to stand on something to peer out. Æva did precisely that, using a wooden chest she found underneath one of the beds to give her a height advantage. The shutters were open, fortunately, but there still wasn't much to see, the inner grounds of the fortress looking quite deserted before her view was obstructed entirely by the curtain wall.

She climbed down from the chest, frustrated, and walked back over to the entrance to put her ear to the crack between the door and its frame. She couldn't hear anything, although she knew for a fact Eamon was in the room right across from her. If he were quiet, there'd be a reason, and she felt it fair to surmise he'd taken the opportunity to rest, knowing well enough any escape attempt would require him to bide his time. She turned back and moved to one of the beds, joining Brandon to sit on it.

It felt comfortable, the softness of the mattress reinforcing the impression this room hadn't been outfitted to accommodate prisoners. That was something, but the cold would be an issue if they had to remain here long. It was winter now, and Christmas couldn't be far off, not that she'd get to celebrate it. She'd heard before how cold Norþanhymbre could be, and from what she'd experienced so far, the rumours were true. This was not like the South, and she didn't think she could bear to spend another winter in captivity. It had taken such a toll on her before.

"Do you think Eamon will get us out of this?" Brandon sounded hopeful. Æva felt it wise to not disappoint him, knowing that being locked up here would be difficult enough without a despairing child for company.

"He'll be thinking of something," she assured him, rubbing his back with the flat of her palm. "We just need to keep our heads. I understand it's upsetting, but, as I said, we need to conserve our strength. Our moment will come."

"Why did that man want to know about you and King Edmund?"

"His name is Uhtred, and I don't know why he wants to know. I think he wants to act against Edmund and thinks I might know something that could help him."

"But Edmund is king, isn't he? Doesn't that mean Uhtred has to be loyal to him?"

"It does, but not everyone sees Edmund as king. In this country, we don't just have our rulers take the throne because they happen to be the firstborn or because they are good with a sword…the ealdormen need to approve of them. They have to gather in a witan, and the witan decides who is king."

"So Edmund isn't really king?" Brandon sounded confused. Everyone who followed Edmund thought of him as king, but technically he was still just an aetheling, and the real King of England remained in Normandy. It was for that reason some perhaps wanted Æthelred back, thinking they'd be pleasing God with his return, but Æva still doubted it. Eamon had been right. Uhtred wanted Æthelred on the throne because he stood to gain from it. She wasn't sure how exactly, but he'd clearly set his heart on the matter, and so Edmund had to go.

"Edmund is not king, at least in the sense we've not had a chance to sit down and make him such," explained Æva patiently. "Yet he has the best claim…he's the eldest of Æthelred's remaining sons…and he's strong. He's good. He loves God. And he cares about us."

"He does?" Brandon asked. "Is that why he came for me in the tunnels under Lundenburg? He came and made Æthelred give me back. He said if he didn't, he'd refuse to acknowledge him as his father and never speak to him again."

"He said that?" gasped Æva.

"He did," nodded Brandon, "and they were both very sad. I could tell. Everyone was sad. They talked about father. They thought I didn't understand, but I did. King Æthelred had him killed, didn't he?"

"Yes," said Æva glumly, weaving her arm around Brandon's shoulders to hold him close. "It wasn't Alaric's fault…the sins of his father came back to haunt us. I'll tell you about that someday, but it does mean we can't go home to Hamptonscir."

"So I'll not see grandfather again?"

"You can…but I can't. Not after what Ulfcytel told me. You'll be free to make up your own mind when you're older. Then you can do as you will. But for the moment, you'll have to trust me."

"I do trust you," frowned Brandon, like the idea of doing anything else was novel and strange to him. "I just want to see grandfather again. Everyone seems to leave. Why do people go?"

"It's not your fault," she said, holding him closer. "These are just difficult times. Nobody wants to leave you, Brandon. Your father died fighting for you."

"And you? What will I do if you go?"

"That won't happen," said Æva firmly, her hand briefly tensing around his shoulder. "Nobody will take me from you. Don't worry yourself thinking otherwise. We'll get out of this and find Edmund, and then everything will be fine."

"Are Ulfcytel and Cenric dead?"

Brandon's question had caught her off-guard. She couldn't think of much to say that would comfort him, given it was more than likely neither of those men had managed to fight their way clear of the ambush. Cenric had saved their lives that night, that was certain, yet as mighty as he was she couldn't think how he could possibly have prevailed. It made her heart ache to think of it. He'd deserved better. They'd all deserved better.

"I don't know," she admitted hoarsely, her emotions suddenly difficult to keep in check. "All we can do is wait. Prayers will help. Let us pray God sends someone to deliver us, that Cenric and the others are alive...and that Edmund be kept safe from those who seek to harm him."

Brandon said his prayers, applying himself to the words as any true believer would. By the time they were finished night was upon them, and despite the cold Æva was actually quite tired, the journey and drama of the past few days having sapped her energy. She told Brandon to get into bed, and she herself took the bed on the opposite side, finding it surprisingly warm despite the lightness of the covers. She was asleep in no time, her repose sure and undisturbed by dream or angst until she was suddenly woken by a sound at the door. It was dark, almost impenetrably so, but she'd definitely heard something. It sounded again. A sharp, scraping noise, like someone was on the other side and tampering with something.

She got up, the darkness yielding just enough for her to spy the form of Brandon, still fast asleep. Panic clutched at her as she heard the sound again, the feeling turning to full-on fright when the door suddenly clicked and opened, albeit just a few inches. A faint sliver of light crept in, but nobody made their presence known and all was quiet. Then she saw something. A head and face, appearing around the door frame. It was male, his hair tousled and unkempt, the bruises on his...she breathed a sigh of relief. It was Eamon. He'd escaped.

"Come on," he whispered, leaning further into the room lest the sound carry. "The locks here are worthless...but we're not out of trouble yet. Get your boy and keep quiet, and I'll get us out and away from here."

Æva moved fast, waking Brandon and whispering for him to remain silent. She dressed quickly, urging Brandon to do the same, before joining Eamon in the corridor. It was almost dark, the only light coming from a guttering torch attached to the wall over by the intersection they'd been hauled past earlier.

She felt beyond tense, fearing that whatever Eamon had in mind would only spell disaster, yet a quiet confidence settled over her when she beheld the door to his chamber. It was partially open, and she could see he'd broken the lock, picking it with a wooden tool of his own contrivance. He was oddly at ease, like he'd done all this before, and when he began to sneak away down the corridor she could only follow. Brandon and Æva tried to imitate him, watching the way he moved, slowly but surely and almost entirely without noise. They retraced their steps, following the route back to Uhtred's chamber. They stood motionless in the dark for a while, observing the two guards standing vigil by the doors just around the corner. There was no way past, and despite Eamon's apparent expertise at this sort of thing, they couldn't think of a way to proceed without being spotted. They decided to return to their rooms, Eamon whispering that he wouldn't give up and they'd plan a way to escape.

They blundered into a pair of wandering guards less than a minute later. Eamon had been quiet, but he'd been powerless to stop them from being spotted in the corridor, for the guards had their own torches and would have needed to be blind to somehow miss them skulking through the shadows. They called out, ordering them to stop where they were, only for Eamon to rush the nearest and seize his spear. The second guard began roaring for assistance, and Ǣva could only watch as another patrol came running, their demands and threats making little impression on Eamon now he was armed.

He tried to fight. He disarmed one of their captors with a quick jab to the wrist, but yet more men soon appeared, ensuring Eamon was not only trapped but impossibly outnumbered. They shouted and brandished an assortment of spears and axes, demanding Eamon drop his weapon. Ǣva was about to urge him to do just that when she heard another voice, the very sound of it hateful to her ears.

"Let go of the spear, or I'll have the boy killed."

They stared at Uhtred, all of them, captives and guards together, his terrible threat appalling all who heard it. He'd obviously only just woken, for he was wrapped in a single plush fur cloak, his bare feet suggesting he'd leapt out of bed on hearing the commotion. Eamon looked back at Ǣva, his eyes wide and pleading, unsure of what to do. She nodded at him, just once, and he dropped the spear, letting it fall to the ground with a clatter. Ǣva wasn't about to try and call Uhtred's bluff on this. From what she'd seen so far, he was a cold and serious man who was not above shedding blood to achieve his goals. If he made a threat, it would be wise to pay attention, and she wasn't about to gamble with Brandon's life. Their escape attempt had failed. They'd pray and hope Uhtred would now be merciful.

He wasn't. He had his guards seize Eamon; two men, one holding each arm. Uhtred then hit him, again and again, striking him repeatedly across the face with loud, sharp slaps. Brandon bellowed an objection, but Uhtred didn't relent, merely smiling at the lad as he this time punched Eamon squarely in the solar plexus. Eamon let out a violent groan and slumped forward, the men still holding his arms tightly so that he remained largely upright. Uhtred suddenly brandished a seax, the narrow, polished blade glinting in the torchlight, and held Eamon's chin in place with his left hand. He then looked to Eva.

"Tell me now, lady…what are you to Edmund? What do you mean to him?"

Ǣva glared back at him, but before she could reply, Uhtred lifted his seax to rest, edge down, just above Eamon's ear. The threat was obvious. Ǣva was to give Uhtred an answer that pleased him, or Eamon would lose his ear.

"I'm what you'd expect," said Ǣva, hoping she didn't sound as anxious as she felt. "I'm daughter-in-law to the Ealdorman Ǣlfric…and so Edmund values my presence when the ealdorman can't be with him himself."

"A half-truth," said Uhtred simply. He sliced his seax downwards. Eamon struggled and howled in his captors' grasp, blood gushing from his head. Ǣva watched his ear flop to the floor, the sorry piece of tattered flesh landing next to his discarded spear. This wasn't just, nor in any way rational. Uhtred was a maniac, and a sadistic one at that.

"What do you want from me?" Ǣva wailed, suddenly aware that Brandon was now standing like a statue and frozen in place. He wasn't crying, nor was he angry, but his face was blank, like he was either shocked or had fallen back into himself in light of the horror he witnessed. "Don't hurt him anymore!" Ǣva shouted again, hoping if she made some kind of emotional display, Uhtred might think he'd made his point and cease tormenting them.

"It'd be a shame to leave our friend here all lopsided," said Uhtred. "One ear would look terribly strange…I should really relieve him of both, to even things out."

Eamon hurled himself forward. The guards at his sides were unprepared for it, such was the suddenness and ferocity of his movement, and so they were powerless to stop the top of Eamon's head from connecting squarely with Uhtred's jaw. There was a sharp crack, like a stone falling upon another from a height, and Uhtred staggered backwards, his seax still gripped in his right hand. All of the guards present then did what was expected. They attacked Eamon, reducing him to a heap curled up on the floor, their fury unceasing as they kicked and punched him into a bloody stupor. Æva bade them stop, but her words were of no avail, and the beating continued until Uhtred himself ordered it to cease.

She looked at him, discerning with more than a little satisfaction how Eamon's surprise blow had split his bottom lip. Strangely, he didn't seem angry, but there was a redoubled coldness to him, like the drawing of his blood had somehow made him even more deadly and unpredictable than before. He had his men haul Eamon up and pin him against the wall. Uhtred scrutinised him, seeming to dwell upon the various bruises and blemishes that covered his face. He then held his seax to his throat.

"Last chance, Æva," he said, still focused on Eamon. "Tell me of your full relationship with Edmund, or your man dies here. If you attempt to lie to me, I'll kill your son too."

"He…he…" Æva was stammering; a new experience for her in all her years upon the earth. She looked down when she felt Brandon squeeze her hand, wondering if he was trying to draw her attention to something. He was doing nothing of the kind, but his eyes were hard as he stared up at her, imparting a strange strength she'd not known before. "I am with you," he seemed to say. "I'm not a child, and you need not face this evil alone." Whether Brandon had indeed intended to convey such a message, she couldn't tell. What she did know was she felt calmed by his presence, and she knew exactly what she needed to do.

"Edmund is kind to me," she finally said, her voice low and even. "He showed me and my son mercy when we were held captive…he brought him back to me when the king tried to take him away…and he saved me when Thorkell's brother sought to do me harm."

"That's better," said Uhtred, his blade still at Eamon's throat. "Do continue."

"I don't know what else to say…he took us from Lundenburg just before it fell to Svienn…he helped me bury my husband. He made me a promise."

"Oh?" Uhtred was looking at her now, but his blade hadn't moved. She had his attention, at least.

"He promised me he'd be a better king than his father. That he'd protect his people."

"And you believed him?"

"I did."

"And did he appreciate your faith in him?"

"I don't know. We moved south shortly after to retake Hamptonscir. I've been looking for him ever since."

"Since you left Hamptonscir?"

"Yes."

"Why did you leave?"

Æva took a deep breath, realising she had little choice but to explain to Uhtred her falling out with Ælfric. She did so, keeping it all brief and avoiding specific details about her son, Alfred, and how Ælfric had drawn his sword on Ulfcytel before demanding they all leave him. By the time she'd finished, Uhtred was still looking at her, but he didn't appear remotely surprised by anything she'd said. Ælfric's many sins must be common knowledge in certain circles.

"So you've been attempting to reunite with Edmund so he can make everything better?" He was mocking her now. She couldn't rise to it. That blade was still too close for comfort.

"It is what it is," she said.

"Why are Ulfcytel and this Cenric not with you?"

"We were attacked. I don't know what happened. I fear they may be dead."

Uhtred finally returned his seax to its proper place somewhere within his cloak. "At last, you say something of real interest," he said, his guards behind him allowing Eamon to slump to the floor, still unconscious. "I've not heard anything about Ulfcytel other than that he was supporting Edmund…if he's dead, this will be a grievous blow to Edmund's campaign."

"He'll keep going," said Æva. "The people love him. I know that from the way they spoke of him in Euerwic."

She realised as soon as she'd finished her sentence that she'd made a mistake. Euerwic was Uhtred's domain, and to state that the populace there might have any affection for Edmund clearly wasn't what he wanted to hear. "You'll forgive me if I don't share those sentiments," Uhtred said icily. "But I'll thank you for confirming your feelings for Edmund."

"I don't have any…"

"It's irrelevant anyway," Uhtred interrupted. "If he's off saving your son and defending you against Thorkell's own brother, no less, then I'll say it's fair to surmise he's doing it all for a reason. You have a hold on young Edmund's heart, my dear. And for that, I'm very, very glad."

"Why?" spluttered Æva, confused and annoyed that he should imply there was some kind of budding romance between her and Edmund.

"Because I therefore have a use for you," Uhtred replied, his bloodied lips curling into a cold grin. "We are heading south come morning…an army…my army…is to march on Lundenburg to help our RIGHTFUL king, Æthelred, retake his capital. I fully expect to encounter Edmund, and I fully expect he'll make a nuisance of himself. You'll help convince him to behave."

"How?"

"I have to spell everything out with you, don't I? I'll make it clear to Edmund that if he doesn't disband his army and be ever compliant to his father…then I'll hurt you. And I'll keep on hurting you until he agrees. Try to rest now, Æva, you and your boy. We have a long journey ahead of us, and you'll certainly need all your strength for what's ahead."

XX

Hereward leaned back, his hands gripped on the oar, allowing it to rise and then fall into the freezing waters below. He shifted his weight again, pulling his arms towards his chest with all his considerable might so the oar was heaved through the waters. He felt strangely satisfied at how he was able to keep time with the rest of the crew. He'd been a stranger to all this, but he felt in this moment he was perhaps born to be an oarsman; a man of the sea rather than the warrior he'd ultimately become.

Their ship ploughed on through the surging Temes, its flourishing white sail stark and vivid against the deep, starry blackness of the night sky above. A cold, sharp wind was coming on strong, sweeping across the deck and the men. Hereward couldn't speak for the others, but he wasn't feeling remotely uncomfortable. Despite everything, including the injury he'd sustained in Rouen, he was just too damned excited to feel put off by something as irrelevant as the weather. Great deeds were afoot, and he was to partake in them. He couldn't ask for much more than that.

A figure, dark and featureless in the pale starlight, approached from the prow and beckoned for him to rise and follow. Hereward stood up, signalling for the man he'd taken over from to take his post at the oarlock and resume rowing. It was a shame. Hereward had been enjoying himself. Unfortunately, he had other business now, and Olaf wasn't a man who would appreciate being kept waiting. He'd best hurry.

Hereward made his way towards the front of the ship, trying to keep any limping to an absolute minimum. His leg was healing fast, but there was still pain, and he didn't want people noticing his injury and assuming it had been a mistake to bring him along. It hadn't been. Hereward lived to serve, but he'd grown beyond frustrated during his time at Rouen in the company of the perfidious Normans. It had been a relief, if anything, when violence had erupted and blows had been shared. He'd been wounded, but had dealt out far more punishment than he'd received. He was glad of that. With any luck, what happened here tonight would see him similarly blessed.

"You're limping."

Hereward felt deflated at the words, although he suspected if Olaf had meant any ill will, he'd have put more of an edge on his voice. Hereward drew himself up alongside, following Olaf's gaze out across the dark waters. Olaf was an impressive man, physically, at least. He was young but strong, his well-muscled arms and torso seeming to barely fit inside the notably stretched confines of his mail. He was dressed for battle, as was Hereward, and the shaft of his axe was visible as he leaned upon it, his palms pressing downward upon the head like it were some huge and weighty walking stick.

"Are we close?" Hereward asked, not wanting to talk about his injury. Olaf had been reasonably pleasant to him this entire time, and Hereward knew it was a rare thing to be allowed on board his ship. Despite that, he didn't really care for the honour, and he hadn't wanted to be friends with the Northman, nor get too close to any of his crew. Joining them at the oars was all he was inclined to do, and he'd only done that because he'd wanted to try his hand at it. He didn't know what any of them thought of him, and he didn't much care. They were Norsemen, and worse than that, they were Thorkell's men. Hereward would love to kill them all, should he receive the order. After all they'd done to this country, he'd go about the task with enthusiasm.

"So who wounded you?" asked Olaf, ignoring Hereward's question in favour of his own. "Was it the Normans?" he inquired further, something in his voice suggesting he knew well enough that it had been.

"I will fight anyone who lays a hand on my king," said Hereward tactfully, still hoping Olaf would drop the subject.

"A noble sentiment," said Olaf. "So it was indeed the Normans who fought you? Why? What did you do?"

"Is this a necessary conversation?" Hereward asked, unconcerned now if Olaf took offence.

"It's not, but I like to know these things…you and I are alike, in some ways. We both care about Æthelred. He means something to us."

That made little sense, Hereward thought. Olaf was a murderous killer, and he'd always remain so, despite his recent and much-talked-about conversion to Christianity. "What can he possibly mean to you?" Hereward growled, annoyed that Olaf might think he stood a chance of bonding with him just because he'd apparently decided he admired Æthelred. That in itself was strange. Hereward didn't even "admire" Æthelred, and as far as he knew, most people felt the same. He was the rightful king, that's all, and so Hereward would fight for him. It was about honour and duty. Nothing else.

"He brought me to Christ," announced Olaf solemnly. "I know that sounds strange…but something happened when I entered Lundenburg just before Svienn attacked the city. I felt…different. I visited one of your churches, and the feeling there…I…it was like something within just woke up, like a part of me was finally being nourished after a lifetime of neglect. I can't explain it."

Hereward stared at him, noting how he was still looking out into the darkness with those wide, thoughtful eyes. He decided he didn't know what to make of Olaf at this moment. His words were pious, and Hereward understood them perfectly, for he too had enjoyed such experiences in church and at prayer. The Lord spoke in the silence, Hereward often thought, and it was when a man cleared his mind of all pretensions and simply opened his heart to God that He was most inclined to make His presence known. There was nothing strange about that. What was unusual was that a Northman would claim to have experienced it.

"I think you've explained yourself well enough," Hereward eventually said, still unsure if Olaf was being entirely sincere. "Are you ready to lead these men in the attack? This was your idea."

"It was, and I am," said Olaf. "And as King Æthelred's representative here…what say you of our chances?"

"It's a good plan. If the duke's spies are correct, then Cnut will have much of his army down south fighting this rebellion. Destroying the bridge across the Temes will cut them off from Lundenburg. We can then hit the city hard."

"Something tells me you're the type of man who is accustomed to hitting things hard," said Olaf. "Is that why Æthelred asked me to take you with me when I first broached this plan? He must trust you a great deal."

"I saved his life when Thorkell overran our flank at Bernecestre," said Hereward, a hint of anger rising in his throat at the recollection. "He's my king, and I'll always fight for him against anyone who threatens his realm."

"Anyone at all?" asked Olaf, giving Hereward a strange sideways glance. "We've all heard the claim that his son, Edmund, might like very much to make himself king. Will you take up arms against him if…"

"Stick to discussing the plan. I'll not be baited into a conversation about my king or his family. It's not my business. Nor yours."

Olaf finally turned to him. He wasn't upset, and Hereward soon realised he wasn't even looking directly at him, his gaze instead shifting to something just over his shoulder. Hereward angled his head, seeing the five ships just off their stern, their sails full and their oars rising and falling in rhythm. Six ships, including their own, were all they'd been given for their task tonight, but it would be enough. There was no way the enemy would be expecting what they were about to do. Nobody could. It was completely insane.

"It's almost time," Olaf said quietly. "Would you like to attach the first rope? It seems fitting that a servant as loyal as you should enjoy such an honour."

Hereward grunted in acknowledgement. He'd do what had to be done, yet in his heart of hearts, he didn't much care if Olaf "honoured" him. He was here to do a job, as were they all, and any honour would be gained from loyal service rather than personal aggrandisement. That was a major difference between the English mindset and the Danes, Hereward thought. These people would fight simply because they stood to gain from it, whereas a man like Hereward would only take up arms in service to a higher ideal. He considered explaining that to Olaf, thinking it might help him on his spiritual path if he were indeed sincere in his claims to be a Christian. Then he thought otherwise. Olaf was almost certainly a charlatan, despite his devout words just earlier. Hereward wouldn't waste his breath on him.

He instead stared out from the prow, narrowing his eyes with effort, knowing their objective was likely getting close. A few seconds passed, and then he saw it, the outline faint yet discernible. The bridge. Lundenburg's bridge. The one they'd come to destroy, and by doing so, seal off the enemy armies in the South and prevent them from aiding the capital. It was clever, very clever, but cleverness wouldn't be enough to secure victory here. Courage and fortitude were their best assets now.

He began to appreciate its size as it came further into view. It was huge, connecting both sides of the vast Temes, its solid wooden form supported by a half-dozen equally solid piers rising out of the water. These, in particular, were vital, for the bridge was simply too wide and heavy to bear much without them. Hence their plan. Hereward grinned at the thought of it.

Their ships began to slow, the men easing up on the oars and furling their sails to let the current draw them in. All was quiet now, the familiar splashing, heaving sound of oars hitting and leaving the water fading into silence. Hereward kept his eyes on the bridge, hoping to detect if anyone was up there who might spot them and sound the alarm. It seemed clear. There was nobody there, as was usual for this hour of the night, and the river remained empty. This was perfect. The longer they remained undetected, the more time they'd have to do what they'd come to do.

Hereward stripped out of his armour, ditching his mail and leathers on the deck behind him. They were suddenly enveloped in darkness, the bridge now directly above them blotting out the meagre starlight. They slowed and then stopped altogether, the other ships joining them in the blackness. A Northman Hereward had never spoken with passed him a rope, thick and gnarled, the length of which trailed across the deck before terminating at a point he couldn't discern. He hoped they'd tie this to something secure. What they were about to do would really test what this ship was made of.

New problems immediately presented themselves. There wasn't much room for manoeuvre here, since great mounds of jagged, moss-covered stones had been placed around the piers in an effort to hold them in place against the current. It was a sound idea, of course, lest the entire bridge be swept away in a storm, but it made their task tonight a little harder. They couldn't just lean over and make fast their ropes as they saw fit. The stones made that impossible. They'd need to climb.

Hereward moved to the side of the ship as it bobbed and shifted next to the closest pier. He reached out with one hand, touching the hard, damp surface of the stones, feeling he should somehow make contact with them before he dared attempt the climb. He made a leap for it, his feet leaving the deck to hurl himself at the pier, rope in hand. He succeeded, relief flooding his heart, and began his ascent, grappling upwards towards the underside of the bridge.

He didn't have to climb far, but the tricky part was now upon him. He had to attach the rope, tying it around the bare wooden pier so it wouldn't come off no matter how much pressure was applied. Hereward wasn't sure if he could do that, but he did his best, although he almost panicked when he realised there was someone else just below him on the opposite side. He stared at him, wondering what he was doing. Then he saw him attaching his own rope, tying it securely with great and practised care. Hereward sighed with relief. That would be two ships they'd have hauling away at this thing. He hoped it would be enough.

He finished up and slithered downwards, noting how the man below had also completed his task and leapt back over onto the deck of his own ship. Hereward had some difficulty letting go, fearing for a moment that if he did he'd simply plunge into the water. Olaf reached out to him, offering his hand, and despite his better judgement, Hereward took it and flung himself clear. He landed just fine, although he nearly knocked Olaf over, such was his weight and trajectory. Hereward gave him a nod, hoping that would suffice as thanks, before turning to examine their handiwork.

It was too dark to see properly, but he could tell his rope, and that of the man he'd seen join him, was firmly attached. If the other ships had been able to do their job, that would mean at least two other piers were similarly tethered. All they needed to do now was get underway and hope for the best.

They started, the oarsmen really putting their backs into it as they recommenced rowing. They'd switched positions, facing towards the prow as a means to propel their vessels back the way they'd come. There was no point in heading further upriver, for if their plan worked they'd only trap themselves and be easy prey for whoever might come looking for them. That could not happen. Not if they wished to survive all this.

The stars were again revealed when they came out from under the bridge, allowing Hereward to get a good look at the other ships. They'd all been successful, each vessel sporting one or more rope cables as firmly attached as Hereward's. The ropes had been tied around the masts of each ship and were growing tauter and tauter as they moved further away, the ships themselves creaking under the pressure. Their crews rushed to hold on, grabbing at the ropes to fix them in place and heave so it would be the bridge, not their masts, that would be the first to yield. Hereward ran to help, taking a length of rope in his own rough hands and bracing his feet upon the deck. He pulled on it, the men around him doing likewise, trying to put as much strain on the bridge as possible. For a second or two, Hereward began to feel foolish, thinking their scheme unlikely to succeed and the bridge simply too strong to be bothered by their exertions. Then he heard a crack, and then another. A third. Something was giving. And it wasn't them.

The first pier suddenly exploded in a flurry of splinters as the ropes half-tore, half-sawed their way through it. The bridge groaned ominously, its great weight shifting haphazardly to those piers still standing. Voices sounded from somewhere, crying out in alarm, and a hail of arrows erupted from atop the bridge to pepper their struggling flotilla. He couldn't see how many men were up there, dark as it was, but they were there and they were eager, their rate of fire unrelenting as they did their best to fend off whatever it was they thought was happening.

The man in front of Hereward fell, an arrow buried in his neck. Hereward picked up the slack, pulling with all his might to finish this and send the bridge and those on it crashing into the Temes. He looked to the oarsmen, seeing the perspiration on their faces as they worked the waters back and forth, back and forth, each man knowing he had to apply all his strength if they were to succeed. Another groan sounded, this time from the mast. That wasn't good. He shouted, commanding others to come help him, imploring them to seize and pull at the rope before the mast simply snapped in half. They did so, Olaf himself coming to his aid. They heaved and growled, their hands red and trembling, hoping to offset the pressure and save their ship. It worked. In the most dramatic way imaginable.

The pier they were attached to suddenly blew outward with an almighty snap, at least three others doing likewise as the entire bridge buckled in on itself. Hereward stood dumbstruck as this great, dark edifice began to collapse, the cracking, groaning cacophony of it all cutting through the night's stillness to undoubtedly awaken everyone for miles around. The men upon it cried out, their screams abruptly ending when they were crushed into the waters amidst the deluge of collapsing timber. Great waves of froth and foam were hurled outward in all directions, buffeting their ships and speeding them away. Nobody caught in the collapse appeared to have resurfaced. A miserable fate, Hereward thought. Then he remembered they were most likely Danes from Svienn's army. They'd had it coming.

Yet they were not alone. Shouts could be heard from the city, and before long, a number of men could be seen rushing into position along the river's northern bank, the light from their guttering torches making them easy to spot. They pursued the ships, firing arrows for the sake of vengeance. Most of them just hit the water, although one tore through the sail of Olaf's ship, causing it to flap about erratically whenever it caught the breeze. The arrows kept coming, but the ships soon outpaced them and continued eastward, the shouts of those on shore growing fainter and fainter until silence was again their most welcome companion.

"How do you feel?"

Olaf had asked a strange question. People had never really inquired about how Hereward had felt in the past, and he himself didn't care much for his own emotions, thinking them troublesome and best avoided. They'd also just performed a feat of extreme daring and valour that had all the same cost the lives of several of Olaf's men. Why he was concerned about Hereward's feelings was thus a bit of a mystery.

"I think we did a good job," he eventually replied. "With the bridge destroyed, Cnut will have issues calling his army back to Lundenburg."

"So we've completed our task," nodded Olaf. "But how do you really feel? Joyful? Grateful? I'm curious."

"I don't see why," said Hereward, frowning. "Who am I to you?"

"An ally, of course, and I'd like to know the English heart. You are English, and you have a heart. What does it tell you?"

"That I'm relieved. That could have been a lot more difficult. If we hadn't had such a clear night for it, we wouldn't have been able to see what we were doing. Your plan, Olaf, was a good one. Is that what you wanted to hear?"

"God is with us," Olaf said abruptly. "He was with us tonight. We were his instrument. Now we need simply meet with King Æthelred as he lands with his army…"

"A Norman army," said Hereward, cutting in. "It's not our king's army. It's under the control of Duke Richard. As is our king."

Olaf frowned, confused. The poor man was completely in the dark as to the character of the nefarious duke, and Hereward hadn't been of a mind to tell him. He had a few reasons why. Hereward didn't trust Olaf, despite his obvious bravery and rather inventive strategies, and he couldn't imagine a time coming when he might. He remained Thorkell's man, and Hereward couldn't wait for the day when Thorkell did the decent thing and keeled over - or better yet - gave Hereward an opportunity to relieve him of his head.

"Don't worry yourself about any of that," said Hereward, trying to suppress a smile at Olaf's continued confusion. "Let's focus on war rather than politics. We're making good time, but let's not be complacent. Cnut's people will be aware something serious is afoot. We must hasten to Beamfleot to meet with the rest of the fleet."

"And then what?" asked Olaf.

"Then we get ready to fight on dry land."

Hereward's words turned out to be prophetic. By the time they'd travelled back to Beamfleot, the sun was just starting to rise, yet there was no peace or beauty to enjoy here. King Æthelred's fleet, or what should be more accurately described as Duke Richard's fleet, was in the river, as expected, but they were under attack from the fortress on the northern bank. This was peculiar. When Olaf and Hereward had rowed past here just hours ago, there'd been no sign of life on the walls. Nobody had even raised a shout, let alone fired on them, making them assume Svienn hadn't bothered to garrison the place after Æthelred had used it to stage his flight to Normandy just last year. That had clearly been a mistake. The place was very much occupied. And judging from the clouds of arrows directed towards the river, they were not pleased to see them.

Olaf had their ships head towards the bank, wanting to join the disembarking Normans now rushing to assail Beamfleot's walls. There was no sign of Æthelred, and all the vessels presently jostling for position looked very much the same, their brute, ugly construction contrasting sharply with the more shapely, decorated hulls of Olaf 's flotilla. Hereward leapt overboard when the prow of his ship came crashing out of the water and onto the flat, muddy shore, Olaf and his men eagerly following in pursuit.

The beach was thick with Normans, their roars reverberating in Hereward's ears whilst they charged onward, their kite shields held high. The fortress was about a half-hundred paces ahead, much of it nestling on a rocky salient that partially extended outward into the Temes. The walls were ancient and looked it, appearing more moss than stone as they rose out of the mud and shallows. The men atop the battlements, however, were not so venerable, and Hereward could see they'd already taken a toll on the invaders, their arrows and thrown spears tearing into the Normans struggling ashore. Hereward sprinted forward, bellowing for Olaf to follow, only to find himself face to face with his king, a scowling Norman at his side doing his best to shield him from any incoming projectiles.

"Did you destroy the bridge?!" snapped Æthelred, wasting no time with pleasantries.

"We did," answered Hereward, noting how the aged king still looked somewhat impressive in his ring mail byrnie, the silver circlet upon his head also giving him an unmissable authority.

"Good! So then will you tell me why Beamfleot is full of angry Danes? Were they here when you rowed past in the night?"

"It looked abandoned," said Olaf, raising his voice over the surrounding din. "Nobody fired on us, and nobody challenged us. There wasn't even a single light from the walls. I cannot explain this, good king."

Æthelred grimaced, his greying teeth sharp and unpleasant in the morning light. "Then I will ask you both to support Thorkell and his people as they seek a remedy for what ails us. Beamfleot has to be cleared, and I don't want anyone escaping to warn Cnut in Lundenburg about what's coming for him. Press the southern walls, Hereward. Secure the battlements. Am I clear?"

Hereward gave a firm nod, both he and Olaf then bowing in due deference to their king and his commands. Hereward shot Olaf a glare, wondering what such a display might mean to a Norseman and mercenary who'd not so long ago been killing Englishmen rather than bowing to them. He dismissed the thought when he left Æthelred's side, joining yet more Normans splashing ashore to charge the fortress walls. The past didn't matter now, only the present. They had a battle to fight, and they'd not win it by dwelling on things that could wait.

They rushed on, Hereward, Olaf's men, and the Normans forming one great screaming mass of metal and fury. It was heavy going, and several men close by caught arrows in the throat and chest, their fearsome cries cut short. Hereward was suddenly alarmed to think he'd left much of his armour back on Olaf's ship. He'd been a fool to leave it there, so taken had he been with the drive to rush into the fray, and now his life was doubly at risk. He then noticed Olaf move up alongside him, his shield extended out and forward so as to protect the pair of them. Hereward kept moving, suppressing the urge to turn and thank Olaf. It didn't mean anything. The foreign bastard probably just didn't want to lose an ally. Hereward wouldn't mistake the gesture for something more than what it was.

They reached the base of the walls, several more men unfortunately falling to arrows. Hereward looked about and behind, thinking he saw some ladders being brought up from the ships, but he didn't want to wait for them. He didn't like such things, thinking them unstable and prone to tipping over if the enemy had the strength to repel them. Hereward had his own methods. He'd put them to the test here.

It was hard climbing, but he now realised it had been a boon leaving his armour behind, as he was far lighter on his feet than he would have been otherwise. Some were following him, the braver Normans trying their luck, but Hereward was way ahead, finding the aged, weather-beaten stones of the wall remarkably easy to scale. The Danes above were sounding off and had started hurling rocks down into the crowd below, but none struck Hereward, and he was free to continue. When he reached the battlements, he simply rolled over them, allowing his weight and momentum to carry him along. The Danes were surprised to see him, almost like they'd never laid eyes on a scantily clad Englishman scaling a fortress wall before, but they reacted fast enough, and Hereward soon found himself facing three foes at once.

He killed the first man, drawing his sword to slash open his throat, but the second Dane came on howling and gibbering like his kind often did, the furious swipes of his axe driving Hereward back. He fell when a Norman scrambled over the wall and impaled him through the neck, the single remaining Dane screaming in alarm at the sight of yet more Normans surmounting the battlements. Hereward dealt with him quickly, using the distraction to cut his legs from under him and finish him as he fell.

He chanced a look back over the wall's edge. A few more warriors were clambering towards him, and he heaved one up when he came within reach, his great strength carrying the man over the parapet with relative ease. Several ladders then thunked into the wall, and the great swarm of men below began their climb, apparently unconcerned with how rickety those things really were.

Hereward turned in time to see more hostile Danes come running up the steps from the courtyard below. The entire southern side of the fortress soon descended into bloodshed, the enemy garrison doing its best to retake their fortifications and dislodge the ladders before more Normans could swamp them. Hereward admired their enthusiasm, but they'd made a fatal error, the nature of which was soon made clear.

A small gatehouse along the eastern wall was hit, its timbers splitting as it was struck and then struck again from without. Hereward had just killed another Dane when he saw the gate collapse inward, the fury of what was almost certainly a battering ram proving impossible to resist. It seemed that the garrison hadn't expected their attackers to try this, for the warriors now rushing to contain the breach were few and far between. Hereward knew they were dead men. What happened next confirmed it.

Thorkell came on, charging through at the head of his men to cut a bloody swathe through the defenders. This was beyond brutal, and the courtyard below was soon awash with gore, the savage spectacle of Dane versus Dane drawing the eye of both Englishman and Norman alike. Men died in droves, their limbs severed or chests and heads split open under the weight of terrible axes. Thorkell strode through it all, his great skill and ferocity seeing him best any warrior with the courage to oppose him. It was a terrible thing to watch, but Hereward couldn't help but think how Æthelred had made the right decision in sending Thorkell to assault the gate whilst the enemy was distracted with the attack on the walls. It made tactical sense. Now if only Thorkell could find a way to get himself killed, then Hereward's day would be complete.

Sadly, there was no such blessing to be had. Thorkell and his brood finished up in the courtyard just as Hereward and the Normans finally cleared the walls, their roars of triumph oddly uniform as they hammered their shields and thanked whatever gods they worshipped for their good fortune. Hereward remained quiet, instead walking down the steps that ran alongside the inner wall to join Thorkell and his men below. It was an absolute mess here, and some of the bodies from the garrison were barely recognisable as human after the sheer savagery meted out to them. This wasn't war as Hereward understood it. Thorkell and his men were something apart. Theirs was a dark and evil craft, without mercy or honour. Hereward would always despise them for it.

He made straight for Thorkell, wanting to get a good look at him. He was with his warriors, of course, and they were still carrying on like men possessed, howling and cheering after their sudden and total victory. Thorkell, however, was strangely still, yet he looked up when Hereward approached, revealing those peculiarly dead eyes from within his dark iron helmet. Hereward remembered them well. He'd seen Thorkell in action at Bernecestre. He'd also seen how he'd almost been killed, only surviving a one-on-one brawl with one of Æthelred's royal guards by sheer luck. Hereward often thought about that fight. Had he made a mistake by rescuing his king instead of facing Thorkell? If he'd leapt into the fray and killed him when he'd had the chance, how would things have ultimately turned out? Would England have somehow been spared the invasion of Svienn Forkbeard? Would anything really be better?

Hereward stopped in front of Thorkell, his bloodied sword still grasped firmly in his right hand. Thorkell was looking straight at him, the evident tension between them suggesting neither wanted to be the first to break eye contact. Thorkell was immense, taller and broader than Hereward, and the axe in his hands was terrifying, looking like it was just as capable of splitting the hull of a ship as the skull of a man.

"Do you remember me?"

Hereward waited for a response, Thorkell's men falling into silence to behold him with wary, suspicious gazes. Thorkell took a single step towards him, his axe still held menacingly in his hands. "Should I?" he asked, his voice rough and unpleasant to the ear. "You are King Æthelred's guardian? But should I know you? I have not seen you distinguish yourself in battle until today."

"I fought at Bernecestre."

Hereward's admission got a reaction. Thorkell's men flinched, forming around their leader as if to prepare themselves for yet more combat. Thorkell continued to stare, those blank eyes as hard and unsettling as always.

"So did many men," Thorkell said, his voice still a low, jagged rumble. "You lived whilst others fell. Does that make you fortunate, or just a coward? Or perhaps a fortunate coward?"

His men laughed, the sound of it grating on Hereward's already fractured nerves. "Call me a coward again," he said evenly, daring Thorkell to take the plunge. The laughter died down. A few seconds passed. Nobody made a move, and Thorkell, as yet, hadn't taken up Hereward's challenge. Each just stared at the other, unwilling to stand down and yet uncertain of where things might lead.

"I believe the king is looking for you, Hereward."

He'd not seen Olaf appear, thinking he'd left him at the base of the outer wall before he'd made his climb onto the battlements. He looked concerned, perhaps anxious to diffuse the situation before it spun out of control. Hereward shot Thorkell one last look before he followed Olaf through the ruined gate, the towering heathen thankfully remaining silent.

That had been close. Hereward was well aware that to fight Thorkell would have likely ended in his demise, even if he hadn't been surrounded by his men. Despite that, he didn't regret confronting him. Thorkell was a man who deserved death, and Hereward sincerely hoped he'd get to perform such a service in the not-too-distant future. God willed it. Of that he was certain.

"Your climbing of the walls was impressive," Olaf said, the pair of them strolling through the smashed and splintered gates of the fortress and back out onto the northern bank of the Temes. A number of Danes lay dead in the grass, the arrows, rocks, and other detritus hurled from the top of the gatehouse having made their mark. The ram that had been used to break down the gate was also here, discarded now it had completed its task. Hereward ignored it and looked to his right, towards the river, seeing that much of the army was now disembarked. The Normans were strange to Hereward, their banners equally peculiar and almost flamboyant as they fluttered in the morning breeze, but he didn't doubt their capacity to fight. He'd seen it first-hand today.

"It came as if by instinct," Hereward said, Olaf nodding slightly. "The rocks along the wall were easily surmounted, and I didn't see any point in stopping there. I hate ladders too, and I didn't want to wait."

Olaf merely nodded again, the two men drawing themselves to an uneasy stop as Æthelred and several others emerged from the throng of Normans along the bank. Hereward could see the man who'd been shielding Æthelred previously, as well as the puffed-up, belligerent, and distinctly unlikable captain that Duke Richard had sent to "advise" them on the correct use of his forces. Hereward didn't respect the bastard, thinking him cold and arrogant in a way that almost matched Richard's own insufferable manner. Godfrey was his name, if Hereward recalled correctly, and they were stuck with him, at least for the time being. He hoped that would soon change.

"You did well in securing the fort so quickly."

Hereward bowed, low and deep, in acknowledgement of his king's praise. "It was a foregone conclusion," said Godfrey, his bitter tone implying he didn't want the English getting any credit. "My men tell me the fort's garrison was significantly under-strength. Svienn or Cnut obviously failed to understand the importance of this place."

"And what do you think of that, Hereward?" asked Æthelred, an eyebrow raised as if he were expecting him to contradict Godfrey.

"I believe there is some truth to what he says," said Hereward diplomatically. "Once I'd scaled the walls, I could see the men up top were few in number, and when Thorkell made his breach, it was all over. It would also explain how Olaf and I managed to slip past in the night, as the few men they had were probably not even awake then...Svienn underestimated the strategic value of Beamfleot. That doesn't mean he'll have done the same for Lundenburg."

Æthelred nodded, a grim smile emerging on his otherwise taciturn face. Godfrey, however, remained as he was, his thick, fleshy brow furrowed in a frown. "We should get everyone back on board," said Godfrey suddenly. "We'll need the speed of a water-borne assault if we are to still take Lundenburg by surprise. If we..."

"The enemy will know we're coming," interrupted Hereward, disregarding Godfrey's redoubled look of irritation. "We destroyed the bridge. There was no keeping that quiet. Cnut, or whoever is in Lundenburg, will know something is wrong, and even if he's unaware that we've taken Beamfleot, he'll have scouts active and on alert."

Hereward turned to Æthelred. "We should march, in full force, by land, my king. Confining your army to its ships will…"

"This is the duke's army!" cried Godfrey. "And it remains under my authority as his representative here! Do not presume!"

"Be quiet!" snapped Hereward, his temper flaring. "I know this is the duke's army and you are his lackey! I speak to my king, and if you are wise you will listen! An assault on Lundenburg from the river will see us pressed against the walls and trapped between them and the water. It will then be an easy matter to sally forth and hit us in the flanks whilst we're vulnerable. Defeat will then be staring us in the face."

"And so what would you do, Hereward?" asked Æthelred, ignoring the now gaping, red-faced Godfrey.

"An overland march, in force," said Hereward without hesitation. "We'll enjoy greater tactical flexibility and be able to respond to threats as they arise. The most likely scenario is that Cnut will remain in the city and attempt to recall his forces from the South. Without the bridge, that will take time. We can then lay siege to the capital and breach the walls before reinforcements arrive."

"And what if they arrive before?" asked Olaf.

"Then things will get more complicated. But the destruction of the bridge will have made an impression. The Danes…the enemy…will know they are cut off. A single, determined assault on the eastern walls could carry the day. The men have had a taste of victory here. They'll want more."

Æthelred managed another pained smile, yet Hereward could tell from his hollow eyes that he was far from happy. The old king parted from Godfrey's side, instructing him and Olaf to wait whilst he walked awhile with Hereward. They wandered for a time in complete silence, exchanging no word as they strolled along the banks of the river, Hereward ever alert for potential dangers.

"We don't have enough men to storm the city in a single assault." Hereward nodded, silent in the face of his king's statement. "We'll use the tunnels that lead under the city, the same ones we used to flee," Æthelred continued. "There's no way Cnut can know of their existence…for him to see us emerging inside the walls without knowing why…it could provoke a panic in the enemy ranks and force a surrender."

"Just how often have you known the Danes to surrender?" Hereward didn't mean to confront his king on this, but the question was a fair one. He'd never heard of the enemy just giving up. If you locked swords with Northmen, you'd better be prepared to kill them. That was the only way you'd win.

"I understand your concern," Æthelred said gently, "and I'm more than aware of what a difficult situation we're in. The duke has given me an army, yes, but it's not of a size that would allow us to assume certain victory. A sneak attack through the tunnels alongside a frontal assault on the Ald Gate is our only option. With any luck, the Danes will be surprised, confused…and then crumble under the sheer pressure of it."

The two men paused, looking out across the waters lapping lazily upon the muddy shore. The sun had fully emerged over the eastern horizon, lighting up the now clear grey sky with an almost painful radiance. The river sparkled at its touch, the light reflecting across the surface like it was one single beauteous expanse of cold, shimmering blue. Their warriors were still celebrating, both Norman and Dane joyous in victory, but from the look on Æthelred's face he was far removed from it. Hereward could guess easily enough what he was thinking about. His daughter, Godgifu. It must be hell for him, being in this situation. It was monstrous, unjust, unfair…all of it, and Hereward didn't think he'd ever find the words to express just how much it sickened him.

"I can't imagine what you must be feeling right now," Hereward said, surprised at how he'd spontaneously put his thoughts into words.

"What do you mean?" asked Æthelred, his question merely curious rather than angry.

"What the duke said…that you are to rule as a puppet on his behalf…and that should you defy him, he'll hurt your daughter. You must be…"

"Go on," asked Æthelred, still sounding far from offended.

"I can't describe it. I've never even heard of such a thing taking place, let alone been involved in it myself. It's…evil is the word. Duke Richard is evil."

"He is what he is," said Æthelred sadly. "This is how the game is played…yet I will confess the duke has adopted measures I've rarely encountered before. He means business. I'm just glad I have you with me, Hereward. It would be so much more of a trial if it were not so."

"Me?" asked Hereward, surprised at his king's admission.

"Yes, you. You threatened the duke when he announced his plans for my daughter…at any other time, I would have considered it impertinent, but your loyalty was a marvel to behold. You also frightened him. You know that? I can read the bastard. He was scared of you."

"Good," nodded Hereward firmly. "I'll have words with any man who makes such threats. I'm just sorry I couldn't fight us clear of his keep. My wound…"

"Is healing well," said Æthelred, "and don't think I'll just forget the service you tried to render me that day. I may be a most unfortunate king, with a fractured family and a bastard of a brother-in-law…but I don't forget loyalty. It's a rare thing in these times, so when it's seen, it's all the more precious."

"I don't know what to say. I am in your service, and so I behave as such. You are my king. That's all that matters."

"I've heard that kind of talk from many others before. I rarely took it seriously. In your case, though, Hereward…you've proved it. And I appreciate it. I'm very much alone now. But it's good to have at least one friend in all this."

Hereward suppressed a frown. His king had honoured him, but he felt a little uneasy at the admission he was "very much alone". From what he remembered, the king had been close to his wife, always, but that had changed when she'd decided to support the duke. Hereward couldn't fathom her reasoning, but it pained him to think Æthelred had now lost even the comfort of having a loyal woman at his side. Emma was a foreign bitch, he decided, and one completely unworthy of the prestige afforded her as Queen of England. He would, of course, keep that opinion to himself, at least for now.

"Will the North rise in your favour?" Hereward asked.

"Uhtred has sent word," said Æthelred, "as has Archbishop Wulfstan. They promise an army, but who knows when it will arrive? We'll have to move fast and not take anything for granted. My subjects are notoriously disloyal. I can't count on them."

"And Edmund?" Hereward felt like he was pushing his luck with that last question, but he had to ask. He didn't know much about the aetheling, but he'd been impressed with how he'd confronted them, alone, in the tunnels under Lundenburg.

Hereward felt he could recall every word of that fateful meeting, especially how Edmund had spoken of his goal to keep on fighting Svienn Forkbeard. There was a real boldness there.

"He's been fighting, as he said he would," answered Æthelred. "Wulfstan didn't go into detail in his letter, but Edmund has an army and apparently did not take kindly to the decision to invite me home."

"Is this something we need to worry about?" asked Hereward. He didn't want to fight Edmund if the young man had indeed decided to meet his father's return with force, but he would if he had to. Æthelred remained the rightful king, and no one could say otherwise and be truthful.

"Time will tell, my friend. I don't think Edmund means me harm, but the prospect of power can do strange things to people. That's all I'll say for now."

They turned away from the water and began walking back the way they'd come. Hereward felt heartened that his king had taken him into his confidence like this. It was a pleasant change from his usual remoteness, but he noticed Æthelred's manner became more and more tense the closer they came to the fortress. He didn't want to be back with the Normans. He didn't want to be king. He'd much rather stay by the river, talking as men do whenever they're afforded such pleasures. Hereward wasn't sure what to do with that realisation. For the moment, all he felt was sadness.

Olaf appeared, with Godfrey and Thorkell, informing them their respective forces were ready to begin the march on Lundenburg. Hereward could see they'd brought some order to the ranks already, their commanders no doubt deciding to cut their victory celebrations short in preparation for moving on to a yet greater prize. The Normans looked as they always did, formidable and yet unlikeable beneath their equally unsightly banners, but the Danes looked disappointed, undoubtedly because they'd not been able to secure much in the way of loot.

All that changed when they again laid eyes on the king. A cheer erupted, starting with the Danes and then spreading through the Normans like a wave. They honoured him, this strange, mixed army, and Æthelred did his part, raising his right arm above his head in a gesture of triumph and respect. Hereward stood by at his side, silent, but his eyes caught Æthelred's when he turned back to confer with Godfrey and the others. He saw into him, right into his very soul, discerning something they'd only just spoken on but was now all the more painful to witness.

The king was surrounded by people, many of them jubilant in the wake of their first victory in the campaign to take back his kingdom. That would normally stir the heart of any man, but not now, for Hereward could see, in that single instant of understanding, that there was only one thing Æthelred felt. Loneliness.

XXI

He'd been waiting for this, dreaming of it on recent nights every time he laid himself down to rest. He'd seen the city before, many times over, but in his visions it was all the more magnificent, its high walls seeming to welcome him in as they stood, sheer and majestic, against the setting sun. He'd race towards them on his horse, his cloak billowing out behind him, and make his way to one of the magnificent gates, knowing his men were following. He'd then enter the city, and its people would rush to him, their faces lit up to see that their king had returned to deliver them. It was all so glorious; a perfectly just beginning to a perfectly just reign.

Edmund stared at Lundenburg's walls now, wondering what had happened and how he could have been so outmanoeuvred. There were men massing around his city on its eastern side, their forms grim and soldierly in the grey, cold light of day, but they were not his own. They were not even Danes. Something strange had happened, and as much as he tried, he couldn't comprehend how it had come to pass.

"Those are Duke Richard's men," said Wulfnoth. Edmund looked to him, still confused, hoping he'd elaborate a little more. They were watching from a fair distance off, their army stationary just behind them, the rank and file of their forces also likely alarmed at what they were seeing. Wulfnoth was on horseback, as was Edmund. Wulfhild, Sigeferth, Morcar, Ulfcytel, and Osbert had joined them also, all atop steeds of their own, and together they stared out from the wooded rise they'd chosen as their vantage point.

"Why didn't our scouts mention any of this?" asked Ulfcytel, confused on how this mystery force had snuck in on their prize without them noticing.

"Because this army has only just arrived?" suggested Morcar. "They are not fools, either. They've destroyed the bridge leading back south. Impressive."

"They are Duke Richard's men," repeated Wulfnoth. "I can tell by the banners. This force is from Normandy. Your father, Edmund, has responded to Wulfstan's summons to return home, and the duke has seen fit to assist him."

Edmund frowned, wondering if they really were Normans up ahead and, if so, whether the duke himself was present on English soil. There were plenty of banners on display, that was true, but Edmund couldn't get a good look at them from this distance, and the men bearing them had fortunately not decided to come any closer.

He soon had cause to regret that thought, for suddenly a whole host of mounted riders detached themselves from their siege lines and began moving towards them. The Normans were aware of their presence then. Edmund hoped they just wanted to talk.

Wulfnoth bellowed a few commands as he saw what was happening. The men behind him acted fast, deploying just in front of Edmund and company so that if anyone tried to charge them, they'd run into an interlocking wall of shields and pointed spears. Edmund approved, but they'd allowed a sizeable portion of their army to come out into the open, forsaking the protection of the trees to stand in full view of whoever was coming. It wasn't a foolish decision by any means, but Edmund felt it would be wise to conceal his forces lest the Normans realise they had the advantage of numbers. In that spirit, he issued a few commands of his own, ensuring their entire line, himself included, stepped back a few dozen paces, the remainder of their army retreating further into the woods behind them.

His jaw dropped when the riders came closer. There were about forty of them, but not all were alike. Some were Danes, that was clear, their less-than-uniform appearance marking them out from the more consistent and disciplined attire of their Norman allies. That wasn't what had Edmund so shocked. At the head of them, flanked on either side by armed and fearsome men, was his father. King Æthelred had come home. Archbishop Wulfstan must have been quite persuasive.

Æthelred slowed his steed and soon stopped, signalling for those around him to do likewise. He looked tired, Edmund thought, but then again he always did, for it would take more than some fancy mail and a fine silver circlet to make his aged father really look like a king again. Edmund realised the man next to him was attired as a Saxon warrior, but apart from that, his force was entirely foreign, and not one of them looked remotely pleased to see them. Aside from his father, oddly enough. He was smiling. A genuine smile. Edmund had not seen the like in years.

"I knew you'd make a good show of it, my boy. You told me you'd keep on fighting Svienn, and I believed you. Let us join forces now, you and I, and put an end to all this."

Somebody cleared their throat, the sound harsh and disagreeable in contrast to Æthelred's honeyed words. Edmund suspected it to be Ulfcytel, and he wasn't surprised when the ealdorman spoke up, for some reason thinking it best he speak before Edmund.

"We recognise Edmund as our king, and I would know what Duke Richard stands to gain by gifting you this army. I doubt he did it for the sake of charity."

"Would you allow an ealdorman to speak on your behalf when you are addressed by your own father?" Æthelred had ignored Ulfcytel entirely, not even glancing in his direction. Edmund, for his part, was seething that Ulfcytel had decided to speak before him. It wasn't right, but they couldn't show disunity now. Ulfcytel was one of his most valued supporters. He needed him on side.

"He does raise a good point," said Edmund. "Just what does the duke get out of all this?"

"Really, Edmund? After so much has happened, you want to talk politics with me? What about you, Wulfhild? Are you not pleased to see me?"

"I am," admitted Wulfhild carefully. "Just know that we all support Edmund. All of us here and more. We'll not fight you, but..."

"I will speak on these matters, sister." Edmund hadn't wanted to cut her off, but she was getting into deep water by presuming she, too, was somehow able to speak for him. "I have an army," said Edmund after turning back to his father, "and it's made up of Englishmen rather than foreigners. You don't want to be king, father, we both know it. Do yourself a favour and help win Lundenburg for somebody who actually wants it."

"You do have an army, as is to be expected," replied Æthelred. "Yet my troops are of better quality...and I have Thorkell. I have..."

"You still keep that murderer on a leash?!" spat Ulfcytel, his horse shaking its head violently as if sharing his outrage.

"Do you have a voice of your own, Edmund?" asked Æthelred, content to ignore Ulfcytel once again.

"His question is valid," Edmund fired back, "and I'll warn you that if you bring Thorkell anywhere near us, I'll have him killed. We did the same for his brother."

"You told me," nodded Æthelred, "and you'll be glad I've kept that a secret from him. He'd be here if he knew, and I wouldn't be able to control him."

"Let him know I'm here, Æthelred!" thundered Ulfcytel, angry at his ongoing refusal to answer him directly. "Let him know I'm still alive and that Alaric killed his brother! I'll do the same for Thorkell if he comes sniffing for vengeance!"

"Is this really the best you can manage, father?" asked Edmund, wanting to get a word in before a fully-fledged argument broke out. "Do you really expect me to fall into step behind you just because you wish it? Do you think my men will fight for you just to...what? Go back to the way things were?"

"Will you ride with me, Edmund?" asked Æthelred, still unruffled by Ulfcytel's threats.

"Don't do it," hissed Wulfnoth suddenly, looking like he feared for Edmund's safety. Edmund stared back at him, wondering if he knew something he didn't. He didn't trust his father, but he found it hard to imagine that he meant him harm. Edmund could tell something was off with him, but it didn't involve malice. There was a weight upon his shoulders, and it wasn't just from his armour. Something was bothering Æthelred, and as much as Edmund resented his presence here, he still wanted to know if he was all right. He was his father, after all.

Edmund made a gesture, beckoning for the humble Osbert to come ride at his side. They then joined Æthelred and his English bodyguard as they parted from their Norman escorts, Edmund doing his best to ignore the ripple of protestations from his allies. They moved south towards the river at a gentle trot, their four horses grumbling to each other in apparent greeting. Edmund had a feeling his father was waiting until they'd covered some distance before speaking, lest the ever-tempestuous Ulfcytel somehow hear it and insist on bellowing out some insult or objection. Edmund would have words with the ealdorman after this. He understood his anger, but he needed to learn prudence, especially when it came to shooting his mouth off.

Edmund looked over at Osbert, giving the young man a respectful nod. He'd chosen him for a reason, mainly because Osbert knew his place and wouldn't try to constantly interrupt when they were talking. He was also a good and faithful man, since he'd stayed loyal when he'd been captured and then gone to some considerable lengths to rescue Ulfcytel and Eadwig. Edmund was deeply sorry it had cost him so dearly. The lad's face was severely burned, giving him a fearful, terrible look, one quite at odds with the noble soul that lay within. Edmund had no notion how such a thing might be remedied, but Osbert so far hadn't offered a word of complaint. That was to his credit, he supposed.

"Where is Eadwig?"

"He's back at my camp," answered Edmund, glad his father had asked. "He's unwell, nothing serious...but he's resting. He's been through a lot. We all have."

"You'll send him my good wishes?" asked Æthelred.

"I will," nodded Edmund. "So what did you wish to discuss with me? You should be quick, because I have not the patience for any int..."

"The duke has Godgifu."

Edmund gave his father a hard stare, his expression troubled. "What do you mean? I thought you'd taken all of Emma's children with you to Normandy."

"I did, and Alfred and Edward are here with my army…or the duke's army. He's sent one of his lackeys to make sure I don't get any ideas about misusing it…and he's kept Godgifu hostage to ensure my future good behaviour."

"Good behaviour?"

"I am to be a puppet king," replied Æthelred, slowing his steed to a halt. The grass was thinning out, the ground softening as it crept closer to the flowing Temes just a hundred yards away. There were a few fishing boats out there, surprisingly, and the fishermen didn't seem bothered by the sight of the collapsed bridge, thinking perhaps their hungry families took priority over whatever latest strife had now come calling. They were quite correct in that, Edmund thought. Family mattered. Godgifu was his half-sister, but that was enough, and he'd take up arms against any man who sought to wrong her.

"You mean he intends to harm her if you prove disobedient to Norman interests?"

"That's it," nodded Æthelred, sounding relieved at how Edmund had cut straight to the heart of it. "When he told me what he had planned, I tried to act…Hereward here threatened the duke and tried to make a fight of it…you should have seen him, Edmund! Unfortunately, it all came to nought, and here we are. I'm a captive, intended to play a part I never should have been entrusted with."

Edmund looked at this "Hereward" who rode at his father's side. If he really had taken up arms, alone, in a bid to save both Æthelred and Godgifu, then Edmund had nothing but respect for him. He'd been through hell by the looks of it, but he still exuded a fierce prowess, and the sword at his belt had certainly been used just recently. He nodded in Edmund's direction when he sensed his eyes on him. There was sincerity there. His father had chosen well in keeping this man close.

"Is that really how you see your kingship, father?" asked Edmund, confused over his admission that he may not be suitable as a monarch.

"It is. You know I spoke with Alaric before I left for Normandy…everything fell into place after that. I came to the throne because of a plot set in motion by others…I was powerless. And I return to it for the same reasons."

"None of that justifies what you did to Alaric!" said Osbert suddenly. "None of that justifies all the other things you've done, to us in Eastengle and beyond! You were our king. You had power. And you abused it!"

Edmund might have thought to chastise Osbert for speaking out of turn. It wasn't pertinent, and he'd chosen Osbert to accompany him precisely because he'd felt he was the least likely of his companions to try and settle old scores with his father. But the young man had spoken the truth, and Edmund wouldn't punish somebody for being honest in a world of lies. Judging from Æthelred 's response, his thoughts were not too far from Edmund's.

"If you'd said that to me in any other time, I'd have had you flogged for it," he said, Osbert bristling visibly. "Yet those days are past. I think you're being a little unfair, young man, but I can't blame you for despising me. Many do, and I've finally learned to understand why."

Æthelred turned back to Edmund and raised his hand to his mouth before clearing his throat. "Now we are on the subject of Alaric," he said, trying to stifle a slight cough, "I think it's important I again stress why I had him killed. It wasn't just about him. It was about his father, the Ealdorman Ælfric. He's not to be trusted, Edmund, despite the fact he's apparently declared his support for you."

"I've not seen anything with my own eyes that would cause me to distrust him," said Edmund, "but his reputation is...less than ideal. He serves me, that I do know. Even now, he fights to hold off Cnut's armies in the South. We'd not have been able to march on Lundenburg if he had not."

"Which makes what we do here all the more important," said Æthelred. "Even with the bridge destroyed..."

"So that really was you?" interrupted Edmund, nodding towards the tangled, waterlogged ruins still straddling the Temes.

"Hereward and Olaf led a sneak attack to destroy it, yes," said Æthelred, "but even with that accomplished, there's a good chance Cnut's forces in Hamptonscir will learn of our presence here and return. With Uhtred still on his way..."

"The Ealdorman Uhtred is coming to assist you?"

"I'm sure you worked that out for yourself, Edmund. He's marching south with his army for my sake, but I don't know how long he'll be. Neither do I know where Cnut is. I was hoping you'd be able to help me with that."

"I attacked him at Gainesburg," said Edmund, his mood lifting with the thought of his victory. "He wasn't killed, but we put his army down like the dogs they are. We think he escaped by ship, but there was some talk of him receiving support from Lindesi."

"What kind of support?"

"Food, shelter, I think. We marched through there on our way here, but the local lord didn't present himself, and the men in his fortress refused to let us in. I suspect Lindesi is actually loyal to Cnut."

"Did you punish them?"

"No," said Edmund. "As I couldn't tell for sure. Many of the commoners joined us as we passed. It's the same everywhere I go. People come to me. They think I'll be a king worth fighting for. I hope to not disappoint them."

"Then you do intend to fight me here? The duke will kill your sister, Edmund. Please don't make this harder by defying me. I do what I must."

Something had truly changed in his father, Edmund could tell. He looked as hard-bitten as always, but there was a gentleness to him that he'd not seen before. If he was telling the truth about Godgifu, and Edmund didn't see why he wouldn't be, then it was a terrible problem for them all. Edmund would not see her harmed, but the only way to prevent it was to submit to his father and allow him to take the throne Edmund and his supporters had been fighting to secure. He didn't want to do that. Too many would think he'd betrayed them. Yet he couldn't put Godgifu at risk. He only had one choice, and it wasn't an easy one. As such, he almost couldn't believe his own words when he next spoke.

"What do you need me to do, father? If helping you take Lundenburg will secure Godgifu's safety in some way, I shall do it. Godgifu is my kin. That can't be ignored."

"You've again proven yourself a man any father would be proud of," said Æthelred. Edmund had no idea what to say to that. He couldn't remember the last time his father had spoken to him like this. He felt awkward. But his heart softened.

"I'm set to attack the eastern walls and carry the gate," continued Æthelred. "You are, of course, aware of the tunnels under the city. I intend to use them in my assault. If you can deploy your forces at my signal to clear Watling Street and attack New Gate, it'll provide a good distraction."

"How many of my men do you expect to die in all this?" Edmund didn't want to think about such things, but he must. He had about fifteen hundred warriors with him, but, as was to be expected, they were not all professional fighters and were not equipped as such. An assault on the walls would cost them dearly.

"There will be losses," said Æthelred solemnly. "Although, with luck, the Danes will start to panic once attacked from the tunnels as well as the eastern and western walls. Cnut is a fatherless boy. I'm counting on him succumbing to his anxieties once he realises his situation."

"That might not work out as well as you think," Edmund cautioned. "He and his people made us fight hard at Gainesburg. I also have to tell you that the Ealdorman Eadric has been assisting him."

"You have proof of this?"

"He attacked us at Sancte Eadmundes Byrig. Svienn had decided to burn the place down. We almost had him and Cnut both. Then Eadric suddenly swept in on our flank with his own men."

"Those are very serious allegations, Edmund. I'd like to think you'd not lie to me..."

"Oh come on!" Edmund shouted, annoyed at Æthelred's continuing inability to see Eadric for what he was. "He's a snake, father! Always has been! Just ask Wulfnoth!"

"Wulfnoth the traitor? I think not!"

"How do you know he's a traitor?! Because Eadric's fat bastard of a brother said so? I believed you when you told me about Godgifu, father, so believe me now! Eadric is working with the enemy!"

Æthelred slumped in the saddle, for the briefest second appearing as a man who truly had the weight of the whole world upon his shoulders. "He served me faithfully when nobody else would," he said, sitting up straight, "but it's only right that I take you seriously, too. If Eadric is indeed working with Cnut, I'll see him punished."

"And who else?" asked Edmund. "You have a lot of enemies, father, real and imagined. I'll need assurance you won't go looking for vengeance in the wrong places once you return to power."

"You're referring to the Ealdorman Ulfcytel? He is disrespectful."

"He's also married to your daughter, in case you forgot. But I don't want assurance for just him. You can't move against Sigeferth and Morcar, either. In fact, if you really do want my support, you'll have to back up your promises, right here and right now. There'll be no seeking to settle old scores. You always saw enemies where there were none and sought to befriend those who were foes. That has to change."

"And then you'll help me get Godgifu back?" asked Æthelred, his voice hopeful. "If you do...you have my word I'll formally name you my successor. Emma won't like it, but she will just have to understand. You'll be king, Edmund. You just have to help me here."

"I will, if you give me your word you won't harm Sigeferth, Morcar, and Ulfcytel."

Edmund kept his eyes on his father in the silence that followed, hoping that whatever he was thinking would, for once, lead him to make the right choice. "I give you my word," he said, finally. "This will be a new dawn for England. Let us come to an accord here, you and I. All will be forgiven. I'll be better this time. You'll see."

Æthelred reached out to take his son's hand. Edmund allowed it, gripping his father by the wrist, noticing now how his own heart was hammering in his chest. He couldn't believe he'd agreed to this. Some would see it as a mistake, but any honest man would see there was no hope of defeating Cnut if Edmund took to fighting with his father. Such a thing might also get Godgifu killed. Edmund wouldn't have that on his conscience. He couldn't stand before God one day and just explain that away.

"You won't regret this, Edmund." Æthelred still held him, his grip surprisingly strong for a man of his years. Edmund stared back at him, unsure of what to say. When his father relented, he still had no words, finding the enormity of his commitment too difficult to comprehend. He also couldn't stomach his father's continued reticence to denounce Eadric. Neither had he mentioned Edmund's uncle, Æthelstan, and how he and Eadric had played a role in his death. Edmund could never forgive that, and he'd never fully trust his father again because of it.

"What happens now?" asked Edmund, feeling more ambivalent than ever about what he'd agreed to.

"I'll send a messenger to inform you when we're about to start our attack. Be ready, and hit those walls hard. I know you can fight. So let's get to it."

Edmund turned away, eager to end this exchange and get back to his people. Osbert followed after him, both men moving across the grass to rejoin their companions. Their horses protested a little, annoyed, perhaps, at having to part company with Hereward and Æthelred's mounts, but they cooperated, moving at a slow gait back to the tree line and the army Edmund knew lurked beyond. He looked over his shoulder when his father suddenly called out to him, but as he listened, he dearly wished he'd just said nothing. He didn't want to hear such words. He just wasn't ready for them.

"I knew you'd do well here, son. I'm proud of you. Your brother would be, too, and your mother…and your uncle. Always remember that."

Edmund spurred his horse into a gallop, unable and unwilling to respond. Osbert hurried to match him, but they said nothing to each other whilst they sped along, their thoughts taking up much of their attention. Edmund knew an argument was waiting for him on his return. Ulfcytel would be outraged. Sigeferth and Morcar might be easier to handle, but Wulfnoth would not be so passive, and there was a real chance Edmund's army could start to break up unless he explained exactly why he'd agreed to Æthelred's plan.

It wouldn't be easy. It would be bloody difficult, in fact, but there was yet another challenge that Edmund couldn't think how to resolve. His father wanted forgiveness. He could tell. There was something in his voice, his manner, his look. But Edmund just couldn't. He couldn't get over what had happened to his uncle. There was no way. And the sad thing was, he didn't think that would ever change.

"I can't do it," Edmund said fretfully, ignoring Osbert's concerned glance as they rode on into the confrontation they both knew awaited.

XXII

The tempest never came. He'd been braced for it, expecting them all to erupt in outrage, confusion, or both. Instead, they just stood there, staring at him. He wasn't sure what was worse. He'd been prepared for anger. He could handle anger. Dumbstruck silence was something else, and the longer it went on, the more uncomfortable he felt.

They were back in the forest, Edmund, Ulfcytel, Wulfnoth, and all the rest. Edmund had gathered them here to break the news of his deal with his father, thinking the relative seclusion might lessen the risk of them being disturbed. They were not so far off to be vulnerable, and the smoke and flickering light of their camp's cookfires was still just about visible up ahead. Edmund felt reassured by the sight, despite the awkwardness of his present company. He was proud of the army he'd gathered here, and they were in good spirits now the walls of the capital were near. He hoped they'd understand his decision. Even if Wulfnoth and the rest of them did not, Edmund felt it would somehow be harder to lose the confidence of the common soldier. They'd already given up so much to follow him. He didn't think he could stand it if they grew to resent him.

"Do you understand what I've said to you?" Edmund hoped they did. He couldn't quite believe it himself when he'd told them, and yet he'd had to. Refusing his father was not an option.

More silence. More stares, not all of them alike. Wulfnoth looked like he was barely holding it together, his face suggesting he was caught somewhere between fear and incredulity. Sigeferth looked sad, as he often did now, and Morcar looked vaguely akin to Wulfnoth, only angrier. Eadwig was pale, but that was probably because he'd spent yet another night throwing his guts up, so there was no telling what he really thought. Wulfhild looked worried, but not for Edmund. Her eyes were on Ulfcytel.

His reaction was the most surprising. Edmund had expected him to rage, unleashing expletives and oaths as to how stupid Edmund was and how he'd never have agreed to follow him if he was just going to capitulate to his father at the first opportunity. Instead, Ulfcytel appeared merely thoughtful. There was no anger. Or dismay. Just thoughtfulness. Edmund would have paid money to find out what was going on in that great shining bald head of his. Fortunately, the ealdorman told him before he could broach such an offer.

"I understand why you've done this," said Ulfcytel, everyone else looking at him like they were almost shocked to hear him say that. "The bond between a father and son goes deep…and there is no military solution to be had here without joining with Æthelred. We either withdraw and allow Cnut to keep Lundenburg, at least for now…or we honour the deal you've struck. You made the right choice, my king."

"I'm not sure you understand," said Edmund carefully. "If we do this, I will not be king. My father will reign once more. I'll be his announced heir, as he promised, but we will all be back under his authority."

"I understand that," replied Ulfcytel. "But you'll be my king, Edmund. Æthelred need not know what I really think of him, although I think he can make a good guess at it. I'll never forgive him for the things he's done…for what he did to Alaric…and so I will continue to think of you as king. Your taking of the throne, whenever that may happen, will just be the completion of what is already fact. You're a king. Your father is not."

"Why such confidence in me?" Edmund asked, bewildered still at Ulfcytel's reaction. "I mean…who am I to you? What did I do to deserve such loyalty?"

"You've asked me something similar before," said Ulfcytel, "and yet I will answer you, as always. It's simple, really. You didn't give up on your country. Your father did. More than once. You have not, and you could have done easily. Instead you fought, with your sword and with your head. And you've suffered for it. I see that, but you've kept on and taken us as far as you can go. That is all I have to say."

"As shocked as I am, I'm in agreement with the ealdorman," said Wulfnoth. "I find it distasteful, and there are still dangers ahead, but the deal you've struck is the only one possible if we are to defeat Cnut and also avoid civil war."

"You think there'd be a civil war?" asked Edmund, horrified. "Who would follow me against my own father? He has the support of all of the North, not to mention Normandy."

"We would," snapped Morcar without hesitation. "I don't want to go back to the bad old days of your father's reign, Edmund, and I'm also more than aware of just how badly you feel we let you down when we gave in to Svienn. If you commanded it, the Five Boroughs would fight Uhtred and anyone else to put you on the throne."

"That's quite a change of heart, Morcar," said Edmund. "You were full of excuses not so long ago. You'll have to forgive me if I wonder about your intentions."

"I think our previous concerns may shed light on this," said Sigeferth nervously. "We spoke before about how your father will seek to blame us for the death of your brother…and so I'm very concerned about this decision you've made, Edmund. How can we know Æthelred won't try to wreak some kind of vengeance on us?"

"Because I made him give his word."

There was murmuring now, from all of them. None of them held Æthelred in high regard, and the idea that he'd keep his promise not to harm them was difficult to digest. Eadwig was safe, as was Wulfhild, but Sigeferth and Morcar had good reason to worry. So did Wulfnoth. They were all marked, and Ulfcytel's sudden conversion to stoicism didn't change that.

"I suggest we focus more on the immediate situation rather than what may or may not happen in the future," said Eadwig, his words drawing an appreciative nod from Edmund. Eadwig was a wise man, and he was quite correct here. Planning for the upcoming battle should take priority. Lundenburg had to be retaken, and the immediate threat, that being Cnut, dealt with. They could worry about politics later.

"So you say it was Æthelred who destroyed the bridge?" asked Ulfcytel. "That was a bold move for him. Cnut's forces will be cut in two, most likely, but not forever. Time remains of the essence."

"It wasn't him personally," corrected Edmund. "He claims somebody named Olaf, most likely one of his Danes, did it, alongside a fellow called Hereward. I saw the latter with my own eyes. He strikes me as a good man. But as to Olaf…"

"Now that is a sore point," growled Ulfcytel. "If your father really does have Thorkell with him…"

"I know," said Edmund, glad in some way that Ulfcytel was now behaving a bit more like his old self. "I told him to keep him away from us. You heard me say that. And I meant it."

"So we now do as father desires?" asked Eadwig, still sounding a little frail from his illness. "We attack the western walls? We don't have the equipment."

"On the contrary," announced Wulfnoth, pleased with himself. "We have several scaling ladders, and I ordered the making of a ram as soon as we pitched camp here. We'll have something, at least, to make the enemy feel threatened. Which is the whole point, isn't it, Edmund?"

"My father does indeed wish us to make a distraction," Edmund confirmed. "It'll confuse the enemy, or make them unsure where to commit their forces once attacked from several directions. It's a good plan."

"It'll cost us," said Sigeferth, "and this is another problem, Edmund. Our army may not fight the same once they learn that Æthelred, rather than your good self, is to take the throne."

"But if we don't do this, then my father may fail in his assault," replied Edmund flatly. "And we know what that means…Cnut will hold Lundenburg long enough for his army down south to get back here. And if I impede my father? Well, Duke Richard may take action then…against my sister. That's not something I can entertain."

"Can we be sure the duke would do that?" asked Wulfhild, disgusted that anyone, even a Norman, would be capable of such dark deeds.

"We can," answered Wulfnoth confidently. "Richard's reputation isn't the most savoury…and as much as I don't trust Æthelred, he's been quite consistent in his attitude towards Emma and their children. He cares for them a great deal. A man like Richard will have sought to exploit that, and he has. Godgifu is in great danger if we don't keep him placated, and the only way to do that seems to be to help Æthelred win this battle."

"I didn't know you were close to your siblings? I mean the ones your father sired with Emma?" Ulfcytel looked more curious than anything, which was just as well, as Edmund didn't want to assume the ealdorman was somehow suggesting he might allow Godgifu to die simply because they didn't share a mother. That would be a grotesque decision to make. Godgifu was a child, unjustly held captive by a man who sounded like a real monster. Edmund would do everything he could for her. His right to call himself a Christian depended on it.

"I barely know her," Edmund said with a shrug. "But she's blood, and she doesn't deserve to be a pawn in some political game. I may dislike her mother, but I won't throw her life away just for the sake of my desire to be king."

"And will you be king?" Sigeferth asked. "Has Æthelred definitely said so? Queen Emma won't like that. She'll want Edward to have priority. You'll have made an enemy of her today, Edmund."

"Let her froth and rage all she likes!" Edmund exclaimed, feeling slightly amused at the thought of it. "She never liked me or Æthelstan, anyway. I have the measure of Emma, and I suspect her hold on my father has been weakened, given the actions of her bastard of a brother."

"That brings another loose end to the fore," said Wulfnoth ominously. "Eadric. He's long desired to influence the queen and thus gain a hold over her children. What does your father say about Eadric? I assume you told him he's a traitor?"

"I did, yet he wants proof, or isn't convinced or some such. I could never understand why he can't see Eadric for what he is."

"If he turns up again, I'll kill him," said Ulfcytel simply. "I'm being serious," he added, as if anyone thought otherwise. "I'll kill him and Thorkell too. There's no coming back from what they've done. There's no redemption for Æthelred either, in my opinion, but I'll play along with him for your sake, Edmund. He'll answer to God, one way or another."

"He's changed," Edmund replied, hoping he didn't sound as ridiculous as he feared. "I know it sounds odd...but I sense something in him. He's not the erratic, unstable man I knew. I believe he does intend to rule us more justly."

"But as a Norman puppet?" asked Sigeferth, his silver eyebrows raised in alarm. "Æthelred may perhaps be a changed man...but Duke Richard wouldn't have sent him back here with an army if he intended to just leave him alone once he's on the throne. We could be driving out the Danes just to hand over England to the Normans."

There was a lot of consternation following that last comment, and rightly so. Edmund tried to think fast, hoping some words would come to him that could perhaps allay their fears and keep them focused on the upcoming battle. He could tell he was losing them. Ulfcytel looked dismayed, and Sigeferth too, although he generally did these days, and Morcar was angry, his harsh tones sounding over the others as they argued among themselves. Edmund didn't know what to do. The prospect of England becoming some kind of client state of Normandy was truly horrifying. Could Duke Richard take things that far? Would he really lower himself to hurt a child if Æthelred resisted?

"We'll just have to get Godgifu back!" Everyone felt silent, their eyes on Eadwig. "You heard what I said," he simmered, holding their gaze well. "If Godgifu is the leverage the duke has over us, then we'll just have to take it away."

"A rescue of some kind?" mused Morcar, to himself as much as Eadwig.

"It's preferable to the alternative!" said Ulfcytel irately. "We've been so fixated on your father's return, Edmund, that I didn't really consider what the duke could force him to do should he regain power. Is it worth it?"

"You mean to fight the Danes so the Normans can rule us by proxy?" Edmund asked rhetorically. "I would say that's a poor deal. Which is why my brother is right. We'll need to take away the duke's advantage. We'll need to get Godgifu back."

"Emma. Emma is the weak link, and Richard was fool enough to send her back here. If we can make it known that we'll do her harm if Richard doesn't give us Godgifu..."

Edmund's eyes widened at what Wulfnoth was suggesting. He saw then that there were many differences between them, and not all because he was Edmund's senior. He was cold, and what he'd suggested was cold. Judging from the way everyone else was looking at him, Edmund was not alone in thinking that. It wasn't right. They wouldn't win this by using the duke's methods against him. It would sully them. Edmund would have none of it.

"We're not doing that," he said sternly. "Don't even think it, Wulfnoth. Emma is a bitch and a fool, but I'm not holding her hostage. I doubt it would work anyway. Richard wouldn't have allowed her to return here if he held her in high esteem. We could end up threatening him over something he doesn't even care about."

"Would he really not care for his own sister?" Wulfhild sounded shocked. She was new to all this, and likely still didn't comprehend just how dark the world could be. She was blessed, in a way.

"Emma was always a bargaining chip," nodded Ulfcytel. "The duke wanted her married-off to Æthelred, not because he thought anything of us, but because he wanted some half-Norman offspring in the equation so he could stake a future claim on England."

"This is getting better and better," said Morcar. "Is this something else we have to worry about now; the Normans using Emma's children, at some future date, to claim they have a right to our entire country?"

"It may be so," answered Edmund, wondering if Morcar really meant to ask such a question, given he was normally so astute at politics and the possibilities that came with it.

"Then I say it's all the more important we win here," piped up Eadwig. "If we smash the Danes, and I mean utterly smash them, we'll give them the impression England is no longer fit for tormenting. Svienn is dead. Now let's kill Cnut. Then Thorkell next. Eliminate Denmark from the game. Get Godgifu back, and then Edmund rules after our father. A strong king. A warrior king. Ironside!"

Everyone nodded, Ulfcytel, Sigeferth, and Morcar following Eadwig's example by repeating the word "Ironside!" with boisterous enthusiasm. Edmund couldn't help but grin. It wasn't out of pride, and he wasn't yet a major fan of his new name, since every time he heard it his mind went back to that monastery and the sight of Æthelstan as he lay dying. It was Eadwig that had made him smile. His brother was continuing to surprise him.

"That's possibly the best sequence of ideas I've heard in some time," laughed Edmund.

"Then let that be our plan," affirmed Ulfcytel with a jab of his finger. "We bloody the Danes here and make them again regret they ever dared think us easy prey. That is our priority. We can work out a way to rescue your sister from Normandy once the dust has settled."

"Be aware the duke could react badly to his sole bargaining chip being snatched from him," cautioned Sigeferth. "He could respond in any number of ways. He's shown he can get troops here...we could end up looking at another invasion."

"Then we'll kill them, all of them," answered Edmund, his hand falling to the pommel of his sword. "Understand this," he continued, looking to each of his companions in turn. "The dark days of humiliation will soon be over. When I am king, there'll be no more intrigue, no more plotting, no more turning on our own...anyone who threatens England, for whatever reason, will be punished. Severely. That is how I will rule. That is how..."

Memories leapt unbidden into Edmund's conscious mind. He remembered the grave, Alaric's grave, and those of all the other men they'd buried back in Eastengle. Æva was kneeling in the grass, barely discernible in the twilight, but the sadness radiating from her was difficult to miss. Edmund had gone over, hoping to say or do something to help. Then she'd asked him to make her a promise. That he'd be a good king. That he'd keep people like her and her child safe. He'd agreed to it. He'd meant it. He still did. And yet Æva was lost to him now, dead for all he knew. The pain of it still shocked him. His cheeks flushed, and his eyes stung. He shouldn't feel like this, but he did.

"Are you alright?" Sigeferth's inquiry was genuine and gentle. He, of all people, knew Edmund's heart, although no one knew of how Æva seemed to have ended up there. Edmund didn't even know that himself. It wasn't his choice. She just seemed to have wandered in without him noticing and wouldn't leave. It wasn't acceptable. He was supposed to be inspiring his men right now, not becoming tearful over recollections of a widow he'd hardly known.

"I'm perfectly fine. Forgive me. Old memories crept up on me. Let us ponder the battle ahead. My father said he would send word when he wants us to begin our atta…"

Newcomers appeared, a man on a horse and a warrior, one of Edmund's own, walking alongside. They approached, Edmund's companions parting to allow it. The warrior spoke, explaining that the man he was escorting claimed to be "a messenger from King Æthelred", who apparently had a note for him. Edmund extended his hand towards the horseman, allowing him to pass a small piece of paper into his fingers. Edmund read it. The instructions were clear enough: "Attack at sundown." His father had put his seal on it, so it was genuine. Æthelred was making his move. It was almost time.

Edmund thanked the messenger and the warrior before dismissing them. He turned back to the others and took a deep breath. "This is it," he announced, feeling a wave of excitement pass through him. "My father's army will be attacking the eastern walls. Now is our time to move. Now is our time to win! Let us prepare our men and take New Gate by storm!"

Their gathering broke up, each man aware of what was at stake and what would be required of him. Edmund caught Ulfcytel as he was striding purposefully back to camp. "I must speak with you a moment," Edmund said, gesturing towards Wulfhild to signify he'd prefer to talk with her husband in private. She moved off without complaint, soon losing herself in conversation with Eadwig.

"What is it?" Ulfcytel asked, both concerned and curious.

"It's about Alaric's widow," Edmund confessed, his voice hushed lest anyone hear him. "Do you know if there's been word from the men we sent to Euerwic to track her down? I've heard nothing."

"Me neither," replied Ulfcytel, "and just so you know, she's been on my mind also. I wanted to keep her safe, Edmund, believe me. It was the least I could do after Alaric. Her absence weighs heavily on my heart."

"And what of Cenric and the others who were with you when you were captured?" asked Edmund, suddenly fearful over the realisation that Cenric was likely dead. "Did he escape? Was it just you who was seized?"

"I didn't see what happened to any of them. I wish I could be of more help. The Danes were out for blood that night, and the only thing that saved me was them thinking I'd be worth something as a hostage. My sword gave it away, you see. You know how it is."

Ulfcytel patted Edmund on the shoulder, the look in his eyes suggesting he somehow knew what he was feeling. He then turned and headed off after Wulfhild, leaving Edmund amidst the trees. The sun was going down, the fading dusk casting deep shadows that seemed to shift with the swaying of branches and the flickering light from their cookfires. He felt sad. Sad for Cenric, but also for Æva and Brandon. He knew he couldn't be feeling like this. He had to snap out of it. He put one foot in front of the other, forcing himself to follow Ulfcytel back to camp. He had an army to lead and a battle to win. That's what mattered. Not the past, nor his aching heart. Nothing could get in the way of what he was about to do. There was too much at risk.

But even as he addressed his men, bellowing for them to form up and follow him to victory or death, he still couldn't shake that feeling. His friend, Cenric, the man who'd saved his life in Lundenburg, was dead, and Æva and Brandon were still missing. If they were dead also, he didn't know what he'd do. He'd tried his utmost to protect them, defying his own father to do it, and yet from the looks of things he'd still failed…and if that were so, he didn't think he'd ever get over it.

XXIII

The wine was good, of a year and vintage that he didn't know and didn't care either. His people hadn't ever made wine, for their climate was entirely unsuitable, but they'd treasured it whenever they'd been able to acquire it. He savoured it now, swishing it around his mouth to further ponder its myriad flavours. It was no good. He couldn't fool himself. It was a drink like any other, used for soothing the nerves or rendering oneself insensible. He swallowed it, finding the sharp, bitter tang vaguely distasteful. Why anyone would choose this over mead was beyond him. People must drink it to appear sophisticated, he supposed. He wondered why he'd felt like imitating them.

Cnut stretched his legs and leaned back in his seat at the banqueting table. He was in old King Æthelred's hall, or what was now, in fact, his own throne room, and he was alone, which for the time being was precisely how he wanted it. A fire was roaring away in the hearth, bringing a little warmth to the otherwise chill chamber, but Cnut felt no particular need for comfort, and it was only idle curiosity that had prompted him to dip into Æthelred's wine. He had more serious business to ponder tonight. Like defending what was his.

He'd watched the Norman force as it approached, wondering why Duke Richard had decided to move against him. It wasn't the largest army he'd ever seen, but it was disciplined, and their commanders had shown themselves capable and cunning when they'd destroyed the bridge over the Temes just a couple of nights before. Cnut had been confused when he'd heard about that, as his men kept insisting the vessels that had attacked there were Norse longships. All had become clear when the messenger from Æthelred had arrived, demanding they surrender the city "for the sake of England's true king." Thorkell and what was left of his men must still be under Æthelred's sway. It had been they who'd attacked the bridge. He should have known. That kind of reckless bravery wasn't exactly common.

Cnut didn't know where Æthelred had managed to obtain a spine, but it would do him little good. He wasn't going to give anything up to him, "true king" or no. He'd have to fight for it, and all Cnut had to do was hold the walls until Eadric returned with his army from the South. Cnut had already sent out riders with orders for him to do just that, and it was of little consequence that his journey would be delayed by the absence of the bridge. Time wasn't much of an issue. Nobody would be taking the walls by storm. They were too high, and Cnut had more than enough men to defend them. Æthelred would be stuck outside until Cnut and Eadric together could deal with him. Then they'd turn their attention to Duke Richard. His treachery would not go unpunished.

He took another sip of wine, turning it into a full swig as he finally gave up attempting to savour this "special vintage." He finished his cup and poured himself another, feeling he deserved some small indulgence in light of what he'd been through of late. The worst thing about being king, he'd decided, was the isolation. People didn't look at him the same anymore. He'd always received deference and respect, as was only right, but this was something else, and Cnut didn't think he'd ever get used to it. People feared him, and not just the English. He had all the power he'd ever wanted, but in many ways, he'd never felt so helpless. He missed his family, but there was a whole sea between him and them, and with his father dead he felt like he really didn't have too many people to even talk to, not that Svienn had ever really bothered to keep him company. Even Østen was remote, acting like he was suddenly afraid to speak his mind, and the others, most particularly that "Lord of Lindesi", were just downright sycophantic. Cnut hoped it wouldn't always be this way. It would drive him mad.

This Edmund "Ironside", also, continued to trouble him. Cnut wasn't used to being bested in anything, really, but this man had defeated him handily at Gainesburg and sullied his reputation by doing so. Cnut knew he only had himself to blame, as he'd wallowed for too long in the North without proper reinforcement, although he wasn't of a mind to give voice to such a thought. Edmund was a great warrior, and if Cnut was to learn any lessons from the experience of being defeated, he knew he had to afford his enemy proper respect. The English were no longer the frightened lambs they'd been for years. Not under Edmund.

Cnut was thus understandably alarmed to witness Edmund's arrival from the north west. He knew he'd been coming, but what surprised him was the fact he and Æthelred now seemed to be working together. Cnut had always assumed Edmund wanted the crown for himself. Lord knew he'd fought for it, whereas Æthelred hadn't fought for anything in his life. They must have come to some kind of accord, the nature of which was a mystery, at least for now. That left Cnut with only one option, which was to wait. The enemy was almost certainly aware that Cnut awaited reinforcements, otherwise there was little reason for them to have attacked the bridge like that. An assault was coming, and it would be poorly planned and rushed when it did. Cnut would then have every advantage. Lundenburg would remain his, as would England.

He'd have felt comforted with that last thought were it not for the noise now intruding from the corridor outside. Something was going on – an argument or a drunken brawl – the cause of which was presently a mystery. He got up and drained the last of his cup, his haste causing some spillage into his beard. He wiped his mouth on his sleeve and approached the doors, checking his belt in the process and feeling a little uneasy when his fingers brushed against the dagger that hung there. He'd been trying to relax or at least think, and he wasn't attired or equipped for a fight. When the attack came, he'd expected to have the time to change into his armour before rushing to the walls, but from what he could hear the enemy had decided to start trouble right away, and within his own halls, no less.

Cnut soon saw how true that presumption was. When he'd managed to haul the doors open and step outside, he felt like he'd been caught in a nightmare. There were Normans, lots of them, pushing up the stone corridor towards him, their swords and kite shields already wet with blood. Several of Cnut's men were dead and trampled 'neath their feet, and the few Danes still fighting looked like they had only moments before they'd be overwhelmed. Cnut was stunned, unable to tear his eyes away as another of his brethren fell, their blood spraying across the walls. Several Normans began rushing towards him, roaring in their strange language. Cnut did the only thing he could. He ran.

It was shameful, beyond shameful, and if he'd had any other option he'd never have considered it, but there was no point in dying here and handing his enemies an easy victory. His lack of armour turned out to be a blessing, for he was far lighter on his feet than any of his pursuers, who thundered after him with all the grace and finesse of an enraged ox. He outpaced them, but he couldn't lose them, and there didn't seem to be any limit to their numbers. None of this was right. There was no way they could have breached the walls without him being alerted. There was trickery afoot.

He'd almost reached the exit to the stables and prison tower when the doors ahead were flung open. Østen was there, his face twisted in horror upon beholding what was happening, the men at his side likewise freezing to the spot in surprise. Cnut sped towards them, bellowing for them to come to his aid. Østen and his escorts got over their shock and charged into the fight, cutting into Cnut's pursuers with axe and spear. It was a brave effort, and Østen hacked down at least two men on his own, but there were yet more Normans rushing in, their weapons bared and bloodied. They couldn't retake the place like this. They needed help.

"Fall back now! With me!" screamed Cnut. Østen nodded and began a fighting withdrawal, a scything blow from his axe almost parting a Norman's head entirely from his shoulders. Cnut managed to reach the doors and get a look outside. It was dark, as was to be expected, but there were no enemies about, and the gate into the fortified compound was closed and secure. The Normans had not overrun the walls to begin pouring in to get at him here. If anything, it looked like they were coming from the inside rather than out. Just what exactly was going on?

Østen was hurrying to Cnut's side when a shove from a pursuing Norman almost caused him to lose his footing. Cnut acted on instinct and threw his dagger, hoping by some fluke to catch the Norman in the throat or eye and give Østen a chance to get away. The blade didn't hit home, instead bouncing off the rim of his enemy's kite shield, but the distraction made them flinch and cease their attack, permitting Østen to reach Cnut. They both knew what had to be done. They stepped out into the night air and closed the doors, ignoring those still alive and fighting within. Cnut didn't want to die here, and Østen was the only one who he felt to be indispensable. He'd let the others pay with their lives so that he might live. He'd avenge them later.

Cnut looked about in a panic, hoping to find something to seal the doors. A clutch of warriors came running from elsewhere within the courtyard, each of them looking concerned, yet all carrying something that at this precise moment could mean the difference between escape and death.

Spears. They had spears, humble things made from iron and ash, and yet for all their simplicity, they were inestimably useful now. Cnut snatched one from the nearest man and slid it through the heavy iron rungs that served as handles on the double doors. He took another and did the same, the twin spears serving to fasten the doors closed. Something began pushing from the other side, and there were muffled, angry shouts, but by now the other Danes had worked out what Cnut was doing and moved to assist him. They stood back, admiring their handiwork, the bundle of six spears looking like it might hold the doors in place, at least for a time. Then Cnut heard the hammering, heavy and persistent and growing in intensity. There must be many men on the other side to make that kind of noise. They had best move.

"What is going on?" snapped Cnut, striding with Østen and the others towards the stables.

"I know not, my king," replied Østen as he hurried several horses out into the open, his hand gripping one by the mane so Cnut could mount. "We are attacked from both east and west. Yet last I saw, the enemy had not breached the walls. I do not understand how they could have gotten into your halls."

"So we have deception here?" asked Cnut, knowing it likely Østen had no means to answer to his satisfaction. The man didn't reply immediately, for he was busy climbing into the saddle of his own horse, the few guards who'd assisted them with the doors finding mounts of their own.

"Like I said, I don't know how they got in," said Østen, their little group of horsemen hurrying through the courtyard's exterior gate and into the streets beyond. "They must have planned something we didn't foresee...attacking from some secret place whilst others hurl themselves at the walls. That's why I came for you...Thorkell leads the assault in the east just as Edmund presses from the west."

"Thorkell himself?" asked Cnut, trying to suppress a flinch at the sudden crash sounding from behind them. The Normans must have finally broken through back there. Cnut kicked his horse, bidding it press on faster and away from the compound. He wasn't dressed for any of this. He wasn't armed, either. His men followed him like the faithful bunch they were, but this was turning out to be a very, very bad night. He had to find some way to turn this around.

"It is indeed Thorkell," confirmed Østen, the hurried hooves of their horses clattering haphazardly upon the stony surface of the street. "When I left to collect you, he'd not breached the gates, but I received word on my way here that Edmund is hitting us hard on the other side of the city. With what I saw back there...my king...even if we hold the walls, we'll be attacked in the rear by those who just surprised us! What shall we do?"

Cnut tried to think. If Æthelred had found a way to get his Norman mercenaries inside whilst Thorkell and Edmund attacked the gates, that meant he undoubtedly intended to rush the defenders by surprise. How he'd been able to do that would have to remain a secret for now, but Cnut didn't see why he shouldn't be able to push these sneak attackers back so they'd be confined to the royal halls and unable to make mischief elsewhere. He'd then be free to concentrate on holding Thorkell and Edmund at bay, safe in the knowledge that Æthelred had likely run out of tricks. That was a good enough plan. Cnut now just had to collect the men and lead them himself in the counterattack.

A great roar suddenly tore through the air behind him. He turned to see the Normans were emerging from the gate and into the city. There were hundreds of them, far more than could have been the case had they been some advance force that had carried the walls by stealth. Cnut's hope of trapping these men in the hall was now moot. It would take an army to drive them back, and he didn't have one to spare, not with the walls under attack. Their situation was indeed grim.

One of the warriors who'd fled with them suddenly cried out. Something had struck his helm, the crash of it making Cnut wince in apprehension. He heard others shouting ahead and to the side of them, and then something hit him in the back of the shoulder, the blunt force almost causing him to slide from his horse. More projectiles clattered around them, the deluge seeming to come from the doors and windows of the buildings on either side of the road. Cnut looked up, trying to shield himself with one arm, and spied the twisted, angry faces of those looking out from their homes. The populace had turned on him. They were furious, and throwing everything they had at his men, as if they somehow knew the battle had turned against the Danes and now was the time to rise up. It was pathetic. These people had called for his father back when he'd first come here to drive Æthelred into exile. Now they had switched sides yet again.

Cnut led his companions in a gallop down the street to the south, outpacing both the charging Normans and their local tormentors. More people began to emerge from their dwellings, however, and they cursed and spat at Cnut as he rode past, hurling insults and objects whenever they felt brave enough. The Danes soon reached an intersection, presenting Cnut with the choice to either ride west, to face Edmund, or head east to try and fend off the ferocious Thorkell. He could hear the fighting from here, low and muffled, terrible images of brutal hand-to-hand combat filling his mind. He could also hear the Normans thundering after him, undeterred and indefatigable. A decision had to be made, and he had to be the one to make it. If he didn't, this battle was already lost.

"We head west!" Cnut shouted, again spurring his mount into motion and taking off at speed down the wide road towards New Gate. More people shouted after them, brandishing fists and cudgels, all denouncing him as a "foreign usurper" and other things he didn't care to think about. They'd suffer for their insolence, if not now, then someday soon. He'd enjoy the spectacle when the time came.

The fighting at New Gate wasn't entirely as he'd expected. The English were swarming the walls, using ladders they'd rushed into position to try and climb up and overwhelm the battlements. Cnut's men were fierce and committed, as he knew them to be, but from the looks of it, Edmund's forces had already been partly successful in capturing a portion of the wall adjacent to the main gatehouse. The garrison were fighting back hard, trying to dislodge them and push their ladders away from the parapet before too many English could scale them, but it wasn't easy and both sides were taking serious losses. This would all be a lot easier to deal with if they didn't have a force of hostile Normans about to rush in and make things more complicated, thought Cnut. He'd have to find some way to turn things around.

He looked to the gate. It had been closed and sealed, as was wise, and there were hundreds of his men braced behind it, their shields raised at their chests and their spears pointing forward. The enemy were hitting it from the other side, most likely with a ram, causing the gate's timbers to shake and crash as they were struck, again and again, in a slow, steady tempo. It was hard on the ears, but thus far the gate was showing little sign of damage and didn't seem likely to fall. If it held, and he saw no reason why it wouldn't, then the men standing ready behind it were just idling to no real purpose. That was a waste, as far as Cnut was concerned. He'd find a better use for them.

He rode closer and cried out to them, his right arm raised in the air so all might see him. Everyone turned, defenders and attackers alike, transfixed by this bellowing horseman. Cnut called his men to him, ordering them to rush to his aid and prepare for "the most treacherous foe" he knew couldn't be too far to their rear. They obeyed him, forming a stout line of shields facing away from the gate to block off the street from where Cnut had emerged. It was just as well they'd reacted so quickly. The Normans were already upon them.

Cnut circled about, trying to manoeuvre his horse to get a good view of the battle unfurling around him. The fighting on the walls rumbled on, the English taking as much punishment as they were giving out, but the Normans were smashing into Cnut's hastily formed shield wall in real force, trying to punch through to take the gatehouse and open the city to the men hammering away outside. That couldn't happen. The Normans had to be beaten back. There was no alternative.

He snatched a spear from someone and joined the fray, Østen and his companions accompanying him. The Normans were overconfident, as they'd rushed the Danes in a hurry without first cohering themselves into a workable formation. They'd enjoyed the element of surprise back at the hall, but now they'd met organised resistance it wasn't going entirely their way. Cnut thought it very probable their plan had been to assassinate him in his chambers, thus decapitating the Danish garrison before it could put up much of a fight. They'd failed in that. Cnut would take pleasure in making them pay for it.

He speared a man, impaling him through the shoulder and then again through the neck. The Danish line was holding, and Cnut and Østen soon lost themselves in the fight, drawing blood and taking lives with a grim enthusiasm. The Normans pressed in, roaring and screaming up at them, and Østen was almost knocked from his horse, so furious was the contest. More Danes in the shield wall fell, their bodies pierced by spears or slashed open by the Normans' terrible broadswords, but overall the defenders were determined to stand their ground and were killing Normans just as they killed them.

They'd been fighting for some time when a great shout suddenly sounded from the gate. Cnut turned, trying to ascertain what was happening. There were still men on the walls, of course, but any hope that his warriors had contained and repulsed the English foothold was soon dashed when the gateway itself began groaning open, allowing a sudden deluge of furious men to pour in and attack. Cnut couldn't believe it. The English had fought clear of their ladders and seized the gatehouse to open the city from within. That shouldn't have been possible. His men were warriors all and skilled at what they did. For them to have been overcome whilst he struggled in the streets below was difficult to comprehend. And yet it had happened. In any other time, Cnut might have been inclined to afford the English a certain grudging respect for that. As it stood, he was just too shocked to comprehend it.

He soon saw how they'd been able to prevail. Dark as it was, he could see Edmund by the gate, his sword held aloft whilst he roared encouragements to his men now charging on through. Cnut might not have been sure it was him, but his features were seared into memory ever since they'd first encountered each other on that terrible day at the monastery. He must have climbed the ladders himself, leaping straight into the fray and capturing the walls with that same frenzied malevolence Cnut had seen him display twice before. It would be easy to dismiss this Edmund as a monster; a savage and terrible foe who fought simply for the joy of shedding blood, but Cnut knew in his heart it wasn't so. Edmund drew strength from something else, and for the first time in his life, Cnut felt he could comprehend the sheer depths of the hatred the English held for the Danes. It was understandable, in a way. His father had been so terribly hard on them. They had all been terribly hard on them, all Norsemen, for centuries. It had been foolish to think there wouldn't be a price to pay.

The English breaking in from the gate charged Cnut's men from the rear. The fighting now spread out as far as could be seen, the walls, gatehouse, and the wide, open square immediately behind turning thick with struggling bodies. It was an eerie sight, since much of the fighting remained wreathed in shadow, the flickering light from the braziers upon the walls only catching on the helms and metal scales of the combatants' armour. It was thus hard to tell who was who, so chaotic had things become, but one thing was gradually becoming more than clear. Cnut's people were losing, and if he didn't do something, he'd again have to endure the shame of defeat.

He heard something over the screams and cries, like some great roaring beast had appeared and was adamant about making itself known. In a sense it was true, for the man presently fighting his way towards him could have passed for a bear, such was his ferocity and dimensions. His face was hidden, thanks to his helmet, but the Englishmen around him seemed to know who he was and fought all the harder because of it. It wasn't Edmund, which left only one other man as a possibility. Ulfcytel. So the Ealdorman Ulfcytel had survived Gainesburg and joined with his rescuer, Edmund. That was a most deadly combination of men. The number of slaughtered Danes at Ulfcytel's feet demonstrated that well enough.

Cnut ushered his horse into another charge, Østen and his companions following him as they and whoever was left standing made a last-ditch defence of the gate. Cnut rode an Englishman down, his body jerking and snapping under the great hooves of his mount. Another leapt aside at the last moment only to be caught and split asunder by Østen's axe, the blow disintegrating both helm and skull in an outpouring of blood and disintegrating brain matter. Cnut stabbed and thrust his weapon into the melée, hoping to somehow get close to Ulfcytel and make a show of defeating him in as bloody and unpleasant a way as possible.

The sound of battle was now doubly intense, and Cnut wondered if he could take it for much longer, so overpowering was the din made by hundreds upon hundreds of men all doing their utmost to end the other. It was worse because of the walls and buildings, he thought. In the open, sound could carry uninhibited, but here it was hemmed in, creating an echoing hellscape that hammered the ears without pause. Men were dying all around, and Edmund had now joined Ulfcytel amid the riotous brawl, the presence of these two heroes driving their people into a Dane-killing frenzy. Cnut fought on, as did Østen and every Dane still living, but he felt a certain feeling creeping up from his stomach. He knew it well, sadly. It was the same feeling he'd experienced at Sancte Eadmundes Byrig. Fear. He'd have to do something about that.

"We have to get you away!" screamed Østen, his axe broken and bloodied from raining down blow after blow upon their most insistent foe.

"I'll not flee!" bellowed Cnut, whirling his horse around to face him properly. "This is my city! I won it! And I'll keep it!"

"Just look around you!" howled Østen with a frantic gesture, hoping Cnut might see the situation for what it was. He did, and it was beyond dire. There were yet more Normans pouring in from the east, their numbers unchecked, and with the gate open the massed ranks of enraged Englishmen couldn't be stopped. Danes were falling everywhere he looked, yet Cnut's eyes somehow focused in on a single man, someone who gave him redoubled pause.

He was hurt, like he'd been through some horrific ordeal by flame or heat or some such, but Cnut recognised him well enough. Osbert. The little bastard was still alive and fighting alongside his master, Ulfcytel. He was good, Cnut gave him that – a survivor and warrior both – and he fought well, killing one Dane and then another with a cold efficiency that was easy to admire. He locked eyes with Cnut. There was recognition there. Osbert was coming for him, with Ulfcytel and Edmund, and with the Normans behind...

"Let's go!"

Cnut's horse suddenly lurched into a spirited gallop towards a narrow street winding north. Cnut almost fell, so sudden was the movement. It was Østen who had spoken, and he'd somehow gotten a tether around the neck of Cnut's steed, forcing it to keep pace with his own. There were other men with them, Danes, thankfully, some mounted and some on foot, and they were all rushing along, fearful and eager to escape the bloody nightmare behind them.

"What are you doing?!" Cnut wailed, grateful yet dismayed at being taken away from the battle.

"This day is lost!" shouted Østen, to those men who could still hear him as well as Cnut. "We must escape through one of the northern gates! Flee!"

"Do not presume to order me around!" Cnut roared back. "As long as I live, I will give the commands here!"

"You will die if you remain! For Odin's sake, boy, we were undone as soon as the Normans surprised us! If they bested us here, it will be the same along the eastern ramparts! Thorkell is coming for us!"

Cnut didn't bother to reply to any of that. He kept on riding, sneaking a fearful glance back the way he'd come. More Danes were fleeing after him, doing their best to disengage from the fighting and follow their king to whatever sanctuary he might provide. The English and Normans killed any who stood fast, and they began to jeer at those fleeing, their collective mockery soon shifting to a massed, screaming cacophony of victory and jubilation. Cnut couldn't see Osbert, but he spied Edmund easily enough, for he made for quite a spectacle. His men had lifted him up onto their shoulders, and they were all bellowing his name, the familiar chant of "Ironside" repeating over and over across the bloody ground to echo through the streets. A hateful sound. Better to be dead than have to hear that again...almost.

They were about halfway to one of the northern gates, Cnut couldn't recall which, when a rider almost knocked into them at speed. They all brought themselves to a halt, their pause allowing the survivors on foot to catch up, their breathing ragged and desperate.

"The eastern gate is breached!" blurted the rider, Cnut assuming correctly this must be a messenger dispatched by Jarl Knud. Cnut had given him command of his forces there, and that "Lord of Lindesi" - or whatever his name was - had joined him, apparently eager to do battle with his former king. Cnut hadn't known whether to feel impressed or disgusted, but the "lord" seemed sincere enough. What the messenger said next made all that irrelevant. Defeat was to be their due this night. That could not be denied.

"Thorkell has broken through, and Æthelred and his mercenaries are entering the city. We were attacked..."

"From behind?"

"That's right, my king! I know not how, but we need assistance. Knud suggests we pull whatever forces can be spared back from the western defence and use them..."

"It's all over," said Cnut. "The same thing just happened to us. The enemy has outthought and outfought us. We've lost Lundenburg."

"What do I do? What do I tell Jarl Knud?"

"Fly back to him and tell him to withdraw to the north," Cnut ordered, each word bitter and raw upon his tongue. "We'll have to be quick, otherwise the enemy will move to prevent our breakout."

"And what then?" asked Østen, a little incredulous.

"I don't know," admitted Cnut. "We need to regroup. Give me time to think and..."

"What about what's left of our armies down south?" interrupted Østen. "What about what's left of our fleet? Even if they were caught by Æthelred's ships, they could still..."

"There is no time!" Cnut cried. "I sent too many of them back with my father's body...too many ships, too many warriors...now this is the result. I thought God would smile on me for honouring my father, but all I have had since then is defeat. I'll not die like this, Østen. I will yet be proven victor over the Ironside!"

Cnut rode on, waving for those behind to hurry and keep pace. The messenger galloped ahead, intent on delivering new orders to Knud, if he was still alive. Østen followed, as did all those who could keep up, and by the time they'd reached what Cnut had been told was known as the "Alders Gate", he had a couple of hundred men with him. Cnut didn't wait for news from Knud. He had the gate hauled open and rode through, the bedraggled column of survivors following after him.

The air was fresher here, and it whipped about Cnut's face as he progressed, his pace slowing to a shambling trot so his men could again catch up. There was no sign of enemy riders nor anyone else looking to impede them, so he could afford to take stock of the situation rather than just flee headlong into the night. It wasn't good. His men were hobbling after him, spread out in a disorderly line along the road leading out from the city and very vulnerable to attack. There were some others emerging from another gate to the east, and from what Cnut could see they were in a similar plight, the events of this terrible night having reduced those who were left to mere shadows of men. All the same, they flocked to him as best they could, desperate and out of breath, some looking like they wouldn't survive the journey. Knud didn't appear to be among them. It was just Cnut and Østen and this ragtag force that had managed to escape. It would have to suffice.

They continued north, not a single word passing between them. Cnut chanced a look back at Lundenburg, wondering if Edmund and the others might decide to pursue them. The walls still stood, less imposing now distance and darkness lay between them, and yet something could be heard on the breeze that troubled Cnut more than he'd care to admit. Celebration. Not just from the invaders, but the whole populace. The people were glad to be rid of him. They'd learned to hate Cnut, and for that, Cnut would learn to hate them. It was all he could do for the moment. In time, he'd ensure he'd do more, and when that day came, he'd see England and Normandy both pay dearly for what they'd done this night.

XXIV

The clouds parted, revealing the full moon in all its glory. Its rays fell upon the city in a pale light, dispelling much of the darkness that had only just blanketed much of everything. Normally this would have been a blessing, as nobody in their right mind cared for the dark, thinking it a nuisance or a menace in its own right. Edmund wasn't so sure if he felt that way now. The night had been bloody, that he knew, but to see the consequences of it so revealed gave him pause. It was just as well they'd won here. It made things easier to stomach. A weaker man might have already emptied his guts.

There was blood everywhere, layered in long, messy streaks and congealing in pools out from the breach and into the streets beyond. The space atop the walls too was a mess, the choke of tangled bodies serving as a grisly carpet for anyone unfortunate enough to still be up there. Some Danes were alive and expiring upon the hard ground in and beyond the gatehouse, their eyes wide with fright as they beheld their slain brethren lying in their multitudes around them. Edmund looked down at one, placing his boot on the wrist of his sword arm lest he be foolish enough to try and strike him. The man simply groaned, baring a set of broken, blood-flecked teeth. He peered up at Edmund, holding his gaze, resigned and fearful. He didn't speak, and in an instant it was over, whatever spark had been lingering behind those brilliant blue eyes fading to nothing with his last breath. Edmund couldn't say he felt sorrow. This man had come here to do harm, and likely had done harm, but now he was dead, cut down in answer for his great crimes. That was a good thing.

It was harder when it was one of his own. They'd taken some serious losses here, and for a time Edmund had almost despaired, thinking their efforts to scale the walls nigh on impossible. The Danes had possessed every advantage, raining rocks and spears and arrows down on them from up high. So many had been killed just trying to get over the battlements, and Edmund was forced to remember his own defence of the Ald Gate just last year. That had been a hard affair, but he'd been on the other side of the walls that time. He could now appreciate just how difficult it was to be the man climbing those ladders. He was fortunate to have survived.

Edmund leant down and hauled a man to his feet. He was Norman and couldn't speak a word of English, but Edmund felt he understood "thank you" in any language, especially when said with such obvious appreciation. Edmund carried him along, the Norman's arm across his shoulder, and deposited him on the ground at a makeshift field hospital being set up in a barn just a hundred paces from the gate. The monks here were busy, and they'd come quickly, as if they'd been waiting for the fighting to die down before making their move. It was a noble endeavour, and their hospital was already full to capacity with wounded, both English and Norman lying flat on beds of piled straw.

He looked about, making sure the Norman got something to drink without spilling it all over himself. A man close by began to fit, spittle and blood fountaining from his bared teeth to cover his already gore-soaked armour. Several monks rushed to aid him, but they were unable to do much, and the warrior continued to twist and writhe upon the floor in what could only be his death agony.

Edmund could see that he was English, one of his own, and the left side of his head was an absolute mess, looking like it had been dented inwards by the sheer force of whatever had struck him. He then expired, noisily and messily, both dignity and comfort lost to him. Edmund crossed himself and said a prayer, imploring Christ to show mercy to the heroic soul coming to join Him. He blinked his eyes open at the sound of a strange language, hushed and heavy with reverence. The Norman was praying too. Edmund nodded in gratitude.

He wandered through the hospital, doing his best to keep out of the monks' way. Some of the wounded recognised him when he came near, and he was astounded at how their faces lit up at the sight of him. He exchanged a few words with those who wished him to linger, praying also with whoever requested it, but he felt desolate inside. He'd hidden the truth from these men. They'd all fought for his sake, yet all they were doing was speeding his father's return to the throne. He'd not really had the chance to make any announcement about the deal he'd struck before they'd attacked the city, and he feared to bring it up now. They'd think he'd betrayed them. Not one of them had left their homes for the sake of Æthelred. They'd all done it for him, thinking he'd free them from the Danes and then rule wisely. A return to the years of misjudgement and ignominy was not what any of them had envisioned. Neither had Edmund, in truth. But he couldn't abandon family. He wouldn't sacrifice Godgifu for his own ambitions.

Edmund found himself back outside, overlooking the square leading in from the gatehouse. His warriors were milling about amidst the bodies and detritus, some sitting at rest or idling in conversation. A few had fallen asleep at the foot of the walls, but the majority of the hundreds present were yet full of energy, the battle and victory giving them a kind of frenetic vigour that Edmund understood well.

A man on horseback approached, attired in the same grey, no-nonsense mail of the Normans. He had a note for Edmund, written in his father's own hand. It was a simple enough statement: "Victory is ours. Enemy routed everywhere. Come find me. Let us sit and discuss."

He folded the note and handed it back to the Norman messenger before bidding him return with word of his acceptance. He then began the walk back across the square, trying to avoid stepping on any bodies as he went. Wulfnoth was up ahead, finishing off a captured Dane he'd been questioning, his blade making short work of whatever life yet remained in his mauled and broken body. Edmund approached quickly, wanting to talk with Wulfnoth and perhaps distract him from any further attempts to extract information from the enemy. Edmund had little regard for the Danes, viewing them rightly as murdering savages, but his honour wouldn't allow him to brutalise anyone incapable of defending themselves. It was not his way, and he wouldn't suffer being lectured on how that should change.

Wulfnoth saw him coming, the moonlight still strong enough to permit them to see almost as if it had been daytime. "So it's done then?" he asked, looking unnaturally pale in the wan light. "The city is ours? Or Æthelred's, depending on how you look at it."

"Keep that to yourself," Edmund commanded. "I have yet to think of how to broach this to the men. I'll let them enjoy their triumph here for a time whilst I ponder a way to soften the blow."

"You realise you had no choice, even if Godgifu's life wasn't at risk? We didn't have the numbers to attack on our own. Striking the deal you made was the only way to get us this far."

"And where are we, Wulfnoth? The men who died storming the walls did it for my sake, not that of my father. I feel like…their faith in me was misplaced. I feel…"

"Too much," said Wulfnoth. "You do, Edmund. It's time to think, not feel. Your heart does you credit at times, but it wouldn't be right to let it bother you about what was undoubtedly a correct decision. Believe it."

"So what happens now?" Edmund asked, unsure if Wulfnoth was trying to comfort or belittle him with those last remarks. "I mean…I'm no king. My father is, and has an army to back him. Do I go to him?"

"It would seem appropriate," said Wulfnoth. "We may learn much. Allow me to accompany you. Leave Ulfcytel here. I fear if he sees Æthelred again, it won't go well…and if he lays eyes on Thorkell…"

"I understand," muttered Edmund, annoyed Wulfnoth felt the need to state the obvious. He could see Ulfcytel now, leaning against the great stone wall that abutted the gate, a clutch of men headed by Osbert lingering likewise. They all looked like they'd just fought their way through hell and back, the sweat, grime, and blood clinging to their flesh and armour like a second skin. Ulfcytel caught Edmund's eye and stood up straight, his expression pained, his red-streaked sword raised above his head. Osbert and company followed his example, all raising their weapons towards Edmund. He nodded in reply. They honoured him. That's all they ever did. As uncertain as things were, he was still so very grateful to have the loyalty of these men.

It was time to go face his father. Edmund gathered some warriors, assigning around eighty or so to accompany him and Wulfnoth in a march to the eastern ramparts. They assembled quickly, and nobody questioned Edmund's decision to leave Ulfcytel behind, the ealdorman himself probably guessing he'd be seen as a liability were he to come. Edmund had wanted Eadwig and Wulfhild to come also, thinking their presence might have a good effect on their father, but it would take too long to collect them from their camp beyond the walls. Time was of import here. He needed to know what his father intended to do with his newly retaken prize.

They moved out, marching through the wide, cobbled avenue into Westceape. It hadn't improved since Edmund had last seen it, and Svienn's cruel reign and the recent fighting had done little for its appearance. The people, though, were jubilant, and they called out to him from their doorways and windows, hailing him as "Dane killer" and "righteous son" and a variety of other titles that almost made him blush. It was hard to take in. Part of the reason Lundenburg had originally fallen to Svienn was the popular uprising that had taken place behind the walls. Many of these people would have been a part of that. They'd called for Svienn then, thinking he'd get them fed, only to learn the hard way that Danes were not to be trusted. Edmund couldn't take them seriously as a result. They were fickle and foolish, and whilst their situation had been desperate, there was no overlooking treason. He remained aloof as he walked, his men following in reserved silence despite the festivities around them.

They passed St Mildred's church, its bells ringing out in triumph, and crossed the stone bridge over the Walbrook to make their way into Cornhill. Edmund was soon again lost in thought, remembering the scenes when he'd been here last. He'd had

Wulfhild with him then, and they'd been eager to petition their father, hoping to secure Ulfcytel's release following his alleged capture at Canterburie. An old man had accosted his sister, or so he'd thought, upon crossing the bridge, and Edmund's heart had gone out to him on witnessing his desperate poverty. He'd resolved then to get his father to do something about the poor, but of course he'd not listened, and Svienn's arrival outside the walls had spelled the end of his reign, at least for a time. Edmund wondered now if his father would ever return to his arrogant ways. He hoped his recent hardships would ensure it would not be so.

Other memories came to the fore. He again thought of the Ald Gate, that same place he, Cenric, and Ecgberht had defended when Svienn had tried to force entry in the dead of night. It had been a hard fight, and Edmund knew, if he were honest with himself, that they'd only prevailed due to the surprise intervention of Thorkell. He felt his heart grow heavier when he again realised both Cenric and Ecgberht were almost certainly dead. It was a tragic loss, and with Æva also gone, he…that was enough. He forced his sorrows down. His father awaited him. And it looked as though he'd brought an awful lot of company, precious little of it respectable.

He caught up with Æthelred as he was moving towards his old halls along the main thoroughfare heading north from Fenchurch. He was marching at the head of his Norsemen, about five hundred strong, a similarly numerous force of Normans bringing up the rear, their number trailing out behind him like some great grey metal serpent. There was no celebration here, and the inhabitants remained shut up in their homes, the sight of the Danes no doubt scaring them witless. They looked terrible, like they'd been bathed in blood, and the one leading them was doubly frightening, appearing as though he'd hacked his way through a thousand men and would do it all again just for the sheer joy of the fight. This would be Thorkell, then. Edmund had only seen him twice before, and never for long, but he could tell it was him. He stank of death. And there was no soul behind those pale eyes. He was a monster. One whose demise was long overdue.

Æthelred wandered over to Edmund, the column of warriors halting close by. Thorkell moved to Æthelred's side, as did that Hereward fellow and an intense-looking Norman Edmund had never met. Edmund gazed upon his father, noting how he'd dressed like he'd intended to do some fighting himself, although the state of his armour and his obvious lack of injuries suggested he'd been kept well clear. It was for the best. If Æthelred died, Duke Richard would have no further use for Godgifu, and God only knew what would happen then.

"So here we are, Edmund…back in our home, a blessed return to normality after so much hardship. What say you? Will you drink with me now?"

Edmund was silent for a time, finding it difficult to compose himself, what with Thorkell's overbearing presence. He was huge, unnaturally so, and the sheer malevolence he gave off was doubly disconcerting given that his face was entirely blank. He just stood there, as motionless as a statue, but he absolutely REEKED of evil. Edmund didn't know how his father had ever gotten used to it. He hoped they'd find some excuse to be rid of him soon, preferably by tying a rope around his neck and hurling him from the walls. It would be quick. Which was more than he deserved.

"Here we are indeed," Edmund began, thinking hard on what to say. "You'll remember my friend, Wulfnoth?" he then asked, gesturing towards the man himself.

"As you said to me, father…you won't be trying to settle old scores now that victory is yours? Why not give us assurances now that Wulfnoth is here? I'm sure he'll appreciate it as much as I will."

"Of course, of course," muttered Æthelred, his eyes narrowing momentarily as he took Wulfnoth in. He mustn't have recognised him, Edmund thought. Wulfnoth had been on the run for months before he'd joined up with Edmund, and in all that time, he'd not really bothered much with his appearance. He looked half-wild, or just like somebody who'd gotten used to hard living and hard fighting, which was quite different from how he'd appeared during his time at court. It didn't matter. Aside from a few arguments, Wulfnoth had served him well. He'd have his father's assurance that he wouldn't be harmed.

"It's a pleasure to see you again," Wulfnoth said, looking like he was almost as bothered by the presence of Thorkell as Edmund.

"I wish I could say the same," answered Æthelred coolly, "but I have given my son my word that I will not be looking to "settle old scores", as he says. So I welcome you, Wulfnoth. Your lands and titles are hereby returned to you…assuming I have your loyalty?"

Wulfnoth shot Edmund a sideways glance, looking for approval. Edmund nodded once, knowing he had to do what must be done. Wulfnoth accepted the gesture and knelt down on one knee. "You have my loyalty, King Æthelred," he said, "and I take this opportunity to yet again state my innocence concerning the charges originally brought against me…I never conspired with Thorkell, not ever. Will he not confirm this?"

Thorkell glanced down at Wulfnoth. There was no recognition there. He didn't know him, and was entirely in the dark about what was being discussed. Edmund almost had to suppress a smirk. He'd always thought the accusations of Eadric's brother, Beorhtric, to be quite ridiculous, and the claim that Wulfnoth had intended to aid Thorkell before he could even land on English soil was doubly so. It was all proven now, as clear as day, from the bemused look on Thorkell's face. Wulfnoth was a total stranger to him. It was good to see another of Eadric's lies exposed for what it was.

"Is he supposed to mean something to me?" Thorkell rumbled, Edmund wincing at the harshness of his voice. "I've not laid eyes on him before. Is he some underling in one of your schemes, king?"

Æthelred paused a few moments, thinking things over. "I'd say that's clear enough evidence of your innocence, Wulfnoth," he eventually said, although Edmund noticed he offered Wulfnoth absolutely no apology whatsoever for believing the lies Eadric and Beorhtric had originally spread about him. Wulfnoth didn't seem offended, and he soon rose from his knee to resume his place at Edmund's side.

"So, how did you fare in the assault on the west?" Æthelred asked brightly, changing the subject altogether.

"The Norman attack from the tunnels was invaluable," Edmund said. "They arrived to hit Cnut's forces in the rear and provided enough of a distraction for us to seize the walls. Once we got the gate open, it was all over."

"You fought yourself?" Thorkell asked, his dead gaze grating on Edmund's nerves.

"I did. What else would I have done?"

Thorkell didn't reply, and Edmund was bemused by the question. He didn't want Thorkell to respect him or think they'd develop some kind of warrior's rapport after sharing the battle here. That was never going to happen, and Edmund was almost relieved at what Thorkell said next, despite the obvious menace in his tone.

"Did you kill my brother?"

Edmund had to think on that. He remembered the repulsive Hemingr and how he'd ended, but it was no lie to stress that Edmund hadn't killed him. He hadn't. Alaric had, or he'd at least inflicted the wound that would have carried him off had Æva not opened his throat. Edmund didn't see any harm in a simple statement of the truth, despite his father's look of alarm.

"I did not kill him."

"Then who did?"

"Alaric."

"Who is Alaric? One of your men?"

"No. He fought in Eastengle and Canterburie."

"One eye?"

"That's him," nodded Edmund, suddenly remembering Alaric's face in vivid detail. He couldn't recall exactly how he'd lost the eye, and Alaric hadn't told him during their first and only meeting, but he'd been impressed with how he'd borne it. A true stoic, that one. And he'd somehow even made an impression on Thorkell, by the looks of it.

"He was a great warrior," Thorkell said. "We fought in Canterburie. He wounded me. I admired him. What became of him?"

"He's dead," replied Edmund.

Thorkell breathed out slowly, apparently satisfied. "There is no dishonour in my brother losing his life to such a man. Did he die well? You saw him?"

"Yes. He and Alaric killed each other. That's all I have to tell you."

That got a reaction. Thorkell smiled, but it wasn't anything like a smile Edmund was accustomed to. It was brutal, as if his beard had suddenly been rent into some broken cleft displaying rows of slab-like teeth flashing out of a mouth framed by chapped and twisted lips. It was all so very disturbing to look at, but it thankfully did not last, and before long Thorkell's face was once more a blank and stony facade.

"A great battle then," Thorkell nodded, unaware of Edmund's thoughts. "One I would have liked to see."

"For certain!" said Æthelred hurriedly, clearly wanting to speak on something else. "Yet there is only one man I'd like to see dead, and that's this Cnut…did you face him, Edmund? He did not come out to fight us when we attacked."

"I didn't see anyone announcing themselves as Cnut, no."

Wulfnoth sniggered slightly, amused by his words. He didn't think what he'd said was funny. He really hadn't seen Cnut, and nobody had turned up and claimed to be him either. Battles were chaotic things, and it was sometimes hard to tell who was who. His father would know that, or should. He'd been on the field at Bernecestre. That had been a fight, and then some. He'd have learned right there just how bad things can get.

"Then he's either dead somewhere or fled the city," mused Æthelred, "and if the former is the case, then I think it's more than likely we'll find his corpse in my halls. Godfrey's men did an excellent job navigating the tunnels at such short notice, don't you agree, Edmund?"

"They did," Edmund affirmed, assuming the Norman still standing at his father's side was indeed this "Godfrey" he'd mentioned. The man kept staring at Edmund, like he was expecting praise, but Edmund wasn't of a mind to offer any. Godfrey hadn't fought his way through the tunnels, and those Normans who'd aided Edmund in his own assault had his thanks, and they knew it. He wouldn't offer gratitude to a man who was almost certainly a pawn of the duke and very much aware of his nefarious plans for Godgifu. It wouldn't be right.

They made it to the royal halls without any further need for conversation. They could see the front gate was in ruins, like it had been smashed open from the inside, but the courtyard within was reasonably intact, the dreaded prison tower looking even more foreboding than usual as it loomed out of the night. This was not a happy place. Alaric had died here, fighting to free himself and his family from the clutches of Thorkell's wretched brother. The remnants of that particular battle had been cleared away, but Edmund still felt mournful just being back here. He'd rather not tarry.

Something caught his eye. A horse stood out in the open, looking like it had escaped the nearby stables. There was something familiar about this animal, the moonlight highlighting a certain conformation that jogged Edmund's memory. He approached, his joy increasing with every step he took. He knew who this was.

It was his old horse, Bede, the very same loyal animal he'd ridden into battle at Bernecestre. He could tell it was him, since he still had the grey and white dapples running up his neck. Edmund had sadly left him behind when they'd all fled the city last year, and at the time the abandonment had been yet another sorrow that had lain heavily upon his heart. He must have remained here ever since. Svienn's people must have fed him, assuming correctly that he was a good animal who would undoubtedly come in useful. He recognised Edmund almost immediately and came closer, grunting in what sounded like both surprise and affection. This was a blessing Edmund had not foreseen.

Everyone else stood back, his father, Thorkell, Wulfnoth, Godfrey, and all their warriors looking bewildered as Edmund placed his palms on Bede's neck and pressed his forehead to his. They stayed like this for a few moments, the two friends enjoying their reunion. Edmund kissed Bede on the forehead, the horse still huffing and rumbling to himself in apparent contentment. Edmund then moved to rejoin the others. He didn't care what they thought of him, and he'd return soon. Bede wouldn't be left alone for long. He was better company than most.

The interior of the halls was horrifying. There were bodies scattered about the place in various states of dismemberment, most of them Danish, some armed and some not. The Normans had really surprised them here, fighting their way up from under the earth to kill anyone they could get their hands on. Navigating the tunnels under the city was no easy task, Edmund knew that personally, and so he suspected the Normans must have been given a guide, although when he asked his father about this he remained tight-lipped. There was also no trace of Cnut, or anyone appearing to be of a regal rank, the corpses that littered the stone passageways appearing either as warriors or underlings of some description. Edmund cared not for the warriors. They'd been invaders, they all had, but killing an armed man was very different from slaughtering those incapable of defending themselves. And yet these Normans appeared to have made no such distinction when they'd stormed this place. That wasn't to be admired.

A noise suddenly split the silence from just up ahead. Edmund moved forward, blade in hand, Hereward and several others alongside him. They were outside Æthelred's old throne room, and from the sound of it, there was somebody on the other side of the immense doors and attempting to get out. They went quiet when Edmund and the others came closer, quite possibly in alarm at the prospect of being discovered.

That would mean whoever was in there was very likely an enemy, maybe even Cnut himself. This would be perfect. To kill so many of his worthless kind and then go on to capture him in the throne room would be a perfect end to an otherwise hard-fought battle. Edmund relished the thought of it. Justice was about to be done.

They burst through the doors, Hereward, Edmund, Wulfnoth, Thorkell, and several of his men all applying their great strength to hurl them open and charge within. They then all stopped, blinking and confused, their hopeful expectation of finding Cnut dashed within a heartbeat.

Before them stood a snivelling wretch of a man, overweight and pale, his great fear-stricken eyes gazing at them like he were a rabbit caught in the path of a fox. Thorkell rumbled something and brandished a torch, the light of it driving back the shadows to reveal his face. He was scared, and he was fat, and he surprisingly wasn't blond or blue-eyed, but none of those things explained who he was or what he was doing here.

"I had not thought to see you," said Æthelred, taking up position along with Godfrey just behind Edmund's left shoulder. "You seem strangely out of place, Leafstan. Did Lindesi not agree with you?"

"It's not what it looks like!" came the response, Edmund wondering how it was possible for a man's voice to have such a high pitch. "I was kidnapped! And I was brought to this place..."

"Don't bother," sighed Æthelred, bored of the spectacle already. "We captured some of your men when we took the walls. They told us everything. But I will ask you...just how much aid has Lindesi given Cnut? Just how much did he pay you to betray me, your true king?"

"I don't know what you mean!" shrieked Leafstan, looking so agitated Edmund thought he might pass out. "And it wasn't just me!" he cried, waving his arms about as if attempting to point out his accomplices. "We all took an oath to Svienn! He made us! And then Cnut came in person to Lindesi! You weren't here to protect us! I had no choice!"

"I don't see any other thegns here," replied Æthelred dismissively. "Why is that, Leafstan? Could it be because, despite whatever promises they gave Svienn, many of them had little affection for him? But here you are, in Lundenburg, alive and well just as we've finished fighting our way inside. Looks a little strange, don't you think?"

"How come the Normans didn't catch you?" Edmund asked, wanting to get to the heart of the matter. "You must have been here when they attacked and killed everyone else. How did you manage to linger undetected?"

Leafstan's face paled even more, his double chins quivering slightly when he tried to shake the sweat from his brow. "It was terrible," he whispered. "I don't know how they got in...but I hid...then when they'd all gone, I tried to find Cnut. Last time I saw him, he'd been here. I..."

"Possibly the worst defence I've ever heard in my life," said Æthelred acidly. "So you are a traitor? You admit it yourself?"

Thorkell growled something indecipherable, the sound hinting he'd sooner just kill Leafstan rather than stand here listening to this back and forth. "Tell us where Cnut is," Edmund said, hoping the fat fool might sense the opportunity to save his skin.

"That's a good idea, Edmund," nodded Æthelred, sounding a little sarcastic. "Do tell us, Leafstan, where Cnut is. It's a chance for you to remain among the living for a while longer. Otherwise, I'll leave you alone with Thorkell here."

Leafstan fainted, his considerable bulk collapsing to the rough stone floor with a wet thump. They got him to his feet again and splashed some water in his face, Edmund feeling genuinely sorry for the man when he squeaked in panic at the sight of the towering Thorkell. "I don't know where he is!" he exclaimed, more terrified than ever. "Believe me! Please! He was here, and now he's not! He must have left to fight you! That's all I can say! I was hiding! That's all!"

"You gave my enemy aid," corrected Æthelred, "and had your people lend their strength to his. I hereby deal with you as is only proper for a traitor. Kill him."

Edmund wasn't sure who his father was issuing the order to, but he wondered if any of this was right. He was about to ask him to reconsider and pause for thought when Thorkell rendered his concerns moot, moving like lightning to split Leafstan's head open with one swing of his axe. Edmund was sprayed with blood, as was Hereward, and they both dropped Leafstan at the same time, allowing his ruined corpse to fall to the floor in a sorry heap. Edmund held his hands to his face, inspecting the gore that now marred his fingertips. He'd been covered in sweat and blood already, but there was something downright disturbing about all this. This wasn't an execution. It was just malice unleashed. Thorkell didn't care who he killed, just as long as he got to do it. That made him forever dangerous.

"Dispatch a force to Lindesi, say about five hundred of your men," Æthelred commanded, the Norman, Godfrey, turning to take his instructions. "I want a full account of what happened there," continued Æthelred, "and don't hesitate should any of Leafstan's remaining people challenge you. From what I can see, Lindesi was the only region to swear allegiance to Svienn and actually mean it. There'll be consequences for that. Am I clear?"

Godfrey nodded, a dark and unpleasant smirk on his face, and strode back through the doors and out into the passageway beyond. Edmund could hear him shouting to his men outside, but he was speaking in his native tongue, and so for all Edmund knew they could be talking about anything. "Do you intend to punish Lindesi?" Edmund inquired, wondering if this decision meant he'd been wrong about his father adopting a more restrained approach to ruling.

"I intend to find out what happened, Edmund," said Æthelred soberly. "As I said…no other Englishmen were fighting in Cnut's ranks aside from them. I was shocked to see it, and I am not easily shocked. If I am to rule, I would have a full picture of what happened in England whilst I was away. This is wisdom, you will agree?"

"I do," said Edmund hesitantly. "But none of this helps us with the more immediate task…Cnut's whereabouts are unknown, and there is still a Danish army in the South. You'd spare five hundred of your Norman mercenaries to charge north when they are needed here?"

"You speak sense," Æthelred conceded. "Yet we received word just before our attack of some most welcome news. Uhtred is almost with us. Five thousand men. In three days, at the most, he'll be here and able to join his forces to ours should the Danes try and challenge us. I can afford then to spare some men in pursuing other…projects."

"Olaf and I will go after Cnut," Thorkell suddenly said, his great bear of a voice echoing off the walls.

"I need you here," Æthelred cautioned, a hint of alarm upon his face. Edmund understood. He didn't want Thorkell and Olaf getting out of his control, especially if it meant going after one of their own kind, if he was even still alive. They'd not really considered the possibility that Cnut had simply been killed in the fighting and nobody had yet noticed. Was that such an absurd idea?

"I can catch him, if he has indeed fled," Thorkell pressed, Æthelred seeming to shrink back in the face of being contradicted by such a man. "I have a nose for these things, and my gut never lies. Cnut is alive, and he will remain dangerous until he is caught."

Hereward stepped away from Edmund to position himself between Æthelred and Thorkell. "The king has made his wishes known," he said sternly, Edmund's admiration for the man going up a notch as he stared Thorkell down.

"The king can speak for himself!" objected Thorkell. He had a dangerous undercurrent to his voice, like he was close to unleashing something terrible. This wasn't good.

"And he has done so!" Edmund barked. "Leave us and return to your men. I would discuss things with my father. Go! NOW!"

Thorkell glowered between Edmund and Hereward, his eyes low and hooded, the look reminiscent of some kind of wild animal. Æthelred made no attempt to argue, and so Thorkell turned and barged his way through the door, shouting for his men to join him outside. That had been a close call. Thorkell had thought to kill Hereward, Edmund could tell, and he'd only relented because Edmund had spoken up. That was curious. Did Thorkell respect him somehow, possibly because of his link to Alaric? And did he respect Alaric because of how he'd fought at Canterburie? He must have killed a significant number of Danes to achieve that. Edmund wished he'd seen it.

Æthelred lumbered ahead towards his throne. Edmund followed at a slow pace, as did Wulfnoth, although Hereward vaulted on, ensuring he remained on the king's flank. They eventually made it past the still annoyingly long banqueting table that dominated much of the chamber, and Æthelred was soon climbing the steps to his throne. He paused when he reached it, as though he was resentful or fearful of what he was about to do. He eventually sat down, one leg crossing over the other, his lips briefly curling upward in what Edmund took for displeasure. He looked exhausted. Tired, worn down by the weight of his armour, but also drained from the realisation of what had just happened. He was King of England again. And he hated it.

"I would speak with my son awhile," Æthelred said weakly, making a few feeble hand gestures that Hereward correctly interpreted to mean he should depart. He nodded to Edmund when he passed by, Wulfnoth also following and closing the doors behind them with their customary clamour. They were alone, Edmund and Æthelred. Like the old days, sort of, albeit without Eadric, which was welcome, but with Thorkell on the loose outside, which was just plain awful. These were very strange times.

"Do you remember when we were here last?"

Edmund thought a moment before responding. "I do," he said sadly, "it was when I came to you with Wulfhild to ask you to help Ulfcytel…but then he barged in here with all those followers of his and…"

"I wasn't referring to that," Æthelred said bitterly. "I was referring to the time before…with you and your brother? The feast we had, all of us, as a family."

"You threw a cup of wine at my head because I dared mention Alaric."

Æthelred shook his head slowly, like he was making some effort to either recall the incident or expunge it from memory. "I'm sorry," he breathed. "I really am. I've done much in my time...not been as strong as I should have been. I have to be strong now. For Godgifu. And you must listen to what I have to say."

"I will if it means my sister is kept safe. Be warned, though...I won't tolerate any further nonsense from either Eadric or Thorkell. Why you keep the latter around like that is a mystery. He's evil, father. Don't you see it? Don't you FEEL it?"

"I do, son. I do. He's a weapon, available to the highest bidder, who, for the time being, is me. Which brings me to my next point...my funds ran low keeping Thorkell placated. I need more. We need more. There must be another tax. A one-off this time, but..."

"What?!" Edmund exclaimed, taking a step back from the throne in surprise. "After all this...after all your assurances...you'd repeat the mistakes of the heregeld?! It ruined us! It ruined your people! And just for Thorkell?!"

"If we don't pay him, he'll turn on us," Æthelred said grimly. "He'll start attacking anywhere he pleases, like he did before, and his men will follow him. I have to keep him under control."

"Just have him killed! I'll do it right now!" Edmund placed his palm on the pommel of his sword to emphasise his intent.

Æthelred laughed, the sound dry and bitter. "I respect your gumption, Edmund. And yet I think you know in your heart that Thorkell is not...right. He's not like other men. If you attack him, you'll die. And if you died, I don't...I don't think..."

"Then attack him and his men, tonight, with our combined armies! He's just a man, father, an evil one, yes, but just a man. He can't even have that many warriors left after all the fighting. We could have his corpse by morning."

"I need him!" Æthelred snapped, his hands falling to grip the armrests of his throne. "As I said, he's a weapon! A good one! By God, Edmund, you should have seen him earlier when we charged the gate! He killed and killed and killed again, and nothing and no one could stop him! I need him! I need him on my side to settle accounts with Richard!"

"So you'll ruin the kingdom, again, to pay Thorkell to help get Godgifu back from the duke?"

"I would, Edmund. Richard has many an advantage...but he doesn't have a man like Thorkell. Or Olaf, for that matter."

"But what use can he possibly be in this situation? If Thorkell attacks Normandy, he'll just be put down. We need other methods. Brute force won't serve us."

"No offence, Edmund, but you don't understand. I was quite prepared to unleash Thorkell on Normandy when I learned of the duke's plans for Godgifu. I would have seen his whole country in flames if it had meant he'd relent and give me back my daughter. That, unfortunately, came to nought, but in the meantime, I won't be denied the options our Danish allies provide. Trust me on this."

"You'd kill innocent people for the sake of your child?" Edmund was incredulous, yet again. He didn't have children of his own, and he felt if he did he'd do anything to keep them safe, but committing himself to what his father had just suggested was going too far. There was love there, of a sort, but a black and twisted one, selfish and terrible. It was not wholesome. It was not Christian.

"Do you seriously hope to sit on this throne one day?" asked Æthelred. Edmund could see where this was going. He was about to get some lecture on how it was supposedly right for a ruler to do dark and evil things if he deemed it necessary. Edmund would have none of it, and he considered for a moment perhaps telling him of the promise he'd given Æva to be a different kind of king. He thought better of it. It would only escalate things and widen the gulf between them.

"I can't agree to this tax," Edmund said instead. "It won't go down well with anyone. They'll think it's just more of the same from you."

"They have no choice. I have thousands of men here and more on the way. Once we defeat the last enemy host in the South, my reign will be unassailable."

"You yourself admitted you were not suited to rule," Edmund said, a little desperate now. "This just proves it. You're crushing people yet again just to serve your own agenda."

"Agenda? You mean helping us free your sister? Yes, I am, if that's what you mean. If you were in her situation, I'd be doing the same."

Edmund didn't know what to say. He turned away, descending the few steps down from the throne so as to pull up a chair from the banqueting table. He sat for a time, trying to think and ignore the baleful presence of his father still illuminated in the unceasing moonlight.

"Have you really changed?" Edmund finally asked. "Have you? Did you mean what you said to me yesterday? That you were not suited to rule, and you'd make me your heir?"

"I meant all of it. The amnesty for my enemies…all of it. I am different."

"And I suppose this difference in you is because of whatever you talked about with Alaric? Remember, father, that you said as much when I saw you before you escaped to Normandy."

"I remember it well. I thought I might never see you again. It hurt."

"So what was it?" Edmund pressed. "What did you and Alaric talk about that changed you?"

"I only became fully cognisant of it on the trip across the sea," said Æthelred. "My dreams…they had more than one meaning. I thought people were accusing me, and it drove me to madness. Alaric had a different perspective. My supposed accusers were nothing of the kind. They wanted me to help them, to help England, to remember my duties as king. And there was more. Your grandmother…"

"Queen Ælfthryth? What does she have to do with any of this?"

Æthelred took a deep breath and then hunched forward, peering at Edmund from on high as if he were about to try and whisper something to him. "She killed Edward so that I would be forced onto this throne," he said softly. "She killed my brother…and sought to be forgiven. For that and more."

Edmund was agape. He'd heard the rumours over and over, and he knew the story of their "martyred" King Edward and how he'd been killed in circumstances that were beyond suspicious. He also knew how it had weighed so very heavily on his father, the angst and guilt wearing down his resolve.

"So it was indeed the queen?" Edmund asked, his voice hushed like he feared he might somehow be discovered by her and punished. "How do you know this? She told you?"

"She always appeared in my dreams. Always, heading straight for Edward's body. It terrified me into wakefulness every time…until Alaric. He was right, his interpretation was right, I mean…I had failed my people, and by confessing that to them, I gained strength. I could face my mother."

"And then what?"

"She asked Edward to forgive her. She then asked me to forgive her."

"For killing Edward?"

"Yes, and much else," sighed Æthelred, his face hardening with bitterness. "She was not…kind to me. She had ideas of her own about what kind of man I was to be. She tested me. Tried to mould me. And when I wouldn't fit into the shape she desired…she…tried to force matters."

"You never told us any of this," Edmund breathed. "Not a word. Not to me, nor Æthelstan. Does Emma know?"

"She knows nothing about anything. Nobody knows. I've carried this, all of this, for years. I was broken, even before my mother's time as regent ended. I took the throne as a frightened, beaten, and resentful child. And I've remained as such ever since."

"You go too far, father. There was a way back. There IS a way back. The things you've done…the things grandmother did to you…you forgave her in the dream? So it's over now?"

"It will never be over for me," said Æthelred, the pained finality in his voice cutting right to Edmund's heart. "I was forced onto this throne for the sake of my mother's plans, and now I'm forced back here by a foreign scoundrel with plans of his own. They'd get on well, Ælfthryth and Duke Richard, I think. Either way, I'm to suffer a little longer."

"What can I do?!" Edmund cried, getting to his feet with a suddenness that toppled his chair over. "Tell me what you need, father! Tell me how to help you!"

"You can help me with what we've already discussed, as in gaining your sister's freedom. And something else too…you can forgive me."

"For what?"

"Your uncle, Æthelstan. I hadn't wanted him to get hurt. I'd wanted Ulfcytel killed, yes, as I thought him an enemy…I saw so many enemies. Your uncle wasn't supposed to get in the way. I grieved for him. I do still."

Silence fell, one so deep and heavy it was like the whole world outside had ceased to be. Edmund's heart surged in his chest, a torrent of conflicting emotions assailing him without mercy. He should forgive his father. He wanted to, and yet something resisted that wouldn't relent. It cried out to him, over and over, telling him to be careful, telling him not to listen, telling him his decision to again support Æthelred would lead to death and calamity for all involved.

Had it not always been so? Was his uncle not dead because of him? Was his own brother not dead because of his ill-advised decisions? Was he not also set to repeat history with this new tax of his, something that would again line Thorkell's pockets, just as Edmund and Æthelstan had originally tried to prevent? Did the revelations about Ælfthryth somehow make up for all that and every other grim deed he'd committed over the course of his reign? His uncle, his brother…Alaric…all these men had died because of Æthelred and the events he'd set in motion. Could that just be ignored? Was that justice?

Edmund lifted his head, unashamed of his tears, and looked his father straight in the face. He then turned and walked away, slipping through the double doors of the chamber and out into the beyond. Æthelred stayed as he was, a lonely figure upon his throne, unwilling or unable to object. The clouds in the night sky shifted, concealing the moon, and all was again darkness, the light that had previously shone down on him from the window ceasing altogether. Æthelred could see nothing. He could hear nothing. There was nothing. Then he felt them. His own tears. He let them flow. He'd been denied so much else. He wouldn't be denied this.

XXV

The priest didn't arrive for some time. He'd been away at the hospital he and his brethren had set up across from New Gate, and he was surprised to see Edmund waiting for him just a short distance back from the altar. It was no bother. Edmund hadn't minded the wait. The night wasn't going anywhere, and with it had come a strange comfort. It was a good time for prayer, and with prayer could come solace. God knew he needed it.

The church was still bathed in shadow, the moonlight that had engulfed the city with their victory fading to almost nothing. Only a single candle upon the altar allowed Edmund to discern his surroundings, and that was in danger of being extinguished the longer it went unattended. Edmund couldn't say he minded too much. St Mildred's was beautiful, in more ways than one, and the feeling he got just from being here was all he needed. God spoke in the silence. He didn't need to be seen in order to do so.

"How may I help you?"

Edmund looked up from prayer, his knees aching as he shifted his weight. The priest was only half-illuminated, so feeble was the light, yet Edmund could see the blood stains on his robe and the tell-tale marks of fatigue under his eyes. He'd seen harrowing sights tonight, this priest. They all had.

He otherwise had a regal look to him, his neat, pointed beard and shock of chestnut hair reminding Edmund of some sainted king or other noble sort who'd since been immortalised for their great deeds.

"I felt called to be here," said Edmund slowly, his voice sounding insufferably loud as it broke the silence.

"I understand," said the priest. "You would unburden your conscience? You have the look of one who might need it."

"You read people well," sighed Edmund, getting to his feet. He reached down to rub his knees, his time on the stones having done little for his circulation. "Before we talk, though…what do you think of what I've wrought here? Would you say God is pleased with my actions?"

The priest raised an eyebrow, unsure of his true meaning. "And what have you wrought?" he asked finally.

"I have helped retake this city," Edmund said, stating the obvious. "The heathen is beaten and either dead or fleeing. What would God make of this, if you were to answer?"

"You are the aetheling, Edmund," nodded the priest knowingly, "and am I right in thinking you are wondering if the killing you've done tonight is a sin? That God recoils from what you've achieved?"

"I would like to hear your thoughts, yes," replied Edmund, hoping he wasn't about to come in for some kind of lecture that would make him feel even worse than he did already.

"War is a complex affair," said the priest, stepping over to the altar to tend the candle, his movements quiet and subtle. It seemed to gutter and glow stronger whilst he beheld it, and when he reached down to hold his palms on either side of the flame it strengthened more so, like it was reacting to his presence.

"Many people will say such things are always justified," he went on, leaving the candle to step behind the altar and bend down as if to retrieve something. Edmund then watched him place two additional candles on either side of the altar and light them. "I have a more nuanced opinion," he eventually said, his eyes meeting Edmund's over the three tiny flames set before him.

"Which is?" Edmund wasn't sure how he felt about the light. It stung his eyes. He must have been kneeling in the dark for longer than he'd thought.

"God does not look on the misery wrought at New Gate with a joyful heart," came the reply, "but neither does He look upon the Danes and what they have so long sought to do with anything akin to approval. They are not here to punish us for our sins. They are just lost men, sunk deep in their passions and sin. They are to be pitied."

"And what of men like me?" asked Edmund, glad this priest wasn't of the same opinion as Archbishop Wulfstan on how the Northmen had somehow been sent to punish the English for their admittedly numerous sins.

"You are damaged," said the priest without hesitation. "Just as I am. We all are. This is a fallen world, and we have fallen and will continue to do so. What's important is that we understand that, and then pick ourselves up off the floor again and again, as often as needed."

"So all the men I've killed tonight...I'm just to pick myself up from that? Could it be said I'd even fallen to begin with?"

"You don't fall alone, Edmund. Those who fought against you had made their choice, and it was a wicked one. To have ignored them and everything they represented would have been a greater sin."

"So killing is not a sin, in a situation like ours?"

"It is. Never doubt it, and there is no glory in the doing of it. But to shy away from the darkness...to be apathetic and passive in the face of evil and allow it to run amok among the sheep...God is not pleased with such a man, regardless of how often he might seek to clothe his inaction with pious words. You're a broken man in a broken world, and you've striven to stop it sliding yet further into the darkness that assails it. You will not be condemned for this. Do not condemn yourself either."

These were good words, Edmund thought. He wondered who this priest was and why he'd not heard of him. Was this really his church, or was he just passing through? He felt he'd do well to know the truth of it.

"May I have your name?" he asked. "And what happened to the priest who was here before? I think I remember him, by appearance at least."

"He was beaten to death just a few feet from where you're standing. The mob...that starving, piteous mob that so wanted Svienn to come in and help them...well, they came here thinking the priest was hiding things and didn't take kindly to being told to leave."

This was a very bitter memory, one Edmund could sadly relate to. He'd not been here, in this church, during those dark days, but he had been in Lundenburg, and he remembered those terrible riots that had ultimately allowed Svienn to overrun the defences and take the city for himself. Many of those same people were likely out there now, tonight, celebrating the Dane's defeat like they themselves were entirely innocent of any wrongdoing. It was a troubling thought, and one he did not care to dwell on.

"And what do you think of my father's return?" Edmund asked, wondering indeed if anyone in the city had much of an idea about what Æthelred was doing here.

"What about him?" inquired the priest, his brow furrowing.

"He's here to be king again," said Edmund, the words bringing shame to his heart. "It was all for him…I gave up my claim to the throne and attacked the city to serve as a distraction for him. He will rule now."

"And this troubles you?"

"Mightily. My men are unaware. I kept it from them, knowing they'd possibly abandon me if they thought I was just fighting for his sake. So many of them died thinking I was to be king. I am a liar."

"Yes, you are."

There was no accusation in his tone. It was neutral, his words conveying a simple statement of fact. Edmund didn't know what was worse. If the priest had raged at him, calling him names and hurling him from his church that would have been bad enough, but having his sins simply confirmed for him, without drama or resentment, was somehow the more painful outcome. Was it fair to call him a liar? Hadn't he only wanted the best? Would they even be here, in this place and having this conversation, if he hadn't done as he had? Shouldn't that be taken into account?

"So what would you have done?" Edmund asked, his pride wounded.

"Probably the exact same thing. Like I said…we're all broken, we all fall, you and I. Our hearts are afflicted, our sins and the sins of our ancestors tearing at us like savage beasts. We're hurt, damaged…fallen…and it shows in our nature."

"So it's in my nature to lie? I never thought of myself like that, father. I don't think it's right."

"Not consciously, perhaps…there's an inclination to sin, yes, but it's also in your nature to do what you think is best, in the difficult situations you find yourself in. You told a lie, or you kept the truth from others because you thought you were serving a greater good. You killed men, again because you thought you were serving a greater good…"

"Was I not?" spluttered Edmund, unsure of where this was going.

"The expulsion of the Danes from England is no doubt a righteous cause," the priest nodded approvingly. "What I would say is…mind your methods. A lie is a lie. It might seem like a slight evil, one used to offset a larger one, but it's still a lie, and from small seeds can come a great harvest. Had you not thought that your men might have trusted you? They followed you this far, fighting all the way. Would the truth really have hurt them so?"

"I don't know. I just think I couldn't have risked losing my army on a single point of principle. I had to think of the bigger picture. I had to win."

The priest was on the move, his footsteps quiet and hushed as he finally came out from behind the altar to stand within arm's reach. "You did, and you have," he said softly, "and it's a good thing. Yet, as I said…from small seeds can come a great harvest…and lies are not the kind of things you want to plough and scatter into the soil of your soul. You understand this?"

"You're suggesting that one lie, even a supposedly noble one, can lead to others? Like one sin leading to greater and greater wrongdoing?"

"That's how it all started, isn't it?" he said with a sad smile. "Adam thought his sin to be harmless enough...and yet he turned the world upside down. He had his excuses, his own prideful reasoning for what he'd done..."

"Come on, father," protested Edmund. "I hardly think...I mean, you know why the truth had to be hidden. We might not be standing here, having this talk, if it hadn't been."

"My comparison is perhaps a little dramatic...I just want you to see how things can escalate. This land is filled with lies, and not just from those like yourself who hold good intentions. Men deceive each other for the sake of expediency, power, material gain...yet not all of them started out like that. Many would have once fancied themselves righteous, only to fall further and further into sin with the repeating of it."

"Are you suggesting I have to catch myself? To make amends? To tell the truth before I become accustomed to falsehood?"

The priest reached out and patted Edmund's arm. "I will not tell you what to do," he said sheepishly. "You are a great man, one of reputation and renown...just listen to your conscience, Edmund. Find a quiet place, such as this one, when you're in doubt, and then just listen. God will come with an answer for you."

"How can you know that? Sometimes I pray...and there's nothing...like He's hidden Himself from me."

"I can understand that. But I will say that when this has happened to me in the past, I'd discover later that I was being pushed towards the right path without knowing. God doesn't always answer prayers with a full-blown miracle that's obvious for all who witness it. There's a subtlety to Him. He sets things in motion, His plans unfurling with the passage of years."

"And may He have set things in motion tonight?" Edmund asked, feeling suddenly comforted.

"It's possible, and you may not even know it. Would it surprise you to know I was also once a man of power and property? That all ended with the heathens. They attacked my lands, killed my family and those under my protection...I was powerless to stop them, and with that feeling came despair. The deepest despair. Enough to break me, almost."

A pang of sorrow welled up in Edmund's chest. The priest's tale was terrible, and not just because he'd lost his family. It was terrible because it wasn't even unusual in these troubled days. There were hundreds, thousands, of people like him, carrying the burden of butchered relatives and missing loved ones. It was another reason why Edmund fought. He'd replace these sorry stories with ones of triumph, and within a generation or two, these times of sadness wouldn't even be a memory. They'd have faded into history, and anyone who might care to look them up would thank God they lived in better days brought about by the actions of good and righteous men. Edmund hoped he'd be counted as one of them.

"So you didn't want to be a priest?" he asked, hoping he wasn't prying into something he wasn't prepared to talk about.

"I was not a priest, no," he said, "but from so much death and hurt, I like to think something came of it. God did not will the death of my family, make no mistake there, but He did decide to use me to bring some good from it. My heart is broken...but in knowing this pain, I can know others who are similarly wounded and bring them comfort. I have a cross to bear, but I am not alone, and neither need be anyone else."

The priest's gaze shifted, his eyes turning downward to look forlornly at his blood-splattered robes. "That's all from my men?" Edmund asked, wondering sadly just how many of his warriors had expired tonight as this cleric did his best to save them.

"Yes," he said softly, "and some from our Norman guests...and some from a Dane or two. They all look alike as they go. The eyes, I mean...English eyes, Norman eyes, Danish eyes...there's fear and panic when they realise they're dying, and then something else...a stillness comes over them, and they fear no more."

"Are you suggesting God comforts the Danes too?" Edmund didn't understand that. God was about justice and mercy both, yet for the Lord to bring the same grace to the unrepentant heathen as He did to His own warriors was difficult to stomach.

"I can't speak for God on this," said the priest, still looking at his robes. "I think God weeps to see what the heathens do to us...what they've done to this country, what they've done to our people...but does He desire us to hate them? Desire their damnation? I don't think so. And this blood here all looks the same. It's all the blood of men, and God does not rejoice to see it."

Edmund turned away, lost in thought. He appreciated what he'd heard so far, and it was no small comfort to him, but he didn't like to assume God was somehow mournful over the violence Edmund had meted out to the enemy in justified retribution. He could be right, this priest, and it was hard to imagine the Lord being pleased with the death of anyone, but the truth was Edmund didn't even like to think of the enemy as human. They didn't behave that way and never had. It was easier to think of them as something else. He didn't need his conscience bothering him as he put them to the sword. It was for that reason he decided to cut this conversation short. The war was not yet over, and his men needed him.

He headed for the exit, the church's interior now a little more discernible as the dark outside gradually gave way to the deep blue of the approaching dawn. When he was about halfway down the nave, the priest suddenly called after him, his voice echoing off the walls with a knowing urgency.

"Something else is on your mind...and I think you should give it voice before you go."

Edmund stopped and looked back. "That's a strange trick you have there," he said, "and I wonder how you can know my mind so well...are you really just a priest?"

"Many people are far more than they seem," he replied, his voice quieter now. "You mentioned your father earlier...you wonder how to relate to him? How to make him a better man? A better king?"

"He expects me to forgive him," Edmund sighed, "and I confess I cannot. He's done too much. I love him, after a fashion...but God help me, I cannot forgive. Not just like that."

"Then don't. Not just like that. Think and pray on it and be a beacon to your father on his path towards repentance. Let your light burn brightly, showing him the way, showing him your virtues so that he might emulate them. Christ himself was not all sweet words and hugs. Far from it! He led by example, and that was how He loved us. Now love your father as Christ loved you. Be an example to him...and in time he may change, and with that...you will find forgiveness comes a little easier."

That was it. That was the way, and Edmund knew it. This was a step on the road, one that just might lead to some kind of reconciliation. The hurt in Edmund's heart went deep, but the notion that he should become a light for his father was deeply moving. Jesus had called upon his followers to be a light for the world…and if that was the case, why could Edmund not include his father in that? Why not be a beacon for him, as best he could?

"Do you think he will even notice it?" Edmund asked, suddenly apprehensive. "So much has happened between us…I could try to burn so bright, only to see him again become lost in shadows of his own making. What then?"

"I don't think that will happen this time," the priest said in return, his eyes giving the impression he wasn't quite focusing on Edmund anymore, despite continuing to look straight at him. "There's a piece of your father in you, and you in him…I'm not just talking about the physical, about the flesh…you will have entered your father's heart the day you were born, the first time he held you, the first time you opened your eyes…there'll always be something there, even if sometimes it seems hidden."

"How can you know this?" whispered Edmund, concerned for a moment that the priest might not hear him.

"I wasn't always as I am now, Edmund. As I said, I once lived a different life, in a different time, so it seems. But my advice stands; be a light for Æthelred, and indeed the world. God wills it for you. God wills it for all of us."

Edmund mumbled his thanks, his mind dwelling on what had been said. Everything seemed somewhat different now. The night was still dark, literally and metaphorically, but something had shifted, allowing a faint light to be revealed that might otherwise have remained obscure. Edmund didn't know how much sense that made, even to himself, but he knew what he had to do. He knew how to be a beacon. And since every journey commenced with a single step, Edmund would start by righting a single wrong.

"What will you do now?" the priest asked.

"What you said," Edmund replied. "I am a liar. I lied to my men. I failed to trust them. I won't have that on my conscience any longer. I can't light the way if I'm burdened by guilt."

"Are you not afraid?"

"Often," admitted Edmund, "but few things worth doing are easy. You yourself said you had a cross to bear. Now I'll bear mine."

XXVI

The army had assembled with the dawn, abandoning the site of their hard-fought victory to muster upon what was left of Watling Street as it trailed out of the woods to approach the western walls of Lundenburg. Edmund could see on his approach, his boots scuffing along the broken stone road, that their numbers were reduced, the assault on the walls having taken an inevitable toll. Not all of those absent were dead, and many of the more seriously wounded were still within the city and being cared for, but Edmund's heart ached all the same. Too many had died, and all of them for him. He'd do the right thing now for their sake.

He scrambled up a couple of haystacks that had been heaped together just off the road. The view was obviously different up here, and his army looked impressive as the sun began its golden ascent across the skyline, their tattered banners and hard, battle-worn faces making it more than clear these were serious men who'd done serious deeds. Sigeferth and Morcar were visible just ahead and to the left, standing at the head of the warriors they'd brought from the Five Boroughs. They looked worried. Edmund hadn't told them what he had planned. He hadn't told anyone. He hoped they'd understand once the dust settled.

Edmund coughed, intentionally emptying his lungs before inhaling deep and full. Ulfcytel was just in front and below him, standing guard with Osbert at the base of the makeshift stage. They looked back and up at him, their faces concerned, but Edmund paid them no mind. He was ready. He'd bare his soul to his men and be done with it, come what may.

"Another night has come and gone…and we greet this dawn with nothing but victory!" Edmund liked to think he knew a thing or two about speechcraft, and the men were predictably exuberant upon hearing his words, a deluge of cheers erupting from their ranks with all the enthusiasm they could muster. It was good to see. If he could lift their spirits like this, they might even forgive what came next.

"And yet I must confess," Edmund said, the noise from the men dwindling into silence. "Our army was always based on trust…you trusted me enough to follow me here, and many of you have given your lives in the process. And so I must tell you…I will not be king. Not yet. You'll have been wondering as to the warriors who came to our aid during the battle…they are from Normandy, and with them comes my father. He is to be king again."

That got a reaction, but not a good one. A low grumbling started, his warriors shifting uneasily and glancing at the other as if to confirm whether they'd heard right. Some exclamations followed, a curse here and there, some even looking to Edmund as if he himself were behind all this. That wasn't fair. He hadn't planned this. He'd just not revealed the full truth when he should have.

"I should have told you all this before," he said, hoping his voice still sounded as authoritative as it had when he'd begun. "I feared your reaction…I thought you'd abandon me, thinking I'd betrayed you. You must know the truth, here and now...there was no way we could have taken back the city from the enemy without my father's help. None. I made a deal that saw the heathen defeated, even if I would not be awarded the laurels we all thought would come. I will be king one day...but not today. Now if any of you feel betrayed or wronged...you are free to leave. Otherwise, I would consider myself a most fortunate man to have your forgiveness."

Edmund bowed his head, hoping to appear contrite. There was a chance some might think he was putting on some display of false humility, but he really wasn't. He felt wretched, and he couldn't shake what the priest at St Mildred's had told him. He was a liar, but he could make amends. Telling the truth was the only way to do that.

He wondered if he'd been clear enough. The men weren't responding as he'd expected. They were just staring at him, their accusatory looks replaced with something approaching confusion, if not indifference. Edmund thought to tell them about Godgifu. It would sway them, perhaps, since there couldn't be a man out there who wouldn't condemn Duke Richard for his dastardly schemes.

He soon thought otherwise. If he told all of them about the situation, rumours would spread, and the duke might hear of it, potentially thinking Edmund was about to act against him. Godgifu would suffer then. Their only option was to remain tight-lipped. That rankled Edmund, and made him feel that what he was hoping to achieve here was almost pointless because of it. These were difficult times to be virtuous. Yet try they must.

"Do you have nothing to say?"

Edmund's words echoed out across the fields and along the high walls to the east, the sound making him appear almost as lonely as he felt. "As I said, I know how this must seem," he went on, "but please know these past weeks have meant the world to me. None of you were forced to join me, and yet you did, for God and country both. Even if you decide to leave me now, I will not begrudge you. You are all free to do as you will, and you have my blessing...and God's, too, I pray."

Somebody stepped forward from the ranks, their armour splattered with grime, earth, and what was most likely blood. He took his helmet off, revealing a face long in years, his greying whiskers and pale, pock-marked skin doing little to diminish the sparkling intensity in his eyes. He was a man of passion, this one. Edmund had a feeling what he had to say would set the stage for whatever happened next.

He looked around, this unknown warrior, taking in the army at his back and the city they'd only just stormed. He then looked to Edmund and spoke, his voice carrying effortlessly. It was a short and simple thing he had to say. All the same, Edmund was surprised by it.

"Will you stay with us?"

Edmund frowned, unsure of the question and the ripple of "aye!"s that followed from the men.

"What do you mean?" he asked, hoping this fellow might expand a little.

"Is this the end?" he asked. "Are we just to go home and live under your father as before? I don't want that. We don't want that. Will you not stay with us? Keep our army here alive...keep our dream alive?"

That was an interesting proposition. It would be irregular indeed for Edmund to maintain a force of his own in peacetime. Then he realised this was his moment. He couldn't just tell them everything they'd fought for was over and that they'd just have to endure his father's bungled kingship as before. He needed an army, this army, and they needed him. It was the only way to finish their campaign. It was the only way to safeguard the realm, from the Danes and from his father. He had to keep them together.

Another man, some distance away and to the right, came forward to speak. "Don't just leave us now," he called. "Don't just let things return to how they were…don't just vanish into some great hall of your father's, Edmund. Stay with us. Finish the fight. And when it's done, protect us from your father's foolishness…and when God takes him, be our king! Say you will!"

"If I understand what you're all asking…" Edmund began, uncertain, "…is that you want our army here to remain intact, and for me to lead it in defence of our people, against anyone who would threaten us, regardless of what deals or intrigues my father stumbles into?"

A thousand and more nodded, almost as one. "I will not ever leave you," Edmund said, the finality in his voice impossible to miss. "Let us stay. Let us finish the job. Let us defeat the Danes, and then fight on against whatever might come after!"

The old warrior who'd spoken first was now grinning, his head bobbing enthusiastically. "I trusted King Edmund to fight the Danes, and so he did," he bellowed, his head half-turned over his shoulder to address those behind him. "And we won, twice, ripping the hands from our tormentors and paying them back for what they've done. I would have followed him into battle last night even if he had told us his father had returned…just as I would have any night! Any day! And I still will!"

Others concurred, shouting words of encouragement, the whole mood shifting in seconds from simmering unease to unashamed jubilation. Edmund tried to speak further, hoping to explain the situation so any lingering doubts would be assuaged, but he couldn't make himself heard, so loud were his men. Not one of them had left. Not one. They all remained, calling his name, calling him "Ironside", calling him king. And he'd not trusted them? He'd thought they'd abandon him? How could he have been so foolish? How could he have been so blessed?

Edmund leapt from the stage, or hay pile or however it might be described. Ulfcytel grinned, both he and Osbert flanking Edmund as they went out into the men. Hands reached for him, and Edmund shook as many as he could, trying to imprint each face upon memory. They were so tired. They were so hurt, some of them bandaged, others limping, but they still loved him, and they all called to him, saying more or less the same thing, that they trusted him, that he'd led them to victory and would do so again, that they'd not leave him, no matter what. He didn't know what to say or do. He was overwhelmed, but he let it wash over him, allowing himself to be so adored as he moved through the ranks. He might not be a king yet, but this morning he was richer than he'd ever been. All the titles and wealth in the world could not compare to this. This was life. This was destiny. His men had made it so. And for that, he'd never leave their side. Not now. Not ever.

****

"Just what did we all just agree to?"

Morcar's left eyebrow was arched upwards like an arrow pointing towards his scalp. That wasn't a good sign. That usually meant he was very unhappy, or amused, Edmund wasn't always sure, but in this instance he must be unhappy. Was he jealous? After all, the warriors from the Five Boroughs had been roaring Edmund's approval alongside all the others. Did Morcar feel he also was entitled to that kind of display because he was their lord?

"What exactly is the matter?" rumbled Ulfcytel, placing his feet up on the table and taking another swig of overly watered ale. The ealdorman was sat on a stool, one barely able to hold him, but he was entirely unconcerned by it. He was also very tired, Edmund could tell. He'd insist he sleep once this meeting was over. The old man would need it.

Sigeferth joined them, moving through the entrance to their rather large and splendid tent to stand at the table with his brother. They were back at their camp, in the woods and well concealed from Lundenburg's walls, their army having thankfully finally ceased applauding Edmund to follow him back here for a well-earned rest. They deserved it, and Edmund hoped to soon close his eyes for a bit too. Yet first, they had business to discuss. Morcar was upset. It was best to deal with this now rather than allow ill feelings to fester.

Wulfnoth stood a short distance away, looking as tired as the rest of them, and Eadwig was here, too, but no Wulfhild. She was asleep, so Eadwig had said. Ulfcytel had been amused to hear it, and Edmund, for his part, didn't feel any resentment. She'd kept pace with them on this journey, and whilst she'd obviously not fought in the battle, there was nothing wrong with her resting whilst they remained at camp. It was all harmless enough. Edmund also imagined Ulfcytel wasn't the easiest man to sleep next to, if the snoring he'd overheard in the past was anything to go by. His poor sister likely needed some peace and quiet.

"The matter, Ulfcytel, is that Edmund appears to have just given the men the impression they'll not be disbanding," continued Morcar, his arched eyebrow now twitching in irritation. "So the men think they'll be remaining as a standing army, one we don't have the money to sustain or even feed. That's a problem."

"What are you talking about, man?" asked Ulfcytel, his nose wrinkling with distaste. "We didn't need money and a note of permission from our mothers to get this force together. We can keep it a while longer. The fight isn't over. The Danes still ravage the South, and Cnut is unaccounted for."

Morcar went to retort, both his eyebrows rising up to the extent he looked halfway comedic. Sigeferth stopped him, placing a gentle hand on his elbow.

"What my brother wishes to convey is that Edmund may not have the authority to keep a force in the field if his father doesn't wish it," he said. "That will be a problem, and so I think we need to think this through rather than getting swept up in emotion. That was a marvellous display there, Edmund, one that moved my heart. But practicalities must be thought of. The men have fields to till and families to return to..."

"Not all of them," interrupted Wulfnoth, his arms folded. "Did you somehow miss the devastation we've seen everywhere, Sigeferth? Many of the men are survivors from some destroyed village or other. They have nothing to get back to. Vengeance was and is all they have. Why do you think they fight like bloody madmen? It's the hate fueling them. We can use it."

"You can leave with the men you brought with you, Sigeferth," said Edmund coolly, knowing he'd be unlikely to take him up on his offer. He and Morcar were right to raise concerns, and their input was welcome, but Edmund couldn't just announce to the men that they were all going home now, not after what they'd done for him not even an hour ago. He had an obligation to them, and promises to keep.

"Let's not be hasty," said Morcar, his eyebrows thankfully returning to their normal position. "So let's say we keep this army together…and let's say what's left of the Danish army comes up from the South and wants a fight. What do we do?"

"We fight them," Ulfcytel said without hesitation, Osbert nodding at his side.

"Edmund, Svienn wasn't messing around when he came here last year," Sigeferth said, seeing fit to ignore Ulfcytel. "His original host was huge, and when united, it was truly terrifying. His mistake was splitting it up, and Cnut's mistake was failing to put it all back together. Divided, they have indeed fallen…but the remnants could still be dangerous."

"I understand that well enough," said Edmund evenly. "Svienn split his forces when he went to keel over and die in Gainesburg, and Cnut sent a whole batch south to deal with Ælfric's rebellion…which reminds me, do we know anything more about the situation in Hamptonscir? Was Ælfric able to hold Porteceaster?"

"There's been no word in some time," said Wulfnoth, knowing rightly that Edmund looked to him on such matters. "Last I heard, the Danes were making a right mess of things around Wincestre, and Ælfric was refusing to capitulate, saying you were the rightful king and he would bow to no other. That's something if it's true, Edmund. Ælfric was never an ealdorman anyone could really trust to stand up for the good of the realm. It would appear he's changed."

Ulfcytel made a peculiar noise, like he'd been halfway in saying a single word only to suddenly force his mouth shut whilst still emitting sound from the back of his throat. Everyone stared at him, Edmund included, Osbert also looking somewhat puzzled. Ulfcytel turned a shade red under their gaze and slowly took his feet off the table before standing up. He actually looked self-conscious, Edmund thought. That was a first for him.

"I think I mentioned before that I became involved in a family squabble between Ælfric and Æva," said Ulfcytel, his hands clasped together in front of him at his waist.

"You said something about that in Gainesburg, as I recall," answered Edmund, his curiosity piqued.

"That's right, and it might explain the behaviour of our Ælfric. I inadvertently wounded both him and Æva by telling her about his rather sordid past…particularly his role in the destruction of Wiltune."

"I think you mentioned this whilst we were in captivity," said Eadwig, Ulfcytel nodding thoughtfully at the memory.

"That's right," he said yet again, "and I'm sad to say Æva didn't handle it too well. Her and Alaric's firstborn son died at Wiltune, so it seems. I should have kept it to myself."

"Why?" asked Eadwig. "Did Æva's reaction somehow shame Ælfric into action? Put some iron in his soul, so to speak? Make him want to make amends by fighting all the harder for my brother?"

Edmund smiled grimly. He liked the image Eadwig had conjured up. He could well imagine Ælfric being distressed in the presence of a confrontational Æva, and by the sounds of it, he'd had it coming. If he had indeed sought to put things right by resisting the Danes so strenuously, then there was something to be admired there. Edmund just sincerely wished Æva hadn't left Porteceaster. He could understand it, hurt as she was, but she'd been safe there. Now she was gone, or missing or lost or something. Edmund still couldn't shake her from his mind. He had to change the subject. He didn't want to appear melancholy yet again in front of his people. It wouldn't convey the right impression.

"Then let's march to help Ælfric," Edmund said, wondering as he spoke whether that was really the best course of action.

"I'd advise against that," said Sigeferth urgently. "The enemy host in the South is a full third of what we originally faced when Svienn landed. We destroyed a smaller portion of it at Gainesburg, and then another just last night in Lundenburg, but we had help to do that. Our force won't be able to do much if we go on the attack so soon."

"We probably won't have to be so aggressive," said Wulfnoth quietly. "Whoever is in charge down there will be aware by now of whatever it was Æthelred did to destroy Lundenburg Bridge...they'll have probably received orders from Cnut, wherever he is, to come back and help."

"You know this for sure?" asked Edmund.

"No, but it's logical. Why waste time besieging Porteceaster when the real prize, as in Lundenburg, is under threat? Cnut can't hold England just by sacking Hamptonscir, regardless of how annoyed he was that Ælfric rose up in your favour. The real fight is here."

"So you say we'll have Danes coming this way?" asked Ulfcytel, his eyes lighting up in a way Edmund didn't find entirely wholesome.

"Yes, although who is even leading the host is an open question," replied Wulfnoth. "Things would be so much simpler if we could confirm Cnut's whereabouts. Whatever the case, we'll be in for a fight. Which is why, Morcar, it made total sense to keep this army. Edmund's contrition was a master stroke...it's boosted morale in a way I never expected."

"I meant every word," Edmund snapped, irked at what he thought was an implication from Wulfnoth that he was putting on some kind of act.

"I don't doubt it, but what I mean is it makes no sense to be worrying about what your father might think when battle may very well soon be upon us. We should prepare. I'd suggest we don't allow ourselves to be trapped within the city...we could try to compensate for our thin numbers by..."

Wulfhild stormed in, her dress almost catching under her feet, such was her haste. She'd come here in a hurry, Edmund could tell, and her headscarf was ill-positioned, exposing a rather scandalous amount of hair that Edmund hoped wasn't actually some new fashion he'd as yet failed to notice.

"Something is afoot," she said, her voice hushed like she was revealing some long-held secret. "There's men approaching, from the north, along the same route we used to get here."

"I thought you were asleep?" asked Ulfcytel, confused.

"I was, but I awoke and went for a ride. I ventured through the woods towards..."

"On your own?!" Ulfcytel again interjected, Edmund sharing his apprehension at the idea of Wulfhild braving the forest without an escort.

"It's not important!" she exclaimed, frustrated. "It's an army! Coming from the north! Our sentries will know about it by now, and I'm sure they'll be here to tell you so you won't have to keep interrupting..."

A warrior bundled through the entrance, nearly knocking into Wulfhild as he came. "King Edmund," he intoned, Edmund suppressing a smile at how his men still insisted on calling him such. "There's an army approaching from the north," he went on, Wulfhild somehow managing to look both pleased and exasperated at being proved right. "It bears the banners of Norþanhymbre...the Ealdorman Uhtred is leading them."

"What do I do?" asked Edmund suddenly, feeling a touch embarrassed at his hesitation.

"We should go to him," said Sigeferth, both Morcar and Wulfnoth nodding in agreement. "With Uhtred here, things just got a lot more complicated. He'll want to speak with your father, and as usual, he'll only be loyal to himself. You should find out his intentions, now."

Edmund wasted no time. He strode towards the tent's entrance, a slight flick of his hand suggesting his present company should follow him. They understood and obeyed, heading out into the open air quickly and with purpose, the soft warmth of the sun filtering through the trees. Edmund took to horse, or took to Bede to be more accurate, his old friend reacting to his sudden presence with a half-surprised rumble. The sentry who had alerted them to Uhtred's presence rode on ahead, Edmund and the others following with a smattering of warriors who'd seen fit to join them. A few people across the campsite called out to Edmund as he rode on through, but Edmund did his best to downplay his presence with a smile and a nod. He appreciated the loyalty of the common soldier, but he had serious business to attend to now. Everything couldn't always be about him.

They made it through the trees to find Uhtred's army encamped upon the open ground to the north east of Lundenburg. There had to be a good five thousand men out there, and they were disciplined and well-equipped, their myriad banners indicating they'd been gathered from all across Norþanhymbre. They'd only just begun to make camp, and Edmund could tell even from this distance that they were tired, their movements having that awkward, heavy manner to them that warriors always displayed when they were exhausted and yet unwilling to let their guard down.

Edmund rode towards them, all his companions and escorts galloping in his wake. Edmund turned to shout some commands to both Sigeferth and Morcar, ordering them to return to camp and prepare their army for a possible clash of arms. They obeyed without question, knowing Edmund to be right and that it would be foolish to leave the men without command or instruction whilst they treated with Uhtred. Edmund thought it very unlikely the Norþanhymbrians would attempt to harm him right outside the capital, but it was wise to be prepared.

It was thus with some regret that Edmund then learned Uhtred had already departed from his army to speak with his father. The Norþanhymbrian envoys were pleasant enough, and they all bowed to him in their saddles after riding with some haste to meet him halfway, but there was no pressing them to give up any additional information. The Ealdorman Uhtred was gone, so they said, and had entered the city after riding ahead of his host with the breaking of day. That meant he must already be speaking with Æthelred. There was only one thing for it, then. Edmund had to get to his father. He couldn't allow him to be manipulated again, if indeed that was what was taking place. There was too much at stake.

Edmund bid everyone but Wulfnoth depart from him, ordering them to return to camp and keep vigil for either an outbreak of hostilities with the Norþanhymbrians or the emergence of the Danes from the south. Edmund and Wulfnoth then rode back through New Gate and the still corpse-strewn streets, taking only a handful of warriors with them for protection. Things had not improved with the full light of day, and Lundenburg would take some time to recover from both Svienn and Cnut's harsh rule and the savage bloodletting it had taken to reclaim it. All the same, the people were again happy to see Edmund, and they resumed cheering him like he was storming the place for a second time. Somebody would have to put a stop to all this, he decided. There was only so much adoration he could take without risking a prideful heart, and he had problems enough as it was without adding to his sins. But it was good to be liked, and he couldn't fault anyone here for being grateful that liberation had finally come, even if it had been in the form of the ever-troubled King Æthelred.

When they reached his father's halls, Edmund could see he'd been wise to leave so many of his advisers behind, Ulfcytel in particular. Thorkell was here, standing like some kind of baleful titan just a few steps down from his father's throne. Hereward stood close by, looking a little uneasy at the towering presence that was Thorkell, and there was another Dane also hovering around, this one apparently called "Olaf", if Edmund's ears did not deceive him.

Edmund shook his head as he approached, already irritated at how his father seemed to be affording this Olaf so much courtesy. There was only one suitable way to treat his kind, and it didn't involve talking. Edmund didn't care how hard they may have fought in the recent battle. None of that made up for everything that had come before. They deserved death, and it would come for them, one way or another, and if Edmund got his way, it would not be from old age.

His mood wasn't improved by the sound of Uhtred's voice. He'd been lurking in the shadows, or at the table since it was partially wreathed in shadow, and he called out to him now, congratulating him "on a victory well deserved." He then droned on for a bit at Æthelred, who was sat close and looking quite unimpressed, telling him how he "must be proud to see a son grow into a man worthy of admiration" and a load of other massively insincere gibberish Edmund was sure nobody within earshot took seriously. Edmund wasn't in the mood for any of this. He'd take the wind out of Uhtred's sails, right now.

"Why have you come here with such a huge army? You didn't send any force, of any kind, when Svienn first laid siege to this city. Why the change of heart?"

Uhtred wasn't thrown by Edmund's question. He'd prepared for it well, giving Edmund more of that tiresome yap about how there'd been "no means of resisting Svienn as long as his forces were so strong." Edmund thought to confront him about some of the things he'd said in Euerwic in front of Archbishop Wulfstan, but he knew it would do no good, and his father was hardly going to be impressed with how Edmund had tried to convince others to abandon their plans to invite him home. He'd look power-mad, and Uhtred would come out posing as the loyal subject and win his father's favour all the more. That wasn't a pleasant scenario, at least for Edmund.

"So what are you going to do now?" Edmund asked, his expression still grim as he beheld Uhtred.

"Whatever my king asks of me," Uhtred replied, although Edmund noticed Æthelred didn't react to his loyal words and continued to look as uncomfortable as ever.

"I've dispatched scouts to investigate the situation in Hamptonscir," interjected Æthelred, sounding as disagreeable as he looked. "Once we're able to gauge the disposition of the enemy forces left in the field, we'll be in a better position to crush them. That is our immediate goal. Nothing else."

Edmund paused, noting how his father had put particular emphasis on his last sentence. He wanted to put a stop to any squabbling between him and Uhtred, that was obvious, but Edmund didn't see how he could focus on the military situation whilst his father still insisted on surrounding himself with bad company. His blood ran cold when he again looked to the horrifying presence that was Thorkell. He was still standing there, motionless, behind Æthelred and yet close to the throne, his face as blank as it always was and yet somehow filled with a terrible promise. Thorkell and Uhtred. Two absolute bastards, and both of them close to his father and very much of a mind to exploit him as much as they could. Edmund was at least thankful Eadric wasn't here. If the grasping Ealdorman of Mierċe were about and looking to get back into his father's good books, it would be too much to bear. In any case, Edmund was powerless to act, at least as long as Cnut was still at large and Godgifu a hostage. He'd have to think of some other way to keep his father protected from any malefactors.

"Why such tension between us?" Uhtred suddenly asked, the smile on his face reminding Edmund of a painting he'd once seen depicting a demon trying to tempt a man into sin.

"I don't trust you," Edmund replied, thinking bluntness was a virtue in this instance, "and I'm irked with the way Norþanhymbre suddenly has the men to come marching south, but couldn't send us any aid whatsoever when that murderous cur currently stood by the throne was ravaging the countryside only last year."

Thorkell stood up straight upon hearing the insult, but that was as far as it went. He didn't react, not really, although he was staring at Edmund with those unnerving eyes of his.

Uhtred rose from his seat. "Let's not insult our honoured ally," he said, his right hand making a vague gesture towards Thorkell. "We have a common enemy," he added, looking at Edmund and Wulfnoth both, "and it makes for good sense to recognise that everyone in this room is an asset to the other, no matter what's happened in the past. Did our Lord not encourage us to forgive?"

Wulfnoth snorted, undoubtedly over the obvious absurdity and insincerity of Uhtred's question. Edmund smiled and shook his head, but Uhtred was acting like he'd made a serious point, which made the situation even funnier.

"Will you not at least break bread with me, Edmund?" asked Uhtred, undeterred. "I'm sure we can settle whatever differences have crept up between us recently. Will you not give me a chance?"

"I would welcome such a thing," nodded Æthelred, and for some reason Thorkell nodded also, making Edmund wonder if the monster thought he was in a position to be giving out advice. Olaf, or whatever he was called, said nothing, as he had for the entirety of this encounter, but he was looking at Edmund in an expectant way now. *They all want me to obey my father*, Edmund thought. Generally, he wouldn't give a damn about what they wanted, but the situation here was quite unique. He needed to get the measure of Uhtred; learn his plans, size him up, ascertain whether he posed a threat to him or anyone else. If he could find any of that out by sharing a meal with him, he'd do it. It would be highly unpleasant, and he'd have to keep his guard up, but he'd do it.

"I will eat with you, Uhtred," Edmund said sullenly, "just name a time and place."

"I think trust between us needs to be restored, so I'm perfectly willing to meet you on neutral ground…say…outside the walls, between our two armies? I can have a pavilion set up to ensure comfort."

"Yes, yes," answered Edmund impatiently, "and the time? We might not have long for sitting about. We're still at war."

"How about this evening?" asked Uhtred.

"That will do," answered Edmund. He turned away almost immediately, his haste causing him to nearly bump into none other than Archbishop Wulfstan and his two rather intimidating escorts. Edmund hadn't heard him enter the room, and he was clearly in some haste, for he skirted around Edmund entirely in a bid to reach his father. Edmund let him go, wondering if the archbishop was still angry with him following the tense scenes of their last meeting. He decided he didn't care. He had other things to attend to for the moment. Like preparing to socialise with a snake like Uhtred.

He and Wulfnoth returned to their camp in short order. Nothing had changed since their departure, and there was no sign of enemy movement from the south nor any sudden displays of treachery from the Norþanhymbrians. Edmund ate a light meal in his tent and snatched a few hours of sleep, but he couldn't rest properly, and the fearful possibility that he may not know how to handle Uhtred kept pressing on his mind. What did the man want? Was he really just interested in winning the war for his father? But what would come after that? More courtly intrigue that would drive his father mad? Did he know about Godgifu? Should Edmund tell him? And where was Cnut? Dead? There was a lot for Edmund to think on, and by the time an envoy arrived to summon him "to a most hospitable repast with the Lord Uhtred", he was almost grateful. He'd prefer having his enemy sat right in front of him. He'd be able to face him then and stare him down, rather than being alone with his frantic thoughts.

Edmund selected Wulfnoth to again accompany him, albeit this time with Eadwig and an escort of a dozen of their best fighters. It was very unlikely that Uhtred might try something violent, but Edmund wanted to send a message, and having such warriors accompany him would certainly do that. Eadwig too would help. He was an aetheling, and for him to be seen at Edmund's side would give Uhtred the appropriate impression that the heirs to the throne were united and all the stronger because of it. The thought pleased him, as did his decision to remain outfitted in his arms and armour. If Uhtred thought he was going to dress nicely for him, he'd be disappointed. Edmund was a warrior, and they were at war. He wouldn't have anyone forgetting that.

Predictably, Uhtred appeared to have done just that. His pavilion was a large, sagging thing with a scented, smothering atmosphere, and it was all finery within, the dining table polished and arrayed handsomely with silver platters and goblets of various shapes and sizes. It had been set up about two hundred yards from Lundenburg's western wall, almost exactly halfway between the Norþanhymbrian army and Edmund's own rag-tag force of hardened Dane killers. Eadwig was the first to sit down, and

Edmund took the spot next to him, happy at least that he'd now get to spend some time with his brother. He hadn't had the opportunity to do much of that over the years. He liked to think one day that might change.

"Where is your lord?" Wulfnoth asked, his words causing the steward he'd addressed to almost drop the basket of bread he was carrying in surprise.

"He's coming soon," said an unknown warrior standing guard at the entrance. The steward didn't answer and instead began dispensing loaves from his basket to each of the platters within reach, the tremor in his hands easy to spot. Edmund suddenly felt uneasy. There were at least two armed Norþanhymbrians in the pavilion presently, along with three of Edmund's men, excluding Wulfnoth and Eadwig. That meant Edmund had at least nine warriors waiting outside, which would make it effectively impossible for Uhtred to try anything peculiar, such as suddenly attacking them unawares. Even so, there was a tension in the air, and this steward was certainly nervous about something.

"Why so pale?" Edmund asked, hoping his words wouldn't cause the lad to become even more frightened.

"He's just like that," said Uhtred as he suddenly sauntered in, three fully armoured men at his back. "He's a good worker, though," he added casually, sitting down at the head of the table. "He's from Eastengle, so I understand. Tell me, Edmund, do you know what became of the Ealdorman Ulfcytel?"

"He's alive," Edmund shrugged, unwilling to give Uhtred anything more than that. He didn't want him to find out just how extensive his support base was. Ulfcytel was Edmund's most significant ally, which for now meant Edmund was eager to keep his whereabouts a secret. He could always mention over the course of their meal here that Ulfcytel was with his army. It all depended on how things played out and whether Uhtred needed to be intimidated. Right now, the presence of Eadwig should send the right message without overawing Uhtred into outright fear.

The meal was actually quite pleasant, consisting of a variety of no-nonsense stews and roasts, all salted so heavily Edmund wondered if Uhtred somehow knew of his preference for the stuff. Wulfnoth insisted on having one of his men test everything before either Edmund or Eadwig touched it, and Edmund felt awkward because of it, hoping the chap didn't object too much to the rather unsettling duties he'd been assigned. Uhtred didn't take offence, and he blathered on predictably about anything and everything, his face only becoming more irritating as the evening crept on and the daylight was replaced with a dozen flickering candles. Edmund soon grew bored of the proceedings and decided to push Uhtred into at least being halfway honest about his intentions. He asked him outright what he was doing here and what he had planned.

Uhtred paused at what had been said, his eyes thoughtful despite the slight smirk on his lips. "You're always so direct, Edmund," he said sourly. "I had a feeling when you left Euerwic that you believed I was only supporting your father's return for my own purposes. I'm sorry to see you still believe that."

"So what are your intentions towards my father?" asked Edmund again, taking the opportunity to deliberately down his goblet of wine in one single motion. All men were impressed with that kind of thing, Edmund had decided, but it was a gesture that could only be repeated so often. Looking like you could handle your drink was a boon, but there was a limit to it, and throwing up all over himself wouldn't convey the best image. He'd pace himself from this point on.

"As they have always been ever since he made me an ealdorman," Uhtred replied tersely. "I serve him. Can you say the same?"

"I can," said Edmund, "and are you suggesting I would somehow turn on my own father?"

"You tell me. After all...you put on a great display in Euerwic. You tried to convince everyone you'd be a better king and that they'd best get behind you. I have not forgotten it, boy. And I have taken precautions."

Edmund scowled, incensed that Uhtred had dared address him as "boy". Wulfnoth was on his feet, his hand hovering over the hilt of his sword, and the men they'd brought inside were similarly tense, each thinking correctly that things were about to turn sour. The Norþanhymbrian guards by the entrance were now glowering over at them like they were eager for escalation, but Edmund found himself bound to his seat despite that. He couldn't believe what he was seeing. Æva and Brandon were here, in the company of a severely beaten man - bound at the wrists like they were - with a missing ear. Æva too had suffered ill-treatment, the bruises upon her face telling their own sad story. It pained Edmund to see it. He was glad when Wulfnoth demanded answers.

"What's the meaning of this?" he snapped, his blade halfway from its sheath. Uhtred ignored him, ordering one of his men to seat Æva, Brandon, and this mystery man who had yet to be named. They were forced into chairs directly across from Edmund, and Uhtred's man then took up position just a few steps behind Æva, the shadow cast from his great mail-clad bulk seeming to almost swallow her up. Æva's eyes met Edmund's. There was relief there, but also sadness. He looked to Brandon. He was terrified. Edmund knew the look. It was the same one he'd worn when Edmund had rescued him from his father just after the battle with Hemingr. Edmund had been resolved then to protect him and his mother, no matter what. That had not changed. He stood up. He had work to do here.

"Explain yourself immediately."

"This is merely insurance," Uhtred said. "I know this woman is dear to you...they told me all about how you confronted your father to bring the boy back to his mother. I wanted to use them to demonstrate a few things, mainly that any attempt by your good self to unseat our current king will result in severe repercussions."

"You'd threaten me with the shedding of innocent blood?" Edmund's voice was deathly quiet, but inside he felt like he could barely control himself. He'd feared Æva and Brandon dead, and to see them again, here, had been the last thing he'd expected. They were so frightened, and Edmund's heart shook with rage at the sight of it. He knew now he had deep and sincere feelings for the woman. It was because of that he also knew Uhtred had made a serious mistake.

Edmund ignored Uhtred whilst he prattled on and wandered over to the pavilion entrance. His men were there in the light of a nearby brazier, but there were also around forty armed Norþanhymbrians. Uhtred wasn't taking any chances. Sadly for him, Edmund was a desperate man now, and he'd behave as such.

He murmured to himself as he made his way to the warrior standing vigil behind Æva. Uhtred was still talking, and in his arrogance, he'd taken Edmund's mumblings as evidence he was taking his threats seriously. He was right. Edmund did take them seriously. Just not in the way Uhtred may have hoped.

"You have made a bold move here, Uhtred," Edmund suddenly announced, his words driving his counterpart into silence. "I do, however, have my own contribution to make."

Edmund moved fast. Æva was sat directly in front of him, but he didn't waste time attempting to free her, as the Norþanhymbrian behind would certainly intervene. Edmund instead drew the seax from his belt and spun around, his wild swing tearing the bastard's throat wide open. He fell, blood and surprise writ large across his face, and everyone aside from the captives scrambled to their feet, Uhtred himself beset with panic.

His warriors were not so afflicted. One of them attacked Edmund immediately, trying to split his skull with an impressively forged axe. Edmund evaded, flipping his seax into his left hand and drawing his sword with his right. He lashed out, opening his opponent up from the groin to the midriff, leaving him tangled upon the ground in an outpouring of his own guts. Uhtred shrieked and produced a sword from his scabbard, imploring the men he had left standing to "subdue our guests!" Edmund wasn't going to let that happen.

He threw his seax, the point of which found the throat of the warrior foolish enough to charge him. He fell, choking on blood and iron, and Wulfnoth killed another, cutting him down with fluid, precise movements of his sword. Uhtred only had one man still on his feet, but he was transfixed with horror and did nothing when Edmund made a grab for his master. Uhtred tried to bring his blade to bear, but Edmund was too fast, snaring the wrist of his sword arm in a vice-like grip. Edmund then smashed his forehead into Uhtred's face, once and then twice, the cartilage of his nose cracking audibly.

Uhtred went limp, his face a mess of blood and mucus. Edmund hadn't expected that to be so easy. All ealdormen were supposed to be more than capable fighters, but Uhtred had miscalculated badly. He really should not have threatened Æva and the boy.

More men tried to enter the pavilion, their voices hot with anger. Edmund flipped Uhtred around and held him in place, his sword at his throat, and roared for the newcomers to back off. There were four of them immediately facing him, but Wulfnoth and company were menacing their flank, which dissuaded them from advancing further. Uhtred squealed something that half-sounded like an appeal for help, so Edmund jabbed him forcefully in the kidneys, reducing him to a pained silence. Eadwig had by this point drawn his own blade and got to work freeing the captives, and the third one - the man with the missing ear that Edmund didn't recognise - now appeared at his side, an axe from the first warrior to die held firmly in his grip. Edmund appreciated the backup.

Shouting sounded from outside, suggesting the warriors Edmund had left there were aware something was up and had become agitated at seeing more of Uhtred's men barge past them into the pavilion. Edmund yelled again at those facing him to back off, and he cut Uhtred to demonstrate he was serious, allowing the edge of his sword to nick the flesh just enough to draw blood. Uhtred whined and again tried to struggle free, but Edmund held him fast, his eyes still on those in front of him. They yet fancied a go at killing him, but they could also see he meant business, and so they retreated a little, allowing Edmund and company to make their way outside.

It was as he'd expected. His men here were facing off against a much larger force of Norþanhymbrians, all of them angry and becoming yet more so when they clapped eyes on Edmund and the very distressed Uhtred. The stars were just starting to come out, and a gentle breeze was blowing in from the north, but that was as pleasant as it got, and Edmund was all too aware they were dangerously close to an all-out bloodbath. Uhtred still wasn't resisting, possibly due to the concussion Edmund suspected he'd given him with the blessings of his forehead, but his men weren't calming down and seemed very likely to make a nuisance of themselves. They'd need a good talking to if this were to go well. Edmund didn't really have any other option.

It was one of the more bizarre feats Edmund had tried to accomplish in his brief lifetime. He was backing away, his men forming around him with their shields raised, and he'd repeatedly shouted to the Norþanhymbrians that any attempt to assault them would result in Uhtred's death. That seemed to prompt caution on their part, yet they still followed, although several had gone running in the direction of their camp, their cries of alarm carrying on the wind. That meant serious trouble. The entire Norþanhymbrian army could be about to come after them. There'd be no surviving that if it happened.

Uhtred had by now found his voice, or a semblance of it, and he was muttering threats as Edmund continued to haul him along, his blade still at his throat. Edmund ignored them, instead informing the ealdorman that he shouldn't have ever presumed to threaten harm on those he cared about. Uhtred kept waffling, claiming he'd "bring ruin and privation" down upon him for his "most treacherous behaviour." Edmund grew weary of his venom, and so he bellowed into Uhtred's ear and threatened to kill him if he didn't "cease his inane prattle!" He did as he was told, and it was with some relief Edmund realised there were more of his men approaching their rear, fully armed and up for a brawl. Somebody must have ridden back to his camp as soon as they'd realised there'd been trouble. That had been wise. He'd be sure to reward whoever had gone for help as soon as this was over.

Regretfully, he realised that might not happen anytime soon. Just as his own men were forming a shield wall at his back, another force came running after them, this one considerably larger than anything Edmund could presently call upon. Edmund ducked through his men, dragging Uhtred with him, and bellowed for Æva and the others to follow, instructing them to keep on going and make for the safety of the camp. They obeyed and hurried off, Wulfnoth leading the way, and as Edmund glanced after them he could see more of his men charging from the tree line to the south, their battle standards raised and a mighty horse-borne Ulfcytel in the lead. This was going to be interesting. If Uhtred's men wanted a fight, they were certainly going to get one.

Edmund called out to his men, instructing them to form a defensive line and make no move unless provoked by the alarmingly large body of warriors currently rushing towards them. Ulfcytel hurried over on his great grey steed, a sparkle of amusement in his eyes on seeing the beaten and defeated Uhtred.

"So I'm to assume your little repast didn't go as planned?"

"Uhtred had Æva and Brandon as hostages," replied Edmund quickly, "and he tried to use them to threaten me. They are on their way back to camp, but I think the Norþanhymbrians might want their ealdorman back."

Ulfcytel gaped in surprise, his mouth then breaking into his typically broad grin. "Then this is indeed a fortuitous day," he said, "and one all the sweeter in that you've given his lordship here a solid beating for his trouble."

"Let me go, and my men won't kill you," Uhtred seethed, his face reddening with frustration as he continued to try and fail to break free of Edmund's grip.

"Tell your army to back off," countered Edmund, annoyed at hearing yet another threat.

"Just let me go and they will!" Uhtred wailed, his jaw gnashing spasmodically like a dying fish.

"You don't get to harm those I care about and just walk away!" snarled Edmund. "I'll have justice for this! Æva will have justice!"

"I can see now I was right to use her," Uhtred sneered. "You care for the woman, and the boy, too, I think. You may have them back, Edmund, but you'll never survive what's coming, not unless you let me go. Your "justice" will have to wait."

Edmund bit back a retort upon seeing the rest of the Norþanhymbrian host come charging out of the dark. There were thousands of them, enough to overwhelm his outnumbered force and likely kill every last one of them. He looked up at Ulfcytel, magnificent and powerful atop his mount, but even he had fallen silent in the face of what approached, and when he finally returned Edmund's gaze, it did not fill him with confidence. This battle could not go in their favour. Not unless something miraculous took place. And from Edmund's own sorry experience, miracles were few and far between in this most unfortunate land.

XXVII

Her every move was irritating, and all the more so in light of how he'd once been foolish enough to hold her in high esteem. Whereas in the past she'd been graceful and refined in her attire, her choice of clothes now seemed pompous and overblown, the regal purple of her dress unjustified and the dimensions of her headscarf scandalous in their limitations.

Even the way she sat irked him, like she was the most august person upon God's green earth. Her table manners seemed unnecessarily exacting, also, as though she ate for the sake of appearances rather than actual hunger. The insincerity of it all repulsed him. He'd get this over with as quickly as possible, and then "Queen" Emma could return to her chambers and away from him. He'd be able to think then. In these doubly trying times, Æthelred valued the company of his thoughts more than ever.

"Is there any word on the whereabouts of this Cnut?" Emma's accent served to almost put Æthelred off his food, so identical was it to her bastard brother. He chewed slowly, working out his frustration on the charred meat between his teeth whilst he pondered whether to even respond.

"We've seen and heard nothing," he finally said, "and it will likely remain so for some time. If he's alive, we'll find him. A man like that won't just slink off and hide."

Emma was silent for a while, perhaps sensing her husband was displeased with her. They were in the throne room, or the elongated, stone-walled chamber that Æthelred had always used as such, and the place was as miserable as it had always been, the air also having an unpleasant tang that made him wonder if Svienn or Cnut's stench was somehow lingering on in their absence. Not even the fire in the hearth across from their table added much cheer, as it was casting long shadows that seemed to dance erratically, making Æthelred think of strange creatures that his mother had told him lurked in the dark waiting to carry off small boys who didn't do as they were told. It was a foolish story from a foolish woman, but it had terrified him at the time, and with all he'd been through lately, he didn't need to be reminded of it.

The only thing remotely pleasing about his situation was the presence of Hereward, who stood vigil behind Æthelred like some kind of armoured statue. He'd only been directly in his service since the battle at Bernecestre, but he was more than glad to have him, especially after seeing how hard he'd fought in Rouen. He was a proficient warrior, no doubt, yet there was no shortage of them around. Loyalty, however, was always in limited supply, and Hereward had that quality firmly in his possession. Æthelred took great comfort in that.

"My brother will be pleased to hear of your victory here," Emma said suddenly, the mention of the duke making Æthelred wince in displeasure.

"I'm sure he will," replied Æthelred neutrally, "as I'm sure you're looking forward to getting back to life as a fully-fledged queen. Exile wasn't your type of thing, was it?"

"What do you mean?" she asked, a certain sharpness in her tone.

"I mean just that," he said. "You didn't like hanging around Rouen knowing you weren't the queen of the castle. Now you are just that. And it only cost you our daughter."

"That's not fair!" screeched Emma, her sudden shrillness making Æthelred's toes curl. "Richard just wants Godgifu to remain with him as…as a safeguard…a way to ensure…"

"A way to ensure I do exactly as he tells me, whenever he wills it. And you not only agreed to it, you let them throw me and Hereward here in a cell just for objecting."

"That's a lie!" protested Emma yet again. "You were not just objecting! You and that hooligan behind you were hurting my brother's men! I had no choice in what happened next. You are responsible!"

"Quiet yourself, woman!" seethed Æthelred, annoyed beyond words at Emma's suspect claim that he and Hereward were somehow both at fault.

"I will not!" she exclaimed, her emerald eyes flashing in the firelight. "You think I don't care about Godgifu…you think I don't care about you…but I do! It wasn't right for us to live our lives in exile! You were born to be a king! I was born…"

"To be a harpy who would sell her own child for the sake of a fancy title and a never-ending wardrobe. Don't you tell me what I was born to be, Emma. You have no idea what it means to rule, nor the pain and suffering I've endured with the doing of it."

"And yet, husband, I have been with you every step of the way. I supported you when people thought you insane because of your nightmares…I supported you when your sons, that idiot Edmund and the so very perfect Æthelstan, were always trying to second guess you. I supported…"

"Don't you ever speak about Æthelstan again in your life."

Æthelred had put his knife down to rest his hands on either side of his platter. He was looking straight at Emma, and he sensed Hereward was glaring at her also. Æthelred had grown used to her resenting his firstborn children, thinking it only natural she'd have issues relating to them, but he wouldn't tolerate that attitude now. Not towards Æthelstan.

Emma muttered something unintelligible and resumed picking at her food, her cheeks flushed pink. Æthelred watched her for a time, noting how cold her eyes seemed whenever she cast a glance at him. He didn't understand why he'd never seen it before. She'd been his rock; the one constant in his darkest days that had stopped him from slipping over the edge into full-blown madness. It had all been a lie. Emma was an opportunist like any other, content and harmless enough when given power and prestige, but as ruthless as any man when denied it. There would have been a time when Æthelred's heart might have broken with the realisation of it all, but not now. He was too angry, and Godgifu wouldn't be helped by him falling apart. He would stay strong.

"He won't hurt her," Emma said quietly, her sullen tones barely audible over the gentle crackling of the fire.

"Say that again," asked Æthelred, knowing he'd heard her well enough the first time.

"I said my brother won't hurt Godgifu. He's just playing politics. He likes to appear fearsome and ruthless to get what he wants. He's always been like that. That's how he got to be where he is today."

"By threatening small children?"

"Like I said, he won't hurt her! You just don't know him! He was different when he explained what he had planned to me. I know him better than you. It will all be well. Trust me…"

"Don't ever ask me to trust you, my queen," spat Æthelred, hoping Emma wasn't so slow-witted she'd have failed to spot the sarcasm in his voice when he'd used her official title. "I know a thing or two about statecraft, and your brother was not putting on some show with me for the sake of acting the villain. He fully intends to use our daughter as he sees fit to force me and England to do his will. You agreed to that. Stop pretending otherwise."

Whatever Emma said in reply was lost in the sound of protesting hinges and the groaning of aged oak. The doors at the head of the chamber were opening, and a single figure hurried through as soon as he was able. He approached Æthelred directly, rushing past Emma to stand before the king. He was Norman, and Æthelred didn't know him, but he appreciated the curt bow before he spoke. Formalities were nice sometimes.

"I apologise for disturbing you, king," he began, Æthelred wrinkling his nose at the sound of his accent. "But there is a great commotion outside the western wall...your son..."

"What about him?" Æthelred demanded.

"He's had a falling out with your northerners. We don't understand what the issue is, but your son's army is facing off against that of Lord Uhtred. Violence is but a heartbeat away! Perhaps the presence of their king might..."

Æthelred was already on his feet and heading towards the exit, the noble Hereward at his side. He'd known there was animosity between Edmund and Uhtred, but he hadn't thought for a moment it would escalate into violence, at least not on such a scale. This was a disaster in the making, and if he didn't assert his authority, he could end up seeing his own forces decimated. He wouldn't know how to continue his campaign then. The Normans he had with him were an asset, but there simply were not enough of them to hold off the Danes if Edmund and his supporters fell to fighting with Norþanhymbre. He had to hurry.

Cuthbert was outside the chamber in the company of several worried-looking Normans, all of whom fell into step beside Æthelred as he strode purposefully towards the main entrance and the courtyard that lay beyond. He stepped out into the night air to see his horse had already been readied for him, and he wasted no time mounting up and riding into the city, Hereward following on a steed of his own. The Norman who'd originally brought him the news rode after him, babbling something about how they "had to hurry", as if somehow Æthelred wasn't doing precisely that. Cuthbert was also with them on a rather nervous grey steed that quite suited his timid personality, and together they made good time toward New Gate, the city streets more or less empty given the lateness of the hour.

That was as good as it got. Æthelred could see for himself how serious the situation was the instant they exited the western wall and emerged onto Watling Street. The stars were shining brightly, illuminating the open ground north of the roadside, but even if it had been the darkest night possible he'd still have been able to locate the trouble, such was the abundance of very angry, heavily armed men. He could tell who was who, since the Norþanhymbrians clearly had the advantage of numbers, which they'd been content to use already by encircling much of the smaller force that had apparently so offended them.

Despite being pressed, however, these men were not cowed, and they were bellowing back at their Norþanhymbrian tormentors with threats aplenty. Their spears too were both ready and sharp. Æthelred had to do something. If they fought, Edmund's forces would almost certainly be overrun, but knowing Edmund he'd still inflict serious losses on the Norþanhymbrians. English blood should not be shed by Englishmen. Æthelred had done plenty of that in the past and regretted it. He also couldn't bear the loss of another son. Edmund had to be saved, no matter what. He'd never forgive Uhtred if something happened to him.

Things became more complicated when he rode closer. He could see that oaf, Ulfcytel, on horseback just behind his own shield wall, and he was roaring and bellowing as was to be expected, his sword circling above his head in a manner that suggested he'd very much like to bring it down upon the brow of anyone stupid enough to test him. The Norþanhymbrians immediately facing him seemed a little apprehensive at the sight, but they hadn't backed off and didn't seem likely to. Then Æthelred heard a voice, familiar in its pitch and timbre. He followed the sound, searching the angry horde before him for its point of origin. His eyes fell on Edmund and the heavily beaten man at his feet. This was foolhardy, even for him. No wonder the Norþanhymbrians were so upset. This had to end now.

Æthelred and his party moved in, the mass of men parting around them. He was just about to call out to Edmund when somebody suddenly grabbed at his horse, the unknown assailant clutching the reins and hauling so his steed reared up in panic. Æthelred fell and fell hard, his back slamming into the grass below with a wet thud. He lay there for a time, wondering if anyone would notice if he took the opportunity for a quick nap. Then he heard more shouting, of an intensity he'd rarely heard in the past. Hereward was angry. And he wasn't being shy about it.

He was on his feet and close by, making straight for the still prone Æthelred and bellowing for all to fall to their knees "in the name of your king!" Æthelred sensed everyone was complying, so quiet had it become, and as Hereward hauled him upright he saw that it was so. It made for quite a sight. Thousands of men, all kneeling in the grass, their previous belligerence fleeing at the sound of Hereward's furious condemnation. All except for Edmund's men. They stood tall, just as he did. Æthelred would knock some sense into the lad's head before this night was over.

"Just what is the meaning of all this?" Æthelred asked, he and Hereward striding through the kneeling multitude.

"This rat here had Æva hostage," replied Edmund, gesturing contemptuously towards Uhtred.

"Who?" asked Æthelred, genuinely confused about who this "Æva" was and how she'd become so important to Edmund that he'd risk a pitched battle with his own countrymen.

"Alaric's wife…widow. Brandon's mother…you know, the boy I asked you to give up in the tunnels under the city…"

"Right, yes," interrupted Æthelred with a flick of his hand. The tunnels under Lundenburg were not common knowledge, and he didn't want just anyone learning of their existence. He remembered Æva and Brandon now, but none of that explained why Edmund had seen fit to spark this confrontation, nor indeed how the Ealdorman Uhtred had managed to capture them to begin with. Why was everyone so intent on making things complicated? This was yet another reason he'd not wanted to come back and be king. Everything was always such a headache.

"If you'll allow me to explain…" croaked Uhtred, still on his knees and looking very much worse for wear. Edmund kicked him in the side, cutting off whatever he was about to say. That wasn't right. Both parties had to be heard if they were to resolve this matter. Violence and more violence wasn't a tenable solution.

"Will you desist and tell me what's going on?" Æthelred asked, more irritated than ever.

"He sought to use Æva and Brandon against me," Edmund hissed, his left hand grabbing Uhtred's hair to wrench his head back. "He hurt them, and was of a mind to continue if I did not obey him. I will not tolerate such dastardly deeds, father. I will NOT be threatened."

"It is a low thing that's happened," Æthelred nodded, "and something that did not need to escalate to this point. What say you, Uhtred? Does my son speak the truth?"

"I merely...sought...to ensure his obedience to your just rule." Uhtred's words were not coming easily, but even had he been hale and hearty, Æthelred would still think to question his motives in all this. Taking hostages was common for parties at war or otherwise generally hostile, but to parade a maligned woman and child in front of Edmund and expect him to submit had been callous and foolish. Uhtred had paid for it with a beating. Æthelred now had to stop any further conflict before it could start. His kingdom depended on it.

"Where is Æva now?" asked Æthelred, suspecting her safety was a priority for Edmund. He wasn't sure what his connection was to this woman, but Æthelred had a hunch it went beyond simple chivalry. It was only natural. Edmund should be married by now, and in the absence of a good wife, his heart must have settled on Æva. That wasn't a match Æthelred would approve of, but he wouldn't blame his son for having feelings for her. There were far, far worse things in this world than youthful infatuation.

"She's back at my camp," said Edmund, waving his sword towards the woods to the south west.

"Then what is your purpose in holding Uhtred here?" inquired Æthelred further.

"I...felt..." Edmund was stuck. He'd probably seized Uhtred in the heat of the moment and then had to use him to keep his ravening army at bay. It was quick thinking, and it had given him what he wanted, but he didn't know what to do next. Æthelred almost felt sorry for him. He couldn't remember romance being this dangerous when he was young, not that he'd ever really had the opportunity to fall in love as and when he might. Politics had always got in the way of that.

Æthelred looked down at Uhtred and fixed him with the most authoritative glare he was capable of. "If my son lets you go, do you give me your word you will march your army back to their tents and trouble him no more?" That was a fair offer, Æthelred thought, at least in the short term. Uhtred would want revenge of some form, but for the moment what really mattered was preventing mass bloodshed. They could soothe any lingering hurts at a later date.

"I will, I promise," said Uhtred, in a manner that actually sounded quite convincing.

"Then let him go," commanded Æthelred, for a brief instant fearing that Edmund, in his rashness, would think it wise to disobey him. Fortunately, that did not come to pass, and Edmund instead hauled Uhtred to his feet before kicking him in the rear. Uhtred staggered a few steps, looking like he was about to lose his balance entirely until one of his warriors reached out and caught him. He looked back, glaring at Edmund with undisguised hatred, but he kept on moving, and with a wave of his hand his great army began to gradually withdraw alongside him, their task completed. They had their lord back. Now Æthelred would have answers.

"You would risk the lives of thousands just for one woman?"

"I had not intended things to go this way," replied Edmund, his eyes still on the retreating Norþanhymbrians. "He caught me off guard and left me no choice. I had to act. It was either that or allow Uhtred to make a pawn of me."

"He did what was right, Æthelred," grumbled Ulfcytel from atop his mount. "Æva is very dear to us, and the least we can do for her, following Alaric's death, is ensure toads like Uhtred can't work their fetid schemes upon her. It is only fair, yes?"

Æthelred stared at Ulfcytel, thinking what he'd said was easily the most polite and civilised thing he'd said to him in some considerable time. In his heart, Æthelred missed his old friend, but a thousand slights and misunderstandings had seen their relationship dashed beyond repair, regardless of how sincere and seemingly correct Ulfcytel's words were now. Æthelred merely nodded in reply, fearing if he spoke to him directly it would only lead to heartache for both of them. A king couldn't have friends, anyway. His mother had told him that, often and with enthusiasm. Æthelred winced at the memory.

"I think we should talk, Edmund," he finally said, hoping they could discuss these matters somewhere warm. It was cold out here, and he didn't want to start shivering in full display of everyone present. It would make him look weak. Or weaker still, since he'd already made a spectacle of himself when he'd fallen from his horse. He wasn't completely sure how that had even happened, but it was beyond embarrassing, that he did know.

"I agree," said Edmund, "but we should do so at my camp. I want to be here in the event Uhtred tries something."

"I think he's learned his lesson, at least for now."

"I can't take any chances, father. If you wish to speak with me, then my tent will suffice. I won't leave my men tonight."

Æthelred grunted and nodded, happy to agree to his son's wishes. He dismissed Cuthbert and the Normans, ordering them back to his halls, and he then followed Edmund south towards the trees that Æthelred assumed concealed his army's campsite. Hereward stayed close, his hand never far from his sword, and it was just as well, since Æthelred felt a little intimidated as he moved through his son's forces. These men had a look to them, the hard, jagged look of those who'd seen a great deal of violence in a relatively short space of time. That wasn't unusual, considering all they'd been through, but there was a certain something to the way they glowered at Æthelred that he didn't care for.

None of them liked him. They didn't like him, and they thought Edmund would make a better king than he. That was the whole reason they'd fought this far south, and now they'd been cheated of that. Æthelred wondered why they'd not deserted Edmund, if indeed his campaign thus far had been waged on the premise he'd take power and reward his supporters. He must have some hold over them still. Loyalty on such a scale…it was a beautiful thing. Æthelred wasn't sure if he'd ever seen the like.

They moved through the woods, taking care lest they stumble or otherwise suffer some misfortune in the dark. There was no need to fear, as before long a warm glow became discernible through the trees, this turning out to be the light cast by the cookfires in Edmund's camp. They headed onward, their path leading them out of the trees and through row after row of tents and the odd horse chewing peacefully at the grass.

Æthelred couldn't help but feel impressed with his son. He'd positioned his forces well, this location ensuring that he'd blocked Watling Street from the east and west whilst granting a decent view of the western and northern approaches to Lundenburg. The camp was also well concealed, making Æthelred wonder if this was how Edmund had been living whilst he was in Normandy. Confronting the Danes directly would have been impossible until recently, so Æthelred assumed Edmund and his men had taken to the woods, never staying in one place for too long and always looking for an opportunity to take the enemy by surprise. It was admirable in many ways, but Æthelred didn't think he himself would be well suited to such a life. He'd never been the fighter or the general some had hoped he'd be. In that respect, Edmund's men were entirely correct. Edmund would be a better king.

They soon entered a fairly spacious, white pavilion, its interior lit by a single candle that was in danger of burning itself out. Æthelred leant on the side of the table within, happy for the opportunity to get his breath back, whilst Edmund ducked outside to issue a sequence of orders to the men filing back into camp. He soon returned and offered Æthelred and Hereward both a seat, although he remained standing. Hereward predictably refused to sit, and he remained at Æthelred's back, guarding him and the exit from the pavilion.

"So what do you have to say to me?" asked Edmund quietly.

"Is this it?" inquired Æthelred as he sat down. "Is it just going to be you and I? I saw you had Sigeferth and Wulfhild and the like with you just a couple of days ago. Will they not join us?"

"You'd want that?"

"I would," nodded Æthelred firmly. "I meant what I said to you. I won't harm them. Forgiveness is a hard thing, and I think you've demonstrated only just recently that you too struggle with it…but I have given you my word that no harm will come to Sigeferth or his people. They are welcome anywhere I have authority."

"I'll pass the message along," Edmund said neutrally. "So what else would you have of me? I'm anxious to see Æva and Brandon, father, so if we could hurry things along…"

"I understand," sighed Æthelred. "I would ask you not to lose your temper over what I'm about to say…but I think you should leave, Edmund. Not for long, but just long enough to allow me to smooth things over with Uhtred. Your presence here will only serve to keep him agitated, and the unity of our armies is now broken. It must be restored if we are to somehow continue this campaign."

"And where would you have me go?"

"Wherever you like. This Æva you are so fond of will certainly need time to recover from Uhtred's rather ill-advised effrontery. Snotingeham has always been a favourite haunt of yours. Why not go there?"

"Those are Sigeferth's lands," said Edmund, his eyes narrowing. "What do you intend, father? You say Sigeferth is welcome, but now you propose I return to his holdings, with him in tow, I'd assume?"

"He is welcome, he and Morcar and anyone else who wishes to stay. You don't have to take your army with you either. You can appoint somebody to lead it in your absence. Ulfcytel is the natural choice."

"I can think of better ideas than leaving you and Ulfcytel in close proximity."

"Those days are over, Edmund," said Æthelred. "I understand we have a past, Ulfcytel and I, but I say again I'm not going to try to settle old scores. All will be forgiven. Godgifu is my foremost concern, not more petty bickering."

"And you wish me gone for the sake of assuaging Uhtred's bruised ego?"

"That's correct. I can spin it so it's what he wants to hear…I can say I've sent you away suitably chastised and that he still has my every confidence…in time, he'll calm down, and we can focus on more important matters."

"So you'll lie then, father?"

"To keep us from the kind of bloodshed and infighting we almost descended into tonight? Yes. Yes, I will."

Edmund rubbed at his great hairy jaw, his eyes downcast. He looked tired, the hollows under his eyes appearing more pronounced, and his beard was long and ragged in a way that reminded Æthelred of Ulfcytel. He was still armoured like he had been when he'd led the assault on the western walls, and his hair was unbound so that it spilled over to hug the sides of his face in a dark, chestnut tangle. The son had become a man, there was no doubt about it, but Æthelred could still see the boy in him whenever their eyes met, and his feelings were hurt. They often had been. Æthelred had rarely had much time for him when he was young. He hadn't thought much of it then, yet he regretted it now. He regretted a great deal. He had much to make amends for.

"I'll march with all my troops," Edmund eventually said, "and make camp close by, or at least close enough for us to send messengers back and forth to each other as required. That way, if this Danish host that's still on the loose makes an appearance, I can head back to assist you."

"I have thousands of men here, Edmund. You have…fifteen hundred, at the most? I think we can afford to let you go for a time."

"That's foolish thinking, father," Edmund said, Æthelred flinching at the rebuke. "In war, those who get complacent and make assumptions about their strength will suffer for it. I taught Cnut that lesson already at Gainesburg."

Æthelred pondered his words, his heart swelling with pride at the thought of Edmund inflicting such a decisive defeat on their ancestral enemies.

"There's a wisdom to what you have said," he admitted, "and I agree to your proposal. Pull your forces back and linger wherever you deem expedient. I will call upon you if anything happens…and in the meantime, I shall try to make Uhtred understand your position."

"Don't threaten me or the people I care about. It's a simple enough position for him to understand, father."

"It is, and you have my backing in this," nodded Æthelred, "but a man like Uhtred will need to have his hurt pride smoothed over. As I have said, I can't do that with you under his feet. He'll need to think I hold you in disfavour for him to calm down and think clearly."

"And whilst you attend to the feelings of a beaten dog, Cnut remains unaccounted for, and what's left of his forces run amok in Hamptonscir."

"You're suggesting I prioritise the military situation?" Æthelred could understand why his son would think that. It was his way, and he didn't really seem to have grasped the importance of diplomacy. Æthelred would not have the army he had if Uhtred wasn't kept content. Politics had to come first, at least for now. It wasn't particularly heroic or exciting, but it was necessary.

Æthelred peered over his shoulder upon hearing someone pushing through the pavilion entrance. Hereward was partially in the way, as he'd moved to block access to whoever was coming through, but Æthelred could see who it was well enough. Two men, dressed for war like Edmund, one dark and deadly, the other softer in appearance, with kind, aged eyes. Morcar and Sigeferth. The two brothers. The two leading thegns of the Five Boroughs. The two men who'd got Æthelred's firstborn son, Æthelstan, killed.

They froze, their eyes flitting fearfully between Æthelred and the towering Hereward. Æthelred stood up and took a few steps forward. Bitterness welled up in his stomach, and he felt the acrid tang of resentment, knowing that if it were not for these two men and their foolish schemes, Æthelstan would still be alive. He wanted them punished. He needed it. Yet he had given his word to Edmund. He would forgive, somehow. Perhaps in time, Edmund would have the heart to do the same for him.

"I'm happy to see you both," lied Æthelred. Morcar bowed slightly, but Sigeferth remained still, looking halfway between defiance and abject terror.

"I would like to make it clear to each of you, in person, that I do not intend to follow up on old enmities," continued Æthelred. "Æthelstan is dead, and whilst it pains me every moment to know it is so, I have chosen to engage with my past shortcomings and begin what I hope will be a different kind of reign. I hope you will support me in this."

"But we didn't kill Æthelstan."

Sigeferth's words cut right through Æthelred's chest. He wasn't sure if he'd intended to be blunt or even rude, but to hear the man divest himself of all responsibility for what had happened was beyond insulting. He didn't know what to think, let alone do, in response. Fortunately, Morcar interjected to save Æthelred any further embarrassment.

"We both regret the outcome of the battle at Bernecestre," he said smoothly, "and I would have it known we acted in accordance with what we thought would be the best interests of the realm. But you, my king, were actually in the right all along...Thorkell was open to negotiation, and whilst your taxes have taken a toll, he did come over to your service. You removed a terrible threat to this kingdom with words rather than arms. That's to be admired."

Æthelred gazed at Morcar, wondering if he were speaking truly or trying to mollify him. He could tell the latter was more likely, since Sigeferth had turned to look at his brother, an expression close to irritated disbelief etched upon his face. Edmund too looked quizzical and had raised a single eyebrow, but Æthelred wasn't about to make a scene, regardless of how insincere Morcar might be. He needed to prove to his son that he'd changed. That was the only way to win his forgiveness, and he yearned for that almost as much as he yearned for Godgifu's return.

"I appreciate what you've said, Morcar," Æthelred lied again, "and I'd like to extend an invitation to you both to attend my royal halls in the next few weeks. I will be issuing invitations to various thegns who may have had cause to doubt me in the past...I want to make it clear things have changed. I have changed. You'd do me great honour if you'd accept."

"Will you not be heading south with your forces to assist the Lord Ælfric?" Sigeferth was too direct. Æthelred didn't like that, but again he was aware he had an audience in the form of Edmund. He'd respond accordingly.

"The situation in Hamptonscir is still unclear, but as soon as my scouts return with something concrete, I will act. Besides, an army doesn't need me to lead it. I have good men who can do that for me. I hope that one day I can count you among them."

"You wish us to lead your armies?" That was Morcar, and he'd misunderstood.

"Not presently," corrected Æthelred. "Yet I would like to think we can bridge any divide between us so that, in time, I can count on you to do so, if needed. What do you say? Will you accept my invitation to break bread?"

They both nodded, Morcar more eagerly than Sigeferth, but Æthelred's heart lightened at the sight. This could be a new beginning, for them and the country as a whole, assuming these men really were willing to work with him on coming to an accord. It was one thing for them to agree to his proposal, especially with Edmund standing there, and quite something else for them to mean it. Æthelred would keep his guard up. He was too accustomed to disappointment to do otherwise.

Nonetheless, he took Sigeferth's hand in his, and then Morcar's, looking into their eyes in turn. He couldn't discern much. They were blank and their motives inscrutable, although there was a slight sadness to Sigeferth that he thought curious. Was he remorseful over Æthelstan? If he were, then that could only lead to good things. From contrition came forgiveness, and from forgiveness came all manner of possibilities. Æthelred had only just started to understand that in his old age. He hoped then that his own resentment towards these two thegns might ease. He didn't like the feeling of bitterness. He'd endured too much of it in his time. He didn't want to let Edmund down by acting on it.

Edmund said a few words, instructing both Sigeferth and Morcar to sit and wait for him whilst he spoke to his father outside. He left the pavilion, and Æthelred followed, Hereward naturally doing likewise. They walked for a time, moving at a slow, leisurely pace through the camp, Æthelred again spotting how every warrior they passed nodded towards Edmund rather than him. A part of him was insulted by it, feeling that as king he was due such respect rather than his son. Another side to him knew better. Edmund deserved the love of these men, and Æthelred did not. He'd like to prove himself to them in time, but for the moment, everything was as it should be.

"Did you mean all that? What you said to Morcar?" Edmund asked as they continued their gentle stroll, the night air crisp and refreshing.

"I did," Æthelred assured him, hoping he at least sounded more genuine than he felt.

"I'm glad to hear it. It was a joint decision to attack Thorkell at Bernecestre. Æthelstan wanted it. I wanted it. Sigeferth and Morcar never pushed us into anything."

"I hope that is the case," said Æthelred. "These have been very painful times for all of us. I hope that before I die, I can play a part in bringing some healing to our people. That has to start somewhere. Forgiveness can be a great…"

"Just give me time, father," muttered Edmund, the resentment in his voice easy to detect. "I know you want me to pretend everything is alright…but there is a lot I need to process, not just in terms of what you and Eadric did to Uncle Æthelstan. You have my support because we need to get Godgifu back, but…just give me time. If you repair your bridges with Sigeferth and Morcar, then it will help. That's all I can say for now."

"I respect your honesty, son. I feared you'd resent me for having you sent away for the sake of Uhtred. I'm glad you're able to put pride aside and see sense. It makes my life a lot easier."

"He's a dog," said Edmund nonchalantly, "and he'll remain so. But I understand you need Norþanhymbre, and alienating the North will not help us when it comes to our business with the Normans. I do what I do for my family. For Godgifu."

They'd stopped on a patch of rough ground, the tree cover ahead intensifying and the campsite behind receding into darkness. A fox called out from somewhere to the north, the sound really quite unpleasant. Another answered, the cry also hard on the ears.

"I'll need to attend to Uhtred now," Æthelred said, hoping that wouldn't be a sore spot for Edmund.

"As I expected," Edmund said, "and I have to prepare my men to move out. We'll be gone by morning. There is, however, one other thing I need to do."

"What's that?" Æthelred asked.

"I have someone to thank."

****

He was too late for vespers, and the main chapel was empty, the light from the customary candles upon the altar flickering unsteadily as he approached. Edmund thought he could detect incense in the air, the sweet smell conjuring up images of the pious assembly that must have convened here only just recently. St Mildred's was a beautiful place, and all the more so now it was quiet and still, the moonlight cascading through its narrow windows possessing a comforting quality that made him feel safe. He knew why. His mother, Ælfgifu, had often taken him here when he was a boy, his brothers and sisters included. It had always been late, but none of them had complained, feeling rightly that there was something wonderful about worship at this hour. Edmund chided himself. Worshipping the Lord was always wonderful. He just had fond memories of doing so at night.

It wasn't long before he heard footsteps off to the west. A figure came into view, their face hidden in shadow, but Edmund had a feeling who it was from the heaviness of their robes. It was only right that he thank this priest. His words had calmed him when he'd needed it, and his advice was sound. If it was God's will, then Edmund could indeed be a light for his father, as was only right and just. Good times could be ahead, times of reconciliation and healing. He knew well enough he wasn't the only man who needed it.

Edmund smiled when the priest came closer, but that vanished as soon as he finally stepped out of the shadows and into the warm glow of the candlelight. It wasn't the same man. This was a priest, of course, and his vestments were evidence of that, but he was old, with hard, flint eyes and a white beard tied into a thin plait at the middle. This was all rather odd. Was the other priest he'd spoken to the night before unwell?

"I'm sorry," Edmund said, feeling oddly nervous before this stranger. "I'd wanted to speak with the priest who was here last night."

"And who was that?" came the reply, this one having a voice even more ragged than his advanced years would suggest.

Edmund described the man he'd spoken with, going into some detail on his appearance and his chestnut beard that had been so well groomed. The priest frowned slightly and then shook his head.

"Nobody of that description has served here," he said slowly, like he was still thinking it over. "I took over from Father Osmund when he was murdered during the riots last year. There has been nobody else."

Edmund paused, unsure of what to say. He asked if the priest could somehow be mistaken, stating again that he'd spoken with somebody else here just the night prior. The priest gave the same answer, his voice gruff but patient. Edmund felt foolish. Something had gone wrong, and now he was gabbling like an idiot, insisting on something this man believed couldn't have happened. He spun around and headed away from the altar, his quick footsteps echoing sharply across the stone-tiled floor. He didn't like embarrassment, and he waved the priest off when he called out to him on whether he needed help. Edmund would not be taken for a drunk or a madman. He had to get out of here.

He stopped by the entrance, observing a single colourful image set into the glass of the majestic window immediately to his left. It was of a man, tall, refined and yet strong, and he was dressed as a king, the gold crown upon his head seeming to sparkle with a light of its own. He was otherwise in dire straits, for he'd been tied to a tree, several fierce-looking men to the left drawing on bows to pepper him with arrows.

Whoever had created all this was an artist of great skill, for the facial features of the crowned man were quite explicit, depicting a regal countenance that struck Edmund as familiar. The eyes gave it away; sharp yet compassionate, and the beard too was distinctive, its chestnut hairs terminating in a single point just prior to meeting the collarbones. Recognition suddenly dawned. This was the priest he'd met with last night. He knew that couldn't be possible. He knew that made no sense. Then he beheld the words that had been worked into the glass directly beneath the image.

Saint Edmund, our Martyred King, Pray for Us.

Edmund shook his head from side to side, his mind reeling at the possibility he was either insane or had encountered some kind of holy apparition. He knew not what to do, but as he dropped to one knee and made the sign of the cross, he remembered some words spoken just recently, and made all the more powerful in light of recent events:

"I wasn't always as I am now, Edmund. As I said, I once lived a different life, in a different time, so it seems. But my advice stands; be a light for Æthelred, and indeed the world. God wills it for you. God wills it for all of us."

"I will," Edmund whispered, his hands meeting at his chest in prayer. "But I will need your help…Saint Edmund, our Martyred King, pray for us."

XXVIII

Ulfcytel emerged from the trees, almost frightening the life out of Æva as she sat huddled by the campfire. He lifted her up off the ground in what was an embrace of a sort, but one she was quite unaccustomed to, even if the good-natured rumble of a laugh sounding directly into her ears still made her smile. He put her down eventually, the huge man looking strangely sheepish at what he'd done. He patted Brandon on the head, his great hairy hand remarkably gentle, and mumbled something about he'd grown and would "be fighting in no time." She knew he meant well, but right now she couldn't bear to think of her son behaving like that. There'd been too much violence. She yearned for an end to it.

Æva's mouth dropped when she beheld the man standing with Ulfcytel. She hadn't recognised him at first, taking him for just another warrior about camp, but she could see it now, that same concerned look she'd grown familiar with, despite the mess of scorched flesh that made up his face. She stepped forward, taking Osbert's hand and asking him what had happened. He shrugged it off, unwilling or perhaps unable to revisit the memory of whatever had befallen him. Then Ulfcytel asked about Cenric. That brought more woes to Æva's heart. If Cenric hadn't turned up here, then that meant he was almost certainly dead. It was hard to imagine anything being able to kill him, so great a warrior had he been, but she just couldn't provide any realistic explanation for his prolonged absence. Cenric must be dead, and Ulfcytel hung his head low at the realisation of it. Now it was Æva's turn to hug him. She couldn't lift him off the ground, but she could provide comfort. In these harsh and brutal times, she felt it was all she could do.

Osbert had by this point moved past her to sit with Eamon, and the two were now exchanging words over the campfire, both men pleased and relieved to see the other. Brandon was sat close by, looking alarmed and curious at the sight of Osbert, but he was otherwise recovering from his ordeal well. She hoped he wasn't just trying to be brave. What they'd been through was truly harrowing, especially for one so young. Perhaps the sight of Edmund humbling Uhtred so decisively had lifted Brandon's spirits. She hoped so. She needed to thank him for that. It had been quite a spectacle, despite the terror she'd felt during their escape and the pitched battle that had very nearly followed. True justice was a rare thing, but she'd witnessed a little piece of it tonight, and it had pleased her. She hoped to see plenty more in the days to come.

"I owe you an apology," said Ulfcytel, his craggy, battle-hardened face oddly soft in the glow of the campfire. "I thought I was doing the right thing by you and Alaric, as in telling you about Ælfric and his past…I didn't expect…"

"I was the one who decided to act on it," Æva said. "You followed me because you cared. That's something I'll always value. And I'd rather you'd told me about Ælfric than keep it all a secret. I deserved to know. For my sake. And for the sake of my Alfred."

Ulfcytel again hung his head in sadness, appearing more troubled than she would have thought at the mention of her and Alaric's firstborn son. "Word is Ælfric took action after we left," he then said, "and soon came under siege for his open loyalty to Edmund. That says something. As dark as his past is...he's doing the right thing in the present."

"I thought the Danes were defeated?" Æva asked, wondering if Uhtred had been lying on their journey south when he'd said the capital had already fallen to Æthelred's Norman hirelings.

"A lot of them, yes," replied Ulfcytel. "Edmund bloodied them up something good at Gainesburg, and we chased them all the way down here...but we think Cnut dispatched a large host south beforehand to deal with Ælfric. It was fortuitous for us. We'd not have been able to take Lundenburg with so many defending it."

"So what are we doing hanging about?" spluttered Æva, wondering if sitting around with this army whilst Ælfric was under siege was part of some grand military stratagem she'd failed to spot. There was no sense in pausing, was there?

Ulfcytel gave her a faint smile, like he'd somehow heard her thoughts and considered them justified. "The king...Edmund even...is awaiting news of the exact size and location of the enemy force. Then we'll act. We remain here because they could be coming north to meet us."

"And Cnut?

"No idea," he shrugged. "The fighting was full on when we stormed New Gate, so he could be dead in the city somewhere. Or he could be on the run...the worst case scenario is he's slipped down south to reunite with what's left of his armies."

"So we just do nothing in the meantime?"

"It might look like that, lady, but we're not. We have won a sizeable victory here, and campaigns often unravel when one side becomes overconfident after winning a major prize. Stopping awhile until we have a clearer understanding of what to do is the right idea."

"But what if Ælfric is about to be overrun?!" objected Æva. "Porteceaster was my home, Ulfcytel, and there are many there I care about! We can't just wait whilst they fight alone against what's left of the Danish horde!"

Ulfcytel sat down by their campfire and beckoned for her to do the same. He looked up when she didn't, his eyes still sad, and so she made the sacrifice of kneeling down upon the drying grass, hoping he'd finally tell her something she'd find useful.

"The only reason for Porteceaster to still be under siege is for the enemy to have not heard about what's happened here," he said quietly. "They'd be foolish to waste men and resources trying to capture it whilst everything they've won elsewhere is taken from them. Lundenburg is more valuable than Porteceaster. It's that simple."

Æva thought on what he'd said, feeling happy at least that Brandon had decided to move closer and sit with her. "You forget what beasts the Danes are," she eventually said. "They could be aware they've lost the capital and decide to vent their blood lust on the good people of Hamptonscir. They have to be stopped!"

"What you say is not impossible, and yet for the time being we await further information. Edmund is on board with it, and besides...plenty of our men need a rest. We've been moving and fighting for weeks. Tonight they must sleep. As should you. You and the boy have been through a lot."

Æva frowned and lifted her hand to the swelling around her left eye. Uhtred had been harsh with her, but such beatings were nothing compared to those he'd meted out to Eamon, who still looked like a walking bruise even now. But was she to just sit and do nothing because of a single bad experience? What she'd endured up north was barely much of anything compared with the ordeal she'd undergone when the Danes had attacked Wiltune. She was stronger than Ulfcytel thought, although she couldn't deny the men in this camp were tired, and with good reason. So many of them were wounded. The fight to retake the capital really must have been something to see. They deserved a rest, at least for tonight. Maybe in the morning, she could take her concerns to Edmund.

The man himself suddenly appeared out of the dark, riding atop some grey, dappled steed and at the head of a fearsome-looking mounted escort. He dismounted quickly, and his warriors did the same, Edmund exchanging a few words with them before they all ambled off with the horses to presumably seek food and comfort elsewhere in the camp. He approached their fire, and Ulfcytel and the others all got to their feet, leaving Æva sitting in the grass until she finally mustered the energy to rise. Edmund was still a king as far as Æva was concerned, and he was due respect, even if she felt like falling asleep right here and right now. It was hard to rest well when you were a captive. Fear did unpleasant things to the mind.

Brandon ran to Edmund and stopped right in front of him. They stared at the other, Edmund looking almost as shy and awkward as Brandon until Æva wandered over and broke the silence.

"My son has something he wants to say to you."

"And what's that?" asked Edmund, his eyes still on the clearly nervous Brandon.

"I wanted to thank you," said the boy, his voice barely more than a squeak. "That's three times you've helped me now. I hope you're not in too much trouble for it."

"Uhtred can't do anything to hurt me," Edmund said confidently, "but you are more than welcome with your thanks, young sir. I appreciate it greatly."

Brandon smiled and turned to Æva, but she was more preoccupied for the moment with how Edmund was looking at her. He seemed nervous at her presence and unable to hold eye contact, which was truly peculiar given how formidable he looked with the firelight dancing and reflecting off his battle-worn armour and that rather remarkable moth brooch he had pinned to his cloak. There was something about his manner that reminded her of somebody else, in a distant time and place, and she wasn't sure if she cared for it. Had something shaken or changed him since they'd last spoken?

"Are you alright?" she asked.

"I am," he said, but she didn't quite believe him. His voice was too quiet, unsure, which again seemed absurd considering who he was and the great deeds he'd only just accomplished. Æva could tell there was something bothering him. Then she realised who he reminded her of. Alaric. He was acting like Alaric, as in when he was young and they were in the early stages of their courtship. He'd been nervous all the time, both fearful and yet desirous of her, and Edmund was giving off much the same air now. She hoped she was wrong. She had absolutely no intention of being with any man now that Alaric was gone, even if that man was as noble and capable as Edmund. Æva's heart was just not in it. She belonged to her husband, and whilst he may have departed to be with God, it made absolutely no difference to her. She was married. That's all there was to it.

"I too wanted to thank you," said Æva, hoping the sound of her voice might somehow change Edmund's peculiar countenance. "What you did…I wasn't expecting it. Uhtred was so cruel and so convinced you'd have to do everything he said because he had me as a hostage. I never thought our liberty could be won so…directly."

She turned when she heard Ulfcytel guffawing to himself behind them. Osbert and Eamon were laughing also, like his mirth was infectious, and even Brandon was smirking, although Æva was quite sure he wouldn't be able to explain why if asked.

"I still wish I'd seen it!" Ulfcytel rumbled joyously. "To have Uhtred acting all smug and thinking he had it all worked out…and then Edmund just bashes his face in and drags him all the way back here!"

Æva smiled and then grinned, unable to hide her amusement. Ulfcytel's description of what had happened was crude but accurate, and whilst she'd been too terrified to consider much at the time other than survival, it was pleasant to think back on how Uhtred's schemes had all combusted so rapidly. The man was a bully, and like all bullies, he'd swiftly come unstuck the moment somebody good and brave and strong had stood up to him. Hopefully, Brandon would see that and draw the right lessons from it. The boy needed a positive male influence in his life now that both Alaric and Cenric were gone.

She turned back to Edmund, relieved to see his previous nervousness had dissipated after enjoying a good laugh. She sensed an opportunity. She could ask him about the situation in Hamptonscir and stress that the Ealdorman Ælfric needed help. He was only in this predicament because he was loyal to Edmund, she could say, and so he was honour-bound to ride south and assist him. It was worth a try. The worst thing that could happen was that he'd say no.

Edmund didn't decline her request, at least not directly. He seemed to be thinking it over, and she fancied she could see some glint in his tired eyes that said he yearned to mount up and ride to face the enemy once more. Then he spoke, and she realised she'd perhaps been wrong.

"I'm afraid the situation is more complicated than I'm at liberty to explain. Rescuing you and Brandon has created another issue that my father needs to set right…but he can't do it with me sitting right here with an army. We must go elsewhere."

"Æthelred sends you away so soon after we've given him victory?" asked Ulfcytel, the bitterness in his question quite easy to understand.

"As I said, it's complicated," Edmund replied. "We'll rest here tonight and move out with the dawn. I have a very specific destination in mind."

"Hamptonscir?" Æva asked, thinking she might try her luck again.

"We're barely twelve hundred strong here, Æva," said Edmund. "We would need more men to lift the siege of Porteceaster, if it is still under attack, which is doubtful."

"But not certain," Æva suggested.

"Of course," said Edmund, "but we will be better able to deal with the remnants of Cnut's forces once our scouts return with more information. Then, lady, you have my word I will do all I can to help the Ealdorman Ælfric."

"So where are we heading to?" That was Ulfcytel, and he sounded almost as confused as Æva. She didn't like the sound of any of this and couldn't understand why they didn't just take some of Æthelred's Normans and smash the enemy wherever they might be. Was war that complicated? Was she missing something, given she was so ignorant of its supposed intricacies?

"Oxenefordscir," said Edmund quietly, the slight shift of his weight from one foot to the other suggesting he'd been giving this some thought. He had a plan and a purpose, Æva could see.

"And why there?" Brandon asked, looking like he'd finally gotten over his nerves.

"You'll all see soon enough," Edmund said. "Let us rest now. These are interesting times, and we'll need to be wide awake to appreciate them."

Æva didn't know precisely what he meant by that comment, and at this point, she didn't care. She was tired, and by the time Ulfcytel escorted her and Brandon to the tent set aside for them, she felt close to collapse. She fell asleep quickly, Brandon also, and her dreams were thankfully few and fleeting, all of them involving a recollection of her time in captivity at the hands of the dastardly Uhtred.

She awoke with the dawn, the sound of activity outside her tent proving difficult to ignore. Brandon was up, complaining about being hungry, so they got dressed and left in search of something to eat.

The camp was now a busy place. Warriors in various states of battle readiness were hurrying to and fro, their bellowed instructions to the other drowning out the delicate birdsong emerging from the surrounding forest. In actuality, this was a very well-orchestrated operation, and in no time at all much of the camp was packed away, the tents and supplies that had been left out all stowed within a multitude of sturdy horse-drawn carts.

Only a few traces remained of what had been here the night before, and even the campfires had been kicked to ash and then covered in earth and leaves for the sake of concealment. Æva was glad one of those things still left was the "cook house", as the men kept calling the tent full of food. They needed breakfast. Brandon wouldn't let her forget it.

She waited in line with a multitude of others, feeling uncomfortable and exposed among so many men she didn't know. Her clothes were in quite a state, muddied and discoloured, and the long sleeves of her cyrtel were starting to fray. Her veil was also dishevelled, and this was by far the worst of it, as Æva's hair was disobedient at the best of times and was now largely exposed to anyone inclined to look. That sent the wrong impression, and her anxiety only increased when she realised many of these men had likely not been in proximity to a woman in months. This had been a mistake. She should have waited in her tent for Ulfcytel or someone to collect her. If only Brandon hadn't been so insistent about his hunger.

Fortunately, nobody laid a hand on her. They were perfect gentlemen, these soldiers, and the worst she received was a few not-so-subtly sideways glances that were obviously intended to get the full measure of her figure. The quartermaster or "cook" or whoever it was handing out porridge also didn't bother her, and he smiled at Brandon before affording him an unduly generous helping. Ulfcytel then decided to appear, flanked by the intense and rather burnt-looking Osbert, and they all ate together on a nearby log, Eamon also dropping in to sit and look as foreboding and unapproachable as always. Æva really wanted to talk to him in private. He'd tried so hard to protect them from Uhtred and ultimately paid for it with an abundance of beatings and a missing ear. She didn't want him blaming himself or thinking he'd failed in his duties somehow. His efforts had been heroic. It was only bad luck that had seen them undone.

Edmund and the dark, hook-nosed fellow called Wulfnoth strutted past, shouting orders for their men to secure their horses and supplies and prepare to march. She glanced at Edmund over her porridge, thinking how confident he seemed as he stood there, hands on hips, his great broad shoulders and huge bearded hammer of a jaw making him look like a man nobody would dare disobey. He suddenly turned, like he'd sensed her gaze, and for a split second their eyes met. He had that same look he'd had last night. The nervous one, but it was only for her. He was a tower of strength and authority for all others, but shy and yielding with her. Just like Alaric in days gone by. She looked away. This was all getting to be rather uncomfortable.

It was fortunate that it did not last. Most of the men had by now formed a long marching column that trailed out behind them to vanish into the woods. Everyone else was taking to horse, and Æva received a steed of her own, as did Brandon. He'd ridden before but was unsure of himself now, so Æva stayed very close just in case she needed to take the reins of the beast he might otherwise struggle to control.

They began to move out, the foot soldiers marching just behind with the baggage train at their rear, the metal of their helms and spear tips catching the morning sun. Æva rode close to the head of the column in the company of Ulfcytel and his wife, Wulfhild. The two women exchanged pleasantries, but neither really knew the other, and Æva presently was too worried about Brandon to be fussed with making new friends. The animal he was on was patient and gentle, it was true, but his lack of confidence didn't bode well.

Edmund appeared and rode towards them, apparently forfeiting his place in the vanguard of the army to assist Brandon. How he'd noticed Brandon was in difficulty, Æva had no idea, but the boy seemed to calm when Edmund pulled up alongside him. They exchanged a few words, Edmund instructing Brandon a little on "how to make friends with horses", and then suddenly they were off, both of them trotting ahead of Æva to take position up front with Wulfnoth and the others.

Æva went to object but then thought better of it. Brandon was getting to be of an age now where he needed the company and instruction of people other than his mother. It would do him good, and from what she could see here, he was actually quite gifted at horse riding now he was more at ease in the saddle. Æva felt a flash of pride surge in her chest. She'd been so intent on protecting her son all this time, and with good reason, but here he was riding alongside a king at the head of an army. It was a strange sight, but no less wonderful because of it.

They were soon well away from their old campsite, the sound of a thousand and more footfalls from the men behind turning to a monotonous, thundering dirge. They were following the flat, aged stones of Watling Street as it trailed north west away from the city, and the day was a pleasant one, the trees to their right and the fields to their left verdant and seemingly joyous 'neath the touch of the springtime sun.

The morning dragged on, and it seemed to take an inordinate amount of time for the sun to reach its height, its golden rays beating down on them with mounting intensity. Æva yearned to get out of these clothes and into something more suitable, but nobody had as yet offered to provide her with anything, and she didn't think any of these gruff, formidable men were of a mind to give her fashion advice.

Only Wulfhild might be able to help, and Æva almost regretted asking her, such was her enthusiasm to assist. Ulfcytel actually looked embarrassed as his wife babbled on about all the clothes she had and how Æva could help herself to whatever she liked. She didn't understand why since his wife was only trying to help, but then Wulfhild herself flushed with consternation and began apologising. Much of her wardrobe was, of course, back in Lundenburg, and she herself hadn't entered the city when they'd retaken it out of fear of encountering the typically irate and unpleasant Æthelred. Æva now felt sorry for Wulfhild. Normally any daughter would leap at the chance to be reunited with an estranged father, especially in times as dangerous as these. She didn't pry any further. With any luck, she'd be able to acquire a change of clothes elsewhere. Somehow.

They eventually turned off Watling Street to take a dirt road heading north, the cool air from the surrounding evergreens providing a welcome respite from the burdensome heat. Brandon was still up ahead with Edmund and looking like he was having the time of his life. He kept glancing back, at his mother but also the marching men behind, and he seemed to draw strength from that, perhaps emboldened with the notion that he was the leader of this army and Edmund merely one of his advisers.

Æva smiled at the idea. It was good for a young man to have ambitions of such a nature, within reason, although she still couldn't bear the thought of him ever being involved in violence. There was always the chance he'd put his energy towards more peaceful pursuits, like life in a religious order. Æva liked the thought of that. He'd be good at it, and there was a poetic justice to it all, given the violence of his conception and the repulsive deeds of his paternity. Perhaps God would make it so.

She turned in the saddle to see Ulfcytel staring straight at her, his expression thoughtful. Wulfhild had ridden on ahead for the sake of speaking with Edmund, leaving Æva and the ealdorman free to talk among themselves.

"The boy seems happy," he said quietly, nodding in the direction of Brandon.

"I hope so," answered Æva. "This past year has been so hard on him. For a time, it felt like we were cursed and that everything was out to get us."

"Well, there's over a thousand double-hard bastards behind us who won't take kindly to anyone or anything trying to get you." Ulfcytel was grinning, but he still had that thoughtful glint in his eyes. Something was on his mind, despite his attempt at humour.

He spoke again, not content to endure the silence. "Brandon has an unusual look," he said. "I can't see anything of Alaric in him, and not a lot of you. Were your parents perhaps gifted with blond..."

"What are you saying?!" snapped Æva, her temper flaring hot and raw. She realised her mistake a second later. Ulfcytel now had a knowing look to him, like he'd made an effort to provoke a reaction and was now closer to the truth because of it.

"I had this conversation with Cenric, you know," he said gently. "He thought I meant harm...that I was suggesting you'd been unfaithful to Alaric and birthed a son not of his lineage. He was very protective of you. He was a good man."

Æva turned away, a scowl upon her face. She thought to end this little exchange and ride ahead to be with Brandon. It would work, in the short term, as she'd be free of her present company, but by her actions she'd simply be confirming Ulfcytel's suspicions for him. She had to face this issue head-on. Brandon had never looked like Alaric, it was true, and it was becoming more and more obvious as he aged that something was off. If Ulfcytel could see it, then others would too, and rumours could be far worse than awkward conversations. She'd endure this one with that in mind.

"You can't tell anyone, especially Brandon."

Ulfcytel nodded at her words, apparently taking them as seriously as she'd hoped. "You don't have to explain anything to me," he said. "I've interfered in your family's affairs enough...I just...I have a big mouth, is what it is. My father used to tell me that.

Told me it'd get me in trouble, and he was right. I'll leave you be, if you wish."

"I don't mind," sighed Æva. "I knew I'd have to talk about this sooner or later. Alaric was dark and broad, and...Brandon isn't. There's a good reason why. You've obviously already guessed it. But it was nothing sordid. When Wiltune was burned... the Danes...they..."

Ulfcytel's eyes widened in shock only to then fill with sadness. "Lord have mercy," he whispered, and crossed himself, his gnarled paw of a hand strangely delicate as he made the gesture. "I don't know what to say," he muttered, "...and Alaric raised him anyway? Had him think he was his true father?"

"He did."

"He must have loved you a great deal." Ulfcytel's statement cut straight to her heart, such was the simple truth of it.

"He did," she again said, her voice quavering. "It was hard for him. For both of us. But he did it, and a fine job he was doing. Not a day goes by that I don't wish he was here."

"You and me both," he said softly. "We all miss him, all of us. Even Edmund, I think, is a little awed whenever I speak of him. This must all be such a great burden for you. If there is any way I can lighten it..."

"You can get me some new clothes," she said quickly. "These are soiled, well, not soiled in the traditional sense, but they are hardly suitable. Uhtred didn't really care if I was comfortable when he was dragging us down from Norþanhymbre."

"I will...and as for Uhtred...I still can't believe how Edmund slapped him silly!" Ulfcytel was laughing again, and Æva joined him. She was determined not to slip into a depression, as talking about Alaric was wont to do, and the memory of seeing Uhtred so insensible was indeed an amusing one. Wulfhild suddenly reappeared atop her chestnut mare, asking what all the laughter was about. Ulfcytel calmed down, claiming it was all "just a joke", as if he'd been caught out doing something he shouldn't. Wulfhild frowned slightly and then smiled. She was probably used to her husband's boisterous antics. Ulfcytel was a good man, and he liked to laugh. Æva could see how he and Alaric had become friends. There was a little bit of Osmund in him, and that could only be a good thing.

They rode through the evening, the men behind still keeping up a vigorous pace. They stopped close to midnight, or what Æva assumed was midnight, since some fast-moving cloud cover had crept in to obscure the moonlight and plunge them into a rather ominous darkness. They had torches, of course, and they used them to make their way off-road and into a thicket of pines, the trees creaking eerily in the wind. A few campfires were then lit and hot food became available, but Æva was again tired and fell asleep beside Brandon whilst he jabbered excitedly about his time with Edmund. She'd have loved to hear all about it, but her eyes were beyond heavy. Tales of horses and armies and how fantastic Edmund was could wait.

She didn't dream, instead enjoying one of the most restful nights she'd had in years. When she awoke, it was past dawn and the forest was full of sunlight, the birdsong carrying clear and far even as the men again hurried about in preparation to depart. She sat up, seeing that somebody had placed a bowl of fresh porridge within arm's reach. Brandon wasn't here. That worried her, and so she took the bowl and ate from it as she walked, asking the first man she came across if he knew where her son was. He made a gesture behind him, a gentle smile upon his face. There was something going on over there. Some kind of gathering. And from what Æva could see, a fair few people found it rather entertaining.

She hurried over, pushing through those men spectating over whatever exactly was taking place. There was a small clearing here, and within it stood Edmund and Brandon both, swords in hand. Æva went to call out, angry and also alarmed at the sight of the boy with a weapon, but she fell silent when she saw his face. He was happy, beyond happy, actually, his look suggesting he thought training with Edmund to be the most wondrous thing in the world to date.

Edmund was very patient, instructing Brandon on how to stand and also move without dropping his guard. Brandon took to it like a fish to water, in part because Æva knew Alaric had already instructed him on the absolute basics some time ago. He was enjoying the attention, that she could tell, and the lesson he was learning would make him feel like a man. He needed that. The days of boyhood would be over soon enough. It was only natural he would want to test his limits.

Æva moved closer, fearing perhaps it was still too soon for Brandon to be holding an actual blade, but as she neared she could see the tips had been blunted, making them effectively useless for anything but training. Edmund looked over and smiled, and Æva nodded back to him, content to allow him to continue. They sparred for a while longer, Brandon now looking like he thought himself the greatest warrior who'd ever walked the earth. It was to his detriment. Edmund knocked him flat on his arse. It wasn't out of malice, and it wasn't a forceful blow, but that was enough. Æva had to intervene.

"I apologise," Edmund said quickly. "I hadn't expected the lad to lose his footing like that."

"Whatever you were thinking, it's gone too far," said Æva, reaching out to haul Brandon to his feet. He refused to take her hand. In fact, he stood up on his own and retrieved his sword, demanding Edmund attack him again. Edmund read the situation well. Training was over. They had a journey to resume.

"You did well today," said Edmund to Brandon, "and we'll try this again later, if we have the chance."

"Why not now?" demanded Brandon.

"We have to prepare to move," replied Edmund, "and I think your mother wants to speak with you."

Edmund ambled off without another word, although his voice continued to carry through the trees, so loud were his shouted commands to the rest of his men. Brandon was frowning, deep and angry, and it was all directed at his mother.

"You shouldn't have interrupted," he said. "Everyone saw it. They'll think I'm weak."

"They'll think you're a boy with a concerned mother," retorted Æva, knowing as she finished her sentence that was the last thing Brandon wanted to hear.

"Exactly! Since when does a warrior have his mum rush in and save him? Father never read me a story like that!"

Ulfcytel appeared from amidst those who'd been watching them. "I know of a story where a mother sought to avenge her son," he said hopefully, "and I think she was even more capable than he was. A terrible foe, indeed."

"What's that story?" Brandon asked.

"It's about a hero named Beowulf," said Ulfcytel. "It's about…"

"I know what it's about," said Æva. "And I don't think bringing up Grendel's mother is particularly helpful. Unless you're suggesting something about me?"

Ulfcytel shrugged. "I'm just trying to help," he said, "and it is a most epic tale…but I'm not attempting to say you're some kind of hideous monster, my lady. Have no fear of it."

Æva laughed, amused at how Ulfcytel looked a shade awkward. He grinned back at her, his face more like a smiling silvered bush, and patted Brandon on the shoulder, informing him that he "had talent" and would one day "slay a thousand Grendels."

They were soon back on the road, Æva this time making sure Brandon kept his horse alongside hers so that he didn't go galloping off to ride with Edmund. He complained, but Ulfcytel provided adequate distraction with a tale of Alaric and how they'd attacked the Danes at Gipeswic and stolen their ships. Æva at first wondered if this was such a good idea, but Brandon hung on every word, and his chest swelled with pride when Ulfcytel spoke on how Alaric had saved his life when he'd been wounded. Æva had heard these stories before when they'd escaped Svienn's siege of Lundenburg, but Brandon had been exhausted then and probably hadn't really understood them, such was his condition. She smiled at Brandon, pleased that he was enjoying himself. It was good he was learning about his father and the hero he was. He could never discover his true lineage. There was no pride to be had there.

It was getting close to mid-afternoon when Æva felt like she recognised where they were. They'd gone off-road a little while ago, the avalanche of men following behind them, and were moving across a wide, grassy plain that was largely featureless aside from the faint outline of a single hill in the distance. It was this hill that gave her an ill feeling, and as they got closer, she felt compelled to ride to the head of the column and confront Edmund. This wasn't a good place, and she'd have answers as to why he'd brought them here.

Edmund was riding in his full armour, and as such much of his face was covered by his helmet, but Æva could still tell it was him from the jutting breadth of his beard and the grey steed he always seemed so fond of. The ever-lethal-looking Wulfnoth was at his right side, as was his habit, and they glanced at her when she rode up on Edmund's left, whatever conversation they'd been having now cut short.

"We're heading for the battle site close to Bernecestre, aren't we?" Æva hadn't felt like wasting time on pleasantries. She'd find out what Edmund intended, and quickly.

"That is correct," answered Edmund. "You know of it?"

"We passed through here when we were heading north to look for you. That place…I didn't want Brandon seeing the remains then, and I don't now."

"They'll all be rotted to pieces," said Wulfnoth coolly.

"But the bones remain," said Æva, "and it's not right for someone so young to see such things."

"He won't be a boy forever," came Wulfnoth's retort.

"He won't, but it's not your place to say that," Æva replied. "He's seen a lot of things, Edmund, and this shouldn't be something else he has to worry about."

"We'll make camp soon," said Edmund, "and come morning, I'll arrange it so you can stay there with Brandon whilst the rest of us search the site. He'll see nothing, but I must confess…"

"Confess what?"

"Like Wulfnoth said, he won't be a boy forever. Many brave and decent men died not far from here, and they were fighting so that lads like Brandon might have a country to inherit. You should impress upon him that reality. Don't shield him from it."

Æva turned away and rode back down the line to resume her spot alongside Brandon, Ulfcytel, and Wulfhild. They continued on in silence, Æva thinking deeply about what Edmund had said. He was right, in a way. Those men had fallen for the sake of a noble cause, and it would be foolish and negligent of her to refuse to inform her son of that weighty truth. She spent some time thinking on this, and when she was finished the sun had nearly dipped below the horizon, leaving the army with nothing to do aside from set up camp close to the base of that accursed hill. She dismounted, Brandon and the others doing likewise, and set to work, feeling she had to pull her weight if she were to continue travelling with these men. She couldn't go home, after all. Edmund and his army were all she had.

They were soon sat by a fire, a forest of tents expanding out and around them in all directions. Wulfhild had arranged it so she'd be able to cook, and something was already simmering away in a great iron pot she'd managed to hang over the flames, the wholesome smell causing Æva's stomach to grumble. Despite this, she still felt on edge. She knew what was out there, as did many of the others, Ulfcytel included. There was a darkness upon these lands now, not the literal darkness they endured presently, but something else. A darkness of the soul. Too many men had died here, and their suffering and hate had left a kind of imprint or echo, one that was still palpable. She'd felt it when they'd come here last time, and she could feel it now. Others seemed to be aware of it, and the men were quieter than usual, like they too were ill at ease over something they couldn't quite identify.

Edmund appeared from out of the shadows, instructing Ulfcytel to come with him, leaving Wulfhild to serve up what had been cooking. It tasted better than expected, and Æva soon felt drowsy. Their tent beckoned, and she ventured into it gladly, yet sleep never came. She tossed and turned, unable to nod off, although Brandon was thankfully free of such burdens and continued to slumber peacefully next to her. She couldn't go on like this. A walk might do her good. She got dressed and slipped outside, as quietly as she could.

The night was cool, and the fire they'd been sitting at had burned down to embers, the red glow shining gently into the surrounding blackness. The camp was quiet, yet something could be heard from a distance off to the west, like men were sporadically calling to each other as they went about some unknown task. Æva strained her eyes against the dark, hoping to discern what was happening, and in time she could make out the outline of the hill, and then something beyond it. Torches. There were men with torches out there, amid the detritus of bones and rusted weapons that made up the battlefield. That didn't make a whole lot of sense. Edmund must be in a strange mood to have left the camp without waiting until morning. She'd find out why.

Ulfcytel wasn't in his tent. Wulfhild was, but she was fast asleep and wouldn't be stirred, despite Æva's rather insistent whispering. She gave up in short order and snuck back outside, noting this time how more stars had thankfully appeared in the otherwise dour sky to provide a modicum of light. Æva made her way through the camp, heading always towards the torchlight beyond. She was soon challenged by sentries posted around the outskirts, but they backed off when they saw who it was, although she wasn't completely sure why. Edmund or somebody must have told them not to bother her, or that she was indeed a lady of noble standing. She requested one of them head back to guard her tent in any case. She didn't want Brandon waking up and finding himself completely alone. It wouldn't be right.

She pressed on beyond the camp, the grass thick and damp and almost to her knees. The ominous feeling she'd felt earlier was present and growing stronger, making her realise she must be getting closer to that terrible place of slaughter. She could see the men just ahead, all of them looking down amid their flickering lights, apparently searching for something. Edmund was there, and so was Ulfcytel and Wulfnoth, wandering hither and thither as if the earth might somehow reveal its secrets simply from being stared at.

She came upon Edmund and reached out for him. That was a mistake. He spun around, his left arm grabbing her by the wrist and bending it back. He realised what he'd done in an instant and released her, his apology repeated and sincere. Æva's heart was hammering, but she wasn't angry. She could see the bones at their feet, and that hateful feeling was now stronger than ever. Edmund would be sensing it too, for she remembered now how he'd fought in this battle personally. It would be difficult for him just to be here, and it was foolish to try and touch a man as he without him being aware. She was the one who should be apologising, and she did. That calmed him. Yet it didn't explain anything about what he'd been doing.

"Are you searching for something?" Æva asked.

"We are," said Edmund, "and I'm sorry if we disturbed you. The work cannot wait. I must finish what we came here to do."

"And what's that?"

"If it's still here, you'll see soon enough."

Edmund wouldn't be questioned any more than that. He waved her off, muttering something about her needing patience, and kept on sifting through the grass, the light from his blazing torch revealing nought but bones and shattered shields. He persisted like this for an hour, ignoring Æva whilst she followed, making her wonder if she should simply head back to camp and try to sleep. If only he would tell her what they were searching for. She could help then. Why shut her out like this?

Despite her better judgement, she remained at his side. Ulfcytel came and went with a search party of around fifteen tired-looking fellows, but he was all business, and once he'd exchanged a few words with Edmund he was gone again. The hours stretched on and on, and nothing seemed to be getting resolved, as this mystery object they were looking for continued to elude them. The darkness was also receding, giving way to a pale, greyish light that brought a blanket of cloying mist rising directly from the earth. Æva didn't know what that was about, but it didn't sit well with her. This was an accursed place, and it didn't look any better with the approaching morning. It was time to go. Brandon would need his breakfast.

She hadn't gone far when she discovered them. They were scattered about alongside more human remains, yet for some reason these bones disturbed her more than anything she'd seen here previously. Animals were so innocent, and horses doubly so, and it was a source of much upset to Æva that men continued to use the gentle beasts for the sake of war. These poor things had certainly endured that sorry fate, and they'd paid for it here, appearing like they'd been either cut to pieces or impaled on spears, such was the state of them.

One of their riders looked like he'd died whilst cradling the head of his injured mount. He was all bones in rusted mail, of course, and his steed was likewise decomposed, but whoever this man had been he'd loved his animal companion a great deal. Æva almost let rip with a sob at the sight of it, the thought of this poor soul giving his last embers of strength to try and help his horse stirring her to tears. A charge had been made here, to break the enemy or stave off defeat for a little longer, she knew not, but it had not ended well. It must have been all so very heroic, as cavalry charges were supposed to be, but that was never much comfort to the frightened animals caught up in them. They'd all rather be off in a meadow somewhere, living their lives peacefully. If only men would follow their example. She couldn't help but think the world would be a more Godly place then.

Æva was turning away from this sorry sight when she fell. The grass broke her fall, but she'd felt a sharp pain across her left shin, making her fear she'd cut herself open on some discarded blade. When she sat up, she could see that wasn't the case, although she had tripped on something, as there seemed to be what looked like a thin wooden pole emerging from the grass just behind her. She rose quickly and tugged at it, but it was held fast, the weight from a nearby horse skeleton pinning it in place. There was something else there, like vivid green cloth, of a different and more vibrant hue than the grass. She took a closer look, discovering that she'd tripped on what appeared to be the banner pole for some kind of magnificent standard. It didn't seem fair to leave such a beautiful thing here, in this awful place. Æva would retrieve it.

She gripped the pole again, this time right at the point she suspected she'd tripped on it. She heaved and heaved, but the accursed wood kept slipping in her grip, and the weight of the unfortunate beast holding it down refused to budge. She thought to call out, thinking Edmund couldn't have wandered too far, but decided against it. Æva wanted to do this herself. Banners like this were usually only carried to signify the presence of somebody of import on the battlefield. That meant this charge had likely been led by such a person, which would explain the intensity of the fighting here. The Danes would have wanted to kill this man, whoever he was, and his banner would have brought them to him like moths to a flame. She wondered why they hadn't recovered it with their victory. Wouldn't such a debased people have wanted to show it off as a trophy of some kind?

Whatever had happened, Æva wouldn't get far if she just stood around thinking. She heaved again, putting everything she had into it, her teeth baring in a most un-lady-like fashion. She was just about to give up and accept defeat when the pole suddenly came free, her own strength causing her to fall sideways as the weight of the dead horse finally shifted. She got up in a hurry and again gripped the pole to drag it further away from the bones, taking the banner with it. She took a step back to look upon it. It was magnificent, and the fabric didn't seem to have been affected at all by its prolonged stay out in the open. It was green, as she'd seen earlier, but of the most brilliant kind, similar to the emeralds her father had once shown her at the market in Wiltune when she was a child. There was something else amidst the green, though, like a stark whiteness depicting some kind of creature, proud and fearsome. She was bending low to get a better look when she heard heavy treads approaching. Edmund was here.

He looked lost, or at least demoralised, but that changed the moment he saw what was at Æva's feet. He rushed to her, calling out for Ulfcytel and Wulfnoth, and they all came running, a gaggle of men at their back. They were tired and breathing heavily, but Edmund had a rare vigour now, and as he stooped to retrieve the banner, Æva could see a certain glint in his eye that confirmed this was indeed what they'd been searching for. He braced his legs and lifted it in both hands, all eyes now gazing upward as the standard fluttered in the morning breeze. It was as Æva suspected. The fabric was entirely without decay, like it had somehow been protected from the elements.

Recognition finally dawned on her as to what this was and why they'd been searching for it. A white dragon upon a ground of green. Not just any dragon, mind. This was the white dragon of Saint Edmund. Only King Æthelred was permitted to carry this, or at least have one of his men carry it for him when he deemed it necessary to take to battle, which was rare enough. But now Edmund had it. That was different. This was a king's banner, and it was now held by a man worthy of it.

"Did you know it was here?" Æva asked Edmund, a little breathless from her exertions.

"I did," Edmund said, his gaze still uplifted.

"How?" she asked. "Did you see your father carrying it when you fought here? And how is it so…untarnished?"

"I saw it briefly," he replied, "and I'm afraid I cannot answer your question as to its condition…I don't know the full truth of it for certain."

"But you do know at least something?" she asked, confused. "How? Somebody told you the banner was still here?"

Edmund tore his eyes away from the dragon on high and stared straight at her, his eyes filled with purpose. "You could say that...and with its retrieval, we are one step closer to something precious."

"Which is what?"

"What else?" Edmund chuckled, the men around him doing the same. "Victory, my lady. We have the banner of England's own saint, unharmed and incorrupt. This is a miracle. And when others hear of it, they will know that God has not abandoned us. They will rise, like the dragon above our heads, and tear England's enemies to pieces."

XXIX

It was just as well Edmund had gone away. Uhtred had taken some calming down, but he'd been relatively easy to deal with, especially when Æthelred had told him his son's absence was a direct result of his "damnable impertinence" towards him. This situation now would be considerably more difficult to handle, and the presence of Edmund and that madman, Ulfcytel, would have rendered it impossible. Æthelred would thank God later if he were somehow able to make sense of it.

The Mercians had come out of the east in some numbers, their banners and assorted heraldry easy to spot from atop Lundenburg's battlements. Uhtred's men had rushed to assemble, presenting a fearsome mass of spear tips and shields towards the newcomers, but Æthelred suspected that was more for show than anything. It was obvious the approaching men were not Danes. The smell would have given them away if they were.

Eadric had then appeared, emerging from the ranks of his host atop a white stallion like he were some kind of returning saviour. Eadgyth rode at his side, and this more than anything got Æthelred's attention. He'd not seen his daughter since he'd married her to Eadric. His heart swelled at the sight of her, and so despite himself he'd rushed from the walls of New Gate, Hereward, Thorkell, and a hundred men-at-arms chasing after him.

A whole litany of questions assailed his mind as he hurried. Where had Eadric been all this time? Had he really betrayed him for the sake of Svienn, and was Edmund right to think he'd actually attacked his forces at Sancte Eadmundes Byrig? If that were true, was Eadric stupid enough to think he could just turn up and ingratiate himself with Æthelred now he'd returned? Was this all some ploy on his part for the sake of winning favour?

Æthelred stopped just in front of Eadgyth's horse. He reached up to take her hand, ignoring Eadric entirely. She took it and allowed her father to help her dismount, her eyes flitting nervously between her husband and Æthelred. He embraced her, and she returned it, albeit with some anxiety, and Æthelred gently put his hands to her cheeks to look her straight in the face. She'd aged, but the lines and wrinkles were not the worst of it. The blue in her eyes had faded. Something was wrong. He'd find out what ailed her and set it right.

"You're shaking," he said softly.

"I'm cold, is all," she replied. "A strange mist settled on the land not a day ago, and it cut right to the bone. I'll be alright."

"I missed you," said Æthelred.

"And I you," came the response, but she said no more than that. Æthelred released her, feeling awkward and a little ashamed in the face of her silence. He shouldn't have fled to Normandy without her. That must have been a bitter pill to swallow, and she'd likely resented him for it. Æthelred understood. He'd try and make amends, in time.

Eadric had by now gotten down from his horse and was making his way over to them like all was right with the world. He fell to one knee, as was correct, and then spoke, his tone suitably obsequious for one looking to address a monarch.

"It stirs my heart to see you again, my good king. Let me begin by explaining..."

"What happened to you last year when we approached Beamfleot?" demanded Thorkell suddenly, his great thunderclap of a voice making Æthelred look back at him in alarm. "You were with us, Eadric, with me and my men as we made ready to get your king to Normandy. Then you vanished. It smacked of treachery. I would have an answer."

Eadric too looked startled, at least for a moment, yet he hid it well, and by the time he'd angled his head to reply to Thorkell, he appeared bereft of fear.

"I could not just flee the country with you all, wise Thorkell," he said, Æthelred frowning at his decision to describe the towering Danish juggernaut as "wise". "For the love I bear my wife, I had to return to Mierċe and see to her safety," he added, breaking eye contact with Thorkell to again gaze up at Æthelred.

"I love your daughter," he said, "but I know I failed you and left you without explanation. For that, I will accept any punishment you see fit to mete out, good king."

"It's true, father," said Eadgyth as she joined Eadric on her knees, her hand clasped around his. "He came rushing back, saying we had to flee lest we be forced to swear allegiance to Svienn. But it was too late. The Danes fell upon us and forced our fealty."

"Did they indeed?" asked Æthelred, his hands upon his hips. "You capitulated to Svienn, Eadric? After abandoning me to begin with?"

"He only sought to protect me," protested Eadgyth, her eyes widening with emotion. "Svienn would have laid waste to Mierċe if we had not feigned loyalty. You know what he was capable of. We had no choice."

"I'm quite sure your husband can answer for himself, daughter."

Eadric stayed as he was, yet he'd turned a shade pale, or paler than he usually seemed at any rate. Chances were he was unsettled by the presence of Thorkell, as was only natural, but he was also perhaps anxious that his reunion with his king wasn't going as smoothly as he may have hoped. Æthelred didn't care. The accusations against Eadric were serious, and his disappearing act wouldn't be justified by claiming he couldn't stand to desert his wife. Eadric had never been the sentimental type. Æthelred didn't think he'd suddenly become so in the past few months.

"It is as my dear Eadgyth says," stated Eadric, finally. "I never intended to leave you, my king, but as our plan to flee the country neared fruition, I found my conscience began to bother me. You gave your daughter to me as wife, and our wedding was one of the proudest days of my life. I could not turn my back on that."

Æthelred frowned, unsure of what to make of his words. "What do you think of all that, Thorkell?" he asked, turning slightly to face the Dane.

"I'm not married," shrugged Thorkell, "and matters of the heart have always confused me. This is your man, king, and your decision. If you wish him dead, then tell me."

Eadgyth suddenly flung herself at her father's feet, imploring him to "show mercy". Æthelred hauled her upright, embarrassed at this increasingly hysterical spectacle, and told her to calm herself. She took a deep, shuddering breath, her cheeks wet with tears, and Æthelred knew then that his daughter had either become an adept actress or was entirely genuine in her concern for her husband. That didn't mean Eadric was telling the truth, but it at least worked in his favour. He commanded him to get up off his knees. There were better ways to discuss these matters, and kneeling in the mud in front of thousands of warriors just wasn't ideal.

They re-entered the city and began the long trudge back to Æthelred's halls. Eadric kept his distance, walking alongside his wife like he was fearful of Thorkell, which was probably true. Æthelred took in his city as they moved, eyeing the inhabitants who eyed him back in return. He'd heard about how they'd cheered Edmund, and for a short time, they'd been happy to see him too, which was quite a novelty for his troubled reign.

He'd enjoyed it whilst it lasted, but the news that a new tax would be levied upon the city and the country in general had brought a subdued mood. Æthelred was, of course, keeping the purpose of the tax a secret, as the notion that Thorkell needed additional payment to help him rescue his daughter from the Duke of Normandy would confuse and anger many. He couldn't be having that right now. He needed Lundenburg secure and its revenues likewise. Once Godgifu was back home, he could reassess. In the meantime, this long-suffering city would have to endure a little more.

Æthelred dispersed his escort as they neared his home, instructing only Hereward to remain whilst he and Eadric talked. They passed through the outer gate and then the courtyard, Eadric looking substantially less uneasy now that Thorkell wasn't with them. When they were inside, he developed a spring in his step, the warmth and familiarity of the place perhaps proving a comfort to him. Eadgyth still looked pale and upset, and she kept sneaking nervous glances at Æthelred and Hereward both, making one think she viewed her father with a great deal of unease. Æthelred frowned at that. He'd been neglectful rather than abusive as a parent. Eadgyth likely just needed time to relax after the hardships of the road. A good feed would help.

Sadly, Cuthbert wasn't anywhere to be found, and the guards standing vigil outside the audience chamber didn't look to be cooks. Æthelred had them open up the doors so that he and his party might enter, and they did so, Eadric marching on past the guards like he still held authority here and couldn't be questioned. Eadric had always been aloof like that with the lower orders, but it was still strange to see him behave as such now. Perhaps old habits just died hard.

Æthelred ambled all the way down the hall towards his throne and took a seat. Hereward moved into position next to him, silent and menacing, and Eadric and Eadgyth simply stood before the throne, as if awaiting judgement. Æthelred bid them sit at the banqueting table. He didn't like how his daughter was looking, and he'd rather she be seated if she were to do anything as dramatic as fainting.

"Edmund tells me you attacked him and his men in Eastengle."

Eadric's lips parted, just a little, perhaps in alarm or at least surprise. "And what would I be doing there? I've been in Mierce much of this time. Why would I be travelling so far afield in difficult days as these?"

"You tell me," replied Æthelred, "but from where I'm sitting, I have two choices, and one of them is to assume my own son is a liar. I'm not willing to do that, so you'll have to think of a better response to his accusation."

"How can I defend myself against an aetheling?" asked Eadric. "And especially when he isn't even here? All I can tell you is that I've not even been to Eastengle since you sent me to Hringmere to ensure Ulfcytel did not survive the ba..."

Eadric's voice trailed off, and Æthelred winced at what he'd nearly let slip. He looked to his right, to Hereward, and it was as he'd feared, for the noble warrior was glowering at Eadric with a mixture of curiosity and contempt. Æthelred thought to kill Eadric, here and now, and thus forever bury the secret of what they'd planned for Hringmere. It might be easier that way. If it became common knowledge that he'd plotted against the legendary Ulfcytel, then his popularity would plummet even further. That wasn't something he could afford in his precarious position. Lips must be silenced.

It was then that Æthelred recalled his own foolishness. Many knew of his troubled history with Ulfcytel, for Æthelred himself had admitted to much of it in these very halls when confronted by the ferocious ealdorman only last year. Edmund had been here to witness it, and so had many thegns and their retainers, all of them shocked to see such an astonishing display. Bloodshed had thankfully been averted, in part due to the actions of Edmund, and he and Ulfcytel had taken off in a hurry, the latter content to leave his vengeance for another day. There would thus be little point in killing Eadric now. The damage was likely done, and it was only the chaos of the months that followed that had probably quashed any further rumours about what exactly had happened at the Battle of Hringmere. People didn't have time for gossip when their lives were at stake. With all the treachery and bloodshed that had assailed them for years, such stories had become stale and repetitious anyway.

"I confess this is a difficult situation for me," shrugged Æthelred, bereft of any option but to state the obvious.

"Then let me help," said Eadric. "You valued my advice once. We kept the realm together, you and I. Do not turn from me now over mere hearsay. Let me serve you once more."

"So you really did swear allegiance to Svienn?" Æthelred had to ask again, as distasteful as it was. He understood many hadn't had much of a choice, but it hurt yet still to think of everyone capitulating just like that. Then again, he couldn't really object. He had fled the country, after all.

"I did, king," replied Eadric solemnly. "For the sake of avoiding further violence and a fight I could not win, I swallowed my pride and took the knee. Mierċe had to be kept safe. Your daughter had to be kept safe."

Æthelred's gaze settled on Eadgyth, and for the briefest of moments he considered going over to her and gathering her up in his arms. It was good to have her back, and he had let her down terribly by leaving her whilst he went away. He'd had few options at the time, what with Lundenburg under siege, yet it still rankled him that he'd done so little and thus forced Eadric to act when he would not. Æthelred was a touch surprised at that. He'd always thought the Ealdorman of Mierċe cold and dispassionate, as these were qualities Æthelred had come to value in contrast to his more short-tempered and vice-inclined thegns. But every man had his vulnerabilities, and Eadric's was his love for Eadgyth. It was a good thing, really. He wouldn't have wanted anything less for one of his daughters.

"You have my thanks for taking care of her," said Æthelred sincerely. Eadric was about to reply when the doors at the head of the chamber again ground open, revealing the rather timid form of Cuthbert. He rushed to the throne, bowing deep and low at its steps. Æthelred interrupted him before the usual grovelling could commence, ordering him to make haste to the kitchens and bring them food and mead. The young steward hurried away, knowing from the king's manner that speed would serve him well in this situation. Æthelred stood up and moved to take a seat next to his daughter. She'd gotten some colour back in her cheeks at the mention of food. It was just as well. He'd been getting more and more worried about her.

Cuthbert returned before long in the company of several others, each man bearing a wooden tray replete with bread and meats and more than a little mead. They set them down upon the table before their betters and stepped back, awaiting further commands. Æthelred waved them off, thanking them for their haste, and they left as quickly as they'd come, the doors closing behind them with the usual cacophony. Eadric ate like he had an appetite, but Eadgyth merely picked at her food, and she soon refused to eat any more, claiming she had no stomach for it. She then turned to her father, her eyes filling with tears. She had something to tell him, and whatever it was, it came from the heart.

"You have to believe him. You NEED to believe Eadric. What he says is true. There was no treachery, none, and there never was, not from him. Edmund must be confused. He always was quick to lose his temper, and if he's been fighting the Danes for so long he could be seeing enemies everywhere. Please, father, you must know how it feels to be so torn inside. I know you loved mother, and no one, not even God himself, could have forced you to abandon her, such was your love. Eadric was in the same position. He…"

"I understand," breathed Æthelred, feeling surprised and emotional over his daughter's mention of his late wife. He could tell she was genuine. This was no act. She loved Eadric, and he loved her, which was something Æthelred hadn't foreseen when he'd originally decided to marry her off to him. Eadgyth had sung a very different song then, claiming the newly minted Ealdorman of Mierċe "had a bad air to him" and that he'd treat her most cruelly. He hadn't cared for her objections at the time, and thinking on it now, Æthelred could see just how different he'd been back then. He was so haunted, by the past and more, and the weight upon his shoulders had crushed him into callousness and sin. He wouldn't be like that with Eadgyth now. This would be a fresh start, for all three of them.

"I have to admit your words have touched me," he said, nodding to his daughter and Eadric alike. "There was so much confusion and hurt when I decided to leave the country…and I can see now that I asked you, Eadric, to do things that were impossible for any man to do without breaking his heart. I only wish you'd spoken with me first. You could have, you know."

"It's a hard thing to approach a king with disobedience," said Eadric as he dabbed at his mead-sodden lips with his sleeve.

"That may be," said Æthelred, "and yet I want you to know that time is over. I'm of a different mind, and I intend to be a different king. I will still ask things of you, Eadric, for there are many matters that will need attending to in the days ahead…but you need to know you can confide in me. You both can."

"And what prompted this change of heart?" asked Eadric curiously.

"Many things have happened since we last spoke in-depth, you and I. Would you believe me, for instance, if I told you that the son of our Ealdorman Ælfric held the key to understanding my dreams? That he helped ease my troubled conscience and close a door on a turbulent past?"

"You mean Alaric?" asked Eadric, a brief shake of his head signalling disbelief.

"Indeed, Alaric," affirmed Æthelred, "and yet that is a topic for another time. Just know that things are different now. I feel…better."

Eadric nodded his head, slow and measured, his attempt at feigning understanding failing miserably, given the confusion in his pale eyes. "But what about Edmund?" he asked, sounding almost fearful. "If he thinks I had some hand in whatever it is he's decided I did, then he could seek to do me har…"

"No, no, think nothing of it," interjected Æthelred. "He's been sent away, and I won't be inclined to call him back until I can correspond with him further and get his assurances that he won't make trouble. He's very dear to me…yet he has much to learn still."

"You can't let him hurt Eadric," pleaded Eadgyth yet again.

"And he won't," soothed Æthelred, sliding his hand across the table to place the tips of his fingers upon hers. "I have everything under control, and many things are to be forgiven and forgotten."

"Oh?" asked Eadric. "There are more things you would discuss with us?"

"Not necessarily with you," said Æthelred, "although Edmund has convinced me to forgive the actions of the thegns, Sigeferth and Mor…"

"They got your firstborn son killed!" blurted Eadric, his eyes turning sharp. "That meeting with Thorkell would have gone smoothly if they'd not come charging in with that army of theirs! It was a disaster, my king!"

"One I have had much time to think on…which is why I say Sigeferth and Morcar are to be left alone."

"I will of course obey you in this, but if I could just understand what has led you to…"

"It's many things," snapped Æthelred, feeling surprised at his sudden anger. "They have always been close to my son," he continued, calmer this time, "and I would not alienate him by taking revenge. I have forgiven you, Eadric, for your disobedience and your capitulation to Svienn, as so many others did the same for the sake of their own survival. I will thus forgive Sigeferth and his brother."

"And what do they make of this forgiveness?" asked Eadric, his eyebrows raised.

"You can ask them yourself," answered Æthelred. "They were with Edmund on his campaign, and he's left them here in Lundenburg, along with Eadwig, so that they can attend the assembly I have planned."

"Assembly? Plans? Can I help somehow?"

"Yes, you can attend and be the gentleman I know you can be," said Æthelred with a smirk. "I've invited so many…all those notables who capitulated to the Danes in my absence. I will lavish them with food and drink and make it clear the past is precisely that: the past. We can start anew. Born again, almost."

"With Sigeferth and Morcar?" Eadric asked, like he was somehow having trouble understanding what was being said.

"That is correct."

"And Edmund?"

"My son may not be there," sighed Æthelred, "for I fear the wounds from his recent altercation with the Ealdorman Uhtred are too fresh. So do not fear, Eadric, Edmund will not be coming to bury his sword in your vitals just yet."

Æthelred leaned back in his chair, chuckling at his joke, if it could be called such, but Eadric and his wife did not see the funny side and continued to stare at him, uneasy.

It didn't matter. Æthelred was king, and he wouldn't be dissuaded from this. If Eadric wanted Sigeferth and Morcar dead, he'd have to wait until nature, or God, granted that request, because Æthelred would have no hand in it. They were lucky, those two, in that they had Edmund to intercede for them. In his heart of hearts, Æthelred still hated them, in part because of what had happened to Æthelstan, sure, but also because of how both he and Edmund had always warmed to them. They'd tried to undermine Æthelred's role as a father, and ultimately the web of influence they'd spun over his sons had resulted in tragedy and death. Æthelred wouldn't be getting over that in a hurry. But there would be no bloodshed. He wouldn't let Edmund down. Æthelred might lose him altogether if he did, and that would break his heart all over again. He needed him.

Eadric finished eating, clearing what was on his plate until nothing remained but crumbs. Æthelred bade them leave, granting Eadric permission to take up residence in the old quarters he'd inhabited here previously. He bowed before departing, all smiles and gratitude, and Eadgyth did the same, but Æthelred rose and embraced her, assurances and words of comfort spilling from his lips. He wasn't sure if it had the intended result, as she kept up with that worried look she'd had this entire time, but it was important to make the effort. She'd soon realise nobody could hurt her husband, and that they were all safe to resume their duties as they saw fit.

They eventually left, and Æthelred sat alone, save for the continuing presence of Hereward. Æthelred looked over at him and smiled, pleased with how he'd handled the situation with Eadric and of a mood to talk, but Hereward appeared very much like a man who was fixated on his duty rather than socialising. It was a shame, but Æthelred understood. They all had their duties, formal and personal, and Æthelred was satisfied, for the moment, that he was living up to his. Challenges lay ahead, yet if he carried on like this, he'd be able to face them, of that he had little doubt.

****

Eadric shut the door to his chambers and locked it. He stooped to the keyhole and listened, his wife waiting patiently beside him. There was nothing. The old fool of a supposed king hadn't even arranged a guard to spy on them. This was perfect. And it had all been so easy. Fortune was smiling on him, and he was elated in the glow it cast.

He turned around, content that they were secure. His old quarters were as he remembered, and they were free of the strange reek that had settled over the rest of the complex. Eadric wasn't entirely sure what that was about, thinking the aroma reminiscent of badly roasted meat and stale sweat, but he suspected it had something to do with the prolonged Danish occupation. This room was unmolested, and his bed was as it should be, as were the rushes upon the floor and the various tapestries he'd arranged here when he'd first ascended to the noble position of ealdorman. All was well.

The events that had led to his return had not been easy. When King Svienn had suddenly died in Gainesburg, Eadric had been disgusted and uncomfortable over Cnut's reaction, and with good reason. The young Dane had moped around, wasting time whilst being nursed by that idiot, Østen. Eadric had no patience for that, so he'd made himself scarce, thinking his talents would be put to better use in Lundenburg. He'd been quite correct, for upon his arrival they'd received word of the vile Ælfric and his rebellion in Hamptonscir. Eadric had leapt at the chance to put it down, and it hadn't taken much wrangling to convince Jarl Knud to hand over a portion of the garrison so that he could lead it south. Victory would be theirs, Eadric had said, and Cnut would be happy it had been won through the joint efforts of Saxon and Dane both. That was the future, as King Svienn would have wished.

But Ælfric had fought hard, and by the time they'd got him encircled in his stronghold at Porteceaster, he was well-supplied and defiant to a fault. Eadric had ordered his Danes forward to assault the walls, but each time they were hurled back with blood and losses aplenty. Eadric hadn't known what to do. He'd raged at his captains, telling them Ælfric was just an old man in a fortress and that Danish honour demanded he fall. They'd spluttered excuses, but then more news had arrived, news that had given Eadric an opportunity to escape his failing campaign and seek advantage elsewhere: Cnut was defeated at Gainesburg, by one "Edmund Ironside", no less, and Æthelred was marching on Lundenburg after seizing Beamfleot. Eadric wouldn't risk his life by fighting the father and the son both. It was time to reassess.

He'd abandoned his men in the darkness of night, taking his best horse and galloping back to Mierċe as fast as he could. He'd known he'd have to again ingratiate himself with Æthelred if he were to survive this, and his daughter was the way to do it. She hadn't wanted any part of it, naturally, but Eadric had soon convinced her. He could be very convincing. Especially when those he wished to influence already feared him.

Eadric ceased his contemplation of recent events and brought himself back to the present. He snapped his fingers at Eadgyth and gestured towards the bed. She responded at once, sitting down upon the mattress to remove her riding boots.

"You did well today," said Eadric, his arms folded and his back against the door. "For a moment there, I thought we might fail," he continued on, uncaring as to whether his wife had anything to say for herself. "But I suppose it went as I'd expected...he was vulnerable to you, and your tears...a perfect display."

"I'm so pleased you approve," whispered Eadgyth, her insincerity stark and obvious. Eadric frowned. He thought to strike her, as he usually did when she displeased him, but decided against it. It was one thing to behave as such when back at home, but as foolish as her father was, these were still his halls and he'd take action if he suspected his daughter was being abused. Caution was the better strategy here. He'd forgo teaching his wife proper respect until they were again in Mierċe.

And what a wife he had. She was a fine-looking woman, blonde and pale, like Eadric, albeit with the usual assets that any lady should possess. He watched her whilst she undressed, noting how long it took for her to remove her hooded travelling robe and her long-sleeved cyrtel. He always made sure she dressed heavily, even in the summer months. He didn't want her attracting the gaze of others, as her face was wont to do, and he had things to hide. The bruises, for one, would draw the eye, and that was a headache he didn't need, least of all now.

He could see them well enough in the present moment. They ran up her back; ugly blemishes that Eadric was all the same appreciative of. She had a mouth on her still, as a daughter of a king naturally would have, but Eadric was owed respect and would never desist until her spirit was suitably broken. He felt like he'd come close to achieving that these past couple of years. He had gotten her to lie to her own father, after all. She'd proven herself valuable. It was perhaps a pity Eadric still wasn't of a mind to reward her.

Eadgyth slipped into the bed and lay on her back, her eyes open and fixed on the ceiling. She was shivering and clutching the blankets over her breasts, but Eadric knew it wasn't from the cold. It had always been like this between them, and as he unfastened his belt and removed his breecs, he wondered if things would ever change. Would she learn to love him someday? What if he became gentle, or experienced some kind of epiphany like her idiot father had? Would she think fondly of him then, or perhaps welcome him to their bed as he'd heard other women did with their husbands?

Eadric decided upon mounting her that he didn't actually care. Eadgyth was an asset, a trophy, one that he'd been awarded, as was just, and that he'd use and exploit as he saw fit. The thought excited him, even more than her pallid touch upon his skin, and Eadric suspected there and then that he was indeed blessed. Everything went his way. It always did. He looked out for himself, and fate rewarded him, over and over, for his strength and wisdom. It would always be thus with men of destiny and power, and poor Eadgyth here, not to mention her gullible father, would always find themselves outmanoeuvred, used, and ultimately discarded.

Something unexpected then happened. Eadgyth looked right at him - a rarity when performing her wifely duties - but the anger in her eyes spoke to something, triggering a memory Eadric would rather not have. Her bastard brother, Edmund. Eadric remembered how he'd looked at him, back when he'd led his men in the attack at Sancte Eadmundes Byrig to save Svienn from his wrath. Edmund had wanted to kill him, as he'd already killed so many, and his fury would not be bound by mere words and platitudes. He'd be back, and so Eadric was in serious danger, despite Æthelred's assurances to the contrary. Something had to be done. If those two fools, Sigeferth and Morcar, were really here, they'd be almost certainly working for Edmund and would report Eadric's presence to him the moment they learned of it. That wouldn't do. Eadric would strike first.

He pulled away from Eadgyth and sat upon the edge of the bed, his shoulders hunched and troubled. She ignored him, likely relieved to be free of him. He cared not. He had to get to work now. Everything he'd done in his years at court had been focused on one goal: isolating the king from those who might help him, his sons included. Svienn's invasion had disrupted that long-term stratagem, and in facing the fire and bloodshed that followed, the aetheling, Edmund, had proven himself a man with an iron resolve. He was too much of a threat, and so he must be isolated, step by step, until his power could be constrained. It was all so clear. Eadric knew what he must do.

He rose and got dressed, his breecs still damp from their long journey. He left the room, locking Eadgyth within lest she get any strange ideas and go wandering. Eadric couldn't afford any mistakes now, not with her and certainly not with her murderous brother. Action was required, and Edmund's long reach had to be cut back, permanently if possible. Eadric would start with his allies. He'd start with Sigeferth and Morcar.

XXX

They pushed and pushed again, the splinters from the hull cutting into their hands. They kept at it, giving it their all to force the great wooden hulks backwards into the churning waters. Their weight ground against the shingle, the sound harsh upon the ear, yet not one man uttered so much as a single complaint amidst their labours. They knew what was at stake. Either they got these ships back into the water, or they were all dead. Those pursuing them would make certain of it.

Cnut glanced up, blinking the sweat from his eyes. He could see the smoke to the south intensifying, spreading out from beyond the long grasses and the old coastal road, which meant the Normans were getting yet closer. He'd suspected at first that they were solely after him, as was only logical, but as he and his band of survivors pressed further into Lindesi, he could see their pursuers were eager to vent their frustrations upon the local population. Æthelred must have discovered how Lindesi had assisted them after the battle at Gainesburg. Now he was having his Norman hirelings take revenge. Cnut understood. He would have done the same.

The first of the ships had reached the water. The men roared in triumph and pursued it, pushing it further out as the sea crept up to their knees and then waists. Cnut smiled at the sight of them, sharing their joy. When they'd fled Lundenburg, they'd been in disarray, and for a time he hadn't known how to proceed, thinking a proper course of action would be to somehow sneak past Æthelred's armies and reunite with the Danish host allegedly led by Eadric in the South. The Normans behind them, however, had not let up, and Cnut's people had been pushed further and further north in a bid to avoid detection. It had been humiliating, exhausting, and he and his band had spent more time hiding in ditches or skulking in pine woods than he cared to admit. It was almost all over now. Cnut would escape. Then he could plan anew.

His back felt like it was breaking by the time they'd got the second and final ship into the sea. The vessels were now both bobbing up and down amid the surf, almost like they were raring to go after having been left here when Cnut had been shipwrecked on this very beach after escaping from Gainesburg. It was fortuitous how they'd been undisturbed and unharmed in their absence. The locals must have worked out who they belonged to, and in their loyalty decided to leave them be. It was unfortunate they were paying for it now.

"Let us make haste," said Østen breathlessly, the sea up to his thighs. "We may have just two ships, but once we're back home, we can prepare revenge! The English will come to regret our escape, that I tell you, my king!"

Cnut grinned, pleased by Østen's brave words. The others felt the same, and they all rushed into the sea to haul themselves aboard their ships. Cnut grabbed an oar and began rowing, his rhythm naturally synching with the rest of the crew, their course taking them out east and away from the beach. They had lost much, a whole kingdom, and many of their brethren would never return home, but they were alive. Cnut could work with that.

He realised then that was the only thing he had to feel happy about. The swiftness and sheer enormity of his defeat weighed heavily on his heart, and the more he thought about it, the more blame he was inclined to put on his own shoulders. He'd made mistakes. He really had, and his first had been in sending so many warriors away on the flotilla that had borne his father's body back to Denmark. His second had been letting his grief blind him to how vulnerable he was in Gainesburg, and his third had…well…he likely couldn't be blamed for the loss of Lundenburg. The enemy had done something, some trick or treachery, that had allowed them inside the walls, and Cnut couldn't have been prepared for that. It should have never gotten to that point, anyway. The Norman fleet should have been intercepted before it even reached the Temes. Somebody had made a mistake with that, and it wasn't Cnut.

He spied a figure towards the stern, seated yet hunched over. Whoever it was wore a full robe, heavy and hooded, their face largely hidden. The warriors rowing nearby were ignoring him, like he'd never come aboard and was now invisible, which in itself provoked Cnut's interest. He didn't think he'd seen him on the journey up here. He'd solve this mystery right now.

Cnut stood up, allowing another to take his place at the oars. He strode towards the back of the ship and stopped in front of the hooded figure, his hands upon his hips.

"Who are you?" Cnut asked, a few of the men peering back at him at the sound of his voice. The figure looked up, the motion revealing at least some of his face. Their eyes met. Sharp eyes. Very sharp, possessing a hint of either brilliance or madness. Cnut reached forward impatiently and wrenched the man's hood back. Dark hair, or at least darker than most others on the ship, reaching down to his shoulders and very much needing a wash. Cnut recognised him. This was the abbot, or something of the kind, that Eadric had always been so fond of. Cnut remembered him from when he'd interrupted their supposed execution of Osbert. Ælfmær was his name. Abbot Ælfmær. The traitor, to his own kind anyway. Cnut would have words with him.

"How did you even end up here? I did not see you in the flight from Lundenburg."

Ælfmær twisted in his seat, everything about him suggesting he was more than a little uncomfortable. "I'm good at keeping a low profile," he said quietly, the answer entirely unsatisfactory as far as Cnut was concerned.

"That doesn't tell me anything, so you will tell me now how you came to be with us. Otherwise, I will have you cast into the sea."

The threat worked, for Ælfmær began to tremble, his body shaking so violently Cnut wondered if they should throw him overboard anyway lest he cause them to capsize. "I-I-I-I w-wasn't in Lundenburg when it fell," he finally blurted out. "I left when Eadric went south…I-I didn't feel safe there, with my own…"

"Your own kind?" asked Østen, appearing at Cnut's side.

"It is true," Ælfmær replied grudgingly. "Many of my people wish me dead for what I did at C-C-Canterburie. I could not be surrounded by such men, as I would have been in Lundenburg. Your father saw fit to guard me…he saw my value, but…"

"But I don't?" Cnut couldn't recall his father speaking of this man, but he had heard elsewhere that the abbot had done something to ensure Canterburie fell to Thorkell, which meant every Englishman with a scrap of honour would want him dead. Just what schemes this Ælfmær had worked to ensure the city's capture was presently a mystery. Cnut felt that he'd like to find out.

"What exactly did you do at Canterburie?" he asked. The abbot smiled slightly, the look base and unlikeable, as if he were reliving fond memories that were a source of pride to him.

"They were fools," he said quietly, Cnut leaning forward slightly so he might yet hear him. "They wouldn't listen to me…the archbishop…that great stupid ox, Ulfcytel, and his one-eyed Dane killer, Alaric…none of them understood how we were being punished for our sins. It was up to me to make them see. It was up to me to allow Thorkell in."

Cnut's face curled into a scowl. This man was insane, and so he wondered how useful he could possibly be, even if his father had apparently seen some utility in him. "Get to the point," he barked. "Tell me how you helped Thorkell overcome the walls! What did you do?!"

"Canterburie's defenders could not be bested by brute force," said Ælfmær, still with that disturbing smile. "Thorkell tried, once and then twice, and each time he was forced back. I had supporters. Men who knew the will of God, and men who knew how to establish contact with the Norsemen. A deal was made, you see…we'd open up the city from the inside, and Thorkell would come in and take the garrison by surprise."

"And you managed that?" asked Østen, his disbelief obvious. "How? Wasn't the place brimming with warriors all up for the fight? With the mighty Ulfcytel leading them?"

"Most on one side, defending one direction, facing the horde," said Ælfmær. "No gate was unguarded, true, but I knew ways…secret ways…into the city, and we opened them, and on our signal, Thorkell came sweeping in. For a time, I thought…the defenders…they…even when attacked from behind, they…"

"They fought on," said Cnut, feeling a flash of admiration. "Even when your treachery bore fruit, they fought on. That disturbs you?"

The abbot frowned at the question, his eyes darting from side to side in anxious confusion. "They were sinners!" he reiterated. "And all of them deserved judgement, and judgement came! My conscience is clear. I did the Lord's work. Your father saw that. That's why he protected me."

Cnut stared at him a little longer in silence, wondering just what was to be done with this "man" who was so very treacherous. Was it all an act? Was he actually mad enough to think he'd done the right thing by his own people, or was this a facade for something else? And how had he joined up with them as they passed through Lindesi? That question also warranted an answer.

"You hid out in Lindesi, then?" Cnut inquired. "And when you saw us fleeing the Normans, you snuck in among us? Why?"

"Lindesi was loyal to you and your father," said Ælfmær. "I felt I'd be safe there and able to find some solitude. But when I heard about Gainesburg…and then Lundenburg…and then I saw you…and with the Normans burning everything…"

"You feared for your life, yes," acknowledged Cnut with a nod, "but that still doesn't explain how I failed to even notice you join us."

"I did," said Østen suddenly, "and I'm sorry if this has created any confusion between us. As the abbot admits, your father did see a use for him, as he did for any Englishman willing to come over to his side. He'd originally given me the task of seeing he remained alive…Eadric took an interest in him, and we agreed to stash him in some abbey in the middle of nowhere. I thought he'd be safe…but that Osbert fellow somehow found out about it and tried to kill him. I admit I lost track of the abbot after your father died. My mind…my judgement…it was on other things."

"But you allowed him to join us and didn't see fit to tell me?" Cnut wasn't trying to be harsh on Østen. He just wanted to be clear on what had happened.

"I honestly didn't think it was an issue," he replied. "As I said, your father was always eager to build bridges with any man who would at least submit to him. He thought they'd help bring reconciliation between our people and the English…"

"This lunatic who everybody hates? He thought the English would see him with us and follow his example?"

"It does seem strange when you put it like that," shrugged Østen. "I obeyed your father's wishes, that's all I can say. If you are of a different mind, then command me now. I will see it done."

Ælfmær began to shake again, his eyes widening with panic at the prospect of being thrown into the sea. Cnut thought about it for a while, wondering also what his father had really seen in this man. He could understand bringing Eadric on side, as he held a level of power and influence they couldn't afford to discount. Ælfmær, however, was something else, and it wasn't just because he'd betrayed so many. He genuinely believed God wanted to punish the English, and that his instrument was Thorkell. Cnut wouldn't presume to speak for God, but he knew Canterburie had been a great and holy city, and so for God to decide to have it levelled just because he was annoyed at the general sinfulness of the population was more than peculiar. It was a madman's kind of logic, and there was no telling what other notions a madman might develop and decide to act on. Ælfmær was therefore dangerous, and he had no place at Cnut's side.

Cnut looked west, across the stern and towards the rapidly receding shoreline. More smoke lay over the horizon, signifying Æthelred's ongoing wrath upon Lindesi. The English king would reduce the region to rubble, he suspected, undoubtedly to set an example to others. None of that could be helped now. Their ships were making good time, and the weather was otherwise temperate, which bode well for the journey ahead. Cnut waited a while, ignoring both Ælfmær and Østen as they stared at him. He'd let them ponder what was on his mind. When they were a suitable distance from the beach, he'd make his thoughts clear enough.

A few more minutes passed before Cnut deemed it was the right time to strike. He made a lunge for Ælfmær and heaved him up by the scruff of his neck, the poor man protesting profusely. Østen said something, out of surprise rather than anger, but Cnut ignored him, and with a little effort, he'd soon wrestled the struggling Ælfmær over the side of their ship. He made a more than sizeable splash as he hit the water, and Cnut initially wondered if he'd been wearing something heavy without his knowledge, so rapid was his disappearance beneath the waves. He resurfaced quickly, coughing and gabbling, his repeated shrieks about not being able to swim falling on uncaring ears. The men at their oars laughed, amused by the spectacle, as did Cnut. It was good to rid themselves of those who were useless. Only the strong would be of worth now.

Østen, however, was uneasy. He kept looking at the abbot and then at Cnut, his frown pronounced as though he didn't agree with his king and what he'd done. Cnut shook his head, uncaring as to what his friend thought. Ælfmær was a treacherous fool, and it was no great loss to dunk him into the sea where he'd at least have the comfort of knowing his body might eventually wash up on English soil. Cnut could think of far, far worse ways to deal with men such as he. This method, if anything, was a mercy. It was certainly less dramatic than what the English would do to him, should they have ever caught him.

Then Ælfmær said something of note. He'd ceased his raving and begging and begun howling something quite specific, over and over, even as the waves endeavoured to wash over him. Cnut peered back at him and angled his head against the breeze, hoping to discern the abbot's words. He kept mentioning a name, that being Edmund, but also something about "his remains" and where to find them. Cnut shook his head again and turned to Østen, confused. Østen must have had sharper ears than he, for his expression was very much alarmed.

"He's saying he knows where the remains of Saint Edmund are! This is too good an opportunity to miss, my king! If you wish to re-conquer England, having such knowledge could be invaluable!"

Østen spoke the truth. This really was too good an opportunity, especially if Cnut were to return to England, as intended, and settle scores with its people. He thus gave the order to his oarsmen to reverse their rowing so their vessel could double back and retrieve the now very much drowning Ælfmær. By the time they'd got him back onboard and had resumed course, he was weakened by his ordeal, his words proving difficult to comprehend whilst he insisted on coughing up yet more seawater. Cnut didn't have the patience for it. He again laid hands on him and flipped him over, wrapping his arms around his stomach in a reverse hold. He then pulled the unfortunate man into him, rhythmically, so that any water in his lungs or anywhere else had little option but to vacate through his mouth. It made an awful mess, and by the time it was over the abbot was again on the deck, his lips and beard flecked with watery vomit. Cnut kicked him before he could pass out. He'd have his secrets, and then decide his fate.

"You treat him harshly, my king."

Cnut glared at Østen, annoyed by the criticism. He was just formulating some kind of reprimand when Ælfmær suddenly spoke, his voice wet and sickly. "I know where Saint Edmund is buried," he said, slowly between breaths, "and I will help you find him…if you permit me to remain at your side."

"How did you know the saint's remains were of interest to me?" asked Cnut. His father had never taken this man with them when they'd accosted Sancte Eadmundes Byrig. There was no way for him to know.

"Everyone heard of the battle at the monastery that you'd been told housed his remains," replied Ælfmær. Cnut now felt foolish. Of course rumours would have spread, particularly after they'd set the place on fire and several hundred angry Englishmen had tried to kill them for it. It was the way of things, and Ælfmær hadn't needed to be physically present to understand what had happened.

"And what do you expect me to do with these remains, should I find them?" asked Cnut.

"Whatever you wish," spluttered Ælfmær, now hauling himself into a sitting position. "Many of the English will think them lost thanks to your father's actions…if you discover them intact, it could help legitimise your claim as king."

"My claim is dust and ash," snapped Cnut bitterly. "No Englishman will follow me…they must be broken, by force, before they accept me as their rightful ruler, and even then, many will die before they can be made obedient."

Ælfmær chuckled, his mouth twisting into a cruel, lopsided grin. "Some yes, perhaps many, and yet others will be in awe if you rediscover the saint…they will take it as a sign from God that you are favoured."

"A sign?" asked Cnut. "They'll think I discovered the saint's bones because it was God's will? That would be a lie, wouldn't it?"

"If it helps you achieve your goals, why would you object?" Ælfmær shrugged with that last comment, and Cnut stared at him, knowing now more than ever that this man was about as holy as any other grasper and liar he'd been unfortunate enough to meet. It repulsed him, and for a few moments, he seriously considered taking his head, such was his offence. Østen then leaned in and spoke gently into Cnut's ear, his wisdom, as usual, proving difficult to argue with.

"He's a snake, it's true, but I detect no lie in him. Obtaining the bones of Saint Edmund would indeed make an impression on the English, one that couldn't help but strengthen your claim to rule them."

Cnut nodded and turned back to Ælfmær. "Why was the saint not at the monastery where he was supposed to be?" he demanded, thinking Ælfmær should have the answer if he already knew so much on the subject.

"It was the Ealdorman Ulfcytel," answered Ælfmær weakly. "He had them sent away from Eastengle just before Thorkell invaded his lands. He tried to keep it a secret, but people in the Church gossip like any other."

"And he was the only one involved?" asked Østen.

Ælfmær shook his head. "No, he had help…the two thegns, Sigeferth and Morcar, assisted him in relocating the saint to an abbey in the Five Boroughs. They tried to keep it to themselves, but…like I said…"

A memory began to form in Cnut's mind. He remembered his time at Sancte Eadmundes Byrig, specifically how his father had questioned the monks there prior to execution. One monk had cried out, mentioning Ulfcytel and Sigeferth both, although the name of the former had only served to enrage his father and speed the monk's rather untidy demise. Cnut could recall thinking the bloodletting was foolish and unnecessary, and he was pleased he'd now been proved right. He then realised his pride was unwarranted. It had been his father who had conquered England to begin with, just as it had been Cnut who had lost it. There was no escaping that, even with this new knowledge brought to light.

"You do me a service with these insights," admitted Cnut grudgingly. "So serve me yet again, good abbot, by telling me where exactly Sigeferth and his ilk put Saint Edmund's remains."

Ælfmær's eyes widened, his lips parting in apparent shock. He began to stutter, and by the time he'd finished his reply, Cnut was again angry and very much inclined to throw him back into the sea.

"I-I-I c-c-can't," he said, "n-n-not without assurances that you won't just k-k-k-k-KILL m-m-me once I tell you!"

"And if you don't tell me, I'll kill you right now."

Cnut's wasn't messing around. He wanted that information, and the abbot's whining was getting tiresome. Unfortunately, the threat must have been more terrifying than he'd thought, or the abbot was weaker than expected, as he was now passed out, flat on his back, a trickle of something that certainly wasn't seawater emerging from between his legs. Cnut wrinkled his nose in disgust.

"I suppose that settles matters for the time being," chuckled Østen.

"Does it?" asked Cnut, turning to face him. "When I ask somebody a question, it's because I desire an answer. His fear of me is irrelevant, as is his desire to keep his life."

"Not to him, clearly."

"Just what are you suggesting, Østen?"

Østen looked Cnut straight in the eyes, his expression now serious. "The abbot values his life, as all men do. There is nothing unusual in that. If he has the information he claims to have, then we must get it from him in a way that ensures we receive the full truth, and nothing else."

"I'm not sure I understand."

"What I mean, my king, is that we can't threaten or torture it out of him. There'd be nothing to stop him from simply lying to us then, especially if he thinks we're going to kill him anyway. This is one instance where a gentle touch will prove more fruitful than a clenched fist."

"Are you suggesting I don't know that?" Cnut demanded.

Østen broke eye contact to nod in the direction of Ælfmær. Cnut turned to look at him, seeing there and then what a ruin of a man he was, and partly from Cnut's hand. Østen was right, again. If the abbot really did know the location of Saint Edmund's remains, he'd need to feel like he had a good reason to share that information. Force wouldn't help, as in his panic and resentment, the man could give them any number of falsehoods just to see them thwarted. A gentle touch, as Østen said, may very well be the better choice here.

By the time Ælfmær was back on his feet, the day was spent, the darkness that fell on them as black and impenetrable as anything Cnut had seen in years. They ignored the abbot and rowed on, allowing him to rest and regain his strength, his habit of screaming, sobbing, and wetting himself now thankfully a thing of the past. Cnut looked up at the sky, hoping to spy the stars, any stars, that might aid them in their efforts at navigation. There was nothing there. Just a blanket of clouds, impenetrable, or what Cnut assumed must be a blanket of clouds, given it was so dark they couldn't even see that. It was like there was nothing up there, what had once been the sky instead replaced with a void, inscrutable, enveloping, pressing down upon the whole world. He didn't like it, and morning couldn't come soon enough.

When the sun began to thankfully rise in the east, they were still no closer to having a clear idea of where they even were, let alone where they ought to go. The grey, unwelcoming sea stretched on and on around them in all directions, expanding to the horizons in apparent perpetuity. Their second vessel was still with them not far off their port side, but they also were largely clueless on their location. All they could agree on was that they were east of England, which given the location of their departure, would mean they'd just need to keep heading east and south to reach Denmark. Cnut gritted his teeth and again pondered his humiliation, wondering whether he really wanted to return home and confirm to everyone, his brother especially, that he'd been defeated. It didn't sit well with him. But if he were to live, he had no choice.

Their supplies were also an issue. In their hurry to escape the Normans, they'd had little time to gather food or water, and both vessels were empty of such things. Cnut wasn't hungry, and a lack of bread was no issue considering how long he knew men could go without it, but the absence of water was a serious worry. They had to reach land, any land, and soon, or they'd rapidly start losing people to thirst. That wouldn't be just. These were warriors all, men who'd fought both Edmund and Æthelred's Normans and lived to tell of it. To have them meet their end lying flat, desperate and dried out, upon the deck of a ship was a fate they in no way deserved. They would die as they had lived; with honour. Cnut would see to it.

They kept on rowing, their sails also unfurled until darkness again began to fall and a harsh wind started blowing in from the north. Cnut quickly had their sails furled in and secured, knowing by experience that the storm breaking over them wouldn't hesitate to do all the damage it could. They stayed on course, hoping to outlast or outpace the wind and waves now howling and raging about them, but it wasn't long until things got even worse. The wind wouldn't let up, and both their ships had begun to rise and fall in the water, the ocean beneath them seeming to coil and flex with displeasure at their continued presence. Water was now spraying across the deck in considerable abundance, soaking the men and their very frightened-looking abbot. This wasn't going well. It was time to bail, and bail furiously.

Cnut gave the order, at times struggling to make himself heard over the piercing gale and ever-crashing waves. The men leapt to it, grabbing anything they could that might be used to carry water. They were working fast, and the deck showed no immediate sign of flooding, but it was arduous work, and as Cnut leant his strength to theirs he wondered how long they could keep this up. It was now a contest of wills, he decided, pitting his men against the storm and sea combined. They were enemies, like the English, but unlike the fearsome Edmund Ironside, this storm was but a thing of nature that could be tamed or at least endured. Stout hearts would see them through. Their aching shoulders were nothing compared to what awaited them should they fail.

The wind soon began blowing stronger than ever, and the sea got even rougher with it, tossing their vessel about like it were nought but a child's toy. A huge wave emerged out of the dark to smash into them head-on, ensuring the snarling dragon's head at the front of the ship was almost entirely submerged. It didn't last, and the slope of the sea soon saw them tossed upwards, the prow erupting from the water in giddy triumph before plunging back down again. As dramatic as it had looked, their ship's impromptu acrobatics had seen them take on yet more water, the flood knocking several men down in the process. This was beyond dangerous. If something was not done rapidly, they'd risk being submerged completely and permanently when hit by the next wave. The men began bailing faster than ever, and Cnut was moving to join them when something heavy smashed into him from behind and pitched him onto his face. He went to get up, trying and failing to shift himself even in the slightest. He was trapped, and he was immobile, and he found both things terrifying.

Østen knelt at his side, gabbling something, and several others joined him, each straining and growling as they tried to shift something from his back. Cnut couldn't so much as turn his head around, such was the weight, but he'd worked out what had happened. The mast had broken and fallen and pinned him in place. It hurt, he knew that for sure, and he spluttered and sneezed when the water sloshing back and forth across the deck began filling his mouth and nose. He couldn't die like this. They had to get him free. They had to…

He opened his eyes. His vision was blurred, yet it was now quiet, the crackle of burning wood the only sound to intrude upon his senses. He blinked, over and over, thinking seawater must have obscured his sight. He raised his hands to his face, noticing then that his beard and skin were dry. Things began to clear a little; he perceived his palms, lined and supple, his fingers long yet muscular. He looked down at himself, noting with surprise that, of all places, he was tucked up in bed. It was his bed, in his old room, the fire in the hearth not ten feet away burning lazily and the wolf skin rug before it as plush and enveloping as he remembered. This couldn't be right. He couldn't have just been plucked from his ship and deposited in Roskilde, in bed, no less. Was he so favoured by God that he'd go to such efforts to save him?

He tried to sit up, yet it wasn't easy, and he nearly bit his tongue simply from the effort of overcoming the pain in his back. He put his hands on his knees, his breathing heavy and his head hanging. The door then opened. Somebody was standing there, of that he was sure, and they rushed to his side, their features coming into proper focus. Cnut couldn't believe it. God must have been with him, for he felt truly blessed now. Estrith had come.

"I thought I heard you cry out," she said anxiously, her sapphire eyes lit with concern. She was a handsome woman, like everyone in the family, her pale features bearing that chiselled, narrow look that was customary among their people and Cnut's relatives in particular. She was his sister, and Cnut had always been fond of her. She'd been one of the few tender things in his life. He was glad to see her now because of that.

"What happened to me?" he croaked, the strength of his voice failing him.

"Østen brought you here, said you'd been in an accident on the journey back. He wouldn't tell me anything apart from that, so we just tended to your wounds and let you sleep."

"For how long?"

"What do you mean?"

"For how long have I been asleep?" He felt tense and vulnerable. Sleep was necessary, for obvious reasons, yet to have been unconscious for so long would have made him look weak. That was not ideal.

"About a week," she said timidly. "Harald had Father Erik come and do what he could...I think it worked? I mean, you sat up on your own..."

Cnut nodded, grateful for her explanation but more than agitated at the thought of his brother, Harald, presiding over his care. This was a critical time, any fool could see that, and for Cnut to appear helpless before his older brother would only imperil his chances of convincing him to lend support for a second invasion of England. That would not do. Something had to be done. Cnut would start by getting out of bed.

It was harder than he could have imagined. His legs were trying, yet they moved like they were encased in mud or tar or something of that sort, and he had to physically grab them just to shift them out from under his blankets. Estrith was all in a flutter and warbling about how he had to "take things easier", but he ignored her, knowing she couldn't possibly understand the situation for what it was. Cnut wobbled as he planted his feet on the floor, his right arm firmly grasped around his sister's shoulders for support. Her aid was welcome, yet it presented problems of its own. He couldn't just walk out of his room like this. If Harald were to learn to respect him again, having his sister carry him around was a non-starter. They'd have to think of something.

A humble stick was the solution. Cnut tried it out, using the thin ash rod to balance his right side. He didn't know where Estrith had obtained such a thing, given that she certainly wasn't of an age to need it, but it was more than helpful and certainly preferable to clinging to her. He took a step forward and then another, the rod clacking against the wooden floorboards. He felt silly, like an old man, yet it was better than the alternative, which more than likely would involve falling flat on his face. He'd accept this blessing for what it was.

Getting dressed, however, remained an issue. If he'd felt like an old man before, he now felt as a child, incapable of doing anything and requiring a woman to help him. Estrith, thank God, didn't seem to mind, stressing over and over how she was "glad to help" and that he'd soon "be stronger than ever." He looked down at himself once she'd finished and passed his stick back to him. He wasn't in his armour, thankfully, since the weight of that would likely end him, but he felt better now he was at least back in his linens and furs. Estrith had also combed and tied his hair, just like she had before he'd left for England. He'd always kept that a secret. As far as anyone else need know, Cnut wasn't concerned with his looks, nor did he have a soft spot for anyone. It was better that way.

They'd made it beyond the door to his room when he almost fell. His sister caught him, somehow, but Cnut's heart was racing with the shock of it, his cheeks flushing pink with embarrassment. He leant against his door for a time, the surface hard and uncomfortable against his back, trying to catch his breath and focus on what lay ahead. Just one foot in front of the other. That's all he needed to do. He had his stick. That would see him right. All he had to do was concentrate.

His determined optimism soon paid off. His legs gradually became more obedient, and by the time they'd reached the main chamber of his brother's hall he felt relatively secure, at least in terms of falling over or otherwise making a fool out of himself. Harald was there, sat at their long table, his words quiet yet stern whilst he held conversation with what was none other than Østen. The latter stood up and bowed when he saw Cnut coming, his eyes twinkling with what looked like affection and relief. Østen was always so loyal, Cnut thought, to his father and now to him. He'd reward it fully someday.

"What happened?" Cnut asked, wanting to get straight to the point.

"The storm broke the mast…and it fell on you," replied Østen. He sounded embarrassed, like somehow Cnut's misfortune reflected poorly on him.

"I was injured that badly? Over a mast?"

"There's a real weight to them," nodded Østen. "Just ask any shipwright. Yet when we couldn't wake you even after we'd gotten you clear…I feared the worst."

"What about the rest of the men? They made it?"

"Both vessels, yes, through the blessing of the Gods…or just God…but they made it. Ælfmær too. All is well."

Cnut's eyes flitted towards his brother. He'd remained seated, his elbows resting on the table before him and his head angled to look upon Cnut. His long, blond-bearded face was blank, as were his stereotypically blue eyes. Cnut stared back at him, taking in his appearance and wondering if he'd done something to cause him upset.

Harald was a few years older than him, the firstborn son, in fact, of their father, the late King Svienn, but they were very different in quite a few ways. Cnut was tall and almost lanky in his appearance, whereas Harald was stockier, with a visible paunch from too much soft living. They both wore their flaxen hair long, too long, some might say, and their temperaments were often at odds, something their father had sometimes remarked on. Cnut was tempestuous and daring, which had pleased Svienn, whereas Harald was far more reserved and in the habit of concealing his thoughts more often than some might like. Cnut had never found out for certain, but he'd assumed that's why his father had taken him with him to England. He didn't need a stoic when it came to conquest. He needed a warrior.

Cnut wasn't happy to see Harald, and by the looks of things the feeling was mutual. He hobbled over anyway, his sister still close, and sat down at the table, Estrith joining him. Harald persisted in staring, blank as usual, and Cnut glowered for a moment at the thin gold circlet upon his head. Did Harald think himself a king? Of what exactly? That had not been their father's wish, and so for Harald to just take such a mantle upon himself, if that's what he was doing, was beyond impertinent. Cnut thought he might as well say so.

"That thing on your head, brother…does it have a function aside from making you look pretty?"

Harald leant back in his chair, his eyes hooded. "That was good of you to send father's body back to us so quickly," he muttered, his hands now folded in his lap.

"How was the funeral?" asked Cnut, hoping his peculiar brother had at least put on a proper display. Svienn was a king and their father both. He deserved to be honoured.

"It was as you'd expect," said Harald. "It was sad, and a shock with the suddenness of it all…I did wonder why you'd sent so many warriors to escort him home. You clearly needed them."

Cnut flinched with that last comment. It had been a low blow, and he knew Harald well enough to know he was attempting to infer something by uttering it. This wasn't, however, the time for arguments, so Cnut decided to opt in favour of humility rather than pride.

"If you're suggesting I could have used those men better had I kept most of them in England…then I would agree," sighed Cnut, resigning himself to face facts, no matter how uncomfortable.

"Just what happened over there, brother? One moment we'd received word that the English were beaten and their king fleeing…and the next, our father is dead."

"It's hard to explain," muttered Cnut, his eyes lifting briefly to behold Østen as he laid a bowl of stew and a tankard of mead before him. Cnut took a drink, enjoying the sharp tang of the liquid splashing over his tongue. The English mead had been too sweet. The stuff made at home was far more suited to his tastes. He'd missed it.

"Go on," implored Harald, his manner still unreadable.

"It was at a place called Gainesburg," said Cnut, talking his way around half a mouthful of stew. "He'd called all of the thegns and ealdormen to himself…"

"The what?"

"Ealdormen, brother. Like our jarls. Men of standing and prestige."

"Oh," shrugged Harald, unconcerned at his ignorance of England. "Please, continue."

Cnut spooned a few more mouthfuls of stew into his mouth before speaking again. "As I said…the place was called Gainesburg…"

"In the North?" Harald again interrupted.

"Yes…father wanted to make a show of things, like he wanted everyone to see him as victor and serve him accordingly. He…"

"This will be because of the old balance of power, yes? He wanted to make it clear he intended to honour our old sphere of influence around Jorvik, rather than just rule from the South like any other king of Westseaxe."

Østen cleared his throat and resumed his place at the table. Cnut looked around, wanting to gauge the reactions of those present to his brother's uncharacteristic display of knowledge. Estrith looked as expected, concerned for Cnut, but certainly not fazed by Harald. Østen appeared as one who would rather be elsewhere, but that could be for any number of reasons, and so Cnut could only conclude that he was the only one particularly surprised here. So their father had indeed wanted to rule from the North, as others had said. Gainesburg had not therefore been chosen by accident. The question remained, though, as to why he'd not told him.

"Who told you that?" asked Cnut, "and how can you know so much about English politics without even knowing what an ealdorman is?"

"And so father died after this gathering?" asked Harald, ignoring Cnut's question.

"Suddenly, yes, whilst he was at table," said Østen, his eyes troubled with the recollection. "Raving something about an English saint, so he was, like he feared him…he…"

Østen seemed to partially wilt under Cnut's gaze. He fell silent, his eyes cast down towards the table, knowing he'd misspoken. "It is as my man has said," muttered Cnut darkly, still irked that Østen had mentioned his father's humiliation.

"And was there a saint?" asked Harald.

"I don't understand it myself," Cnut sighed, "yet as you can guess, no such man was present. Father had recently attacked the resting place of England's patron, Saint Edmund. I don't know why, and I thought it ill-advised, but he did it and we barely escaped. Some might say the saint came for him out of vengeance. I don't know the truth of it. No one does."

"What do you mean you barely escaped, brother? This saint sounds quite formidable if he came for you both."

Cnut shook his head, wondering if Harald was toying with him. "That's not what I meant," he said testily. "The English attacked us when we made a move on the saint's remains…they fought well. Too well."

"And this is why you're sitting here, in my hall, rather than ruling such people?"

Østen stirred uncomfortably in his seat, Estrith doing likewise. Cnut looked over at them; Østen in his resigned and very hairy dutifulness and Estrith in all her delicate finery. Harald was different from both of them. There was little that was good about him, at least in his present mood. He was set to humiliate Cnut, and wouldn't be satisfied until he'd done so.

"Do you seek to wound me?" asked Cnut at last.

"Humble you, perhaps," said Harald quickly. "I know what you think of me and how father saw us both. You think he left me here and took you to England because you had his confidence, and I did not. You are wrong."

"How else was I supposed to take it? England is the grand prize. If he thought little of me, he wouldn't have arranged a place for me at his side."

"He thought a lot of you," admitted Harald. "And yet, just because he did doesn't mean he wanted you to succeed him. He left me in Denmark because he knew I had wisdom and could govern his country in his absence. You still had much to learn, which is why he made sure you'd be kept close to him so you could be instructed."

Cnut laughed, the sound bitter and brittle within his throat. "Do you seriously want to have this conversation now?" he asked, holding his hands up as if to signify the foolishness of it all. "Father no doubt thought himself blessed to have two sons. If he left you here, it's because he valued...he loved..."

"I think you're being too charitable there, brother. Father didn't love us. Father didn't love anyone, just as he wasn't loved by grandfather. He made it so that he'd have no weaknesses to exploit. Ever."

Harald, sadly, had a point. Svienn had been hard on his children, all of them, and when he wasn't pushing them to their limits he was aloof, remote, or just downright uncaring. Cnut had been distressed by that in his boyhood, and there'd been times when he'd wondered if he were but a tool to be utilised to achieve his father's own purposes. Cnut had once dared speak of such things and instantly had cause to regret it. He didn't want to think on those memories now. The past was the past.

"What would you have me say?" asked Cnut, genuinely confused as to what his brother could want from this exchange.

"I want you to understand a few things," said Harald. "I rule here. I am King of Denmark. You might have been King of England, or one King of England amidst several contenders, but you failed in that, and you are back here. In my domain."

Østen stirred from his previous awkwardness, his look fierce. "I knew King Svienn's mind better than most," he said sternly. "And I know he favoured Cnut and desired him to rule after him. No disrespect, Harald, but you overstep and..."

"But you DO disrespect me!" shouted Harald, his fist suddenly hammering the table. Heavy treads came closer, the sound drawing Cnut to his feet. Several warriors had appeared from one of the side passages and were standing not five feet away, their axes gripped tight in their gauntleted hands. Cnut had a feeling what this was about. These men weren't just responding to a raised voice heard by accident. Harald had told them to come running if he gave a signal. He was trying to intimidate him. It wouldn't work.

"Call your men off, Harald," said Cnut. "There's no need for this...Østen speaks his mind, and only a fool would discount his knowledge and experience. We can discuss which one of us was most favoured later. For now, let there be peace between us."

Harald was unmoved. "You know, brother," he said, his expression again blank, "I have a feeling if our situations were reversed, you'd not be so accommodating. I know if you were king here and I the one returning in disgrace, you'd do with me as you saw fit, with no thought of the "peace between us", as you say."

Estrith suddenly intervened, unsettled by how things were going. "How can you say that to him?" she asked Harald. "You are my brothers...you grew up together, you fought together...father may have been a hard man, but he did care for you, in his way. Get your men to stand down, Harald. Cnut knows and respects you. That is enough."

Cnut looked back at his sister, grateful for her words. Harald had visibly softened, his tense manner easing slightly after hearing Estrith's plea. The warriors across from them had also relaxed, at least a little, looking more like they were just vigilant guards on duty rather than the men of violence they'd appeared as mere seconds earlier. Sadly, Harald was not entirely finished yet, and his verbal barbs continued to lash Cnut, humiliating him further.

"Your men hate you, you know that, Cnut? They've been drifting in over the past week…small groups of ships carrying clutches of ragged survivors. They say you sent them south to put down some petty rebellion only to be suddenly deserted by the Englishman appointed to lead them. What say you to that?"

Cnut sat down, his legs paining him once more. His back ached, and it was getting worse with Harald's provocations, making him want more than anything to retire to his bed. He could not. He wouldn't back down to him. Not now.

"I didn't know," said Cnut, his voice faint. "Jarl Knud sent those men to Hamptonscir and placed the Ealdorman Eadric in charge of them. I was making haste to Lundenburg at the time after our defea…after the battle at Gainesburg."

"Well, whoever this Eadric is, they say he left them in the night after word reached them of Æthelred's return. You should not have trusted this man, Cnut, and you should not have gotten complacent whilst your conquest was still incomplete. How did you use the ships father left you, as in the ones you didn't send back with his body? Did you use them to patrol the seas, to watch for an invading force?"

Silence fell, at least in terms of human speech. The fire still crackled, burning away in the hearth on the far side of the room. The wind also could be heard outside, high pitched and yet reassuring in its intensity. Cnut had missed Denmark and its harsh yet predictable weather. England had been grey and damp, seemingly in perpetuity, neither of which had suited him. He'd get outside again as soon as he was able and take in the sights, assuming his bastard brother was of a mood to let him. Judging from how this was going, Cnut wouldn't be surprised if Harald thought to make him a prisoner. He didn't want that. He'd suffered enough.

"I admit I neglected naval matters," Cnut finally said, still quiet. "I wasn't expecting Normandy to turn on us, and there was no reason to think they'd suddenly intervene with such force. Everything looked so secure. We'd won. And then we hadn't. It all just…unravelled, so very quickly."

"What do you think father would have done? Would he have let things unravel?"

Østen rose from the table, his face thunderous. "I'll not sit here and listen to any more of this!" he snarled. "You rush to judge your brother, Harald, but you know nothing of the hardships he's faced. The English are no longer the weak and confused people we've grown accustomed to. Under Edmund Ironside, they are different creatures…different beasts!"

Harald scoffed, "Edmund Ironside? Who bears this fearsome name? Surely not an Englishman?"

"That's what Østen is trying to tell you, if you would but listen," said Cnut. "He's the son of Æthelred, but you would not think it if you saw him. I don't dare guess at how many of us he's killed. England is different now. Very different."

"And you would return to this land?" Harald asked. "You'd go back there to fight that monster?"

Cnut levelled his gaze with Harald's, looking deep into his eyes. "I would," he said. "Right now, if I were able. Father would have wished it. I wish it. I will see it come to pass."

His words were again not taken seriously, as expected. Harald smirked to himself, his pale lips twisting in a manner Cnut had always found so very disagreeable. Østen scowled at the sight of it and moved for the doors, his footsteps quick and energetic upon the rough wooden flooring. He paused, turning back to face Cnut before speaking.

"Your wife is here, my king. You may like to visit her, or I shall bring her to you, if you would command me…I should tell you, also, that she is with child."

Cnut hesitated, for a brief second wondering just what exactly Østen was even talking about. Then he remembered, feeling doubly foolish he'd somehow forgotten his own wedding. It all seemed like a lifetime ago now, when his father was alive and the English could do nothing but grovel, but married he'd been and married he remained. He'd sent her away from England, thinking she'd prove a hindrance to his campaign, but he was glad to hear she'd made it across the sea safely. Ælfgifu, she was called. A horrible name, for certain, yet she was fair to look upon. And if Østen was right, she may have just blessed him with an heir.

He rose, feeling a little giddy as he reached for his stick. His sister helped him, concern on her face, and they both headed towards Østen, who was still waiting patiently not a few feet from the doors. Cnut's heart leapt as he considered what lay beyond. Roskilde, in all its frigid beauty, and with it, his wife and unborn child. He may have been defeated in England, but he'd returned home to blessings he'd not expected. He'd make the most of it.

Harald, unfortunately, called out to them one last time, his threatening words dispelling Cnut's newfound optimism.

"Be warned, brother, lest you get any ideas about gathering your surviving men or trying to assemble some kind of force to return to England. That was our father's dream. It is no longer valid. I rule here, and Denmark only has one king. Remember that, for you forget such things at your peril."

XXXI

Everything was smashed, the detritus left by the Danes' assault covering the earth like a carpet. The walls had held, as was only proper, and yet the whole area north of the fortress had been crushed flat, scorched, or otherwise ruined, any tree, hedge, or farmhouse suffering much the same fate as the other. Yet the walls still stood; those great, grey, strong Roman walls of antiquity. They remained, as they always had. That's what counted. Porteceaster had endured.

And yet from appearances, it had been a close call. There were bodies covering the approaches, their number increasing the closer you got to the fortifications. Some had been killed by arrows and the like, but others had been slashed or stabbed whilst scaling the walls and come crashing down to their deaths. They lay in groups upon the ground, broken and bloody and caked with flies. It was hard to look at, but ultimately Osbert cared not. They were Danes. Their fate was much deserved.

None of that helped explain their current predicament. Osbert was currently on horseback and alongside his lord, Ulfcytel, who was predictably alongside Edmund, who was, in turn, beside Wulfnoth. Eamon was just behind, the great and blessed banner of Saint Edmund held keenly in his grip. Alaric's widow, Æva, was close by and with her son, Brandon, and all were atop a steed of their own, the beasts snorting and huffing to themselves in the afternoon air. The rest of their army spilled out to their rear, some two thousand men if their last estimate was accurate, their spear tips pointed upward en masse towards the overcast sky. It was a reassuring sight, but even that failed to put Osbert's mind entirely at ease. Something was wrong here, and he yearned to find out what.

Edmund called out again, announcing his presence to anyone on the walls. There was no reply, save the echo of his typically robust voice. All was quiet, the battlements remaining mysteriously empty. He repeated himself again and yet again, calling for the Ealdorman Ælfric to make himself known. Nothing. There were no sounds from Porteceaster, none. The place was a tomb, sealed up from within and devoid of life, or so it looked. That made no sense. The Danes had not carried the walls, as Edmund's own scouts had seen them take to ship from here just a week prior. They'd failed to take the place, so went the word, and had simply left, disorganised and defeated. Edmund had been elated, as was natural, and they'd swarmed south in force, ready to congratulate and embrace the venerable Ælfric for his most determined resistance. Osbert felt they should have done this earlier, whilst there was still fighting to be done, but that was just his opinion. He wasn't the strategist Edmund was, and so he'd held his tongue. Perhaps he shouldn't have.

Edmund called out one last time. Again, nothing. Osbert saw the concern in his eyes as he leant over and whispered something to Wulfnoth, imparting some sentiment or instruction. Wulfnoth sprang into action immediately and began riding towards the walls, a clutch of men following. He turned a moment, his eyes drifting to both Osbert and Eamon. He nodded to them and made a gesture, signalling that they should follow. Eamon handed the banner to the man beside him and went after Wulfnoth. Osbert looked to Ulfcytel, and the ealdorman nodded, granting him permission to aid Wulfnoth in whatever had been assigned.

It didn't take Osbert long to work out what was to be done. Wulfnoth dismounted from his steed and began scaling the walls, going from handhold to handhold, his movements almost unnaturally proficient. Somebody had passed him a rope beforehand, and it trailed after him now, the bulk of it tied around his waist for convenience. He reached the summit within a half-minute; a feat that would be truly remarkable were it not for the fact Osbert already knew how adept he was at such antics. He'd done the same at Canterburie, scaling the walls and infiltrating the city to search for survivors. Osbert owed Wulfnoth his life for that. He'd not forgotten it.

Wulfnoth tied one end of the rope around the nearest crenellation, his movements quick and precise, as expected. He let the rope dangle over the parapet, allowing Eamon to go scrambling up after him. Several of Wulfnoth's men had begun climbing the sheer surface of the wall unassisted, and Osbert was considering following them until Eamon hissed an order at him from above. He'd stick with the rope. It was safer that way, and he didn't fancy falling off the wall. It would be embarrassing with all these people watching.

By the time he'd made it up top, he was sweating a little, his breathing also irregular after his exertions. Everyone who was supposed to be here was now staring into the fortress interior. Osbert had never been to Porteceaster before, but Alaric had spoken of it during their time together, mentioning how he'd been blessed to make his home here. He could see an impressive tower tucked back towards the southern wall, lonesome and forlorn 'neath the dark, heavy clouds, and there was what looked like a great hall beneath it, its sizeable stone and timber arches putting the more humble buildings to shame. The rest of the settlement otherwise looked intact and functional, if tightly packed, providing comfort and shelter to what Obsert estimated would be in the figure of several hundred people. It then occurred to him that was precisely what was odd about all this. People. There were none. Nobody was here, either upon the battlements or in the streets below. Porteceaster was empty.

Wulfnoth was already moving, descending a narrow stairwell into the settlement proper. Osbert followed, Eamon and the rest close at hand, and before long they'd made it to the sealed gatehouse immediately facing Edmund and his army. They worked fast, unbarring the gate and hauling its doors open, the groaning and creaking of iron and timber harshly discordant as it broke the silence.

Edmund came striding through, his grey horse for the moment remaining outside. Others were with him, as usual, and Ulfcytel gave Osbert a wink and a smile as he came closer, several hundred men following at his back.They all spread out, moving through the streets with great caution, each man holding either spear or axe at the ready lest they encounter any sudden surprises. When they reached the great hall, Osbert had noticed that Æva was with them, always following at Edmund's heels and always looking a touch fearful. Osbert couldn't quite recall what had caused her to leave this place after Ulfcytel had helped retake it for the sake of her father-in-law, but he could remember Ulfcytel speaking on it a little and how it had apparently involved something about Ælfric inadvertently causing the destruction of Wiltune and the death of her and Alaric's son. It was a shame. This should be a happy occasion for her. She was undoubtedly missing Alaric too. Osbert could sympathise with that. It was something they had in common.

It was then Osbert realised they were not alone here. An old hound had appeared from a particularly sorry-looking barn and was wandering over to them, its wide eyes lit with hope. Eamon sat down on his haunches and whistled, beckoning the poor thing over. It came at a trot, and the boy, Brandon, rushed to Eamon's side, his enthusiasm for meeting this wayward beast impossible to hide. Eamon handed Brandon a piece of bread he'd retrieved from his knapsack, and the boy gifted it to their new friend, his tail wagging at such a rate it was almost a blur.

Osbert turned upon realising Edmund and Æva had approached from behind. They were both smiling, which put Osbert at ease, since he at times found Edmund's intensity to be more than a little intimidating.

"What will you call him?" asked Edmund, his question for Brandon.

"Dog Face," said Brandon without hesitation, the honesty of his answer causing everyone who heard it to burst out laughing.

It was strange seeing Edmund laugh, thought Osbert. He had a blunt, perhaps even brutal face, and his throat was more accustomed to roaring orders on the battlefield than giving voice to mirth. He was terrifying whenever the fight came upon them, and everyone had seen how even the Danes seemed to wilt in the face of his fury, but here he appeared like anyone else, enjoying a moment and very much glad to be alive.

Osbert smiled at him when he caught his eye, and he again saw something there that reminded him of precisely why they should all continue to follow him wherever he might lead. Edmund was a friend. He didn't put on airs, and he didn't put himself above others, despite the nobility of his bloodline. That was refreshing, and it was no wonder people continued to flock to him, especially now word had spread of their miraculously incorrupt banner.

He was also happy Edmund hadn't flinched when looking back at him. The monks at Gainesburg had told Osbert the burns to his face would never fully heal, and so he was stuck like this, with one half of his visage scarred up and red raw. For a time, he'd feared others might struggle to look upon him, but Edmund had no such problem, nor did anyone else in this army. They were as brothers, and Osbert would always be glad of it.

"Dog Face" followed when they entered the great hall, the beast staying close to Brandon. It was marvellous in here, worthy of a king rather than just an ealdorman, and Osbert and Eamon alike were taken aback at the wondrous tapestries of great deeds and the great men who'd performed them. Osbert stopped underneath an imposing image of none other than King Alfred of Westseaxe. He was stood tall, his sword held aloft in one hand and his shield at rest and facing forward. Osbert had never seen such an image before, and to view it now made him feel like he was playing a part in some kind of saga that had begun long before his birth and would continue on long after he'd ceased to be. It was a realistic notion, he supposed. King Alfred had dealt with dark days of his own, and won through with glory and honour both. Osbert saw no reason why they'd not enjoy the same. They had Edmund, after all, and Edmund had Alfred's blood in his veins.

"It's supposed to be at Ethandun," said a stern yet feminine voice. Osbert turned and saw Æva, her eyes on the painting. "Just after his victory there?" she asked, as if unsure whether Osbert even knew of the Battle of Ethandun. "It was when he gave us back our hope…when he brought us back from the brink and set things right."

"This image means a great deal to you?" asked Osbert, having heard the reverence in her voice.

"Of course," she said. "Now more than ever. Alaric always loved King Alfred. He sought to emulate him."

"He succeeded," replied Osbert immediately. Æva smiled and nodded, pleased by his words. They moved on. The past could remain the past, for now. For the time being, they had a mystery to solve.

Sadly, the rest of the hall yielded few clues. Everything was as it should be, claimed Æva, it's just that nobody was here. "Dog Face" was unable to shed light on things, given that he was unable to talk, which left Edmund with little to do other than order yet another search of the hall and its environs. There had to be something here, he kept saying, although what he expected to find Osbert wasn't sure. Fortunately, things became more interesting once they'd reached the ealdorman's living quarters.

They were small, consisting of two chambers, one for sleeping and the other presumably for entertaining guests or holding meetings. Æva didn't look enthused to be back here, and Osbert wasn't about to ask why. He'd seen something. Hidden in plain sight, as it were. He had no idea how they'd not spotted it immediately, but there it was. A single piece of parchment upon the table, held in place with a knife thrust downward through its centre. He removed it carefully and began to read, his lips mouthing the words as he struggled with the flowing text of an unfamiliar hand:

I held this place, my home and sanctuary, against the armies of Svienn for the sake of King Edmund. I now abandon it and go into exile out of fear of King Æthelred. Do not attempt to find me. You will not succeed. Æthelred will not take what little family I have left. Should Æva resurface, I'd consider it a kindness if she be told that I miss her and that I regret the past more than she could ever imagine.

Ælfric, Ealdorman of Hamptonscir.

Osbert finished reading and handed the letter to Æva. She read fast, faster than Osbert, and then left via the door they'd used to enter. Osbert followed, wondering what any of this could mean and how it might affect their campaign. Edmund was by now sat at a great long table in the main chamber of the hall, looking very much like he'd decided to settle in. Æva approached quickly and handed him the letter. He read fast too. Then he looked at her and spoke.

"Ælfric deserved better. I should have had us come here sooner, as you suggested, Æva. I am sorry."

"What do we do now?" Æva asked. "It's like he took everyone with him… everyone, every single person, not just his warriors. I have no notion as to where. He could be anywhere, land or sea."

"He left the dog," said Osbert, feeling foolish at mentioning it.

"He did," said Edmund, his smile faint. "An oversight on his part, but it does us good. If this fortress had been entirely devoid of life, I fear the men may have been spooked by it. They'll be pleased it wasn't so. Our hairy new friend is most welcome."

Wulfnoth emerged from somewhere, his sudden appearance making Osbert wonder if he'd been intentionally sneaking about. He ignored everyone aside from

Edmund, speaking in his usual crisp, direct manner on how the men had finished searching much of the fortress and discovered nothing of note, dead, living, or otherwise. Edmund drummed his fingers on the table, lost in thought.

"What do we have in storage?" he asked.

"Foodstuffs of some description," said Wulfnoth. "Not all that much, probably as much of it was consumed during the siege, but if you intend to stay here a little longer, the men will appreciate it. There's proper shelter here, although given our numbers…"

"We won't all fit inside the walls," nodded Edmund, understanding the obvious. Ulfcytel lumbered over, several warriors with him, and took a seat at the table. He went to give Edmund more or less the same report as Wulfnoth had given, but Edmund bade him quiet and instead began to read aloud the letter from Ælfric. Ulfcytel's face reddened from behind his great beard, his sad eyes upon Æva.

"I cannot say where the ealdorman may have gotten to," said Ulfcytel, looking back to Edmund, his voice hoarse with emotion. "There are no ships in the harbour, so if you ask me, he would have used everything he had to evacuate to who knows where."

"Didn't Cenric say that the ealdorman once escaped this place to seek refuge in Suthhamtunam?" Osbert wondered if he'd been wrong to speak, but he felt he might have an advantage in this situation given he was far removed from it, emotionally speaking.

"That's very true," confirmed Æva. "We did indeed flee there to get away from Eadric."

Edmund twisted in his chair to face Wulfnoth. "Head out with a force of riders and evaluate the situation in Suthhamtunam," he ordered brusquely. "Even if Ælfric isn't there, somebody could know something."

Wulfnoth nodded once and turned on his heels, departing from them with no undue ceremony, a handful of men following.

"I would say we also investigate the Isle of Wit," said Ulfcytel suddenly, like the idea had only just dawned on him.

"Didn't you say the harbour was empty?" asked Edmund.

"That's true," said Ulfcytel, "so we should make it a priority to scout the coast for something seaworthy. Once we find a ship, I can lead an expedition to the island to see if the locals know something we don't."

"Are you sure you're up to it?" Edmund asked, concerned.

"What wouldn't I be?" replied Ulfcytel, almost offended. Edmund stared at him for a moment or two, possibly to ascertain his emotional state and whether assigning him a new mission was for the best. Osbert felt concern of his own now. He didn't like to see the ealdorman in pain, and whatever the truth behind recent events, Osbert could see they troubled him.

"I would accompany you, of course?" Osbert asked, not wanting to be left behind.

Ulfcytel's eyes snapped up to behold him, as if he'd somehow forgotten he'd been standing here. "Of course," he said gently. "Where else would you be? Your place is always at my side."

Osbert smiled slightly, pleased with what had been said. Edmund stood up, saying something about how he intended to remain in Porteceaster with the army until the mystery of Ælfric's disappearance had been solved. He paused when Brandon appeared from somewhere, Dog Face wandering after him. Edmund seemed to take him in, and then Æva too. Something was on his mind.

"I am forgetting myself," he said quietly. "These lands belong to Ælfric, and the eldest member of his family presently here is you, Æva. In that case, I would ask you for permission to take up residence in your halls."

"Are you serious?" asked Æva, like she thought Edmund was perhaps trying to be funny. Something strange then seemed to happen. Edmund looked awkward. Osbert had never seen that before. Nobody could make him feel that way, until now, that is. He wondered how Æva had even managed to do it. Was Edmund just shy with women? It wasn't unheard of, even among those who were otherwise confident in any other situation.

"I am serious," said Edmund, still appearing a little self-conscious. "These lands belong to your family. With everyone else gone, authority rests with you."

Æva shook her head, as though she thought this scenario surprising and perhaps even a tad silly. "Then in that case, my king," she said with a slight bow, "I welcome you to Porteceaster, and put its resources at your disposal."

Edmund seemed mollified by that, although Osbert wondered what his reaction would have been if, for some strange reason, Æva had decided to refuse him. He was being courteous to her, as was only right, since he was about to use her home to house a considerable number of very smelly, very tired men. She'd done the gracious thing by accepting, even if she really had no choice in the matter. It wouldn't have made sense for her to refuse, anyway. Her fate was tied to Edmund's, and the more Osbert thought about it, the more he felt Edmund had tied himself to her.

In any case, Osbert didn't have time to stand around and hypothesise on the emotions of others. Ulfcytel had work for him, for they had to get a party together, horses too, to scout the coastline for ships they might use to get to the Isle of Wit. Eamon came with them, and they soon gathered a score of mounted warriors well suited to their task. Æva had retreated to the tower with Brandon and Dog Face, apparently willing to allow Edmund to do whatever he liked with the rest of the fortress, which he did, billeting several hundred of his men outside the great hall to man the walls and serve as a garrison.

The rest lurked outside, making camp on Edmund's orders about a quarter mile north east. Edmund himself remained in the great hall, yet for what reason, Osbert was unsure. It seemed a little ostentatious for him, as all he'd really known of the man was the rough and ready persona he put on when they were either marching through the wilderness or fighting in some battle. He had things to prepare, Eamon had said, and that was undoubtedly true. Edmund was always thinking, always planning. It was a strength that would continue to serve them well.

Ulfcytel had them ride out into the encroaching night, their flaming torches stuttering in the breeze. He'd sent another search party in the opposite direction, claiming the entire coast was likely littered with hamlets and fishing villages that would almost certainly host something seaworthy for them to acquire. Osbert asked if they intended to compensate the owners, which got a good-natured laugh from Ulfcytel. They would, he assured him. They were not thieves. They would treat the locals fairly, as justice demanded.

Luck seemed to smile upon such sentiments, or at least they thought. They'd ridden about ten miles when they discovered a hamlet, tucked tight beneath the beginnings of a chalk cliff that went on at some length before jutting out into the sea. The waters surged around it, splashing up its pale surface as if intending to surmount it. The hamlet, however, was almost entirely burnt, the ruins of what must have once been quite serviceable shacks appearing vaguely sinister when illuminated in the flickering light of their torches.

Ulfcytel mumbled something, cursing the Danes for their cruelty, and made his way down to the beach, the "crunch crunch" of his heavy treads echoing across the cliff face. There had been ships here, but they'd been burnt to ruin, their hulls charred to the brink of disintegration. Cnut's men had done a thorough job. The only positive was the lack of bodies. The fishermen must have fled in time. Perhaps Ælfric had saved them.

They'd ridden on about another ten miles when Ulfcytel bade them halt. They made camp amidst a clutch of rocks not far from the beach, the sound of the sea rolling in their ears. At least some of the rocks were of a size to provide shelter from the wind pouring in across the water, and so the ealdorman decided to bed down next to one, using his cloak to cushion his great bald head. He said something before he dozed off, claiming they'd "rest here until dawn" and instructing them to wake him when it was his "turn to stand watch and keep an eye out for any massive bastards who might murder us." The rest of the men chuckled to themselves whilst they too lay down to rest, amused by Ulfcytel's rather blunt and open style of command. Osbert was used to it. He wasn't tired either, so he took the first watch, scrambling up atop one of the larger rocks to give himself a decent view of the area.

There wasn't a whole lot to see. The cloud cover was still dense, and so what moon and starlight they had didn't illuminate much. He had a view of the beach from here, and could just about see the white froth of the waves impacting upon the shingle. Eamon appeared and swiftly scurried up to join him. They sat for a time, Osbert savouring the freshness of the sea-borne breeze as it snatched at his cloak.

"Do you ever think about the Abbot Ælfmær?"

Eamon seemed to tense up at Osbert's question, his frown implying this was an unwelcome topic he'd not expected to be broached. "Sometimes," he said quietly, "but only in the sense I still don't understand what happened. It should have been an easy kill for us. Lord knows the man deserves it."

"It was Eadric's doing," said Osbert. "He wanted to use the abbot as bait...lure us in so he could capture someone."

"Who?" asked Eamon. "Who are we to Eadric? And how would he know we were even about the place?"

"Not us...Eadric wanted Ulfcytel...he knew he'd command others to come and settle scores with the abbot. He was right."

"Good for Eadric," said Eamon, sarcastic.

"What happened after I went into the abbey?" Osbert asked. "I mean, I know what happened, from my perspective, I just want to know what it looked like from the outside. You fled when you saw things had gone awry?"

Eamon angled his head to stare at Osbert directly. "I'm no coward," he said firmly, "and I only withdrew because one moment all was quiet…and the next there were Danes suddenly everywhere. I saw you with them, unconscious, but I knew I'd only throw my life away trying to get to you. I had to rethink and plan."

"I'm sorry," replied Osbert, saddened Eamon thought he was implying something. "I meant nothing by it, and I'm sure you did what you could. But there was more than one Dane? I was only attacked by one in the abbot's quarters."

"More than one, yes," nodded Eamon, "and so I concluded King Svienn was serious about protecting Ælfmær. It's a moot point now, what with Svienn dead. All's well that ends well, eh."

"Did you speak to Edmund about this? I told him what I know when his army came to Gainesburg. It all seems strange to me still, and Ælfmær is still out there, somewhere. At some point, he'll need to be taken care of."

"I agree, and I gave Edmund a full report after he freed me from Uhtred. That's a whole other story, and I'd rather not..."

Eamon lifted a hand towards the side of his head and his notably missing ear. Osbert had heard that Uhtred had mistreated Eamon, and it was obvious to anyone who looked upon him now that the rumours were true. He'd not dared ask him for details. Some things were best left alone, at least until those who'd gone through them decided they wanted to talk. Osbert was, however, curious on what Edmund might have said to him about their failure to kill the abbot.

"So what did Edmund say to you about Ælfmær? He didn't seem troubled by what I said, but he had so many things on his mind. He always does."

"He didn't say much when I spoke to him," said Eamon, "but I do think he was disturbed, at least a little. Skulking about and murdering people doesn't seem to be his kind of thing, but I think he understands the situation called for it. He'll be looking out for the abbot, I think, him and that Wulfnoth he keeps so close."

"What do you make of Wulfnoth?" asked Osbert. "As you said...Edmund keeps him close. He must have his uses."

"You can say that again."

"What do you mean?"

Eamon fixed him with a look like he thought he was being intentionally thick-headed. "He got us out of Canterburie. It was nicely done, all stealth, killing only when he had to...we owe him our lives. So much could have gone wrong, but Wulfnoth got us out, quick and clean."

"It might not have been so clean," said Osbert, sniggering slightly. "You remember what happened when he first got through the door of that wretched shed we were locked in? Alaric started a brawl with him right there."

Eamon grinned, seeming to recall the memory with a degree of fondness. "That he did. He wasn't to know. We thought we would all die there. There was no way of knowing we'd have a mystery rescuer just waiting for the chance to come help us."

"Do you ever think much about Alaric?"

"I do. He's with me, in my heart, and I'll never forget him...but I fear if I speak of Alaric now, my emotions will get the better of me."

"Why not let them?" asked Osbert. "Surely it's better to let these things breathe rather than keep them bottled up?"

"That's easy for some to say. You're a young man, Osbert, and youth allows the emotions to run free, strong and potent. You might think there's a freedom there, but you'll come to regret that in time. The memories of those we've lost...they stir up so much feeling...feelings that can be more trouble than they are worth."

"What do you mean?" he asked, annoyed. It wasn't fair to make out he was just a kid. Eamon may have a good decade or more on him, but Osbert had proven himself enough times now. He wasn't delicate, nor did he lack self-control.

"Please don't take that as a criticism," Eamon assured him quietly. "If anything, it's my problem. Let's just say that if I'd endured what I've been through this past year when I was your age…I'm not sure if I could. I don't think I'd have been able to. I think it would break me. So I count myself blessed I was already broken. That way, I can't be broken again. Does that make sense?"

Osbert nodded thoughtfully. He didn't want to pressure him, and in truth, that was easily one of the deepest and most involved statements he'd ever managed to get out of him. Eamon had a point, the more he thought about it. He'd marched with Alaric from Hamptonscir with hundreds of others and fought in almost every battle since…but he was now completely alone. Everyone else that had been with him that day Osbert had seen them thundering up the road into Ulfcytel's war camp was gone. Alaric, Osmund, Bana…they were all dead. Only Eamon remained. Alive, yes, but alone. Osbert understood what he meant now, and if he were honest with himself, he didn't think he'd be able to handle it if he were in a similar situation. Perhaps it really was fortunate that Eamon had been hardened by life already. It was an interesting perspective. Interesting and tragic.

"So you spent time with Cnut?" Eamon asked, catching Osbert off guard with his question.

"I did," he replied, unsure if he wanted to talk about it.

"And you were freed when Edmund took Gainesburg?"

"That's correct."

"What's he like?"

"Who?" asked Osbert.

"Cnut. We know all about Svienn, but his son remains a mystery. He's good at losing battles, that seems true. I expect he was shaken by his father's death. That worked in our favour."

"He's…" Osbert wasn't sure how to describe him. He hadn't spent all that much time with Cnut, not enough to really know him, but the man had made an impression, and it wasn't as just another murderous Danish thug, although that aspect was undeniably present in him.

"He's not entirely as I thought," he finally said. "He has an interest in us, partially. He questioned me in Æthelred's study. He seemed to like the books."

Eamon started to laugh, an unusual sight, and he smothered it with a hand lest he wake the others. "What?" he asked, his voice again quiet. "Books? Cnut? These are the people who've been murdering us for years and burning everything…and he wants to read our books now?"

"If he does, it's only because he sees power in knowledge, or something like that. He's a sadistic monster, that I can tell you, and he has the same violent temperament as the rest of his kind. There's just something else there. A mind. A will. I can't explain it. It worries me."

"It's just as well he's dead then," sighed Eamon, like he was somehow sure of the matter.

"We can't know that. I saw him fleeing Gainesburg, and I saw him again when we charged New Gate. He was alive, and he remains so. I can feel it."

"I believe you," said Eamon.

Osbert looked at him, wondering if he was being mocked. Eamon saw his expression and spoke again. "I'm serious…it's unusual that we never recovered Cnut's body. Kings on the battlefield...let's admit we all know battles can be confusing, but when kings die, it tends to make an impression. Cnut may very well still be out there, somewhere, but if he is, his men have fled these lands. He's toothless. He has no way to strike at us."

"If he escaped to Denmark, he'll not sit idle," said Osbert. "He'll never give up on his ambition to rule us. I saw it in him."

"Then if he comes back, we'll defeat him again," said Eamon, the determination in his voice music to Osbert's ears. "Only this time, we'll be more thorough. No stragglers, no remnants fleeing, no hesitation...we kill every last Dane, and hang Cnut from the walls over the Temes so all passing by road and river may see him."

That would be a pleasing sight, thought Osbert. Everyone would know what they'd achieved, and word would spread across Europe of the Danish king who'd again tried his luck subjugating the English only to be met with dishonour and defeat. Nobody would dare lay another hand on them after that. It could herald a new epoch of peace, brought by the sword, admittedly, but peace all the same. It was a wonderful concept, and something Osbert had never known in his life, but he yearned for it despite its strangeness. War was not man's natural state. It was a product of humanity's fall, when they'd become cut off from God, and sin had entered their hearts and the world in general. It was not right, and it was not the Lord's original intention for them to live like this. There had to be something better. There could be something better. They just had to believe it. Faith would see them through, and Osbert had faith, in God and in his king, Edmund. It would always be so.

But would they really be able to defeat Cnut if he resurfaced now the foolish Æthelred was again in charge? Osbert was not so sure. Æthelred had won his throne back, for certain, but a lot of that was owed to the thousands of Normans he'd brought with him, not to mention the army Edmund had put at his service. The Danes were also much easier to deal with when forced to defend static targets, as they had been at Gainesburg and Lundenburg. Manoeuvrability had always been their strength, and England's woes over the past several decades had largely stemmed from the fact there were few places in the country that weren't relatively close to a river. This had allowed the Northmen to strike from their longships pretty much as and when they desired, leaving any armed response dependent on racing across country to confront them before they could withdraw to their vessels. It was difficult, and the nation had bled as a result, by a thousand cuts, until they'd been too weak to resist any longer. That had been Svienn's method, and it had served him well. Osbert saw no reason why Cnut wouldn't adopt the same tactics, and Æthelred wouldn't be able to stop him if he did. They needed Edmund for that. He'd think of something. He'd put things right.

Eamon suddenly tensed, his shoulders hunched and his head held at an angle as if listening. Osbert glanced about, looking down from their vantage point to spy the sleeping forms of Ulfcytel and the others. All was well. He was just about to ask Eamon what was wrong when he heard it. A sound, not from the night-shrouded countryside ahead, but behind them. He stood up and looked out across the beach and the oncoming waves. The noise sounded again and then again, like something was slapping upon the water, rhythmically, and getting louder with the doing of it. It was soon joined by a shape, dark and indistinct, but getting closer by the moment. He knew what it was. It was a ship, its prow cutting through the surf, its heaving oars rising and falling in a well-practised tempo.

Osbert's heart upped the pace when several figures became visible on deck. He'd hoped when he'd first spotted the vessel that it might be friendly, or have something to do with the fishing village they'd passed that very evening. It was not so. The men on deck were armed, their axes and spears ready and deadly, their flowing blond hair and coarse, dark armour marking them as their enemy. Danes. The reports of their flight from Hamptonscir must have been premature, or these men had, for whatever reason, decided to return. None of that mattered now. What mattered was that they kill them all.

Osbert let loose with his voice, the sound of it thundering across the shingle. "TO ARMS! THE ENEMY PRESSES US FROM THE SEA! AWAKE, AND LET US SHED HEATHEN BLOOD ONCE MORE!"

XXXII

The people were frightened and numerous, their number trailing away from the gate in a shifting column of wretched impoverishment. They weren't calmed by the presence of Edmund's warriors, and some kept flicking their eyes up towards the battlements, as if afraid of being suddenly attacked from above. They had endured much, the people of Hamptonscir, and not just in recent weeks. These lands had been under attack for a long time, and the cost had been great. They'd need time to heal from their wounds, physical or otherwise. Edmund would help them with that.

He strode out beyond the northern gatehouse, the wind tugging at his cloak. He stopped about twenty paces from the closest refugees, a bodyguard of a half dozen warriors formed up around him.

"I am the Aetheling Edmund," he boomed, his hands upon his hips and his chest puffed out for the sake of appearances, "and I welcome you to Porteceaster. Be assured I will do all in my power to see you fed and sheltered. The Danes are gone. Let this land be at peace."

It didn't have the effect he'd hoped for. The people still looked nervous, and not one of them seemed inclined to so much as take another step forward. That was strange, Edmund thought. They'd come to him, and they'd be able to see themselves that he was neither a Dane nor of a will to do them harm. They must have been through a great ordeal, he surmised. Fear did terrible things to a man, especially when they perceived themselves powerless to resist. He should be patient.

Somebody finally emerged from the crowd to speak with him. He was a priest, if his robes were anything to consider, and yet by appearances he'd endured as much as anyone. He was haunted, it was in the face; the tightness of the jaw and width and intensity of the eyes making it clear he'd seen sights he'd rather forget.

"You'll have to forgive our reticence," he said, his voice dry and hoarse, "as the last time we saw so many men under arms, they did not have such noble words for us."

"I understand," nodded Edmund, "which is why with the Danes gone…"

"They are not gone," the priest said. "They may have ceased assailing the very impressive stronghold behind you, but they are not gone. They attacked us just a couple of nights ago. Hence why we came here."

"My scouts told me they'd lifted their siege and taken to ship," answered Edmund, confused and concerned.

"I believe that is the case," said the priest, "for here at least, but the raiding continues. They came to us over the water, just a few, but enough, and burned Mideltune. I got out with those who would follow. And here we are."

Edmund thought for a moment. Mideltune was a reasonably short distance to the east, on an island that, sadly, would leave it quite vulnerable to any enemy ships still operating close by. It was typical of the Danes to make hit-and-run attacks to weaken an opponent before launching a more sizeable strike, but this contradicted the news his scouts had brought him. The enemy was supposed to be defeated, so why would they waste time continuing offensive operations elsewhere? Then he realised the truth of it. They were acting out of spite, attacking softer targets as they fled to Denmark just to let the English know they were still capable of hurting them. It was disgusting, in more ways than one. Edmund would see such men killed on sight.

"I am sorry for your troubles," said Edmund sincerely. "My offer still stands. I will shelter you here, and you will enjoy the protection of my men for as long as you desire."

"That is kind," said the priest, "yet we wish to rebuild. If you could perhaps let us rest here for a few nights, we'll then move on, back to our homes and commence reconstruction."

"I wouldn't recommend you go back so soon," said Edmund. "Let me dispatch a force...we'll secure what's left of your homes and act as a deterrent against further raids. Any Dane we catch along the way will feel the weight of justice falling most heavily upon him."

The priest smiled, broad and sincere, as did some of the others within earshot. "A fair offer," he said, "and one we are delighted to accept. Yet I must ask...did I hear you right just now? Are you really an aetheling?"

"I am. Edmund. Ironside."

Everyone was aflutter at his words, their fear dissipating with the hearing of them. That made Edmund smile. They'd heard of him, not just in terms of who he was, which was obviously common knowledge, but what he'd done and what he might yet be capable of. It pleased him beyond measure.

"May God bless you," said the priest, still smiling. "We're grateful to you, and heartened the Lord has sent a man like you to aid us in these times. Lead on, my king."

Edmund turned with his bodyguard to walk ahead and allow the refugees to follow them through the gates and into the fortress. He tried to hide it, but he could feel his face had flushed pink, such was his elation at the fact the priest had referred to him as king. He'd heard these things before from his own people, but it felt different to hear it from these poor souls who now looked to him for protection. Edmund would repay such fealty. Not a single hair on their heads would be harmed, and anyone who tried would die, preferably with Edmund's sword through their gullet. He smirked at the image.

He barked orders to one of his waiting adjutants, a new man by the name of Edgar, instructing him to get word to the kitchens to begin cooking up a suitably vast quantity of broth. The fortress interior was also to be prepared, he said, so that the people would be able to take shelter in conditions at least somewhat comfortable. Edgar nodded and hurried off, his raised voice echoing across the walls as he commandeered the necessary men to aid him in his task. Edmund headed back to the great hall, instructing the sentries at the gate to alert him if there were any problems with the newcomers. He needed to think awhile, and for that he needed quiet.

He made it in record time, or so he fancied, having proceeded at a jog for the sake of livening himself up. The warriors on duty outside the hall flinched when they saw him coming, but Edmund waved them off with a smile, thinking it likely they'd noticed him running and feared he was being pursued. He slowed upon passing through the double doors of the hall's entryway, his eyes once again snatching glimpses of the great tapestries and paintings lining the walls within. Ælfric had been wise to secure these treasures, thought Edmund. He'd see they were provided with proper care and reverence for as long as he remained here.

Edmund was sat alone and at table close to the main hearth when he saw her. He'd not thought to bother her, knowing she preferred her solitude in the tower, yet she'd chosen to appear now, dressed in an emerald-coloured cyrtel that reminded him of the green of the sea. She'd covered her hair, as was only appropriate, but her headscarf looked tight to the point of discomfort, making her pale, narrow face appear severe and anxious. Edmund smiled, but she didn't return it, instead sitting down just across from him. Æva was troubled. She always was. Edmund wished he could do something for her. He had the will for it, but didn't know if there was a way.

"Is Brandon…"

"He's fine," she said quickly. "He's upstairs, and he doesn't want me forcing him to cling to my side at all hours. He's too old for that."

"What brought you down here?" Edmund asked, hoping she wouldn't take offence given that, morally speaking, this was her home.

"I saw people from the tower," she said. "Where are they from, and why did you let them in?"

"They are survivors from Mideltune," he answered. "They came here in search of aid. I intend to give it to them."

"Noble," said Æva, "but what happened at Mideltune? You know that's where Cenric was from?"

"They were attacked by enemy raiders. I'll be dispatching men soon enough to deal with them, should any have been foolish enough to linger…but no, I didn't know Cenric hailed from there. Is he on your mind? Is that why you look so sad?"

Æva sighed and shook her head. "It's not just him," she muttered, "it's everything here. Everything has a memory attached to it, even the stones. I feel lost, like a solitary echo of what was…now condemned to fade with time and isolation. Does that make sense?"

She had an interesting way with words, Edmund thought, but in truth, he felt he could understand where she was coming from. "I think I may have experienced something similar," he said. "In Snotingeham…I spent a winter always at my brother's graveside. We'd both spent so much time in that town when we were young. So many memories, yes? But then one day Æthelstan was gone and I…I just remained. An echo of what had been."

At first he thought he'd wounded her, such was her expression, but then she spoke, with tears too, but of relief as well as sadness. "That's it," she said breathlessly, "that's it exactly. Alaric is everywhere here. He permeates everything, as does Cenric…Osmund…but all are gone now. All dead, and those who may be alive are elsewhere, leaving me with nothing but an empty shell of memories to contemplate. What do I do?"

"I had good friends to help me during my own time of sorrow. Sigeferth, and his wife, Ealdgyth, and of course my sister, Wulfhild. Yet I'll be honest with you, Æva…there was a time when they couldn't reach me. They tried, but my grief was still too pronounced. I had to address that first and wait things out. Then my friends were able to help me."

"So that's what I must do?" she asked. "Just endure the pain until it gets better, and I can somehow find comfort in the company of others?"

"You tell me," Edmund said. "You came down from your chambers. You're sitting here. If you want my opinion…that means you're already feeling a little brighter. Otherwise, how could you be putting up with me now?"

She laughed, amused by his self-depreciation. "Where is Wulfhild, anyway?" she asked. "It occurs to me that I still barely know her."

"She's around, reading something in Ælfric's chambers, I think. She's upset I sent Ulfcytel away."

"I think she must miss him," remarked Æva.

"She does, but I had need of her husband, and he is always willing. We have to find out where Ælfric went."

"Why? If I'm honest, I'm surprised you'd care…nobody came to help him when this place was under attack, and he was never a popular man before that."

"I should have come earlier, I see that now," sighed Edmund, feeling suddenly guilty. "The strategic situation was…well, I've explained all that to you before. I just feel I owe it to Ælfric to find him and help him. Hamptonscir would never have been attacked like this if he'd sat quiet and submitted to Svienn like everyone else. He chose the hard path for my sake. I will not forget it."

"Are you not afraid of your father? Æthelred wanted Ælfric and I dead."

"He's given me certain assurances," said Edmund. "He's to let things lie; no more vendettas. So far, he seems eager to keep his word."

"You'll forgive me if I'm not inspired with confidence," muttered Æva, her expression bitter.

"I understand," said Edmund, remembering well enough how Æthelred's orders had cost her husband his life. "I just want you to know, Æva, that…"

He couldn't find the words. His heart was beating in his ears, and he felt suddenly warm, too warm. There was anxiety, also, the stuff frothing up from his stomach like a swarm of angry insects.

"You want me to know…?"

"That…I wouldn't let anything happen to you or Brandon," he blurted, his words quick, haphazard almost. "I would never…when I look at you, I feel…it's like I…"

A sudden crash sounded through the hall, making Edmund wonder if the doors at the entrance had been forced open from without. He could hear shouting and hurrying footsteps, all of which were getting closer. He stood up, interposing himself between Æva and whatever was heading towards them. There must have been some kind of trouble with the newcomers. He'd use reason and dialogue as his first option, but if anyone thought to harm his people, they'd realise their folly soon enough.

Ulfcytel stormed into view, a single unconscious warrior draped over his mailed buttress of a shoulder. Others followed, all of them dishevelled and battered, a couple having to be supported by their brethren as they limped or shuffled along. The man with one ear, Eamon, was with them and assisting a wounded comrade Edmund didn't recognise. These must have been the men Ulfcytel had taken with him in his bid to scout the coast and obtain a ship. Something bad had then happened. Edmund felt like he could guess as to what.

"We were attacked!" exclaimed Ulfcytel, striding past Edmund to deposit his wounded compatriot onto the table. Æva stood up, her eyes concerned as she beheld the man who now lay there. It was Osbert, and he was not in good health. His byrnie was ruined, the metal rings around the chest having split open after what was most probably a blow from an axe swung with both arms. Blood was flowing freely, and from the pallidness of Osbert's skin, it had been doing so for some time. Edmund had seen enough battlefield injuries to know the poor lad probably wasn't coming back from this, but it didn't matter. They'd do everything they could to save him.

The priest who'd come with the refugees suddenly appeared, as if he'd followed Ulfcytel after realising his skills would be needed. "We have to get this man out of that mail shirt first," he said calmly. "Just be gentle about it. That's a serious amount of blood he's already lost, and we don't want to shake him about more than necessary."

Edmund nodded and set to work, Ulfcytel assisting. The rest of the wounded had sat or lain down upon the floor to wait their turn, as none of them were as severely wounded as Osbert. It took more time than Edmund expected, but they eventually managed to get him out of his armour so that the priest could inspect his wound properly.

"What happened?" Edmund asked Ulfcytel, content to leave the priest to his work for the moment.

"Bastard Danes happened!" Ulfcytel thundered. "We'd gone east, looking for a ship, as agreed. There was nothing, just a burnt-out fishing village with burnt-out fishing boats, but when we bedded down, a bloody great longship suddenly came out of the dark and unloaded a score of scumbags right on top of us!"

Edmund grit his teeth, thinking on where exactly Ulfcytel's party might have been located at the time of the attack. His knowledge of Hamptonscir was limited since he'd rarely had reason to come here, but if Ulfcytel had headed east from Porteceaster, that would have put him in some kind of proximity to Mideltune. It wasn't, therefore, unreasonable to suspect he'd run into some of the raiding party that had put so many people to flight just a couple of nights ago.

"You killed them all?" Edmund asked, feeling he knew the ealdorman well enough to know the answer already.

"Too bloody right!" he said. "We left none alive, but they didn't go quietly. They fought hard, and we made sure they died hard."

"And their ship?" Edmund asked.

"Damaged," he said. "From the looks of it, they were caught in a storm or some such. The mast was practically splintered in half, and the sails were all shot to hell. They were taking on water too, but the deck was strewn with random crap, like coins and jewellery, all of it looking like it were from around here…methinks they'd been raiding only to have God send them some bad weather."

Osbert let loose with a hacking cough, leaving flecks of blood splattered across his beard. Eamon and Æva had rushed the priest an assortment of supplies whilst Edmund had been talking, giving him clean water and also some bandages that looked like they'd been made in a hurry from an old cyrtel. Osbert kept coughing whilst his wound was compressed and bandaged, but he soon began to fit, his entire body shaking like it was being assailed by some malevolent spirit. Ulfcytel hurried to his side and held his arms to the table, the ealdorman twisting his own body at a peculiar angle so the priest still had room to work.

Wulfhild appeared, approaching quietly to put an affectionate hand to Ulfcytel's shoulder. He looked at her briefly and turned back to the still convulsing Osbert, his face and arms tense as he did his best to keep him from tumbling off the table. Edmund moved to help, repeating the Jesus Prayer in his mind so that Christ himself might show mercy to the much-maligned man lying before them. Osbert coughed again, and his body then stiffened with such violence he vomited a stream of blood and stomach acid up and outwards all over Edmund and Ulfcytel both. Edmund could see Ulfcytel was weeping openly, his lips moving frantically with a litany of whispered prayers. Edmund had only ever seen him like this once, after Alaric had died. He'd been an absolute mountain of a man since then, unflappable and unstoppable, but it was not so now. Osbert must really mean something to him.

The man himself finally calmed, his convulsions easing into stillness. He was breathing, shallow and light, but it was better than nothing at all. The bleeding had also subsided, and with a little effort they managed to get his entire upper torso bandaged, Ulfcytel assisting with a gentleness that was distinctly paternal. He mumbled his thanks to the priest once they'd finished. The man bowed slightly, but the ealdorman himself remained still, his eyes lowered towards the unconscious Osbert, his front and face covered in a patchwork of sweat, tears, blood, and vomit.

Edmund saw something in him, something he'd not spotted before. He knew he and Wulfhild wanted children. They'd tried, with tragic results, and Edmund had been grieved to hear of their stillborn and the heartbreak it must have caused them. He didn't know much about Osbert or how he'd come to be in Ulfcytel's service, but he could tell from observing him these past minutes that the ealdorman cared for him with a depth and sincerity that was unmistakably fatherly. Edmund had no children of his own, of course, and his father had largely ignored him when he was a boy, but he'd often thought of fatherhood in an idealised sense, and Ulfcytel had personified it here.

It would be hard to put it into words, but it was like Ulfcytel's great heart had opened, displaying the love that lay within for any who might care to look. Edmund respected him all the more for it. It gave him hope, also, that perhaps one day his own father might look upon him the way Ulfcytel now watched over Osbert. Was that a foolish dream? He knew not, but he was clear about one thing: Osbert couldn't be allowed to expire. Ulfcytel wouldn't survive it. He could see it in his eyes and the tears that still welled there. Ælfric and his disappearing act could wait, for the moment. Edmund had more important things to focus on. Ulfcytel needed him, and he'd not be found wanting.

XXXIII

The flames from the candles flickered and danced in the stone alcove, their light a soft, golden glow amidst the deepening purple of twilight. Æthelred sat before them and bowed his head, allowing the evening breeze to tousle at his thinning locks. This was a special day. Saint Alban's day, but that was not the sole reason he was now sitting in prayer. It was the birthday of his departed son, Æthelstan. He missed him. He wanted him to know that, if God, in his mercy, would make it so.

Æthelred had spent much of the day at St Mildred's, as was expected. He'd inhaled more than his fair share of incense, and Father Chad had been quite enthusiastic with the censer, swinging it back and forth like he were hoping to hypnotise them. Despite the irritation to his nostrils, Æthelred liked the tradition, thinking it touchingly appropriate for the priest to venerate the congregation just as he'd done with the altar and icons. He hoped the custom would never fall out of style. It was important that people feel cared for by both Church and God. Worship should not be some remote spectacle. People had to feel like they were participants, not passive accessories.

He opened his eyes, the Jesus Prayer continuing to spill from his lips. He was in his garden in Lundenburg, one of his favourite places to be, just as it had been with his children. He was facing away from much of it, his attention towards the wall and the alcove he'd used on and off for years for the sake of prayer. An icon was ensconced there, bearing the likeness of Christ, his hand raised in a blessing. It was a simple thing. It was also the only gift his father, King Edgar, had seen fit to bestow on him. As such, Æthelred would always treasure it.

His prayers ceased, and he looked around. The shadows had deepened, but he could still see well enough, and the sound of the wind rustling through the leaves of his fruit trees was like a salve for his troubled mind. This was a beautiful place, and it was full of beautiful memories. Æthelstan had loved it here as a boy, and the same went for his brothers and sisters. Æthelred would do anything to have him back with him, here and now. Fate, however, had decided to deny him such simple pleasures, as it had done with so many of his other children. Æthelred felt like weeping openly at the thought of it.

There was, unfortunately, little time for such release. He instead stood up and crossed himself, using the sleeves of his crimson threaded tunic to dry his tears. He had other business to attend to, which sadly couldn't involve him being open with his emotions. Thegns and ealdormen had come, and they awaited him in his banqueting hall, all apparently eager to reaffirm their allegiance to him as King of England. There was no way Æthelred could be himself in front of such men. A facade must be thrown up; a projection of power and dignity. It was everything he'd wanted to avoid. He'd wanted a simpler life. Fate had again conspired to deny him that.

He reached out and took one of the candles, using it to light his way back to those familiar double doors and the revelling "notables" he knew awaited him. The guards bowed when they saw him and allowed him entry, the stench of mead and roast meat assailing his nose as he passed within. The doors shut behind him, and all was quiet, the sound of conversation fading to nothing. A dozen and then three dozen more pairs of eyes fell upon him, some anxious, some relieved, others unreadable. He hoped they found him impressive. He'd dressed for it, and the golden, bejewelled circlet he was wearing conveyed a certain image, as did the sword and scabbard at his belt. He'd look like a warrior king tonight, even if he weren't one in actual practice.

Æthelred made his way through the throng, the obsequious multitude parting to let him through. Emma appeared and moved to his side, dressed in a predictably flamboyant gown of purple-dyed silk. He almost scowled when she clasped his elbow, finding her touch repulsive now he knew the nature of her heart and the blackened soul that dwelled there. Many a thegn bowed their head when he moved past them, even Sigeferth and his bastard brother, Morcar. They were all here, from every corner, at least those who still saw fit to come in person, which excluded snakes like Ulfcytel and Ælfric and the ever-enigmatic Wulfnoth. Æthelred would have done something about them, had he been able. But that just wasn't possible. Edmund's influence protected them. He'd not risk offending him. He had to see that he'd changed. His actions would prove it.

He and Emma reached the throne, and Æthelred stared at it for a moment, his mind awash with images of that bastard Svienn sitting here like he somehow owned the entire place simply by merit of his own murderousness. He snapped out of it, turning back to behold his audience from his newfound vantage point.

"I want to thank you all for coming," he announced, projecting his voice across the whole chamber. "I've said it before, and I'll say it again…the past is the past. Svienn is dead, and those who gave him allegiance out of desperation are no enemies of mine. Let there be no further need for discord. I have returned, and I accept your renewed fealty in the spirit of magnanimity. England has its king. All is well."

A round of applause followed, some more enthusiastic in their contributions than others. Archbishop Wulfstan was beaming, despite his age and stretched leather purse of a face, and Æthelred couldn't help but return it, so earnest was the old man in his appreciation. Eadric was close by with his fat brother, Beorhtric, the latter bellowing something about "God and country" as if he really cared about either. Eadric's wife, Eadgyth, was at his side, looking up at her father, Æthelred, like she expected something more from him. Eadwig was there too, appearing thoughtful as always, as were Uhtred and Æthelmaer, the two ealdormen appearing very much at ease in the company of the other.

The rest of the assembly was made up of various thegns and their retainers, and Æthelred could name most of them by sight, although there were a few newcomers he didn't recognise. Hereward, of course, had moved up to the throne, his armoured, square shoulders and barrel chest on full display. Æthelred appreciated it. A projection of might and physicality was always important when dealing with his people, especially these snakes presently arrayed before him. Æthelred couldn't do that himself, old as he was, but Hereward could, and he did it well, every time. It also wasn't just for show. Hereward could kill anyone present. Æthelred had witnessed him do such things several times now, as had Emma, which would explain the anxiety in her eyes whenever she looked at him. Æthelred smiled. He was in control. This evening might just turn out well.

His guests came forward, one at a time, to kneel before the throne and affirm their loyalty to him as "King of England, by the will of God and men" and all the rest of it.

It took a while, and by the time they'd finished, night was upon them, prompting somebody to light a line of torches tucked into the alcoves along the walls.

A whole throng of stewards then entered, led by Cuthbert, Æthelred's long-faithful servant. They began clearing away the platters and tankards that littered the table, replacing them with fresh delicacies and copious amounts of wine and mead both. Cuthbert himself hurried up to the throne to place a single cup of wine into Æthelred's hand, a few whispered words assuring him that it was his favourite vintage. Æthelred frowned and took a sip, unsure whether he even had a favourite vintage, but it was palatable enough, the stuff tasting pleasantly fruity as it sloshed across his tongue. Cuthbert refilled his cup and bowed before skittering off, leaving Æthelred to survey his guests. They were gorging themselves, again, and drinking, again. He'd leave them to it. If they were happy, they'd not be of a mind to make trouble. Æthelred didn't want trouble.

He finished his wine and got up, observing with incredulity how Emma had stayed standing at his side for the entire time. He looked at her and jerked his head towards their audience, implying she should depart from him and go do something that didn't involve looking like an overly dressed statue. She obeyed, a brief scowl marring her features upon moving past him. Æthelred then descended the steps to survey what was offered at table, the noble and distinctly intimidating Hereward at his right hand.

"Your words were most gracious, my king," said Sigeferth, the fool having emerged from the throng to engage him in conversation. He looked old, Æthelred thought, and the finery of his attire didn't hide it, nor the hint of unease that lingered in those tired, puffy eyes. He'd brought his bitch of a wife, Ealdgyth; too young and too pretty for an ageing clown like Sigeferth, but her smile was enchanting, and she seemed to have a genuine affection for her husband if her body language was anything to go by. Æthelred should have married her to one of his sons. Edmund would be a good match, since he apparently loved the Five Boroughs so much. Sigeferth didn't deserve her.

"Did you hear me?" Sigeferth asked, his impertinence grating.

"I did," snapped Æthelred, "and what of it? You wanted to tell me I'm gracious to my face? Why? Don't you have drinking to do? Æthelstan would be doing that right now, if he were here."

Sigeferth took that well, like he'd been expecting the barb and had prepared for it in advance. "I never got to tell you how sorry I am about Æthelstan," he said. "Morcar and I were both there with Edmund when he passed. He spoke to Edmund before he went. He gave him his blessing and confidence. Called him Ironside. A name others, in their love for him, have been quick to embrace."

"What does that even mean?" asked Æthelred, annoyed and saddened at the thought of his dying son.

"It was something of a private joke between the two of them," said Morcar, appearing now to stand with his brother. "Æthelstan would note at times that Edmund was very difficult for him to knock over when they sparred. He quipped, more than once, that he must be made of iron. Given that Edmund was visibly wounded in the side at Bernecestre and kept on fighting…well, you can see how Æthelstan got the notion."

"Why would you say this to me?" seethed Æthelred, allowing a returning Cuthbert to refill his cup. "What do you hope to gain? You intend to throw me off balance? Make me sad and distracted by making me think on the death of my son?"

"No, not at all," said Sigeferth hurriedly. "It's just I'd never gotten to tell you…and with it being Æthelstan's birthday…"

"Get out of my sight, the three of you."

They all obeyed, quickly and without comment. Æthelred gripped his cup harder, fancying he might be able to break it if he vented enough of his rage upon its surface. It held firm, which was just as well, and he drank again, long and deep, hoping to calm himself and blot out the images Sigeferth had placed in his mind. He was irked that they'd known it was Æthelstan's birthday. They probably knew Edmund's too. They were always entertaining them, fussing over them, like Æthelred himself wasn't a good enough father. Bastards, each of them. Once this night was over, he'd be glad to see the back of them.

More conversation followed, thankfully from persons more palatable to his senses. Eadric banged on for a bit, talking about how he intended to attract a greater influx of trade into Mierċe by improving the roads and settling accounts with the Welsh. Æthelred frowned whilst he continued with some story about how he'd had them punished by mounting an armed expedition, which was news to Æthelred, and not really of the most welcome kind. He'd of course ordered Eadric in the past to press the Welsh for tribute, most particularly after the Battle of Hringmere when he'd needed revenues to pay Thorkell, but he hadn't been aware he'd opted for such a violent solution to their problems. Eadric had best calm himself. Æthelred needed the Britons placid, and rampaging across the border to burn them out of their homes wasn't the way to do that. He told him as such. Eadric nodded. That would have to do.

The Ealdorman Uhtred made himself known, his twin bodyguards eyeing Hereward as they approached. Æthelred didn't pay all that much attention when Uhtred began to talk at him. It was boring stuff; just pleasantries and waffle, but he was glad Uhtred had gotten over his rude treatment at the hands of Edmund, and he was also happy he didn't mention him once.

Æthelred knew Uhtred had by now sent much of his army home to tend their fields, which was a shame, as for a time he'd enjoyed watching the combined armies of Norþanhymbre, Mierċe, and Normandy all milling about beneath his walls. There must have been close to ten thousand warriors out there. A formidable force, one that he could have used not so long ago when Thorkell had been hurling himself at Canterburie. It was typical that his ealdormen hadn't seen fit to assist him then, but had appeared with all their men and retinues when they felt it served them. That would have to change.

Just as he'd thought of Canterburie, a man appeared, one Æthelred had thought long dead. Ælfweard was his name, and he'd once held the rank of reeve, given to him by Æthelred himself so that he might oversee Canterburie and the financial concerns that came with it. His position was now moot since Thorkell had destroyed most of the city, which left Æthelred curious on how the reeve had even escaped. He was no fighter, and he wasn't particularly clever either, except with numbers.

"I greet you, King Æthelred," said Ælfweard, as if the two were somehow not even acquainted.

"I thought you dead," said Æthelred, unashamed of the surprise in his voice.

"Not yet," replied Ælfweard. "And if you are referring to the destruction of Canterburie…there were many brave heroes who sought to defend my city when no one else would. I owe them much, even if we were ultimately defeated."

"And what heroes were these?" Æthelred didn't like where this was going. There was something in Ælfweard's eyes; a certain look that was too close to contempt. He didn't favour it.

"You know as well as I do," he said. "Everyone knows, everyone heard of the siege and the battle and the destruction and murder and rape and desecration that followed. Those who stood, arms in hand, to prevent that will always be remembered, in the minds of men and angels both. In any case…congratulations on your return to power. You should know I have been helping in the reconstruction efforts at Canterburie. If you do intend to rule wisely, my good king, we would appreciate your aid."

Ælfweard didn't wait for a response. He turned and left, like he'd expected nothing from his king to begin with and couldn't be bothered to hear him prove it. Æthelred didn't know what to make of any of that. The reeve was bitter over the destruction of Canterburie, that was obvious, and Æthelred couldn't say his feelings were unwarranted. What had happened there had been a disgusting affair. He'd heard the stories. Women violated and then impaled on spikes, their children, too. Æthelred couldn't imagine such scenes, but he believed it. Thorkell would need to answer for that, but not in this life. He was too useful. Æthelred would leave it to God, and there was no doubting that the great and mighty Thorkell the Tall would burn in hell. Æthelred hoped he wouldn't be condemned to follow him.

He drank more wine, Cuthbert again assisting him with yet another refill. It tasted better than ever, which was typical for alcoholic beverages when they started to work their magic upon the senses. This type of drunkenness felt a little different, though. He felt angry, which he generally didn't expect from wine. He wanted solitude, yet couldn't get it, since everyone expected him to remain here and listen to their self-serving prattle. Even worse, Godfrey, that Norman bastard sent by the duke to oversee his armies, had by now appeared, which made Æthelred very, very uncomfortable indeed. His presence sent the wrong message. It reminded everyone of Duke Richard's part in his return. People would think on it, and then gossip. It was the way of things. Unfortunately, he could do nothing about it, and by the smug look on his face, Godfrey knew it.

The irritation soon became too much. His own nobles were an annoyance, yet to have Godfrey here reminding everyone of their debt to Normandy was intolerable. Æthelred hurried to the doors, the crowd shifting around him, and made an exit, answering any queries as to his intent with a withering glare. He didn't slow in his escape, instead taking a left turn and striding down the corridor towards his garden. He could think there, and there would be no Godfrey, nor Sigeferth either. That in itself would be a blessing.

He sat on the stone bench he'd prayed at earlier. Hereward had followed, yet he was keeping a respectful distance, no doubt from reading his mood. It was dark, and the candles he'd lit before had burned themselves out, but there was a clear sky above, the stars appearing as a blanket of lightly veiled diamonds sparkling on high.

Hereward tensed when footsteps sounded from the way they'd come. Æthelred twisted around in time to see his daughter, Eadgyth, emerge from the shadows, her eyes wide with what he took to be anxiety. She wasn't with her husband, Eadric. That was strange. The two were generally inseparable.

"Can I talk to you?" she asked, her hands trembling.

"What is it?" Æthelred asked, gesturing for Hereward to let her pass.

"I was hoping we could speak in private, father."

"I have things to be doing, daughter. I'm just taking a break. Soon I'll have to return to that viper's nest and endure until all the serpents have passed out from drink."

"I have something I need to tell you," she pressed. "I can't...please, will you not just..."

"Just tell me here, Eadgyth! I don't have the time for fuss, and anything you can say to me you can say in front of Hereward." He drank again from his cup. It was bitter now. It hadn't been before.

She said something, but it was hard to hear, and then yet more footsteps, hurried this time, could be heard heading towards them. Hereward moved to bar Eadric's path as he emerged into the starlight, thinking perhaps that Æthelred wanted time alone with his daughter without her husband butting in. It wasn't so. Eadric had something on his mind, if his flushed countenance was any indication. Æthelred would hear it spoken.

"Is everything alright?" Eadric asked, his eyes upon his wife.

"Yes, yes, we're all fine," snapped Æthelred, another hurried gesture seeing Hereward step back from Eadric so that he could approach. Eadgyth looked truly uncomfortable now. She'd begun to fidget, rubbing at her thumbs frantically like she had a painful itch to soothe. Just what was all that about?

"Would you care for some more wine, my king?" Eadric asked casually, his worried look easing somewhat.

"Yes, get Cuthbert to bring more, but I think Eadgyth wanted to tell me something. You feel safe speaking in front of your husband, don't you, daughter? A wife shouldn't keep secrets."

"She should not," agreed Eadric.

Eadgyth stared for a moment, her face unreadable, as if she'd made some sudden effort to get control of herself so she'd give nothing away to anyone who might care to judge her. "I'll go and tell Cuthbert to bring more wine," she said neutrally, and headed back the way she'd come, leaving Eadric standing there. This was all rather odd, thought Æthelred. She'd clearly had something to say, but Eadric's presence had robbed her of the inclination. He'd have to ask her later and...

"The wine is indeed a pleasant one, is it not?" asked Eadric, his voice cutting through Æthelred's train of thought.

"It is," he replied with a nod. He drained his cup with one long swig, ignoring how some wine seeped into his beard. He was drunk, he knew, and it didn't really matter. He was in too dark a mood to be bothered by such things.

Cuthbert appeared, as expected, yet Eadgyth was not with him. Æthelred wondered about that whilst Cuthbert refilled his cup, thinking she'd perhaps been caught up in conversation with some of the untrustworthy reptiles back at the banquet. It would be just like Sigeferth and Morcar to try and woo her. They'd done that with Edmund and Æthelstan. Why not try it with his daughter?

He drank from his now full cup. He didn't care about how it tasted, since his intention was to make himself insensible so the evening might speed itself on to a conclusion that didn't involve him having to talk to anyone. Sigeferth, unfortunately, remained in his thoughts, as irritating as if he were here in person. He could picture him back there, blathering on at Eadgyth, always acting so noble, like he were some kindly grandfather, not that he was that old. He'd be talking about Æthelstan, most likely, trying to impress upon Eadgyth how sorry he was that he'd gotten him killed. Æthelred wouldn't stand for it.

"Bring Sigeferth and Morcar."

Eadric turned quickly and hurried away, his eagerness to comply with his king's wishes always so very refreshing. Æthelred drained his cup in the meantime, and Cuthbert again refilled it, mumbling about how he'd have to go and fetch another wineskin. Æthelred made a noise in the back of his throat, both irritable and impatient. Cuthbert made himself scarce. He'd understood.

Eadric soon appeared, and Sigeferth and Morcar were with him, the two brothers looking a little uneasy. They didn't like Eadric, and Eadric didn't like them. Æthelred knew why, for they were related to a certain Ælfhelm that Eadric had killed on Æthelred's orders. He felt bad about that at times, when he was alone and in low spirits. He didn't now. He was too angry. He was king and could do as he willed. Anyone who dissented from that deserved to be punished.

"What have you been saying to my daughter?" he demanded, standing up, cup in hand, to confront his guests. They looked confused, staring at the other and then at Eadric and back to Æthelred.

"I believe we may have misunderstood," said Morcar, stoic as always. It only angered Æthelred further.

"Don't play your stupid games with me, Morcar," Æthelred simmered. "You both know it's Æthelstan's birthday, and you both doted on him, trying to extend your oh-so-wholesome influence over him. Did you hope to do the same with Eadgyth? Is that why she's so troubled?"

"We've not spoken with her all night," protested Sigeferth.

"Not so," said Eadric coolly. "I saw you speaking with my wife not an hour ago. She'd been happy before then. Now she isn't. As her husband, I'd have your answer as to why. As will the king."

"Hold your lying tongue!" spat Morcar, his previously calm bearing crumbling in an instant. "We've not spoken with your wife, on any matter, and you know it! You speak falsehoods, in front of your own king! The shame of it!"

Eadric angled his head towards Æthelred. "I'm afraid I must insist to you, my king, that the noble Morcar here is attempting to mislead us. He and his good brother did indeed speak with Eadgyth, and the effect was as I said. She became troubled."

"Call for her then!" demanded Sigeferth. "Call for the lady Eadgyth and let's have her opinion on our conduct!"

"Don't make demands of me!" Æthelred shouted, slurring slightly. "You dare vex me, on today of all days?! I was gracious enough in allowing Edmund to leave you here so that you might prove your loyalty, yet I see now you have not changed. You remain as you are. Snakes!"

Sigeferth looked at Morcar, and Morcar looked back, each of them unsure. "Silence does not help your case," said Eadric quietly, "and so I will remind you that you stand before the King of England. You are obliged to be honest and answer…"

Sigeferth spun to face him, his face twisting in anger. "What a joke!" he boomed. "You'd lecture us on honesty?! The biggest rat in the country?! Eadric of bloody Sciropesberie?! A liar and murderer both!"

"You will do as he says!" bellowed Æthelred. His throat felt sore, so he took more wine.

"Obey the likes of Eadric?" sneered Morcar. "A man who conspired his way to the top and left a river of blood in his wake, often on your orders? We'll not stand for this! Command as you will, king, but we have done nothing to upset your daughter, and I won't be baited by Eadric the Grasper!"

Æthelred could feel his face reddening, the heat of his anger rising upward to overpower his reason. He spoke, his voice raw and hot with malice, uttering words he'd long ached to unleash.

"Even after so much time has passed, and you have done me so much wrong, you are defiant. You got my son killed…you manipulated Æthelstan and Edmund into attacking Thor…"

"No!" snapped Sigeferth, loud and sharp. "That's not right! Thorkell had to be stopped, and you had failed to act, again and again! It fell to better men to come to the defence of the kingdom, and your sons rose to the occasion, as Edmund still does! You dishonour Æthelstan's memory by bearing such ill-conceived grudges!"

It wasn't entirely clear what happened next. There was a moment of shocked silence, and Sigeferth most of all was afflicted by it, his expression suggesting he'd only just now realised his folly. Æthelred could hear his heart hammering in his chest, and his eyes were wet, although if they were tears of rage or just grief, he was not sure. He did know that he'd dropped his wine, the contents discharging across the earth like a streak of freshly shed blood. His sword was then in his hand, the blade shimmering slightly upon catching the starlight. He felt the desire to kill, and his legs acted on it, propelling him forward towards Sigeferth even as his vision remained clouded with tears.

Somebody cried out as he paused to wipe them away. There was a shout, and Sigeferth went down, hard and heavy, like he was dead already and whatever had assailed him was of such a force as to kill him instantly. Æthelred stared on in shock at the sight of Morcar locking swords with Eadric over Sigeferth's prone form, Hereward lumbering to intervene. He was too late. Morcar was now on the ground, his hands held to his throat in a futile effort to contain the fountain of blood erupting from between his fingers. He gurgled and thrashed, his eyes filled with hatred, gazing up at the triumphant Eadric. Then he was still, his soul departing to join his brother in judgement.

Æthelred blinked. His vision cleared. Eadric returned his sword to its scabbard, unconcerned at the blood that now soaked his tunic. Hereward was dumbfounded, looking in disbelief to Eadric, the dead brothers, and then Æthelred. Somebody gasped, the sound barely audible, but Æthelred's eyes looked to the source of it. Eadwig, his son, was there, gazing out from the archway leading back to the throne room. He'd seen everything. That wasn't right. None of this was right. Æthelred had to do something.

"It-it-it's not as bad as it looks," he stammered, his excuse truly pitiful in light of the cold reality. Eadwig looked at his father, his eyes filled with regret. He then turned and fled the way he'd come, the sound of his flight sharp and frantic. Æthelred took a step forward and then another, thinking he might pursue. The lad shouldn't have seen this, whatever it was. Nobody should have. Nothing good could come of this.

"Be still, my king," said Eadric calmly. "Sigeferth attacked me for a reason. He knew he'd gambled and lost in attempting to manipulate my wife. I can only conclude he sought to wipe the slate clean by killing me and anyone else who might accuse him, you included."

"He sought to kill me?!" Æthelred breathed, unsure and unsteady. He'd not actually seen Sigeferth attack Eadric, as his eyes had been full of tears at the time. Only Morcar had done so.

"Oh yes," replied Eadric. "He drew a weapon, didn't he? Drew a weapon on his king…I had to defend us. I had no choice."

"What say you, Hereward?" asked Æthelred, desiring a second opinion. Hereward still looked uncertain, something Æthelred had rarely seen. It did not inspire confidence.

"I'm afraid I looked to you as soon as you drew your sword," he finally said. "I was also not at an angle that would allow me to see Sigeferth's hands, if he was attempting to ready a weapon. It…"

"He was doing just that," Eadric interrupted firmly. "His hand went to the hilt of his sword, and his eyes were fixed on me, alive with hate. I know the look; it's the look any man has when he's made the decision to kill, and anyone who doesn't act on such a thing will usually end up dead. I'd prefer to remain alive. And we are, all of us. All is well."

"I'm drunk," Æthelred said feebly. "I don't know what to think…why am I so angry? Wine is normally so calming…Eadwig! Where is Eadwig!? Hereward, you must go after him and bring him back. He won't understand any of this. I have to talk to him. Please, go!"

Hereward didn't need to be told twice. He headed off in pursuit of Eadwig, his movements potently fast despite the weight of his armour. Æthelred fell to his knees by Sigeferth's side, his hand releasing its hold on his sword. It clattered to the ground, forgotten and unused.

"This wasn't how it was supposed to be," wept Æthelred, his tears returning in abundance. "I promised Edmund…I promised him I'd not harm them, and now I have. He'll never forgive me now! Not for this, and not for his uncle!"

Eadric placed a hand upon his trembling shoulder. "All will be well," he soothed. "You have your queen and the other children, Edward and Alfred. Edward will make a fine heir. You don't need…"

"No!" protested Æthelred, drawing away from his touch. "I promised Edmund he'd be king after me! I might have failed to keep my word in its entirety, but I'll not fail in this!"

"My king, I must inform you that if Edmund believes himself your heir and is sufficiently angered by what's happened here tonight, then you may be in danger. He could make an attempt on your life, not directly, but from the shadows, knowing that with your death, he'd be able to…"

"You don't know him, you fool! My boy has more nobility in him than you or I or anyone else in England! He'd never stoop so low! He is his mother's son, through and through!"

"Then I fear we have yet more concerns," said Eadric, still strangely calm. "Sigeferth's wife is back there and likely wondering where her husband is. They have no sons between them. With him dead, she will be the most powerful person in the Five Boroughs. If she escapes to lead an uprising…"

"Have her seized then!" Æthelred spluttered, suddenly afraid. "Get Cuthbert in here to get rid of these bodies, and then get her away from the banquet so you can sequester her somewhere for the rest of the night. Be quick, and don't make a spectacle of it! Go!"

Eadric vanished in a flash, or what seemed like a flash, given Æthelred's vision was again blurred with tears. He was frightened and miserable, which was nothing new, but the anger was still there, hot and vital, telling him over and over how justice had been done. He wasn't so sure. This rage was a strange thing, novel and unwelcome, and in his heart, he knew the truth. This was a tragedy, one that should never have happened. He continued to weep, images of Edmund and Æthelstan both upon his mind. They'd loved these two men, Sigeferth and Morcar, and now Æthelred had taken them away. Consequences could only follow. Blood would call out for more blood, and Æthelred had the unsettling notion that Edmund would be the one shedding it.

"I'm so sorry," he whispered. "I'm so, so sorry."

The two dead men did not answer. Æthelred was alone with his grief. As he always had been.

XXXIV

Eadwig had never been a very physical man. He wasn't fat or unhealthy, but he'd neglected his body, thinking the mind and the knowledge it contained was the only thing that mattered. He'd learned these past months what a mistake that had been. Trying times required men of action, and now was his time to act. If only it were not so difficult.

His chest was heaving by the time he'd made it to the doors leading to the banquet. He kept on running, nearly knocking over several drunken thegns as he sped past. They called after him, asking him to stop and share a drink, but he ignored them, focusing instead on his breath and what lay ahead. This whole place was like a warren, the passageways twisting and turning seemingly at random, yet Eadwig knew it well and had a good memory. The exit wasn't far off, and nobody on guard duty would be looking to stop him, considering his rank and status. This nightmare might soon end.

He was pushing his way past the outer doors to the hall when it hit him. Sigeferth and Morcar really were dead. That hadn't been for show, and there was no way they could survive the injuries they'd been dealt. Eadwig was no warrior, yet even he knew that a blade to the throat wouldn't work wonders when it came to health and longevity. The murderer, Eadric, might look like a girlish fop, but he obviously had more than a little skill with that sword of his. He was practised and ruthless, traits Eadwig might be inclined to value if possessed by a man of virtue. In Eadric's case, it was just horrifying.

The night air whipped past his ears as he made it through the courtyard and towards the stables. He needed a horse, a fast one, if he were to make haste to Edmund and tell him of what he'd seen. His brother had sent word a while ago, saying something about how the Danes had apparently fled the South and that it was now expedient to aid the Ealdorman Ælfric. Eadwig knew his father didn't think much of that since he hated Ælfric for myriad reasons, but Eadwig thought it a noble gesture, of the kind his brother was wont to do. Edmund was most likely in Porteceaster then, with that red-haired woman, Æva, for him to dote on. Eadwig could spot the signs. Edmund was like a nervous puppy whenever she was near, and Eadwig wasn't about to forget his explosive reaction that night Uhtred had sought to threaten her. Edmund cared for her a great deal. It was nice to see. If he were sensible, he'd find the courage to act on it.

Eadwig obtained a horse; a dun nag that rumbled at being awoken and kept bobbing its head about like it were nervous. They rode out, passing through the courtyard gates and into the city at some considerable speed. He suspected his father would have sent people after him, so he made sure he didn't slow, thinking it a blessing the streets were clear and most of the population had retired for the night.

He'd just reached the broad intersection to approach New Gate when he noticed something was wrong. There were some men out on the street and to the east, attired like Danes, and they were dragging something heavy, a chest or crate of some sort that Eadwig couldn't quite identify. They kept looking about the place, their expressions watchful, like they were expecting to be accosted or challenged over whatever it was they were doing. They were heading south, following the road down from Fenchurch Street and towards the Billings Gate. That struck Eadwig as odd. The only purpose of heading in that direction would be to load something aboard a ship docked at one of the wharves jutting out into the Temes. Hauling cargo around here was hardly unusual, but at night it was peculiar, especially when the people doing it were fully armoured and equipped for a fight. Eadwig dismounted, leaving his horse to its own devices, and became one with the shadows. Something was afoot here, and he'd find out what.

He crept along, staying within the almost impenetrable darkness that hugged the edge of the street. He reached a corner just as the men he'd been pursuing passed from view, their course taking them further south on a more direct route through the thickening patchwork of thatched hovels and shabby-looking storehouses. Eadwig followed, his footsteps careful and quiet, and caught up with them again, spotting this time how there were yet more of them dragging several more crates, each of them alike. The men grunted and cursed, complaining about the weight, their accents unmistakable even at this distance. Danes. These must be Thorkell's men. Eadwig had wondered why he hadn't been at the banquet and terrifying everyone with his mere presence. The murderous bastard was up to something. Eadwig would know what it was.

Before long, they'd reached the southern walls and were indeed approaching the Billings Gate, as Eadwig had suspected. It was lit up by several braziers burning on either side of its wide, stone entrance, the flames casting great dancing shadows across the approaching broadway. Eadwig's heart rate increased when he came closer. It would be harder to sneak about here, what with the light, and if he continued on he risked detection. He decided it was worth it. The Danes were just passing under the gate anyway and looked entirely focused on their task, their earlier caution now absent. They thought they'd gotten away with whatever it was they were doing. That meant they must have a ship or two out there, waiting to take on what they'd acquired.

Eadwig waited until they'd all passed from view before he made his move. He hurried towards the gate, staying within the meagre shadows cast by the buildings on the eastern side of the street. Eventually, he had to leave them, emerging out into the light and scuttling towards the gate. He came up alongside one of the braziers, the heat from the flames reassuringly pleasant, and pressed himself up against the hard stones of the gatehouse. He ventured a look around the corner and out into the night beyond, hoping to catch sight of his quarry. There was nothing, just more darkness. The Danes had vanished into it without a trace. Then he heard it. They were still talking among themselves, and laughing too. They must be happy, thinking the hard part of their journey was over. Eadwig would see about that.

It was then he saw the foot, poking out from underneath a pile of hay just a few meters back from the stairwell leading up to the battlements above. Eadwig crept over, trying to keep low lest he be seen. It was a man's foot alright, booted and sturdy as was typical, yet none of that explained what this individual was doing underneath all this hay. Eadwig took a hold of the boot and pulled gently to slide him out from under his burden. He suppressed a gasp. This must be one of the sentries assigned to watch the gate or patrol the walls. He was dead, and as Eadwig glanced about in alarm he saw more to his left, their bodies piled up under the shadows of the wall. He knelt down, inspecting the unfortunate man at his feet. His throat had been cut, and something sharp and long had smashed its way through his mail at the sternum. The Danes could only have done this. They didn't want anyone to see them passing through with their cargo. This was the grim result.

He returned to his previous spot by the brazier and slipped around the corner to head under the gate. He walked on through, passing beneath the great walls of Lundenburg's southern facade, doing his utmost to soften his steps so they didn't echo. He soon emerged on the other side onto what he knew was the gravel and dirt road approaching the riverbank and the docks and jetties that lay upon it. This place would be bustling during the day, with sailors and workmen of all types busying themselves with their vessels and cargo, but now it was all darkness; the only sound heard the muttering of Danes and the scraping racket as they dragged their prizes ever onward. He could see their shapes moving up ahead and the outline of something large down by the water. A ship. A longship, and then several others moored with it. There wasn't much time.

Eadwig flinched when somebody ahead lit a torch. He must have been moving quicker than he thought, for he was now way closer to the Danes than he'd estimated. They saw him, and he saw them, all forty of them, with at least eight chests. They were surprised, and a few of them dropped the chest they'd been carrying, allowing it to crash to the earth and flip open. Coins spilled out, in their thousands, gold and silver both. That couldn't be fair payment for the role they'd played in taking back Lundenburg. It was an excessively vast sum, something that could only have been obtained through theft. The bastards must have emptied what was in the treasury just as Æthelred had started to refill it. Somebody had to know about this. Somebody had to answer for it.

"An inquisitive one, you are. I knew it as soon as I saw you. It's in the eyes."

Eadwig liked to think he'd met many a character in his time, yet Thorkell the Tall was by far the most memorable, and not purely because of his physical appearance. His voice was unmistakable, and anyone who heard it would never forget it, such was the rumbling menace it conveyed. He turned around, his heart again quickening at the sight before him. It was him, Thorkell, as bold as anything, with the strangely vacant eyes and the beard like a silvered torrent erupting from his anvil of a chin. He was dressed for war, as always, and he had that huge axe of his, the long one with the excessively large head, yet he was content for the moment to leave it strapped to his back. That was something, Eadwig thought. Perhaps he'd yet survive this encounter.

"It is indeed in the eyes," Thorkell repeated, a brutal, heavily muscled hand reaching out to grip Eadwig by the chin. Other Danes appeared around him, their expressions hard. They really hadn't wanted anyone following them. That confirmed it, then. They weren't just transporting monies paid to them for services rendered. This was a heist, timed to coincide with the royal banquet. Thorkell must have given this some serious thought.

"Do you think your father is proud of you?" asked Thorkell, his hand still gripping Eadwig's chin.

"What do you mean?" Eadwig breathed, frightened and also confused at the question.

"If I'd had a son like you," Thorkell rumbled on, "I'd not have been proud. Æthelred's firstborn…what was his name?"

"Æthelstan," mumbled Eadwig.

"I remember seeing him. Riding atop his horse, cutting into my men, all his warriors following after him. That was a son worth having. He died a good death, as he deserved. What kind of death do you think you're owed, Eadwig?"

"What do you want from me?! Why are you doing this? My father paid you well to serve him, and yet now you steal even more of his wealth! When is enough ever enough for you people?!"

"When I say it is," replied Thorkell, his grip tightening to the edge of real discomfort. "I made my wealth as and how I chose. Nobody could stop me, and you were all fools to forgive and forget so quickly and allow me into your confidence. Doesn't your Christ tell you to forgive?"

"Yes," groaned Eadwig, his eyes watering as he tried to bear the pain in his jaw.

"A mistake. Only a fool would talk that way. Forgiveness means nothing, not in a world where the strong take and the weak endure as they must, if they endure at all. What say you to that?"

"I say you should let me go…if you kill an aetheling, there'll be consequences. My father will hunt you down. M-m-m-my brother, Edmund, will hunt you down."

"That would at least be interesting," he nodded. "Edmund is another son of Æthelred who is worth something, at least. He fights, like Æthelstan fought, and yet the Gods must favour him since he is still alive whilst his brother is dead. Do you think the Gods favour you tonight, Eadwig?"

"God!" Eadwig protested. "There is only one God, He who was made flesh so that He might dwell among us and save us from our si…"

"You bore me," interrupted Thorkell. "Scholarly types are always boring. You should have taken the path of the warrior. Then you might have grown strong and worthy, like your brothers. It matters not now. I will do King Æthelred one last service by ridding him of his weakling son."

Thorkell suddenly let him go, but Eadwig gained no respite. A fist hammered into his jaw, leaving him sprawled at Thorkell's feet, his vision blurring over. It cleared briefly, permitting him to see Thorkell place a knee upon his chest to deliver another blow and then another after that. Eadwig couldn't breathe, so immense was the weight atop him, and he tasted blood as the beating continued, a short, sharp snap announcing the breaking of his nose. He tried to lift his arms to protect himself, but he felt like his own limbs were now resisting his commands, as if they themselves were terrified of Thorkell and wouldn't dare defy him.

Thorkell's fist again smashed into his mouth, knocking his front teeth loose, a second and then a third strike causing some of them to shatter altogether. Time seemed to slow, and all the memories of Eadwig's past faded into obscurity in the face of the agonising present. His pain had always been here, so it felt, just as he'd only ever existed in these few terrifying moments as he was beaten to death on the hard, unforgiving ground. Eadwig tried to lash out, and his fist did connect with something, but all that followed was laughter, from Thorkell and the others. Then the beating resumed.

Thorkell stood up, removing his knee from his chest, but there was no mercy to be had. He stamped on him, bringing his boot down upon Eadwig's skull, the crack from the impact sharp and loud. He couldn't see now. Only the pain remained. And the sound. Laughter. He was being mocked in these final moments. Let them enjoy themselves. They'd all face a grim and terrible judgement when it was their time to stand before the Lord. Eadwig was sure of it.

He was on the verge of unconsciousness when the figure of a man, wreathed in shadow, hurried through the gate, a sword drawn and a challenge upon his lips. Thorkell stepped back from the prone aetheling and turned, he and his fiendish brethren all wondering who this brave stranger might be.

"Get yourself away from the king's son," the newcomer demanded, "and give yourself up so that you may face his justice."

"Or what?" Thorkell laughed, the sound of it wet yet brittle, like the cracking and grinding of joints in their sockets.

"Or face my own justice, here and now."

Thorkell's men moved into position beside their leader, their axes held ready.

"You are brave," Thorkell said, his great axe now held in his scuffed and bloodied hands. "I will make you this offer. We only want the money, and it's too late to stop us getting it. Turn around and walk away. I grant you this boon, one warrior to another."

"And if I should decline?" asked the stranger.

"You will die here," said Thorkell, "and be remembered, briefly, as just another fool of a Saxon fighting against what couldn't be helped. Decide."

"I've decided," said Hereward, stepping forward into the torchlight, his sword held aloft in both hands. Thorkell nodded in recognition. Hereward charged.

XXXV

The beast came after him, its mighty pincers clacking in anticipation. Edmund stumbled backwards across the shingled beach, knowing he had to think fast if he were to avoid dismemberment. The sea crashed and rumbled behind him, impacting on the stones at his heels. He continued to fall back, and the foul creature advanced, knowing he'd run out of options. He felt the cool waters filling his boots, the reach of the waves extending up past his ankles. This was it. Either he swam out into the depths – a dangerous prospect at any time – or he make a fight of it here and now. Edmund inhaled deeply, steeling himself for the contest.

Brandon stuck a bucket over the crab, trapping the thing and hiding it from view. They could hear it clicking and scrambling as it endeavoured to break free, but for the moment it was very much out of the fight. Edmund took a few steps forward, his boots now sodden with seawater, and placed his hands on his hips before giving Brandon a low bow.

"I thank you, my noble friend, for saving me from this most dastardly foe. Ask anything that is in my power to give, and I shall give it."

Brandon smiled, delighted at being addressed so formally. He paused as he thought, a multitude of options rushing through his mind on how to respond.

"Can I have… Wincestre?" he asked.

"Then it is my most regal pleasure to award you the city of Wincestre," answered Edmund. "At least until we find your grandfather. I think he'll be wanting it back, what with being Ealdorman of Hamptonscir and all."

They both looked down at the bucket. The crab was still in there, raging to itself, which made Brandon appear a little apprehensive. He wasn't a cruel boy, and they'd only begun this game as the crab had seemed way too interested in the lunch they'd been sharing just a few meters further up the beach. Ulfcytel was sat there now upon a blanket, his manner sullen and reserved despite the occasion. Æva was next to him, smiling at Brandon as she so often did. The fortress's southern wall was close by, rising up behind like some great grey behemoth, and the sky above was a pristine blue, free of clouds or anything that might lower their spirits. The sun hadn't let up despite the approaching evening, its gentle rays cascading over the sparkling waters for as far as the eye could see. This had been a good day. Edmund didn't want it to end. But first, he had to do something.

He bent down and removed the bucket, holding it in both hands. The crab immediately lurched into action as soon as it was revealed, for some reason believing Edmund was the one who'd been responsible for its predicament. It came after him again, its legs clicking and clacking and its pincers held high. There was only one way out of this. They had to give in. They had to give it what it wanted. Submission was a hard thing, but Edmund had no choice. He reached into the pocket of his breecs and found what the monster had long desired. Cheese. He dropped a morsel at his feet and moved off, Brandon following, the crab now entirely content as it feasted on its tribute.

They wandered back over to Æva and Ulfcytel. "You'll be glad to know the beast of Porteceaster has been placated," Edmund announced to them both, "and because of my great bravery..."

He slipped on something, the pebbles shifting under his weight to send him tumbling onto his arse. Brandon laughed, and so did everyone else, Ulfcytel a little grudgingly, it must be admitted, but it was still a laugh. Edmund stood up and patted himself down, embarrassed at the spectacle he'd made of himself.

"That wasn't me at my finest," he said bashfully.

"I promise I won't bring it up at your coronation," grunted Ulfcytel. "Unless I'm drunk, which is likely, in which case I will. So yes, I'll be bringing it up, just when you're not around. It's the least I can do, my king."

"I'd expect nothing less," replied Edmund, resuming his seat between the ealdorman and Æva. Brandon had stopped laughing and moved off on his own, apparently deciding a slick of seaweed down by the waves was of vital importance and must be inspected. Æva went after him, her hands pinching up the length of her dress at the waist so its edges didn't trail across the shingle. Edmund felt momentarily sad. He couldn't help but feel she was sometimes uncomfortable in his presence, especially if he was physically close. It troubled him to think she thought ill of him.

"You're good with the boy," said Ulfcytel quietly as they watched Brandon now jabbing at the seaweed with a stick he'd retrieved.

"I am?" asked Edmund. "Why? Because we outwitted a crab?"

"No," chuckled Ulfcytel, "because you make him laugh. You make him feel...involved. The worst thing we can do for the lad is make him think he's a burden. Or irrelevant."

Edmund had a feeling Ulfcytel was speaking from experience, but he didn't want to pry. He was on edge, and this had been the first and only time they'd managed to get him to move from Osbert's bedside since his wounding. Wulfhild was watching over him now, as otherwise Ulfcytel would have never agreed to leave. He'd been like a parent, obsessing over his wounded son and blaming himself for what had happened. Edmund had tried to convince him otherwise. He'd failed, and so he'd decided to at least try and get him outside into the fresh air. It seemed to be doing him good.

"My father was like that," Ulfcytel continued, interpreting Edmund's respectful silence as an invitation to speak more. "He was a brave man, and good in many ways...didn't care for his children, though. I always resented it and saw it as a mistake. A father should always rejoice at having children. It seems unnatural for it to be otherwise."

Edmund shifted his weight, trying to ease out the ache that still assailed his rear after his earlier tumble. "You turned out alright," he said. "So somebody must have gone to some effort with you to teach you right from wrong."

"Worked it out myself," said Ulfcytel with a sigh. "I had many examples not to follow, you see. Other lads picked on me, as I was sad at home and so sad anywhere else...that draws the bullies. They can smell sadness, and they want to add to it. I resolved never to be like them."

"You were bullied?" Edmund asked, incredulous that anyone would dare mistreat the mighty Ulfcytel.

"For years. Stopped talking and everything. You work out ways to avoid drawing attention to yourself, so I stopped talking, laughing...smiling even. My parents just ignored it. I wasn't worth the bother, I suppose, and my brothers saw it as an excuse to be yet crueller, like they wanted to get a rise out of me. All that did was give me more examples of how not to be. I then set myself the task of being different from them. Let them own their own sins. I'd be a different man, with different values."

Edmund felt he understood. He'd not gotten into trouble much when he was a boy, for his status as an aetheling ensured hardly anyone ever so much as dared speak to him in a discourteous fashion. Æthelstan had also been fiercely protective of his younger siblings, and nobody but the most thick-headed buffoon had ever crossed Æthelstan.

He remembered somebody had tried once, the brattish son of some thegn or other. They'd chanced upon Eadwig and pushed him into a pond, throwing the book he'd been reading in after him. Edmund and Æthelstan had found Eadwig sometime after, soaking wet and in tears, his trembling hands leafing through the sodden pages of his ruined book. The two older brothers hadn't appreciated that. They'd gone out looking to get even, and as luck would have it, they'd stumbled upon the guilty party soon enough.

He'd been bragging to his mates, acting like there was something impressive about what he'd done. They'd given him a split lip for his trouble, and when he'd tried fighting back, he'd gotten a bloody nose to go with it. Some of his friends had objected quite forcefully, but their courage left them after a few seconds of frantic scuffling and the realisation that the two brothers weren't going to back down.

Nobody had ever bothered Eadwig again after that, and word had spread fast. Edmund and Æthelstan were not just royal fops, and anyone who messed with their studious younger brother would come out worse. It was true then, and it was true now, even with Æthelstan gone. Edmund wouldn't let anyone hurt Eadwig. He'd put a sword through the man who tried.

He turned back to Ulfcytel, pondering what he'd said about his own childhood. "Is this why you've always fought so hard against the Danes?" Edmund asked, thinking aloud.

"What do you mean?"

"You don't like bullies, Ulfcytel. The likes of Svienn Forkbeard, Thorkell, Cnut...biggest bullies we've ever known."

"Never really saw the connection," shrugged Ulfcytel. "I mean, who needs an excuse for a fight with the Danes? They've always had it coming. Yet now that you mention it...I think there's something to what you say. Maybe there is something lurking in my soul that equates them with what I went through as a boy. Interesting notion."

They paused awhile, watching Æva and Brandon paddling about. Æva had hitched her dress up even more to avoid the water, exposing a scandalous amount of calf in the process, but she looked determined to assist her son in whatever it was he was looking for, shells most likely. Brandon was happy, in any case. Edmund was glad to be a part of it.

"Osbert is on the mend, you know," said Edmund, repeating what he'd been telling Ulfcytel for the past week. There was no falsehood in it. He wished Ulfcytel would see that.

"So people keep saying," he answered. "Don't mistake me; I'm grateful for the prayers of, well, everyone. God must have plans for Osbert, as I tell you..." he paused, letting out a deep, shuddering sigh. "I tell you...I thought that cleft in his chest was it.

That'd be the thing to carry him off. I saw it as it happened. I thought, "That's it. My lad's gone. I can't handle this. I won't get better after this. I'm done for." Does that sound silly?"

Edmund shook his head, feeling strangely emotional at Ulfcytel's choice of words. "And the man who struck the blow?" he asked. "What happened to him? I'm assuming you arranged for a suitable response."

"Eamon killed him. Cut his bloody arm off and then half his head. Fearsome bloke, that one. One of Alaric's boys he brought with him back when we were all gathering at Hringmere. He survived that, and then the big fight when we stole Thorkell's ships...and then Canterburie and whatever Uhtred was trying to do to him. Stern stuff in him. Real backbone."

Ulfcytel spoke the truth, as he always did, yet Edmund sometimes sensed a certain strangeness from Eamon. He'd never given him reason to mistrust him, but there was a coldness to him, something that triggered an instinct Edmund couldn't ignore. Eamon had a story, as everyone did, and chances were it probably wouldn't be the most jovial narrative imaginable, should he ever decide to share it. There was a darkness, a pain, a trauma in his eyes, and despite his many brave and valorous deeds, Edmund wasn't of a mind to discount it.

He leaned back, letting his elbows rest upon the blanket as he gazed out to sea. The sun was going down to the west, illuminating the water like it were one great expanse of sparkling, liquid bronze lapping against a far distant backdrop of darkening orange and fading, blueish pink. Ulfcytel continued to sit in silence beside him, his mountainous bulk a reassuring presence in its own right. Edmund saw him smile slightly at the sight of Brandon and Æva laughing and playing in the shallows. This was a good moment, thought Edmund. A peaceful moment, one where he felt content in the company of a good friend whilst watching over the woman he lo...

A horn blast, loud and sharp, split the air, the sound repeating twice and then three times over from the direction of the fortress. Edmund and Ulfcytel were on their feet in an instant, both looking for the source of alarm. Somebody was shouting from the walls, the urgency of their voice filling Edmund with apprehension. Longships. Longships had been spotted to the east and heading towards them. That could mean only one thing. The Danes had returned.

Edmund turned in time to see Brandon and Æva splashing ashore. He called to them, commanding them to hurry, sporadically shifting his gaze back to the eastern horizon and the apparently inbound vessels. He couldn't see anything yet, for the coast curved inward at about a hundred yards ahead as it opened up into Porteceaster's harbour, but that did not mean they were safe, nor did they have time to waste. They had to get inside, and quickly. Only then could Edmund make a proper analysis of the situation.

Æva finally reached him, her dress soaked from the knees downward. She kept hold of Brandon's hand as they all ran the length of the southern wall - the sound of blasting horns still pealing out from above them - to access the narrow gatehouse on its most easterly end. They made it and passed within, Edmund and Ulfcytel then assisting those on watch with sealing the gate, each man grunting with effort as they pushed the heavy, solid oak doors closed.

"Get back to the tower," Edmund told Æva, making his way toward an adjacent stairwell to access the battlements above. She obeyed, hurrying away with Brandon, their otherwise pleasant time on the beach now just a memory. Edmund vaulted up the stairs, Ulfcytel close behind, and came out atop the southern ramparts, a dozen warriors turning to look at him as he appeared.

"What's the situation?" Edmund barked, but as he asked, his eyes revealed all he needed to know. There were three ships, unmistakably Norse in appearance, skirting the edges of the harbour and on a direct course for their position. Edmund bellowed for archers just as Ulfcytel joined him, his breathing heavy and his eyes wide upon spotting their uninvited guests. The enemy were fools to have come this close to their fortifications. Edmund would exact a heavy toll for their hubris.

He was proud of how quickly his men rose to the occasion. He'd only given the order about a half minute ago, but there were already another two score warriors atop the walls around him, their arrows nocked and ready to unleash. The ships were coming on fast, their sails puffed outward with the evening breeze, and they could see the glitter from the armour and weapons of those on deck as they caught the sunset. There were a lot of them, filling each ship to capacity, almost. Edmund raised a hand. He'd let them come a little closer. Then he'd give them a suitable welcome.

Edmund's attention was suddenly drawn to the prow of the lead ship. Somebody was standing there, as far forward as they could possibly be without falling into the sea, and they were waving a white piece of cloth like their life depended on it. They began to shout, yelling over and over in perfect English about how they apparently meant no harm. Edmund's curiosity was roused further when they came yet closer, allowing him to pick out certain details as to his armour and appearance. He was English, that seemed certain, and Edmund felt he recognised him, although from where he knew not. Then it struck him. This was Hereward, as in the bodyguard who had until recently been inseparable from his father. Just what the heck was he doing here, leading a flotilla of enemy ships, no less?

"Stand down, lads," yelled Edmund, repeating the order a second time so everyone fully understood. The men all stared at him, their bows now tilting downward yet still nocked and ready.

"Who is that man?" Ulfcytel asked, a deep crease upon his brow.

"It's my father's bloody bodyguard!" spluttered Edmund, like he still couldn't believe it. "Hereward is his name, I think."

"What on earth is he doing?" exclaimed the ealdorman. "Did he capture those ships himself? But there's loads of arse-faced Danes right behind him on the deck. Do you think Æthelred has sent some of Thorkell's lot down here to treat with us?"

Edmund narrowed his eyes, his attention still on Hereward and his frantic gesturing. He was close enough now that there could be no mistaking his identity, although what he was even doing here remained an open question. Edmund raised his right hand in greeting, which seemed to mollify him, as he'd stopped waving his little flag around, presumably realising he wasn't in danger of being shot full of arrows. Hereward then turned and gestured to the rest of the crew, and their ship began to curve to port, bringing it closer to the beach where Edmund had only recently been whiling away his evening.

Hereward shouted something up at them and moved back from the prow to momentarily disappear amidst the crew. He re-emerged a few seconds later with what looked like a human person slung over his shoulder, the weight apparently of little concern to him. He jumped overboard, landing waist-deep in water, and began to make his way ashore, his movements slow and purposeful as the waves lapped at his sides. Another man joined him, leaping off the port side of the ship with measured confidence, and followed after him. They emerged on the beach in short order, the pebbles crunching under their heavy treads, and began to follow the same route Edmund had taken under the southern wall so they could perhaps access the gatehouse below them. Edmund wasn't about to let them just walk on up to his front door like that. He'd have an explanation from them.

"Explain your presence here!" he yelled, his stomach protesting a little as he leaned over the battlements to project his voice downward.

"Hurry and open the gate!" Hereward shouted back, his impressive dash eastward ensuring he was now directly below Edmund's position.

"I can't just let you in!" Edmund protested. "You're lucky I have not peppered you all with arrows. Just what are you up to?!"

Hereward skittered to a halt just a few feet from the sealed gate. "It's an emergency, Edmund!" he said through ragged, gasping breaths. "Something has happened with your father! And your brother, Eadwig, he's…"

A gust of wind suddenly blew in from the west to assault Edmund's right ear and prevent him from hearing whatever it was Hereward was saying. He ordered the gate opened regardless, but as he moved to greet their guests, he made sure he had Ulfcytel and at least a dozen warriors with him so they'd be well prepared should the newcomers try anything. Hereward lumbered on through, passing under the gatehouse and into the fortress interior, his mystery companion following.

Edmund scrutinised the latter as he came closer. His armour marked him out as a Northman of some description, but his helmet was presently masking much of his face, which made it impossible for Edmund to identify him from any other of his father's Danish lackeys. Hereward stopped a few feet from Edmund and looked about, his breathing laboured as he and his companion took in the forest of spears pointing right at them. Nobody moved. Then Hereward spoke.

"I'm so sorry," he said, his grief genuine, and put the man he'd been carrying down upon the ground. Edmund came closer, wondering who this unfortunate soul might be. He was bandaged like he'd suffered some kind of extensive head injury, and he was yet breathing, but for how long Edmund could not tell, given his situation and the fact he was as limp as a fish. Edmund knelt next to him and…

"Eadwig!"

He reached out, pulling his younger brother into his arms and holding him tight. His face was a mess, his eyes swollen and dark, his nose bent in and to the left and his lips scabbed over. Tears came unbidden, and Edmund began to gently rock Eadwig back and forth, hoping to coax some semblance of life into his bruised and bloodied form.

"Please talk to me," pleaded Edmund, "please answer me! Don't you leave me too, brother!" Eadwig's eyes fluttered, but no words came, although he still had his breath, slow and shallow, but breath all the same. Edmund fancied he looked up at him, his eyes welling with tears upon beholding his older brother. The sight broke his heart.

"Be careful with his head," said Hereward urgently. "I wasn't there when Thorkell first attacked him, so…"

"Thorkell?!" snarled Edmund, looking up at Hereward as he held Eadwig tight. "What about Thorkell? He tried to kill my brother?"

"He did," said the helmeted fellow who had accompanied Hereward. "I was aboard ship in the Temes at the time, with the rest of my men. I didn't see the start of it, otherwise I would have done something."

Ulfcytel drew his sword and stepped up, positioning himself to Edmund's right and facing Hereward and his associate directly. "You're saying Thorkell attacked Eadwig?" he asked, his tone hostile. "Why? Did the wretched dog get sick of Æthelred and decide to take it out on his son?"

"It was a robbery," said Hereward. "Thorkell's men emptied out the treasury whilst the king was drinking with his thegns…they must have planned it all in advance. Eadwig caught them at it. I would say Thorkell didn't appreciate the interruption."

Edmund looked over his shoulder to command one of his men to bring their resident priest with all haste. He turned back as Eadwig emitted a low moan, and Edmund rested his head in his lap before reaching for his hand. He smiled when Eadwig returned his squeeze, albeit feebly. Not all was lost.

"And who the hell is this then?" Ulfcytel asked, flicking his blade to the stranger Hereward had brought with him. The man didn't answer, instead lifting his hands up to remove his helm and reveal his face. Young, blond, bearded, with blue eyes…a typical look, yet Edmund had a good memory. He'd met this one before. He couldn't say he was overly pleased to see him.

"Olaf," hissed Edmund. "So you were in on Thorkell's plan to rob my father? Why come here, then? Why help Hereward?"

"I wasn't "in" on anything," said Olaf defensively. "Thorkell told me to prepare my men and ships at the Billings Gate, saying he needed us for a special enterprise. I didn't know what he had planned and only became aware when I heard the shouting and…"

"Eadwig was shouting?" asked Edmund.

"No, Hereward attacked Thorkell on his own," replied Olaf. "He wouldn't have lasted long, and normally I would not have acted, but…Hereward and I shared the task of taking down Lundenburg's bridge not so long ago. I respect him. I didn't understand why he and Thorkell had come to blows, but I rushed to investigate."

"And Thorkell attacked you? Why?"

"He didn't, not at first," said Olaf. "I tried to break it up, but I then saw Eadwig upon the ground and understood that Thorkell was looking to murder him. I didn't like that. I may have originally come to England as Viking…but I'm Christian now. I couldn't allow Thorkell to just murder the son of the man who brought me to Christ."

The priest they'd sent for had appeared from behind Edmund and began seeing to Eadwig. Edmund had several men take a hold of him, gently, and carry him back to the great hall, instructing them to assist the priest with whatever he needed. Edmund looked again to Olaf, an angry sneer on his face.

"You're a Christian, are you?" he said mockingly. "You're not the first of your kind to claim that title, yet it always seems to have minimal effect on your behaviour. Tell me, Olaf, when you and Thorkell were rampaging across England not so long ago…just how many churches did you sack? How many good men did you kill?"

Olaf broke eye contact, his cheeks flushing with shame. "I admit I have done many wrongs," he said quietly. "When I first set foot on English soil, I was a murderer and continued to behave as murderers do. Thorkell was my guide in that…but then something changed in me, and…"

"Were you at the battle at Bernecestre?" snapped Edmund. "Were you at the battle where my older brother was killed?"

"I cannot lie," Olaf said sorrowfully. "I was indeed there. Yet I never chanced upon such a man as he, nor did I kill him."

"How many Englishmen did you kill then?" rumbled Ulfcytel. "And were you at Canterburie too? How many did you slaughter there? How many women did you rape?"

Olaf hung his head, uncomfortable and perhaps anxious under Ulfcytel's accusatory gaze. He took a step back in alarm when Edmund drew his sword, yet he didn't go for his own weapon. Hereward just watched, unwilling to intervene in defence of a man who'd undoubtedly committed great crimes against his people. One charitable act did not make up for everything Olaf had done, Edmund thought. He'd make sure he understood that.

"Tell me where Thorkell is," said Edmund sternly, pointing the tip of his blade directly towards Olaf's mailed chest.

"Gone," said Olaf. "I didn't see where. We had to get out of there in a hurry. I'd say he's fled back to the Baltic with his loot. It would make little sense to stay."

"This is where his Jomsvikings operate from?" asked Ulfcytel. Olaf nodded. Edmund would make a note of that. It wouldn't hurt to keep such things in mind should the opportunity arise to strike back at Thorkell someday. For the moment, though, he'd deal with Olaf.

"You helped save my brother," said Edmund, "and for that, I will not kill you. Yet I would have you depart these lands, never to return. If you do, I will hear of it, and put you down like any other Dane."

"I am from Norway."

"I care not! Begone, if you value your life and those of your men! Otherwise, I'll carve my name into your flesh!"

These were strong words, and Edmund meant them. Olaf shot Hereward a look, perhaps asking for support, but Hereward simply shook his head. If Olaf had hoped to find assistance from that quarter, he'd been mistaken. Hereward was loyal to England. He would not be coming to his defence.

"So be it," said Olaf to Edmund and Hereward both. "May God be with you. You will not be seeing me again."

He turned and strode back through the gate, vanishing from view. Edmund had his men seal it after him before he set out for the great hall, Ulfcytel and Hereward in tow. They arrived just in time to see the weather turn, a light drizzle emerging from a batch of rain clouds speeding towards the reddish glow of the still-setting sun.

Edmund hurried inside, eager to see his brother. Hereward gazed up at the works of art displayed in the entrance hall, his eyes wide with wonder as they hurried past towards the main chamber. This place had once served as a means for the Ealdorman Ælfric to hold assemblies and banquets, but since Osbert's wounding, Edmund had converted it into a makeshift hospital. Osbert was there now, sound asleep in his blankets, several of his wounded compatriots doing likewise.

Eadwig had been deposited on the long, sturdy table Edmund had previously used for dining. The priest had removed the bandages, revealing his head so that he could examine it. Edmund fought back the urge to weep as he came closer. It was a mess there, like one giant scab extending downwards from his crown. Eadwig had closed his eyes, so Edmund again took his hand, hoping he'd squeeze back once more. Nothing. He hoped he was just asleep. He couldn't bear to consider the alternative.

"I'm afraid this man is in the hands of God," said the priest.

"So prayer is our only recourse?" asked Edmund, feeling a little impious upon hearing his own question.

"A most potent recourse," corrected the priest predictably. "His skull is fractured, so once I've cleaned away what needs to be cleaned, I'll apply a fresh bandage to try and hold it all together. Otherwise, I fear what may happen. I suggest we don't attempt to move him again."

"So he really is in God's hands?" asked Ulfcytel.

"As are we all."

The priest began dabbing at Eadwig's skull, using a rag he kept wetted from a small wooden bowl. He was gentle and precise, although Edmund winced whilst he watched, fearing every move might somehow spell the end of his brother before they'd even had a chance to help him.

"There is more I must tell you," said Hereward quietly. Edmund looked over at him, his expression pained.

"It was no mere coincidence that I stumbled upon Eadwig as he was attacked," continued Hereward. "Your father had sent me after him once he'd run from…he'd…he'd witnessed a most ignoble act. That is why I brought him here rather than stay in Lundenburg. It's not safe."

"Why?" asked Edmund. "What did he see?"

Hereward inhaled deeply before speaking. "The thegns from the Five Boroughs, Sigeferth and Morcar? They were known to you?"

"Like stepfathers, almost," said Edmund. Hereward's face seemed to grow darker upon hearing his words. Something wasn't right here.

"Then brace yourself, for I fear this news will grieve you all the more. They have been murdered, right before the king. I saw it, but it all happened so fast I was powerless to stop it."

"They are dead?" breathed Edmund, feeling suddenly numb. "You saw this? My father willed it?"

"He drew his sword first, yes," nodded Hereward. "They were arguing. The king was drunk, and he blamed the two thegns for the death of your older brother. Sigeferth must have had something to drink, too, for his words were…defiant. The king then made a move like he intended them harm, yet the Ealdorman Eadric…"

"What about him?" demanded Ulfcytel.

"He was fast. Very fast. He'd killed Sigeferth before I'd even noticed he'd pulled his weapon from its sheath. Morcar tried to fight, and I tried to get between them, yet it was soon over. They are dead." He lowered his head, averting his eyes from Edmund. "I'm so sorry."

"And my brother saw this?" asked Edmund, gesturing towards Eadwig.

"He did," acknowledged Hereward. "And then he fled. I expect he thought to inform you of what had transpired. I was sent after him. He was quick, and I nearly lost him twice over. I only wish I'd been faster on my feet. Thorkell might never have had cause to harm him then."

"Thorkell is a brute animal," growled Ulfcytel. "Nobody is safe, anywhere, as long as he's alive, and it's no surprise to me that he's betrayed us. He'll be out recruiting again, I'm sure, using the money he took to hire more warriors. It won't stop until he's in the ground."

"Then I'm sorry I only cut off his hand," said Hereward, patting the dark leather scabbard at his thigh.

"You did?" asked Edmund.

"He was overconfident. He's good, and his men would have killed me had Olaf not intervened...but still overconfident. He overreached with one of those wild swings of that axe of his. I imagine he regrets it now."

Despite everything, Edmund smiled. "So he could have bled out somewhere," he mused, hoping it might actually be the case.

"It's possible," grunted Ulfcytel, "yet as pleasing a prospect as that is...I somehow doubt it. Thorkell has survived much, including me ringing his head like a bell when we fought in Canterburie. I've a hunch he's alive."

Ulfcytel nodded to Hereward. "That doesn't take away what you did, my friend," he said. "You clearly have great skill, and you did the right thing in bringing Eadwig to his brother here. If Eadric is now confident enough to kill people right in front of Æthelred..."

"Then he's acting openly on whatever his long-term goal is," said Edmund. "That's the only explanation I can think of. Eadric is rattled...by me, I think. He knows he was seen assisting Svienn when I attacked him at Sancte Eadmundes Byrig. He may also be aware of the deal I made with my father to allow me to take the throne once he's gone. He'll know once I'm king, I'll have him executed, so he's made a move to isolate me. He probably engineered the situation that night so he'd be able to kill Sigeferth and get away with it."

"Sigeferth was more than just a political ally, though?" asked Hereward. "Morcar, too? They were close to you, personally."

"They were," nodded Edmund, his voice heavy with sadness. "I can't believe this has happened. After every chance...every assurance my father gave that he'd changed...he does this. I can't get past it. There can be no turning back. I have to confront him at once."

"What about Sigeferth's family?" asked Ulfcytel quickly. "He had sons? Heirs? Remember, Edmund, that if anyone wants to deprive you of supporters, simply killing them isn't enough. They have to control their families, otherwise their power and property simply passes down to the next man in line."

An ill feeling again settled on Edmund. "No, no sons," he said, deep in thought. "Just daughters...and his wife, Ealdgyth. She'll inherit everything, all of it, all of Snotingeham and much else for miles around. She'll be the second most powerful woman in England."

"Eadric will know that, count on it," said Ulfcytel. He again turned to Hereward. "Please tell me that Ealdgyth is alive? I'm assuming she'd accompanied her husband to attend the king and his festivities."

"I believe so," said Hereward. "I saw her, or a woman I'd been told was the wife of Sigeferth. She wasn't present to witness the murders, thank the Lord. As to where she is now..."

"I need to get back there," Edmund said firmly. "I need to confront my father. His actions are unforgivable. A settling of accounts between us is long overdue. I was a fool to think he'd have the sense to redeem himself."

"And what of Ealdgyth?" asked Ulfcytel. "Remember, Eadric won't take kindly to your presence if you encounter him. He'll be moving against Sigeferth's family already, most likely."

"Then I'll kill him," glowered Edmund, his hand at his sword hilt. "I mean it. I'll kill the bastard, and if he's laid a hand on Ealdgyth, I'll make it last. I'll bleed him dry."

Hereward cleared his throat, as if desiring to make a point. "I hate to have to say this," he began, "but I remain loyal to the king. The killing of the two thegns was wrong, but upon my honour, I cannot turn against him. I would accompany you to Lundenburg, Edmund. I do not want matters to escalate between you."

Edmund thought fast. He was grateful to Hereward, and he spoke words of duty that were easy to admire, but he couldn't have him getting in the way. If he were to confront his father and force him to hand over Eadric and Ealdgyth, he couldn't have Hereward as an obstacle. He'd deal with him here and now. He called for his guards.

Hereward went for his sword, but he hesitated, like he couldn't quite believe how rapidly his luck had changed. That was a mistake, for it left him exposed to the strength of Ulfcytel's right hook. He fell down - his limbs tangled and his eyes furious - and was then disarmed, the guards binding his wrists to lead him away. Edmund watched him go, his guilt heavy and pronounced at what he'd done.

It couldn't be helped. He couldn't have anyone putting themselves between him and his father. "King" Æthelred had made his final mistake. So many people were dead because of his foolishness, including Edmund's own uncle, not to mention long-missed heroes like Alaric. Now he'd murdered two prominent thegns, all for the sake of avenging something that wasn't their fault to begin with. Edmund would not stand for it any longer. His father's time was over. England needed a new king. Edmund would rise to the challenge.

XXXVI

"A ruler should not be distracted."

His mother's words echoed in his head, as real as if she'd been standing right next to him. She'd drilled that lesson into Æthelred from a young age, and he liked to think in the years that followed he'd allowed relatively few things to affect his focus. Emma had been the first, back when he'd thought her a good and noble soul. His fear and guilt over the death of his predecessor had been a second. Today he was distracted by a third, one so absurd his mother would undoubtedly see fit to scold him, had she been around. It was just as well she was not. Her absence was always something to be grateful for.

These tiny chicks didn't feel the same way, at least about their own mothers. Æthelred didn't know who had decided to have this coop installed in his courtyard, but he was transfixed by it now, finding the behaviour of the hens and chicks absolutely fascinating. The tiny beasts somehow knew which hen was their own, and they in turn knew each of them, despite the fact they all looked identical with their puffed, yellow feathers and earnest, haphazard gait. Æthelred could see other hens inside the coop, each sat on their own nest of eggs and crooning to themselves in apparent satisfaction. They were all so gentle, so caring, and so completely dedicated to their progeny, despite the seeming unimportance of their lives. For some reason, he'd never really seen it before, but today of all days it was a marvel to him. He wasn't entirely sure why.

A memory rose to the surface. He was twelve, and sat on his throne, the same one he used to this day. His mother was lecturing him, her pale, unhealthy face shoved in his, her eyes ablaze with wrath. She jabbed him in the chest, over and over, making him wince with the sharpness of her fingernails. She didn't relent. She never did. The Queen Regent had a lesson to impart, and he had best listen. It was how it had always been back then.

He smiled when he remembered his defiance. He'd pushed her away, telling her he was king and she was just his mother. He'd paid for that, over and over, and he still bore some of the marks across his back, but he was glad that in his old age he could still recall a time when he'd hoped to stand up to her and her "advice". It had never been advice. She'd sought to break and control him. She might have eventually succeeded with the first part. He wasn't sure she'd achieved the second.

Some of the chicks had wandered over. He didn't dare move, lest he frighten them away, and they kept up that "cheep cheep" sound, even in the presence of a king such as he. He smiled at them. Theirs was a simplicity that was difficult not to admire, and when their mothers ushered them from his feet he felt only disappointment. They were just being protective, he supposed. Maternal instinct. He was aware of the concept. He wished he'd experienced it himself. In that respect, these chicks were better off than he, a King of England no less, and their mothers were far wiser than his had ever been. It was a strange thought. He decided he'd have to give some unusual orders after this. Nobody was to harm these chickens. He liked having them around.

A warrior approached, his helmet catching the afternoon's light. He gave a quick bow before giving his report, informing Æthelred that Eadwig was still unaccounted for, as was Thorkell, Olaf, and Hereward. Æthelred nodded in acknowledgement and ordered him to return to his men and continue the search, inside and outside the city. He'd leave no stone unturned when it came to his son. There had to be some trace, and they would find it.

Thorkell was the only part of this mystery that made sense. The treasury had been emptied, and a number of guards had turned up dead, particularly around the Billings Gate. There was only one man in the city who had the nerve and physical prowess to carry off such a thing, so Thorkell was their number one suspect. Æthelred had realised the bastard was likely already halfway to Denmark by the time they'd discovered his treachery, but he'd ordered Godfrey and the Norman ships to sea regardless. If there was any chance of catching that rat, they had to take it. Honour and justice demanded it.

What was worrying was the way Thorkell's disappearance had coincided with Eadwig's. It was very possible there was a relationship between the two, and in Æthelred's experience coincidences were quite rare, especially when it came to events of such magnitude. It had occurred to him that Eadwig had somehow discovered Thorkell's scheme as he fled, prompting the heathen scoundrel to take him hostage or kill him. Hereward might have attempted to intervene, as was his duty, which left Æthelred facing the very real and distinctly awful possibility that both his son and faithful bodyguard had come undone at the hands of their former ally. That left Æthelred with only one option. Thorkell had to be found, and he'd search land and sea until it was done.

He turned upon hearing heavy footsteps approaching. Edmund had come, entering the courtyard via the main gate. Æthelred's heart upped its pace when he saw him, realising his presence and quick, purposeful stride could only mean one thing: Edmund had somehow found out about Sigeferth and Morcar. This was not going to be easy. It was just as well Eadric wasn't here. Æthelred didn't think he'd be able to control his son if it was not so.

"Tell me what happened."

Æthelred paused, uneasy over Edmund's command. He'd not heard him speak in such a fashion to him before. It was improper, his tone akin to what he used to instruct his soldiers, minus the respect.

"How did you find out so quickly?" asked Æthelred, unwilling to play games with the truth.

"My sources are my own affair," said Edmund, his face blank and inscrutable behind his dark, thick beard. He'd been growing that thing out for some time. It made him look fierce, even as the rest of his face remained impassive.

"Morcar is dead, as is Sigeferth," admitted Æthelred, trying to keep his voice as flat and unemotional as he could. It wasn't easy.

"And you had a hand in this?" asked Edmund, his eyes like dark, piercing orbs. "I was told you drew your sword first, and your revolting pet, Eadric, finished it."

Æthelred frowned, disturbed at the accuracy of whatever information Edmund had been given. "The Ealdorman of Mierċe killed them both, that is true. And despite it all, I am so very sorry, son. I want you to know that..."

"You will not address me in that fashion again." Edmund let his words hang in the air, allowing them to sink in. Æthelred did his best not to gape, but his mouth hung open anyway. This couldn't be. He had to get control of the situation. He had to make him see sense.

"Let's talk inside," pleaded Æthelred. "I know once you hear the full story, you'll..." He'd stepped forward, his hands reaching out for Edmund's, but as he did so he was pushed back, the flat of Edmund's palm pressing into his chest. The guards at the gate saw what was happening and rushed over to take up position alongside Æthelred, although they wisely refrained from making any attempt on Edmund's person without express orders. Edmund wasn't fazed. He was comfortable with the situation. Æthelred felt nothing but sorrow with the realising of it.

"Did you punish Eadric?"

"I confess I did not," said Æthelred.

"Why? He killed two thegns, powerful ones. If you had not wished it, you'd have taken action against him."

"They did kill your brother, Edmund. Let's be honest about all this. You've always seen Sigeferth as a father figure, I know that, but they were players in this game like any other. They used you. They used Æthelstan. It cost him his life. I had to give answer for that!"

"Still prattling out the same pathetic delusions, father," sneered Edmund, his contempt quite repellent to behold. "Æthelstan died because you preferred to talk with an inhuman bastard like Thorkell rather than aid the likes of Ulfcytel in fighting him. Had you helped Ulfcytel at Hringmere, as we suggested, none of this would be happening. Æthelstan and countless others would be alive. They are dead because of you."

"Harsh words!" exclaimed Æthelred, his efforts at fighting back tears proving largely futile. "Is that really how you see me? Am I really such a fool in your eyes? Is there nothing left between us?"

"You gave me your WORD!" roared Edmund, his anger firing from his mouth like a bow shot aimed straight for Æthelred's heart. "You said you would be different! That you'd forgive! And the moment my back is turned, you start killing my friends!"

"I know it's tragic, and I know you're hurt, but as I said, I had to give answer for the death of Æthelstan. If you'll just listen..."

Something flashed in Æthelred's peripheral vision. Emma had emerged from the hall, dressed in that ridiculous purple gown again, and was coming closer, her arms gesticulating as she prattled objections at Edmund. She moved between them both and got in Edmund's face, demanding he "grow up and be a man" and "remember who your father is" and all the rest of it. It was brave, in a way. Then she made the mistake of telling Edmund his mother would be ashamed of him.

Æthelred winced as she fell. Edmund had slapped her with the back of his fist, putting enough force into it to knock her down. She rose to her knees after a few seconds, her right hand upon what would undoubtedly turn out to be a very bruised cheek. One of Æthelred's men helped her up and took her back behind her husband, her movements slow and awkward in her likely dazed state. Æthelred wasn't sure he really blamed Edmund for that. Emma had shown some valour here, but she'd underestimated the gravity of the situation and the extent to which Edmund would indulge her. He might be inclined to feel pity for her, if he didn't despise her so much.

"Are you content now?" Æthelred asked Edmund. "Have you expelled your pent-up wrath, after humbling my wife so?"

"I do not regret my actions concerning your Norman whore," stated Edmund, his brazen disrespect drawing a gasp from at least one of Æthelred's guards.

"What would you have of me then?" asked Æthelred. "Do you want me to beg, is that it? Beg you to listen to reason? This is what you desire?"

"Tell me where Sigeferth's wife is."

"What?"

"You heard me. I wager you sent Eadric to either kill or incarcerate Ealdgyth so she won't inherit Sigeferth's lands. Am I correct?"

Æthelred sighed. His son was clever, cleverer than he'd thought. Eadric had indeed been dispatched with the captive Ealdgyth to a nunnery at Malmesberie; a place suitably far from her base of support up north. Eadric had advised they simply murder her and her daughters, but Æthelred wouldn't tread such a dark path, not anymore. Ealdgyth could live out her life in service to God and ideally be kept well away from the tumultuous events that had led to the death of her foolish husband. As a captive nun, she'd also be less inclined to get any silly notions in her head, like leading the Five Boroughs in rebellion. Æthelred was doing her a service, really. In time, perhaps, he might even allow her to see her children.

"You have a sharp mind," nodded Æthelred soberly. "Yet I must again disappoint you. If you catch up with Eadric, you'll kill him."

"So I'm right in thinking he has Ealdgyth?"

"You think right."

"That means you are not of a mind to kill her," mused Edmund. "You'll hide her away then? Until you can set in motion some scheme to acquire her property? Or force her into marriage with some stooge of yours?"

"I have to consider all options," answered Æthelred. "If I'm to avoid civil war, Ealdgyth must be kept under control. I regret the death of her husband, I really do, but it cannot be helped now. Too many lives are at stake."

"Tell me where she is!"

"I will not!" screeched Æthelred.

Edmund drew his sword, the movement catching everyone present off guard. "You WILL!" he half-screamed, half-roared, his voice staggeringly loud. "Ealdgyth must be returned to her daughters! You will NOT destroy another family! I WON'T let you!"

Æthelred could tell they were rapidly approaching a point of no return. Edmund wasn't making idle threats, not if the look in his eyes told him anything. Æthelred's men were still standing, tall and solid at his side, but he suspected they would much rather witness a peaceful resolution than actually try to fight Edmund. He had a reputation now. "Ironside", he was known as. It suited him. It also made him that much more terrifying.

"Ealdgyth is to be handed over to the nunnery at Malmesberie," said Æthelred, a tremor in his voice. "She is to live a good life there, serving God and…"

"It's a prison," snarled Edmund. "One she's to be confined to so she doesn't make trouble."

"I have to keep the peace," said Æthelred, feeling a little guilty at his deception. He was feeding Edmund a morsel of information to try and mollify him, but he had no intention of just letting him head off to Malmesberie and act the hero. He'd have riders surround him once he was outside the city, of a number that he couldn't just fight through. Then he could calm down in a cell. He'd see sense in time.

Edmund went to turn away, like he was satisfied and would indeed be leaving for Malmesberie or whatever it was he thought he was doing. He hesitated, pausing to think for a moment or two, his eyes hard. He turned back to Æthelred and spoke, his words as bitter as they were painful.

"Eadwig may not survive, you know."

"What?!" gasped Æthelred.

"He came to us, your man, Hereward," continued Edmund, cold and unmoved. "He told us you'd sent him in pursuit of Eadwig once he'd fled after witnessing the murder of Sigeferth. Apparently, Eadwig got into some trouble down by the docks…and Hereward arrived just in time to see Thorkell beating his skull in."

"Hereward is with you?" Æthelred spluttered. "As is Eadwig? How did they escape Thorkell? And where IS Thorkell, for that matter?"

"I don't know where he is," answered Edmund, "and if I ever find him, I'll have him scourged, gelded, and then hung with his own entrails. Eadwig survived because Hereward attacked Thorkell, despite knowing it might mean his death. Olaf, of all people, came to his aid. They delivered Eadwig to me in Porteceaster."

"So, how is he?"

"It's as you can imagine," said Edmund. "His skull is broken, so I'm told. He doesn't speak. He squeezes my hand if I take his in mine, and I can see in his eyes that his soul yet remains, but that's it. That's what your monster, Thorkell, has done. That's what YOU have done!"

Edmund jabbed a finger at him with that last statement, his eyes flashing with undisguised menace. Æthelred tried to reply, but words failed him, such was his dismay at what he was hearing.

"I was told to be a light for you, you know that?" added Edmund, quieter this time. "I was told to be a light, as Christ commanded of His followers. That was the way to help you, so they said. I was to be an example you might follow."

"There's still time," implored Æthelred. "Whatever has happened…we can get through this. Let me come with you to see Eadwig. I can't bear to think of him as you describe. He needs me!"

"To Porteceaster?!" asked Edmund, incredulous now. "Do you forget the family that rules there? As in Ælfric, the man you wanted killed? The man whose son, Alaric, you DID have killed, even as he fought to his last breath for the sake of his wife and child?! You think I would seek to be so cruel to the lady Æva by having you walk into her own home?"

"I AM KING!" snarled Æthelred. "And I will go where I please, in my own realm, as I choose! If I wish to see my son, so be it! Do not deny me, Edmund!"

"But I DO deny you, father!" Edmund bellowed, this time jabbing that finger into Æthelred's chest. "I deny YOU! You killed Uncle Æthelstan! You killed Alaric! You killed Sigeferth and Morcar! And how many sons have you lost because of your stupidity? Æthelstan was the first…will Eadwig be another?"

Æthelred held his hands up to his ears, trying to shut out the cruel words cascading around them.

"No," he mumbled tearfully, "that can't be…you have to…please, Edmund, just let me…"

"Goodbye, father," said Edmund, his voice suddenly sorrowful. "I told you once, back when you were fleeing Svienn, that I'd part ways with you. I now do precisely that. You are lost. Always have been. And you will never get better. You will never learn mercy. You were always the ill-suited king. Always unready. That is how you'll be remembered. Æthelred the Unready."

Edmund turned his back, his head held low as he strode through the courtyard gate and into the city streets beyond. Æthelred went to call out to him, demanding, begging, that he return. No words came, just a noise that sounded like a bass, half-strangled growl. Something then splashed at his feet. Red, like blood but…it couldn't be. He lifted his hand to his nose. He felt wetness. He held his hand out in front of him. Red, lots of red, splashed across his fingers and palm, fresh and vital. He tried to speak again. No words came. Just a mournful moan, twinged with panic.

He fell backwards, his men reacting quickly to break his fall. He let out a pained gurgle as they lowered him to the earth, their mouths aflutter with questions on what was wrong. Emma knelt at his side and took his hand, her green eyes filled with concern. He tried to pull away from her. Nothing. His strength had left him. He couldn't speak. He felt fear, which only mounted when yet more blood began to pour from his nostrils to saturate his beard and tunic. He could still see, and as his head lolled to one side he saw something, a sight just past Emma's shoulder catching his eye.

The hens. They were back in their coop and gathering together in one great feathery mass of clucks and squawks. They were anxious after witnessing recent events, yet their chicks were huddled against them and apparently content. He wanted to go to them. He needed it, to be away from all this, to forget his past life and be as simple as one of these chicks, safe in its mother's embrace. It was absurd, ridiculous, and anyone who might one day know of such a yearning would think him insane. He didn't care anymore. The hens had it right. They loved their children, no matter what. They were motherly, always, and protective, always, expecting nothing from their offspring and grateful for their mere existence.

"If only I had been given such a mother," he tried to say, succeeding only in another low, sorrowful moan. Perhaps then he wouldn't have been so sad. Perhaps then he wouldn't have been such a disappointment. Perhaps then he wouldn't have been so…unready, as Edmund had said. He closed his eyes, one of the few things he could still manage, and allowed the dark to claim him, hoping he might finally find peace.

XXXVII

Æva gripped the sword by the hilt and held it, point-first, towards the far wall of her bedchamber. She felt the tension in her wrists, forearms, and shoulders too, so unused was she to the weight. She couldn't remember if she'd ever held it like this. It felt strange. Alaric had taken many lives with this blade, of that she was sure. She didn't know what to think of that now she was holding it herself.

"It's a fine weapon," said Ulfcytel, observing at her side. "May I hold it?" He held out his hands, palms facing up like he expected her to say yes.

"Of course," she answered, angling herself to pass the sword hilt first so he wouldn't cut himself. Ulfcytel reached out and took it by the blade, his fingers placed in the fuller so as to not slice open his palms. He then gripped the hilt with both hands, extending it outward like she had done. He took a few swings through the open air, his movements slow and measured.

"It's light," he finally said. "Lighter than most swords. That can be a bad thing for an unskilled warrior inclined to use his weapon as a cudgel. Fortunately, Alaric was no slouch with a blade. We were lucky to have found it."

"I confess I didn't really know what to do with it when we came here," said Æva, her eyes following the sparkle and shine of the metal as Ulfcytel continued his practice. "The plan was to give it to Brandon when he's old enough."

Ulfcytel stopped, letting the sword hang down towards the floor. "Is he not old enough?" he asked, an eyebrow raised. "I knew a thing or two about fighting when I was his age. Best to start early rather than late. His life might one day depend on it."

"He's too young," said Æva irritably. "I can barely hold that thing for long. Brandon will only hurt himself or somebody else if he goes swinging it around."

"That's not what I was thinking," Ulfcytel said absent-mindedly, his eyes now upon the finely worked pommel. "Alaric, by the looks of it, already made a start in his training. If we..."

"How do you know that?" asked Æva, still annoyed at the prospect of unsolicited advice. She hated that. Sometimes she felt that everyone she met was of a mind to give her their opinion, for some reason assuming she was some little lost lamb who couldn't think for herself. It was beyond tiresome.

"I saw him practising with Edmund that time," Ulfcytel said, still studying the pommel. "I could tell he wasn't a complete novice. He knew how to stand. His footwork was good. Alaric must have given him a few lessons, no?"

Æva thought back, accessing memories. It was true Alaric had given Brandon some points of advice on how to hold himself with a weapon, but she couldn't recall anything particularly involved. She'd never enjoyed seeing the boy like that, as though he himself was a fighter like his father. It didn't feel right. It wasn't in his temperament. She'd told Alaric that, but he'd never taken her seriously. It was one of the few things they'd ever had cause to argue over.

"He did instruct him a few times," she finally admitted. "It was nothing major. I always thought Alaric had the skill to fight his way through a thicket of Danes if he wanted to..."

"I can confirm he was very much capable of doing so," grinned Ulfcytel.

"...but I never got the impression Brandon was of such a mind," continued Æva, ignoring the interruption. "He's too gentle. He's not got a warrior's spirit, it's obvious. He doesn't even hurt insects, for goodness sake. He saves them from being squished underfoot and puts them outside."

"I do that," said Ulfcytel, frowning. "Why wouldn't I? A gentle heart does not preclude one from rising to the challenge of defending one's country."

"It's just different," sighed Æva, folding her arms across her chest. "...do you really save insects?"

"Aye! And why not? They are fascinating things. I like the funny little armoured bastards with all the legs."

"Woodlice."

"That's them," he nodded. "But seriously, Æva, if I may be so bold..."

"That depends on what you're being bold about."

"...Brandon wants to learn," he said. "I know it's not my business, but he was inseparable from Edmund on the road to Bernecestre. He's inseparable from Edmund whenever he gets the chance. He wants to imitate him. There's a reason for that."

"Because he has no father?" she asked sadly.

"That's part of it," said Ulfcytel, slightly deflated. "The other is that Edmund is a natural role model, and the fact Brandon has chosen him to look up to says a few things."

"A few things about Brandon? Like what?"

"That he's a good lad, for a start. He sees a nobility in Edmund that he can relate to. And he sees a courageous spirit, which is again something he can relate to. I can spot these things from a mile off...which is why I say Brandon should be trained. And in time...he can take possession of this."

He held up the sword and extended it out towards her, hilt first, like he'd just made a point that was impossible to argue with. Æva took it in both hands and deposited it back into the chest at her feet, closing the lid.

"Does everyone think I require a lecture on my own son?" she asked, twisting the key in the lock until it clicked twice. She then slipped the key back into the coin purse at her belt and turned to Ulfcytel.

"I apologise if you think that's what I'm doing," he said timidly. "I only speak my mind. Since I have caused offence, I shall beg your pardon and take my leave."

He made a move for the door, his eyes downcast. She said nothing at first, but as he lumbered out into the chamber beyond she called after him. "I'm sorry," she said. "You didn't offend me. It's just...it's not easy being in my position. Things are always on my mind, especially when it comes to Brandon."

"I can't imagine what it must be like," said Ulfcytel, looking back at her from the doorway.

"Surely you and Wulfhild must have children?"

Æva regretted her words almost immediately. The ealdorman's face seemed to sag, his eyes taking on a despairing look that spoke to the fact she'd clearly hit a nerve. "I'm sorry," she said hurriedly. "I didn't mean to pry."

"Don't be sorry," he said softly. "It is what it is. Now I had best go check on Osbert and Eadwig."

"I would like to come," said Æva hopefully. She enjoyed tending to them. She hoped it brought them comfort.

Ulfcytel grunted something in the affirmative and turned to head off towards the tower staircase. Æva followed, and they were soon making their descent down the familiar, well-worn stone steps, the surrounding shadows ensuring the ealdorman was a broad, hobbling silhouette in front of her. They emerged into the main hall to find it brightly lit, the fire in the hearth blazing away like it were mid-winter rather than late summer. Æva understood why. Eadwig wasn't far off, atop the table Edmund had not so long ago used to dine. It was important he be kept warm. His condition was simply too fragile to risk anything else.

Wulfhild saw them coming and stood up. Brandon was with her, with his hound, "Dog Face", as he was known, and they'd been feeding Osbert, who really looked quite content upon the floor, his straw bed and sheepskin blanket seeming to serve him well. They'd put him close to the hearth at first, but he'd complained a fair amount, saying he was too warm and didn't need to be "coddled". Ulfcytel had begged to differ on that score, but he'd granted his request to be moved, shifting him and his bed a half dozen paces into the north east corner. Osbert had then spent much of his time asleep. It was understandable. His wound would take time to heal. Æva was surprised at the progress he'd made already. God was indeed good, she thought.

"All I can do is wet Eadwig's lips," said Wulfhild when they came within earshot.

"He still won't eat anything?" Ulfcytel asked, giving Eadwig a quick once over to make sure he hadn't decided to start bleeding again.

"He wants to," Wulfhild said, "or at least I think he does, but he doesn't seem able to chew. He swallows a little water but then starts to choke. I can't risk that again. His head…it's…"

Ulfcytel grunted, understanding what she meant. Eadwig's injuries were terrible, and when Æva had heard of how he'd received them, she'd been almost too afraid to look. It wasn't as bad as she'd feared, given the abundance of bandages, but there was something so incredibly sad about seeing him like this. He never spoke. He never moved. He responded when Æva took his hand, and his eyes also rolled slightly in their sockets as if trying to focus on her, but that was it. Edmund must have been devastated by it all. It was no wonder he'd left in such a hurry. She hoped he'd be alright.

"What about some kind of soup?" said Æva, thinking the solution to Eadwig's inability to chew might be quite easy to solve.

"That's a good idea," answered Wulfhild. "Can you cook it or…shall I…"

"I can do it," said Æva, wondering why Wulfhild seemed so unsure of herself. "Something easy on the digestion will be best. He's probably used to richer fare where he's from, but that won't serve him now. I'll keep it simple."

"But nutritious," smiled Ulfcytel.

"Of course," she replied, wondering what purpose there'd be in making a soup that was somehow otherwise. She hurried off in the direction of the kitchens, leaving Brandon with Wulfhild. She felt unusually optimistic as she sauntered through the hall, and at first she couldn't work out why. Then it hit her. She felt useful. The prospect of making soup to feed Eadwig had given her a purpose, and as absurd as that sounded, it was far better than how she'd felt previously. She'd perceived herself as a burden for so long now, always needing help or chasing after Edmund and his army, which had left her dispirited and aimless. That wasn't the case tonight. Eadwig was going to get his soup, and Æva would be the one to make it happen. That made her smile.

The kitchens were not quite as she remembered them. They were a mess, and from the looks of things a whole lot of people who didn't know how to cook had recently used them, which probably meant somebody from the garrison had decided to add some literal spice to their rations. Æva cleaned up a little for the sake of hygiene and got to work, chopping vegetables and boiling water to make a soup fit for a king, or at least an injured aetheling at any rate.

The broth she concocted had been one of Alaric's old favourites, and the smell stirred pleasant memories as she wandered back through the hall, a large wooden bowl held snugly in her hands. Eadwig was still there when she returned, his eyes closed in what looked like a reasonably peaceful slumber. She pulled up a stool and sat next to him, the soup and spoon in her lap, and waited, allowing it to cool. Wulfhild, Ulfcytel, and Brandon went to come over, but Æva asked them to give her a moment, knowing that Eadwig, despite his state, would feel embarrassed at being fed with an audience present. They agreed and understood, and so only Brandon remained, his eyes pained as he looked upon the unfortunate aetheling. He was a kind boy, and very sensitive to the misfortunes of others. Æva would have to think of a way to cheer him up. Helping Eadwig would be a good start.

He'd opened his eyes, as if able to smell what was on offer even if he couldn't voice any appreciation. It was a bit of a nightmare at first since he couldn't even part his lips fully, let alone lift his head, but they managed it, getting the first spoonful of cooled broth into his mouth with the minimum of fuss. Brandon dabbed at his face with a cloth, clearing up any spillage, and Eadwig, to his credit, actually swallowed, his Adam's apple bobbing up and then down quite beautifully. Æva smiled at him. He smiled back, the corners of his mouth lifting ever so slightly. The feeling then returned. She felt useful. It was wonderful.

Eadwig managed to finish half the bowl of soup before he signalled satisfaction. It was, of course, difficult to know whether he'd had his fill, what with his inability to talk, so Æva took his shaking head at face value. Brandon again cleaned up, having manifested a fresh cloth from somewhere to wipe Eadwig's beard and lips.

The boy then did something unexpected. He passed Æva a book, one familiar to her in appearance and yet surprising, considering she'd thought it confined to the study. It was a Bible, the one she used to read to her brother-in-law, Ælfgar. It was a beautiful old thing, and the calligraphy inside was as she remembered, the letters so artfully crafted some might think they were the work of angels rather than men. Brandon stared at her whilst she flipped through the pages, his look expectant.

"Will you read?" he asked. Dog Face had again appeared and wandered over, his shaking tail and earnest expression suggesting he too wanted her to recite something.

"Is that what you want?" Æva asked Brandon.

"I think it might help. Eadwig might like it. He must be very bored."

Æva looked over to find that Eadwig was staring at her, his eyes hopeful. She resumed her seat on the stool and began to read aloud, the act bringing back memories of her times in the tower with Ælfgar. Brandon sat on the floor, Dog Face nestled at his side, and listened attentively to the beginnings of the Gospel according to Saint John. Eadwig likewise kept his gaze on Æva, seemingly content.

"Why did Jesus turn water into wine?" asked Brandon, confused at what he was hearing.

"It's a metaphor," Æva said. "It signifies Christ's ever bountiful care and mercy towards us."

"A metaphor?" Brandon asked. "You mean he didn't really do the miracle?"

She thought on that for a second. She'd heard it said that the Bible contained different levels of truth, not all of which could be understood literally. In her experience, that made things easier to understand, as some of the older narratives confused her otherwise, especially when it came to talking snakes and God losing His temper over the consumption of an apple. Things had to be interpreted properly, with their meanings fully understood, which required learned men to scrutinise the text and draw out the higher spiritual lessons that lay within. You couldn't do that just by reading it yourself and thinking you'd somehow obtain its real meaning in one sitting. The Bible wasn't that kind of book.

Æva assumed the same logic applied to the story of Jesus at the wedding in Cana. She suspected there were metaphors in play here, since it seemed strange to her that Christ would use his power to make something as potentially troublesome as wine. A priest had once told her that Christ's wine wouldn't have been like the stuff drunk today and wouldn't have gotten you intoxicated, which Æva assumed meant he'd performed a literal miracle as described. Another priest had told her, however, that nobody could be certain if such a thing had taken place, or if it had, Jesus had meant it to be interpreted as something deeper; the wine, perhaps, serving as a means to demonstrate the outpouring of his love upon the world. She liked that explanation better. She just wasn't entirely sure which one was true.

She was thinking on how to explain this to Brandon when she heard the outer doors of the hall groaning open and then closing. Heavy treads were heard, the sound echoing off stone as they came yet closer. Wulfnoth appeared from the shadows, looking grim and fatigued, much of his cloak and armour caked with mud. He had that spear of his slung over his shoulder, the one with the red tassels, and from the looks of it he'd seen combat just recently, the bloody residue upon its tip catching the light. Ulfcytel rose to meet him, but Wulfnoth suddenly stopped when he drew close to Æva, his dark eyes troubled.

"What in God's blessed name has happened?" he breathed, as if in shock. "Eadwig? Can you hear me, lad?"

"He's been injured," said Æva, feeling a little awkward at her statement of the obvious. "Thorkell attacked him in Lundenburg and…"

"What?" snapped Wulfnoth, shaking his head in disbelief. "Thorkell? Why? He turned on Æthelred?"

"It is as the lady says," rumbled Ulfcytel, now at Wulfnoth's side. "Thorkell was in the process of robbing the treasury, and poor Eadwig here discovered him in the act. Eadwig would have died if it wasn't for Hereward."

"The king's thegn, Æthelred's bodyguard?"

"That's correct," Ulfcytel nodded. "We had to detain him once he'd brought Eadwig to us. It's a sad thing, but Edmund didn't want him getting in the way."

"In the way?" asked Wulfnoth. "Where is Edmund?"

"He's gone to Lundenburg," said Æva. "He went to confront his father over..." she paused, the words catching in her throat. She'd never met Morcar, but Sigeferth had been kind to her when she'd come to his door, cold and desperate, after Eamon had found her and Brandon wandering the woods. She'd been sincerely grieved to hear of his fate.

"Sigeferth and Morcar are dead," Ulfcytel announced. "Æthelred had them killed, or at least Eadric did it and he wasn't of a mind to stop or punish him."

Wulfnoth frowned, his spear now gripped in his right hand, its bloody tip pointing towards the rafters. "But you remained when Edmund left?" he asked Ulfcytel. "So who went with him?"

"Nobody," sighed Ulfcytel. "He insisted on going alone. Said he needed to speak with his father one on one, without anyone else around to rattle him."

"That's insane!" exclaimed Wulfnoth, his tone sharp with outrage. Eadwig murmured to himself, disturbed at the altercation. Æva took his hand in hers. She didn't want him getting upset.

"Do you understand what is likely taking place?" asked Wulfnoth, quieter now. "Eadric will have killed Sigeferth and Mocar precisely because they're allies of Edmund. That means he's decided to take action against Edmund himself, possibly from finding out that Æthelred promised him the throne. It's always been about the succession. Eadric wants Emma's boy, Edward, as king."

"How do you know that?" asked Æva.

Wulfnoth looked down at her, the angle of his hooked beak of a nose making him look vaguely peculiar. "I think I had this conversation with your husband once," he said solemnly. "We'd just escaped Canterburie, he and I, and understandably he wanted to know who I was and what I was doing breaking him out of his prison. I will tell you as I told him...Eadric wants power for himself, but he worked out long ago that Æthelred's boys," he gestured towards Eadwig, "are too headstrong for him to control. The young Edward, Alfred, and Godgifu...that's a different story."

"So he wants a child king on the throne for him to push around?" Ulfcytel asked, his voice thick with contempt.

"Yes," said Wulfnoth, like it was somehow so obvious. "One he can mould and threaten and manipulate. Eadric wouldn't have been able to do that with Æthelstan or Edmund. Can you imagine that little bastard trying to take advantage of either of them? They'd have knocked his teeth out on the spot."

They all paused as Eadwig began to make a curious noise that, to Æva's ears at least, sounded like it were somewhere between choking and crying. She looked over in alarm, fearing he was having difficulties with the soup she'd served him. She then saw the amusement in his eyes. There was nothing to fear. Eadwig was laughing, in his own broken, tragic way, but a laugh nonetheless. He'd heard what Wulfnoth had said, and the thought of Eadric getting a beating from his older brothers amused him. Æva couldn't fault him on that. It would make for quite a spectacle.

"Which makes Edmund going off alone so much worse," continued Wulfnoth, apparently having no time for laughter. "Eadric will be expecting him to make a fuss over Sigeferth's death and will have planned accordingly. He could be in great danger!"

Ulfcytel inclined his head forward and lifted his hands to his beard, exasperated. "I can't believe I didn't see it," he wailed. "I did say to Edmund that he should take an escort, but…" he looked over his shoulder, his eyes on Wulfhild. "Why did you marry such a bloody fool?!" he demanded, turning back to face Wulfnoth before she could answer. "I'm so sorry," he said. "I should have thought about it more. It's just Edmund can be so headstrong, especially when he's angry."

"I know what he's like," admitted Wulfnoth. "He's hard to argue with, but when he's like that it's all the more important we try. He gets odd notions, lets his emotions get the better of him…" Wulfnoth looked at Æva for a brief second, "…and tends to favour his heart over his head."

"So what shall we do?" asked Ulfcytel, having entirely missed Wulfnoth's rather strange glance towards Æva.

"I'll go after him," Wulfnoth said. "I have people in Lundenburg who can assist me when I arrive. If Eadric has already made his move against Edmund…I can always avenge him."

Eadwig made another sound, like a half-wail combined with a sob. Æva squeezed his hand again and whispered a few comforting words, none of which seemed to have much of an impact. It wasn't right that they were having this conversation in front of him. Grief would not speed his recovery, if a recovery was even possible. There was no sense in causing him needless distress.

"Can we not talk about such things here?" Æva asked. "Eadwig has endured enough as it is. Let's be sensitive about all this."

Wulfnoth again looked down at him, his face blank and impassive. "I apologise, my lord," he said, his formal tone directed at Eadwig. "Be assured that I will do my utmost to put things right. You have my most solemn promise that if it is at all possible, I will bring your brother back to you unharmed."

Eadwig predictably didn't say anything, instead closing his eyes like he wanted to shut everything out. "Why not just march on Lundenburg?" Ulfcytel asked. "If we're serious about doing this, then having an army at our back will help."

Wulfnoth shook his head, the two of them apparently content to continue their conversation despite everything Æva had just said. "Throwing all we have into this might not be the best idea," he murmured. "Æthelred will still have his Normans, and Uhtred and his people may still be around. That would leave us massively outnumbered if it came to a fight. A more subtle approach is what's needed here."

"And you are indeed the most subtle master of subtle things that need mastering?" smiled Ulfcytel.

"Somebody has to be," Wulfnoth said with yet another shake of his head.

Ulfcytel didn't seem fazed by the veiled insult. "I don't suppose now is a good time to ask if you found any trace of Ælfric in Suthhamtunam?" he asked quietly. Æva felt her heart beat a little faster at the mention of her father-in-law. Despite everything, she was anxious to learn of his fate.

"The town is in good order and willing to continue in their fealty to Edmund, but no, old Ælfric wasn't there," answered Wulfnoth. "We don't need him presently in any case. He fears Æthelred, if his note to us is anything to go by, and he's not wrong in doing so. Let him recover his wits wherever he's taken himself off to, and let us focus on what's in front of us."

"I would like to come with you to Lundenburg," asked Brandon suddenly, everyone turning at once to look down at him.

"Why would you want that?" Wulfnoth inquired, his eyes narrowing into slits.

"Because Edmund is the rightful king, and I don't want anything to happen to him."

"Can you wield a sword?" Wulfnoth had raised a single eyebrow, suggesting he was playing games with Brandon. Æva didn't like it.

"I was learning! I can get better."

"Noble sentiments," said Wulfnoth. "Keep practising. Perhaps one day you and I can serve our king together."

Brandon looked deflated as Wulfnoth and Ulfcytel moved off towards the outer doors, their conversation gradually fading from earshot. "It's good advice," said Æva reassuringly. "If you practice with your father's sword, you'll be as good as anyone by the time you're their age."

"Father's sword?" asked Brandon, his eyes lighting up. "Where is it? Can I have it?"

"Not now," said Æva swiftly, hoping she hadn't inadvertently started an argument.

"When then?"

"When Edmund comes back," she answered, having to think fast. "He'll be able to teach you."

"Ulfcytel is around, he can teach me," replied Brandon, sounding a little surly.

"Everyone is very busy, Brandon. When things calm down a bit, we'll have more time. Then Edmund or whoever you like can teach you swordcraft."

"With father's sword?"

"Not at first," Æva said firmly. "It's a very potent thing, that is. I don't want you to hurt yourself."

Eadwig made another noise, a low grunt mixed with the beginnings of a gurgle. He had a slight smile now, making Æva think he agreed with what she'd said. Hearing others speak seemed to be doing him good. Interaction was an important part of recovery, so she'd heard, and in Eadwig's case she felt it might be vital. He must be absolutely despairing, trapped as he seemed within his own body. She'd do anything she could to lighten his burden.

"Can I get you anything?" she asked, still sat at his side. He shook his head, the movement almost imperceptible, and let out a contented sigh before closing his eyes. He was fast asleep in no time. Eating must have exhausted him. At least he wasn't fretting over the news about Edmund. Æva didn't think she'd be of much help to him on that score.

Yet that didn't absolve her from the duty to aid Edmund if she could. They'd become close in their time here, in a way she wasn't always entirely comfortable with, but if his temper was likely to get him into trouble, she could be of some use in making him see reason. She should have really stopped him before he could rush off to Lundenburg on his own. It had been an obvious mistake, but everyone, including her, had been so overwhelmed by recent events they'd not been thinking as they should. That would have to change.

She called Wulfhild over, asking her if she'd mind keeping Eadwig and Brandon company whilst she ran an errand. She agreed, and so Æva headed off in search of Wulfnoth. It then occurred to her that she'd actually just asked a member of the royal family, as in Wulfhild, to watch her son like she were a common serving girl. The thought made Æva wince. She hoped Wulfhild hadn't taken offence, but even if she had, it was too late now. Æva wanted some answers from Wulfnoth, and she wouldn't get them waiting around by the fire.

Evening was almost upon them when she made it outside into Porteceaster's walled interior. The refugees from Mideltune were still in evidence, and she could see several of them close by as they cleared up whatever work they'd been doing for the day. Æva had wondered how they'd occupy themselves during their time here, thinking that people who'd just been burnt out of their homes would do little other than recover from the shock. She'd been wrong in that. These people may have lost much, yet they were very industrious, setting themselves the task of repairing any part of the fortress that needed it as well as tending to the vegetable gardens both inside and outside the walls. It kept them distracted, she supposed, yet it would also keep them fed. That was obviously important. These were very dramatic times, but in the midst of it all, they had to find a few moments for the simple things, like remembering to eat. It was easily forgotten, in Æva's experience.

She wandered through the old market square, knowing the squat, stone barracks would be just up ahead. The sun was dwindling fast when she reached them, causing her to squint as she tried to ascertain who was inside. She threw caution to the wind and opened up the front doors, knowing the worst-case scenario would just involve her interrupting a bunch of Edmund's warriors whilst they sat eating their evening meal. True enough, they were there, at least thirty of them eating from bowls at long, narrow tables, yet they paid her little attention when she came on through, which in all honesty was something of a relief to her. She asked one of them if Wulfnoth was here. He nodded and pointed at a door towards the back of the chamber. She turned cold. Wulfnoth must have headed to the cells. She could guess why. He'd be wanting to talk to their new guest.

Her instincts had been quite correct. It had taken her a little while to get down here, what with the need to descend several flights of stairs, and the dark had been a problem until she'd entered the underground prison proper and been able to take advantage of the light cast from several small braziers set into the walls. All the cells were empty, their stout doors hammered shut, aside from one, which contained their "guest". Both Ulfcytel and Wulfnoth were facing him from the corridor, alongside a third man Æva assumed was tasked with standing watch. She got a bad feeling from all this. There was a certain tension in the air, one that set her on edge.

"So you refuse to tell us anything about Eadric's return to Lundenburg?" Wulfnoth said, his hard eyes on the prisoner. Æva's breath caught in her throat as she laid eyes on him. He'd been beaten, his bruised face speaking to some considerable abuse in the not-so-distant past. Wulfnoth, if his scuffed knuckles were anything to go by, was the one behind this, and that did not sit well with her.

"You've hurt him?" she asked, looking to Ulfcytel for confirmation. He didn't look too happy with the situation, but he'd obviously done nothing about it for whatever reason.

"He had to be made compliant," he replied hesitantly. "He did try to draw his weapon on Edmund, Æva. I had to put him down."

She scowled, finding Ulfcytel's answer elusive. "That was days ago," she said, again peering at the prisoner through the open cell door. "He's bleeding now, so who did that? Was he a threat even whilst divested of his weapons and armour?"

"Why are you even here?" Wulfnoth asked, turning to face her.

"I want to talk to you about a way to somehow help Edmund…but now I'm here, I think you'd better explain yourself."

"And I think you'd better leave," replied Wulfnoth, turning back to the prisoner.

"And I think you'd better remember who rules here," said Æva sternly, her hands upon her hips. "With my father-in-law missing, I'm the only member of his family present in Porteceaster. It belongs to me."

Wulfnoth's face twisted into a particularly irksome smirk. "Are you trying to make us laugh?" he said, his voice echoing slightly off the surrounding masonry. "Edmund is king, and I act on his authority. It would…"

Ulfcytel cleared his throat awkwardly. "I remember Edmund was quite eager to stress we were here with the lady Æva's permission," he said. "She is right in reminding us that this is her family seat, and with the Ealdorman Ælfric gone…"

"I don't care," snapped Wulfnoth. "We have business with the prisoner, and I won't desist from that just because Edmund is soft on a woman."

"And I'm that woman?" asked Æva, annoyed.

"Of course you are," said Wulfnoth, not bothering to meet her gaze. "And it's of no consequence to me. What is of consequence is that Hereward will have direct knowledge of Eadric's recent activities in Lundenburg. That knowledge can help us. Don't you agree, Hereward?"

Æva again looked to the beaten prisoner, or Hereward as Wulfnoth had called him. He was sat down, cross-legged on the cold earth floor, with nothing but some rather sorry-looking undergarments to cover his bruised flesh. Despite his battered state, he still looked capable, leading Æva to wonder how they'd been able to capture him so easily. He stared up at her from the shadows, his eyes deep and sorrowful, his lank, unkempt hair cascading down either side of his face. This wasn't a bad man. He didn't deserve mistreatment.

"I would have helped you, you know," Hereward said, turning his gaze towards Wulfnoth. "Eadric is no friend to me…and most importantly, he's no real friend to the king. But this?" He lifted a hand to indicate his beaten face. "There was no need for it. I came here to do Edmund a service and hopefully allow his brother to recover from his wounds in safety. I was not expecting such…treachery."

"It's not like that, and you know it," Ulfcytel grumbled. "You made it quite clear that you were loyal to Æthelred above all else. Edmund couldn't go and do what needs to be done and have you snapping at his heels. Your incarceration was a necessary evil."

"And what has Edmund gone to do exactly?" Hereward asked spitefully.

"You already know," Ulfcytel replied. "Which is why you have to tell us what you know of Eadric's recent activities. Any snippet of information could help us."

"I told you. He killed Sigeferth and Morcar, and I was sent to retrieve the fleeing Eadwig. I came straight here once I'd found him."

"But you must have seen Eadric around before," said Wulfnoth. "Does he still cling to the king's side? What about the queen? The children? Has he made any attempt to get closer to Edward?"

Hereward shook his head wearily. "Eadric is a rat, in the company of other rats," he said. "He sticks close to the king, undoubtedly to get back in his favour. That's all I know."

Wulfnoth stepped forward into the cell, the sudden movement catching Æva by surprise. Before she'd had a chance to do or say anything, he'd already seized Hereward, drawing him to his feet to press him against the back wall.

"There's got to be more!" Wulfnoth cried, his voice staggeringly loud from the confines of the cell. "How often does Eadric meet with the king? What do they discuss? Do they talk about Edmund? The Normans? Are there Normans present when they meet? Tell me!"

"Often, sometimes, maybe," said Hereward, unimpressed with the theatrics.

"Eadric would have known that Edmund would come for him if he hurt Sigeferth," Wulfnoth barked, his hands still on Hereward. "Tell me what he has planned. He'd be a fool not to have prepared anything. Speak!"

"What the hell do you want me to say?" Hereward shot back. "Do you think Eadric just walks up to the king and says "I have a dastardly plan to discuss, let's do it right in front of Hereward here." Is that how you think it works? I thought you were supposed to be clever?"

Wulfnoth wouldn't relent. "I know you almost never leave Æthelred's side," he snarled into his face. "You will know something! Anything! Something that could help us! Tell me, or I'll see to it that you suffer!"

"And just how do you know that?" demanded Hereward. "You have spies in the capital, right? So why should I trust you? Why should I help you?"

"Because Edmund may be in danger," Ulfcytel said irritably. "And if you care about this kingdom, you will care about its future. Edmund is that future, but only if we protect him from the likes of Eadric."

"Æthelred is king," intoned Hereward, to Ulfcytel and Wulfnoth both. "He has my allegiance. I only brought Eadwig here as I didn't think it safe to have him around Eadric. Had I known this would be the reception I'd receive, I'd have thought of something else. I'm loyal to the king. That's all I have to say."

Wulfnoth's hand dropped to his belt and pulled a narrow seax from its scabbard. He held it up to Hereward's face, the tip pressed just under his eye with enough pressure to draw a trickle of blood.

"Do not hide behind noble words," hissed Wulfnoth. "I've broken many a Dane, you know that? They are all so full of defiance at first, but it all ends the same way. They tell me what I want to know…through blood and broken teeth as they writhe at my feet. Don't think it won't be the same with you."

Hereward said nothing, his expression implacable despite the pain he must surely feel. Æva, however, did NOT like where this was going. Wulfnoth was a cold man, she'd worked that out just from laying eyes on him months ago, and she could very much believe his boast that he'd tortured Danes for the sake of their secrets. That was hardly a Christian thing to do, and this was even worse. Hereward had done nothing wrong. In fact, he'd shown great courage in bringing them Eadwig. Æva would not stand to see him harmed.

"You'll not be hurting this man," she said, putting on her best "stop it and come here" voice that she generally only used with Brandon.

"Don't interfere," replied Wulfnoth, his eyes still glaring into Hereward's.

"I will, though!" snapped Æva. "I am the authority in Porteceaster! These lands belong to my family, and in the absence of the Ealdorman Ælfric…"

"Edmund indulges you," said Wulfnoth, still refusing to turn and look at her. "This is a matter of import, one that will not be interrupted. Stay and watch, if you can stomach it, although I suggest you leave before it gets too messy..."

"That's enough," said Ulfcytel. "We won't be doing this, Wulfnoth, not now. Edmund had Hereward incarcerated here purely out of necessity. It will weigh on his conscience, I know it. I also know he'll not have you torturing the man who saved Eadwig's life. Relent."

"I must..."

"Relent, damn you!" howled Ulfcytel, his voice ricocheting back and forth across the walls, quite painfully.

Wulfnoth looked at him over his shoulder, as if trying to ascertain whether he could still argue his case. He thought better of it and instead sheathed his seax, a second later stepping back into the corridor to rejoin Ulfcytel. Hereward stayed on his feet, his eyes defiant, but he otherwise made no move to retaliate. Ævа could understand the need to find out everything they could about Eadric, but the ends couldn't justify the means. It also made no sense to be wasting time here when Edmund himself could be in danger. Surely his safety, rather than physically accosting Hereward just in case he might know something, was the priority?

"Are you happy now?" she asked Wulfnoth. He acted like she'd said nothing, instead turning to address Ulfcytel.

"I'm going to ride out in search of Edmund," he said. "I'll take my own men, whilst you remain here with the army."

"Wouldn't it have been better to do that before?" asked Æva, indignant at being ignored. "You've wasted time here questioning a man who doesn't know anything. Edmund could be riding into a trap as we speak."

"Enough," said Wulfnoth, his eyes flashing with anger. "Do not presume you know my craft, and do not presume to think you know enough to give me advice. I have waged a long war against the likes of Eadric the Grasper, and I have yet to learn all his tricks. Any information I can uncover on his plans, intentions, schemes...it all matters. More than someone like you could know."

"What do you mean someone like me?" Æva was scowling. She'd had enough of this man and his ill manners.

"In that case, I will say something," Hereward suddenly announced. "Eadric brought his wife to Lundenburg. That's something I've not known him to do before."

"Why didn't you say that earlier?" snapped Wulfnoth, irritated.

"Because you hit me," said Hereward, "and then you threatened me with a blade. The lady there," he nodded at Æva, "she's the only person to act like I'm even human ever since I've been thrown in here."

Wulfnoth scowled even more, like he thought he was being toyed with. "So because of her supposed kindness, you'll give up a little information?"

"It's not even information, just something I remembered," Hereward said. "But yes...civility and decency matter to me. You could have cut me all night, Wulfnoth, and I'd never have told you a damn thing. Why? Because you'd have proven yourself an evil man. And I'll resist evil until the end."

"We can debate how evil I am some other time," sighed Wulfnoth, exasperated. "Just tell me what you observed about Eadric's wife...it's Eadgyth, isn't it?"

"Yes," confirmed Ulfcytel. "One of Æthelred's daughters. I've not seen her in bloody years. When I heard she was to be married off to Eadric…I…let's just say I doubt it's a happy marriage."

"That's the odd thing," said Hereward. "She seemed very loyal to Eadric. Kept saying to the king about how Eadric had tried to do the right thing…I thought it looked strange at the time. Like she was stressing it a little too much."

"An act, most likely," nodded Wulfnoth. "If Eadric has only recently seen fit to bring her back to Lundenburg, it's because he wants her as a mollifying influence on Æthelred. Chances are he forced her into that performance. She would have complied, knowing the consequences of defiance and all."

"You think he hurts her?" asked Æva, her stomach twisting in apprehension.

"I can almost guarantee it," said Wulfnoth grimly. "Eadgyth would have been a prize to Eadric at one time, since she binds him to the royal family, but that's the only regard he'll have for her. She's a resource, an exploitable one. I can only imagine the horrors she's endured in Mierċe."

"That's another thing," said Hereward. "She was upset the night Sigeferth was killed. She tried to approach the king when he was alone in his garden…well, alone except for me standing watch, of course. She was acting like she wanted to tell him something, but then Eadric came running over. Like he was nervous of what she might say."

"And then what?" asked Ulfcytel.

"Oh, Eadric seemed to get control of the situation, and fast…but I got the impression the wife had wanted to tell the king something in private…and she'd thought twice about it as soon as her husband appeared. If he's hurting her, that would explain it. She's scared of him."

"Anything else you can tell me?" asked Wulfnoth.

"There was a strange accusation from Eadric, now that I think of it. He accused Sigeferth of upsetting his wife back at the banquet. Sigeferth wasn't having any of it, and from what I'd seen that evening, the man had never even approached the woman. But it really got the king angry. He took it very personally, and everything spun out of control from there."

Wulfnoth paused for thought, his fingers drumming along the edge of his scabbard. "I think I know what that is," he murmured. "Eadric thinks fast…he'll have been aware his wife was about to expose his abuse of her to Æthelred. Claiming Sigeferth had somehow upset her would explain away her behaviour…and also antagonise the king. He was always dismayed by Sigeferth's influence over Edmund and Æthelstan. If he thought the man was now trying something with his daughter…"

"So is that what drove him into a murderous rage then?" asked Ulfcytel.

"He wasn't happy about any of it," shrugged Hereward, "and he took everything Eadric said like it was the unvarnished truth. Sigeferth and Morcar must have had a bit to drink as they weren't taking it lying down…and then the fate of the Aetheling Æthelstan came up. I think that was the main sore spot for the king."

"So he killed them just for that?" Æva had first-hand experience of how unstable Æthelred was, but even so, this all seemed quite strange.

"He drew his sword and made a move," said Hereward, "but as I said to Edmund…Eadric was fast, and finished the job before the king could get near them."

"Had he been drinking?" asked Wulfnoth.

"Yes, wine. Everyone had been, apart from me. But the king had wine."

"From the same supply as everyone else?" Wulfnoth had a look to him now, like he felt he was on to something.

"No, his own special vintage or something. His steward, Cuthbert, kept bringing it over. I didn't see him do that for anyone else."

"Are you a drinking man, Hereward?"

"I was," Hereward nodded, "in my youth. Not so much now. It's bad for the body and mind both. In my role as guardian to the king, I like to stay sharp."

"You've seen the king drink wine before?"

"Yes."

"Did it ever have that kind of effect on him? As in rage? Murderous rage?"

Hereward thought for a moment. "You're suggesting Eadric had tampered with his wine?"

"Indeed!" said Wulfnoth, a little too enthusiastically. "Why would he not? He's pulled off a serious win here...get the king drunk, but not just any kind of drunk...a certain something in the wine that affects his judgement more than usual. Then he gets him to think Sigeferth is up to something with his daughter. Then he brings them before the king, knowing that tensions will flare and that the king, in his compromised state, will simply not be able to handle an argument over his dead son. The rest is...well, we know what happened. Eadric had a plan. And it worked."

Ulfcytel sighed, his exhalation long and slow. "He's even worse than I thought," he said quietly. "I thought the plan to have me killed back at Hringmere was bad enough...but the man has a capacity for intrigue that's tough to comprehend. I think it's almost certain that he's got plans for Edmund. This is all about him. Sigeferth and Morcar were a means to weaken Edmund, and Eadric will be expecting him to come charging up to Lundenburg. I shouldn't have let him go!"

"It was my fault too," soothed Ælva, her hand reaching up to rest reassuringly upon Ulfcytel's arm. "We were all so shocked about Eadwig, and Edmund was so tempestuous. All we can do now is try to help him."

The door to the cell suddenly slammed shut, the abruptness almost causing Ælva to jump back in fright. Wulfnoth then motioned for the gaoler, who had until now been largely still and silent, and had him lock the door, Hereward staying entirely quiet from the other side.

"You're just going to keep him shut up in there?" asked Ælva, confused and appalled considering Hereward's newfound willingness to cooperate.

"Of course," said Wulfnoth tersely as he barged past her on his way to the exit. "He's been useful," he said over his shoulder, "but I won't trust him not to get in my way."

"Where are you going?" Ulfcytel called after him, his voice again reverberating about the place.

Wulfnoth paused at the door leading to the stairs and looked back at them, his expression blank, the flicker of torchlight playing across his face. "To gather my men," he said. "To help Edmund before Eadric can strike."

"And what if he already has?" asked the ealdorman.

"Then I'll do my utmost to thwart his plans...or avenge Edmund, should Eadric have succeeded in bringing them to fruition."

Wulfnoth turned and passed through the doorway, his echoing footsteps faintly audible from his hurried flight up the stairs and into the barracks above. Æva stepped towards the now closed and locked cell door, hoping to perhaps speak with its occupant despite not being able to physically lay eyes on him. Ulfcytel saw what she was doing and ushered her away and down the corridor, her objections making little impression on him.

"Not now," he said. "I understand you feel sorry for Hereward, but now is not the time."

"Time for what?" she asked, irritated at how he'd laid his hands on her. He let go when she stopped resisting, and they began climbing the stairs together, the shadows almost swallowing them up as they ascended.

"We need to keep our heads clear," Ulfcytel finally replied, leading her out of the darkness and back into the barrack room dining hall. There were still some warriors loafing around, content with the meal they'd just put away. She was glad at least somebody was in good spirits. She wished she could count herself among them.

"I just wanted to talk to him," Æva said, following Ulfcytel out through the main entrance and into the open air. The evening had nearly turned to night, and the heavens were just starting to become visible in the clear twilight skies above. The breeze had picked up, unfortunately, and Æva felt a slight chill creep across her skin. She wrapped her arms about herself, her discomfort obvious.

"Hurry back to the hall," Ulfcytel told Æva, his eyes on Wulfnoth as he and several others prepared a batch of horses to ride out.

"Why is everyone suddenly disrespecting me?" asked Æva, her arms still folded. "Did you forget who owns this place? If Edmund is in trouble, then I want to go with Wulfnoth and help him."

"What?" exclaimed Ulfcytel, his face creased with irritation. "And just what do you think you can do against the Ealdorman of Mierċe that Wulfnoth cannot?"

Æva stammered, her words refusing to take shape. "I-I-I-I-I can be there to advise Edmund on…"

"And if he's already fallen into the trap Eadric has likely set for him? You're going to talk your way out of it?"

"Why so harsh with me, Ulfcytel?" she asked, her feelings hurt. "Am I really so stupid to you all? For what reason?"

"It's not that we think that," said Ulfcytel, his hands now upon her shoulders. She shook him off. She wouldn't be patronised.

"I'm sorry," he said quickly. "It's just you're involving yourself in things you have little experience of. Wulfnoth was wrong to threaten Hereward with harm, and you did the right thing in objecting. But don't assume you know our business better than us. This is warrior's work that's ahead, Æva. Leave Wulfnoth to handle it."

"You're saying that because I'm a woman, I should just shut up?"

"Put it this way…you saw Alaric when he returned from battle, at least once?" She nodded. "Can you really say you understood him then?" he asked. "Can you really say you knew what he'd gone through? That you could advise him on anything he'd just experienced and might encounter again in future battles?"

Æva sighed and shook her head. He was right. She knew little of war, and there had been times when she'd almost feared Alaric after he'd returned from some violent encounter or other. There'd been an odd energy to him, dark and aggressive, one that seemed completely at odds with the gentle, compassionate man she'd first met all those years ago. She knew it had its place. They needed warriors, and likely always would, but it was a world she knew nothing of, and only pride had caused her to presume otherwise.

"I'll go back to Brandon," she said, embarrassed over the whole conversation. "Will you promise me something, though?"

Ulfcytel nodded, his beard swaying a little in the breeze.

"Don't let anyone hurt Hereward. I may be no great war leader like yourself and Wulfnoth, but I know right from wrong. Don't let it happen."

He nodded again, a grunt the only answer he seemed inclined to give. Æva took her leave, her path taking her past Wulfnoth and his now-mounted men as they made ready to depart.

"That is what we need, Æva," Ulfcytel suddenly called after her, his voice sharp and clear. "Despite everything I just said…we still need that concern of yours, that compassion, that softness. Men of war can become lost, can become changed with the rage, the fury…a compassionate touch…a reminder that there is such a thing as gentleness…it can bring us back from the brink."

"The brink of what?" Æva asked.

"From becoming what we reviled to begin with…from losing ourselves in hate, bloodlust…from becoming like the Danes. Becoming less than men."

She didn't respond, instead turning to watch when Wulfnoth and his men spurred their horses into motion and headed off at a trot towards the northern gate. He was a strange man, this Wulfnoth, and after tonight she'd not warmed to him, thinking him ruthless to the point of cruelty. Ulfcytel, however, had spoken some wise words. Men like him did need a check on their baser instincts, something to pull them back before they went too far. She could well believe she was capable of being that restraining force, as she had earlier when Hereward was in peril. Then it occurred to her she'd only been able to do that because Ulfcytel had spoken up in support. If he'd not been there, anything could have happened, and that worried her.

Æva's anxiety didn't relent, staying with her even after Wulfnoth and his men had ridden through the gate and vanished from view. That was it then. He was out there now, on his way to hopefully catch up with Edmund before Eadric could ensnare him in whatever plan he'd formulated. She could well imagine Wulfnoth and his methods could be very useful in thwarting such schemes, but she still felt unsettled and upset over it all. His was a dark path, and for the life of her, she hoped Edmund would not be too heavily influenced by it. He'd made a promise to her once that he'd be a good king, one far removed from base violence and the kind of cold pragmatism she'd seen tonight. She'd pray that he'd always remember that promise. The consequences of him doing otherwise did not bear thinking about.

XXXVIII

The bag was suffocating, the cord sealing it around his head cutting into his neck. The fabric too was rough, the sensation of it against his skin sharp and unpleasant. His head was still aching fiercely, making him suspect he'd been struck from behind. Judging from how wet the back of his neck felt, he'd not yet stopped bleeding. That was concerning.

Edmund flexed in his seat, hoping to get some blood flowing into his wrists. They were tied behind him, the feeling of rope against flesh unmistakable, which also adhered him to this chair, or whatever it was he was sat on considering he couldn't see. It creaked underneath his weight in any case, but he'd been unable to get it to do much else, nor could he find a way to free his arms. He'd been in a fair few predicaments in his life, but this was by far the most frustrating.

From what he could tell, he was not alone. He'd heard snatches of conversation, barely audible at times, that confirmed his captors were close by. He couldn't make out much, but by the sound of it they were fretful about what to do with him. That would mean they'd either known he was an aetheling in advance or had worked it out after accosting him. Chances were they feared retribution of some sort. Edmund would use that fear to his advantage, assuming they ever came in to introduce themselves.

At that very moment, he heard a door creaking open not a dozen paces in front of him. Two sets of footsteps approached, the sound dull and heavy upon what could only be solid stone flooring. They were arguing, and their accents gave them away as Lundenburgers, or at least persons who'd spent a lot of time there. Edmund fought the urge to flinch as they came closer. It wouldn't take much to end his life in this situation. He hoped that was not what they'd come here to do.

Rough hands seized at his face. The cord around his neck came loose, and a second later the bag was snatched from his head, revealing his surroundings in all their dismal glory. He was in a small room, some kind of cellar, dark and windowless, and there was a single door just ahead of him, slightly ajar. He was sat on a narrow pine wood chair, as he'd suspected, and as he angled his head around, he could see his wrists were indeed bound by a rope attached to the chair's frame.

The two men before him were not thegns, nor anyone of note or property. They were filthy; their faces smeared with grime, their otherwise practical attire of hardened leather and starched linen looking similarly unkempt. Edmund, though, had long learned that appearances could be very deceiving, and he didn't doubt that was the case here, as whoever these men were, they'd been able to sneak up on him and take him off of Lundenburg's streets without being detected. That spoke to a level of competence that shouldn't be disregarded. These two were dangerous, of that he was sure.

"Look at the state of him!" exclaimed one, his face a mass of freckles and his hair one long, ginger tumult. "I told you we should have seen to him earlier. The ealdorman won't be happy if we let him croak down here."

His associate, a larger man with darker hair and more conventional features, did not reply. He instead reached out with his right hand to grip Edmund across the crown of his head, his left bringing up a waterskin of some sort to splash its contents across his face. Edmund gasped as the cool water hit him, doing his best to catch and swallow the droplets before they soaked into his beard. He'd not realised how thirsty he was. Just how long had he been here?

"He's got plenty of life in him," said the one who'd just hit him with the water. "Look at the way he drinks. I've never seen a dead man do that."

The ginger chap frowned, his look unfriendly. "Just how long are we going to have to keep him here anyway? If the ealdorman…"

"Stop saying that, you bloody idiot," snapped the other, his teeth flashing. "This isn't just any other job for us. This bastard is bloody dangerous, and clever with it too."

Edmund took a deep breath and spoke. "Am I right in assuming this ealdorman you speak of is called Uhtred?" he asked, finding the act of speaking a little painful, given the dryness of his throat. Uhtred must have sent these men, he surmised. He must still be unhappy after the beating Edmund had given him a while back. This was a strange way to take revenge, if that's what he was looking to do.

"Uhtred?" asked the ginger, looking genuinely confused. That struck Edmund as odd, although it narrowed down the range of suspects quite nicely. If Uhtred wasn't behind this, then there was only one other who could be, assuming these two were even using the title of "ealdorman" correctly and it wasn't just a code name for somebody else. Eadric. Eadric must have sent these men. Edmund should have expected it. Coming to Lundenburg alone had been foolish.

"We're not supposed to talk to you," said the other, less freckly fellow, almost apologetically.

"Why not?" Edmund asked.

"Just orders," he shrugged. "We follow orders. We get told to grab a man, we do it. Kill a man, whatever."

"I was glad to catch up with you, though," sneered Ginger as he glowered down at Edmund. "I saw you back when we were under siege from Svienn Forkbeard. You started giving some high and mighty speech, trying to get us to stay loyal and resist to the end. You remember?"

Edmund did indeed remember. It was on the same night that Svienn had made his first attempt to storm the Ald Gate. He'd failed, but not by much, and Edmund had almost lost his life in the melee, so unprepared were they for the attack. Cenric had saved him, and when victory had come, he and Edmund had tried to return to their hideaway elsewhere in the city to plan their next move. They'd then chanced upon a most unexpected gathering. Hundreds of people had been present, all transfixed by some fat loudmouth preaching treason and surrender. Edmund had tried to intervene. His temper had gotten the better of him. The mob had not appreciated it. He and Cenric had barely made it out alive.

"I remember a bunch of ingrates turning on their own," muttered Edmund bitterly. "Were you one of them? Did you want to kill me then, is that it?"

Edmund blinked as he felt the sting from the slap. "We were starvin', you bloody bastard!" spat Ginger, his hand still held aloft like he intended to strike him again. "I'd been living on the streets for months, and then you appear acting like you know what we're going through and what's good for us!"

"And what would you have had me do?" asked Edmund. "Ignore you? Just let people open up the city to Svienn? How did that work out for you, living under Svienn?"

"We got fed! It was an end to war! And then you went off and made a new war to bring to us!"

"Are you serious?" Edmund asked, agape at what he was hearing. "You preferred peace and a few crumbs living under the man who'd been preying on us for years? You'd choose that over being ruled by your own kind?"

"MY own kind?" squeaked Ginger, still angry. "What did MY own kind ever do for me? What did YOU ever do?"

"Give me time," replied Edmund. "I can understand your frustration. These past years…I know they've not been gentle, on any of us. But I will be king. Things will be different then. I swear it."

Everything suddenly went dark, the abrupt change catching Edmund off guard. The other man had intervened, putting the bag back over his head and fastening it tight around his neck. "You won't be doing much," he heard him say. "They'll be no kingly future for you, so says the ealdorman."

"What's Eadric paying you?" bellowed Edmund, his voice annoyingly loud within the confines of the bag. "If it's money you want, then name your price. There's a way out of this, and it doesn't have to end with your deaths."

Laughter erupted around him, the sound of it making his toes and fingers curl with indignation. The two men left, guffawing all the way, the ginger one repeating Edmund's own words back at him in mocking imitation. The door slammed shut, leaving Edmund alone in silence and darkness. He hung his head, resigning himself to another spell with nobody to talk to. His stomach grumbled. That was a worry. He couldn't afford to weaken from hunger. It would only reduce his chances of escape.

Hours passed, or what Edmund assumed to be hours, his head hanging even lower towards his chest, his eyes closing in the hope of sleep. He dreamed of Cenric, or at least thought on him awhile as he tried to will himself unconscious, but it didn't work, and thinking of lost friends only made him sad. It'd be a fine thing to have Cenric with him now, he thought. He'd get them out of this. Those two idiots beyond wouldn't stand a chance. Neither would Eadric, for that matter, if he really was behind all this. Cenric would kill them all.

Voices, muffled and anxious, sounded from somewhere. Footsteps were then heard, and they grew yet louder, the noise suddenly ceasing just outside the door. A few seconds passed, Edmund straining his ears for the slightest sound. The door opened. His captors had returned, yet there was something else. A third person, most likely. They'd brought a friend.

The bag was again yanked off his head. Ginger and the other fellow were stood there, and true enough there was a third man between them, his expression cold and impassive. He was well dressed, his dark blue kirtle and matching breecs appearing to be of the finest quality, as were his boots and gold embroidered cloak. He had a sword too, sheathed in a black leather scabbard, the tip just about visible from beneath the outer edge of his cloak.

There was something special about this one, and not purely because of his attire. It was in the face, that narrow, pale face with the gentle eyes and admittedly fine auburn beard. Edmund felt he knew this man. He just couldn't for the moment think as to where from.

"Just where does the ealdorman expect us to take him?" asked Ginger, his question directed towards the stranger.

"You're not being paid to worry about such matters," came the response. "Just untie his hands and get him up."

"I still don't understand why Eadric didn't come himself, though," said Ginger as he moved behind Edmund's chair and snipped the ropes holding him in place. Edmund immediately brought his arms around in front of him, his hands frantically rubbing at his wrists. They'd gotten so sore being tied back like that. This was a lot better.

"I gave you his letter," said the stranger impatiently. "It bears Eadric's mark. Is that not enough?"

"None of us can read right," said the non-ginger fellow. "But I don't see how a fancy pants thegn like you would even know where to find us if Eadric hadn't sent you."

"What a clever chap you are," said the stranger, his condescending manner somehow failing to provoke. He reached out towards Edmund, offering his hand. Edmund took it and was hauled upright, the pins and needles in his feet making him wince. They hobbled out and through the door, Edmund and this "fancy pants thegn", and into the next room. They were definitely in a cellar, of that Edmund was now sure, as there was a narrow wooden staircase over in the far corner, a sliver of what looked like daylight pouring down from above.

There were three more men in here, ones Edmund didn't recognise, and they all looked as bad as the other two, as if they were all participants in some kind of contest where the point was to look as disreputable as possible. They had weapons, each man bearing either a short axe or seax of some description, and there were several worn-looking spears leaning against the wall by the door they'd just come through. The stranger made for the stairs, his manner confident, and Edmund followed, thinking that even if he were not yet free of danger, it would at least be good to get himself out into the fresh air. Then the trouble started.

It began with a thundering sound, the heavy treads cascading down the stairs filling Edmund with dread. A larger man with a vivid scar cutting across his mouth and cheeks came hammering down the steps towards them, dressed in the same rough and ready fashion as the others. He looked unfriendly like the rest, but there was a greater air of menace to him, making Edmund suspect he was the one who held authority here. He demanded they stop, a single piece of parchment held in his oversized hands.

"You said this is the ealdorman's signature?" He'd growled the question, thrusting the parchment into the stranger's chest.

He took it, looking irked over how crumpled it was. "That's exactly what it is," he said, like all was tedium. "You can read, I hope? That's all written in Eadric's own hand. Tell me it's not so."

"It looks to be so," nodded the brute, "but tell me now why Eadric wants him moved outside the city? I'd have thought once he finished with that woman and her girls, he'd want to be right back here to do the job himself."

"What woman and what girls?" demanded Edmund. They were almost certainly referring to Sigeferth's wife and their four daughters. That meant Eadric either had them already or would very soon. That wasn't good. Edmund had better do something.

"Shut up!" spat the brute, his eyes flashing with anger as he snapped his head towards Edmund and then back to the stranger. "As I was saying…explain to me why Eadric wants him moved…and why he'd send somebody I don't even know with a letter bearing his mark. It's a strange choice to me."

"You only just thought to ask me this?" inquired the stranger. "Why let me in if you think me an imposter?"

"I didn't let you in. That ginger idiot and his half-wit mate did. I'm in charge here, and I say," he jabbed a finger at the stranger's chest, "that you, with your very fine accent and very fine letter, are up to no good."

"What woman and what girls?" repeated Edmund, his hands balling into fists.

"Shut it! Or I'll be explaining to the ealdorman how we killed you early for being an arse!"

Edmund saw red. It was fear as well as anger, since he was now beset with images of Eadric and Ealdgyth, the former laughing to himself as he forced her to give up the location of the rest of her family. He could recall his father saying Ealdgyth was to become a nun at Malmesberie, but Edmund wouldn't put it past Eadric to simply kill her and then lie to his father about what had happened. That's why he had to act. That's why he'd just planted his boot in the nether regions of the bastard in front of him.

He dropped like a stone, a surprised, high-pitched cry squealing from his throat. Edmund immediately felt the hands of his two gaolers trying to restrain him, their shouts raw and angry in his ears. He spun around, using his weight and momentum to deliver a right hook to Ginger's face. The fool staggered backwards and, to Edmund's amusement, somehow managed to knock himself out on the edge of the still-open door behind them. His associate pulled out a blade he'd had concealed somewhere and made a move, his teeth bared as he did his best to ram the point between Edmund's ribs.

Edmund leapt away, landing on the man he'd kicked earlier. He made a peculiar noise, caught between a growl and a sob, so Edmund kicked him again, the blow to the head silencing him altogether. Edmund felt fear upon seeing the stranger suddenly draw his sword, and from the roared expletives from the three men behind, they too were far from pleased. He was surrounded, facing five separate opponents, all armed, whilst he had nothing but his fists. At least he'd humbled two of them. It was just a shame his chances of besting all of them were so distressingly slim.

It was with that thought the unexpected happened. The stranger suddenly attacked the gaoler who'd just tried to stab Edmund, his sword cleaving his throat out with one single slashing sweep. The poor bastard collapsed, choking on his own blood, and the stranger called to Edmund by name before tossing his weapon in his direction. Edmund reacted fast, leaping to pluck the blade from the air. He managed it and spun around to face the three ruffians to his rear, sword in hand.

It was all over in seconds. These men may have been good in tavern brawls or smashing people over the head from behind, but they were wheat to the scythe now he had a sword. He bested the first man with a single flick of his blade, its keen edge slicing his hand clean off, the axe it had once gripped clattering to the floor.

He fell down, sobbing with shock and pain, his remaining hand clutching at his bloodied stump. His friends rushed to avenge him, their faces twisted with aggression. Edmund avoided one wild axe swing and ducked in low, his counterattack seeing his assailant's guts come pouring out from his ruptured belly. The last man screamed something and made a rush for the stairs, hoping to escape this mad killer who'd only just earlier been entirely at their mercy. Edmund was on him in an instant, slashing both his hamstrings and heaving him backwards off the steps and onto his back.

"What is Eadric planning?!" Edmund screamed, his boot on the man's throat. "Tell me!" he roared, holding the tip of his sword a mere inch from his left eye. "Tell me what he has planned for Ealdgyth! Does he mean to kill her and her daughters?!"

"I don't know anything!" came the strangled, desperate reply. "I'm just the muscle! I don't know anything, didn't do anything! I just hit people!"

"Was it you who smashed me over the head?" Edmund asked, his left hand probing delicately at the back of his skull. It still felt wet, yet he had his wits about him. Hopefully, that meant the damage was at least superficial, even if it were enough to initially knock him out.

"I'm sorry! God as my witness, I just do what I'm told!"

"Who tells you?!" snarled Edmund, the point of his blade creeping yet closer to the soft tissue of his eyeball.

The man made a gesture toward the unconscious form of the brute Edmund had kicked in the nuts at the start of the fight. "Check him," said Edmund to the stranger, who had turned slightly pale at the surrounding carnage.

"As you wish," he said curtly, and knelt down on the brute's right, his fingers resting gently at the side of his neck. "He's alive," he muttered. "And yet…wait…"

The stranger leant down further, inspecting the head wound from where Edmund had kicked him. "That doesn't look good," he said, reaching to lift the brute's head up an inch or two so Edmund could see. His head was bleeding, and not just a modest amount, either. Edmund had really kicked him hard, even more so than he'd first thought. He couldn't say he was overly sorry for that. Yet it did mean this man wouldn't be waking up anytime soon, and even if he did, he might not be of much use to them.

"Let's go," Edmund told the stranger, ignoring the terrified man at his feet and vaulting up the stairs to whatever lay above. He'd left three survivors; the one he'd just questioned, the one still sobbing over the loss of his hand, and the ginger fella who'd done the decent thing and sparked himself out. Some might say that was a mistake and that these men would come looking for him, but Edmund didn't care. They were hired thugs, employed by Eadric for reasons they likely didn't understand themselves. He didn't hate them, not like he hated the Danes, and he wouldn't kill them if he didn't have to. He'd be a better man than that.

He made it to the top of the stairs and looked around. He was in a house, a residence of some kind, and daylight was pouring in from the unshuttered windows, a slightly ajar door also revealing the alley beyond. Heavy thatch spread out above him, held in place by crisscrossing rafters of solid oak. Several passages branched off from here, the closest leading to a kitchen and what looked like some sort of pantry, yet he didn't have time for any of this, and his escape wouldn't be expedited by making himself something to eat. He took a step towards the door, his sword held at the ready. It caught the light, the blood-splattered iron reminding him of something. His own sword. The one he always used. The one Æthelstan and then Alaric had fought with. Where was it?!

The stranger cleared his throat as he emerged from the staircase. Edmund turned, seeing he was holding something out towards him that he'd balanced atop his palms. A scabbard. His scabbard. And within it, his sword.

Edmund hurriedly took it, making sure to pass the stranger's blade back to him. "How did you find this?" he asked, attaching the scabbard to his belt. He then drew the sword out from within it. The blade was reassuringly heavy in his grip. It felt right. He was whole again.

"It was down there," said the stranger, gesturing lazily towards the stairs. "They must have taken it off you and decided to keep it for themselves. I once knew a man who fought with such a weapon. I thought it was one of a kind."

"What was his name?" asked Edmund, oddly curious.

"Alaric."

"What? You knew Alaric?"

"I did, but I…oh…"

The stranger's voice trailed off, his eyes widening in alarm at something just past Edmund's shoulder. Edmund turned in time to see several hooded men come barging through the front door, blades and spears at the ready. Four of them, now five, with even more outside by the looks of it. Edmund wasn't sure as to their capabilities, but he wasn't going to let himself get killed here. If these newcomers wanted a fight, then…

"Edmund?"

He recognised the voice from the lead figure. He'd pulled his hood back, revealing dark hair, darker eyes, and the tell-tale nose that only one man in the whole world possessed.

"Wulfnoth! What are you doing here?"

"I was hoping to savagely murder the men who I'd been told had abducted you," said Wulfnoth, a little too casually. "I should have known you'd break free on your own…Ælfweard? Is that you back there?"

"Is it indeed I," said the stranger, or Ælfweard or whoever he was. "May I suggest we make haste to somewhere hopefully more hospitable? I'd love to catch up, but these are not the most civilised of environs."

"Come on," said Wulfnoth, turning to bundle his men back out the front door. Edmund followed them, Ælfweard bringing up the rear, and they emerged into a narrow alley trailing haphazardly between twin rows of rather sorry-looking thatched houses. Edmund blinked and blinked again, hoping the sting from the daylight might ease off, only to see that Wulfnoth and his men were already hurrying away and impatient for him and Ælfweard to follow.

They chased after them, the buildings on either side casting long, threatening shadows. Wulfnoth and his lads started to slow, appearing quite casual whilst they wandered out of the alley and into a broad, bustling street. Edmund recognised it. The buildings, the dilapidation, the rotten thatch, wattle and daub walls and mud slicks upon the road…all of it. This was Westceape. They were close to New Gate here. They could escape Lundenburg and be on their way to Malmesberie in no time. Eadric might yet be thwarted in his plans for Ealdgyth.

Wulfnoth suddenly turned when Edmund tried to follow them out into the open. He ushered him backwards, and Edmund obeyed, knowing the man's instincts were rarely wrong and that danger may be close. Wulfnoth whispered something to one of his men, who promptly divested himself of his cloak and handed it to Edmund. This made sense. Edmund put it on, pulling the hood up and over his head, the pain from his wound making him wince. The others could show their faces around here easily enough. Nobody was out looking for them, and Edmund had been downright foolish in thinking he could just wander around the city alone, especially after confronting his father. Hiding his face until they were beyond the walls was a wise choice.

Anxiety then seized him. He'd left Bede at a public stable just east over the Walbrook from Lodeburec, which meant they'd have to head further into the city to retrieve him. Wulfnoth objected, telling Edmund it wasn't worth the risk and that Bede was just any old horse. Edmund would have none of it. Bede would be escaping with them. He'd leave no man behind. Even the one with four legs who couldn't talk.

They retrieved Bede easily enough. The thugs who'd captured Edmund had taken any money he'd been carrying, so Ælfweard gave up a few coins to keep the peace and ensure the stable master didn't cause a stink. Bede rumbled to himself whilst Edmund led him through the streets back into Westceape, the sound of his clattering hooves strangely reassuring. Edmund grinned at him from beneath his hood. Bede stared back, his dark, almost black eyes somehow appearing both empty and yet full of meaning.

Everything went quite smoothly after that. They made it through the western walls, the sentries on duty appearing half-asleep, and got out onto Watling Street, the autumn wind blissfully refreshing as it blew in from the south west. Wulfnoth and his people had apparently tethered their horses close to the forest campsite Edmund had chosen back when he'd come here with his army, and so they headed there in all haste. They paused a moment upon arriving, taking in the emerald grove and the familiar, swaying columns of ash and oak surrounding it. Edmund pulled his hood back and down, allowing the breeze to tousle at his hair. The sound of the wind in the trees was heavenly, stripping him of all previous anxiety and granting him clarity of purpose. He began issuing orders, telling Ælfweard, Wulfnoth, and his men to mount up and follow him. It was a long way to Malmesberie, and there was no time to waste.

They only stopped when night came on, the red and pink rays of the setting sun fading to deep blue and then black. Edmund didn't want to wait, thinking a night ride would hasten matters, yet Wulfnoth's people were fatigued to the point rest had become a necessity. They'd galloped up from the South after Wulfnoth had learned how Edmund had gone to face his father alone. Edmund appreciated their haste and dedication to duty. He'd endeavour to not repeat the mistakes of the past few days. It was all well and good to rush into danger, wanting to put things right, but he couldn't keep doing that on his own. He wasn't invincible, despite apparently having sides of iron. He also didn't want anyone being put at risk because of his reckless behaviour. It wasn't right.

A very spartan camp was set up a few hundred yards off-road, the forest heaving and groaning to itself as the same wind continued to assail it from the south. The stars shone from above, the swaying of branches and a few wisps of cloud failing to obstruct the otherwise awe-inspiring view. Most of Wulfnoth's fourteen men were asleep, yet he remained awake, sitting with Edmund and the mysterious Ælfweard upon the fern and bracken floor. An owl hooted from what sounded like a short distance off, and all was peaceful, the feeling a welcome one after the drama of their escape.

"How did you know Edmund was in trouble?" Wulfnoth asked, his voice soft and his eyes upon Ælfweard.

"More to the point," interrupted Edmund, "who are you? You look familiar. I just can't place it."

"I'm quite forgettable," Ælfweard said with a smile. "But you may remember me from when you came to the village of Offetuna just after you'd escaped Svienn Forkbeard's assault on Lundenburg."

"Of course!" said Edmund, his mind finally clicking. "You were a reeve, in Canterburie? You fought alongside Ulfcytel in the defence of the city?"

"I'm not much for fighting, but yes, I was there, and I was captured along with Alaric and the archbishop. 'Course the Danes murdered the archbishop…and later did the same to Alaric, I was sorry to hear."

"Where did you go after that?" asked Edmund. "I thought you'd stay with us."

Ælfweard leaned back on his elbows, looking like he was trying to get comfortable whilst keeping his very fine clothes free of blemishes. "Like I said, I'm not one for fighting. I was wounded…a wound of the heart, so it is…I'd been reeve in Canterburie for so long, known its people, known every inch of it…and then Thorkell took it all. We looked to Alaric in those dark days when we were prisoners. He kept us going. A friend of mine died during our escape also…do you remember Leofwine, Wulfnoth?"

"The injured warrior you brought with you over the walls? Yes, I remember him well."

"Alaric carried him on his back," nodded Ælfweard with another sad smile. "He'd been cut up in the fighting, badly. Alaric wouldn't give up on any of us, though. Neither would the archbishop. They were a right pair, those two. Strong. Overbearing, sometimes. But good. Always good."

Edmund sat patiently, appreciative that Ælfweard felt comfortable enough around him to open up like this. "So you didn't want to take part in our campaign after that?" asked Edmund. "I'm not judging you," he added quickly, not wanting Ælfweard to think he was accusing him of anything. "Not everyone is a warrior…but we did need good men. Still do."

"I returned home," breathed Ælfweard, like it was a fearful thing to admit. "There was not much left…just ruined streets and a few ragged groups of survivors. I tried to help patch things back together. I was better at that. I'm no good at killing."

"And how is Canterburie now?" asked Wulfnoth.

"Surviving. Just about. We'll rebuild, but it will take time. The king…your father, Edmund…when I'd heard he was back on the throne and wanting to make peace with all those who might have failed him…well, I had to attend him. I wanted to see if it was all true."

"So you serve him still?" Edmund asked.

"He's the king, what can I say? I spoke to him at his recent banquet, but it was a hard thing for me to do. He seemed angry, but I was too, remembering how he didn't send us aid when we needed it most…and then later he looked so troubled, so caught up in things…I know about Sigeferth and Morcar, Edmund. I'm sorry."

"That does not explain how you knew Edmund had been abducted."

Edmund shot Wulfnoth a look, thinking his tone a little improper. This was not an interrogation, and he had no desire to see it turn into one.

"I could ask you the same question," said Ælfweard to Wulfnoth. "After all, you came storming in, right through the door, just as we were leaving. How did you know where to go?"

"Eadric's ship leaks," said Wulfnoth cryptically. "Lundenburg is a sieve… information flows in and flows out. It's up to people like me to catch it…and not everyone Eadric employs is as loyal to him as he thinks."

"So you have spies in Lundenburg?" asked Edmund. "Double agents? People working for Eadric and yourself?"

Wulfnoth nodded.

"Isn't that terribly dangerous?" asked Edmund. "How do you trust them?"

"I don't. Double agents are delicate things to handle…you have to apply a mixed approach…money, threats, violence, blackmail…it all served a purpose. I found you." He looked to Ælfweard. "That still leaves your role in this a mystery," he said. "Would you care to enlighten us?"

"I had to do something," Ælfweard said defensively. "I saw you, Edmund, when you confronted your father. It was harrowing, and it was not my place to intervene, but when you hurried off, and Æthelred collapsed…"

"What? My father is ill?"

"Confined to his bed. The queen kept me away, hissing something about me being "just another vulture", whatever that could mean. So I went after you, thinking you should know. Then I saw you being followed."

"So you followed the followers," nodded Wulfnoth, a hint of admiration in his tone.

"That's right. They were being quite subtle about it, enough so that you didn't seem to notice. Then they hit you from behind," he winced, like he was feeling it himself. "I admit I wondered if you'd survived it. Then they took you away to the house I found you in."

"But you turned up claiming to have a letter from Eadric?" Edmund asked, confused as to Ælfweard's otherwise successful ruse.

"Yes, I heard them mention "the ealdorman" at one point. Seemed to me fairly obvious what was going on. Sigeferth and Morcar were two of your most important allies, and you left them in Lundenburg to demonstrate your support for your father's reign…is that correct?"

"Kind of," said Edmund. "I wanted him to reconcile with them, as he promised. I thought things were looking up. I was wrong."

"I wouldn't beat yourself up about it," said Ælfweard gently. "But as to Eadric and Sigeferth and all that…I could tell something awful had happened when I saw Eadric accosting Ealdgyth outside the banquet…"

"What did he do?" Edmund didn't like the sound of this. If Eadric had actually hurt Ealdgyth, he'd cut off his hands, not that he'd intended to ever go easy on him anyway. Much was owed to the Ealdorman of Mierċe, and none of it pleasant.

"Oh, he tried to keep it quiet," replied Ælfweard. "He waited for her to leave the main hall, probably to look for her husband, and had her seized and bundled off somewhere. She was objecting, good and loud, so I heard that. Then I saw Sigeferth and his brother being carried away, dead as anything. It was obvious Eadric was involved in it all."

"So, what's the business about this letter?" Wulfnoth asked. "The one Edmund just mentioned? This helped you gain access to where they were keeping him?"

"That it did. I forged Eadric's signature. I've seen him sign a couple of charters before, so I know what it looks like. I have a strange mind. I remember things, sometimes so exactly it's like a picture in my head."

Wulfnoth stirred in his sitting position, uneasy at what he was hearing. "So you forged Eadric's signature on a letter…saying what?"

"That the prisoner, as in Edmund, was to be moved, and I was the one to do it. It got me past the two idiots who let me in. I think I overawed them, being all important and whatever. It's not like people who look, talk, and act like me just wander in off the street, is it? Well, except when I actually did."

Edmund smiled, grateful and also amused at the sheer audacity of Ælfweard's rescue plan. "Why didn't you just return to my father's halls?" he asked. "His men might have assisted you if they thought me in trouble."

"It didn't feel right," replied Ælfweard without hesitation. "Eadric puts down roots everywhere, black and poisoned. I didn't know who to trust, especially with the king out of the equation. For all I knew, those I might ask for help could be agents of Eadric and inclined to stick a blade between my ribs just for bringing it up. Do I sound paranoid?"

"You're not paranoid," said Wulfnoth, quietly yet confidently. "That's exactly how Eadric operates. You did well acting on your own initiative."

"Were you scared when that big bastard came thundering down the stairs with your letter?" asked Edmund, thinking he knew the answer already.

"Oh yes," chuckled Ælfweard. "He was the clever one, and I think he saw through it all. Then you kicked him in his…masculinity…and of course, you know what happened next."

"I don't," said Wulfnoth. "What happened?"

"Edmund killed everyone."

"Not everyone," Edmund said. "But some people are going to be waking up with sore heads…and maybe missing hands too."

"You think that's funny?" Wulfnoth asked.

"I do not," said Edmund. "Those men were just pawns. That's why I left some alive when opportunity presented."

"But that's what I mean," Wulfnoth persisted. "You left witnesses. They'll be able to get word to Eadric that you escaped."

"Had I simply massacred everyone, Eadric would have worked out what had happened soon enough. Either way, the situation would be the same."

"It's not the same," said Wulfnoth, shaking his head. "We left enemies at our rear, ones that could be moving to alert Eadric as we speak. You should have…"

"Should have?" Edmund asked, frowning in irritation. "I appreciate all that you do for me, Wulfnoth, but do not presume to tell me what I "should have" done. I extended some mercy to men who, for whatever unfortunate reason, had made themselves my enemies. I will not kill unless I have to. Not our own. Not Englishmen."

"What confuses me," piped up Ælfweard, "is why would Eadric use street thugs to apprehend you? They only had any success at all because you were caught by surprise."

"Because if he'd decided to kill Edmund, he wouldn't have wanted any witnesses," said Wulfnoth.

"What do you mean?" asked Ælfweard.

Wulfnoth took a deep breath before answering, rattling off the individual points of Eadric's plan, as he saw it. "Hire people unknown to anyone that matters…get them to sequester Edmund somewhere nobody will look…Eadric arrives, questions Edmund, tortures Edmund…then has the street thugs kill Edmund…and then Eadric kills all of them to make it look like he was avenging the death of an aetheling. That way, Eadric wins, with all loose ends tied up, and also looks the hero."

Everyone paused, their silence broken only by the wind in the trees and the shuffling of their horses grazing and resting a few paces behind. Wulfnoth had summed it up well, yet it was disturbing just how good he was at predicting the goals and ambitions of their enemies. It was like he was as dark as Eadric, or he'd been fighting Eadric in this battle of wits and intrigue for so long they'd somehow become alike. Edmund didn't feel comfortable with any of that, and the more he thought about it, the more he was certain the warm, chivalrous Wulfnoth of his youth had been absent for too long.

"I suppose now you're going to tell us why we're not heading back south to Hamptonscir?" Wulfnoth suddenly asked, interrupting Edmund's train of thought.

"As I said before…Eadric has taken Ealdgyth, on my father's orders, to the nunnery in Malmesberie. My father wants her to keep quiet and live out the rest of her life in prayer. I don't think that's fair."

"You've obviously considered how important she is now, with her husband dead?"

"I have, Wulfnoth. She's the power in the Five Boroughs, in wealth and property. My father sees that. He wishes to remove her from play. I'll not let him."

"You should consider the possibility that Eadric has simply killed her and her entire family," Wulfnoth said, his voice flat. "He'll no doubt have some puppet of his lined up to take their place, if he has."

"We'll find out when we get there," said Edmund. "Because if he has done so…I'll pursue him to the ends of the earth. He and my father both have done so much harm, and I tried to forgive, but no longer. Great changes are on the way, and I intend to speed them along."

"What changes?" whispered Ælfweard, a little anxiously.

"Changes in kings," said Edmund. "We've suffered enough under the corruption and incompetence of my father. Killing Sigeferth and Morcar was the final straw. Abducting Ealdgyth…there's no coming back from that. I intend to save her and her daughters. It'll be my gift to my departed friends."

"And then what?" asked Wulfnoth. "You mentioned a change in kings? Am I right in thinking "

"You are," nodded Edmund, his tone grave. "I will use Ealdgyth to rally the Five Boroughs to my banner. I have Hamptonscir through Æva, and Ulfcytel gives me Eastengle. With the Five Boroughs, I will have seized half of my father's kingdom from under him. I'll then face whatever happens. Because there is no way I'm letting him just get away with what he's done. England deserves better. As king, I'll ensure that she gets it."

XXXIX

Æthelred had long thought there could be few things worse than his nightmares. He'd endured them for years, that dark chapel and his dead brother and mother haunting him incessantly, and for a time he'd despaired, thinking he might never be rid of them. Losing children had been a worse experience. Fighting in battle, also, had always frightened him, and when he'd fallen from his horse at Bernecestre only to have Thorkell grab him by the throat, he'd been convinced his death was at hand. It was a miracle he'd gotten through that. Hereward had been that miracle.

And yet Hereward wasn't here now, and his current predicament was worse than his nightmares had ever been. At least they'd ended, or had been limited to his night-time hours, whereas this was unceasing, intolerable, terrifying. He wanted more than anything for it to stop. His prayers, as yet, had gone unanswered.

He was almost entirely immobile, on his back and in bed. They'd hurried him in here after he'd first fallen, the blood flow from his nose taking a full hour to stop. They'd poked and prodded him for days, an assortment of monks and healers filing into his bedchamber to try anything and everything to cure his mystery ailment. He'd been bled, had a poultice upon his head, been steamed in a bath, massaged, rubbed down with oils, and prayed over incessantly. Of all those things, only the prayers had made Æthelred feel anything approaching hope. If God would not help him, then he was surely lost. It's not like anyone else had even a smidgen of love for him. Edmund had made that clear.

His eyes filled with tears at the thought of it. His son had been so angry, as Æthelred had expected him to be, yet the news about Eadwig had taken him completely by surprise. He tried not to think on it, but certain images kept pushing into his consciousness. He could see Eadwig now, beaten and bloodied, that treacherous bastard, Thorkell, standing over him. Darkness closed in, obscuring Thorkell, leaving Eadwig alone, his battered, broken body immobile except for the blinking of his eyes. Æthelred pictured them as he remembered, deep and thoughtful, yet now filled with sadness. He needed his father. The boy needed his father, yet Æthelred could do nothing, as his own body had rebelled against him, confining him to the prison of flesh he presently endured.

It wasn't right. None of it was. Nothing like this was supposed to happen. Was this to be his destiny now, trapped whilst his children learned to hate him and one of his beloved sons, Eadwig, suffered as he did? What kind of monster would will such a fate for a man? Was there no mercy? Was there no justice?

Somebody was dabbing a cloth at his face and clearing his eyes of tears. Emma was here, again, sitting at his bedside with that impatient look to her, like somehow this was all his fault. He glared back at her, hoping she'd get the message that her company was neither requested nor welcome. For some reason, he retained a little motion in his right arm, so he raised it now, taking her wrist in his grip and pushing her away. She frowned, annoyed by his defiance.

"Will you not even let me touch you?" she asked, her voice hushed and resentful.

Æthelred went to reply, but all he managed was a low, wet growl. It summed up his attitude well enough, he supposed.

"Are you hungry?" she asked, brighter now. He shook his head. Feeding him was a complete nightmare for all concerned, and he didn't need the humiliation. Peace and quiet were what he desired. If only she'd get that through that decorative head of hers.

Emma rose from the stool she'd been sitting on and began to shift Æthelred's pillows so he might sit upright with some degree of comfort. He objected, or made some angry, guttural noises, but she succeeded in positioning him with his back against the wall, his blankets tucked up around his waist. He must have lost weight, he thought. There was no way a woman of such slender dimensions would have been able to do that otherwise. The realisation did not please him.

"I've noticed you can still use your hand," she said as she placed a thin, rectangular board made of slate into his lap. He stared at it, wondering what he was supposed to do and why she'd even bothered. She passed him a piece of chalk, inserting it gently into his right hand. He immediately set to work, inscribing his deepest, most heartfelt feelings onto the slate.

"GO AWAY"

"That's not nice," she said patiently, gently rubbing away his fine work with the cloth she'd used earlier. "Tell me what you need, Æthelred. Tell me how to help you."

He wrote again, more specific this time.

"HELP EADWIG"

"I wish we could," she sighed, "and yet Edmund has the power in this situation. I still cannot believe the things he said. What a cruel man he is!"

"SHUT UP"

"You can do better," she said, exasperated. "I'm going to just rub out anything you write that's rude. I don't like it." She wasn't joking. She'd already erased everything he'd written. He scowled at her, or as much of a scowl as he could manage.

"Are you hungry?"

"NO"

"Thirsty?"

"NO"

"Would you like to see Edward and Alfred? They are waiting outside."

"YES"

"I thought so," she said, smiling, and rose to approach the door. She opened it, and his two boys came in, both of them looking like the perfectly presentable young aethelings they were. Alfred bounded over to Æthelred's side, but Edward hesitated at the foot of his bed, his expression worried. Æthelred tried to give him a reassuring smile. Judging by Edward's reaction, it didn't help.

"What happened?" he asked. "Is this some trick? Why is his face so uneven?"

"It's just a little illness," said Emma, apparently at ease in her own lies. "It's quite normal for a man of his age, especially when they have such wicked sons who insist on breaking their hearts."

Æthelred went to scrabble something down in response to that, but thought better of it. He didn't want to expose his boys to foul language.

"Was it Edmund?" asked Alfred, his concerned eyes on Æthelred. The boy was holding on to his hand, the one he couldn't move. He looked sad. Æthelred reached out with his right and patted him on the head. Alfred smiled.

"It was indeed Edmund who upset him so," said Emma, now standing with her hand upon Edward's shoulder. "He spoke some cruel words, and had bad news that he delighted in sharing. It's no wonder your father had a tumble after."

"Edmund was cruel?" asked Edward, looking to his mother. "I've never seen him be cruel."

"War changes a man," answered Emma. "And Edmund thinks he's to be king. He doesn't understand that only good men get to be kings. He thinks he's owed it and that he can do what he likes to get it."

Æthelred went to object, succeeding only in making a noise akin to a horse impaled through the lungs. "That doesn't sound like Edmund," said Edward, looking even more worried in light of Æthelred's peculiar utterance. "Edmund always seemed to care more than most...he didn't put on airs either. He was honest."

"It was an act," said Emma dismissively. "He wants power. One day you'll understand. Now it's time to go."

Edward went to object, as did Alfred, but Emma wouldn't tolerate any dissension and ushered them back through the door and into the hands of one of their minders. She then turned to face Æthelred, her back to the now closed door. "Edward thinks too much," she said quietly. "I don't know why he can't ever just accept what I say. It's like he doesn't trust me."

Æthelred scribbled something on the slate and held it up to her.

"HE'S A CLEVER BOY"

"That's not nice," she said, approaching his bedside to again wipe his slate clean. He tried to resist, but she forced the issue, ignoring him entirely as he grumbled with dissatisfaction.

"But that reminds me of something we need to discuss," she said, again sitting on the stool at his side. "If Edward is such a clever boy...perhaps it's time...perhaps it's time you declared him your heir?"

Æthelred bared his teeth and made a hissing sound, his right arm rising and failing in what he hoped would signify annoyance. "Don't be like that," she pleaded. "Just try to look at the situation as I might see it...Edmund is lost. He hates us. He's so angry and so violent and dangerous...just look what he did to the Danes when we were away in Normandy!"

"HAHA"

It was a sincere enough statement. Edmund's conduct in his campaign against Svienn and Cnut had been exemplary. The fact that Emma seemed to be trying to use that as a point against him was really quite humorous. What a fool she was.

"It's not funny," she whined. "He won victories, yes, but can't you see what a threat that makes him? Men follow great warriors! Yet do great warriors make great kings? Ask yourself that, husband."

"ALFRED"

"You want Alfred to be king? But Edward is older."

"KING ALFRED OF WESTSEAXE"

"I don't understand," she said, frustrated. "What does he have to do with any of this?"

Æthelred groaned to himself and wrote something else.

"KING ALFRED. GREAT WARRIOR. GREAT KING."

"Yes, but he was an exception!" she persisted, rubbing his slate clean yet again. "And wasn't Alfred a scholarly king? A Godly king? Edmund can barely read, and he has no love for Christ!"

"LIAR"

"Stop it!" she yelled, her shrill outrage lashing the walls. "What are you even trying to tell me? That you want Edmund to still be the heir, even at this late hour? What about our children? What about me?!"

"AND SO THE MASK SLIPS"

"What does that mean? An English expression? Something unkind, yes?"

Æthelred didn't bother to write anything else. He just stared at her, his face still somewhat lopsided, any effort on his part to straighten it out coming to nought, as usual. She'd get nothing from him. There was no way he was going to turn on Edmund. To some, that would make no sense, given their recent altercation, not to mention the murder of Sigeferth and Morcar. Æthelred wasn't even sure if he understood it himself. He just knew there was a limit to what he'd do and what he'd allow himself to be manipulated into. He'd given his word to Edmund, promising him he'd not seek vengeance on those who had wronged him and that he, Edmund, would be king after him. Æthelred had failed on the first part. He'd not fail on the second.

"Is there nothing I can say to convince you?" asked Emma.

"NO. EDMUND WILL BE KING."

She stood up, looking down at him, an annoyingly imperious look on her face. "In that case…I must write to my brother in Rouen, telling him you are unfit to rule…and that your designated heir may be a threat to Normandy's interests in England."

Æthelred lashed out with his right arm, his hand extended to claw at Emma with his fingernails. She stepped back out of reach, and Æthelred fell, sliding out of his bed onto the cold stone floor below. That didn't seem right. He must have put an awful lot of force into that swipe to carry him off like this. He hadn't thought he'd had it in him.

Emma, sadly, was unmoved. She walked away, leaving him on his side despite his rumbling moans for assistance. "You can stay like that," she said coolly when she reached the door. "You may have been right about me, to an extent. I do seek power, but not as an end in itself. Edward must rule, and England's future lies with Normandy. Our son will understand that far better than a mad dog like Edmund. You'll see that in time. Until then…sleep well, husband."

She left, closing the door behind her, leaving Æthelred alone and without aid. There was a draught coming from somewhere, which for the moment was going right up his nightshirt; a piece of bad luck he wasn't exactly surprised by. He gave up trying to move, knowing there was little point in flailing his arm around when no other part of his body was inclined to respond. Darkness came, inescapable and impenetrable, and all was quiet, the silence so thick he wondered if there would ever be an end to it.

That came soon enough. His door opened, slowly at first, the creaking and scraping of aged wood upon stone drawing Æthelred out of his morose slumber. Light flooded in, erratic and unsteady, like somebody had a lit torch. Then he heard a gasp, followed by a concerned word as somebody pawed at his shoulder to ease him onto his back.

"What happened, father?!"

Æthelred blinked, the intensity of the light obscuring his vision. Three figures were present, one large and bearing the torch, the other two of a smaller stature and kneeling at his side. His eyes soon adjusted, revealing his two sons, Edward and Alfred. He didn't recognise the torchbearer, as his helmet hid much of his face. Somebody must have assigned Edward a guard. In these troubled times, that was certainly a good idea.

In any case, this mystery warrior had Æthelred back in bed in no time. His sons sat on the mattress with him, one on either side, both very much concerned. "How did you fall out of bed?" Edward asked. He got no answer, but Æthelred managed to make a few imprecise gestures towards the chalk and slate scattered across the floor. The guard retrieved them, placing them in Æthelred's lap before stepping back, his head bowed slightly in respect.

"THANK YOU"

They read it, Alfred's lips moving slightly as he comprehended the letters. "Is mother angry?" Edward asked, sounding uncertain. "She said you'd both argued…and then I couldn't sleep. Everything feels just…wrong. What happened to you, father? Why can't you move?"

Æthelred felt his heart stir as he beheld his son. He was troubled and genuinely concerned for him; a real comfort to a man who'd only recently been left to spend the night on the floor by his harpy of a wife. He had to find a way to answer his question. He had to find a way to help him understand what had happened. That was a tall order, considering Æthelred himself didn't know what was wrong with him. Even so, he would try.

"ARGUMENT WITH EDMUND. EADWIG HURT. MY HEART CAN'T TAKE IT."

"Just tell us what you need," said Edward. Alfred nodded in agreement.

"BRING INK AND PARCHMENT? LETTER MUST BE SENT. FOR EDMUND."

Edward's eyes narrowed as he read the words. "Of course," he said. "What would you say to Edmund?"

"FORGIVE ME. HELP ME. BE A LIGHT FOR ME."

"What is the meaning of this?!"

Everyone looked up to see Emma standing in the doorway. Nobody had heard her approach, her bare feet and light nightdress having reduced the sound of her steps. She glared at all of them, her green eyes catching the light like chipped and jagged emeralds.

"Get to bed, both of you," she said. "And you," she pointed at the guard. "Do not allow them to wander again, especially to see their father."

Æthelred looked at the man, hoping to see some sign that he might be inclined to disobey. He instead nodded towards Emma, mumbling something in affirmation, and helped her gather the boys up, escorting them away from the bed and out through the door. Æthelred wrote something on his slate and flapped it about, hoping they'd see.

"STOP"

Emma snatched the slate from his hand and waited. The guard closed the door upon leaving, ignoring both Edward and Alfred and their many protestations. It was dark again, too dark, which made Æthelred more than uneasy considering Emma was still standing over him, her breath just about audible as she inhaled and exhaled in obvious irritation.

"I should not have left you on the floor," she finally said, the voice coming out of the blackness as if disembodied. "And yet, husband, you do test me. I was never just the pretty face you thought I was...but I am also not the cold monster you believe me to be now. I am not without mercy...I am not without love for you."

Æthelred grunted disagreeably. It was the best he could manage.

"You will only be given the means to write when I am present," she announced, her tone hardening like brittle ice. "I do not want you to upset the boys, and they will not be permitted to visit. This situation...this illness that has come upon you so suddenly...think of it as a gift from God. It will give you time to rest. To think. To see the situation clearly. Edmund will be a disaster for England. God has given you the opportunity to contemplate that. I suggest you seize it."

She left, her footsteps soft and hushed as she crossed the room to make her exit. Æthelred lingered on, immobile amidst his blankets. He was still awake when the first trace of birdsong sounded in the dark, heralding the approaching dawn. He had not slept. He couldn't. There was only one single option left to him now, and it didn't involve sleep.

He couldn't clasp his hands together for prayer, so he simply placed his right palm upon his chest, hoping the gesture would serve as the next best thing. "I am a sinner, Lord," he thought, "and many men are dead because of me. I have reigned for years, trying and failing, sinning and falling, a disappointment to many and a burden to all."

He breathed in, slow and deep, trying to marshal his thoughts so that he might confess further. "I had men killed...I usurped and stole, always to cement my own power...I lied, I tried to bribe and pay off the heathen rather than face them in battle. I had a hero murdered even after he'd helped me just so that he wouldn't be a threat to me at a later date. I have sinned, Lord. And the weight of it is more than I can bear."

Tears began to trickle from his eyes, wetting his cheeks with their passing. "Yet as sinful as I am, if this is to be my end...let my errant children find it in their hearts to think of me from time to time. Let them find some small memory of me that is good and pleasant and kind...let them remember that, rather than what I am today. A failure. Inept. Unready."

A feeling of peace descended, the stress and tension draining from his body with a suddenness that defied comprehension. He sensed something, some presence, benevolent and pure, that was somehow there and yet was not, like it was on the edge of his awareness and its existence surpassed his understanding. It spoke, without disturbing the silence, as if its words were a part of that silence and couldn't be understood without it.

King Æthelred closed his eyes, unexpectedly content, and slept, his dreamless slumber the most blissful he'd ever known.

XXXX

"I never thought I'd have cause to say such a thing, but…that is the most heavily fortified nunnery I've ever laid eyes on."

Edmund held his hand to his mouth, trying to stifle his mirth. Despite the humour of his delivery, there wasn't anything inaccurate in what Ælfweard had said. The abbey had been fortified, and it seemingly wasn't for the protection of the nuns. Something wasn't right here, and Edmund had a good enough idea as to why.

"There's got to be around forty of the bastards," said Wulfnoth quietly, as serious as ever. "Look at how they are equipped…look at how they carry themselves…Eadric must have called for his own hearthweru to meet him here. I think he knows we'll be wanting to get inside and is taking no chances."

Edmund nodded, all thoughts of laughter now very much forgotten. He was tired. They'd been on the move for some time, their spirited ride taking them dangerously close to the boundaries of old Mierċe. They were still in Westseaxe, but barely, and Eadric's influence over Malmesberie and its abbey was obviously quite pronounced. The heavily armed men below were testament to that fact.

Malmesberie otherwise looked fairly typical. He could see most of it from where they were crouched, the forested rise they were ensconced on affording them a decent view. The abbey was quite impressive, being one singular, squat stone hall, the length of which sported several protruding annexes that Edmund assumed were side chapels or living quarters. It had a thatched roof, as was typical, and a pair of tall, curved double doors set into a high stone archway for an entrance. If there were any other entry points, Edmund could not tell.

The town seemed to have been built around it, the more modest buildings looking like they'd been fashioned from local timber without any undue fuss going into their construction. There were not too many people about, as was only natural given that evening was creeping on, but from the manner of those present they were fearful. They kept glancing towards the abbey, or more specifically, the fearsome men around it. Edmund took that as a sign that Eadric hadn't come here as a friend, and nobody here had been foolish enough to take him as such.

The men Wulfnoth had brought with him to Lundenburg were still with them but concealed in the trees about fifty yards back, along with Bede and the rest of the horses. Edmund and company had opted to dismount and do some scouting, some instinct telling him it would be foolhardy to stay on the road and ride into Malmesberie like any other traveller. He could see now his hunch had been correct. Eadric's men wouldn't have given him a warm welcome.

"So what's the plan?" Edmund asked, his question put to either of his companions. "There's seventeen of us against forty…I think brute force isn't going to work here."

"It won't," nodded Wulfnoth. "And that's just the Mierċians we've seen so far. There could be more in the abbey. Guarding Ealdgyth, perhaps. Ready to kill her, even."

Edmund's eyes widened at the thought of it. If what Wulfnoth said was true, it made their job considerably more difficult, as even if they managed to get inside, it would be impossible to get Ealdgyth to safety if Eadric had ordered his men to kill her if a rescue was ever attempted. If it were anyone else, he'd have told Wulfnoth he shouldn't give voice to additional problems they had no way of knowing even existed, but this was Eadric they were dealing with. He was a clever bastard, and completely evil to boot. Trouble awaited them inside, of that Edmund was sure.

"What about a nice distraction?" asked Ælfweard.

"Nice?" asked Wulfnoth. "Can't it be some other kind of distraction?"

"...something that draws a lot of those men away," Ælfweard continued, ignoring Wulfnoth. "Like one of us sets a fire...or pretends to attack the town."

"Why not both?" asked Wulfnoth. "I can take my men back onto the main road...and then we can come screaming up on our horses, full speed, making a bloody great noise and..."

"You can't hurt anyone," said Edmund. "The people of Malmesberie have done nothing wrong. Chances are Eadric's already threatened or wronged them in some way to get them to cooperate...we can't attack them in their own homes."

"I won't shed a drop of blood," said Wulfnoth. "I mean, look there..." he pointed towards a rather large, rundown building far from the abbey on the western outskirts. "What's that place even used for? It's abandoned, surely. Me and my lads can set that on fire and then rush the abbey only to pull away..."

"So the hearthweru will chase you?" asked Edmund, thinking this plan was actually quite appealing.

"We can hope," said Wulfnoth. "If we're out of luck...Eadric will have given his men specific orders not to come to the town's defence. But why would he do that? He can't think of every contingency, and as for us attacking Malmesberie..."

"Pretending to attack Malmesberie," corrected Edmund.

"...well, he won't be expecting it. I don't think so, anyway. He probably thinks the king never told you Ealdgyth was even here." Wulfnoth paused, his eyes thoughtful. "Just how did you get Æthelred to tell you about any of this?"

Edmund shrugged. "I just kind of shouted a lot. I drew my sword at one point. I lost control. I won't be including it among my most precious of memories."

Wulfnoth clicked his tongue. "I suppose there are some benefits to being an aetheling then," he said. "Were anyone else to draw a weapon on the king..."

"I understand," said Edmund, impatient. He didn't want to dwell too much on his last encounter with his father. It upset him, and he'd been thinking a lot on what Ælfweard had said as to him falling ill. As angry as he was, Edmund didn't want his father to suffer, despite everything he'd done, and despite the fact Edmund was still fully committed to seizing his throne. He wasn't a cruel man. He was just doing what justice demanded.

"So you'll take your men and do this distraction?" asked Edmund of Wulfnoth.

"Let's hold here awhile," Wulfnoth replied. Edmund nodded, aware that their chances were improved if they waited for darkness to fall. It was dusk, and the whole western horizon was one layered, glowing mass of fading orange emerging from a backdrop of ever-darkening blue. Edmund stayed as he was, allowing himself the small luxury of watching what was left of the sunset, both Wulfnoth and Ælfweard silent at his side.

"What about now?" Wulfnoth whispered, causing Edmund to almost jump, so relaxed had he become. It was now virtually night, almost but not quite, but that was good enough. It was time to go to work.

"Use all of your men," Edmund instructed. "We'll need to make it look like you're a real raiding party, or at least scary enough to get Eadric's men to think you're a threat and follow you. I will then..."

"What about me?" asked Ælfweard, nonplussed. "Won't I be given something to do?"

"Just stay up here," said Edmund, "but if anything happens...if more warriors appear and look to be of the unfriendly type...start yelling. We'll hear you."

"Won't that just draw a lot of attention on myself?"

"Yes," said Wulfnoth, "although you should be happy...think of all the attention I'm going to be getting!"

"You have horses to escape," said Ælfweard. "I just have..."

"You have your own steed," said Edmund, gesturing back towards the trees and the men and horses concealed there. "If all goes wrong, by all means, get out of here and ride for Porteceaster. Ulfcytel is there. He'll be glad to see you again."

Ælfweard nodded once, looking content enough with his assigned role in things. Wulfnoth then started back towards the tree line, staying low for precaution. Edmund waited. And waited some more. He was just wondering if something had gone wrong already when he heard hoofbeats on the road to the south and west, the sound growing louder and closer with every second. There were shouts now, jubilant and fearsome, of the type Edmund had grown to associate with Danish raiders with murder and mayhem in mind.

He turned his head to his left, looking down towards the main approach to the town. He spied Wulfnoth and his men a moment later. They were riding at full speed and making a real racket with it, several of them brandishing lit torches that Edmund suspected were about to be put to good use. Sure enough, the first fire was lit, the thatch of the building Wulfnoth had previously pointed out igniting with a speed that was quite alarming. Shouts were heard from elsewhere, panicked and fearful, which almost certainly meant the townsfolk believed they were under attack and had best defend themselves. Edmund said a silent prayer, imploring God to safeguard the innocent. He'd feel beyond guilty if any of the inhabitants were killed in all this.

Edmund stood up and began moving down the hillside at a jog. He could still see Wulfnoth and his men, riding at full pelt through the town and, like Edmund, on course for the abbey. Several of the warriors on guard were already chasing after them, but without mounts of their own they simply couldn't catch them, and none of Wulfnoth's lot were about to stop and exchange blows. Eadric obviously hadn't bothered to leave his people with any horses. Why would he? All they had to do was guard the nuns. Being set upon by Wulfnoth and his crazy mob wasn't something they'd prepared for.

Not everyone was fooled by the distraction. There were two men still guarding the main entrance, the entirety of which was presently illuminated by a rather imposing brazier just adjacent to the doors. Edmund didn't slow, instead rushing towards them at full speed, his arms waving frantically above his head.

"We are beset!" he called, doing his best to sound frightened. "The Danes are...the Danes...they..."

"Stop!" commanded one of the men, holding his hand out, palm facing forward. "Stay where you are and…"

Edmund still didn't slow. In fact, he sped up, continuing with his "frightened villager" act until the last possible moment. He careered into the guard, head first, his skull connecting with the underside of his jaw. He fell down, hard, and Edmund just carried on, storming past and then through the double doors beyond and into the abbey.

The second guard chased after him, but he'd hesitated over the sudden violence, allowing Edmund precious time. He put it to good use, ducking inside and holding the doors closed, the man just beyond hammering away to no real effect. Edmund looked about, hoping to find something to brace the doors with. They were capable of being barred from here, but Edmund lacked the means to do so. He'd have to improvise, and quickly.

A sharp crack rent the air, and Edmund found himself stumbling backwards, his vision obscured by tears of pain. The guard must have thrown his full weight into the door, causing it to open straight into Edmund's face. He was on Edmund in a heartbeat, striking him twice about the jaw with a closed fist. He then twisted him around and shoulder charged him into a wall, the sudden, brutal impact forcing the air from his lungs. The bastard kept on at him, hammering him in the chest and stomach and reaching for his throat. Edmund wouldn't allow that.

He slipped his hands behind his attacker's neck and pulled, forcing his head downward at a tilt. He then hauled his right knee upwards, smashing the man full in the face. He released him as he weakened, allowing him to stagger away a few steps, a torrent of blood pouring from his nose. Despite the punishment meted out to him, the villain was still in the mood for fighting, and he soon pulled a long, narrow seax from a scabbard at his waist, a wicked, broken grin spreading across his otherwise bloodied mouth.

Surprisingly, he didn't attack immediately. He instead took a deep breath and began to yell down a side passage to the left of the main entrance, his voice echoing sharply across the stones. "KILL THE LADY!" he thundered, Edmund's eyes widening in horror as realisation dawned. He went to shout again, but Edmund was moving fast, smashing the hilt of his sword into his face with enough force to knock him flat onto his back.

Edmund laid into him, kicking him repeatedly across the head and chest. He went to get up, twisting around onto his front and trying to push himself up with his hands, but Edmund wouldn't relent. He heard a rib or two snap as his boot again found its mark, another kick seeing his opponent suddenly spit blood onto the flagstone and slump, face-first, into his own fluids. He wasn't moving. That was enough.

All was quiet, save for the confused and alarmed shouts that continued to sound off from outside. Edmund looked around, alert for any other enemies that might decide to reveal themselves. The abbey stretched out before him, the antechamber he was standing in leading into what looked like a significantly large chapel. It was empty, such was the hour, and he couldn't really see much, again for the same reason, although he could see a few points of light up ahead that he assumed would be candles atop an altar.

This was no time for taking in the sights, however. The bastard he'd just laid low hadn't shouted something so specific for no reason. Ealdgyth must be close, and from what he'd just seen and heard, Eadric's men had orders to kill her if they thought a rescue was likely to succeed. Edmund thus hurried to the same passage the guard had yelled down, thinking it logical that if Ealdgyth was anywhere, she'd be down here.

He kept on, his breath hot and heavy from his exertions. He'd made a real mess of things thus far. There was nothing subtle about any of this. This was a ridiculous situation he was in, and perhaps more so because of his rather brutal approach in gaining access to what was, in the final analysis, a house of God. He continued running, occasionally ducking into side chambers as and when they presented themselves, his eyes ever alert for any trace of Ealdgyth. There were none, but there was still time. He also couldn't hear any sounds of pursuit. Perhaps the Lord was yet smiling on him.

What happened next put paid to that notion. A monster appeared from the archway up ahead, its skin unnaturally pallid and its eyes ablaze with rage. Edmund skidded to a halt before it, his face flushed and his breath ragged. "What is the meaning of this?" the beast demanded, her voice like fingernails upon a slate board. Edmund was in serious trouble now. There were not many things he feared in life, but he counted ancient, angry nuns among them. There was nothing a man such as he could do in the face of their fury. They were relentless.

"Ealdgyth!" exclaimed Edmund. "Is there a lady named Ealdgyth here? I must find her!"

"Just who are you, young man?!" demanded the wizened old witch. "You should know no man is permitted within this place. We have sworn ourselves to lives of chastity, poverty, and…"

"And permitting Eadric of Mierċe to kidnap an innocent woman and imprison her here!" thundered Edmund, unwilling to allow this abbess or whoever she was to waste his time. "Just tell me where she is! Her life is at…"

Somebody called his name. He couldn't work out precisely where it was coming from, but there was only one reason for somebody to be shouting "Edmund" around here, and it wasn't because they just happened to like how it sounded. True enough, Ealdgyth appeared up ahead and past the nun's shoulder, dressed as if she were just another sister. She smiled upon seeing him, yet that quickly passed, her look suddenly turning to outright fear. There was somebody behind her, in the shadows. And judging from their bulk, it wasn't just another nun.

Edmund brushed past the old crone in front of him, her shrieking protestations ringing in his ears. The figure up ahead stepped out into full view, his long chain byrnie and menacing axe making it clear enough he wasn't here for the sake of nightly prayers. Ealdgyth made a dash towards Edmund, and Edmund, for his part, broke into another run, his sword again drawn as he made straight for her. He reached Ealdgyth, but there was no time for greetings, for the armed man at her rear came on with some urgency, his axe swinging straight for Edmund's head.

He fell back, bundling Ealdgyth behind him, hoping to secure some space to put this bastard down. He was skilled, and quicker than his bulk and armour would suggest, making Edmund suspect he must be one of Eadric's chosen elite. They continued to exchange blows, the stone passageway now ringing with the sound of combat.

Such bedlam had, of course, woken up every other nun in the vicinity, prompting something of a general panic. Edmund ignored them as several looked on, their eyes wide with fright. He didn't need the distraction. He had to win this. He wasn't just fighting for himself. If this man killed him, then he thought it certain Ealdgyth would be next. Edmund wouldn't have that. He'd triumph here and be away from this place as intended.

He got part of his wish, just not in the way he'd initially envisioned. His opponent smashed him in the ribs with the haft of his axe, sending Edmund reeling with pain. The fiend made another swing for him, a disembowelling strike if ever there was one, but he'd not been prepared for Edmund's unusual capacity to absorb punishment and recover. Edmund stepped into his swing, bypassing the head of the axe, and rammed the point of his sword through his throat. He fell like a sack of rocks, his neck reduced to one weeping ruin of torn flesh and splintered bone, the watching nuns all scattering in panic.

Edmund ignored his fallen, twitching opponent and turned to Ealdgyth. "Are you alright?" he asked, more breathless than ever. "Was he supposed to kill you? Did he hurt you?"

"I'm alright," she replied, her face deathly pale. "And yes, I think he was meant to if need be. I heard your voice and ran from him…you should know, Edmund, that Eadric…"

Her voice faded to silence, her fearful gaze fixed on something to Edmund's right. He twisted around, sword ready, thinking another foe was about to attack him, only to come face to face with the Ealdorman Eadric himself. Their eyes met, if only for a second, Edmund all rage and bluster and Eadric as surprised as any man could be. He looked as unsavoury as always, his skin still soft and his eyes that unpleasant shade of grey, but he was clearly very, very unhappy to see Edmund.

"You killed my friends."

Edmund wasn't asking a question. It was a simple statement, albeit imbued with hate. Eadric did not reply, at least not with words. He attacked in a heartbeat, his blade flashing straight for Edmund's throat. It was parried, just about, but Eadric wasn't fazed and kept up the assault, his fast, precise strikes proving increasingly difficult to defend against.

It was then Edmund noticed a weakness. Eadric was good, very good, but his was a skill obtained through practice rather than experience. He had what felt like a largely academic grasp of swordcraft, one that focused purely on the blade itself rather than the brutal, unpredictable art of using whatever you had at your disposal to take your opponent down. He was thus surprised when Edmund smashed another of his lightning strikes aside only to kick him square in the stomach, the force of it sending him staggering backwards several paces to finally collapse, awkwardly, onto his rump.

He recovered and rose quickly despite his shock, and Edmund advanced upon him, grinning malevolently and eager to dish out more punishment. Eadric wasn't up for that. He spun on his heels and fled, likely thinking he'd come out worse if their exchange continued. Edmund gave chase, Ealdgyth too, knowing they had an opportunity here to bring some much needed justice. They ran out into the chantry of the main chapel Edmund had seen earlier, the sound of their echoing pursuit carrying far and wide. Eadric was moving fast, vaulting over the altar and deliberately knocking a brass crucifix and several candles into Edmund's path. He leapt over them, a growl escaping his throat at Eadric's casual disrespect of holy things and this holy place.

Several warriors from outside had now entered the abbey via the main entrance and were making straight for them. They were yelling, demanding Edmund stop and promising bloody retribution if he didn't. Edmund continued to pursue Eadric, chasing him out of the chapel and then north through a sequence of drafty corridors and one very spartan dining hall. Ealdgyth followed at his back, and Eadric's men followed her, yet the ealdorman himself hadn't stopped, possibly as he knew Edmund would likely be able to kill him before his men could intervene. Eadric was light on his feet and agile with it, and he continued to try and knock things into Edmund's way as they rampaged through the abbey, at one point even shoving a nun towards him like she'd prove useful as a human obstacle.

The poor woman screamed, terrified and confused and struggling to regain her balance. Edmund caught her before she could fall, an apology on his lips, and continued on, but Eadric's ploy had worked and he'd lost time. There was only so much abbey they could run through, also, and they'd come to the end. Eadric stood in the doorway of what had to be a rear entrance Edmund hadn't known about. He looked back at them for a brief second, smug and triumphant, the night air snatching at his hair. He then stepped beyond and slammed the door shut, a thumping sound following as something heavy was heaved into place from the other side.

Edmund came to a halt, Ealdgyth too. He turned to look behind him, back the way they had come. It wasn't just three warriors coming after them. There were at least five, now six, then seven, all of them with murder on their minds if the noise they were making was anything to go by. Edmund was a good fighter, that he knew, yet he didn't feel comfortable with these odds, especially in such narrow confines and with an unarmed woman who was dependent on his protection. There was only one thing for it. He'd gotten in here through brute force. He'd be leaving the same way.

He made a run for the door and tried to fling it open, using his weight to do the job. It held fast, whatever was on the other side pinning it in place. He pushed again, putting his back into it. That got a better result, the door opening by perhaps half an inch and then holding. This wasn't good. Edmund would have to go for a more inventive approach.

He stepped back a few paces and made another rush for the door, his sword held aloft in both hands. He'd bash his way out, using his weight and strength to break the thing to pieces if need be. He wouldn't have long, but it was preferable to fighting alone against insurmountable odds. He loosed a roar from his throat as he charged, intending to use all his rage and momentum to smash his way to freedom.

The door flew open before he could strike. Edmund tumbled on through into the night air, his arms all a tangle. Ealdgyth followed, as was wise, and Edmund turned to see none other than Ælfweard shutting the door, his expression anxious upon seeing what was chasing them.

"I thought you might need some assistance," he said nervously, bending down to heave a seriously hefty stone bench back into position in front of the door. Edmund helped him, both men sliding the bench up tight against the door frame as Eadric had presumably done just a minute before. It was relatively easy to move when gripped or dragged at one end, but when placed directly across something it was nigh on impossible to shift. Edmund could vouch for that, and so could the men now attempting to hammer their way out to get at them. It was time to go.

"Did you see Eadric?" Edmund asked, noting that Ælfweard appeared to have brought both Bede and his own horse along with him. Edmund leapt atop Bede, gesturing for Ealdgyth to join him. She did so, Ælfweard also mounting up with all necessary haste.

"Eadric?" he replied, now in the saddle. "You of course mean that bastard over there?"

Ælfweard had pointed at something over to the north and west. Sure enough, Eadric was there, atop a horse and glaring down at them from a grassy rise overlooking the abbey on its northern side. Edmund roared and went after him, and Eadric made a truly pitiful noise whilst spurring at his horse, like he was somehow begging it to get him out of here and keep him safe. He briefly vanished from view as they rode up the hill, but they caught sight of him again when they crested the summit, riding north in considerable haste.

There was only one thing to do in response. They gave chase, the sound of hooves hammering the earth. Bede was a strong horse, and he bore his double burden well, but there was no denying they'd struggle to catch up with Eadric unless something changed. Ælfweard stormed on ahead atop his own beast, Eadric glancing back at him in panic as he came yet closer.

They were now on a narrow, overgrown trail heading north out of Malmesberie and into Mierċe. This was a dangerous situation, since if they continued this way, Eadric would almost certainly chance upon more people under his authority and use them accordingly. Trees and then more trees came looming out of the night, their skeletal limbs reaching out to form one tangled, crisscrossing mass above them. They rode faster and faster, the trail taking them further and further north, the leaves from low-lying branches whipping about their heads.

It became clear enough that the sooner this ended, the better it would be for all of them. Eadric was a good rider, and Ælfweard, whilst almost on him, had not yet been able to get close enough to do anything decisive. Edmund would settle this right now. He spurred Bede on, and he rose to the challenge, his hooves pounding onward and his breath thundering from his flaring, shuddering nostrils. He was doing it. Despite everything, he was closing the gap. Eadric was almost within reach.

Edmund had never been more surprised in his life. Bede suddenly reared up, sending both him and Ealdgyth hurtling backwards. The ground rose to meet them, the impact sending a dull shock wave of agony up the length of Edmund's spine. For a time, he could do nothing but groan, such was the pain, but he forced himself through it, opening his eyes and crawling over to check on Ealdgyth. She was conscious, but shaken.

With some effort he managed to help her up, the pain in his back making his teeth grit, only to see that Ælfweard had fallen also and was only just managing to rise. Bede was rampaging about, his whinnies pleading and desperate, as was Ælfweard's steed. Edmund saw something on the road, glinting in the faint starlight. A metal token, so it appeared, or perhaps a coin. Ealdgyth appeared at his side and bent down to look. She picked it up and handed it to Edmund.

He gasped when he realised what it was. He threw it away, hurling the wretched thing into the undergrowth. He went over to Bede, trying to soothe his agitation. Ælfweard was now up and rubbing his head, his expression both pained and confused. Bede eventually relented, at least a little, allowing Edmund to reach down and grip his front ankle so that the beast might raise his foot. He saw it then, the metal glinting just like the other had. He reached out and pulled on it, Bede thankfully retaining a measure of control whilst the cruel device was removed from his hoof.

"The bastard threw bloody caltrops at us," said Edmund bitterly, finding another in Bede's right foot. Ælfweard was having trouble calming his horse, so Edmund finished up with Bede and applied his own magic touch, bringing the poor creature back to some level of normalcy. All in all, they removed a good six caltrops from their horses, none of which had thankfully done any serious damage. Edmund wouldn't remount Bede in such a condition, though. There was no way he could be made to move at any reasonable speed, and it would be cruel to try. They'd have to think of something else if they wished to continue the pursuit.

"So that's it then?" asked Ælfweard glumly. "Eadric throws these horrible spiky things across the road and just gets away? I suppose he'll be halfway to Mierċe by now, which means..."

"Which means he'll be a lot harder to root out if we go after him," interjected Edmund. "I just can't believe the little bastard actually did that. Caltrops! Of all things! Not even the Danes fight like that!"

Ælfweard went to say something but paused. They could hear hoofbeats in the distance, and they were rapidly getting closer. They then saw the lights, bobbing and weaving from the direction they'd come. Edmund drew his sword, but there was no need, and he let out a sigh of relief when Wulfnoth and his men rode into view, their torches burning brightly. Edmund strode forward, his arms held up over his head so they'd hopefully see him and stop. He didn't know how many of those caltrops were around. There was no point in seeing any more horses hurt.

They spotted him and came clattering to a halt, Wulfnoth at their head. "So we are successful?" he asked, nodding his head towards Ealdgyth.

"More or less," said Edmund. "And yet I have let an opportunity slip from grasp. Eadric was here, and we were on his tail."

"I had wondered if he might be present," replied Wulfnoth. "He has slithered away then?"

"He has, but not for long," announced Edmund gravely. "You and I are going after him...have half your men here take Ealdgyth to Snotingeham. The rest come with us. I'll have Eadric's life before dawn breaks!"

Wulfnoth shook his head. "Edmund, I must advise against this. The men we faced in Malmesberie will be after us, and if we cross into Mierċe, essentially everyone we meet will be Eadric's pawn and looking to stick a knife in our flesh. Dividing our forces invites disaster. Let's do what we came here to do. Let's get Ealdgyth home."

Edmund thought on it, allowing his anger to cool. Wulfnoth was right. There were only eighteen of them, including Ealdgyth, and there were over forty men in Malmesberie who would certainly be searching for them presently. Eadric was a coward, obviously, but once in Mierċe, he'd have Lord knows how many warriors to call on and make their life miserable. It was a fool's errand to try and chase him down in such circumstances. They'd achieved the task they'd originally set themselves. Edmund would be content with that, for the moment, anyway.

He sighed, his mind made up. "You are right, Wulfnoth, as you so often are," he said. "It is time we left this place...after one more thing. Eadric has covered the road ahead of us in caltrops. I say we brush them off into the grass. Leaving them here could be a disaster for any beast."

Wulfnoth looked at him like he was half-insane, but the rest of the men had already dismounted to assist Edmund, leaving Wulfnoth little choice. They cleared the road, making sure it was safe once again for anyone or anything that might care to tread it. Ealdgyth looked on approvingly, pleased at this display of compassion. Edmund didn't see it as anything to make a fuss about. There was no sign of hostiles, as of yet anyway. They had time to do a good deed here, and so they'd do it.

They finished up, and Edmund commandeered a fresh mount from one of Wulfnoth's men so that he and Ealdgyth could still ride together. The man he'd dispossessed mounted up with another, as did Ælfweard, although they made sure to have Bede and the other injured horse tethered so they could bring them along. They then set out, off the trail and north east into the tangled forest, the shadows cast from their torches dancing erratically through the trees. They didn't move too fast, since Edmund could tell Bede was having difficulty, and his heart went out to him when he noticed his limp. Eadric had done many terrible things in his life. Hurting Bede was just another to add to the list.

Fortunately, the rest of the night went far more smoothly. The thugs from Malmesberie didn't make themselves known, and there was no sign of trouble coming from Mierċe, which likely meant they'd given Eadric a good scare. Edmund looked back at Ealdgyth as they continued on, thinking she'd appreciate a sympathetic ear after everything she'd been through.

"How are you feeling?" he asked, believing it to be a better question than asking if she was alright when she almost certainly wasn't.

"Tired," she said, her voice so hushed he could barely hear her from over his shoulder. "I thank you, though," she said after a long pause. "When Eadric took me from Lundenburg, I thought he intended to murder me too."

"It was my father's will that you become a nun, whether you liked it or not," said Edmund.

"I don't think Eadric was too happy with that arrangement," she replied. "Otherwise, why handle the situation himself? Why assign a man to follow me about the place, armed as he was?"

"Indeed," affirmed Edmund, remembering the brute he'd killed inside the abbey. "Eadric is calling the shots now, and as always, my father is foolish enough to let it happen. I suspect he wants me out of the way. And you, of course. Both he and my father don't want any trouble from the Five Boroughs."

"They should have thought of that before murdering my husband and brother-in-law!"

Edmund nodded at her words. "Fear not," he said, "for I have taken matters into my own hands."

"I got that impression earlier," she chuckled slightly.

"Not just that," smiled Edmund. "I have decided my father cannot be left on the throne. I made him give his word, did you know that? I made him give his word that he would not hurt Sigeferth or Morcar. He's let me down for the final time."

"What are you saying?" Ealdgyth asked, apprehensive.

"I need you with me. I need you to use the property and influence you now possess to rally the Five Boroughs to my side. I will be king, with your help."

"You would really do this, Edmund? You'd really rise against Æthelred?"

"It's not as daunting a prospect as you might think. I have an army, I have the South, or much of it anyway…and I have Eastengle. With your support, I'll have everything north of Lundenburg and up to the borders of Norþanhymbre."

"An impressive amount of land, Edmund. And yet I fear there are certain dangers…Sigeferth told me that Duke Richard has your sister captive as part of some effort to manipulate your father. Won't you…"

"I cannot sit and do nothing," interrupted Edmund, annoyed and fearful at the mention of the dastardly Norman duke. "The longer my father is left in power, the more harm he's likely to do, either through Eadric or his own ill judgement. The realm has suffered like this for years now. It's time it ended."

A ripple of agreement sounded from the men. They were with him, and Edmund felt stronger from knowing it. He wouldn't leave his sister to die, not ever, but he couldn't just do nothing now his father had decided to go back to ruling as ruthlessly as he'd done before. There was a line, and it had been crossed.

"We'll think of some way to resolve the situation with the duke," said Wulfnoth thoughtfully. "If he harms Godgifu because he thinks you'll resist his influence, then he'll have simply made an enemy…a formidable one."

"Do you seek to flatter me, Wulfnoth?"

"I'm stating facts. The duke will know of your campaign against Svienn, and if you do indeed rise against your father…"

"I WILL rise, Wulfnoth. It's not a remote possibility."

"Of course, my king. What I'm saying is Richard would be a fool to execute his hostage just because you came to the throne. He'll approach you soon, I foresee. He'll want certain assurances. He'll want to manipulate you. He'll use Godgifu as a bargaining chip as he has certainly done with your father."

Edmund sighed, his exhalation turning to a low growl. "Let me worry about one thing at a time," he said. "Now that we have you, Ealdgyth, we're in a far better position than we were. With the Five Boroughs in my possession…"

"Is that what I am, Edmund?" she asked, a touch dismayed. "I'm just some asset of yours? To be used in your feud with your father? Please say it's not so."

"I misspoke," said Edmund, genuinely regretting his words. "Everything I have done…everything has been because…I tried to forgive my father. I did. Sincerely. Truly. But when I heard he'd murdered Sigeferth…"

He paused, the grief seizing his voice. To lose a friend was bad enough, but to lose a father also because he was the one who'd had them killed was simply horrific. It was not out of greed that Edmund acted. He was doing what he had to do for the sake of justice and for the sake of the realm. He needed people to see that.

"I think I understand," said Ealdgyth gently. "And rest assured, now that I have my husband's authority, I will lend my strength to yours. I just wanted to be sure, Edmund. Thank you for again proving yourself a good man."

"Again?" Edmund asked, craning his neck in the saddle so that he might see her. "When have I proven myself before?"

"Why do you think Sigeferth favoured you and your brother?" asked Ealdgyth. "He saw something in you. A substance. A goodness. Something that needed to be nurtured and nourished so that it could come to a proper fruition. When your brother died, and you were beset by grief…you proved it again. No base or selfish character would ever grieve like that. You were wounded, and you proved yourself a good man with the bearing of it."

"You think I'm good because I grieved?"

"Absolutely," she said emphatically. "You have a heart. You've experienced pain with it, of course, yet that suffering was born out of your love for another. We are to love one another, as Christ loves us, remember? To love is to suffer, sometimes, and England does not need a king who does not love. Love is patient, love is kind. It does not envy, it does not boast, it is not proud. It does not dishonour others, it is not self-seeking, it is not easily angered, it keeps no record of wrongs. Love does not delight in evil but rejoices with the truth. It always protects, always trusts, always hopes, always perseveres."

"You have a most excellent memory," muttered Edmund, secretly awed by Ealdgyth's command of Holy Scripture.

"And is it not so?" she asked. "Have you not sought to protect, trust, hope, and persevere? Is that not why you fought so hard against Svienn and Cnut? Is that not why I am with you, right now? Eadric would have killed me, even if you had not come, I think. I am alive now as you could not stand to see me join my husband. That double injustice would have been intolerable to you. Am I wrong?"

"You are not," said Edmund quietly, his anger rising at the thought of Eadric murdering Ealdgyth just as he had Sigeferth. He knew then that Ealdgyth had been right to ask him what he'd intended with her rescue. If he were forced to think on it, he had at times been fixated on the political rather than the moral, seeing Ealdgyth as a means to an end rather than an end in herself.

That wasn't right, and it wasn't who he was as a man, let alone a king. Rescuing Ealdgyth couldn't be just a way of obtaining the power and prestige she commanded. Everything Edmund did now had to be for the sake of Sigeferth and his memory. He'd be wise to remain focused on that and comport himself as his old friend would have wished.

Edmund hoped God would aid him in this. For even if he did stop his father from doing any more harm, if he became king only to be corrupted by the position then all would have been for nought. He'd be no better than Eadric then, or Uhtred, or any number of power-obsessed malefactors propping up his murderous father from behind his throne. Edmund would not suffer such a fate to befall him. Scripture would again be his guide in this. For truly, what does it profit a man to gain the whole world and yet lose his own soul?

XXXXI

The smoke hung thickly over Snotingeham, turning the already ashen sky yet darker. The fire was out and had been for at least a half hour, so Edmund had been told, but that didn't detract from the tragedy they faced. The sight of Ealdgyth was enough to prove that. All her daughters had been inside the hall when it had gone up in flames. Only one had made it out. Edmund had no words for her. No one did, and the only man who might have been able to comfort her in this was dead. This was not how Edmund had envisioned his return to the Five Boroughs. He would find out the truth of what had happened here. Justice would then follow.

"It happened very fast."

Edmund turned at the sound of the voice to behold the head of Snotingeham's garrison, a man he knew as Ælfnoð. He'd been a loyal servant and ally of Sigeferth over the years, and Edmund could see from his eyes the pain he was in now. He'd been close to the family, and undoubtedly thought what had happened to be a failure on his part. He couldn't blame himself. From where Edmund was standing, it was a minor miracle they'd been able to stop the blaze where they had.

He looked out across the ruins. Sigeferth's hall was largely eradicated, its once generous dimensions now collapsed and charred to virtually nothing. Several score of Snotingeham's citizens were present, each proud of their timely efforts in fighting the fire and yet sorrowful over the lives that had been lost.

"Foul play?" Edmund asked Ælfnoð, still struggling to ignore Ealdgyth's wailings as she sobbed, on her knees, in the street, her single remaining child wrapped up in her arms. It was a hard sight that called for gentleness. Yet answers had to be obtained.

"I've ordered the palisade gates sealed," affirmed Ælfnoð. "It's all too suspicious," he said, gesturing towards the ruins. "Fires have happened here before, but for my Lord Sigeferth's hall, specifically, to just combust like that, so soon after his murder..."

"Newcomers?" asked Wulfnoth, breaking his silence. He'd been staring at the ruins for some time, his expression unreadable, unlike Ælfweard and the rest of the men, who all looked genuinely mournful as they lingered just behind.

"What do you mean?" asked Ælfnoð. "Have we met before, my lord? I'm not sure I know your face."

"This is Wulfnoth," said Edmund. "He's of great help to me. We can trust him."

"THE Wulfnoth?!" asked Ælfnoð, disbelief upon his aged and distinctly hairy face. "The one who was accused of conspiring with Thork..."

"It's all nonsense," said Ælfweard, his voice raised. "I owe my life to Wulfnoth, and it's poor form to take rumours at face value."

"Our friend the reeve speaks true," said Edmund. "And you should know, Ælfnoð, that the one who tried to frame Wulfnoth during the incident you speak of may have had a hand in what happened here."

"Is that so?" asked Ælfnoð. "And you wish to know if any strangers have come here of late? Ones that may be in the employ of…who are we talking about exactly?"

"Eadric of Mierċe," said Wulfnoth, without turning to face Ælfnoð. "He and his brother framed me. He also killed your Lord Sigeferth. What you may not know is that Edmund encountered him when we sprang Ealdgyth from captivity. He will not have been pleased."

Ælfnoð had turned a little pale. "So all of my Lord Sigeferth's family is the target?" he asked, his voice pained. "You thwarted his schemes with Ealdgyth, so he turns his ire on her daughters?"

Edmund scowled at the thought of it, but what had been said was very likely true. Eadric had probably arranged for Sigeferth's children to be killed weeks ago, thinking them loose ends he couldn't afford to leave in play. With Ealdgyth out of his grasp, he'd probably decided to expedite matters. His timing, however, meant the men who'd set this blaze could still be around, and with a mind to open Ealdgyth's throat and that of her sole remaining child. It was utterly unconscionable. And, sadly, very believable.

"It is likely so," nodded Edmund. "So I would ask you to keep Snotingeham sealed. Have your men search everywhere, and I mean everywhere. Look for strangers, anyone suspicious. There must be some clue on the whereabouts of a guilty party. We have to find it."

"It won't be obvious," said Wulfnoth. "Eadric won't have hired anyone from Mierċe. The accent, the look…it'd give them away. It'll be a local, is my guess. Somebody you may actually know. Eadric has spies all over. It won't have been too much fuss to make a spy turn assassin."

"We'll get to searching then," said Ælfnoð. "It's just…" he stopped, his gaze drifting to the grieving Ealdgyth. Tears welled up in his eyes, and he went to dab them away, his great soot-stained paw doing little other than smear his already dirtied face.

Edmund put a hand to his shoulder. "I feel for you," he said. "This is a terrible shock, for us all."

"I served my Lord Sigeferth for years," said Ælfnoð weakly. "I did everything for him, he and his family…and now he's gone and…"

"Yes?" asked Edmund.

"I failed him. I failed my lord. I should have gone with him when he left to campaign with you. I should have been with him in Lundenburg. I should have…"

Edmund squeezed his shoulder. "You can tear your heart asunder thinking of all the things you might have done," he said. "Just think on this…you still have an opportunity to serve Sigeferth. Catch those who did this. We'll then have justice. You have my word on it."

Ælfnoð nodded and inhaled deeply. He began walking over to a clutch of his men, instructing them to begin their search. Edmund took the opportunity to speak with Ealdgyth, clearing his throat upon his approach so as to not startle her. He needn't have bothered. She was in a world of her own now, one of overwhelming grief, and she was still kneeling down and sobbing fitfully towards the ruins of her home. Her daughter, her youngest by the looks of it, still clung to her, but her expression was blank, making Edmund wonder if she'd simply shut down to better process the horrors she'd only just witnessed. Ælfwynn was her name. He remembered her well enough. Sigeferth had always doted on her. He'd doted on all his children.

Edmund knelt, hoping his reduced stature might make him seem more amiable. "We should go inside," he said softly, his eyes on both Ealdgyth and Ælfwynn. "The smoke here…it's still too thick. It won't do us any good to linger."

"I. Can't. Leave," wheezed Ealdgyth, barely able to form words. "We. Can't."

"For Ælfwynn's sake?" Edmund asked. "Please, Ealdgyth, the air here is no good. Let me help."

Ealdgyth nodded slightly and rose, slowly, to her feet, Edmund standing ready lest she fall. She held Ælfwynn's hand as they moved down the street towards the stables, inhaling great strangled breaths between sobs. She was covered in ash, for she'd gone running into the ruins when they'd arrived, screaming for them to follow and help. It had been too late by then, and Edmund had been forced to haul her back, fearing the heat and fumes would overwhelm her. She'd not gone willingly, but she'd been powerless to resist. Edmund had felt guilty about it at the time, yet he knew he'd done the right thing. Ealdgyth had endured a shock unlike anything anyone should ever have to experience. Nobody could be expected to behave rationally under the weight of such terrible pain.

They moved past the graveyard, Edmund sneaking a look in the hope of spotting Æthelstan's headstone. It was there, way towards the back and partially obscured by wisps of smoke. They kept on walking, following the muddied street westward. Snotingeham's buildings rose up around them, tightly packed as always, their damp and dilapidated exteriors appearing doubly forlorn amidst the still drifting smoke. Ealdgyth and Ælfwynn walked hand in hand, their heads hanging low. Edmund stayed close and led them to the front entrance of an inn he and Sigeferth had frequented several times in the past. It wasn't open at this early hour, but he rapped on the door anyway, knowing he had to get Ealdgyth and her daughter somewhere they could rest and recuperate. This was as good a place as any.

The door suddenly opened just as Edmund was about to knock for the seventh or eighth time. The owner, Wystan, was a thin man of advancing years, and seemed a tad suspicious until he realised who his guests were. He let them in then, a smile on his lips like he was sincerely pleased to see them.

Inside was as Edmund remembered, consisting of a single expanse of rush-littered floorboards leading to a stone hearth built into the north wall. Tables and chairs of various sizes and conditions were cluttered about the place, fashioned from the same cheap pine that was so common in this area. A stout wooden staircase could be seen up ahead and to the left, allowing guests to ascend to the upper storey and sleep once they'd drunk their fill.

The bar, if you could call it that, was close to the entrance they'd come through, the storeroom behind it no doubt filled with kegs of all sizes for Wystan's typically thirsty and boisterous customers. It all stank, quite badly actually, the stench of stale ale and suspect mead filling his nostrils. Edmund didn't care. He wasn't here to have a good time, and he didn't think he'd be able to even if he tried.

He led his two charges to a table tucked out of the way in the corner. They sat down, Edmund finding it odd to see the place so empty. The last time he'd been here, the whole ground floor had been one mass of drinking, raucous men. It was sad to see it so deserted, the hearth also unlit and the air uncomfortably chill.

He asked Wystan to bring them porridge, assuming he were willing. He was, and he didn't complain at being ordered around, having rightly gotten the impression something terrible had happened and Edmund had good reason for being here. He seemed entirely ignorant of the blaze, which seemed strange, as a fire of such size and intensity would have surely awoken everyone across town. Perhaps he was just a very heavy sleeper. It wasn't unknown. Æthelstan had been the same.

Ealdgyth didn't eat. She just sat there, inhaling and exhaling, her wet, mournful eyes fixed on nothing in particular. Ælfwynn managed a few spoonfuls, which gave Edmund some hope that the child may yet recover from her ordeal. That must have been a serious amount of smoke she'd inhaled, and it remained a mystery how she'd escaped whilst her sisters had not. Edmund didn't think it fair to question her on it, at least not yet. She'd talk when she was good and ready.

The whispering, harsh and persistent, was unwelcome. He looked up, trying to ascertain where it was coming from, thinking there was something strangely unpleasant about the sound. He left the table and began to move, treading softly across the rush-strewn floor, his eyes and ears alert for anything unusual. The whispering kept on. Someone, somewhere, was having quite a conversation, albeit without wanting to be overheard. That made him suspicious.

His instincts were soon proven entirely correct. The thrown knife barely missed him, instead sailing past his head to clatter against the far wall. It had been a close call, and the man responsible appeared from the storeroom a heartbeat later, his look a venomous one as he was joined by Wystan and two others Edmund didn't recognise. So this was it then. They'd found their assassins, and as Wulfnoth had said, it appeared at least one of them was a local. Edmund had thought it odd the way Wystan had denied all knowledge of the fire. He'd been putting on an act, buying time and trying to get them to drop their guard whilst he summoned his fellow evil-doers. It wouldn't help them now. He drew his sword.

"Stop eating the porridge," said Edmund, keeping his eyes on the men in front of him. It seemed improbable that Wystan had an assortment of poisons just lying around, but it was better to be safe than sorry. It would be truly tragic for Ælfwynn to have survived all she had only to die choking on some porridge laced with who knew what.

"It's a shame you came here," said Wystan, like he was indeed genuinely sorrowful. "You could have gone anywhere else in town, but you came here, and sealed your fate with it. We only wanted to kill the girls, you see. Now you've gone and changed all that. We'll be killing all of you and getting a good tidy bonus, I'd say."

"Just listen to yourself speak, man," hissed Edmund. "You used to drink with Sigeferth, back in the day. He always liked it here. And now you throw your lot in with Eadric?"

"It's not a personal thing," said the unpleasant-looking fellow who'd thrown the knife. "It's just money. It's all about money. Always has been. Always will be."

"If you give up now, I won't kill you," said Edmund. They laughed, all of them, the three men Edmund didn't know revealing an assortment of knives, seaxes, and cudgels. Theirs was a cruel mirth, and Edmund wouldn't stand to hear it. He rushed forward with a shout, his sword raised and ready.

They were better than he'd expected. The one who'd just been waffling on about money was fast, and he managed to parry Edmund's sword at least twice before his head was cut from his shoulders. The other two were just as good, and one scored a solid hit on Edmund's chest with the edge of his blade. Edmund didn't pause, knowing his byrnie had absorbed the damage, and killed him seconds later, breaking his skull to pieces with all the fury he deserved. Only one assailant was left standing, not counting the terrified Wystan. This would be over quickly.

The third man, however, wasn't inclined to just give up and die. He drew a knife, similar to what had been hurled at Edmund earlier, and made ready to throw, looking like his intent was to pierce him through the throat. Edmund rushed him, hoping to intervene before that could happen, when his opponent's upper torso suddenly splintered outward, the head of a spear protruding from his chest. He fell, revealing the spectre that was Wulfnoth, Ælfweard hurrying to join him from the now open front door. Edmund hadn't heard them come in. It was good to see them, Wulfnoth in particular. He'd come in useful when it came to getting information from Wystan.

Sadly, the man himself didn't look like he was in the mood for talking. He tried to make a break for it, vaulting back over his own bar and into a side room. Wulfnoth and Ælfweard were on him in a second, dragging him backwards towards Edmund. He struggled, but Wulfnoth and the reeve together were by far the stronger, and they threw the old fool to the floor with ease. All three of them loomed over him, the points of their weapons resting upon his throat.

"You'll be telling me now where Eadric is," growled Edmund.

"I don't know where he is!" came the predictable response. "He never comes in person! He just sends me orders from time to time…asks me to do things. This was like any other task."

"Burning innocent children is just another day's work for you?" Edmund didn't expect him to answer that, not really. Wystan had proven himself a man without conscience, and so appealing to any sense of innate goodness on his part was a wasted effort. He just wanted to see him try and justify himself.

Wystan spat, his look suddenly furious. "Why did you even have to come here?! I don't understand…was there something here you wanted? Why would you, of all people, darken my door again?"

"This was once a happy place for Sigeferth and I," said Edmund. "You remember him, of course? He was your rightful lord. That woman over there?" He pointed to the still-seated and doubly shaken Ealdgyth. "She was his wife. You knew that. You still killed his girls. Why?!"

"It's just life! Life ends! You make a bit of money and see where it takes you! I've known you haughty do-gooder types all my days! You're all hypocrites! You can't judge m…"

Edmund's boot silenced him. His head lolled back, blood seeping from his mouth, but he was still breathing, which meant they'd be able to resume their little discussion soon enough. Wulfnoth would likely be looking forward to that.

"You knew this man?" asked Wulfnoth, casually inspecting the bloodied tip of his spear.

"I came here a few times with Sigeferth. I thought they were friends. I thought this would be a safe, welcoming place for Ealdgyth to rest in."

"Probably why Eadric chose to employ him then," said Wulfnoth, wiping the blood from his spear on the unconscious Wystan. "An inn is a great place to pick up information…and if Sigeferth was known to drink here? Even better. I'm sure Eadric learned all kinds of things from this berk. Those days are over, at least."

"Can anyone be trusted?" asked Edmund, feeling suddenly vulnerable at the sheer abundance of treachery he'd encountered.

"Yes," said Wulfnoth without hesitation. "Ignore all that yap this idiot said about money and life...evil bastards always talk like that. It's always the same noise they make when they have to justify themselves. They try to convince you everyone is as rotten as they are, which, conveniently, makes their own rottenness somehow less terrible and your virtue the aberration. It's pathetic."

"He's right, Edmund," said Ælfweard, having found his voice after their impromptu wrestling match with Wystan. "This will hardly come as a shock to you or anyone else who knows me, but I'm a sensitive man, and many have long sought to shame me for it. When I was held captive in Canterburie, I almost lost my mind at the barbarism meted out to my people. I've always been pained by the sufferings of others, and some have mocked me because of that, thinking me a lesser man, thinking that because I hurt when others hurt, that because I feel, that because I care, I'm somehow foolish or weak. Their barbs bother me little. I have a gentle heart...and I know the Lord would rather have me as I am than turn cold and cruel like these men at our feet."

Edmund nodded, knowing his friends spoke the truth. "Why did you both follow me here?" he asked. "Your appearance seems quite timely. Not that I couldn't have handled it myself..."

"I had a bad feeling," replied Wulfnoth. "That's all. That's all it takes. I learned long ago I get little...hunches...and when I do, I had best follow them. That and it's not like you could retire to Sigeferth's hall like you normally would. You had to go somewhere else, and there's only so many places in Snotingeham that offer hospitality."

Edmund made a gesture, indicating the bloody business around them. "Hospitality?" he asked, a dark chuckle escaping his lips.

"Alright, a bunch of scumbags in some dive of an inn," shrugged Wulfnoth. "What do you want me to do with this one?" he asked, poking the innkeeper with his spear. "When he wakes up, I reckon we'll have to chat with him some more, if you know what I mean."

"Just bind his hands and hand him over to Ælfnoð and his people," said Edmund wearily. "We can question him later. Right now," he turned to look at Ealdgyth, "...right now, I have other matters to attend to."

He went back over to the two ladies. That had been a difficult thing for them to witness, especially for Ælfwynn, who had turned even paler than she had been previously, if that was even possible. Wulfnoth read the situation well, and he and Ælfweard began hauling the corpses behind the bar so they'd be out of sight. It wouldn't do much good, since the poor child had seen Edmund killing them to begin with, but it was a nice touch. Wulfnoth finished and lifted Wystan up over his shoulder, giving Edmund one last nod before proceeding outside. Ælfweard lingered, like he was wondering if Edmund might need him for something, but it was not so, and he departed with a gesture from Edmund, his face downcast after witnessing yet more terrible deeds.

"We should leave," said Ealdgyth, her arm around Ælfwynn's trembling shoulders. "This is an awful place. Is there nowhere safe?"

"It is now," said Edmund firmly. "Nobody can hurt us, and we'll soon have some answers once that cur wakes up. We should count ourselves lucky."

"Lucky?!" said Ealdgyth. "My husband is suddenly murdered and I'm abducted, only to return home to find all but one of my children slain?! Where is my luck, Edmund? How is that good fortune?"

"I misspoke. I apologise. I merely wish to stay true to our purpose."

"I'm not sure if I even want anything to do with that purpose," whispered Ealdgyth, her eyes again glazed with tears. "I never wanted any of this…I didn't want to go to Lundenburg. Life was complicated enough being married to a thegn of such standing. I never wanted a complicated life, Edmund. I never wanted…"

"I understand," he said in reply, saddened by the grief in her voice. "What can I do? Just tell me what I need to do to help you, and I will see it done."

"There is only one thing to be done," she said, her eyes suddenly clearing. "The Five Boroughs must have justice. I must have justice. Let's do what we came here to do. I'll have word sent to all who would hear me to gather and listen to what you say. I will support any measure you propose, provided it brings me closer to vengeance. Is that what you can offer?"

"Vengeance?" asked Edmund, finding her sudden vigour unsettling. "I can," he nodded. "Justice, that is. We'll bring Eadric and my father to justice."

"Vengeance…justice…whatever…just tell me you'll kill Eadric." She still had that look. There was a darkness to it. It didn't suit her.

"Eadric will die," said Edmund, deep and low. "It's him or me. I intend for it to be him."

"You mean that? You won't just come to some compromise or agreement with him?"

"What agreement can possibly be reached between us?" he said, a little breathless that she could even ask him such a thing. "He killed my friends…he tried to kill you and all your family. There is no greater fiend in all of England. I WILL have his head."

Ealdgyth smiled, a subtle motion, but it was there. "Then consider the Five Boroughs yours," she said.

****

Edmund kept Ealdgyth's words in mind over the next few days. He was busy, very busy, ordering the summoning of every thegn now answering to Ealdgyth to attend him here for a most important gathering. He also took the time to send a few of Wulfnoth's men back down south with orders for Ulfcytel to bring the army up to meet him. He wanted his supporters here. He needed them. An impression had to be made, and having his army march in, fearsome and ready, would do it.

The local thegns did not take long to arrive. They wandered into town, often atop splendid steeds, accompanied by various retainers and bodyguards that naturally had to be housed and catered for. Edmund had taken over Wystan's inn, using it as living quarters for both himself and Ealdgyth. Wystan himself wasn't in a position to object. He'd not told them anything useful in captivity, although he had confessed his crimes in quite some detail, like he was expecting clemency. Edmund hadn't been in the mood for that. He'd dragged him to the market square and beheaded him himself in front of anyone who cared to look. Let that send a message, he thought, to any others who would dare stoop so low.

He'd then gathered the thegns to where they now stood, in the inn, with the hearth thankfully lit to dispel autumn's mounting damp. There were quite a few of them, and some faces were known to him, as they'd attended Sigeferth back when Edmund and Æthelstan had fought one another for their entertainment. A great many had also later mustered their fyrds to assist them with their attack on Thorkell the Tall at Bernecestre. They'd seen Edmund fight. They'd respected him then. He hoped they'd respect him now.

Edmund stood before them, the heat from the blazing hearth behind him warming his back. He'd made sure to clean himself up for this, allowing Ealdgyth to trim his beard and cut his hair. She'd passed him her mirror after, and he'd marvelled at the job she'd done. He looked civilised, like a man at court, but not too refined, his beard still possessing that wedge-like quality he'd always been eager to cultivate. His armour too had been cleaned, the dirt and congealed blood washed away so all that was left was shimmering metal. He liked the way it glimmered whenever it caught the light, the effect making him look like he was made of silvered scales. It was important they see him for what he was. A warrior. A defender of the Faith. A King of England.

If he were indeed projecting such an image, nobody would have been able to tell from the reaction of the thegns. They looked impatient, dissatisfied, like each had been stirred from slumber before daybreak without explanation. Edmund had a feeling he'd have to really make an impact with his words if he were to win them over. He had Wulfnoth, Ealdgyth and also Ælfweard at his back, these three combined conveying both authority and martial prowess, but nobody here looked likely to be swayed by anything other than a herculean effort. He'd start with something simple. He'd start with humility.

"I want to thank you all for attending us at such short notice," said Edmund, hoping to look each man in the eye as he spoke. "I understand you all lead busy lives, and you all certainly have difficulties of your own, despite the recent defeat of the Danish usurper. And so I am most honoured to have you as guests."

"Do you want to make yourself king?"

Edmund was startled by the question. It had come from the thegns, but he couldn't tell who had spoken. Then a man stepped forward, long in beard and years both, his face like a battered shield with a red nose for a boss. Edmund knew this man. He'd fought alongside them at Bernecestre. Alston was his name. He wasn't a fan of wasting time.

"You're as direct as I remember, Alston," said Edmund, a ripple of laughter spreading throughout his audience. "And to answer your question…yes, I will be king. My father gave me his word it would be so. He promised something else, also. That he wouldn't harm your lords, Sigeferth and Morcar. He broke his promise, as you know. I say we deserve better."

"And you are to give us better?" pressed Alston. "On the condition that we overthrow your father and seat you in his place?"

The whole room stirred, those present sounding quite taken aback at such a dramatic proposal. "A costly enterprise, no doubt," nodded Edmund. "Yet I ask you, all of you…just how many men do you think were unlawfully killed during my father's reign? Sigeferth was not the first. And if we do nothing, he won't be the last."

"So this is a rebellion?" asked a red-bearded man Edmund didn't know. "You would have us declare you king and wage war against your father?"

"I would have you do what's best," said Edmund. "I would have you do what is just. Was the murder of your Lord Sigeferth for the best? Was it just? Can any of you good men here tell me it was a one-off, either? That my father hasn't done anything like this before and isn't likely to do it again?"

The room descended into murmuring, each thegn looking like they were in partial agreement yet wouldn't do Edmund the service of openly admitting it. Ealdgyth stepped forward to stand at his side. She'd prepared for the occasion just as Edmund, and she was quite a sight as a result. Her cyrtel was long, very long, extending out behind her heels to partially trail across the floorboards. It was black, as was the veil upon her head, all of it done to signify her grief and newfound status as a widow. Her eyes, however, hadn't lost that spark they'd gained just the other day. She had words she would share, ones of depth and importance.

"I have given Edmund my allegiance," she stated simply, speaking over the continued mutterings. "And he is the one who had my husband's confidence. He is the one who saved me from the predations of Eadric and Æthelred. Without him, I would not be here. I will honour him as my king."

"That's all well and good," said Alston, his head bowing an inch or two towards Ealdgyth. "But what is being discussed here is treason. Many of us have the respect and friendship of Archbishop Wulfstan...many of us supported his decision to have Æthelred return from exile. To turn against him now, to turn against God's king..."

"He is NOT God's king!" said Ealdgyth, the mettle in her voice drawing a few gasps from the crowd. "A Christian king is to be good and generous and truthful with his subjects...they certainly don't make promises of forgiveness only to commit base murder when it suits them. Æthelred has failed this land, failed its people, time and again. You know it! I know it! Let us not be so foolish as to pretend otherwise!"

"What you are saying IS treason!"

Edmund scanned the crowd, unable to discern who had spoken. They revealed themselves a few seconds later, the others parting to let him pass. He stood at the head of the throng, eyeing Edmund and Ealdgyth, his face strangely angular, like his features had been somehow sharpened by his own hand. Even his beard was pointed, the tip extending slightly forward and down, suggesting he'd applied wax or oil to make it so. It was the eyes, though, that gave Edmund pause. There was a fire to them. Of the same kind he'd seen in Ealdgyth.

"I would ask you to be careful with your words," said Edmund, feeling he had to assert his authority over this man for there to be any chance of gaining his respect. "I do not take this action lightly, and it breaks my heart to have to commit to it. I love my father, let no man doubt it, but I cannot allow him to escape justice. Not after Sigeferth. Not after Morcar."

"It's still treason," muttered the thegn with the pointed beard. "Why do you come here, Edmund, to demand we follow you in this? What do the Five Boroughs stand to gain through war with the crown? And it WILL be war, be sure of it."

"I will remind you, my lord, that I hold authority here," said Ealdgyth, her hands upon her hips. "If I give Edmund my confidence, that means I expect all of you to follow suit. When you see me, you see Sigeferth. You see my husband. Now honour Edmund as my husband would have."

Pointy beard laughed, as did those next to him. It spread around the room, even the gruff Alston soon succumbing. Edmund could not believe it. They were laughing at Ealdgyth. They were laughing at the widow of their own rightful lord. Such disrespect would not stand.

"What is your name?" asked Edmund, his question directed at the still guffawing pointy.

"I am Sigebryht," he replied, having stilled himself enough to respond, "and I must say, Edmund, that coming here with nought but a widow's authority to back you up wasn't the best idea. Just what did you expect? That we'd all declare you king because a grieving woman demanded it?"

Edmund found himself moving, his legs compelling him forward on a direct course for Sigebryht. To his credit, the man held his ground, and he remained quite calm even as Edmund grabbed him by the scruff of his cloak to bellow into his face.

"You would dare disrespect the lady Ealdgyth?! At a time like this, just days after her children were murdered and weeks after her husband was taken from her?! You would do all of this and still call yourself a man?!"

The thegns immediately adjacent to this exchange had stepped back, wary and unnerved by the sudden escalation. Sigebryht still wasn't flustered, and his voice was calm when he formed words, his eyes never diverting from Edmund's.

"I remember you, and your brother," he said quietly. "And I remember how you led us all into battle against Thorkell. I respect you for it…yet this is too much, Edmund. Many of us fell at Bernecestre, fighting the heathen, as was right. Many of us will fall if we follow you…except this time, we'll be fighting Englishmen. That's an entirely different scenario. One I would certainly not look to rush into."

Others agreed, a sequence of affirmations and nodding heads greeting his words. Edmund let Sigebryht go, but he didn't step away. He was still angry at what had been said, and Sigebryht's otherwise valid concern about fighting Englishmen would not placate him. He'd given great offence. It was only right that he understand that.

"If you were at Bernecestre, you'd remember Sigeferth," Edmund began. "You'd remember how he fought with us, to the last, even as we were pushed back into that accursed valley. Did he not gain your respect that day? Did you think so little of the man you'd think it proper to disrespect his wife?"

"Not at all," said Sigebryht, still annoyingly calm. "I respected Ealdgyth as his wife, just as I respect her now as a widow. But she is a woman, and I will not have me and mine pushed into outright treason just so she can get even with the king! That's the truth, Edmund, and nothing you can do will change that!"

His words provoked another outburst of agreement, some of it so enthusiastic it was like the thegns thought Sigebryht the true authority here. Edmund turned away and headed back over to the hearth, resuming his place next to Ealdgyth. Ælfweard was stood by the flames, apparently unwilling to speak since he was a stranger here. Wulfnoth lingered close by, silent and deadly, but there was nothing a man such as he could contribute to this situation. Words were not working, but violence would only seal their fate entirely. If the thegns would not listen to Ealdgyth, then Edmund was really just a rootless aetheling with no real say in anything. The thought made him yet angrier. He'd have them know it.

"So this is it then?!" he asked, his ire forcing everyone back into silence. "You'd continue to live under an unjust king...a king who murdered your own lord...just because you were too afraid of the consequences of defiance?"

"No, Edmund," said Alston. "We refuse to follow an errant aetheling who, whilst brave, has no real stake in these lands. You hold no authority here, and the nearest you've come to it..." he gestured towards Ealdgyth, "...well, what can we say? She's grieving. Understandably, and I would have justice for her. But I will not find myself hip-deep in English blood for the sake of a widow's vengeance. You are not my lord, Edmund. If you were, it would be different, but you are not! You cannot compel us, and we won't be intimidated!"

The room erupted into cheers. The thegns were joyous, reacting like Alston had just given some epic speech in defiance of a bloodthirsty tyrant. That was the last thing Edmund was. So much of this seemed to be because Ealdgyth was a woman. They didn't trust her, and as much as Edmund would hate to admit it, he could somewhat understand their position. She was grieving. Justifiably so. But was that enough cause to start a war? Would anyone really commit to what they were asking just for the sake of one woman's revenge?

"Hold a moment, all of you," said Ælfweard, moving up from behind Edmund to stand at his left. He'd been silent this entire time, but now he'd decided to speak, looking like he'd been angered by the thegns and had finally found the courage to express it.

"This behaviour of yours is shameful," he said, his audience quietening down, although his words had already drawn a few scowls. "My name is Ælfweard, and not so long ago, I was reeve of the once great city of Canterburie. You'll all have heard what happened there, and yes, it was as bad as they say. It became a charnel house, a hell, an earthly one, and King Æthelred did NOTHING! He sent not one warrior, gave us not one coin, and when all was done and the city burned, all he could do was send his pet, Eadric of Mierċe, to pay the Danes to give up our dearly missed Archbishop Ælfheah. But that was all! He didn't care about the rest of us! He didn't care about the thousands of others who'd died!"

"Is there a point to this?" shouted some thegn, another Edmund wasn't sure he recognised. Others nodded and sounded off in support. Ælfweard's cheeks flushed a little. He was still angry.

"The point is, the king you're so eager to support let the Holy City burn!" he snapped, spitting his words like they were sharpened shards he hoped would cause harm. "The Ealdorman Ulfcytel...Alaric..." Ælfweard turned and gestured to Wulfnoth, his voice softening, "...my friend and rescuer here, Wulfnoth...they came to help us! And they, at least those of them still alive, now stand with Edmund. Does that not say something to you? Does that not tell you of the kind of men Edmund has backing him? Does it not tell you of the kind of man he is? Does that not tell you of the kind of king he might yet be?"

Edmund had to hand it to Ælfweard. He'd spoken from the heart, a heart he'd recently said was soft and sensitive, although from his display here it was certainly far from weak. The thegns were moved also, but not necessarily in a good way. They looked shaken, but resentful, as though they'd taken Ælfweard's admonishment as an injustice they'd prefer to have never heard. They gave voice to that impression, saying that Canterburie's unfortunate fate had nothing to do with them and shouldn't be used to push them into supporting treason. Ælfweard's cheeks flushed yet again, his anger unspent, but Edmund bid him step back. He could see how this was going. These men would not listen to them, and little could be done to change that.

"I would have you leave us," said Edmund, his voice again prompting silence. "You have disappointed me. I would have thought you'd be eager to do right by your Lord Sigeferth…to do right by England…but I can see none of you hold such a thing close to heart. Leave me now to think on what must be done."

They all shifted on their feet, uneasy over his attempt to shame them. "Then we shall leave," said Sigebryht lightly. "Yet just remember, Edmund…many of us followed you and your brother into war with great eagerness because it was just. Coming here to demand we follow you again, but for revenge…and getting this stranger to yell at us about Canterburie…I'd say think on your position. If you were my lord, I'd follow you anywhere. I'd have to. Honour would demand it. But you are not. And so I will look to the best interests of my people."

Sigebryht turned on his heels with that final word and began moving through the crowd, intent on reaching the exit as speedily as he could. Most of the others gradually began to follow him, some lingering a little, awkward and perhaps ashamed to be just walking out, but they too eventually left.

A few stayed, waiting for the others to leave, and approached Edmund, declaring their loyalty to both he and Ealdgyth and whatever course of action they thought best. Edmund thanked them sincerely, but he had to ask why they'd not spoken up beforehand to persuade their peers. Their answer was fairly predictable, all of them agreeing that the other thegns would not suffer to be led by a woman and would not be swayed otherwise unless something changed. Edmund nodded, still sad at what he'd witnessed, and bid them leave, although he thanked them again for their loyalty. The door slammed shut as the last thegn departed, and the inn was again plunged into silence, the crackling fire the only thing to disturb it.

"I honestly did not expect that," said Wulfnoth. "I usually like to think I'm good at politics and the like, but…that was unusual. I'd have thought they'd all be up for settling scores, especially after the…"

His voice trailed off, yet they all knew what he'd meant. The wrongs that had been committed against them were extreme, and nothing was more extreme than burning children in their own homes. Edmund had hoped the locals would be baying for Eadric's blood after that, but it was not so. They cared, at least on some level, but it wasn't enough to win their allegiance, an allegiance few of them felt was even owed to Ealdgyth. That was troubling, and for the moment, Edmund had no idea how to proceed.

"I feel like I should apologise," said Ealdgyth, both Edmund and Wulfnoth frowning at her statement. "I just assumed they would follow me, obey me…it seemed right that they would. They were always so devoted to Sigeferth. Would that I could inspire the same devotion."

"This has little to do with you," said Edmund, trying to spare her feelings. "They were right in what they said…I am an errant aetheling, with no roots in these lands. What I asked of them was considerable. I should have thought harder on it."

"You have my support," said Ealdgyth, suddenly severe, "and that should have been enough for them. It would have been, had I been Sigeferth, or if he'd had a male heir to take his place, rather than a grieving widow. The thegns want to see strength, that's the real issue here. And I have none."

"Was it my fault?" asked Ælfweard suddenly, having retreated to lurk by the hearth to stare into the flames. "Did I go too far? Was it a bad idea to bring up Canterburie?"

"No!" said precisely everyone, all shaking their heads as one. Ælfweard looked back at them from the hearth and smiled, amused and heartened by their reaction. "I thought we needed a dose of reality," he said. "The reality of how we live, the reality of what the Danes did to us under Æthelred."

"Hold that thought," said Wulfnoth, raising a single finger in emphasis. He wandered over to the bar, obtaining four flagons of something before returning. He passed one to Edmund, then Ealdgyth and Ælfweard. He eventually drank deep of his own, acting as if he were a man who'd not had a drink in some considerable time. Edmund sipped his in turn, noting the slightly stale aroma of crushed berries and aged honey. It was good enough. Mead was mead, he thought, and after the day he'd had, he felt like he was entitled to a tipple.

"You speak of facing realities," said Wulfnoth finally, "and strength," he added, nodding towards Ealdgyth. "These are both points well made. We don't have our army with us, but we will soon, and led by the fearsome Ulfcytel, no less. That's bound to make an impression on the thegns here. We'll have strength. Real strength."

"You think they'll just change their mind?" asked Edmund, unsure. "That they'll take back everything they said because Ulfcytel and a couple of thousand men turn up?"

"With that magic banner of yours, too," said Wulfnoth. "Don't knock it," he said, extending a hand like he thought Edmund would object. "Your discovery of the incorrupt banner has been taken as a miracle, at least by the men. When others see it and hear the story behind it, then it will make a difference. Trust me."

"I'm not so sure," said Edmund, taking another sip of mead. "I think it's all about power with these men, power and practicalities. The retrieval of my father's banner from Bernecestre will be taken as just a fable. They won't think it's incorrupt. They'll dismiss it as hearsay."

"What are you both talking about?" asked Ealdgyth, Ælfweard nodding in support of her question. "You mean to say you witnessed some kind of miracle? That this banner of yours is special? How?"

"It's complicated," sighed Edmund, "and I don't think I even understand it myself. I've not told anyone this, but…something strange happened in Lundenburg. I had a conversation with a man in St Mildred's church who…"

"Yes?" asked Wulfnoth, wanting him to continue.

"He wasn't quite a man, or he wasn't who he seemed," said Edmund. "I can't explain it. I thought him a priest. He gave me advice. I went to return to thank him before we left, only for another priest to be in the church with no knowledge of who this man was. I then…"

He fell silent again, wondering if he would lose respect by just declaring that he believed he'd encountered an apparition of Saint Edmund. "I just had an inkling, is all," he finally said, "an inkling that told me I needed to get to Bernecestre. That my father's banner would be there. That it would help."

Wulfnoth was staring at him, his eyes hooded. "Are you quite sure you don't want to get anything else off your chest?" he asked, his voice halfway between tenderness and suspicion. The man knew he wasn't telling the whole truth. Wulfnoth had a way with such things, but Edmund wasn't going to let on about his conversation with the saint, nor the premonition, the drive, the instinct that had come later that told him he simply HAD to find the dragon banner at Bernecestre. They might think him insane or possessed, and he didn't need the added stress right now. They were the only allies he had, presently. He'd be wise to keep them as such.

Edmund shook his head, deciding to hold his tongue for the time being. They ate, preparing a meal in the tiny kitchen sequestered off from the inn's store room. Ælfwynn joined them after they'd dragged a table back into position by the fire, the girl looking like she was a touch more alive now she'd had some time to process her harrowing ordeal. Edmund smiled at her whilst they sat with their stew, the warmth from the hearth a welcome luxury. She smiled back. Ealdgyth saw it and was glad. Edmund was glad too.

Night came on, and Edmund retired upstairs, taking a single room that was at least reasonably free of the stale ale stench that pervaded the inn elsewhere. Ealdgyth opted for a larger room containing an additional cot for the sake of Ælfwynn, whereas Ælfweard bedded down by the embers of their fire, saying he'd gotten used to sleeping by campfires and didn't want to be without one.

Wulfnoth, typically, headed off outside, intent on organising night patrols across town. He didn't trust the thegns, and he'd been eager to secure the town ever since they'd arrived in case anyone or anything tried to make trouble. Edmund couldn't blame him for that, but he insisted he work with Ælfnoð and the rest of the garrison as much as he could. The locals were good people, for the most part, and it wouldn't be fair to them to have Wulfnoth, an outsider, turn up and start assuming he knew best when it came to their safety. A little cooperation was in order.

Edmund couldn't sleep. He'd have normally been annoyed at that, but tonight it was different, as being wide awake allowed him to hear something, soft and yet audible. Whoever was outside was trying to be quiet, but they'd obviously been counting on everyone being asleep at this late hour, which simply wasn't the case with Edmund and his troubled mind. He sat up and slid out of bed, creeping over to his door, sword in hand, to peer through the cracks. It was all darkness outside. Then he heard the noise again, like a footstep, followed by the clicking, discordant sound of a door handle being tugged at. Somebody was outside Ealdgyth's room. Edmund had been foolish not to have posted a guard. He'd make up for that mistake right now.

He heaved his door open and burst into the corridor, roaring a challenge as he went. A light flashed up ahead, faint and flickering, the candle revealing a hooded and cloaked figure, too tall to be Wulfnoth and certainly too broad to be Ealdgyth. Edmund could see the shutters overlooking the landing had been forced, allowing this intruder to climb on through without alerting anyone outside. He wasn't sure how he'd been able to do that without Edmund hearing him before he made entry, but it was all moot now. He'd have answers from this man. And for his sake, they had best be edifying.

The intruder wasn't so obliging. He dropped his candle and went to flee, heading for the open shutters and the sliver of moonlight protruding through them. Edmund gave chase, but the man was fast, outpacing him easily and making a leap for the window. Fortunately, he'd misjudged the distance in the dark and fell short, managing to wedge himself between the shutters as they suddenly blew inward. He reacted quickly, kicking them open and trying to simply climb through. It was too late. Edmund was already upon him.

He began hauling the intruder backwards, his hand clutching tightly at the tail end of his cloak. He struggled, and Edmund soon saw the glint of the seax. He didn't fancy dying here, not now. He took action. The scream was loud, the pitch and intensity making Edmund's ears ache. The assassin's hand flopped to the floor, the seax clattering with it, Edmund's own blade once again red with blood. Edmund then bashed him in the face with the hilt, hoping to stun him and also dissuade him of any foolish notions like attempting to kill him. He fell, and Edmund reached out and flicked his hood back, revealing a face both surprising and familiar.

Red hair, with a matching beard, and cold eyes. This was one of the thegns who'd argued with Edmund just earlier. And from his presence and antics here tonight, he'd been hoping to kill Ealdgyth.

Wulfnoth came running, vaulting up the stairs with two of his men and a freshly-woken Ælfweard, their swords at the ready. "What happened here?!" demanded Wulfnoth, confused at the sight before him.

"Why don't you tell us?" said Edmund, his eyes still on the would-be-assassin. "Go on," he persisted, "tell us why you sneaked in here and wanted to get at Ealdgyth. Answer me!"

A door opened further down the landing, and Ealdgyth appeared, bleary-eyed from sleep. "What's happened?" she asked, a nervous-looking Ælfwynn peering out from behind her voluminous nightgown. "Who is this…" She paused. She'd recognised him. This was about to get interesting.

"Why, Harold?!" she wailed, looking down upon the injured thegn. "Why would you do this? You wanted to take our lives? For what reason?"

"I'll not say anything," said Harold, his expression pained and his bloody stump tucked into his rapidly reddening cloak. "I'll not say a word, you'll get nothing out of me, not a…"

"You're with Eadric, aren't you?" asked Edmund knowingly. "How many of the other thegns have signed on with him? How many of the others want Ealdgyth dead?"

"Not a word, not a word," repeated Harold, breathing in and out rapidly. "Not a word, not a word, not a…"

Edmund kicked him, his foot intentionally aimed at Harold's stump. "Tell me, you bloody bastard!" he snarled, ignoring the agonised wailings now assailing his ears. "Tell me why you wish her dead! Answer!"

Harold might have looked like he was on his way out, but he still moved fast, his single remaining hand procuring a knife from somewhere within his cloak. He twisted around towards Ealdgyth, his arm arching back like he intended to throw the blade. Edmund reacted as his instincts demanded, and Harold died with a sword through his throat, his eyebrows raised in agonised surprise. The knife clattered to the ground, and all was then quiet, save for the sound of Ælfwynn's sobbing. The poor girl had again seen it all. This couldn't go on. They had to think of a way to stop these assassination attempts, and fast.

Wulfnoth bent low, rifling through Harold's clothing in an effort to find anything of interest. He stood up, looking nonplussed, his hands empty after his fruitless search. "Can you think of any reason why he might mean you harm?" Wulfnoth asked Ealdgyth.

"No," she said, kneeling to try and calm the still tearful Ælfwynn. "I never thought him a good man, but I also never thought he'd want me dead. I don't have answers."

"I must apologise," Wulfnoth said, to both Ealdgyth and Edmund. "I placed men on watch at the front entrance, of course…but this rat still got through. It's not good enough."

"He scaled the wall and came through the shutters, somehow," said Edmund, not wanting Wulfnoth to blame himself. "There was no way we could have known a man capable of climbing like some kind of spider would come for us. I thought the danger had passed once I'd executed Wystan."

Wulfnoth shook his head, the motion slight but rapid. "Wystan was Eadric's man, no doubt," he said. "He fit the profile; an innkeeper who would hear all kinds of things…but a thegn? Usually, such men are harder for a dog like Eadric to manipulate, especially so far outside of his own sphere of influence."

"Then perhaps there's another reason why this Harold acted?" Edmund wasn't sure what that could be, but he wanted to keep Wulfnoth engaged. He had a fine mind for this sort of thing, and if he couldn't work it out, then no one could.

"You may be right," nodded Wulfnoth, "but my instincts are telling me we should prioritise our safety. Snotingeham may not be the best place for us to wait for Ulfcytel. If the local thegns are murderous rather than merely disobedient…"

"I have a solution," said Ealdgyth, having by this point convinced her tearful daughter to step back into their room and shut the door. She then came towards them and stopped, a look of rare contempt on her face as she eyed the dead Harold. She was growing cold, thought Edmund. All the death, all the loss…it was hardening her. It wasn't a good thing.

"And your solution?" asked Wulfnoth, sounding sceptical.

"It's one thing to kill me," Ealdgyth announced, looking both men in the face, "but another to kill a member of the royal family. I have my husband's property, yes, but as recent events have shown…nobody will obey me just for that, and me and my daughters can apparently be murdered on a whim. I would have that change."

"How?" asked Edmund, wondering if she really had a point or was just thinking aloud to calm her nerves.

"Do you care about me and Ælfwynn?" she asked, a tremor of grief in her voice.

"Of course," nodded Edmund, reaching out to caress her shoulder. "You're all I have left of Sigeferth. Never doubt you have a place in my heart."

"Then marry me," she said simply. "You want Sigeferth's lands and wealth? You'll have them for your own, with all the authority that comes with it. But more importantly, Edmund…you'll be saving me and my Ælfwynn. Because after tonight, I don't think this is going to stop. Eadric…or whoever else wants me dead, will keep going. But they'll think twice about hurting us if you make us royal. If you take us into your family. If you make me your wife."

XXXXII

The days and nights both seemed to blur into one. He was trapped, hemmed in and confined by bare stone walls and a locked, imposing door fashioned from solid, unyielding oak. It wasn't much to look at, and his prayers for deliverance and the safety of his king had gone unanswered. Hereward knew he was perhaps being unfair on that last point. He had no means to know how Æthelred was faring. He hoped God was watching over him, as would only be right, but he somehow doubted it. The king had always been a troubled man. Hereward could attest to that. That was just yet another reason why he had to escape. Æthelred needed good men at his side, and despite his many sins and failings, Hereward considered himself one of those.

"So they've all gone then?" asked Hereward, directing his inquiry towards the man he knew was lingering outside the door. He himself was sat on the hard ground, his back pressed against the wall and his knees hugged tightly to his chest. It was the most comfortable position possible in his situation, which wasn't saying much. All the same, he'd endure.

"Oh yes, they have, 'tis true," came the reply, old Bertram sounding about as animated as he usually did. Being tasked with guarding these cells had him bored silly. No wonder he wanted to talk so much. Hereward was the only company he had.

"So Edmund will be marching to overthrow the king?"

"I don't know about that," said Bertram, still sounding flat. "Something big is afoot, for sure, bigger than what first brought us here. Bigger than what caused me to join up with Edmund to begin with."

"Why did you join with Edmund?" Hereward could guess the answer. He smiled when Bertram proved him correct.

"To fight back," he said. "To kill Danes. They killed my brother, and my father, and my sister. I owed them a proper hiding after that. Gave them one, too, at Gainesburg. I told you about that, right?"

"You did," nodded Hereward, still smiling. Bertram was very proud of how he'd fought there, and from what Hereward had heard, it was no wonder. It had been a great victory. And the Danes had indeed needed a "proper hiding". Of that, there could be no doubt.

"So if you want to know what I think," continued Bertram, "I reckon Edmund wants Ulfcytel and the army with him for something major. That's the only reason I can think of for the ealdorman to just march out of here like that."

"He left a garrison, though, surely?" Hereward expected he had. Porteceaster was a serious win for Edmund, and Ulfcytel would be a fool to have taken all of his men and left it to whoever might happen to come along. And Ulfcytel was no fool.

Bertram coughed and then sneezed, sounding like he'd somehow managed to combine the two actions at once. "'Scuse me...I've got a bit of a sniffle from being down here so much...but to answer your question...no, there's still a garrison, otherwise I wouldn't be here talking to you, would I?"

"There's a logic to what you say," nodded Hereward. "And the lady, Æva?" he asked, "does she travel with the ealdorman and his army?"

Hereward didn't really know Æva, but he'd been impressed with what he'd seen of her. She'd been kind to him, raising her voice in his defence when that malevolent Wulfnoth had seen fit to harm him. She was an honourable woman, and apparently one who held some kind of authority here. He wished he'd had the good fortune to meet such a lass, back when he was young.

"She's gone," said Bertram. "Along with that lad of hers, the one who looks like a Dane."

"Who?"

"Æva's lad looks like a Dane," repeated Bertram. "She acts like nobody else can see it, or perhaps wants to act like nobody can, but we do. It's obvious. It's unfortunate. Nothing good can come from such stock."

"What do you mean?" asked Hereward.

"Put it this way…poor Æva isn't the first English girl to have had a Dane force himself on her. There's little blond twerps bawling all across the land because of things like that. And nothing good ever comes of it. Rotten seed gives rise to rotten fruit, if you know what I mean."

"I wouldn't let Ulfcytel hear you talking like that."

"What do you mean?"

Hereward chuckled to himself, wondering why Bertram hadn't put two and two together. "Do you not know?" he asked. "Ulfcytel is from Eastengle. It was settled by Danes, in part, after they'd taken it from Saint Edmund. How Saxon do you think the name "Ulfcytel" sounds anyway? The man has Danish ancestry."

"No?! Really?" Bertram sounded genuinely surprised.

"I think it's very likely," said Hereward. "I mean, how many people have you met previously with such a name?"

"A couple of lads, actually."

"Were they from Eastengle?"

Bertram fell silent, perhaps thinking it over. Then he laughed, the sound good-natured. "Alright then," he said, still chuckling. "I suppose maybe it doesn't matter anyway. The Eastenglians are a good and Christian people now. That's what matters, right?"

"I'm glad you think so," said Hereward, wondering now as to Æva's child and whether Bertram was right in what he'd said about him. If it were true and he had indeed been conceived by force, then it was a terrible thing, yet the lad himself wasn't at fault. He was a boy, like any other, regardless of the crimes of his father. It would be monstrously unjust for anyone to think otherwise.

"So, are you going to let me out?" Hereward was smiling again, knowing Bertram appreciated his sense of humour.

"Ah yes," said Bertram. "Just give me a couple of decades to find the key, and we'll have you out and chasing after King Edmund in no time, aye?"

Hereward laughed, but there was a note of bitterness in it. He felt on some level that he could understand what Edmund was doing, especially after the murder of Morcar and Sigeferth, yet all the same he could not support it. The son should not turn on the father, especially in times as unpredictable as these. Æthelred was still king, and Hereward would serve him until death. It was just a shame his loyalty had landed him in gaol.

He looked about his cell again, noting how the ambient light had diminished to the point night couldn't be far off. "They've gone and forgotten to bring me my dinner again," said Bertram suddenly, confirming Hereward's suspicions in regard to the time. "If I go get myself some grub, do you promise not to go wandering whilst I'm gone?"

"You'll bring me back something?" asked Hereward hopefully.

"What would you like, my lord?" laughed Bertram. "Roast pork with parsnips? Salted crab cakes? How about some fresh salmon and…"

"Yes to all of that," said Hereward.

"Or a punch in the face?"

"Ulfcytel already gave me one of those."

"So you told me," said Bertram, somewhat mournfully. "It's a sorry affair, you having to be locked up. King Edmund needs every good man he can get…and you seem to me to be a good man."

"I'm glad you think so," said Hereward, "but Edmund is not king. As I have said."

"That you have, and for the sake of avoiding an old argument, I'll be going to get some food. Don't go anywhere whilst I'm gone and…"

"And what?"

"I'll bring you back a barley cake. I think we have some. I'll be sure to make sure it's buttered so the thing doesn't just dry up in your mouth like they usually do."

"Thank you," said Hereward, sincerely touched by Bertram's decency. He waited whilst he wandered off, listening to his footsteps grow fainter and fainter until there was nothing but silence. Now was the time. Hereward hadn't wanted it to come to this, but he wasn't sure if he'd get a better chance. He'd take this opportunity for what it was.

It wasn't easy. Hereward hated throwing up, as it reminded him of a particularly bad illness he'd had when he was young where he seemed to do little else. Nevertheless, he plucked up the courage to jam his fingers down his throat, his face contorting with displeasure. Nothing came up. All he'd done was make himself feel uncomfortable. He tried again. Still nothing, although he now had a hand covered in mucus, which wasn't ideal. He tried a third time. That was better, but not enough. A fourth attempt did it, the fingers down his throat prompting him to unleash the contents of his stomach all over his chin and chest. It stank, and he felt quite disgusted with himself for doing it, but it was necessary. He lay down on the floor and closed his eyes. Bertram would hopefully be back soon.

As luck would have it, he was. Footsteps sounded on the stairs, faint and echoing, and before long Bertram could be heard outside, chewing and slurping on something like he were half-starved. He called to Hereward, but there'd be no reply, unfortunately, as Hereward was busy pretending to be unconscious. Bertram called out again, reminding him he'd returned with his barley cake. That was a tough thing to ignore, but Hereward still managed it. Bertram began fiddling with the lock of the cell door. He was coming in to check on him. It wouldn't be long now. Hereward was ready.

"What the bloody hell?!" said Bertram, his voice as alarmed as anyone would expect given the sight that greeted him. Hereward was lying down on his back, his eyes closed, right on the hard, cold floor of the cell. He was, of course, covered in his own vomit, which made Bertram almost gag himself, such was the odour. He nudged Hereward's side with his boot, asking him what he was playing at. Hereward said nothing. He needed him to get closer. Then he'd strike.

Bertram eventually did what was needed. He knelt down, hauling Hereward up into a sitting position against the wall. He splashed some water in his face, the action thankfully washing some of the sick out of his beard. Hereward opened his eyes, speaking words he sincerely meant, despite what he was about to do.

"I'm so sorry, Bertram. I really am."

Bertram let go of the waterskin as Hereward's fist ploughed into the side of his jaw. He took the punch well, barely a grunt escaping his lips, so Hereward hit him again on the opposite side. He fell backwards, splaying out flat in the cell doorway. Hereward got up and straddled his chest, gifting him with a third punch when he made a move to sit up. Then he was still. Bleeding, but still. Hereward leaned in, placing his ear close to Bertram's mouth. He was breathing just fine. That was a relief. Hereward would have hated to have killed him. The sight of the barley cake he'd brought, squashed and discarded on the floor, was mournful enough. It was a cold deed that had been done here. Hereward hoped to one day somehow earn his forgiveness.

He nonetheless stripped Bertram of his clothes, removing his helm – a rather flimsy, open-faced thing made of tarnished iron – as well as his long ring mail shirt, breecs, and distinctly worn, grubby boots. Hereward put them all on, thankful to be looking somewhat like a warrior again, finding the weight of the mail reassuringly heavy. The boots were a bit tight, for Bertram was a smaller man than Hereward, but he couldn't complain too much on that score. Bertram had also carried a short, stout axe designed for close-quarter combat, in addition to a quite decent-looking seax tucked away in a leather scabbard inside his left boot. Hereward took the latter. He'd never liked axes, thinking them imprecise and brutish. The seax, however, was a weapon he could respect.

He used the last of Bertram's water to properly wash his face, thinking quite logically that walking around stinking of vomit would only draw attention. He stepped out and shut the cell door when finished, although he didn't lock it, and he left the key he'd found in Bertram's breecs right outside. Beating a man unconscious was no trivial matter, and Hereward didn't want anything to get in the way of Bertram receiving aid. It made his escape effort a lot riskier since Bertram could wake up and alert the others, but he still felt it was the right thing to do. Hereward couldn't bear the thought of Bertram just expiring in a locked cell with no one able to help him. He'd make sure that scenario didn't come to pass.

The next part was easier than he'd feared. The gaol was small, consisting of a half dozen cells all aligned in a single row leading to some stairs heading upward into the main barracks. Hereward made it up there just fine, and nobody made any issue of his appearance in the dining hall, so fixated were they on their evening meal. Hereward took the time to help himself to another barley cake, feeling quite sad with the doing of it. If Bertram had been a sadistic monster like Wulfnoth, all this would have been a lot easier. Instead, he'd been kind and gentle, appearing to almost respect Hereward's decision to remain loyal to King Æthelred, despite ultimately disagreeing with it. In any other time, they'd have been friends. Necessity, unfortunately, had made it otherwise.

Hereward ducked outside, the shock of the evening chill quite unpleasant after his time in the well-heated barracks. He needed a cloak, a nice thick woollen one, but for the life of him he had no idea where to obtain such a thing, and he didn't fancy wandering back into the barracks and asking. He headed east, moving down towards the curtain wall and the small gatehouse he'd passed through when he'd first come here with Olaf. It was closed, and there were two unfriendly-looking chaps with spears standing watch. Hereward didn't fancy conversing with them, so he turned and headed north, following the length of the eastern ramparts and doing his utmost to remain within their shadow. It didn't amount to much, considering the sun had almost set entirely, but it made him feel safer. He hoped it didn't make him look too suspicious.

What he assumed to be the main gatehouse was a short distance from here. It was large, all rough-cut stone and forbidding archways, the burning metal braziers on either side lighting the whole thing up like it was still daytime. There were lots of men here, all of them armed and armoured, but most of them were up on the walls above and facing out into the coming night. Some seemed to be patrolling, wandering up and down the battlements with flaming torches held aloft, these same men sometimes coming down into the interior to converse a little with the guards on the gate. They were relaxed but capable. Hereward could always tell a veteran warrior from the untested. They had a certain air to them, and these men definitely had it. They were Dane killers, like all of Edmund's men. He'd best be careful.

He took a deep breath and approached the gate. Confidence was key, so Hereward's father had often said, and it had served him well in many instances throughout his life. He hoped escaping from an ancient Roman fortress would be no different. He made straight for the men standing guard, wandering past them and out through the open gate like he was completely at ease with himself and had every right to be doing what he was doing. His heart was hammering away, but the guards ignored him, although one nodded respectfully when he passed by. Hereward kept on, putting one foot in front of the other. He was almost beyond the walls now. Just a few more paces, and he'd be free.

He froze when someone called out from behind. He turned, seeing a single guard advancing hurriedly towards him. "You'll freeze to death out there, mate," he said, divesting himself of his cloak and wrapping it around Hereward's shoulders. "You going after Æbbe's lot, is that it?"

Hereward nodded in thanks, adjusting the rather grimy, well-travelled cloak so it fell properly across his back. He had absolutely no idea who Æbbe was, but he couldn't just say that as he'd blow his cover. He then realised he had an even chance of getting this right by either saying "yes" or "no", and answering in the affirmative had a better feel to it. He'd take his chances. It's not like he had any other option.

"Yes, I am," said Hereward, feeling bad about the lie.

"On your own?" asked the guard.

"Yes, I don't want to wait," said Hereward quickly. "Others are coming to join me, once they've finished eating."

"Ah, I see," replied the guard, like he was actually convinced. "Just be careful when you get to…wait…is that a barley cake in your hand?"

Hereward looked down, seeing that he was still holding the fresh barley cake he'd retrieved from the barracks. Why he'd forgotten to eat it was beyond him. He must have gotten distracted thinking about Bertram. Hereward said the only thing that seemed appropriate.

"It is…I meant to give it to Bertram. He's not feeling well. I was just getting him this cake from the barracks when I was called to go assist with Æbbe."

"Bertram? Older bloke? Likes to talk? Goes on about how he killed a Dane with his bare hands at Gainesburg?"

"That's him," nodded Hereward.

"I'll give it to him," said the guard pleasantly. "He's still doing his shift in the gaol? I can make my way over there once I'm finished here."

Hereward handed over the cake, thinking it rather odd that anyone would want the thing now it had been passed around between multiple different men. The guard smiled and wandered off, passing back through the shadows of the gatehouse to resume his position across from the flickering braziers. Hereward hurried on, escaping the fortress entirely to trudge east along a dirt and gravel road he hoped would lead him away from this place as rapidly as possible.

Porteceaster remained visible for some time, its great grey walls looming out of the night. Hereward couldn't relax with such a sight at his back. He ducked off the road, heading north through some woodland he hoped would conceal his movements. It was still cold, and there was a faint mist clinging to the forest floor, the stuff chilling him further. It wouldn't be long now. Bertram would either wake up and sound the alarm, or that guard would discover him whilst attempting to give him Hereward's cake. Both scenarios would lead to men looking for him. He had to hurry and make as much progress as he could before that happened.

Angry shouts sounded from behind him. The alarm had almost certainly been raised, meaning he'd likely soon be hearing from men on horseback. He lumbered onward through the misted pines, the ground wet and uneven, hoping the forest might make it harder for any mounted search parties to pursue him. He could hear hooves pounding the earth, still a distance off, and there were more shouts with it, but for the moment it didn't seem like anyone was in direct pursuit. If he kept on and avoided doing anything stupid, he could get out of this.

A light source was approaching from behind. Hereward turned his head, trying to discern exactly what was happening. He couldn't see much, but the light was there, far back where he'd first entered the wood. It was bobbing up and down, flickering unsteadily between the spindled trees, making him suspect it was a torch held by a man now entering the forest. They must be following his tracks. Hereward should have known something like this would happen. Edmund's men were too good for this to have gone otherwise.

Speed was his only recourse. He broke into a full sprint, smashing through fern and bramble alike. His armour and helm took the worst of it, but something soon cut him across the cheek, drawing blood and making him wince. He kept up the pace, charging through the woods like an enraged boar, his stamina still thankfully high despite his time in captivity. It wouldn't do much when it came to their ability to track him, since the trail he was leaving was more evident than ever, but it would give him time. That in itself was a precious commodity.

Sadly, his speed soon became a liability. Hereward had completely failed to spot the sudden drop ahead, and he flew off the edge of the precipice like a thrown rock, his legs still working frantically in mid-air. He hit the ground, or what seemed like the ground, a great splash of something saturating his entire lower half. He checked himself. His feet ached from the fall, but the stream he was in had softened the impact. The water was up just past his thighs and moving fast, heading off to the east to who knows where. Then he realised what a blessing this was. If he moved against the flow, the stream would take him west and then north, effectively erasing any trail he might leave and ensuring he was impossible to track. He could escape. God was smiling on him this night.

It was hard going. The current was strong and persistent, and it wasn't about to ease up now that Hereward had decided to work against it. The water was cold, and he soon started to lose any feeling in his feet, making it seem like he was walking on two solid stone blocks. He couldn't detect any sign of pursuit, which made him think Edmund's men had likely lost his trail back at the precipice. That would make sense, yet it also didn't mean he was safe. They'd have worked out what had happened and almost certainly come to the very sensible conclusion that he'd ended up in the water. He hoped they'd assume he'd decided to go with the current and head east. It was the logical thing to do, from their perspective. Hereward, however, liked being unpredictable.

His gamble paid off. He'd been struggling on for hours, the water as uncooperative as always, and yet there'd been no sign of anyone, at all, that might mean him harm. Dawn wasn't far off when he finally decided to leave the stream, the earthen banks around him having thankfully flattened out so he could extricate himself with ease. He sat down in a rolling patch of ferns and caught his breath, his limbs heavy and fatigued. The water had soaked through his boots and breecs, its chill touch numbing his legs. There was no chance of making a fire, and it would be foolish to try, so he just removed his wet clothing, exposing his feet and legs to the damp forest air. He began to massage himself vigorously, trying to force the cold from his flesh. Some feeling started to creep back in, and before long he could wiggle his toes quite energetically. That was enough. He'd not tarry more than he had to.

The next few hours of his journey north were uneventful. He carried his soaked clothes in his hands and across his shoulders, uncaring as to the occasional pine needle he stepped on. The forest seemed to go on forever, stretching out into eternity like some great bark and needle carpet. Dawn eventually came, the birds erupting into song about an hour before the first rays of sunlight began to filter through the trees. The woods started to thin, and soon Hereward was walking on grass again, the dewy softness a real comfort after the persistently spiky forest floor.

By the time he'd reached the bridge over the Temes, he was an absolute ruin of a man. He'd gone days without eating, and whilst he was a stronger fellow than most, it had still taken a toll. He'd managed to get his clothes dry some nights prior when he'd eventually got a fire going, but that was as far as his luck had held. He was exhausted, yet as miserable as his journey had been, it didn't come close to what he felt now. There was no way across the river. The bridge was destroyed. He'd know that. He'd done it himself.

He stood there for a time, staring at the mass of rotting timbers from the edge of the southern bank. It rose out of the river like some kind of monster from pagan myth, the tangles of wood and stone strangely unsettling as it all lay, half-submerged, in the dark, flowing waters. He could remember how elated he'd been when he and Olaf had brought it all crashing down. It had been a daring ploy, and it had sealed off Lundenburg from the Danish armies in the South, allowing them to retake the capital. He'd been joyous, and rightly so. It was a great victory, one he'd been happy to help win for his king. He didn't feel like that now. His king still needed him, but now he was stuck, trapped on one side of the river by the fruits of his own hand. Some might call that ironic. Hereward just thought it depressing.

He sat down on the grass, his stomach again grumbling in protest at his ongoing fast. He began to think, pondering his recent ordeals and the decisions he'd made to overcome them. The way he saw it, he'd still made the right decision in taking Eadwig south to Edmund. It wasn't safe in the capital, not with Eadric around, and Eadwig was a witness to the double murder Eadric would no doubt want to keep hidden. Hereward was loyal to the crown, beyond loyal, in fact, and so he'd always look out for the royal family, even if it sometimes meant using his own initiative to ensure their safety. Æthelred was undoubtedly displeased that Hereward had made the decision he had, but he'd still stand by it. He'd face his king's wrath, knowing he'd done what he judged to be right. Eadwig was alive because of him and Olaf. That might not have been the case had they taken him home to Eadric.

A shout sounded from across the water, making Hereward leap to his feet. He looked around, wondering if Edmund's men had somehow tracked him this far north. Then he saw the boat. A fishing boat. Heading towards him with two crew, both of whom seemed eager for his attention. He raised his arm in greeting, hoping they were friendly. He'd managed to avoid shedding blood so far. It would be a sincere shame if he had to start now.

"Are you alright?"

"I'm doing better than this," Hereward called, gesturing towards the ruined bridge. The boat was still a way off, which meant both men were having to raise their voices a fair degree in order to be heard.

"Do you need to get to the other side?"

"I do!" shouted Hereward, excited now, although he fully expected this mystery saviour would want paying.

"Are you English?" The man was full of questions. Hereward would answer them, assuming they let him aboard and speak to him properly. All this yelling would exhaust him further if it carried on for much longer.

"I am!" he shouted enthusiastically. "And you have nothing to fear from me! I'm no Dane! I kill Danes!"

The two fishermen nodded to the other, smiling, and finally rowed their boat close enough to the bank for one of them to disembark, the grey waters coming up to his thighs. Hereward could smell him already, but it was fresh, like the fish they'd obtained in those nets had only just been caught. His stomach again grumbled. He tried to push the thought of fish to one side. He was only partly successful.

"So you'll be wanting us to row you across?" The fisherman sounded quite genuine. Hereward had a way with people, and this one didn't strike him as the dishonest sort.

"If you can," he replied. "But if you're wanting payment, you'll have to wait a little while. I have nothing on me, but I give you my word I'll be able to reimburse you once I reach the king."

The man stopped, the water now just to his shins. "The king, you say?" he said, uncertain. "And who am I addressing that's so fortunate to keep the company of a king?"

"I'm Hereward."

"Who?"

"Hereward. I guard his majesty. Have done since Bernecestre."

"Bernecestre?" said the fisherman, again advancing towards him. He exited the waters, plodding through the sucking mud to stand a few arm's lengths from Hereward.

He was a strange-looking man, with a lumpy hooked nose and dark, dark eyes, but again Hereward couldn't sense anything off about him. He was trustworthy, as any man should be.

"That's correct," said Hereward. "I fought at Bernecestre and…"

"My son died there," said the fisherman suddenly. "My other son," he turned and pointed towards his associate still in the boat, "…he's all I have left now. Did you know the name of Osgar?"

"I never knew such a man," said Hereward carefully, "but if that was your son, then I am sincerely sorry to hear of his demise. Many a brave man fell that day. I hold every one of them in my prayers."

The fisherman nodded; a slow, melancholic gesture, his face flushed and his breath slightly rapid. "Well, we'll give you a ride, then," he finally said. "If you are who you say you are, then far be it for me to delay you. Don't worry about no payment either. If you fought alongside my Osgar, then…"

His voice faded, but Hereward understood, and he followed him over to his boat, wading out with him so they could climb aboard. They rowed him across alright, and they made conversation as they did, but Hereward was careful not to let slip anything relating to recent events involving Edmund. That man had a way with commoners, and everyone had heard of his furious resistance to Svienn and Cnut. For Hereward to admit he'd made an enemy of him might not go well. These were good people. He didn't want to antagonise them.

When they reached the northern bank, Hereward disembarked, thanking both men for their service and inquiring whether they frequented this section of the river on a regular basis. They said they did, so Hereward promised them he'd return here within a few days with payment. They tried to argue, stressing it wasn't necessary, but Hereward wouldn't be dissuaded. They'd done him a favour here, just when he'd needed it most, and he'd see them suitably rewarded.

Lundenburg's streets were just like he remembered. They were poor and getting poorer, the buildings dirty and dilapidated, many of them still in ruins from the chaos and carnage that had preceded Svienn's conquest last year. The inhabitants were much the same, looking nervous and malnourished, their faces tired and marked with worry. They'd been so jubilant when the city had been retaken and the Danes cut down. Now it was different. Life had gone on much as before, and nobody had much confidence in anything getting better. Hereward wasn't sure he could entirely blame them.

Trouble found him soon enough. The guards on the gate to King Æthelred's compound had recognised him as he approached. That wasn't unusual, for he was hardly a stranger, but one of them had fled from him and vanished into the main hall like he was hoping to alert someone. Hereward continued on, walking through the gate and heading straight for the hall, his stomach grumbling yet more in anticipation of the meal he'd soon enjoy. He didn't get that far. Emma wouldn't let him.

She stormed out in the company of four armed Normans and the guard who'd fled from Hereward previously. She was dressed rather modestly, it must be said, her gown having none of the peculiar flamboyance of days gone by, but this certainly wasn't indicative of any positive change in her. She was scowling, excessively so, and all of it was meant for Hereward. He had no idea how he'd managed to offend her. He had a notion he was about to find out.

"What do you want?" she asked pointedly, her face still scrunched up and her arms folded. Two of the Normans had moved to flank Hereward on his left and right, their spears pointed directly towards him.

"I am returning to serve my king," said Hereward neutrally. He wouldn't be baited by the queen. She had his loyalty, but that would only go so far. Æthelred was his lord. Emma was just the spouse, and a Norman one at that.

"Why did you flee?" she asked. "I'm told you were sent to retrieve Eadwig. Where is he?"

"I took him to Edmund."

"I know!" Her eyes flashed. There was a real wrath there. It wasn't pleasing to look upon. "Edmund himself told us," she spat, "yet that doesn't explain your lack of loyalty. Why did you leave Lundenburg with Eadwig to start with?"

Hereward eyed the Normans around him, wondering if they really intended violence or if this was some kind of scare tactic. "It was not safe here. Two thegns were dead…Thorkell had attacked Eadwig. I had to get him somewhere secure. Where he might heal undisturbed."

"Your king's own hall is not safe?" asked Emma, still venomous. "Have you any idea of the stress all this has caused him, Hereward? He lies inside, in his chambers, unable to talk. I don't know how long he may last, but your foolishness has only contributed to his poor health."

"What exactly is wrong?" asked Hereward, alarmed. "You must let me see him…" He went to step forward, his concern for his king compelling him to move. Emma reacted badly, recoiling like he somehow meant her harm. The Norman to the left seized at him, clutching his arm. Hereward dropped him with a single punch. The one to his right launched himself forward, tackling Hereward around the waist and bringing him down. They struggled in the dirt, but the other Normans were already on him, their strength and weight pinning him to the ground. This wasn't going well at all.

Hereward wouldn't give up, and he kept struggling whilst he was hauled upright, yet he was weakened by hunger and fatigue. They beat him, splitting his lips and bloodying his nose, and took him to the prison tower, dragging him up the long winding stairs and hurling him into a cell. Emma snarled something at him about "traitors" meeting their "much-deserved end" before departing, the Normans slamming the heavy oaken door shut before he could so much as grunt. That was it then. A prisoner he was, again, and just when his king needed him most. He'd not expected a warm welcome, but this was something else. Hereward would not take this lying down.

It was with some considerable displeasure he realised he had to do just that. There was a cot in the cell, and his condition demanded he rest upon it, his famished and exhausted body giving him little choice. His bruised and swollen eyes closed of their own accord, and he slept, dreaming of recent events.

Eadwig was there, just as Hereward had found him upon interrupting Thorkell's attempt on his life. The Danes flew at him, seeking to end Hereward before he could intervene. He fought back, as he had in reality, his sword cleaving through them like they were but wheat at harvest time. He killed them all, and he broke Thorkell, too, forcing him to his knees and bending him to his will. He made him confess, his sins pouring from his smashed and bleeding mouth, the tip of Hereward's sword resting at his throat.

Eadwig rose, fit and well, and they both listened to Thorkell baring his soul. He admitted to everything, all his crimes, in England and abroad, everything he'd done, at Bernecestre and Canterburie and Hringmere, all of it. He then died, falling face first into the grass, the Lord taking his soul for the sake of judgement. Hereward turned and walked with Eadwig back to Æthelred's hall, satisfied that justice had been served. Eadric wasn't there when they arrived, nor were the recently murdered Sigeferth and Morcar. The only one present was the king, and he embraced Hereward as a son, telling him he'd done well, telling him how proud he was and how he'd kept them all safe. Everything was as it should be. Hereward had done the right thing, and all that was left to do was…

He awoke with a start, the sound of something at the door stirring him into consciousness. He dismissed his foolish dream, feeling vaguely embarrassed at the memory of it. He wasn't the warrior he'd been in his dream, nor had he succeeded in keeping everyone safe as he so desired. He'd failed. If it were otherwise, he wouldn't be in this cell.

The noise sounded again, as though somebody was knocking all too delicately on the other side of the door. Hereward stood up, his eyes gradually acclimating themselves to the dark now twilight was upon them. The cell didn't have much in terms of windows, but there was a single barred opening built into the outer wall, of the type that might barely allow a man to look out upon the city. Hereward ignored it for the moment, instead approaching the cell door so that he could listen. He had no idea if anyone was out there, but if it was yet more Normans, he couldn't fathom why they'd not just come on in and given him another beating. Scratching about outside served little purpose.

Somebody spoke, the sound muffled and indistinct. Hereward knelt down, his ear close to the keyhole in the door. "Are you there?" said a voice, young and unsure and yet familiar. Hereward did what felt natural. He talked back.

"I'm here."

"Hereward?"

"Yes. Who is this?"

"Edward!"

"The aetheling?"

"Yes, of course! Are you alright?"

"I'm beaten and starving," said Hereward, matter-of-factly. "But just what is going on? Why did you come here? Is your father safe?"

"I can't tell," blurted Edward, sounding suddenly close to tears. "I saw him, after his…fall. He was so ill he couldn't talk. We came back that night when mother wasn't there, and he was on the floor by his bed! We helped him, but then mother appeared and forced us from his chambers. She hasn't let us see him since."

"Why?"

"I don't know! She won't answer our questions and spends all her time with that Norman, Godfrey. I know she's written to Uncle Richard in Normandy, but she won't tell me why."

That didn't sound good. If the queen was communicating with her brother whilst the king was incapacitated, there'd be a good reason for it. Richard wouldn't want to waste this opportunity. Hereward had already witnessed his dastardly plan to manipulate Æthelred through Godgifu. If he'd been made aware that Æthelred was in poor health, the Norman duke would want to take advantage of the situation, for his own benefit, of course. It was always about him. The man was a bastard, through and through. It would be the same for his descendants, most likely.

"Your mother has turned on me, Edward," said Hereward. "We have to think of some way to..."

"She did that?" squeaked Edward, sounding startled. "Why? My father needs you."

"He does. But you must take care. I fear what your mother might do if she knew you'd come here."

"I'm not afraid," said Edward firmly. "She's just the queen...she has no right to stop me seeing my father, nor any business having good men like you locked up. Just let me..."

"You have to be careful," said Hereward, interrupting. "There are things being set in motion that make me afraid. A great danger is about to come over us."

"What danger? Something worse than what's been happening here?"

"I'm afraid so. You have to try and get to your father, Edward. Tell him...tell him Edmund is rising against him. Tell him also I did what I thought best with Eadwig. I remain loyal. Always loyal. That's why Edmund had me imprisoned."

"You were imprisoned? You escaped?"

"I did," nodded Hereward. "And was rewarded for that with yet more imprisonment. It's not right. But don't fret. Ultimately I don't matter. What does matter is getting to the king. If Edmund starts an uprising, thousands could die. Others will see it, the Northmen...the Normans...they'll swoop in and take our country from us whilst we fight each other."

"Would Edmund really do that?" Edward didn't sound convinced. He likely understood, like Hereward, that Edmund was a good man. That made all this harder. An evil man would be easy to handle. You could just fight him and defeat him and leave it at that. Edmund was certainly not evil. Just misguided. He needed his father. They had to reconcile before it was too late.

"Edmund is in pain," said Hereward diplomatically. "Some good friends of his...well...they are no longer with us. That's why I went away for a while. I had to get Eadwig somewhere safe."

"What happened to Eadwig?" Hereward sighed at Edward's question. The poor lad really was in the dark. He felt for him.

"It's complicated. Just know he's safe. I made sure of it. What we have to do now is get word to the king. You have to do it, Edward. Tell him I'm imprisoned here. Tell him what Edmund intends. But also..."

"Yes?"

"Tell him I never betrayed him. Tell him I did what I judged to be right. Tell him I always sought to do that. For his sake. For Eadwig's sake. For all his family. I never broke my vow to him. And I never will. He's my king. Until his last breath or mine."

Edward didn't reply immediately. Hereward stayed hunched low, his face still hovering around the keyhole. He couldn't see anything through it, but he imagined Edward was there, wrestling with his fears and trying to make sense of them. None of this should be happening. Emma was a cruel woman to be doing this. Hereward had never liked her. He'd bring her to justice for all this as soon as he was able.

"I lied before," said Edward sullenly.

"What do you mean?"

"When I said I wasn't afraid…it wasn't true. I'm scared." Edward had stated the obvious. Hereward could hear it in his voice, but the admission still made him ache with sympathy.

"I know," said Hereward softly. "As am I."

"You're scared? But you're Hereward. You're like…invincible or something."

"No, that's not so. I'm scared a lot. Every time I fight, and then other times too."

"How do you get past it?" Edward sounded surprised.

"I just think on what I'm fighting for…what might happen if I don't…who might get hurt if I don't step up and do what must be done. You can understand that, Edward?"

"I think so."

"Do you want to be king someday?" He knew he was putting the boy on the spot with that question, but it served a purpose. He had to be emboldened to his task. He had to have courage.

"Mother wants it," said Edward. "I don't know if I…if I'll be any good. It looks so hard. Everything feels so…dangerous."

Hereward nodded. "I understand. Now let me ask you another question…what do you care about?"

"How do you mean?"

"What do you care about?" Hereward repeated. "In your life…what is it that draws your affection? What would you see nurtured, protected?"

"My family. And my faith…my country too. England has suffered so much. I want to see an end to it. I pray for it, all the time. If I become king…I'd see it done."

"Then keep that close," said Hereward. "Keep that vision of an England free from suffering foremost in your mind. It's a good image, a good dream, something you and I share. Because one thing is clear to me, Edward…if your mother is allowed to continue like this, England will suffer yet more. Your uncle, Duke Richard, is looking to gain power over us…and if we don't stop him, I fear future generations will know nothing but the Norman yoke for centuries to come."

XXXXIII

There were hundreds of them, marching out of the sea of pines, their shields held tight to their chests and their spears reaching up towards the pale grey sky. Their armour and helms caught the sunlight, making them appear as a sparkling wave of glittering metal emerging from the swaying green of the tree line. He saw their faces as they came closer, all bearded, all fatigued, but all possessing a certain light in their eyes that wouldn't be extinguished by mere hardship. They were warriors, dedicated and driven, but with the hearts of men, gentle and decent and determined to defend their homeland and people to the very end. Edmund loved them for it. He always would.

Ulfcytel rode at the head of them, his armoured bulk perched atop his dark, heavily muscled steed. The mighty dragon banner of St Edmund trailed behind him, held by a man upon horseback at his rear, and Edmund gazed upon it, relieved and inspired all at once. This would make a difference. Any Englishman worth his salt would be swayed by such a majestic sight. It was glorious, and with the army advancing alongside it was doubly so. Good things could come of this, and those thegns who'd recently doubted him would now have cause for regret. Or so he hoped.

Ulfcytel kept his eyes on Edmund as he rode closer, the masses of men following just behind, an almost imperceptibly slight smile creasing the corners of his mouth. The ealdorman was pleased to see him. Edmund could relate to that. He'd missed his friend. He'd missed all of them. Great deeds were now afoot, and he needed great men at his side to help him see them through. Ulfcytel was certainly one of those.

Yet Edmund's heart upped its pace when he beheld Æva. She was with the army and upon a horse of her own, Wulfhild and Brandon riding at her flanks. The wind was tousling her hair, pushing back her headscarf just enough for that sunset waterfall she always kept hidden to come into view. She didn't seem bothered by it, and like Ulfcytel, her eyes were on Edmund, although not in the way he might have liked. There was a determination there, strong yet cold. That made him nervous. He needed to talk to her about the future. He needed to talk to her about Ealdgyth's proposal. Edmund couldn't marry if there was the slightest chance Æva might one day return his affections. He had no choice in that. His heart compelled him.

Edmund's heels suddenly left the ground. Ulfcytel had dismounted and embraced him in a bear-like hug, which for the moment meant Edmund had been pitched forward into the ealdorman's chest. His huge arms were wrapped around him, holding him tight, Ulfcytel's great rumbling laugh now sounding in his ears.

"You're not too full of yourself to refuse a hug, my king?" he thundered, his voice impossibly loud.

"I am not," Edmund somehow managed to say, doing his best to return the embrace. "Yet I would appreciate it if you did not suffocate me here and now. I don't think that would do much for the army's morale."

"Ah yes," said Ulfcytel, letting him go, Edmund's feet now thankfully returning to solid ground. "It would be a sorry sight for them to witness. Regicide is a terrible thing. Unless your name is Svienn or Cnut. Then it's just funny."

They both laughed, deep and sincere, the rest of their army slowly coming to a clattering halt about a dozen paces back. Edmund took a look over his shoulder, spying the still sorrowful form of Ealdgyth and Ælfwynn just behind him. The local thegns Edmund had summoned and largely failed to convince a couple of weeks ago were stood a short distance away, the gates and palisade of Snotingeham itself at their backs. Some of them looked elated. They were impressed by the army and the banner and perhaps awed by the presence of Ulfcytel.

Others were not. Some were nervous, agitated. These would be the thegns who'd made such a fuss when Edmund had come asking them for their allegiance. They likely thought he was trying to threaten them into obedience. That wasn't true, but if they were intimidated, he couldn't say he was sorry for it. These were hard times, and Edmund had a hard task before him. He wouldn't apologise for having men willing to assist him in that.

"So you didn't have any trouble on the way here?" asked Edmund, looking back to Ulfcytel.

"Nothing. The roads were clear, more or less, and no Miercians or Normans or much else saw fit to trouble us. I'd say Eadric and Æthelred both chose not to hinder us, although why I can't say. Perhaps we just got lucky."

"There are things I must tell you in such regard," said Edmund soberly. "But for the moment, I would..."

He paused, seeing that Ealdgyth and Ælfwynn had moved to his side. "You mentioned Eadric?" Ealdgyth asked Ulfcytel, her eyes sharp.

"Aye, lady," said Ulfcytel, lowering his head in respect. "And let me just say how sorry I was to hear of your Sigeferth. I didn't know him well, yet I mourn his loss. We all do."

"It's said you are a great fighting man," said Ealdgyth, her eyes still on the ealdorman.

"I do what I can," he replied. "For God, king, and country. I would serve little else."

"And who is your king?" she asked. Ulfcytel inclined his head towards Edmund.

"Then that means you'll fight against Eadric and Æthelred?" she then asked without hesitation.

Ulfcytel raised his eyebrows and looked to Edmund, clearly hoping for clarification. "My father has gone too far," Edmund said sternly. "It wasn't enough just to murder Sigeferth and Morcar...he moved against Ealdgyth too. We had to break her out of captivity at Malmesberie. Eadric was there. He and his men tried to kill her rather than see her freed."

"That's a bloody awful thing," said Ulfcytel. "And entirely believable too. Eadric is a damned menace. Always has been."

"He tried to kill all my daughters," said Ealdgyth flatly. "He got three. One remains."

"This is why I summoned you," said Edmund, cutting Ulfcytel off before he could respond. "With all that's happened, I think we can both agree my father cannot stay on the throne. Justice has to be done. And Eadric needs killing. It's that simple."

Ulfcytel looked to Edmund, then back to Ealdgyth. He stared at her for a second or two before looking down at Ælfwynn, who appeared a little apprehensive under such scrutiny. "It really is that simple," said Ulfcytel gently, his face softening as he beheld the child. "To think that days like these should be ours. That such things could even be done…to children, no less!"

Ulfcytel's eyes snapped back to Edmund. They'd changed, appearing to shine with an inner fire that Edmund had generally only seen when he was of a mood towards battle and bloodshed. "I'm with you, my king," he said with a firm nod. "Your father has done too much…and will continue to do too much. Enough is enough. Let us have an end to it."

****

It was dark by the time the army had made camp. They'd set up just south of Snotingeham, erecting a forest of tents and cookfires with an efficiency born from habit. Edmund had placed Ealdgyth and Ælfwynn in his own pavilion, knowing the risk of them being assassinated was drastically reduced when surrounded by his loyal warriors. He'd seen them fed, making sure they received both comfort and nourishment, and he'd then left, instructing Wulfnoth to attend to their safety. He couldn't be everywhere tonight, and he had a very particular business in mind.

Ulfcytel was at the inn Edmund had appropriated from the now thankfully dead Wystan. He was eating, as was typical, and Ælfweard had joined him, appearing sincerely happy to see him again. Edmund sat with them awhile, listening to their stories and glad that the reeve and the ealdorman thought so well of each other. They must have bonded at Canterburie, he assumed. He could well understand why.

Ælfweard eventually left, giving Edmund a reassuring look, like he somehow knew something was on his mind. Edmund wondered about that, although he was glad the man had taken his leave. He needed to speak with the ealdorman in private. Ulfcytel was a master of war, and well-equipped to offer advice on anything relating to such. Edmund would now have his opinion on another type of conflict. One of the heart.

"Ealdgyth wishes to marry me."

Ulfcytel raised an eyebrow, his voice cut off by the fact he was taking a long draught from an alarmingly large drinking horn. "So she does?" he finally asked, wiping his mead-flecked lips with his sleeve. "Is it also fair to surmise this has something to do with you inheriting her late husband's lands?"

"That it does," nodded Edmund. He'd sat right across from Ulfcytel, the gentle warmth of the fire cascading down his left side. "I had hoped the local thegns would obey her," continued Edmund, "and see her as a successor to Sigeferth. But they do not…not many, anyway. They won't assist me in any rebellion against my father. We think that will change if I marry Ealdgyth."

"It will help," said Ulfcytel, his attentions now on the unusually blackened toast he'd been nibbling. "I'm not too surprised they wouldn't obey Ealdgyth, at least in something as serious as taking on Æthelred. She's a widow, she's grieving, she's a woman, obviously…if you marry her though…you'll gain Sigeferth's authority, and they'll see it. You'll be his male successor as well as an aetheling. Few here would dare question such a man."

"There's yet more to it," said Edmund. "The men who killed her daughters…there was another assassin who tried to take her life in this very place. One of the disobedient thegns, in fact. I killed him, as he deserved."

"Most certainly!" said Ulfcytel emphatically, a shower of blackened crumbs erupting from his mouth and beard.

"…and yet I have a feeling these attempts to eliminate her will not stop there," said Edmund, ignoring the crumbs. "Eadric will keep trying to remove her from the game. If I marry her, she'll be a member of the royal family. Even Eadric will think twice about harming her then."

Ulfcytel paused a moment, continuing to chew his toast, nosily, whilst thinking on what had been said. "It would complicate matters for Eadric, yes," he mused. "There are no guarantees, though. If he sees you as an enemy, he may not hesitate to try and harm you, regardless of title and family connections and so forth. But it's still worth a try…if he kills the wife of an aetheling…well, that's never been done. He'll be an outcast, a pariah in the eyes of other notables. He's unpopular enough as it is…I think he may not want to risk it."

"Eadric has already tried to kill me," said Edmund, his expression grim in recalling equally grim memories. "We fought in Malmesberie...and in Lundenburg, he had me captured by common street thugs…Wulfnoth thinks he intended to murder both me and the thugs so he could blame my death on them."

"So he'd come out looking like he'd avenged you?"

"That's right. So in that respect, it looks like Eadric is quite confident about making a move against me, at least in secret."

"I'd say that was a one-off opportunity for Eadric then," said Ulfcytel. "It might have worked…but will he get such a chance again? My argument stands, I think. He'll think twice about killing Ealdgyth with you involved. The same goes for anything your father may try. It just wouldn't look good for either of them."

"I agree," said Edmund. "She'll be safe, her daughter too. I owe her that much, but it still strikes me as…"

"You have reservations about marrying your friend's widow?"

"I do," sighed Edmund. "She may be closer to my age than Sigeferth…but they loved one another. I can't imagine…I mean…"

"You don't have to have children with her," said Ulfcytel. "And I understand this may feel distasteful…but this is indeed a way to make sure she remains safe. And it helps us, also. The Five Boroughs are vitally important for what we have planned. Your father brought this on us, Edmund. We do what we must."

"People will expect children, though," said Edmund quietly. "And I won't lie with a woman when out of wedlock, never. There's also no possibility of me siring an heir with another once I'm married. I will not have that stain on my honour. And I'll need heirs once I'm king."

"Is Ealdgyth aware of your concerns? She's already had children. She may not want to…"

"She is willing," said Edmund. "I just…"

"There's something else, isn't there, Edmund? Your head is in this, but your heart is not. Call me an old fool if I'm wrong, but…I think I'm right. What's really bothering you?"

Edmund again sighed, feeling relieved and appreciative that Ulfcytel clearly knew him so well. "You were close to Alaric?" Edmund asked.

"In the short time I knew him, yes. He was a great man. One of faith and integrity."

"And you would see right done by his widow?"

"Always," said Ulfcytel. "Upon my soul, Edmund, I will defend Æva and Brandon to the death. It's my way of honouring Alaric. And I know what you're about to say next…I see it in your eyes. I see it in your manner whenever she's around. You have feelings for her."

"Am I really so transparent?"

"Partly, but you and Wulfhild are quite alike. Your hearts are open. I know your sister, and I know you…and, if you recall, you did seriously batter a certain Ealdorman of Norþanhymbre when he sought to do Æva harm. That told me everything I needed to know."

"Uhtred is an unjust man," answered Edmund. "I did what I did…"

"For the sake of justice, yes," nodded Ulfcytel, "and because Æva is in your very heart. I see it, lad. There's no shame in it. You're a young man, and you mean well."

Edmund scowled a little, fearing he was being patronised. Ulfcytel saw the look and spoke again. "That came out wrong," he said quickly. "Just tell me how you feel…I've spoken enough on this. Share your thoughts, if you will, my king."

Edmund took another deep breath and let it go, his exhalation long and pronounced. He broke eye contact with the ealdorman, instead looking down at his hands clasped upon the table in front of him. "It's something like…" he paused again, struggling for words, "…whenever she's close, I feel…afraid…but also elated. To see her so grieved still…"

"It hurts you?" asked Ulfcytel.

"It does. When I first met her, the first time I saw her…she was in my father's prison tower. She was so…vulnerable, yet also defiant. I could feel it then, like I wanted to stay with her, like I had to make sure she was alright."

"And you felt the same when we defeated Hemingr and his men?"

"I did," breathed Edmund, still looking down at his hands. "She was so wounded by Alaric's death, we all were…but she was in such pain. My heart just…I couldn't let it slide. I had to get Brandon back. I'd never spoken to my father like that before. But I had to do it. I had to ease her suffering."

"I remember," murmured Ulfcytel, sounding like he too was becoming emotional at recalling past events. "And this feeling of yours," he continued slowly, "it grew stronger with time? Was it like…"

"Fear?" asked Edmund rhetorically, finding the courage to again look Ulfcytel in the eyes. "Yes, it's like fear, but also…"

"Hope?"

"That's it," said Edmund. "Every time I see her, I'm afraid of her, like I'll make a total arse out of myself just by being around. But then there's hope. That she'll see me as I see her, that she'll…"

"How do you see her, Edmund?"

"She's so beautiful!" whispered Edmund. "She's so, so beautiful. Like she's the key to everything. My happiness…my future…my…"

"Heart."

Ulfcytel settled back in his chair after uttering that last quiet word. He'd spoken the truth, so Edmund wasn't about to correct him. They instead sat for a few moments, letting the sound of the fire snapping and smouldering in the hearth hang in the air. The light cast from the flames played gently across the room, the dancing shadows falling upon Ulfcytel's face in a way that made him appear somehow more venerable than usual. It was fair enough, thought Edmund. There was wisdom in that great bald head of his, although he did sincerely wish he'd say something more. Anything to break this silence. Anything to give him some clarity.

"You have a decision to make," Ulfcytel eventually said. "And I cannot make it for you. Say you marry Ealdgyth…you'll win the Five Boroughs, and you'll again prove yourself a noble soul by taking her under your protection. But…"

"But?" asked Edmund, not wanting him to fall into silence once more.

"Some might say you'll not be being true to yourself. That you'd be forsaking your heart for the sake of a marriage of convenience. I can't advise you, Edmund, but I reckon that's not how you want to live your life. There's only one way out of this."

"And what's that?" Edmund was excited now. He hoped it didn't show, but he had a feeling the ealdorman was about to give him a clear solution.

"You need to talk to Æva. You need to tell her what you told me. Don't hold back. If you love this woman, then you can't pretend she just doesn't exist. This is a crossroads in your life. Æva must be free to make this decision with you."

"Are you not angry?" asked Edmund, suddenly apprehensive. "It's not been long since Alaric was taken from us. He was your friend, and…do you not feel I'm somehow dishonouring him?"

"In truth, I'm a little sensitive about it, yes. But I know you're a fine man, Edmund. You didn't ask for this, nor would you have ever sought to come between Alaric and Æva had he survived the siege of Lundenburg. Your intentions are noble. Your feelings…sincere."

"Was it like this with my sister?"

Ulfcytel let out a bark of laughter, surprised but also humoured by the question. "Somewhat," he said, still smiling. "Wulfhild was given to me by your father, but we were fortunate. Love came to us in time. It may be that way with you and Ealdgyth, but…"

"But what?"

"I think you'd spend the rest of your life wondering what might have been. You have to find your courage, Edmund. You have to let Æva know how you feel. Don't deny yourself this chance."

"Courage?" Edmund breathed the word, pondering its meaning. "I can find that on the battlefield, but here…"

"I know," said Ulfcytel sympathetically. "Courage comes in many forms. When it comes to the clash of arms…well, you and I both share an affinity for that form of courage. When it comes to the heart, though…it's difficult. It really is."

"What'll I do if she spurns me?"

"You'll have an answer, at least," said Ulfcytel. "And you'll have clarity with the giving of it. And I'll be here for you if it comes to that. Count on it."

"Will you not think it strange to see a king weeping?" Edmund was only half-joking. He didn't want to embarrass himself like that, yet he feared it was very possible should things go badly.

"I've seen many things in my time, Edmund. Many, many things, so let me say this…if your father had ever come to me with his troubles, as you have done tonight, then I would not have sent him away, nor would I have shamed him for his tears. It might have done him good to have such a release. I could have helped him. He chose to make that impossible. So I help you now. And I will always endeavour to do so."

Edmund stood up, moved by what had been said. Ulfcytel rose with him, and before Edmund knew it, they'd embraced, the two men slapping at each other's backs like they were a pair of drums. Ulfcytel eventually released him, and Edmund left without comment, content that no further words were necessary. He was blessed to have such a friend, there was no denying that. No matter what else happened tonight, he'd remember that and hold it to heart.

He found Æva back at the camp. She was with Wulfhild beside a log fire, the crackling flames sending glowing motes of ash drifting upward towards the star-filled sky. They'd donned thick furs against the late autumn chill, and Eamon too was close by, looking menacing and inscrutable, as he generally did. Edmund nodded to the man when he approached, and Eamon got to his feet, a short bow following. Edmund acknowledged the gesture and turned to Æva.

"Where is Brandon?"

Æva gave him a look, like she thought the question a little foolish. "He's asleep," she said. "It was a long journey here, and he was tired."

"Of course," said Edmund, his voice faint. He didn't know how to go about this. He needed to speak to Æva, but he certainly couldn't do it with his sister and Eamon looking right at him.

"Would you come for a walk with me?" His cheeks flushed at having to ask, but he had no choice. He had to get her alone. If he tried to say what he'd come to say out in the open like this, he'd die of embarrassment before he finished.

"Will you not just eat with us?" asked Wulfhild, like Edmund was being intentionally awkward. "There's stew coming, so I'm told."

"Later," said Edmund, feeling a flash of annoyance. "I just need to talk to Æva for a moment."

He turned back to her, his expression uncertain. She seemed to see it, but she stood up regardless and came over to him. He led on, away from the fire and south through the camp, his mind aflutter at what he might say. They stopped just past the outermost edge of tents, the pine forest the army had traversed earlier barely discernible in the enveloping darkness. They could hear it creaking and rustling in the breeze, the sound reminding Edmund of better times from his childhood. He missed Sigeferth. Morcar too. They'd been fond of these woods. It was sad to think they'd never enjoy them again.

"Are you alright?" Æva didn't sound comfortable. She was worried but pained with it, like the rapidly encroaching winter had already gotten the better of her.

"Are you cold?" Edmund asked, thinking it strange she'd be in discomfort under all those furs. He was dressed in little but his armour and still wasn't bothered.

"Slightly," she admitted. "Yet I also wonder why you brought me here. Is there something you'd show me?"

"I heard you've been of help to my brother, Eadwig."

"I spent a lot of time with him. I can tell he likes the company. I hope he's not missing it too much."

"I'm grateful to you for making the effort," said Edmund, sincere in his words. "Many would not be so patient with a man in his condition. Your compassion is admirable."

Æva looked out past Edmund's shoulder, taking in the night beyond. "Is that why you've brought me here?" she asked hesitantly.

"No," he said clumsily. "I just…Ealdgyth and I may get married."

"Sigeferth's widow?"

"Yes," stumbled Edmund, his tongue suddenly feeling thick and unresponsive. "The thegns here will not follow her…if I take her into my family, I'll gain all her lands…Sigeferth's lands, I mean. All he had, and she now has, will be mine."

"A political marriage," nodded Æva knowingly. "I confess I'm glad I avoided such a thing."

"Why?"

She looked at him, a frown marring her forehead for the briefest moment. "There's no heart there. God made man and woman both for the sake of children. Love must be at the centre, the core, of any marriage. To make it all about land and power…"

"I don't disagree," said Edmund, knowing her to be right. "I never thought I'd entertain such a thing…especially with Ealdgyth. I used to look at her and Sigeferth and feel…envious, I suppose. Hopeful too. Like one day I might be blessed with that kind of devotion."

"You wanted devotion?" asked Æva.

"Always," said Edmund, his head nodding emphatically. "I kept it to myself…because I thought my father would make me marry whoever he wanted. But I wanted something more. Something sincere. Something kind."

"Do you fear you won't get that with Ealdgyth?"

"She wants vengeance," sighed Edmund, "and I can't say she's wrong in the desire for it. I have to set things right. The guilty must be punished, and I need the Five Boroughs to be able to do that. But…"

He paused, trying to summon the courage to speak from his heart. "I fear if I do this, I'll be making a mistake. Like I'll be ignoring something precious…something a man shouldn't ignore."

"I'm not sure I understand." She'd said the words, but Edmund wasn't fooled. She knew what he was about to say. He'd best get to it.

"I can provide for you, you know," he said, feeling awkward at his equally awkward words. "You and Brandon…once I'm king, you need never fear anything, you need never want for anything. I'll make this land safe. I'll bring peace, and you can…"

"You're asking me to marry you?" Again Æva sounded like she knew well enough what he was suggesting.

Edmund took a step forward, his hands reaching for hers. "I am," he said, feeling enthused that she hadn't pulled away. "I know I'm not making much sense, but…you're always on my mind. You're always there, no matter what I'm doing or who I'm with. When I feared you dead, I…"

She didn't reply. She just stared at him, allowing her hands to rest in his. He couldn't stop now. He'd say it all and be done with it.

"I can't stand the thought of anything happening to you. This feeling never goes away…it only grows stronger. Marrying Ealdgyth will bring me power and influence in the short term, but…"

Again she said nothing. She kept on staring, still as a statue. It was all a lot to take in, he could understand that. He'd finish and let her decide.

"...I can't pass up this chance," he breathed softly. "I can't let what I feel just fade, because it won't. I need you with me. I need you at my side. Always. Please, Æva, say you understand."

"You wanted a marriage based on sincerity rather than politics?" she asked, her voice hushed.

"Always," he said. "Since I was a boy."

"With someone you love and can't live without?"

"Yes, exactly."

She looked down at his hands, seemingly thoughtful. "Then know this," she said, suddenly looking him straight in the face. "I had that...I was lucky. I don't wish to hurt you, Edmund, but you must understand. I had that love. What you aspire to...I had it. And so you'll understand when I tell you it doesn't just end. It can't. It transcends death. Outlasts it. Alaric waits for me in heaven, just as I wait for him. In faith and love."

Edmund stared, lost in her eyes. There was no deception there. She was being entirely truthful, but that didn't make things any easier. Her honesty had cut him deep, regardless of how noble her intentions might be. She pulled her hands from his, leaving him standing there, silent yet in pain, the night's cold finally seeping into his bones.

"I appreciate what you've said," he mumbled. That was all he could manage. He strode off, away from her and back through the thicket of tents. Some of his men were about, sitting at campfires or wandering on patrol, but he ignored their myriad nods and bows whenever he passed by. He didn't want to speak to them. He didn't want to speak to anyone. He'd made a fool of himself, and was now suffering for it. It had been a stupid idea. Æva had never shown any interest in him, that had always been obvious. She was kind, yes, but she was like that to virtually everyone. Edmund was a prize idiot for thinking he'd ever had a chance.

He stopped suddenly, his efforts to blink back tears coming to nought. He held his hands to his face, trying to make it look like he was blowing on his palms to keep out the cold. His tears didn't relent, so he pressed his palms to his eyes to paw them away before they became too visible. Nobody could see him like this. If anyone were to spot a weeping Edmund Ironside, the resulting gossip would...

"I'm so sorry, Edmund."

He turned, knowing he'd been seen. Ulfcytel stood there, half-shrouded in shadow, the moonlight playing across the silvered cascade that was his beard.

"It cannot be helped," sniffed Edmund, again wiping at his eyes with urgency.

"I know," said Ulfcytel, the old man stepping closer to use his significant bulk to shield Edmund from prying eyes.

"This is embarrassing," croaked Edmund, his voice failing him.

"It's only natural. But don't think this had anything to do with you. You're a fine man. I should have mentioned this before, but..."

"But what?" Edmund had stopped crying, which was a considerable relief to him. Sadly, Ulfcytel's next statement proved more shocking than he could ever have imagined.

"Brandon isn't Alaric's boy," he said, doubly quiet now. "Don't tell anyone," he stressed, "I'm doing her a disservice by telling you this. I just feel that...I can't stand to see you so hurt, lad. I just..."

"Then who is his father?!" Edmund couldn't help but feel alarmed. He had a hard time imagining Æva being unfaithful. That could only mean…

"Some bastard Dane forced himself on her at Wiltune," said Ulfcytel, shaking his head sorrowfully. "At least that's what she said, or at least heavily implied. I don't think she'd want it spoken of again. I only do so now because I fear I should have warned you of this…complication."

Edmund breathed out, long and slow. He felt sick, and angry with it, like he needed to find this Dane and hack the limbs from his body as punishment for his great crimes.

"And Alaric knew?" he asked, incredulous.

"Aye," said Ulfcytel, his voice tender. "He knew. I can't imagine how hard it was for him."

"And he still raised him? Saw fit to act as his father?"

"That he did."

That was something. Many a man wouldn't have done so. They'd have put their ego first, frothing and raging and blaming the mother and who knows what else. Even worse, some would have forgotten their Christian convictions in a heartbeat, perhaps even wishing the child dead as a means to salve their injured pride. Alaric hadn't been such a man, clearly, and Edmund could now understand Æva all the more. Edmund hadn't been rejected this evening. This wasn't about him. Something far more precious was in play here. He'd have her know it.

"I have to go speak to her again," said Edmund. Ulfcytel looked alarmed, as if fearing Edmund was going to go tell Æva they'd been gossiping. "It's not like that," said Edmund, cutting him off. "I'll keep you out of this, rest assured. I just understand things now. Things I didn't before. Thank you for helping me, Ulfcytel."

He headed off, retracing his steps back to the edge of the camp. Ulfcytel stayed as he was, confused but also hopeful that Edmund had somehow drawn strength from his words. Æva was back where he'd left her, looking out into the night and seemingly lost in thought. He cleared his throat, not wanting to startle her. She looked over at him, her face forlorn, like she had indeed been going over old memories.

"I know about Brandon."

She frowned at that, which was no surprise. "And it's not what you think," Edmund said hurriedly. "I just want to ask…I wanted to say…I feel like I understand you now. More than I did. I understand why you refused me."

Æva was silent, afraid perhaps to comment on something that already made her feel vulnerable. Edmund floundered for something to say, knowing he had to explain himself further before she took offence. The moonlight was brighter now, cascading downward to blanket the entire camp. Something drew Edmund's eye, the light causing it to sparkle faintly with a strange relevance. It was his uncle's brooch, the one in the shape of a moth that his aunt had given him when he'd last seen her. It was pinned to his cloak, as was usual, and he took it now, removing it to hold it in his fingers. He looked at it for a few moments, thinking deeply. He then stepped forward, acting seemingly on instinct, and pressed it into Æva's hands.

"This belonged to my uncle, Æthelstan," he said. "He and Alaric fought together. I think you know this?"

Æva stared down at the brooch, turning it over and over. It still looked exquisite, even at night, and Edmund had no idea how its creator had managed to fashion it in the shape of a moth to such an exacting degree.

"It's beautiful," Æva eventually said. "But why give it to me?"

"It feels right," said Edmund. "Alaric and my uncle…it's something that links us together, don't you think? I'd like you to keep it."

"I can't possibly…"

"Please, Æva," said Edmund, feeling again pained. "Please do this for me. I'll not bother you after this…as in bother you with my…feelings. Just please accept this gift, for my own peace of mind, if nothing else."

She nodded, still uncertain, but then pinned the brooch to her furs, just across from her left shoulder. It caught the moonlight yet again, making it appear like a giant and rather formidable moth had just landed on her and was loath to depart. She smiled at it, perhaps thinking the same thing.

"So tell me now," asked Æva quietly, "what makes you think you understand me all the more?"

"Many men would not have raised a boy such as Brandon," said Edmund, getting right to the heart of it. "But Alaric did…and I think I understand now why you feel as you do about him. That's not something that can just fade with time. I'd be selfish, foolish…cruel, to expect it."

Æva just nodded, still silent.

"Will you do one more thing for me, though?" asked Edmund.

"Tell me," she said simply.

"Tell me about Alaric. It helps me understand. It helps me understand you…and it gives me something to strive for. I don't intend for his sacrifice to have been in vain. Men like him, doing what he did, for Brandon, for you, for England…for Christ even…it speaks to the heart, even though they may be absent. Does that make sense?"

She smiled, the motion slight but genuine.

"It makes perfect sense," she said softly.

XXXXIV

"Did I ever tell you much about my childhood?"

Æthelred opened his eyes at the sound of Eadric's voice. He was close, sat on a pine wood chair pulled up to the side of the king's bed, his expression entirely blank as he waited for him to respond. He looked terrible; his clothes caked with mud, his skin pale to the point of ill-health and his normally resplendent locks limp and lifeless. Æthelred had no idea what kind of answer he wanted to his question. He couldn't give one anyway. Eadric must have been told that.

"I see you've not yet recovered from your ordeal," said Eadric, his fingers tapping against the slate board he held in his lap. Æthelred narrowed his eyes at the sight of it. He'd been using that to communicate, writing simple statements down in chalk to whoever might be inclined to read them. Emma had put a stop to that, and he'd thought she'd disposed of it entirely. What Eadric was doing with it was a mystery. It didn't seem right for him to have it.

"You'll know I was born in Sciropesberie, of course," said Eadric, his fingers continuing with their irritating "tap-tap-tappy-tap" upon the slate. "What you may not know much about is my early life there...how I was shaped into the man I am today. Did you ever think to ask?"

Æthelred rumbled to himself, knowing that was the best he could do at present. He did, however, make a gesture with his right hand, imploring Eadric to cease his interminable tapping and pass him the slate board so he could write.

"You want this?" Eadric asked, lifting the board up before letting it settle back into his lap. "You know as well as I, my king, that I don't think your wife would approve."

Æthelred rumbled again, annoyed at whatever game Eadric thought he was playing. He'd never gotten this feeling from him before. Something was wrong. Eadric could tell well enough the power here had shifted, slipping out of Æthelred's hands and into those of his foreign bitch of a queen. Æthelred would have hoped Eadric might have sought to correct that injustice. Sadly, it seemed his hopes had been misplaced.

"I can't say I'm surprised," said Eadric. "It was only a matter of time before something like this happened...the Normans have been eyeing us for years now, hoping the constant invasions from the east might yield an opportunity for them to expand their influence...to make us dependent on them, or subjugate us outright. What with your...condition," he made a lazy flick of the hand towards the bed-ridden Æthelred, "I would say that time has come. A shame, really."

"G-g-g-g-gggiiiiivvvvvvv..." Æthelred slurred painfully, his frantic gesturing towards the slate board now looking vaguely pitiful. Eadric smiled and shook his head.

"That was sort of a word, I suppose," he said. "But I'm told that's as good as it's going to get for you. Your physician has put all this down to stress...I understand you have your son to thank for that. He had some harsh words for you, didn't he? Harsh words about what we did to Sigeferth and Morcar?"

Æthelred shot him a look, his eyes disdainful. He didn't want to hear this. He didn't want to revisit the past.

"I had harsh words to say to my father once," Eadric added. "He was always hard on me. He was quite open about how he hated me. He liked to tell me how he was "giving up" on me...over and over. I think he thought it would hurt me. It did. But he failed to realise that a wounded heart...like any other part of the body...can turn numb. Scab over, if you will. The flesh dies off if left unattended...the heart dies, and with it...all feeling. All sentiment. All weakness. Only the will remains."

Eadric reached out and put the slate board on Æthelred's old desk. He watched him do it, apprehensive and powerless. "I can remember being different, you see," said Eadric, turning back to Æthelred, his eyes strangely hollow. "I can remember being bothered by my father's words...by the beatings...and my mother...approving of what he did. She wanted me to feel guilty, yes? She wanted me to think there was something awful about me, and that despite what my father did, it was somehow because they loved me. They didn't. I see that now. You can't choose your parents. It's a random accident. God doesn't bestow them on you. God doesn't bestow anything."

"These are difficult things to hear, I know," he went on as he settled into his chair and crossed his legs, his muddied boots scuffed and ragged. "But once the old me was burned away, I learned a few things. The "why" that I had on my mind...why do they hate me, why do they hurt me, why don't they love me...it just faded to nothing one day. All that was left, as I say, was the will. The will to escape. To get even. To ensure what had been done to me could never be done again. Nobody is to ever wield that kind of power over me. I am the one with the power, and if I can't have it...I will take it."

Æthelred didn't know what to make of any of this. He knew who Eadric's father was, of course, but he'd always been a quiet, unassuming man, one he certainly hadn't seen as abusive or cruel in any of his undertakings, domestic or otherwise. There was something about Eadric now, though, that told Æthelred he was being perfectly truthful, and the situation was all the more horrible because of it. He didn't feel safe with him. He wanted to cry out, but there was no guarantee if he did anyone would hear him. The best course of action was to simply remain as he was, quiet and still. Hopefully, once Eadric unburdened himself of whatever he had on his mind, he'd get up and leave.

"Edmund reminds me of myself, in a way," he went on, still unconcerned at Æthelred's inability to answer. "I confronted my father one day, much as Edmund did just recently with you. I suppose it was different. I had no supposedly noble cause like Edmund. I just hated my father and wanted him to suffer. And he did. I made sure of that...after I'd made certain he couldn't write me out of his will and my harpy of a mother was entirely powerless to intervene. It was a good day. His last day, of course, but that's what made it so good, at least for me."

"The rest is history," he added after a brief pause. "I set to work doing what was right, or at least right for me. I was the dutiful thegn, but I made sure to stand out, despite how modest my holdings were. And you saw that, didn't you, my king? You recognised something in me, I think. You knew I could do things others might baulk at. That's why you had me kill Ælfhelm."

That was a sore point, at least to Æthelred. He'd had Ælfhelm killed, yes, and he'd gotten Eadric to do it, but it had been necessary at the time, despite how guilty he still felt about it. Ælfhelm had been an ealdorman, and a popular one, at least in the North, but therein lay the problem. He'd had aspirations of breaking Norþanhymbre away from his rule, or at least that was the word, which was something Æthelred couldn't tolerate. England had to stay united. And so Ælfhelm had needed to go. He didn't understand why Eadric was bringing this up now. He'd been made an ealdorman as a reward for his part in their little scheme. It made no sense to drag shameful memories to the surface. Unless…

"But of course, everyone blamed me," said Eadric, sounding suddenly bitter. "It was like you could escape responsibility for giving the order…and me, the loyal servant who simply sought to do as commanded, was found to be at fault exclusively. That Wulfnoth…he'd mock me. Called me "Eadric of Sciropesberie", even after I became an ealdorman, like there was something shameful in my origins. That's partly why I fabricated all that nonsense about him collaborating with Thorkell. That's why I had my brother lie to you so you'd remove Wulfnoth for us and silence his damnable tongue."

Æthelred tried to sit up, both anger and surprise surging in his chest. He failed and fell back onto his mattress, his breath wheezing in and out like an old pair of bellows. He'd come to suspect something was amiss with the accusation against Wulfnoth, as Thorkell himself clearly hadn't recognised the man when they'd met after retaking Lundenburg from Cnut. To hear Eadric openly admit he'd been lying to him was painful beyond words. The man was a snake, just as Edmund had so often said. If only he'd listened then. If only he'd listened more in general. Now he was trapped, a prisoner in his own body, and powerless to resist the serpent he'd thought he'd tamed. It was a terrible feeling. Worse was yet to come.

"You're upset by that?" Eadric asked, surprised. "It's just the way things go. You're not long for this world, Æthelred, so I thought you might as well know. I'm surprised you didn't work it out for yourself. You knew Wulfnoth thought so highly of your sons. That's why he's with Edmund now rather than here with us. You knew he sought to have them take the throne, and would do whatever it took to see it come to pass. I have other ambitions. Ones that certainly don't involve your son, Edmund, becoming king. He'll kill me if he does. I'll have nowhere left to go. Which is why I'm here."

Eadric now had something else in his hands. It was a piece of parchment, and he scrutinised it for a few seconds, his eyes darting quickly from top to bottom. He handed it to Æthelred, allowing him to grip it in his right hand. Æthelred went to study the text, but Eadric's voice cut in, giving voice to his own suspicions.

"All you need do is make your mark," he said. "I've taken care of everything else. Edward will be king. I'll be safe then. You owe me that. I've done many, many grim deeds for you…your queen, also, will be safe with Edward on the throne. Edmund is a madman. I can attest to that. He attacked me just recently. Do the right thing. Let Edward rule."

Æthelred stared at the parchment, doing his best to focus on the dark, smooth ink and the message it conveyed. It was written as if he himself was speaking to the reader, relaying a long, meandering monologue about how Æthelred was apparently "eager to see the matter of succession settled" by "making it clear that my son, Edward, has my every confidence as the one, single, and indisputable heir to the Kingdom of England." Æthelred was temporarily taken aback by the audacity of it all. He knew

Emma would be behind this, with Eadric pushing and prompting her as needed. It made him sick. And it wouldn't do them much good, either. He'd given his word to Edmund that he'd succeed him when he passed. He may have let his son down with Sigeferth and Morcar, but he wouldn't fail him in this. He made it known by flinging the parchment back in Eadric's face.

He took it well, in his way. He didn't get angry, instead retrieving the parchment from the floor and holding it in his lap, his expression neutral. "I understand how you must feel," he sighed, a statement Æthelred found difficult to believe. "I too know what it's like to be powerless…to feel trapped, as though every detail of your life and destiny is out of your hands. But think of it like this…we've come so far, you and I…we've done many things together, for good or ill…this is your chance to reward me properly. This will save my life. Edmund will kill me, as I said. Edward will not. You must help me in this, my king."

Now that was really pushing it, thought Æthelred. Eadric had been well compensated for everything he'd done in his service. To ask him for more, right after he'd admitted to lying to him for some considerable time over the situation with Wulfnoth, was monumentally foolish. Æthelred thought that unusual in itself. Eadric was normally such a smooth operator. If he'd wanted to convince him to let Edward rule, then telling him how he'd framed Wulfnoth seemed like an odd way of going about it. Eadric wasn't himself, or at least he wasn't as assured and professional as he'd been in the past. Æthelred studied him from his bed, scrutinising his muddied attire and dishevelled appearance. He had a haunted look to him. He'd not seen it before, but it was there; a tension around the mouth and eyes. Edmund really must have tried to kill him. Æthelred would have an answer as to why.

He gestured again for him to be given the slate board, an irate moan sounding from his throat. Eadric paused, possibly thinking of denying his request, before suddenly handing him the board and retrieving a length of chalk from the desk. Æthelred took both and commenced writing, noting with some relief how his text seemed slightly more legible than before.

"WHAT HAPPENED WITH EDMUND?"

Eadric again paused, like he either hadn't understood what had been written or was just loath to answer. "He somehow found out about what we had planned for Ealdgyth," he finally said, a hint of bitterness and what looked like apprehension crossing his features. "He attacked me at Malmesberie, he and several others. They burned the town, slaughtering the innocent, the nuns…Edmund himself came for me, the blood of a woman he'd only just killed fresh on his sword. A terrible sight."

Eadric had very likely hoped to be taken seriously. He'd no doubt thought Æthelred too weakened by his condition to discern a lie, thinking his illness would make him just nod along to whatever was suggested. It was either that, or Eadric was so addled by his recent experience his usual talent for manipulation had slipped from grasp. He scowled, perturbed at the sound of laughter, his eyes flashing with anger at the sight of his king giggling hysterically from his bed.

"Be silent!" he snapped, his restrained composure shattering. "You'll do as I ask, Æthelred!" he shrieked, jabbing a finger in his direction. "This is not just some routine matter of political intrigue…this is about my life! Edmund WILL kill me! I will not have it! You will make Edward the heir if you have any sense left in you! Do the right thing!"

Æthelred continued to laugh, finding the notion of Eadric thinking he could speak on what was right and what was wrong to be quite hysterical. Eadric didn't see the funny side. He leapt to his feet, snatching the board and chalk and hurling them away. He then heaved Æthelred upward so he was sat up in bed and thrust the parchment into his lap. A quill was procured, possibly from Æthelred's desk, and thrust into his right hand. Æthelred snarled when Eadric took him by the wrist and tried to physically force him to make his mark upon the page. He resisted. Eadric tried again. Æthelred bit him in the face.

He howled, clutching at his cheek and staggering back. "Sign the parchment!" he roared, advancing again to Æthelred's bedside, his hand still upon his cheek. "Sign it! Do the right thing, for once in your sorry life!"

Æthelred could hear his heart hammering in his chest when Eadric gripped him by the hair and screamed into his face. Despite the sheer volume, he couldn't make out much of what he was saying. It was all so discordant, high-pitched, and furious; a veritable deluge of hatred and frustration pouring out of a twisted, scowling mouth just a few inches from his own. Eadric was unhinged. Whatever Edmund had done to him had brought something out, something that had been buried or at least controlled for some considerable time. Eadric was that abused child again, raging and hateful, demanding the affection of his cruel parents and despairing over the knowledge he'd never obtain it. Æthelred felt nothing but fear, and for a moment, he thought to simply give in and do as he'd been asked. If it would get Eadric to desist, would it be such a bad thing?

A not-so-old memory stirred. He was in the tunnels under Lundenburg, escaping with the others before the city could fall to Svienn. Edmund had caught up with him, demanding he release Brandon into his custody so he could be reunited with his mother. They'd argued briefly, and Edmund had threatened to cut off relations with him, saying he would make it so they never saw each other again. Æthelred had been mortified by the prospect. He'd had to relent. And then they'd spoken on Edmund's mother, Ælfgifu. She'd been the bond that had kept them together as a family. She'd been the one who had kept them united. And if she were here, now, she'd know Æthelred had to keep his promise to Edmund. She'd know that Edmund, not Edward, must be king. She'd know that was the only way Æthelred would ever find any kind of redemption in the eyes of his son. The snarling madman before him presently couldn't be allowed to get in the way of that.

He deceived Eadric. He pretended to be frightened, acting like he was suitably cowed and about to "make your mark", as Eadric kept screeching, upon the parchment. Eadric looked pleased, although his eyes widened with outrage when Æthelred simply stabbed the quill through the centre of the parchment, puncturing a hole right through it. Eadric went to intervene, clutching at Æthelred's arm, and in the ensuing tussle the parchment was quite ruined, the once flowing script torn and defaced.

Æthelred again started to laugh, feeling glad beyond measure that he'd kept his courage and confounded his bastard ealdorman in the process. Eadric was not so pleased. He struck him, slapping him across the cheek, and he repeated the action, over and over, the flat of his palm raining down upon each side of his face in a furious rhythm. Æthelred hissed in rage and pain, but Eadric kept going, spitting frenzied accusations and strange objections as if Æthelred was somebody else in a different place and a different time. Eadric again seemed as a boy, fighting a battle that was long spent and had never had anything to do with Æthelred to begin with. He laughed at that, finding Eadric's instability in the face of a crippled old man vaguely amusing. That was a mistake.

Eadric struck him with a closed fist. It hurt, and Æthelred couldn't remember the last time he'd endured such a thing, thinking perhaps his own mother might have been the only person to ever dare do so. Eadric hit him again, ignoring his moaned objections, and struck him a third time, the action snapping Æthelred's skull backwards so it impacted against the stone wall at the head of his bed. His vision clouded, from tears or pain or perhaps both, he knew not, but he could see Eadric had pulled his fist back, his teeth bared, to strike him again. He looked like he intended to put some real force into this one. Æthelred closed his eyes. He hoped unconsciousness might claim him soon. At least that would bring him a little peace.

"Stop this at once!"

Both stared in the direction of the voice, Eadric's assault thankfully paused. Eadgyth, Æthelred's daughter and wife to Eadric, was standing in the doorway to the bedchamber, looking fierce and fearful both, if that were possible. "What are you doing?" she demanded, her arms crossing defensively across her chest. "You'd hurt an old man in his bed? My father too!"

"Close the door," said Eadric, his voice a low, menacing growl. "This does not concern you, wife. Depart from us and shut the door. You know what will happen if you refuse."

Æthelred didn't like the sound of that. Eadric had essentially admitted to abusing his daughter; something that made him hate him all the more. There'd be no turning back after this, should Æthelred ever heal and become the king he was. Edmund would be the least of Eadric's worries then. Æthelred would set Hereward on him. That would see justice served.

"I'm not afraid of you!" Eadgyth hissed, the tears in her eyes suggesting she wasn't being entirely truthful. "This is too much! I won't have you hurting my father as you do so many others! Leave him, or I'll call the guards!"

"And you think they'll obey you over me?" Eadric scoffed.

"No, but…I…I…" Eadgyth was stammering, out of her depth, unable to argue with the reality that, even after assaulting the King of England, Eadric still had the power in this situation and she did not. Eadric walked over to her, his gait casual and measured, his left hand massaging the knuckles of his right. Remarkably she held her ground, at least until he planted the flat of his palm into her chest, forcefully, to send her hurtling back out of the doorway and onto the stone floor beyond. Eadric ignored her and slammed the door shut. Eadgyth did not attempt another intervention, and Eadric turned back towards Æthelred, his eyes like two rigid, icy orbs set into his skull.

"Apologies for the interruption, my king," he said, a sneer upon his face as he again advanced towards him. "Let us resume our discussion. I just know we can come to some kind of accord."

****

Eadgyth hurried away from the bedchamber, her hand clasped to her aching chest and her cheeks wet with tears. She tried not to think of what was happening now, knowing from experience just how far her husband's fury could go. She'd long hated her father for marrying her to Eadric and thus inadvertently setting her up for years of abuse. Yet something had changed in her when she saw him just moments ago, so pained and helpless, suffering just as she had. She couldn't have it. She WOULDN'T have it.

Eadric should have killed her years ago. He'd been a fool not to. There was only so much a person could take before all they thought of was vengeance and were thus rendered immune to the fear of further punishment. Eadgyth couldn't believe how she'd just confronted him, thinking such courage had long fled from her heart. She was pleased there was still a spark of bravery left in her. It would be of use now.

She pressed on, the long, flowing lengths of her blue and white cyrtel trailing across the cold stones. She wasn't the powerless non-entity everyone thought she was. She knew she wasn't alone in caring for her father, despite everything. If Eadric was set on abusing a dying old man in his own bed, then she'd have something to say about that, regardless of the risks. There was at least one other who almost certainly felt the same. It was in him she would now place her trust, even if she brought the wrath of a queen upon herself by doing it.

Eadgyth smiled as she left her father's hall, resuming that same, quickened pace across the courtyard, and passed into the long, enveloping shadow of the prison tower.

XXXXV

He'd always been one for getting lost in thought. It had been so since he was a child, and others had at times made fun of him for it, mistaking his bouts of deep and sudden introspection for simplicity or outright stupidity. It wasn't right, and Edmund didn't consider it a flaw on his part. He liked to think things through, that's all, and if he were prone to daydreaming on occasion, he didn't see the harm in it. Unless, of course, he did it at inappropriate times. His own wedding, for instance.

He glanced about, briefly wondering why old Father Wilfrid was looking at him so intently. He'd been waffling on for some time, and Edmund couldn't help but drift away. It wasn't a good look. Everyone was staring at him, the assembled multitude shifting uncomfortably at his apparent faux pas. Just what had the priest said?

"Well, do you, my lord?" asked Father Wilfrid, hissing the words from between gritted teeth. "Do you indeed wish to take this good lady as wife? Will you love her, comfort her, honour and keep her in sickness and in health, forsaking all others, for as long as you both live?"

Edmund looked over to his left and the "good lady" that had been mentioned. Ealdgyth looked the part, dressed in an excessively long white cyrtel with matching veil. She was staring back at Edmund expectantly, like she was willing him to say the words and bind them once and for all in Holy Matrimony. Edmund knew it had to be done. But he couldn't help but hesitate. This wasn't what he'd ever wanted, despite having come to appreciate its necessity.

He peered over his shoulder, looking back at their audience. They were in St Mary's church – the natural choice for a wedding since it was the only church in Snotingeham – and the place was packed out, every thegn, notable, and man of rank squeezing their way in to watch Edmund squirm. Ulfcytel was there in the front row, looking strangely different now he was out of his armour and had washed and plaited his beard. Wulfhild stood next to him, dressed for the occasion like her husband, and Æva was next to her, staring awkwardly at Edmund like she was embarrassed for him. Edmund shouldn't have looked at her. It made it all that much harder. He didn't want this. He didn't want to marry Ealdgyth. This had all been a mistake. He'd be honest now and admit to it before he bound himself to an unhappy union. It was better this way.

Then he saw Brandon. The lad was next to his mother, of course, but on his right was the girl, Ælfwynn, and next to her was Wulfnoth. Edmund knew for a fact that Wulfnoth was armed underneath that very fine green cloak of his; a necessary evil in church, they'd agreed, given the security situation and their previous trouble with assassins. Yet the sight of the children alongside the protective Wulfnoth stirred something in Edmund's memory. A promise he'd made. To Æva.

He could remember it like it was yesterday. They'd fled Lundenburg, escaping through the tunnel network beneath the ground, and made it to Offetuna, hoping the priest that had apparently assisted Æva's husband, Alaric, might be inclined to help them give him a proper burial. They'd found the priest dead, and Ulfcytel, true to form, had later succumbed to emotion and stormed off into the forest, taking Alaric's body with him. They'd followed, and he'd led them to the site of a battle, one where Alaric's good friend, Osmund, was said to have fallen. They'd there also discovered the remains of Edmund's uncle, Æthelstan, and all of his men, cut down in some ambush sprung from the duplicitous mind of Eadric of Mierċe. Edmund had been aghast to see it, and he had grieved as was natural.

By the time night had fallen, however, they'd gone some way to putting things right. They'd given the English dead a proper burial, Alaric and Æthelstan included. Æva and Brandon, though, had been beset by sadness, and they'd refused to depart from Alaric's grave, leaving Edmund concerned for each of them. He'd gone to talk to her, huddled as she was in the darkness, hoping to perhaps bring her something or provide some words of comfort. She'd then asked him something specific. She'd told him to become king. Of a different kind than his father. One that would protect. One that would prevent the horrors they'd all just witnessed, for the sake of the children and the children yet to come.

Edmund had agreed, as was right, and as he gazed upon the young Brandon and Ælfwynn now, he knew his promise was still binding. They'd both lost so much. Alaric had been snatched from Brandon, thanks to the brute malevolence of that beast, Hemingr. Ælfwynn, likewise, was now without her father and sisters, and all because of that poisonous reptile, Eadric. It pained Edmund to think his own father had played a deciding role in both their tragedies. That made his task here that much more important. He had to keep his promise to Æva. He loved her, with all his heart, yet she was beyond his reach, and so the only way he could act on that love was to honour what he'd agreed to. He'd become king. He'd stop his father and Eadric both. There'd be justice, for Brandon and Ælfwynn and all the many, many children just like them. His mind was made up. He turned back to Father Wilfrid.

"I do," said Edmund, loudly and clearly. "I do wish to take the lady Ealdgyth as wife, and let no man here dispute my intentions. Let us see it done, in Christ's name."

"And you, my lady?" asked Father Wilfrid, looking quite relieved as he turned to Ealdgyth. "Will you accept this man as your husband, to live together in God's ordinance of Holy Matrimony? Will you obey him and serve him, love, honour, and keep him in sickness and in health, forsaking all others, so long as you both shall live?"

"I will," said Ealdgyth without hesitation, her expression difficult to discern from beneath her veil. Edmund stared at her whilst the priest went on, his voice a monotone as he declared their union to all present. Edmund stepped forward at the appropriate time and lifted her veil, pressing his lips to hers. She returned the gesture, with some warmth it must be said, but Edmund's heart was still cold despite her sincerity. He never thought he'd be on this path. He never thought any of this could happen.

Everything was a blur as he wandered down the aisle with his new wife. Ulfcytel was clapping loudly and baying "God save the king!", and Ælfwynn had scampered to her mother's side to clasp her hand. Ealdgyth took Edmund's left hand in hers, and the three of them walked on into a deluge of thunderous adoration from the enthused crowd. Edmund smiled grimly, knowing many of these thegns only supported him now he was effectively the most powerful man in the Five Boroughs. He'd tolerate and forgive them, as he should, for he needed their loyalty, and if they were willing to give it with his marriage to Ealdgyth, he'd accept it for what it was.

They left the church and paused atop the stone steps leading down into the street. Wulfnoth had appeared close by, and he'd arranged for several hundred warriors to line both sides of the thoroughfare directly ahead. They looked magnificent, their armour polished and sparkling, their spear tips catching the fading light of the frigid afternoon. Edmund felt a pang of sorrow as yet another memory stirred. He'd stood here, at the top of these steps and taking in the view, not all that long ago, with Sigeferth, Morcar, Ealdgyth, and Æthelstan, back when he and his brother had fought a duel at Sigeferth's hall for the entertainment of their guests. It seemed like a lifetime ago now, and three of those men had been taken from them, leaving just Edmund and Ealdgyth with their memories. Edmund looked at her. He could see sorrow in her eyes. He fancied she was thinking much the same as he was.

More warriors had appeared at the far end of the street. They weren't drawn up in disciplined lines like the others, making Edmund think this was some kind of spontaneous gathering they'd embarked on of their own volition. They came closer, cheering and clashing weapons upon their shields, and Edmund smiled at the sight, so sincere was the spectacle. Others joined them, the people of Snotingeham flocking out of their homes to applaud him. Those men who'd been standing guard eventually followed suit, and they cheered Edmund and his new bride with the rest, their cries and faces jubilant.

"God save King Edmund!" they said, over and over, like his father was already deposed and better days were upon them. Then he heard the other chant, that single word, that name, repeated over and over from hundreds upon hundreds of throats. He knew it well. "Ironside." They said it like they meant it, like they had when they'd smashed Cnut at Gainesburg. His brother had given him that name, and his men had taken it to heart. That meant something. He'd tell them that. There was no time like the present.

"You honour me," announced Edmund, the crowd quietening upon hearing him speak. Ulfcytel had now joined him, as had Wulfhild and Brandon even, Æva hovering just behind. "Last time I was standing upon these steps," continued Edmund, "I was with my beloved brother, Æthelstan, and your lords, Sigeferth and Morcar. We'd received word of my father's plan to deliver yet more English gold into the hands of the heathens…and we were rightly dismayed to hear it."

The crowd muttered uneasily at the mention of the much-loathed heregeld, the memory of which was undoubtedly still fresh in their minds. "But we resolved to do something to stop such injustice," said Edmund, "and with the support of the men and warriors of the Five Boroughs, we faced Thorkell in battle rather than see him receive a single coin. Our resolve cost my dear brother his life. I found out later that my uncle had also lost his life thanks to my father's treachery…and now your lords, Sigeferth and Morcar, have been taken from us. And again, my father's hands are red with blood."

More muttering followed, a few angry expletives erupting at the mention of Thorkell and the recent murders in Lundenburg. "And I would no longer have it so," rumbled Edmund, his voice echoing out over the multitude. "I would no longer live under a king who kills his own whenever it suits him. I would no longer live under a king who pays the heathens rather than face them, with sword in hand and a prayer upon his lips. I would no longer live under a king…who breaks his word just to settle imaginary scores with men who are guilty of nothing but loving this land, as any true Englishman would! Even if that king is my father! I will not stand for it! I will act, as I should have long before!"

Cheering sounded from some of the warriors below, and Edmund glanced over to see Ulfcytel applauding, the assembled wedding guests just behind him following his lead. "I AM King of England," bellowed Edmund, turning back to his audience. "Because my father has lost the right to call himself that. He has lost the right to rule…he has schemed, conspired, lied, shed the blood of the innocent…all things a proper Christian king would never do! And we have suffered for it, over and over, through the bitterest years this nation has ever endured! Yet we remain a nation! We remain Englishmen! And we will defend our land! For the heathens will return, and when they do…I give you my vow, here and now, that I will bleed for you, all of you, to ensure our people remain safe! We have suffered and lamented…and been ground to dust for the sake of the greed of foreigners for too long…that will no longer be so. Follow me now, and let us finish what we started! Let us deliver notice to the Danes that England is no longer a cowed and beaten land! That it has risen, and that is united, righteous, and free!"

The crowd erupted, as Edmund had hoped. The warriors hammered their shields, over and over, the great drumming cacophony almost drowning out the frenzied howls of approval from the rest of Snotingeham's people. Wulfnoth was suddenly in front of Edmund and had fallen to his knees. His hands were raised, palms facing up, a majestic sword placed upon them. Edmund knew this blade well. It had been his brother's, originally, before he had made a gift of it to the much-missed Alaric. Edmund had used it these past months, making the Danes pay in blood for the death of Alaric and Æthelstan both. He took it from Wulfnoth and held it up to the light, the people below almost rapturous at the sight. He pointed it to the sky, tip-first, allowing the cold sunlight to fall upon the shimmering, silvered metal. This was his moment. This was destiny. This was the fate he'd seize.

He looked back briefly, his gaze meeting Brandon's and then Æva's. It was a fleeting gesture, but he saw in her eyes that she understood. He was keeping his promise, the one he'd made at the graveside of her husband. This was his service to her. This was how he'd love her forevermore. It pleased him that she saw it. He'd draw strength from that. Enough for a thousand battles. He would not fail.

King Edmund Ironside moved down the steps of the church, his wife, stepdaughter, and friends following, and walked out to greet his people, knowing he would die for them and they for him. He'd repay such loyalty, any way he could, and England, although beaten and bloodied, would see that and rally to his side. Dark days were coming to an end. There was a light now, shining out for all to see, and Edmund would play his part, come what may. A promise he would keep. A nation he would defend. And England would be born anew.

XXXXVI

The cold winds blasted across the icy plains, their keening wail quite painful upon his already tender ears. Cnut pressed onward, his furs clutched tight about himself, his fingers red and swollen from exposure. He could see what he'd come for, just up ahead, the tall, dark outline of the stones becoming visible out of the furious, white-flecked haze of the blizzard. He'd find insight here, if not comfort. He didn't care for the latter anyway. What he needed was clarity. The stones may yet give it to him.

He glanced behind him, taking in the hunched, shuffling shape that was Østen. He was attired as Cnut was, looking like he were half-bear, such was the thickness of his furs, and the same went for the multitude that followed. They endured the storm as the warriors they were, for they were Danes all, and the bite of the wind and the falling of snow was nothing compared to what they'd been through. England and its many hardships hadn't been enough to lay them low. This storm wouldn't succeed where Edmund had failed.

And yet Cnut still had reason for melancholy. The men behind him were barely a thousand strong, strung out in a great meandering column stretching back across the jagged, desolate white landscape towards the forlorn grey of the northern horizon. When they'd left Denmark just last year, he and his father had commanded a host of thousands, one so vast they'd been able to breach the walls of Lundenburg itself. This was all that remained. England had not welcomed them, and her fierce and terrible son, Edmund, had not relented in his lust for Danish blood. Many of those that had escaped him would no longer answer to Cnut, and with Harald upon the throne in Roskilde, they'd opted for the easy path and declared their loyalty to him. Cnut was bitter over it. But at least he still had these men. He still had Østen. He still had his English wife, Ælfgifu, too, heavily guarded amidst the trudging throng and blessedly pregnant with Cnut's child. He even still had the brooding English abbot, Ælfmær. That counted for something. It had to. He wouldn't believe he'd endured all he had for no real purpose. He had to make some sense of all this. With any luck, he'd have such an opportunity before long.

The stones loomed yet closer, emerging from the storm like the gnarled, implacable fixtures he knew them to be. Cnut upped his pace through the thickening snow, excitement and relief spurring him on. He stopped when he fell into the stones' shadow, the howl of the wind seeming to fade into irrelevance in the face of the significance of the moment. He reached out and touched one, his frost-bitten fingers tracing the edges of the runes carved into the solid rock. He knew this inscription. It was familiar to him, to all his family, and with good reason. His grandfather had seen to that. This was one of his stones. King Harald Bluetooth had wanted to be remembered for bringing Christ to Denmark. This here was a testament to that noble legacy.

Cnut fell to his knees, Østen and the others standing at his back. He lifted his hands to his chest, ignoring the pained throb from his fingers as they were forcibly unfurled and straightened so that he could pray. He stayed like this for a time, enduring the blizzard with indifference, his mind fixated on prayer and the resolution he'd long hoped for. He eventually opened his eyes, the wind again wailing in his ears, and stared straight ahead, taking in the stone immediately facing him. He saw Christ there, but this was no holy apparition. He'd been carved into the rock, crucified like he had been, although this time he was surrounded by brambles too, the things seeming to entwine themselves around his limbs to hold him in place. It was a fine depiction, Cnut thought. Yet it was of absolutely no help with his many problems.

He stood up, a little unsteadily in the wind, and ordered his men to start making camp around a sparse outcropping of swaying, skeletal trees about a hundred yards east. They moved off, eager at the prospect of shelter, but Østen stayed right where he was, his eyes on Cnut. "What would you have of me?" Cnut asked after a few moments, his voice raised to overcome the wind. Østen was silent for a time, his eyes drifting towards the stones. He knew this place, that was certain. He'd have come here with Svienn, and from the looks of it, he viewed them with a combination of sadness and reverence. Østen was still pagan, Cnut knew, as were many of their people along with him, but he wouldn't begrudge him for that now. He would, however, like to know what he was thinking. He had a feeling it would do him some good to share his burdens.

"I was here with your grandfather once," said Østen suddenly, surprising Cnut with his admission. "It was a good day, or the worst, depending on how you see things. But when your father moved against him…"

He'd fallen silent. He felt uncomfortable speaking on those days. Many did. Cnut understood. He didn't know why Svienn had overthrown the Bluetooth either, but he had, although he'd not sought to undo the work he'd begun on ensuring Denmark became Christian. Cnut had wondered about that at times, but typically his father had never given him much of an answer when he'd asked. "It was necessary," he'd just say, and leave it at that, like that was all the explanation needed.

The blizzard relented a little, allowing a small stone church to become visible just off to the north and east. Cnut couldn't fathom why they'd not seen it before, but there it was now, emerging out of the freezing gale and looking quite ominous against the swirling, frantic backdrop of the storm. Cnut began moving towards it, and Østen followed, their heavy, half-frozen boots gouging great imprints into the surrounding snow. They reached the narrow archway of an entrance and eased open the frosted doors, Cnut expressing some surprise they'd not been locked or barred from within. They stepped inside, eager to get out of the wind and see if anyone else had sought refuge here.

It was not so. The church was both tiny and empty, consisting of a single, narrow nave leading up to a bare stone altar, an imposing wooden cross fixed to the wall just beyond. Cnut headed straight for it and genuflected before the altar, wondering who might be responsible for maintaining this place and where exactly they'd got to. Østen had closed the doors, reducing the sound of the wind outside to an irksome whine. He pulled the hood of his furs back, Cnut doing the same so they could finally talk properly.

"Did you know about this place?" asked Cnut, his voice echoing slightly. The church had a musty smell to it, making him think they were the first people to come here in some time.

"I did," said Østen. "Your grandfather had it built. Long before your birth, that was. This is your first visit?"

"Not to the rune stones, no," shrugged Cnut. "My father brought me to them when I was a boy...but I have no memory of this place. It's like it just came out of the storm by magic."

Østen chuckled to himself, his arms folded as he leaned back against the doors. "Oh, it's quite real. I can remember your grandfather being so proud the day it was finished. He was the first one to pray here. He felt it important to make a gesture. He thought others would see his sincerity and follow him."

"And did they?"

"Some."

"But not you?"

"No," said Østen, and left it at that. They stared at the other, awkward in their silence. Cnut had never asked him why he wasn't a Christian. He felt like now might be a good time to find out.

"So why?" he asked. "I mean...what is it about the old ways that entraps you?"

"I wouldn't use the word entrapped," said Østen. "I just don't understand how...a people like ours...we're warriors, or at least many of us choose to live as Viking. I'm one of them. From what I know, this Jesus was not such a man. Keeping my distance from him seemed like the only honest thing to do. I can't pretend I'm like him. I'm not. We're not."

Cnut scowled at his words, only for a single thought to rise unbidden into his mind. Østen was right. His people were not Christ-like, and neither was he. They still carried on in the old ways, taking whatever they decided was theirs and offering no apology to anyone left alive to complain. It had always been this way, as far as he was aware. He didn't see it changing. He didn't think he wanted it to. Yet he knew God acted in the world and that he'd allowed the Danes to take England, if only for a time. Cnut would understand the purpose behind that. He would uncover God's will. He would win his favour. Then nothing could stand in his way.

"So you consider my ambitions at odds with my faith?" asked Cnut. "You think God frowns on what me and my father set out to do in England?"

"We are defeated, are we not?" asked Østen. "Svienn died too at the hands of England's Saint Edmund. I was there, my king. I take such things as the omens they are."

"Are you not afraid of offending me?" asked Cnut, annoyed that he'd mention his father's death without prior warning.

"You are not some overly sensitive whelp in need of coddling," replied Østen, his tone neutral. "You are a king, and a king should have honest men at his side. I am an honest man. You know this."

Cnut nodded, somewhat pleased and flattered that Østen took him so seriously. "And honest as you are..." said Cnut, "...will you now tell me what my father would never tell me? Why did he overthrow my grandfather? Why did the Forkbeard move against the Bluetooth?"

Østen's face soured, his eyes seeming to lose a little of their sparkle at the mention of such dark and duplicitous deeds. "It was a grim business," he finally muttered, his remorse obvious. "I didn't want any part of it at first. A son should not turn against the father...but me and Svienn...we were bonded in battle and victory. I had to follow him, even if I didn't like it. Even if we earned the ire of the Gods."

"But why?" asked Cnut, secretly alarmed that Østen had mentioned "the Gods", in church, no less. "Why do it? Did not others rally to defend my grandfather? Why turn Dane against Dane?"

"Because Harald Bluetooth was doing that anyway," sighed Østen. "Your grandfather wasn't a gentle man. That's not uncommon for our people, but he was very…single-minded about how he wanted to shape our country. It was to be Christian, and that left no room for people who believe as I do. And there are still many of us."

"So my father overthrew him to prevent him from sparking a larger civil war through his aggressive evangelising?"

"You cut right to it, my king," said Østen. "That is precisely why Svienn acted and why I eventually followed him. King Harald wouldn't take no for an answer…he wouldn't relent…he shed blood when it wasn't necessary, exiled others, killed men for so much as questioning him…we all wanted to act, but we knew not how. Then Svienn gave us a way out."

"And you weren't surprised that my father would turn on his own? Wasn't he sorrowful for it?"

"I'm not sure. Svienn always was difficult to read, at least to me. I don't think he wanted to do it. On some level, he wanted Denmark to be Christian too, but he wasn't willing to see his people divided by a river of blood to see it done. That's why I forsook my honour and followed him in rebellion."

Cnut frowned, confused at his words. "You consider yourself dishonourable now? Why?"

"Because Harald was king, and Svienn was his son. The son submits to the father, and a subject submits to his king. That's the law, of Gods and men. Always has been. Always will be. To break that law was a hard thing, a terrible thing…but we did it. And Denmark was the better for it, I think, yet scars remain. People remember. It haunts us still."

Cnut had no idea what to say. Østen had let him in on something his father had long seemed to want to hide, and now he knew, he couldn't say he felt much better. He'd suspected in his time that many a jarl somehow thought badly of Svienn, and from what Østen had just said, it seemed likely people still remembered his rebellion and abhorred the memories of it to this day. Cnut couldn't say who was right and who was wrong. He personally couldn't imagine turning against his own father, but people did all manner of things when they felt they had no choice. Family didn't seem to always matter like it should. He'd know that. His brother, Harald, had made himself King of Denmark at his expense. It was why Cnut was here now, shivering in this church discussing bitter memories whilst Harald sat in a warm hall back in Roskilde. Cnut felt his teeth grind at the image.

"Is that why you stayed with me?" he suddenly asked. "You and the rest of the men out there…you had every opportunity to make your life easy and accept Harald as king. Plenty have done so. Why not you?"

"Would you believe me if I said I thought you'd be a better king than he?" asked Østen, smiling faintly.

"There must be more to it than that. Why not tell me?"

"You are correct," Østen nodded. "You of course know that your father and I were friends. Heck, I just told you how I followed him into rebellion…that builds a bond. You're his son. I can't abandon you."

"And you think I need protecting?" Cnut wasn't upset. There was no chance he could somehow argue his position wasn't a weak one, considering all that had happened. It would be foolish to try. He needed men like Østen. If they deserted him, he'd have nothing but shame and bad memories.

"You are King of England, by right of conquest," said Østen gravely. "And I think your father wanted you to have Denmark too. I knew his mind. Harald has taken advantage of the situation to suit his own ends. I don't respect that. I won't follow a man like that."

Cnut sighed, a long, drawn-out thing. "What am I even doing here?" he asked, raising his hands to take in the chill stone walls around them. "I thought once I saw the runes…some insight might be obtained…that something might happen that would tell me what to do nex…"

A horn sounded from outside, high-pitched and shaky, like the man responsible was close to panic. Another followed, and then another after that, each as dour and ominous as the first. Østen turned and stepped back when the doors behind him began to open from without, their aged hinges creaking and grinding. A gust of icy wind came on through, bringing a fearful-looking warrior with it. He saw Cnut and spoke, his voice as alarmed as his look.

"My king, there is a force of armed men approaching from the west. We can't be sure yet who they are, but…"

"Let's go," snapped Cnut, striding forward without hesitation to leave the church and face their uninvited guests. He emerged back out into the snow and ice, the wind again clutching at his furs so as to find a way in. Østen had followed, as had their rather frightened messenger. The rest of the men were here, hurriedly assembling into a shield wall facing away from the church, their spears and axes held ready. Cnut took position at the head of them, sword in hand and gazing out into the storm, wondering if…

He saw movement up ahead. There were men, just a few at first but then hundreds more, emerging out of the biting wind. They were warriors, that was obvious, for they had the gait and bulk of men burdened with thick furs and heavy armour. Many carried spears, but some sported hefty, broad-headed axes, of the type only an impressively strong and experienced fighter would dare presume to use.

The warrior striding at the head of them was one such man. He was huge, tall, and broad across the chest, an axe of considerable length gripped in one hand like it was no burden at all. He led his men onward, wrapped tight in his wolf skins, his face hidden beneath a hefty, burnished helm of battered iron. Cnut noticed some of his men had flinched at the sight of him, so imposing was his presence. He felt their apprehension. He was glad when Østen appeared at his side and began shouting.

"STAND FAST AND IDENTIFY YOURSELF!"

The tall figure ignored him, instead continuing his implacable advance towards them. His men hurried after him, reforming their ranks into one great line of painted shields. There was only one reason for that, Cnut realised. These must be his brother's men, here to kill him and his followers and crush any rebellion before it could even start. It was low of Harald to try this at such a sacred place, but Cnut wasn't excessively surprised. Harald intended to rule, and he'd made it perfectly clear what he'd thought of Cnut's return and his plan to reconquer England. Bloodshed was his answer. Cnut would give him an answer of his own.

He raised his sword in the air, his arm tensed and his teeth bared in a snarl. He'd lead this charge himself, cutting down that tall bastard and taking his head for all to see. They'd win a great victory, staining the snow red with the blood of Harald's men and sending a clear enough message to Danes everywhere that…

"I WOULD SPEAK WITH KING CNUT!"

The opposing force had stopped, forming up behind their leader after he'd suddenly paused in his stride to bark out his request. "I am he," Cnut answered, lowering his sword but still keeping it ready. "What would you have of me? Who are you? My brother's men?"

The tall one stepped forward and let his axe drop to the snow, using his now freed hand to remove his helm. A craggy, overly broad face was revealed, his great grey beard flecked with snow and ice. "I am Thorkell," he said, some of Cnut's men gasping at the name. "And I have come to negotiate with you for…"

"You are no friend to the king!" declared Østen, the venom of his outburst almost making Cnut jump. "You defied his father every chance you had, putting your own interests ahead of those of our people! Why come here? Has Harald paid you to do away with us before we can rally a larger force to oppose him?"

"Your man speaks out of turn," said Thorkell to Cnut. "And yet there is truth in what he says. I did long defy your father, King Svienn. Our interests were not in accord. Now he's gone, I wonder if the son will prove the wiser ruler."

"I am not a ruler," snapped Cnut, angered at Østen for speaking without permission but also irked by Thorkell's inference that his father was a fool. "You know I'm no ruler. My brother is King of Denmark. I am King of England, but in name only. Do not play games with me, Thorkell. You fought against us at Lundenburg. You were seen. Tell me why we should not fight, here and now."

"Because that would be a waste of an opportunity," said Thorkell. Cnut was about to speak again when a few of Thorkell's men suddenly broke ranks, bearing what looked like some kind of wooden chest between them. They approached, moving just past Thorkell before setting their burden down upon the pristine snow. Thorkell stepped forward to stand beside it, and one of his men opened it up, revealing what lay within.

Cnut blinked, wondering what Thorkell was playing at. The chest was full of coins, gold and silver, of a quantity that suggested Thorkell had been enjoying great success even as Cnut fell to misery and defeat. More men came forward, depositing yet more chests, three and four and then five, at Thorkell's feet, all similarly filled with riches. Thorkell reached down to pick up a single coin. He threw it to Cnut, the thing landing just an inch or so in front of him. Cnut picked it up.

He recognised it well enough. It was English, with the face of the idiotic King Æthelred on one side and a cross on the other. Cnut was well acquainted with such coins, for they'd been in circulation in Denmark for some considerable time thanks to the reaving of his father and Æthelred's habit of trying to bribe him to stay away. Cnut finished studying it and let it slip from his grasp, allowing the storm to claim it. Thorkell would have to try harder to impress him, if that's what he was doing.

"Explain to me what you intend," Cnut said. "I doubt you came here to give me all this as tribute."

"I did not," said Thorkell, his voice really quite unpleasant, like dry, dusty shale cascading down a rock face. "I wish to work with you. To return to England. This wealth here..." he gestured to the chests with one hand, his other tucked deep into his furs, "...it's for a new army. Our army. We have enough to hire whoever we want, from wherever...your brother won't be able to intervene."

"You would help me take back my throne?" Cnut was surprised, but he wouldn't let it show. "But why me? You hated my father. You never made him such an offer when he was alive. What's changed?"

"England changed," said Thorkell almost sorrowfully. "Before, they were like whipped and frightened dogs. It was almost embarrassing witnessing them try and stop me from doing whatever I pleased. I grew tired of fighting Æthelred, and I certainly grew tired of serving him once we'd won back his capital for him. But now I think England is different. This Edmund Ironside...that's a fearsome name for a fearsome man. He would kill me if he had the chance, I think. So I come to you."

"To combine forces?" asked Cnut. "You fear Edmund's wrath?"

"I fear no man," said Thorkell. "But I now seek something specific from the English. Something I think I will need help to obtain. I'd hoped you might be able to assist me with this, if I, in turn, assist you."

"What is it you wish?" asked Cnut.

Thorkell suddenly pulled his other hand out from beneath his furs, or he would have done had he a hand left. There was just a stump there, bandaged tight in ragged linen, and Thorkell gazed down at it, his mouth twisted in contempt. That would certainly explain why he'd been carrying his fearsome axe single-handed, thought Cnut. What was truly remarkable was that somebody had been able to injure him to such a serious degree. Cnut had long heard tales of Thorkell's prowess in battle. To see him like this was unprecedented.

"I would see England suffer for this," said Thorkell, his voice now like jagged ice. "I would see the man who did this die, screaming, knowing he'd failed, knowing he was defeated and his whole people with him. I would have vengeance, of a kind that will be retold in saga for generations to come. I would have this...because I can do nothing else. It is what I am. All I know is bloodshed. It's all I want, and to slay the man who took my hand is not enough. I must see him broken. I must see his people broken. I must nourish the raven on the blood of Englishmen."

Cnut pondered Thorkell's words. When he was about to give answer, a sound suddenly emerged from the north, over by the trees where he'd told his men to make camp. He turned, spying something through the snow, a dark cloud rising out of the swirling white. The others looked with him, and the snow parted, allowing them to discern a flock of ravens, large in number, directly above the trees, as if suspended in mid-flight. They began to head west, cawing as they went, the sound of them carrying on the piercing gale to assault their ears with their harsh melody.

They all continued to stare, Cnut and Thorkell's men, watching the birds continue their noisy passing up and over their heads, heading west, always west, out to the coast, out to sea, beyond Denmark and then...England. They were heading for England, staying true to their course towards the horizon, a fading, dark blur upon a backdrop of stark, greying white.

All was then silent, the gale subsiding to nothing, the cries of the ravens fading with time and distance. The snow kept up, but it was gentle now, the easing of the wind allowing it to fall undisturbed, the sound of individual flakes hitting the earth quiet and comforting. Thorkell was looking towards Cnut, his men doing the same, the distraction of the ravens now absent. They knew what that had all meant, just as Cnut did. God, or the Gods, Odin or Christ, it mattered not…they were calling him back to England, and Thorkell would be his aid in this. The gold would give them an army, and with that, Cnut would regain a kingdom. England would be his. He knew it, and nobody, not Æthelred nor this Edmund Ironside, would be able to stop him.

He looked at Thorkell, the giant staring back, his dead eyes empty yet expecting an answer. Cnut nodded once, his lips curling into a cruel smile. Thorkell returned his nod. It was done.

They would follow the ravens, and would indeed nourish them on the blood of Englishmen.

Made in the USA
Las Vegas, NV
25 March 2025

20079700R10285